Tattooed Angel

Tattooed Angel

J.S. FURLONG

Masterful Person Company Publishing

70 Willowmere Pond Road

Stafford, VA 22556

mpcpublishing.com

© 2023 J. S. Furlong

ISBN: 978-1-7369891-5-9

Library of Congress Control Number: 2023904806

This book is a work of fiction. Any references to historical events, real people or real locales are used fictitiously. Other names, characters, places and incidents are the product of the author's imagination and any resemblance to actual events, places or persons living or dead is purely coincidental.

Some of the terms included in this book may be trademarks or registered trademarks. Use of such terms does not imply any association or endorsement by such trademark owners and no association or endorsement is intended or should be inferred. This book is not authorized by, and neither the Author or Publisher are affiliated with, the owners of the trademarks referred to in this book.

Typeface: Garamond 11p. Cover design and illustration by @Kasun2050

This book is also available in hardback, ebook & audiobook formats.

For Char

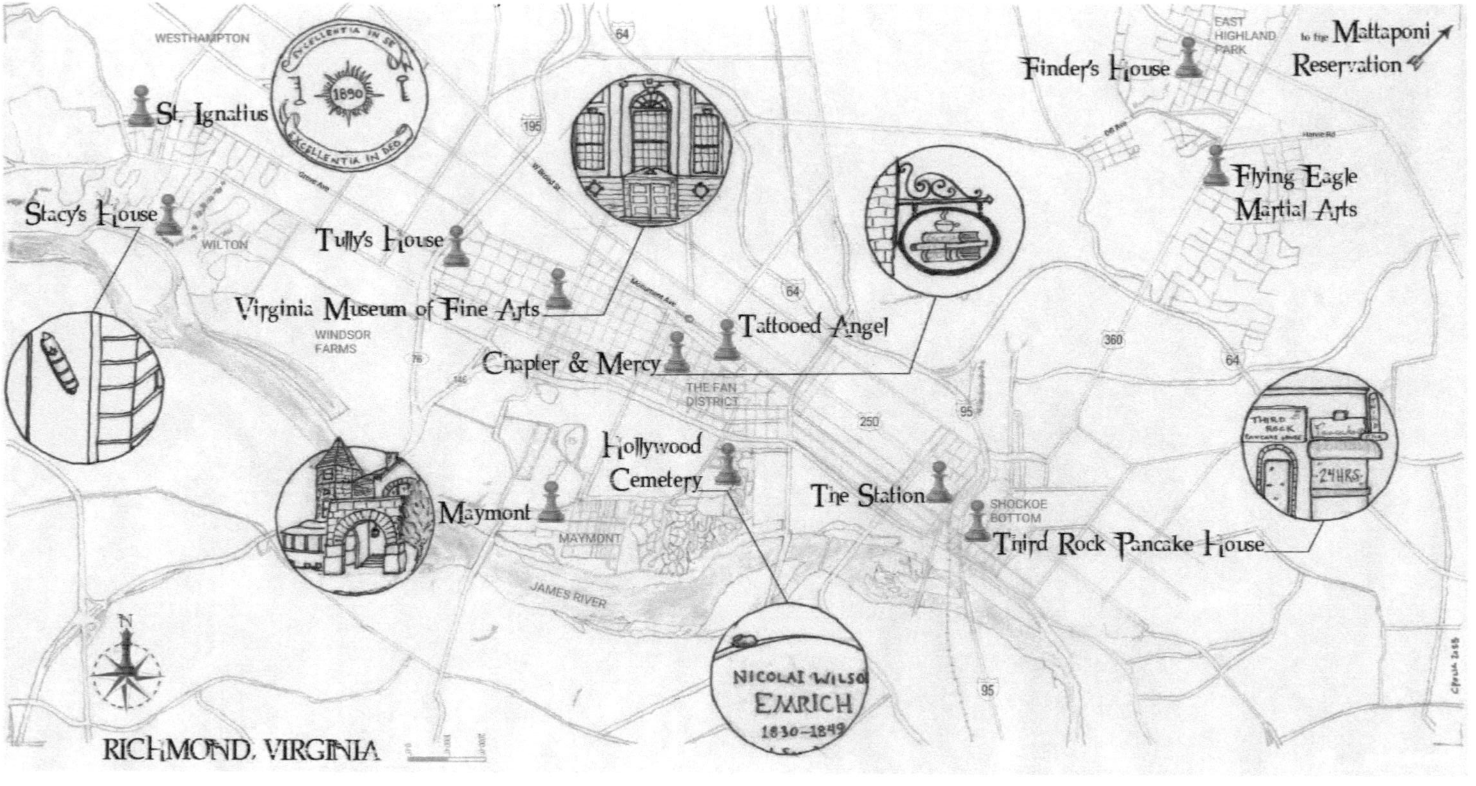
RICHMOND, VIRGINIA
WESTHAMPTON
St. Ignatius
EXCELLENTIA IN SE
1890
EXCELLENTIA IN DEO
Finder's House
EAST HIGHLAND PARK
to the Mattaponi Reservation
Flying Eagle Martial Arts
Stacy's House
WILTON
Tully's House
Virginia Museum of Fine Arts
WINDSOR FARMS
Tattooed Angel
Chapter & Mercy
THE FAN DISTRICT
Hollywood Cemetery
Maymont
MAYMONT
The Station
SHOCKOE BOTTOM
THIRD ROCK PANCAKE HOUSE
24 HRS
Third Rock Pancake House
JAMES RIVER
NICOLAI WILSON EMRICH
1830–1849
N
RICHMOND, VIRGINIA

1.

Friday, November 16, 2001.
7:58 a.m.

An angel saved my life last night. Rather, Finder's opinion is that an angel saved my life. Meredith will probably agree.

I dozed on the gymnasium bleachers, head lolling on my chest like a homeless person on the subway. My thoughts as I snoozed clung to a single three word sentence rolling over and over in my mind.

Vampires are real.

Vampires are *real.*

Exactly nineteen days ago, my family left New York City and moved to Richmond, Virginia. One week to the day after that, I turned fifteen. I went out to celebrate with the only two people at my new school who would speak to me besides the nuns. Then, in a fit of utterly unlike me behavior, I followed a boy out of a diner and witnessed what I thought was a crime.

I'm from New York. I know crime. I also play chess. So when my friends told me they thought what I'd seen was a vampire attack, I did what any National Chess Master from New York City would do. I accepted the match. Checkmate was proving them wrong.

But that game ended last night in a bizarre pawn promotion moment in which Finder claimed I summoned an angel to checkmate the opposition. I do not believe in angels, so I think it's unlikely I summoned one.

This morning, injured, exhausted and probably still in shock from having real fangs embedded in my throat, I warmed the bleachers during my first period class at St. Ignatius College Prep.

A figure materialized at my side. A big figure, tall and built like a Michelangelo statue. Feathery blond hair framed his face. He greeted me with a shrug. Thick, pearlescent arches peeked up from behind his shoulders.

I blinked.

He smiled.

Everyone's pretty upset over at Maymont, he said, tho his lips didn't move. *Especially the Famelicus.*

I squinted at him.

It deserved losing that body. We definitely did the right thing. Go us, right? I did want to apologize about your fall. I wasn't expecting you to pass out or I would've caught you. He tucked his thumbs into a wide sword belt. It looked like Tully's, only shinier. He rocked back and forth on bare feet. A cascade of feathers dipped toward the floor from where they arced above his shoulders.

I had to ask.

"Are those . . . wings?"

Indeed.

"Real wings?"

He squeezed his shoulders and the wings pulsed, a little half-flap. He rose an inch off the floor.

My eyebrows sqwunched together. "So you're for real an ang- "
His eyes brightened as he nodded, putting a finger across his lips.

"Am I not supposed to say- "

It's better if you don't, please. Materializing is against the rules. The nun's coming and you'll want to watch that tailbone when you wake up.

"What nuns?"

Nun. Singular.

"But you're an ang-?"

Sister Mary Gymnasium blew a loud shriek on her whistle. Pain stabbed from my behind to the soles of my feet as I jerked up to a sit.

A little listening, a little faith, said the quiet voice.

"Miss Goldman!" The boxy sister eyed the cushion I sat on, heavy lids narrowed in suspicion. "What is that?"

Okay Goldman, this is it, I said to myself. It's the first explanation, but it won't be the last.

"It's a foam donut, Sister. Because. I broke my tailbone."

Someone snickered.

"It wasn't broken yesterday," said Sister Mary Gymnasium.

"Last night," I said, "I fell down."

A titter went through the class. Sister tapped her sneakered foot. I had never noticed before, but Sister Mary Gymnasium didn't look terrifying up close. Her face was weathered and tan, like she spent a lot of time outside.

She stared at me, taking in what I'd said. "And . . ?"

"I fractured my coccyx."

Sister waited as if there was more. There was not.

It could've been much worse, I thought looking right in her eyes. The Man with No Face could've put his foul tongue in my ear, wrecked my memory and left me writhing in agonizing pain. Finder's dad could've turned her into a vampire, and one or more of us could've become bloodsucker snack packs, or been killed until truly dead.

When I woke up yesterday morning, I thought I was waking up into the day where I would get my checkmate. I was going to prove once and for all that vampires did not exist. It's incredible how wrong one human can be.

It had been a night.

Sister Mary Gymnasium regarded me from under her wimple, tied back like a Catholic pony tail. It could have been the dark circles under my eyes from over twenty-four hours with no sleep, my slumping posture or my flawless impersonation of a broken umbrella, but she took a breath and let it out as if I tried her patience.

"Don't sleep in my class."

"I'm sorry, Sister. I won't let it happen again." And in case you were wondering, Sister Mary Gymnasium, I thought, vampires are real.

As volleyball started again, my thoughts strayed to the one bonus from last night: Nicolai. Nicholas Richard O' Malley, formerly the (fake) vampire Nicolai, also known as Adorable Goth Boy (AGB) and now also known as Nick, was not a vampire. Nick was a real boy. Narrow framed but strong, Nick had a cute shock of dyed black hair that fell into his eyes, deep green eyes flecked with gold like wallpaper in the Macy's holiday window display and framed by long lashes. The sweet little curve to Nick's bottom lip made me forget all about the coffee and wish I was the cup, if you know what I mean. And he was smart. Stitch up your wounds and remember your phone number at the same time smart. Ex-math team, future doctor. I blushed just thinking about it.

However, Nick was not without flaw. He had one noteworthy potential boyfriend downside. I itched with curiosity. How much did one number matter? I sighed and kept my how-old-is-Nick hypothesis to myself. In this case, math was not unlike my dad. One number could change everything. Besides, some questions are best un-investigated. For example, how many teeth does that shark have in its mouth?

Sister Mary Gymnasium's emergency whistle overwhelmed the volleyball noise like a siren through Times Square.

"Back up! Back up, everyone!"

My body jerked in panic. Had Matilda found us? Revenge so soon? But it was daylight! I reached for a cross I didn't have. My heart slammed in my chest; my breath crushed into short panting.

The class spread back from a girl collapsed on the floor like a pile of laundry. It took me a second to recognize her, the Albino Atheist Chick. Sister Mary Gymnasium knelt, fingers on her neck for a pulse. I hadn't seen her send anyone to get the school nurse, but a kid burst in a minute later holding the door for the tallest nun at St. Ig's who wielded a first-aid bag.

"Who saw her fall?" Sister Mary Medical demanded, leaning in to check the Albino Atheist Chick's breathing. No one said a word.

"Not one of you saw anything?" My eyes had been shut, remembering an adorable, age indeterminate Goth boy asking me out for coffee.

Sister Mary Medical exhaled in disgust then shook a small bottle under AAC's nose. The pale girl's eyes fluttered open. I would have to ask Nick if medical school still advocated smelling salts.

The Albino Atheist Chick swallowed hard. The Sisters helped her climb to her feet. Thirty-one percent of St. Ig's sophomores stared at her, some with concern, most with contempt as Sister Mary Medical led her out of the gym, but not toward the locker room. Having been the subject of many who-is-that-freak stares over the last few weeks since enrolling at St. Ig's, I didn't envy her. Still, my classmates' derision lit a fire in my belly. What right did they have to judge her? For all they knew, she'd been up all night fighting vampires, too.

I squeezed my abs like Finder's mama had told me to do before standing up and went for it. Ow. Donut in hand, I walked to Sister Mary Gymnasium as she blew her whistle. The shrill sound made my butt hurt.

Crap. What was the Albino Atheist Chick's name? I reached. Emily? Audrey? Allison? Ugh. Fail.

"The girl who passed out. Her locker's next to mine. She'll need her stuff for next period."

The collective gaze shifted to me. Distaste and disbelief. Maybe relief. Nobody wanted to be friends with creepy Whatshername. I got it. Me neither. But she was sick and in this moment, I got that, too. Michelle Longwarder tossed her ponytail and snickered. I glared back at her. She could kiss my sore, broken butt.

"You can manage it?" Sister Mary Gymnasium's crow's feet wrinkled in concern.

"Standing and walking is better than sitting," I said.

"I'm sure Judy'd appreciate it," she said, still skeptical.

I sighed in relief. Judy! The Albino Atheist Chick's name was Judy. Sister consulted her clipboard, then handed me a hall pass.

"Very kind of you, Stacy," she said.

Ten minutes later I trudged hit-by-a-car slowly through the halls. I wore my backpack in the forbidden position, both straps on. I carried Judy's way too heavy bag slung over one shoulder. Good grief, what was I schlepping? Her anvil collection? I leaned to the side that hurt my behind less in an attempt to balance the bag's weight. In my arms, I held her lunch, and crushed her uniform shirt, blazer and skirt between my foam donut and her shoes. Walking triggered shooting pain down my legs. I stopped every so often and caught my breath. Two quarter pills of pain killers and their companion anti-inflammatories clicked against each other in a baggie in my pocket. One set for lunch time, one for after school or before bed. Today, I couldn't wait for lunch.

When we'd arrived at Finder's house in the freezing pre-dawn, we'd taken showers, eaten a dozen doughnuts and a dozen scrambled eggs between us and gotten the bus on time. Finder's mom had taken our story with impressive calmness considering the deep doo-doo her only daughter had been in for most of the night. I didn't know Mama well yet, but I guessed she freaked out in private.

Working in a pharmacy, Mama seemed to have one of everything needed for a medical emergency somewhere in their tiny, organized home. One failed attempt to sit down, and the foam donut appeared from some corner cabinet. If it wasn't for the half a pain killer she'd given me to go with my breakfast, I might not be walking either. After agreeing that we all felt run over by a bulldozer and would probably suffer serious PTSD later, we decided we might as well go to school. Finder wouldn't miss her Friday Latin quiz, Tully wouldn't lose out on fencing practice, and we'd all be in class to make the most important decision of the entire school year - choosing our science fair partners. Of course, Finder and I had already chosen.

I moved through the halls toward the nurse's office, still in disbelief that a thing I'd believed fictional, a thing that dominated my life since moving to Richmond, a thing I'd tried with all my might to disprove, was true. True as sneakers squeaking on gym floors. True as dogs barking, true as chess. Vampires were real.

It was a dumpster of rats I hadn't wanted to open.

As we drove away from Maymont last night, my mind started to wind up. I had to know. How was it possible? How could they be real? What made them work? Was it something in their cells that got electrified after death, like Frankenstein? How did they become vampires? Could it happen to anyone? Was it a cellular mutation? *Something* made them live after death and able to survive on blood. I had to know what.

Behind me in the empty hallway, the scuff of work boots and the irregular clicking of undone laces on linoleum sent a shiver up my spine.

"Hey, Stayyyy-cee! Need some help?" That southern drawl and heavy step meant only one person.

Bradley Joe Rifkin shambled up beside me, over a head taller and three bodies wider than me. He looked to be about twenty-five, bathed in a swarthy complexion like his ancestors came from somewhere warm and Mediterranean. This good 'ol boy extraordinaire sat at the board beside me at chess practice any chance he got. He did not associate with Joseph Thornton's boys which counted for something. I'd beaten Bradley Joe every game we played, each mate in less than fifteen moves.

"Sister Elizabeth sent me to help you," he said. "We saw you limping slo-mo past the classroom. And Junior's bag looks heavy."

That brought me up short. My eyebrows shot together. "Whose bag?"

"Junior, Sorry, Judy. It's Judy Forest's right?"

"How do you know the bag is Judy's?"

His eyes blinked wide, like I'd trapped his queen. He pressed his lips together and took a breath.

"Stay-cee, would you like to go out with me? You're so smart in chess, I think we'd make a real nice match." If he meant to distract me, it worked.

"Are you joking? You're like twenty-five! No!"

"I'm not twenty-five. I'm nineteen. My daddy died right when I should have started kindergarten and my mom kept me home."

Well, now I felt terrible.

"I'm sorry. That's awful."

"Thank you. So you'll go out with me?"

"No!" His turn around was so fast I suddenly didn't believe him. "Is that story fake? Is it a line you use to try and get dates?"

"No! It's the truth. It's also true that I sure would like it if you went out with me. Please let me help you carry that stuff."

"No."

"Not even the hemorrhoid donut? My grandmother had one of those. Her hemorrhoids were so big she used to- "

"Stop!" I said, my voice echoing down the locker-lined hall. "I do not need help. Go back to class."

"Aw, come on now. I'm not trying to bother you, Stay-cee."

I turned to face him. "I don't need help." Somehow the act of speaking loosened my concentration on holding Judy's junk. Her blouse slipped to the floor. Bradley picked it up, shook it and laid it over his arm.

"I understand. I'm a jerk. I shouldn't have asked you out while your behind is broke."

"How do you know my behind is broke?" It was only first period. Surely the rumor mill hadn't gotten around that fast? He looked at the floor, shifted his weight.

"I apologize. Pretend I never said anything. A gentleman oughta know when to leave a lady alone." He eyed the load of stuff in my arms. "Can I carry her bag for you? Please? I promise I'll be quiet." He indicated Judy's backpack.

"I've got it." I held out my hand, my arm pressing the rest of her clothes to my belly. I opened my fist for the blouse. "Here."

I took a step, one step toward him to get the shirt. The tip of my loafer caught on a crack in the linoleum. A jolt of pain jammed through my tailbone and down my legs.

A waterfall of navy blue cascaded from my arms as my grip on the mad lot of Judy's stuff let go. Her bag slid forward pulling me with it. Bradley reached out a tree trunk arm and caught me. It was like falling against a fence rail. His other hand snagged the backpack. I stumbled forward into his chest. He smelled like cut grass. Not a smell I expected from a hulking teenage boy, not at all.

Shoes bounced across the floor. Judy's lunch landed on top of the uniform, bag opening and spilling its contents. Gently helping me right myself, Bradley Joe checked my stability then let me go. He slung Judy's pack over his shoulder like it weighed nothing, collected the rest of the stuff off the floor and organized it in his hands. I opened my mouth to tell him to give me her stuff, but the look in his eye surprised me. His deep brown eyes were intelligent, clear and compassionate, betraying his lumpy exterior. He offered me the empty lunch sack. He picked up the baggie of carrots and a scratched plastic bottle of water that had fallen out of it. The kind of bottle you aren't supposed to refill. He put them both into the crumpled sack I held open. Maybe the rest of her food had rolled or slid down the hall? A sandwich? Maybe a container full of leftovers?

Nothing else lay on the floor.

Bradley tucked my donut under his arm. I started to protest again, but stopped.

Face it Goldman, you need help. You would do it for someone on your chess team, I told myself. Sighing, I surrendered.

True to his word, Bradley said nothing all the way to Sister Mary Medical's office door. He held it open for me and the Sister greeted us.

"Do you mind waiting and walking Judy to class?" Sister asked me as she took Judy's things from Bradley Joe.

I had twenty minutes before calculus. I could wait.

Bradley Joe planted my donut on the seat closest to the door, the one that looked more comfortable.

I stood still in a moment of decision. Thank him or not? I did not want to encourage him and I certainly did not want him asking me out again. If I said something rude, would he take the hint and leave me alone? On the other hand, I could be civilized and say thank you because he did kinda . . . save my butt. Decisions.

"Thanks, Bradley Joe."

His face lit up. "You're welcome, Stay-cee."

He looked much too happy. I scowled and pointed a finger at him. "That was me being polite. Don't ask me out again. And *don't* take my thank you as encouragement."

He gave me a wolfish grin and turned to go. Then he peeked over his shoulder, good nature twinkling in his eyes. His sigh was like a clean tissue floating to the floor. "Imma tell you truly, Stay-cee, that Yankee accent's all the encouragement I need."

Fifteen minutes later, I stared at the clock and wondered what was taking so long. My head swam with thoughts of vampires, angels, my friends, nearly being killed and the deep unknown of what was coming next. Would Matilda retaliate? Would Darcy Jackson show up to claim Finder since she'd escaped? Would the Man with No Face stay gone for good? My body ached, my brain spun. I needed comfort.

I needed calculus.

Familiar formulas, steady results. Order, certainty, facts. Math didn't change its mind. Math was a peaceful, precious, blissful, consistent, organized, predictable world.

I had a million more questions about vampires now than before I knew the ugly truth. A million, million more. What about my visitor in gym class? What or who was he? I mean, an angel? Vampires were hard enough to believe in and I *knew* they were real. But angels? *Angels?* Real? Not real? Any other explanations? And if vampires were real, what about other monsters? Ghosts? Werewolves? And what *was* the Man with No Face?

We'd been too wiped out to talk much after the fight and I had been preoccupied with pain mitigation.

Speaking of mitigation, I had a bottled coffee hidden in my backpack. I cocked my head and listened to see if I had time to pull my contraband out before Sister Mary Medical opened the patient room door again.

" . . . have to eat. If your mother can't afford food we can get you on a subsidized meal plan here."

Judy's shy voice was so quiet I couldn't make out what she said.

"This isn't the first time, Judy. What if you're on the stairs next time you go down? Or doing a chemistry experiment? Passing out is dangerous," Sister Mary Medical lectured. "Not just for you, but for the people around you. I am very concerned about your nutritional intake. I'm thinking you should see the school psychologist to eliminate the possibility of an eating disorder."

Ugh. Poor Judy. I twisted the cap of Mama's parting gift savoring the perfect aroma of smoky medium roast, sugar and cream. Not food exactly, but nourishment, for my soul if nothing else. I sipped.

In the old days, like a month ago, when I'd walked my daily six blocks to the Lower Manhattan Jewish Day School, a.k.a the JDS, I passed three separate coffee shops on the way. I missed having my coffees hot, but cold coffee was better than no coffee. Shuffling sounds came from behind the door. I took a last quick drink, recapped my elixir and stashed it. I yawned. No one came out. My head began to droop.

I startled awake when the Sister opened her door. Had I fallen asleep? I glanced at the clock. Half past ten. My heart sank. Calculus was long over. One hand flew to Sister Mary Medical's heart when she saw me.

"Oh my goodness! I forgot all about you sitting there!"

Judy came out from the back room redressed in her not-gym-class uniform and carrying her backpack. Sister Mary Medical hurried to sign hall passes.

"What do you have next?" I asked. I couldn't believe the Sister had forgotten about me. Judy stared at me as if I'd said something shocking and stupid.

"AP English. I have AP English next."

Wait. I had AP English next.

Have you ever seen all of your flaws as a human being spilled in front of you like marbles on the stairs? I stammered, "Right. Sorry," trying to find some words, some way to apologize or recover her perception that I was not a horrible person. Which, kind of, I was.

En route to lunch, I detoured to Sister AP Chemistry's classroom, Judy at my heels. The older nun was at her desk holding a fishbowl, students lined up in front.

" . . . random pairings this year," she said, stirring her hand in the papers filling the globe. Finder came up behind me and leaned over.

"What in the name of Santa Claus is this witchcraft?" she said, her 'fro brushing my ear.

"No idea."

Judy came up on my other side and spoke so softly I missed what she said. Judy's volume, on a scale of one to ten, hit maybe a two.

"What?"

"A lottery," Judy said.

"You're kidding." I walked straight, albeit slow, to Sister AP Chemistry's desk. "Layla Jackson and I would like to be partners for the science fair," I said, indicating my tall, athletic friend. "We don't need to draw lots."

"Everyone's drawing this year," said Sister AP Chemistry, mouth turning up into almost a smile. "We've had the same winners two years running." She eyed Finder behind me. "The administration and church board think it's time to even the playing field." I looked over my shoulder at Finder, the punished winner. She lifted her shoulders in a shrug. Wasn't she going to help me fight for this? Sister narrowed her eyes at my friend. "God gets to choose the partners today."

"If you define God as probability distribution," I said before I could stop myself.

"I beg your pardon?"

"Probability distribution. The math function that predicts random occurrences- "

"I know what probability distribution is, Miss Goldman," said Sister AP Chemistry.

"National Science Fair results directly impact Columbia, Harvard and Cornell admissions. Oh, and Yale and Stanford. And U Penn. The whole Ivy League! Random partner assignments are totally unfair to those of us planning an Ivy undergrad in science or research!"

One reach into a bowl of papers filled with dunces could absolutely tank my chances of a solid win. Did she not realize how important this was? A team with Finder would easily sweep a school win, basically guarantee a regional win and give us a significant shot at the state-wide win. Anything less than a state win would be a step backwards and that was no good. I needed to place at Nationals. That needed *both* of us.

"This is the most important high school credential science students have besides an internship," I argued. "Surely the school board knows that. I mean, this school is all about successful Ivy League entry! This is St. Ignatius!"

"So any partner you get will be excellent," Sister said setting her jaw. I heard restless shuffling behind me. Kids were getting impatient. I lowered my voice.

"I cannot take that risk. I can't have just any partner." I squared my feet and stood as tall as I got. "I do very in-depth projects. I won New York *State* last year for a physics experiment on super conductors and I got an honorable mention at Nationals. This year I need to *win* at Nationals. You have to understand." She sighed and started to speak again to the group. I grabbed her arm. "Finder and I are a winning team, surely you can see that!"

"I can," she said. "And if you two and all the other high GPA kids set up your little social squares as work teams, then the kids who need stronger partners for a chance at winning lose out. It's not an even competition if all the strong players go to the same team. It's not fair."

"It's not about fair," I said, too loud. "It's about *winning!*"

Sister scowled. "Then I suggest you take a few moments of quiet prayer before you draw." She eyed the shiny new crucifix on the wall next to her clock. "Ask God to guide your hand in this bowl and if it is His will that you and Ms. Jackson be partners, then so it shall be."

I almost rolled my eyes at Sister and the Jesus hanging on the wall. Instead, I took a breath and dunked my hand into the bowl. The papers inside were soft and light. Like the brush of wings.

2.

November 16, continued.

Face flushed with fury, I seethed all the way to the cafeteria. The ticket crushed in my hand was damp with sweat.

I am alive. I am safe, I told myself. Nothing bad is happening. But it is! I thought. It is!

Squeezing the ticket tighter, I willed the typed black numbers to change. I walked faster to keep up with Finder. Judy trailed paces behind.

"Buck up, sis," Finder said, almost a whisper, as I jogged to keep up. "Think of it this way. At least she's boring. You could do worse than a partner who won't get you into any trouble."

Judy caught up to us as we entered the cafeteria, lunch line curled along the wall. "Do you have a subject in mind already?" Judy said as loud as anything I'd ever heard her say. "Because I have some ideas."

"Why does the sister have it out for you?" I said to Finder as we got in line.

"Every year I win. Every year she thinks I cheat."

"Do you? Let me see your ticket again." I wondered if I could "lose" my number and draw a new one? Finder gave me a withering glance as she handed me her as yet unmatched ticket. I scrutinized the tiny paper one more time. They didn't match. Not even one number.

"She thinks you cheat because how could a poor, Black girl whose father vanished in a big news kerfuffle really be that smart?" Judy said behind us.

Whoa, I thought. Go Judy with the brutal honesty.

Finder kept her eyes straight ahead, looking at the lunch line.

"That's totally ignorant and stupid," I said, even angrier than I had been. "How do we complain? Can we get her to change the decision? Can we, I don't know, protest?" I caught Judy's eye. Her face went soft, sad. She looked at her shoes.

Good job, Jerkface, I said to myself. Kick the puppy, why don't you?

"I'm sorry, Judy," I said. "I didn't mean, um. It's not personal. Finder and I had a project . . . planned."

"It's a stupid system," Judy said, not making eye contact. "If Sister didn't write down the numbers before we got to compare, I would have traded so you guys could work together. A project by you two would be amazing."

Judy pressed her lips together and looked at me like it took effort. I'd essentially said I thought she was dumb and didn't want her as my partner. Still, her gaze held hope and admiration. I'd received that look before, from chess people at tournaments. I got a tray from the stack and when I looked back at Judy, a different expression glittered in her gaze. This one was harder, more familiar. Ambition.

Ambition?

Interesting. Then, it vanished.

"I'll try not to disappoint you, Stacy," Judy said, almost too soft for me to hear. "I know it's important that you win."

I made some generic reassuring comment, but I needed something else, something to make her think I wasn't a completely horrible person.

"Do you like nun jokes?" I had to speak up over the din in the filling cafeteria. "What do you call a sleepwalking nun?" I paused. "A roamin' Catholic!"

Judy giggled.

"How about this one? How do you get three nuns to swear?" I paused. "Make the fourth one yell Bingo!"

Finder sighed and shook her head.

"I'll get us a table and we can brainstorm our project," Judy said with a little half smile. No lunch tray in hand, she turned into the thickening sea of teenagers. Matilda had more color in her face than Judy.

I watched her cross the cafeteria. Guilt at being mean to her swirled in my belly. Maybe I should have told a different joke? In a sudden wash of personal horror, I realized what had just happened. I had just done something exactly like my father.

"I can't wait to hear what those boys have to say about last night," Finder said, stopping at the water fountain with me so I could take my pain pill. I agreed. Our after school rendezvous with Nick and Luke at Third Rock Pancake House couldn't come fast enough.

November 16, continued.
4:15 p.m.

Finder looked over her shoulder as the diner door chimed open. No Tully. She sipped water from a Galaxy-sized water glass.

"Maybe you didn't see the angel because you were still turned evil?" she said. "And thanks for picking us up, by the way. Most gentlemanly of you."

"A ride from school is the least I can do for the ladies who saved my life," said my Adorable Goth Boy Nick.

Finder reached across the wide diner table and drew a smiley face in the condensation on my metal milkshake cup.

"It's badass. Having an angel ready to defend us if we get in too deep? That is a righteous, righteous bonus that we have got to learn to use!"

I hated to crush Finder's excitement, but that could not possibly be what happened.

Oh, it is. Voice in my head, but not in my head.

"I did *not* summon an angel," I said. "I tapped into some kind of cosmic energy field, some kind of epicenter."

Finder smiled a big wide smile. "You did, and we call them angels." She was teasing me! I narrowed my eyes at her. I would remember this.

"Are you sure getting involved with angelic beings, if they even exist, is a good idea?" Nick said, frowning. "They might have opinions you won't like. Or prices you wouldn't want to pay."

"I did not summon an angel."

You did. I should know, right?

"Did you say I turned evil?" Nick said. "Because I don't remember turning evil."

I poked the last of my pancakes, rolling a bite in a pool of melted chocolate chips.

"Oh, you definitely turned evil," I said.

"Mmm-hmmm," Finder agreed. "You sprouted some fangs, and tried to whack Chess Team, here." She sat up and reached across again. This time for my milkshake glass.

Nick, my Adorable Goth Boy, (again, not a vampire) who had gotten multiple hours of sleep since we showed up and saved his lucky gamer life, brushed the shock of hair out of his face, mouth agape. "Say it again? What happened?"

Finder kicked her feet up under the table and crossed them on the bench next to me. She explained to Nick exactly how the Man with No Face had manipulated us into trying to kill each other so he could feed on the blood and power. To what end, we didn't know.

"But instead of gutting you like a voodoo doctor with a chicken, our little Chess Team resisted. Somehow, that resistance summoned an angel and kicked some bad guy booty. It was something to see."

The diner door tinkled open. In strode Tully, avec backpack. He shook rain off his letterman jacket.

"Fencers get varsity letters?" Nick asked as he stood to greet Tully.

"I'm on a team," I said. "I want a varsity letter. Chess players should totally get those." I ate my last bite of pancake. Finder pushed Tully the plates of food she'd ordered for him.

"Oh, lemme go wash my hands," he said.

Nick watched the massive teenager go. "He's a keeper. Cute, athletic and hygienic? Total win for you, girl!" Nick and Finder high-fived. Tully came back, shed his damp outerwear and tucked into his double breakfast, pre-dinner, post-practice snack.

"So," he said between bites, "do we have a plan yet?"

"Other than hide and avoid? Please no," I said.

I wanted to lay as low as possible and hope the vampires' attention on us would pass. Finder spooned the rest of my shake into her empty water glass. I let her. I had eaten a lot of chocolate in the last half hour.

"I've also been thinking," Tully said, polishing off his omelet, "about how that angel showed up, why it showed up, and which one it may have been."

"See?" Finder pointed a long finger at me. Tully went on.

"I suspect it's one of the four archangels and I'd like to figure out how exactly you summoned him and how you can do it again. An archangel's a mighty weapon to have on our side."

"I really wish I had seen that part," Nick said.

"Can we please be realistic?" My voice was a little more pathetic than I meant it to come out. "I did not summon an angel. And I definitely didn't do it on purpose." Had I? Finder and Tully exchanged a look.

"Don't underestimate our Chess Team," Finder said to Nick. "She's got some fire."

Twenty minutes later, I came out of one restroom as Nick was going in to the other.

"Oh, hey," he said, tucking his hands in his pockets. "You know, I'm flying home tomorrow for Thanksgiving, so I'll be gone all week."

Dang. No coffee date. Disappointed.

"My gramma's not doing good so my mom wants me home. I fly back Saturday afternoon. Do you still want to get that coffee?"

Hurray! Yes! Me, all on board the roller coaster of crush.

Be casual, Goldman, I thought. I heard Meredith in my head telling me not to jump too high. Act like being asked out for coffee by a gorgeous college boy was de rigueur.

"Sure." I tried to keep my face from showing too much joy.

"Good! I'll come straight from the airport and pick you up?"

I thought about my dad giving Nick the third degree like he had Finder and Tully when he first met them. There were some significant things I didn't know about Nick yet. An Ern-terrogation at this point might not be good.

"I'll probably be at Chapter & Mercy studying," I said. "Let's meet there. You can take me home after."

"*That's* an offer I can't refuse," Nick said with a very man-like twinkle in his eye. The age gap maw of high school to college yawned opened in front of me.

"Sorry," I said, "I just meant you could give me a ride." Oh no! That was even worse! Shut up, Goldman!

Heat rose to my cheeks. Part of me wished I had at least made the double entendres on purpose.

He blushed, too, and laughed. "I'm sorry! I shouldn't have gone there."

Meredith would know how to handle this and what words to use. I looked at the wall behind him and tried to think of something free of innuendo to say. Nick beat me to it.

"We will travel together in my car from the coffee shop to your house," Nick said, phrasing with care as I failed to force the blush from my cheeks. He ran his fingers through his hair. "My plane lands at 4:00. Meet at 5:00?"

"Sure," I said again as if scheduling dates was something I did all the time.

"Okay, great!" He gave me that big, sweet lip curve smile. "Can't wait! Now, I really gotta pee."

"See you back at the table." I smiled. I wanted to jump up and down and sing I have a da-ate! I have a da-ate! Instead, I walked back to the table and ever so carefully parked my busted butt on my donut.

"Oh my God, did he kiss you?" Finder asked when I slid back into my favorite booth corner spot. "You're purple!"

"No!" I said, "but we are going on a date Saturday night when he gets back from being gone all week." I grinned.

"What's he gonna be gone for?" Tully said. Finder gave him a look. "Oh right, Thanksgiving is Thursday. What with everything else I completely spaced." His plates were all empty. "We're going to the movies next Saturday," Tully said. "You guys should go with us."

Finder nodded. She stabbed the last bite of melon on her plate.

"Don't look so frozen, Goldman," Finder said fork heading for her mouth. She studied my face for a second and the fork froze, enroute. She reached over and grabbed Tully's arm with her free hand. "Teularen, hold the phone."

"What?" Tully said.

"Look at her face. It's not just a date! It's her *First Ever Freakin' Date*! Holy Goth Boy, Batman! Is it, seriously? Your *first* first date?"

"Do you *mind?*" I hissed, looking back toward the bathroom. Clear. "Yes," I whispered.

Finder did a little Cabbage Patch happy dance in her seat. "Go Stacy, go Stacy, oh yeah, go Stacy!"

"Stop!" I balled up a napkin and threw it at her. It bounced off her shoulder. Nick came back to the table and slid in beside me.

"How are we going to get Darcy Jackson to back off?" he said as if Finder's father was who he'd been thinking about since he left. That was disappointing.

The door to the Third Rock Pancake House tinkled open again. Nick got up to hug the newcomer. "I thought you were standing us up!" He sat back down, scooted closer to me and made room for Luke to sit on the end. Luke was Nick's thirty-something gamer friend who we'd also saved last night. Luke's hand was bandaged, and though he'd clearly had a shower, he looked worn and tired.

"Anything . . . happen today?" he said, rubbing his good hand on the thigh of his black jeans as he sat. "Besides me falling asleep on my desk at work? And I drove almost an hour in serious traffic to get here from Midlothian, so one of you please has to tell me the whole story of how you found me and Nick."

Finder did that part, and then told her side of what had happened. Nick and Luke took the stage when she was done. I listened, aware of Nick's thigh pressed against mine.

"What do you think your dad'll do now?" Luke asked Finder. Fine hair brushed the shoulders of his fleece-lined denim jacket.

"Gotta be armed all the time," Tully said. "All of us will." Finder scooted under his arm and leaned her head on his shoulder. A bright headscarf made a border between her face and her hair.

"I probably should've staked him when he was down," Finder said. "We probably should've staked them all."

"We're not killers, Layla," Tully said using Finder's real name. He spoke gently. "Killing isn't what any of us have trained for."

"I'm still not past the I tried to kill Stacy part," Nick said.

"Just let it go, son," Finder said. "The Man with No Face, whatever he or it is, grabbed your mind, shook your smart little shoulders and vamped you out. It wasn't your fault. And to answer your question about what happened to us today while you were responsibly asleep at your desk," Finder said to Luke, "I got Michelle Longwarder as my science fair partner which is a cosmic punishment I definitely do not deserve, Stacy got Judy which is almost funny in it's tragicness, and if there were any justice in the world, we would be partners together."

"She should want unbeatable teams," I said, bitterness creeping into my voice.

"You'd think she'd craft them so she could get that National win," said Nick. "That's what my teacher did in high school." He was so adorable. He understood.

"Y'all have entirely missed the point," Finder said. "Sister Maria Alberta loves science, and she sincerely loves the science fair. She wants to spread the brains around so she can have as many participating teams at the highest levels. If we go together, it's only one win."

"But it would be such a good win!" I said. Finder shook her head.

"If she pairs me with a sort of smart person and you with a sort of smart person then we each bring a win. That's two wins for the price of one even if it's not Nationals. Then there's Ling- he'll place, too." Finder fluttered her eyelashes up at her boyfriend. "And Tully dodged the entire hot mess by being on the super gay fencing team which is about to start competition season and get them all out of everything for three months as they travel."

"The fencing team isn't gay."

"Nope, it's super gay," Finder said. "I'm not saying it's bad. I'm just saying it's gay. Josh Oberton? Sam Spaneker? Dave Brill? Come on, Tull."

"Most of them are straight."

"You are in serious denial, son," she said laughing. "Dave Brill? Not even a teensy bit straight."

"Is that the kid with the fire engine hair?" I said trying to match the name with a face.

"Mm-hmm. The one who keeps advocating to be the captain of the all-girls dance team even though he's a boy."

"Being a dancer doesn't make him gay," Tully said.

"Duh," Finder said. "Being gay makes him gay. At least he's also super athletic. Once a kid in the hall pushed him, calling him a very un-righteous name. This was in middle school before anyone had muscles, but Dave pummeled that kid into smithereens. Now he flames as high as he likes and nobody touches him." Finder nodded as if proud of him. "For real," she said. "Put blood on the floor once. No one messes with you after that."

"It still doesn't mean he's gay," Tully said. Finder snorted and patted his thigh. "You keep thinking that, oh precious one," she said. She leaned up and kissed Tully's cheek. "We try to preserve Tully's innocence around here," she said to Nick and Luke. "It's like a hobby. Keeps him sweet."

Nick pressed his thigh a little tighter to mine. I smelled the leather of his jacket and the pine tree scent of him so close beside me. We weren't being chased by monsters or trying to save anyone's life, the circumstances under which we had held hands before. What would it take to get to hold hands now? I pressed back the tiniest smidge. He felt it and turned to smile at me. I felt a little jealous of the casual intimacy that drew Finder and Tully so comfortably together. Would Nick and I have that?

Finder was talking . . .

"She's gone to Stacy-land, see I finished her shake and she didn't even notice." Finder tapped my now empty glass with her fingers. She looked at the Adorable Goth Boy sitting next to me. The Adorable Goth Boy who had learned real vampires exist while pretending to be a fake one. Who was in college and wouldn't tell me how old he was. And who wanted to take me out for coffee.

"Must be you, boss," Finder said. "Chess Team here is usually a strategy vending machine. Problem in, strategy out."

"Sorry?" I said. Finder was talking about me and I was thinking about holding hands with Nick and how warm my palm would feel against his.

"Never mind," she said. "You stay in college boy daydream-land and I'll ask for the check. I think except for the old men here," she indicated Nick and Luke, "we're about asleep on our feet."

She looked up for our server, then turned sharply toward the window, like someone had called her name. She pressed herself back into the booth and closed her eyes.

"It's too soon," she said. She shivered. And then she cursed.

"Too soon for what?" Luke said.

Tully's eyes met mine. Dread. Panic. We knew what. My belly turned into a ball of ice. Finder opened her eyes and gripped the edge of the table, gaze unfocused. *Finding.*

No, I thought. Not finding.

Counting.

3.

November 16, continued.

"Four," Finder said. "Maybe five."

"Is one your dad?" Tully asked, almost a whisper.

I looked at the giant universe clock above the hostess station. We'd been sitting talking for over two hours. The sun had set, the sky grown dark. Stinkin' winter. Vampire season.

I forced myself to breathe. We needed a strategy. Bully, potentially very angry, stronger-than-us bully, approaching en force. Queen plus bishops and knight was my guess.

Across the booth Finder and Tully shuffled things under the table.

"Here," Tully said, poking my leg with something sharp. I reached under the table and took hold of a stake. Tully looked at Nick and Luke. "You're both going to have to do better than last night. How're your hands?"

"Stitched together in the middle," said Luke a trace of panic in his voice. Nick said, "Can't really use it."

"May not have a choice."

"We can *not* fight!" I hissed. "It's a public place! I'm broken, they're broken- "

"Oh, for crying out loud," Finder said. "Just hold the stakes and be ready to throw them to one of us. Quit looking helpless. You three are all useless in combat, as we learned. We'll fix that, but not right now." She looked at me. "Plan?"

Wait. Was Finder asking *me* to make the plan? A small thread of satisfaction wound through me. She'd had the highest GPA at St. Ig's before I arrived for a reason.

"Avoid confrontation. We need to see what pieces she sent and what tactic she is going to play. I'm guessing a pin. She'll put one of us in the hot seat to force us to give over Finder. We're as safe as we get in here, so we wait. We draw her out. If she wants to engage, she has to come to us. In here."

Tully sat straighter in his seat. "We gotta go in an hour, though. Finder teaches tonight. What if they wait to jump us outside?"

"Bullies hate waiting," I said. "Whoever's here will make a move when they see we're not running. If we're lucky, they'll go home when they realize we aren't coming out to be eaten."

"I like it," Finder said.

"We're all wrecked from last night and lack of sleep," I said looking at Nick and Luke, "and you're injured. So we're gonna pretend like we haven't noticed them." I pulled my Star of David, which maybe I would never take off again, front and center around my neck. "If they want to eat us, they'll have to come in and order like everyone else."

Finder gave me a determined version of her Finder grin. "I like being your partner, Chess Team."

"I like my new nickname." It was true. I liked that it made me not just part of the chess team, but the whole thing. And truthfully, when it came to skills, I kind of was.

"Too bad we can't be science fair partners," she said. "We'd sweep that thing."

"We would," I said. And that was exactly why Sister AP Chemistry had split us up. It was too sad.

I opened my calculus book and Nick scooted closer to look over my shoulder. His thigh pressed mine, warm through written on jeans. His knee peeked through worn denim. A second later my phone rang. We all jumped. Nervous? Who, us?

"I don't recognize the number," I said. Ring, ring. "Should I answer it?"

"What if it's Darcy Jackson telling us to come outside?" Tully said. Ring, ring.

"So don't answer it?" Ring, ring.

"What if it's one of your parents?" Nick said. Ring, ring.

Finder leaned across the table and snagged the phone from my hands.

"Hello?" Pause. "Nope, this is Finder. She's right here." She handed me the phone with a smirk. "It's not vampires."

Was she kidding me? We're sitting trapped in a diner waiting for the other shoe to drop and she isn't going to tell me who it is?

"Did Finder say it was vampires calling?" Judy's quiet voice came over the line. Oh good grief. Not now. Please.

"Hey, Judy. Listen, I can't talk right- "

"I think a project about DNA replication would position us for a win and be super interest- "

"Seriously, I'm busy and can't- "

"-ing. DNA strands recently got proven to have at least one mistake per 100,000 replications which is a much bigger margin of error than researchers previously thought."

"160,000 replications," I said. "I read that article. It is an interesting topic but I've got an idea, too, and I'm not in a good spot to talk right now."

Nick said something that made Finder, Tully and Luke laugh. Judy was talking, but laughter was king. Giving Nick an apologetic glance, I nudged him. He and Luke got up to let me out. I slid out of our booth, away from the comfy pressure of Nick's thigh and my friends, who truly did look as normal as anyone who did not have a cadre of vampires spying on them.

"It's nice that you made friends here so fast," Judy said. "Finder seems really nice."

Was Finder nice? Would she even have said hello to me if I hadn't been a potential excuse to pummel a deserving adversary? Who knows?

"Here's my idea," I said. "I want to do the conditions that allow cells to regenerate or live again after death."

I wondered if Finder's dad would let me swab him for cell samples.

Stacy Rachel Goldman, I thought to myself as Judy started responding. You are *not* asking *Darcy Jackson* for a *favor*. Good grief, could I think of a worse idea?

Any price a vampire would exact for helping me would be waaaaay too high. Judy went on.

" . . . DNA replication has so many real life applications in disease research and genetics. I think the relevancy alone- "

How nice. Judy wanted to cure cancer. Whatever. I needed to figure out how vampires could exist.

"Please, Stacy," she said, her voice dropping so low I had to listen hard to hear. "Think about my idea. DNA mistakes might not seem significant to you, or maybe it's boring, but- "

The pancake house door slammed open. Matilda burst in, a furious swath of lavender velvet flanked by four Bat Suits. Red Goatee Suit, Terminator Suit, a thick blonde I didn't recognize and one livid looking Darcy Jackson. He was the spitting image of his daughter only shorter and more compact. Finder and Tully were out of the booth and in the aisle in one breath, stakes drawn and ready. I reached for a cross I didn't have, a thrill of fear shivering up from my sore tailbone. Had we survived last night only to die now? I avoided Darcy Jackson's toothy snarl, staring instead at the Bat Suit I didn't recognize. How many of those guys did she *have?* Not knowing made me deeply uncomfortable.

Matilda's eyes flashed in fury over my friends' heads. Her gaze landed on *me.*

"THAT WAS UNACCEPTABLE!" Her voice filled the room like she had a microphone.

"YOU TRASHED MY HOME, YOU MURDERED TWO, TWO! Of my Butlers, you attracted the attention of," her eyes bulged in a knowing way, "*Someone* who, despite creating me, almost KILLED me for the third time! I HATE that more than you know. You can't possibly conceive of the pain. Having that thing wind around your brain and drag your life force out like soda through a straw is *agonizing*. And on top of all of it, you STOLE, STOLE! that GIRL!" She pointed to Finder.

My breath stuck in my chest. Why was no one else in the diner reacting to this?

In my ear, Judy spoke louder than I'd ever heard her. "Stacy? Stacy? What's going on?"

That's when I realized the entire population of the Third Rock Pancake House, everyone not in our group that is, stared, unmoving. As if nothing was happening. As if time had stopped. But Judy wasn't in this room.

"Have to go," I whispered.

"Why? What's all the yelling? Are you okay?" I hung up. And quickly flicked the phone's ringer to silent.

"What did you say?" Matilda shrieked. "Are you talking back to me, Miss? You have no right. None! Do you even realize the weeks of effort it took me to lure that one willingly onto the property? How I had to endure that stupid pretender game, and hours, oh so many hours of being oggled by those simpering lumps of flesh, especially *that* one?" She pointed a slender arm at Luke. Then back to me. "YOU OWE ME Little MISS and I am here to collect. Lucky for me, and I am usually very lucky, *you* are highly predictable and here you are at the first place we looked. My boys are so smart, aren't you boys? They found you easy as pie.

"NOW, HERE IS WHAT IS GOING TO HAPPEN. YOU are going to bring me TWO humans to replace my butlers. NOT

ONE. TWO. AND you are going to GET THAT ONE," her arm shot out from her side like a whip aimed at Finder, "to come to me willingly. AND IF YOU DON'T, I am going to come to your house and rip the limbs off every single person you love and don't for one second think this is an EMPTY THREAT. I will come and I will tear them apart while you watch." She swung that pointing arm to me. The aim landed like an electric jolt in my chest. "DON'T THINK I WON'T."

She shook her hair back from her face and released her arm. I could breathe again.

"Ah. I feel better now. That really needed to happen, don't you think?" Matilda looked sideways at Finder. "You can put your little sticks down for now. No staking Mother Matilda when she's on a mission."

Finder lunged forward to attack, but Matilda snapped her fingers. Finder froze. "I am NOT in the mood for back talk, Miss Jackson. Annoy me, and I'll add *your* mother to my list." Darcy stiffened behind her. Not sure he liked that threat. Matilda rolled her eyes at Finder, taunting.

"I know, I know. You're not scared of me, blah blah blah. Well, YOU SHOULD BE. I am a far more difficult customer than your mythical GLEN BACON. Remember that." Then, in a school-yard voice, she said to Finder, "I stole your daddy and now you're mad." She waved her hand in a flippant way. "You should know that he BEGGED me for his gift so he could help you and your little human family, yes he did. BEGGED. He's very rich now you see. I pay very, very well. Did you know that suit he has on cost almost a thousand dollars? It's Armani. Italian, if you didn't know, which you probably didn't and Armani, let me tell you, is one of the finest designers I have witnessed in my copious lifetime if a bit on the simple side. Your father looks handsome in Armani, don't you think?" She ran a delicate hand down his lapel. "I hesitated to concede to his request at first, but he wore me down, my sweet Darcy did."

Finder's dad shrugged. Then he smiled, all fangs. Matilda sank her gaze back into me. My neck burned where the vampire last night had torn it, as if her gaze alone called to her minion's damage beneath the healed over wound. I looked at the hem of my opponent's cling-wrap dress. Get it together Goldman, I told myself. You've seen this before. She's mad because you won and wants a rematch. What would you do if it was chess?

I wouldn't accept. I'd walk away.

She tapped the toe of her pointy satin shoe on the diner floor.

"No," I said, voice shaking more than I meant it to. "I decline the rematch."

Matilda sighed, then licked the points of her teeth.

"I give you until the end of November to pay your debt."

"It was self defense. I don't owe you anything."

I didn't have time to blink. Matilda was across the room before I could react. She slammed me back against the counter. Pain shot through my spine and tailbone. My phone fell out of my hand and clattered to the floor.

"I wasn't asking," she said, those delicate fingers like vise grips on my arms. Her scent filled my nose, lavender and bitters, like mothballs, or hairspray. I turned my head to avoid looking in her eyes. She pressed her body against mine pinning my arms to my sides. She winced, then shook my shoulders hard, once twice. I felt my Star of David slide around its chain. I started to jerk my knee up to try and kick her. Fast like a snake strike, she coiled her hand around my wrists. She dug her nails into the thin skin on the soft underside. My skin split, stinging as she yanked my hands behind me, pinning them to my back over the counter she had me trapped against. She slid one finger under my chain and yanked hard. The necklace snapped and the tiny gold Star of David, the one precious thing I still had from life before Richmond, my one possible defense, flew into the air. I heard the tink as it landed somewhere. I jerked around to see where it fell, but everything was still. Everyone was still. All my friends, even Matilda's Bat Suits, had been put somehow on pause.

"Alone at last," she said. "This is not a game and it is not a negotiation." I leaned as far from her face as I could. "Stop looking for help," Matilda hissed. "This is a private conversation and none of them will remember anything about it. You sabotaged an event I planned, and planned carefully, for months. You stole a victory from me and I am not," she leaned in way too close. Her hair brushed my cheek and she sniffed behind my ear. "I am not happy with you."

I started to struggle and she mashed her foot down on my toe.

"I can break it if you want," she said. "I can smash it beyond repair. Keep struggling and find out."

Not gonna lie, the line between fury and terror is not one I've walked too many times. Though I'm not proud of this, I froze. Trapped. She had more attacks than I had defenses.

Matilda was only taller than me because she had on high heels. She only out weighed me because she had curves.

"Now, you agree to pay the debt you owe me like a good girl," she said softly in my ear, "or I'll take my payment now. In lives. Starting. With. Yours." She ran her fangs along my throat. The skin stung as one tooth cut me, sharp and swift like a razor. Her tongue pressed to the cut.

"Stop." My voice came out weak and scared.

Matilda's lips closed around the cut and her fangs sank deep. The first pull of blood from my throat hurt, making my stomach sling violently upward toward my chest. Serves you right if I throw up all over you, I thought. The second pull hurt more, not just in my skin and muscle, but in my nerves. I gasped in pain. She swallowed purring like someone eating something utterly scrumptious. I pushed my arms against her, trying to break free.

She dug her heel deeper into my toe. I started to cry out, but she relented. Another pull from my neck. My body spasmed against Matilda's, the third pull launching a full body pain so powerful I wondered if I was going to pass out. An involuntary cry broke from my lips. I tried to pull my head forward to knock her off me. She dug deeper with her fangs.

Blood dripped down my neck. Matilda's tongue swept down and caught it. Her free hand went to a spot above my clavicle. She moved my uniform collar out of her way and slid her hand under. Her thumb pressed into the spot by the bone as her cold bare hand anchored my shoulder. The pressure of her thumb felt like she held my heartbeat in her hand. She pulled and swallowed several more times. The pain stole my breath. I writhed against her, even as I ordered my limbs to fight. After a few more pulls, I couldn't think, the pain was so strong. A hot tear rolled down my cheek. My chest cramped and ached. Was my heart going to explode? One more pull. I cried out, the chest pain dragging me toward unconsciousness. Matilda swept the blood again off my neck. She drew back to look at me.

Blood, my blood, wet her lips. Everything moved in slow motion as the pain abated. I gasped in a full breath. Even after the exertion of feeding, Matilda's body didn't move. I breathed in small heaving pants against her marble stillness.

Our eyes met.

Blue as clear ocean water. Blue as the sky. Drawn to them, to their power and desire, their clarity. My body softened.

Stacy! Do not give in! The voice of the probably-not-an-angel leapt loud and strong into my mind.

Matilda's wide eyes held me in their intensity, their beauty. I did not want to look away.

"I can keep going," she said, the voice of what I imagined a lover would be like. With the hand not pinning my wrists behind my back, she stroked my cheek. "I know what it's like to be a young woman," she said, voice crooning sweetness and understanding. "So many thoughts, dilemmas, choices. Their bodies are rough, crass. I prefer," she leaned in so close to my face I smelled my own blood coppery on her mouth. She licked her lips. "I prefer a softer pillow."

DO NOT LET HER KILL YOU.

"I'm not a cruel master," she said. "I will let you stay with me if you ask. Your friend will go with her father and I will take you and your friends. No lives need be lost." She rubbed one finger, feathery light, across my lower lip. "Do you understand what I am offering you? Eternity for your friends, and," she drew her hand up the side of my face and combed her fingers into my hair. She cupped the back of my head in her hand and drew me close. She let her mouth hover over mine so her lips brushed mine when she spoke. "And the most special prize for you. You would be the pearl in my jewel box, Stacy Rachel Goldman. Allowed a life of luxury, gowns, shoes, parties, a maid to bathe you and keep your things, all your needs met." She broke eye contact and leaned in to my ear. "Your will united with mine, your life purpose to bring me pleasure, to learn how exquisite pain can make you feel." She leaned into my throat and licked.

A shiver ran up my spine. Above me, a tissue paper turkey spun like the one Meredith had made with Steve last year. Steve. I jerked back into my body, suddenly aware I'd been half out of it, floating in her eyes and promises. She licked again, another shiver, but not a painful one. She was healing me.

"It's gorgeous, yes? The healing touch?" she whispered in my ear. She licked again. Very slowly. My eyes went wide with where I felt it. That would never do.

"You would have this every night," she breathed. "The more powerful the pain, the more . . . intense the- "

"No."

Matilda froze. I shut my eyes.

"Are you refusing me?"

An unreasonable part of me leaped up to apologize, to do what sweet and beautiful Matilda wanted. The other part latched on to Steve. To Meredith. To my real self. To the voice telling me to not let the monster have me.

"Yes," I whispered. "Let me go."

"You turn down my offer as a beloved part of my household?"

"Yes."

"You would rather I kill you and all of your friends?"

I would rather you let me go, I thought. But no words came out.

"Then you choose to pay your debt. You agree to deliver Layla Jackson to me. I want her willing. You will replace my ruined butlers with two fresh ones."

"Is that my only choice?"

"I can kill you. Though that would be a shame. I admit your blood is somewhat," she ran the tip of her nose along my throat up to my ear, "Intoxicating. If it weren't quite so perfect, I'd probably kill you because you annoy me. I typically don't kill girls. It's against my moral code. I would make an exception for you though since you have caused me so much inconvenience. Or," she ran her lips from my ear down to her bite. She drew little circles with her tongue over the tender spots where her fangs had broken my skin. I shivered. "Mmmm. We can both be happy. You become part of my household and let me spoil you beyond belief. You have only to whisper a desire. Any desire. I will grant it. Ivy League education? Done. Internationally recognized chess partners? Done. A penthouse in New York City? Done. Anything and everything you could possibly want. I will give it to you. Except one tiny thing you may not have. One thing you reserve, and dare I say, preserve for me."

I wasn't considering her offer. I wasn't tempted even a little, but somehow these words came out of my mouth.

"What do you want?"

Matilda smiled. I already felt every curve of her body pressed into mine, but as if she could pull me closer, she drew my head forward. She whispered two words into my ear.

My eyes went wide with the boldness of her request. A sensation I can't explain ran through my body. Outrage mixed with curiosity mixed with the safety and comfort of a life guaranteed mashed into confusion for a brief moment of temptation. Matilda let go of my head. Our eyes met for the second time, but I did not feel her will pressing down like before. She brought her own wrist to her mouth and opened her lips. She bit down.

"Promise me," she said. Blood pooled up as she drew her fangs out. She held her wrist out to me, drops of blood before me. "Promise me of your own free will."

"No."

"Say yes," she said, those wide beautiful eyes looking at me in adoration, the way my mother should have. "Who else will do for you what I can do?"

What was with the Big Bad Evil Guys offering me whatever I wanted? They definitely needed a new strategy.

"Taste it," she said moving her wrist toward my face. I turned my face away. I closed my eyes.

"I'll pay the debt."

Matilda purred against my throat. "That is not the answer I want. Open your eyes."

"No."

"Please."

I stayed put. Eyes squeezed shut. Now her mind pushed against mine from the opening I'd given her before. How could I keep her out? Without even realizing I was doing it, I started saying the only string of Hebrew holy words I'd memorized in my head. Baruch atah Adonai, Eloheinu melech ha'olam . . . In my head it was almost a song . . . Bah-ROOK ah-TA Ah-done-I ello-HAY-new mel-EK ha'oh-LAM . . .

"Fine," she said. "Have it your way." She gave me a little shove as she stepped away.

Score one for the bat mitzvah prayer. I was glad the beginning worked. I wasn't sure I remembered the rest.

She licked her wrist and the wound healed. She straightened her dress. My hand went to my throat. The wound she'd given me was gone, my neck sore, but dry. Blood smeared on my wrists where her nails had dug too deep. Free of her touch, my body started to shake. As she arrived back in her spot by the paused Darcy Jackson, she said, "you should have taken my offer." She gave a little hand wave. With a little pop in the air, my friends and the Bat Suits resumed, not seeming to have noticed anything had happened. Matilda shook her hair back from her shoulders adopting the position she'd been in before attacking me. Now she addressed me.

"I give you until Thanksgiving."

"That's in a little over a week!" Nick said.

"So? You decimated my historically significant home in a little over an *hour*! A week seems perfectly fair."

"You *attacked* us! Out of game!" Nick said. "Your guy stabbed us in the hand for real!"

"Well how else do you stab someone? With a little card that says 'stab' and those silly hand gestures? Honestly."

My mouth was so dry, I thought I might choke. I hoped Matilda couldn't see me shaking as I forced my voice to work.

"I need time." A strategy was forming, but it felt weak, dependent on too many factors. "I need more time to set it up. You know it can take weeks to get things to work smoothly and not attract the . . . "

I hedged. I didn't want to talk about the Man with No Face out loud. What had the maybe-was-but-probably-wasn't-an-angel called him in gym this morning? I reached, but couldn't remember. Matilda's eyes were like coals on my skin, waiting for me to finish my sentence. The sweat of fear and adrenaline flushed my face.

"Yes, yes," she said. "Not attract the attention of those whose attention we do not want. Oh look at us, all agreeing on something at last. Charming!"

Matilda put a finger to her lips and tapped, thinking. After a long pause she put her hand on her hip.

"New Year's Eve. I want a satisfactory conclusion by New Year's Eve. Darcy tells me it's poor fiscal management carrying debt year-to-year. It's inefficient."

I nodded. New Year's Eve was a little over five weeks away. Enough time, I hoped, to figure out how to get out of this.

"Don't even *think* about trying to get out of this," Matilda said. "I see those clever little wheels turning. BUT TRUST me, I will have satisfaction or you will have a SIGNIFICANT January first mess to clean up. And because I'm generous, I also give you until New Year's Eve to make a new decision. It's too bad there aren't any other Bosses like me in town. Then I'd have an excuse. Another claim might incite me to jealous violence. Wouldn't that be fun?"

She turned and strode toward the door. Red Goatee Suit dove forward to open it for her. Two long seconds as Darcy Jackson waved over his shoulder at his daughter before the tinkling diner bells hushed behind them. I didn't even breathe. Then, as if one of her butlers yanked a curtain off the furniture, everything resumed as if the scene that had just occurred had never happened. Silverware clinked on dishes, the diner phone rang. Talk of all kinds took up the silence, banishing it in a blink.

I leaned against the counter behind me, knees weak. I sat, woozy and unsure I could walk across the diner. I didn't want my friends to see me crumple from blood loss. How much had she taken? When I didn't come right back to the table, Nick came over.

I pulled my sleeves down to cover the now dry blood smears on my wrists.

"Are you okay?"

I was not.

"Do you see my Star?" I asked as he picked up my phone. "My necklace broke."

Nick found the tiny gold pendant half way down the breakfast counter under a stool. I slid off my seat and bent to pick up my chain, fallen on the floor right where Matilda and I had stood. She had snapped it in the middle when she yanked it off of my neck.

"You're exhausted," Nick said. "How about I drive you home?"

"Soon," I said, hand going again to my throat. Nothing but smooth skin, tho tender underneath, like a bruise. Did I have a bruise? I didn't want to ask. And being alone, even to wash my wrists in the bathroom? No, thanks. Not until I was sure she was gone. I followed Nick back to our table.

It was a long time before any of us said anything.

Of course Matilda would come after us. Of course she would demand I fix what I broke. Of course she would demand I bring her Finder to be turned into a vampire. I was it, pinned, exactly like I'd predicted. Of course.

Tully spoke first. "In the movies, bad guys go away after you smite them. They don't chase you down, verbally spank you then demand you fix what *they made* you break. If they hadn't been trying to eat us, we wouldn't have touched any of her shiny Bat Suits."

"Why didn't she snatch you?" Luke asked Finder. "Or demand you up and go with them?" He drummed his fingers on the table top.

"I have to be willing," Finder said. Her normally bright eyes were tired, covering sadness. "The fairy-lit arena thing she staged last night? She knew I would never agree to being turned or changed or whatever they call it, so she let her pets beat the righteous dirt out of me. The point of which was to get me to relent."

"And you didn't."

"I didn't."

"Would it really be so bad?" Luke said.

"Yes," Finder, Tully and I spoke at once.

Matilda had been adamant I accept her offer of my own free will, too. Hmm. What was that about? She was capable of forcing any of us to do pretty much anything. But she hadn't. She had bitten me against my will, yes, but she hadn't forced me to taste her blood and accept whatever creepy binding she wanted me to take. All she'd had to do was look in my eyes and tell me to do it. I would have had no choice. And she hadn't let Darcy Jackson vampire-ize Finder either. He'd offered and his daughter declined.

"You have to do a lot worse than whoop me in a cage match to get me to give my life away," Finder said.

"What if she truly is trying to help you?" Luke took a sugar packet out of the little condiment box and tapped it on the table.

"Are you high?" Finder said. She, Tully and I exchanged a look. What was wrong with Luke? Oh, right. He'd never been bitten.

"My father is *enslaved* to her," Finder went on. "Do you not see that? They all are. They might be dressed in Armani, but she *owns* them."

"It's messed up," Nick said.

"Welcome to vampires," Finder said. "Real ones." She pushed her plate off to the side, then rolled her stake over in her lap. "Matilda's not stupid. Last night when y'all didn't chase us, she put me in the building right next to the mansion so they'd be close. In case you set the place on fire or something."

"Told you," I said to Tully.

"She plays like she's hapless, but she's not. She's sharp."

You can say that again, I thought, hand going again to my throat.

"Soon as my dad came and told her you started tracking me, she ran us to the farthest point from the house to waste your time. She wanted to stall until she could get into the game and whack all y'all herself. She hoped once I surrendered, the rest of you would follow." I'd never heard Finder say 'y'all' so many times at once. Her exhaustion was showing.

"She knows who made the plan that caused all the problems last night," Finder said looking at me. "She knows who the brains of this bunch is."

I shuddered as if Matilda's teeth were still on my throat.

"I'm hardly the only brain here, Miss Science Fair Champion."

"I don't think like you do, Stacy. I memorize and translate, but you know *how* to think. You craft strategy from paperclips and string."

"No, I don't."

"Yeah, you do," Tully said. Nick nodded in agreement.

"Class, yo," Finder said to Tully, checking the clock. We started packing up. I put away my calculus while thinking two things. 1. I was desperate to sleep. 2. I didn't want to go home until my family was in bed. The thought of trying to explain any of this, especially my broken tailbone . . . ugh.

"We can figure a way out of this," Tully said as he stood. "There is a way. We don't see it yet, but there is."

I sighed. I saw it.

And there was no way on earth we were going to do it. Not one teeny tiny, eensy weensy way. End stop.

4.

November 16, continued.

The last time I slept like I slept tonight was on September eleventh, except tonight, I slept alone. Hours after the Towers went down, Meredith and I had laid in her full-size bed tossing and turning, unable to unsee what we had seen. For the first time in our lives, safety felt like an illusion, like a lie. We dozed in turns, alternating holding hands and sleeping back-to-back, just to be touching another person. Comfort, real safety provided by each other, and fear of the unknown glued us together. If my apartment hadn't been ruined and we'd spent the night apart, we both would have forfeit our status as teenagers and slept where my little brother Steve had slept, tucked between our parents.

I stood outside Dad and Jill's door looking for that same feeling of comfort and safety when I came in tonight, not gonna lie. A light was on so I peeked in. Dad snored, but Jill was up reading by one of those little book lights. She squinted into the dark as the door opened.

"It's me," I said, super quiet. "I'm home. Sorry I'm so late."

"I heard the alarm when you came in," she said. "And it's okay. I'm glad you called. How was the overnight at Finder's? You guys get your project done?"

I barely remembered the lie I had told to get out of coming home Thursday night.

"Yup."

I mean, what else could I say?

"Good. Sweet dreams," she said and turned her gaze back to her book. Friday night at casa Goldman.

I'd also checked on Steve, sleeping the quiet, comfy sleep of a child who has known only love.

I wanted to call Meredith, but it was too late. I dialed another number.

"Hey Chess, what's the story?"

I didn't have anything to say.

"Are you freaking out?" Finder said.

"More freaked than freaking."

"Yeah. Tonight was bad."

She didn't know the half of it.

"I'm sorry I didn't believe you."

She sighed. "No prob. I wouldn't have believed me either. Maybe. I am pretty trustworthy when it comes to *unimaginables*."

"Nick and I went for coffee after we left you guys," I said.

"Whaaaaat? Girl! A date? Already?"

"It wasn't a date. And I have a story to tell you about what we did, but I'm so tired I think I'll get it wrong. Can I tell you tomorrow?"

"Only if you're still a virgin. Are you still a virgin?"

I smiled. "Yes. Good grief, it's not that kind of story."

"Too bad. And Goth Cuteness is in college so you never know. But okay, tell me tomorrow. Take a shower before you get in bed. And say some prayers or whatever you do to thank that angel that saved us. We seriously owe that dude. Sleep good, sis. You earned it."

I didn't shower. I didn't say any thank you prayers. I put a stake under my pillow and laid down on top of my covers just for a minute, still smelling of lavender and bitters. Sleep came fast and heavy, the paralysis of the injured, exhausted and emotionally drained.

Saturday, November 17, 2001.

"Stacy?"

I shot awake to pain and darkness. I snatched up my weapon.

"Away!" I choked, mouth like sand.

A sudden beam of light blinded me.

"Stacy, it's me."

Steve. Jesus God, just Steve.

"Turn off the flashlight!"

Ignoring a loud complaint from my tailbone, I rolled onto my side then flipped on the bedside lamp. I squinted against its painful brightness. I didn't remember turning it off.

"You smell like . . . " he sniffed the air, then wrinkled his nose. In one hand he clutched the flashlight, in the other he held a box of cheesy crackers. Under his arm, his stuffed monkey dangled as if from a gallows.

"Why are you wearing your uniform?"

I sucked in a dry breath and blinked into the safety of him, of the lamp. My clock read 2:08 a.m.

"What're you doing up?" I said, dropping my stake onto the covers. My hands shook on the blankets. I rubbed my face to clear away the images of Matilda that had been plaguing my half-dead sleep.

"I heard you crying," Steve said, looking small in superhero pajamas. "And shouting."

"In your room?"

"In the kitchen. You smell like vampires. And why is there a Star of David on your forehead?"

*

Nick had drawn the Star on my face. Thinking safety in numbers, we'd walked Finder and Tully to Tully's truck and they had driven us to Nick's massive, antique car. And when I say massive, I mean huge. Nick opened the passenger door and helped me arrange my donut on a bench seat wider than the six-seater diner booth seat we'd just left. The rearview mirror was the size of the copy of Of Mice and Men I'd gotten in English class and behind me, this was the best part, tail fins rose from beside the trunk. I fastened the wide seatbelt across my lap. Then, I did something my father would never approve of. I let a boy who he had never met drive me home.

Except we hadn't gone home.

We'd gone to Maymont.

But first, I'd needed comfort. I needed coffee.

"Tell me something unrelated," Nick said as we settled our backs to the wall at the loft table at Chapter & Mercy, my favorite coffee shop/bookstore in Richmond. "Tell me something about you I don't know."

My hands shook as I lifted my cup to my lips. Was I shaking from blood loss? I set my cup down, hoping future doctor Goth boy wouldn't notice.

"I love the Muppet Show," I said. "My dad watched reruns of it when I was growing up and I love it. He called me Beaker until I pointed out that Beaker is kind of a science disaster." I sipped my amazing coffee.

"At least he didn't call you Bunsen Honeydew."

"He tried. Jill made him stop. Now you. Tell me something I don't know about you."

Nick tapped his fingers against the table. "I love tabloids about royalty."

I laughed out loud, then coughed, unable to get enough breath to keep laughing.

"Are you okay?"

I nodded.

"Fine." I felt awful; dizzy, weak, short of breath. Stupid vampires. Nick put his hand on my forehead.

"You're too cold. I think we should get you home."

"I'm really fine," I lied. "Tell me your story." What I didn't say was: 'I'm terrified she is going to come for me when I am alone, so let's please stay together as long as possible no matter how sick I feel.' After the last twenty-four hours, imagining the little garlic packets hidden all over my house would do anything other than season me for the next vampire that bit me seemed laughable.

Nick gave me a skeptical look, then went on.

"Royalty is my guilty pleasure. I remember being really small, like four or five, and thinking one day I was gonna wake up and poof, be in a palace somewhere, my secret identity as a prince revealed. Once I realized that was unlikely, at like, seven, I started reading about the real British monarchy. I admit I'm still somewhat obsessed."

After two Chapter & Mercy espressos and their accompanying biscotti, my body started to feel less like a milkshake in the blender. I could maybe walk now without wobbling. My mental paralysis started to unlock. I needed to memorize my mistakes and study Matilda's patterns until I could never lose to her again.

"I don't know where she sleeps, who she feeds on, if they can come out in daylight with sunscreen on. I don't even know for sure how a person becomes a vampire. Everything I know is based on assumptions and the Hidden City role playing game stuff I saw you do. I assume they all live at Maymont? I assume they lure in 'willing' victims? I assume there's more to becoming a vampire than being bitten? But I don't *know*. Assumption is so dangerous, Nick," I said. "Anything I assume could be wrong. And wrong could get us killed. I need facts. Solid, real-life, provable facts."

Nick put his chocolate biscotti on my plate. "You need sleep. Your body has been through trauma. Your tailbone is broken. You need to go home. You need to rest and heal."

Beautiful green eyes searched mine. He wasn't wrong.

"Last night was terrifying," he said. "After I left the museum, I kept thinking they were going to sneak up on me, jump me, even though I was in my car. I've never been so grateful for a roommate in my life." Nick's face softened into vulnerability. "You don't want to go home and be by yourself, do you?"

Crap. Was I that easy to read? I looked at my empty cup and said nothing.

"I think we shouldn't count this as going for coffee," he said. "I'd like us to go out when we aren't . . . in the aftermath."

"This is just getting coffees," I said. "Going for coffee is different."

"Going for coffee is a date." A hint of the rock star smile turned up the corner of his mouth. "A date we have next Saturday." The smile filled in. "Now, can I please drive you home? I promise I won't leave until you're safely in the door."

*

I patted the covers beside me, reached over (ow, tailbone) to move my glasses and the sweatshirt I'd fallen asleep on.

"What do vampires smell like?" I asked. Steve climbed onto my four-poster bed. He also reached across me, pinched the tissue box from my nightstand and dumped it on my lap. "What's this for?"

No comment from the superhero. Something dripped off my chin onto my shirt. Good grief.

It hadn't ever occurred to me that a person could cry real tears in her sleep. Odd to know, but *very* weird to experience.

"Old, wet newspapers."

"Newspapers? Not blood or death or something more, I don't know, dramatic?"

Captain Six-Year-Old shrugged. "Evia smells like apples."

"Evia?"

"My friend. The shifter? Who turns into a squirrel?"

Ah. I hadn't realized that Steve and Apple Squirrel Girl were on a first name basis. She was the first "real" unimaginable we'd met, come to think of it. She'd seen the Man with No Face hanging around our house and came up to warn Steve. Now, they were friends.

Steve munched in silence, passing me the cracker box. I would've rather had chocolate, but my stomach hurt in a too much coffee, too many pancakes way. Cheesy crackers were better than nothing.

A doppelgänger for his shrink mom, right down to an interested yet blank you-will-now-be-therapized expression, Steve looked at me. Really looked at me.

"Do you want to talk about it?"

Honestly, I did want to talk about it. I wanted someone to tell me everything was going to be okay. Someone who'd been there, someone who knew. Steve was, you know. Six.

"Do you think angels are real?"

Steve shrugged. "Santa Claus is real."

Hmmm. I weighed that.

"Some of the vampires live in apartments," I said. "We followed one and found out."

"Okay," he said. "Tell me more." Eerie how much he resembled Jill.

"You should go back to sleep," I said. "In your room."

"I want to know about the apartments."

*

"Do you think he saw us?" I said, sliding down in the massive car's front seat. "What if he's a decoy?"

I tilted my head and looked out the car's wide passenger window to survey the leafless trees. No bats as far as I could see. Could we have gone unnoticed? Could Matilda be so confident in her terrorizing of us earlier that she was off her guard? Up ahead, the bright yellow sports car turned right.

"Lights," I said.

"Once we're on a main road. I'd rather he not notice we followed him from Maymont."

"I'd rather he not notice we're following him at all," I said.

Nick turned another corner, headlights still off, and pulled over. "Promise me you will not do this by yourself?"

"Why are you stopping? We'll lose him!"

"He can only go one way from back there." Once the vampire's car was out of sight, Nick turned on his lights and pulled back out.

"Seriously, Stacy," he said. "Please promise you will not come out and try snooping on your own. Me or Finder or Tully should be with you. Preferably more than one."

"I won't," I said, not paying attention. I was focused on the road. Sure enough, Terminator Suit's candy colored car passed us as we reached the end of the alley. Nick turned onto the street to follow him. A white vehicle changed lanes in front of us keeping a car between us and our quarry. We were quiet as the neighborhood we drove through evolved from 'tame residential' to 'lively artistic' by Virginia Commonwealth University.

"That's my med lab building, by the way." Nick nodded to a modern building on the right.

"Wow. It's huge. Speaking of huge, what kind of car is this?" We turned onto West Main Street.

"1969 Dodge Dart." He patted a dashboard deep enough to set dinner plates on. "Bought him from my Uncle. I call him 'The Hulk'."

Except for the limo at Dad and Jill's wedding, I had never ridden in a car this big. The Hulk rode like an ocean liner, cresting lanes like waves.

"He's turning right."

We followed Terminator Suit to a tall, upscale apartment building several blocks off the main road. It looked imported from the Upper West Side, only with less stories. Nick drove past the building, overshooting the turn where Terminator Suit and the white car we'd been following both pulled in. I turned around in my seat. Ow.

"They're parking," I said. Nick went super slow and stopped by the corner. Terminator Suit got out, grabbed a duffle bag from his trunk and went inside the building. The woman from the white car also got out. She hefted a bag of groceries onto her hip. I opened my door to get out.

"Wait. Where are you going?"

"To get information from the doorman," I said.

"This is *Richmond*. There's no doorman."

"That is a fancy building. There is totally a doorman. Or desk person. Whatever."

"Here, I'll drive you. I can't park here. There's a fire hydrant."

"Do you have five bucks?" I searched my backpack for cash.

"Probably. Why?"

"I need a five-dollar bill. A ten is okay too, but a five's better." Nick pulled into the building's half-moon driveway and put the Hulk in park. He dug in his inside pocket and handed me a five. "I'll pay you back," I said.

"What are you doing?"

"You'll see."

I started to open the car door. I was very good at dealing with doormen.

"Wait," Nick said. He dug in his glove box. He pulled out a black eyeliner. "Come here." I scooted closer to him on the seat, very aware of our proximity. Unlike Matilda, where being close felt threatening, sitting this close to Nick made me want to get closer. His beautiful green eyes searched mine just for a second. He anchored his hand gently on my cheek and drew something on my forehead.

"No more leaving the queen undefended," he said.

He pulled down the sun visor and tilted it so I could see his work in the tiny mirror. One six-pointed star centered on my forehead. It was remarkably even and tidy. Like he drew them all the time.

The posh lobby did not disappoint; automatic sliding glass doors, beige settee circling an ultra-modern, gold coffee table, no mailboxes. A high, marble counter encircled the middle-aged, female concierge and mirrored the shape of the settee.

"The gentleman who just came in," I said. "Mr. Jones?"

"That wasn't Mr. Jones," said the concierge, "That was Mr. Lorne."

"Oh my gosh. Of course," I held up the fiver. "He dropped this." I started to walk toward the elevators. "Fifth floor, right?"

"No, ground floor. But you can't go without me calling you down."

I tapped the elevator down button, but it didn't work. It was then I noticed the key card pad. You had to scan a fob to get the elevator to open. Smart.

"I'm sorry, Miss. You can't visit a resident without permission. I'd be happy to call Mr. Lorne up for you. Or, I can hold the money for him here at the desk."

Hmm. What else could I get her to tell me?

"Maybe you could have Mr. Jackson give it to him for me. Darcy Jackson lives here, too, correct?"

She smiled. "Matter of fact, he does! Right next door to Mr. Lorne. How do you know him?"

Oh no. Small talk. I reached for a lie. I failed to find one.

"He's a friend of mine's dad."

"Oh, interesting," she said with an odd expression. "I didn't realize he had a child."

"She's a teenager," I said. "First marriage."

The desk lady looked relieved. I started to back toward the automatic doors. "Did you want to leave that money for him, hon?" she said.

"It's okay," I said. "I'll see him again soon."

Hmm. If more than one of the Bat Suits had apartments here, maybe someone else did, too. What was Matilda's last name? I stood for a second, searching. Bacon? Glen-Bacon? Dooley? Why could I never remember names?

The elevator dinged. I jumped. The doors slid open.

"Perfect timing!" said the desk lady as - no. Oh no. I froze like a deer in the sights of a wolf.

Terminator Suit stepped out of the elevator.

5.

November 17, continued.

Steve ate crackers like popcorn. "What did you do?" he said. "Did he chase you? Did you run?"

"I ran. Maybe never so fast in my life," I said. "It was like a scene in a movie. I was like Drive! Drive!"

"But you got away?"

"Yeah. From what we could tell, he didn't even come after us."

Steve looked at me hard for what felt like a long time. Then he started stacking crackers into a pyramid on the box.

"Did they hurt you?" he asked, focused on his construction. "Did they hurt your friends?"

I braced myself to lie, to make this easy and not scary for him. I failed.

"Yes."

"Did anybody die?"

"Two vampires."

"Did Finder kill them?"

"No." I paused. "I did."

Steve stared at me in disbelief. "Is that why you keep wincing?"

"Because I killed a vampire?"

"Because you got hurt killing a vampire?"

"No," I said. "I got hurt falling down. After the fight was over. It's embarrassing. Nick thinks my tailbone is broken."

"Who's Nick?"

I gave him the short version of the long story. In for a penny, in for a pound.

"In the end, I killed one. Tully got the other."

His eyes got wide. "Did you stake them? Like in Dracula?"

"Tully staked his. I . . . burnt mine. With our mezuzah."

"You *did?* With a *mezuzah?*"

"The main vampire was mad about what happened last night and chased us down at the Pancake House tonight. So we went to where she lives and spied on her. That's how we ended up following the one to his apartment."

"Could vampires come in here?"

The truth was, I had no idea what vampires might do.

"You haven't moved any of the garlic packets I put by your windows, right?"

He shook his head no.

"Good."

Super Steve handed me his monkey.

"Monster will keep you safe from more bad dreams," he said, sliding out of bed to put the crackers on my desk. He left his tower intact, then turned out the light. I waited for the door to close so I could turn it back on, but instead Steve climbed back up in my bed.

"Monster can't sleep without me."

And after telling that story, I can't sleep without the light on, I thought.

Steve curled down into my covers. I turned on my official nite-lite, a pre-9/11 Manhattan skyline snow globe Bubbe had given Steve the day we moved. I had confiscated it while helping him unpack. The Twin Towers stood like candlesticks on the left. I shook it then tried to relax as glowy snow fell over my still perfect New York.

Steve snuggled in and grunted.

"Can I move the stake?"

Right. The stake. Steve cuddled one of my pillows.

A glance at the clock: 2:36. I wondered if Matilda and Mr. Lorne were already plotting their next move based on my blunder.

Or if they were feeding. Feeding meaning killing. And I was lying here in my giant fancy house next to a warm six-year-old and doing absolutely nothing to stop it.

Jill stood in her cream-colored sweat suit flipping a crepe, her back to me, as I walked into the kitchen.

"Good morning, Sleepy!" she said.

Be chill and she'll be chill, I thought. Jill glanced at me over her shoulder. Her gaze went right to the object in my hands. "What's that?"

"Foam donut," I said, über casual. "Finder's mom loaned it to me."

"What for? You're a little young to have hemor—"

"I slipped last night. At Finder's dojo. I kinda hit my tailbone wrong."

Jill slid her crepe onto a plate that matched her dish towels. Still holding the hot pan, she gave me her full attention.

"You fell? Are you okay? Is it broken?" She put down her stuff and rushed to a cabinet. "Here," she said, nabbing a blue plastic tube the size of her thumb. "Start with arnica. Then you need this one, too," she went for a second tube. "Symphonium officinalis, for bone trauma and bruising. Take three of each. Get them out like this- " She turned the tiny vessel upside down and twisted its cup-like top. Three itty bitty, round sugar pills dropped into the cap.

I knew better than to resist Jill when she dove full on into her future role as Jewish Grandmother, so I sat still and tolerated. She dug for another remedy, a toothpaste-sized tube, which she set next to the teensy blue ones.

"This one goes right on the spot," she said. "Rub it in. Do we need to go see a doctor or maybe take you to the hospital?"

"It's not a big deal, Jill. Just sore," I said over the mouthful of little pills dissolving under my tongue. The worry in her eyes triggered me to spill the truth, tell her how much my butt truly stung. Then, I got ahold of myself. "Finder's mom's a pharmacist. She gave me a few co-tylenol in case I need them. It feels okay. Really."

"You're awfully pale. I don't like the circles under you eyes, either. Let's call Saul." Jill grabbed the phone off its cradle. "What's Meredith's number?"

I considered pretending not to remember it for about a half a second. If I suddenly forgot my best friend since kindergarten's phone number, Jill would have me en route to the hospital before she could flip the next crepe.

Jill and Meredith's dad, Dr. Saul Karzinsky, Dr. K. to me, chatted hellos, but Jill got right to the point.

"He says stand up."

I stood. Ouch.

"Yes, she winced. Can you pick up your right leg? Yes, she can. Left? Yes. She just went white as a sheet." Dang. I was failing the play-it-cool part of this test. I walked through a whole battery of small movements with Jill intermittently pouring and flipping crepes while describing my pace and facial reactions to the man who taught me to ride a bike, treated pretty much every ailment I'd ever had and had grounded my best friend from talking on the phone or emailing me for a whole month because she accidentally ate a marijuana-laced brownie at a birthday party. I loved him, I hated him. At last, Jill hung up.

"He says it's definitely broken, but that Finder's mother is right, there's nothing an ER doctor can do for you except give you a script for pain medication. He's faxing one. He says you can have half a pain pill before school and the other half before bed to get you through the week but stop the second you don't desperately need them. I'll pick them up this afternoon, oh wait! Maybe your dad can get them now while he's out." She hit speed dial and explained the whole situation to my father without me having to say one word. Not having to explain my injury, translate: lie, to my father was a massive win. Jill, in this moment, topped my list of great people. She saw a problem, swooped in, took care of it and poof all was well. I wonder if she knew anything about negotiating with angry vampires. Too bad she can't just give Matilda some homeopathics for fury and be like, okay. That solves that.

Seven or eight crepe flips later, Steve burst through the front door carrying a white bakery box and trailed by my father.

"Donuts, donuts, donuts!" Steve chanted as he jumped up and down across the kitchen to Jill. He grabbed my stepmother's pants in one hand as she took the box from him. He kept jumping, and chanting donuts, yanking her clothes.

"Steven! Stop that!" she said, but with a smile that said she thought he was the most adorable, clever thing on earth. She squealed at a bigger jump and then giggled, giving him no reason whatsoever to obey her.

It's not easy to make a sweatsuit look like you'd paid a couple hundred bucks for it, but Jill managed. Her hair was loose with the front pulled back behind her head by a clip that matched the sweats. Elegant on Saturday morning. The exact opposite of me.

I had brushed my teeth, washed my face and dragged on the only clothes it didn't hurt to slide into. Loose sweat pants and my new favorite sweatshirt: one of Meredith's old ones, black, torn by the collar, frayed at the cuffs. It felt like New York.

The phone rang. My dad answered, then offered the handset to me. Steve snagged it from his grip and brought it to me so I didn't have to get up. The little muppet gave me a knowing look.

"Um, Stacy?"

It was Saturday morning. Did the girl have no boundaries?

"Is everything okay?" Judy asked, so quiet on the other end of the line. "I got worried when you didn't call back. I was thinking about our project and I have a few more ideas. My mom has a client up near Carytown and can bring me to your house today if we want to work for a couple hours."

I sighed. I guess the sooner we got this over with the better.

"Can we meet at Chapter & Mercy?" If I was gonna be stuck with an afternoon of Judy, I was gonna need coffee. But first, Meredith was waiting.

"What is the matter with you, not emailing when you got home Thursday night! Don't you realize- "

"Mer. Meredith. Lis- "

"I've been worried sick about you! I almost failed my physics test yesterday because I was worrying about why you hadn't told me what happened. I know I'm still grounded so we couldn't call, but you know I would've gone to the pay phone if you'd sent me an email. So what's the story? Did Aegisthus use his powers? Do you think Nicolai is a real vampire?"

Meredith's voice was loud against the traffic. Even with the phone booth door closed, the Upper West Side of New York City made its voice heard in her background.

"And my father said something about you breaking your tailbone by falling down in martial arts class? That has got to be a lie. I am the best fictionalizer there is, so don't think you can fool me with that."

I dug my toes into the fluffy indigo rug, leaned against my vanity and explained Thursday night to the person who knew me best in the world.

I waited quietly while she processed.

"Vampires are real," she said, a stunned tone in her voice.

"They are."

"And I agree with Finder. It had to be an angel at the end. I mean what else could it be?"

I had no answer for that.

"Stacy, this changes everything. If vampires are real, then anything could be real. Zombies or werewolves or . . . magic. Like you said, maybe angels. Demons. Anything."

"I wish you were here. I feel like you'd know how to handle . . . all of this."

She said nothing. A truck leaned on its horn outside her phone booth. I was full of thinking about Matilda's ultimatum. I had five weeks to think about it. Right now, I had a different, more immediate problem.

"I need you to tell me how to handle my science fair partner," I said.

"Why? Is *she* a vampire?"

"No, my god, Mer. She's just really stubborn. And when we met at Chapter & Mercy this afternoon to figure out our project, she drank, are you sitting down? *A glass of water.*"

"So by stubborn, you mean she's a normal human who thinks coffee is Satan's armpit slime, or maybe lacks the cash to purchase said slime and above all, and truly, how dare she? She won't. Do. Your project. Idea."

I stayed quiet for a minute. Then I spoke.

"Are you jealous I nearly got killed being bitten by a vampire and you didn't? Is that why you're being so mean?"

"I'm not being mean, I'm being honest. You aren't better than that girl just because you're a genius vampire slayer and she's not."

What had gotten into Mer? And then it hit me like a massive, third eye smacking, face palm. This should have been her story, not mine. She was the vampire fan, not me. And she was feeling left out.

"Meredith! What are you talking about? I already said I wish you were here. You would know way better than me what to do."

"I'm not talking about me!"

"You are! Why else would you say those things?"

"Because you left me, Stacy! You didn't just leave, like go to Richmond and everything stayed the same only we're far apart. You left me *behind! You're leaving me behind! I'm* the adventurous one. *You're* the *smart* one. I get us into trouble by being overly adventurous and you get us out by being overly smart. That's how it's always been! And now," she sniffed. "Now you're in Richmond living my dream and I'm here living yours except I'm not even smart enough to take your stupid place." Was she crying? I wanted to hug her. I wanted to shake her.

"You are feeling sorry for yourself in a phone booth about a situation that is completely out of both of our control," I said, suddenly furious. Maybe it was because I was still so tired and on the edge from everything. "I never would have left the City if I hadn't been dragged, you know that." She sniffed, her breathing more ragged that it should have been. "And, I *asked* you if you would help me emancipate and come home, and do you *remember what you said?* You said you *didn't think it was a good idea.* All you had to do was give me one tiny nod of approval and off I would have been, figuring out how to get to come home and live with you."

And there it was. Me being the adventurous one, and her being the smart one. Our roles had reversed and it made exactly neither of us comfortable.

"I have to go," she sniffed.

"Pants on fire, you do not. You just don't want to talk about it anymore. I know all your tricks, Meredith Elena Karzinsky. And I've rescued you from most of them. You brought this up, remember. Not me."

"I have to go."

And, still crying, she hung up.

Sunday, November 18, 2001.

Morning sun bled though my curtains and spilled across dark blue carpet. I'd woken up thinking about Meredith and wondering if I could get special permission from her parents to break her grounding and talk to her. I couldn't really explain she'd sneaked off and called me and we'd had a horrible fight and I needed to talk to her, so that option was off the table. I'd sent her three emails, but had gotten zero replies. Maybe she hadn't opened them. I was halfway through a page of calculus problems when Jill knocked then poked her head around my door.

"Homework?" she said. "Already? It's not even nine thirty."

This situation with Matilda was like a tournament. Rabbi Berman, my chess coach in New York, had taught me a system for tournament prep: five games a day three weeks before a tournament, seven games a day two weeks before a tournament, and nine games a day the week before. The winning jolt occurred the day before the tournament. Zero games. Let your brain rest and recover. I know vampires weren't chess, but Matilda was a real competition and the stakes were high. I needed to show up at school tomorrow with a New Year's Eve strategy to run by Finder and Tully.

Today, I needed to finish my homework, play nine games on the computer to prep for the Richmond After Thanksgiving Team Chess Tournament coming up Friday, then spend my afternoon curled up with a book by our bourgeois, gas fireplace. Maybe make some cookies. I needed to think about anything and everything except vampires. Why had Meredith chosen now to start World War III?

"I have a surprise," Jill said, with a twinkle. "Get dressed and come downstairs. We're going on a family field trip."

I looked up from the Stephen Hawking I'd been reading in the back seat. A thrill of horror ran down my spine.

"Maymont? Wait. We're going to *Maymont?*"

Jill turned in delighted surprise as Dad angled the car into the parking lot.

"You've heard of it?" Panic rose like fire in my belly. "It's a Richmond icon. Plus the nature center and the petting zoo. I have us signed up for the 10:30 mansion tour— "

"*Inside?*"

"Of course, inside. What's the matter?"

I wanted to scream 'There are vampires in there!' but that was not an option. My head rang with nerves. I did not want Matilda or anyone related to her or employed by her to be able to identify my family. Should I fake being sick? My stomach lurched for real.

"Stacy? Are you okay?"

"I don't think I feel good," I said. "Maybe I should go home." My hands shook in my lap.

"Are you having a panic attack?" Jill said. "You need to breathe."

If Matilda found out I had been here, she might decide to change the rules and come eat me and everyone I'd brought. This place was not safe.

"We're supposed to meet two other families from Beth Shamar for the 1:00 carriage tour, but if Stacy isn't okay- "

"She's fine," said Dad. "Just mad we interrupted her chess."

I had plenty to say to that rotten paternal remark, but I was now sincerely trying not to vomit all over the car.

"Tailbone? Carriage?" I said. I couldn't get a deep breath. The world started to spin. I clutched the seat. Steve knew about the vampires, but I'd been careful not to tell him where they lived. He'd smell them once we got in the house. Would he freak out?

"Shoot!" said Jill. "I completely forgot about you being injured. Maybe we can get them to drive you in a golf cart?"

I closed my eyes and tried again to get a deep breath. I did not want a golf cart.

"Not . . . feeling up to this," I said.

It's daytime. You are safe.

The spinning slowed. I regained my grip on the moment.

"Sorry?" I said.

"No one said anything," Steve said very softly.

I assumed that vampires were night creatures only. Could I be wrong? What if I walked into the mansion and there she was, giving the tour? What if the Bat Suits were awake and inside? I lost my breath again. Part of my brain was like, Stacy you're an idiot. If you're in public they can't hurt you. What're they gonna do? Leap for your throat in front of tourists? The other part of me was like, *she can put roomfuls of people on pause.* What if that's how they feed? Snag unsuspecting mansion visitors then erase their memories and return them to their tours? I had underestimated Matilda once. I would not do it again.

In the front seat, my dad was draining his go-cup in denial about me having a bone fide panic attack behind him.

"Mommy's trying to get you a wheelchair," said Steve. Sure enough, the front passenger seat was empty.

What if this is a gift?

"Dad?" I started. "Can you take me ho— "

What if this is an opportunity? said the probably-not-an-angel. I heard him right next to my ear, but inside my head at the same time. It was weird.

Are you for real an angel? I asked.

No reply.

I asked again.

Still nothing.

Rude.

Steve futzed with the dinosaur action figure he kept in the car.

"You are staying and that's final," said Dad. "We'll figure out an option for your broken behind, but these family outings are very important to Jill and she works hard to put them together. Let's be honest, we'd all rather be home. I left the Sunday crossword. Steve was building a castle."

"Not a castle. A keep," said Steve.

My father went on. "But for her to stay calm and happy, she needs to feel like she's contributing and this is how she does it."

"House tours?"

"Day trips. Classes, activities. You know. Jill stuff."

"You love historic house tours," I said.

"I do. But I'm still suffering PTSD from nearly having my children crushed to death at school by falling buildings and my wife being hospitalized from a nervous breakdown also caused by falling buildings and I'm exhausted. I'm exhausted from moving to a new city which isn't really a city as I am accustomed to it. I have to drive a car to get places which is very stressful since I have never had to drive a car daily in my life, and my immediate supervisor has some unknown thing happening in her life which has her out of the office several days every month. Thank god she's good at what she does, or we'd be in big trouble. So yes, I'd rather be home with my slippers and my Sunday Times and a bagel slathered with cream cheese and lox on a plate next to my tea."

"Except there are no bagels here," Steve said a little sadly.

"We do not talk about that," Dad said. "It is my one thing. No bagels is the one thing I cannot manage about this move."

My breath stuck again in my chest.

"I think I'm having a panic attack."

"Unaccceptable," he said from the front seat. "I can only manage one woman with a panic problem. I rely on your steady consistency."

Once upon a time, I had been both steady and consistent. But now?

You could tell him.

What? I said in my head. *Are you crazy?*

I'm divine, said the voice. *You decide.*

A wave of guilt passed over me.

"Are you doing okay, Dad?"

Silence.

"I'm trying to be more honest and open. With my feelings. Since you, well, since," he said. He meant the night a few weeks ago when I'd told a little too much truth about how I felt about moving to Richmond. I'd forgiven him since, but that was a recent development. The Man with No Face offered me everything I thought I wanted for the small price of Nick's life. Don't think I wasn't temped. I could've gone home to New York and my dad would have thought it was his idea. Back to Meredith and Bubbe and my school. And my chess team. A cozy little group not populated by freakazoid sociopaths like Joseph Thornton. One day I'd have to figure out what that kid's deal was. Or run him over with my bike. I had not given in to the Man with No Face, though, despite his temptation. In a flash of insight, I made a most unexpected choice: I let go of my anger and forgave.

Jill came back to the car with news that a wheelchair was available for me if I wanted it, and that the carriage ride would be smoother than a golf cart.

Opportunity, said the voice again. *Stop resisting and letting fear be in charge. You are safe. I am here.*

I felt the brush of feathers against my face.

I wondered for the next half hour if I made it up.

The difference between the Maymont house tour and the countless other historic house tours I'd been on, was the smell. Most historic homes smelled musty or like too much potpourri. Maymont smelled lived-in. The air, even in the rooms that appeared the most fragile, was fresh. The antique rugs were clean and not as worn as they should have been for being originals to an 1890 mansion. The last time I was here, I hadn't noticed the condition of the carpets.

The second we hit the door for tickets, Steve started sneezing.

Jill dug in her purse for tissues. Steve tugged my sleeve. His eyes were wide and scared. He sneezed.

"You're safe," I whispered in his ear. "I'm here." He did not look convinced. He took a tissue and blew his nose. He sneezed again.

"Are you going to sneeze the whole time we're in here?" I said close to his ear.

"It's the wet newspaper smell," he said almost Judy quiet. "The vampire smell. But stronger. Like somebody dosed it with— " He sneezed. "Pepper. Do they— " he hesitated. "Do they live here?"

Jill caught his question and turned to face us. "Not any more honey. The family died a long time ago and left the house to the park service as a museum. There's nobody here but us and the tour guides. What were you hoping for? Zombies?"

I squeezed my little brother around the shoulders. Holding him close made me feel more secure, both for him and for me. No zombies, thanks. Finder's mom had said they were nasty.

When we got to the gentleman's parlor, the tour guide told us the rug was a re-creation. I stood on it, my blood pressure ramping up. I knew what had happened to the original rug. The wood floor had a scorch mark peeking out from underneath it. A scorch mark I had made.

"Look!" Steve said, tugging again at my sleeve. He pointed to a small chess table, wooden with drawers, not unlike the one I had at home. I noticed the white queen didn't exactly match the set. The one that did was at home on my bedside table.

"I bet you'd like to play a game on that, huh?" Dad said nudging my arm. I swallowed. I had saved Finder, Tully, Nick and

Luke's lives on that chess set. Two out of three blitz games. I had won and the vampire had died. The now dead Sloan was one of the two Bat Suits Matilda demanded I 'replace'.

Since Jill and Dad got together, I'd been dragged along on, no joke, probably fifty house tours. Falling Water in Pennsylvania, Washington Inn at New Hope and every other historic house or building where someone famous had slept or died or gotten stitched up in the Civil War. If it had a Historic Landmark plaque on the door and was within a three-hour drive of New York City, I had been there. I should have seen this coming. Of course her first family excursion would be Maymont. Of course.

Every room we entered gave me a new set of chills. My eyes went to the doors, cabinets, corners. Where were the Bat Suits? Were there cameras recording footage that Matilda would watch later picking out victims? I mostly kept my head down, hair spilling across my face. Maybe Matilda and her minions wouldn't notice me. Jill raised her hand with a question. I grabbed her arm.

"What, Stacy?" I let go. I could not explain to her why I didn't want her to ask a question without raising a lot of questions I didn't want to answer. "Sorry," I said. "I thought Steve had to use the bathroom." I tried to melt into the floor.

Our slender tour guide was younger than most house tour docents, not much older than me. Her face came alive when she smiled, hair drawn away from her face by a headband a la Nancy Drew.

"That skirt is very sixties," Jill said eyeing our docent's green pencil skirt. "Don't think I could get away with it."

"Mrs. K. would say you could," I said, referring to Meredith's mom. We followed our guide into the pink parlor.

"Her life is so glamorous," Jill said. "Models and writers and photographers. And designers. I would die if I met Oscar DeLarenta. Or Georgio Armani. Can you imagine?"

I could not. I'd rather meet Gary Kasparov or Judit Polgar.

We paused to listen to Young Docent's spiel about the room and its history. I hung on every word. Anything she said could reveal a clue about Matilda, something to give me an advantage at New Year's. When she released us to wander the room and read about the tea settings and the piano on our own, I beelined for the cabinet housing a few family photographs. Matilda's face, unmistakable yet somber in the style of late 1800s photographs stared back at me. A young woman stood slightly apart from her on one side, and a man in a formal jacket and tightly buttoned collar on the other. Interesting, but not strategically useful. Surely, I couldn't be the first vampire hunter to take this tour. Matilda must have contingencies for that. She must have false information buried everywhere. What did I really need to know?

Excuse me, Miss, but where do the vampires sleep?

"Does this house have an interior cellar entrance?" I asked as our Young Docent passed close to me. She regarded me, gaze steady, eyes bright. There was something familiar about her this close up. Did she go to St. Ig's? "The buildings on Maymont don't have cellars," she said. "Mr. Bacon wanted the most modern features for this house so he had his food storage rooms built into the same level as the kitchen."

"Is there a separate ice room?" Jill's voice, actor-loud and clear, echoed through the space.

"Why, yes. It's been open for tours in the past, but it's currently closed to the public due to its fragile nature."

Or because it's currently blood storage? I wanted to ask.

When some other members of the tour looked over, the docent went on, describing the kitchens, food storage and the dumbwaiter that allowed food to go from the lower level kitchen to the butlers serving in the main floor dining room. She showed us the talking box, a tube that the servants could speak and listen through from level to level. The vampire Sloan had shown it to me.

"Do you think Meredith is Goth because her mom is so high fashion?" Jill said, admiring the china in the dining room cabinet.

"Is this just now occurring to you?" I asked. "Remember the summer I was eleven?"

"Was that the summer she held you prisoner learning all the couture terms?"

"She was going to be a fashion writer like her mom and wanted me to be her editor. She had her own magazine all laid out and everything. Completely ignored how much I hate writing and how English is like, my worst subject."

"At what? An A without a plus?"

"That plus is significant," I said. "It has points. Mer did great until her mom made some comment about her fashion sense being like the Marines. She bought her first pair of combat boots the next week."

"That's so sad," Jill said. "Meredith is incredibly creative."

Understatement. I missed my other half. I wanted to ask Jill's advice on how to handle Meredith being so upset with me, but it was too much to explain. Maybe Finder would have some advice.

My breath stuck a little in my chest as we re-entered the main hall. We stopped in front of the stanchioned-off stairs to hear about the art and fireplace. The last time I'd interacted with this staircase, the Bat Suit who had first bitten me was staked to it. Tully had delivered the killing blow, but the stake had skewered the monster and gouged a chunk out of my thigh. It was a chunk the size of my thumbnail, but it had hurt. It had also healed when the angel (or whatever) had taken over my body and gifted us with the healing of our wounds. Too bad I'd broken my tailbone *after* the healer had left.

Jill grabbed my arm as she turned away from the fireplace. I jumped, stifling a scream. Steve dove behind me, ducking for cover.

"Amazing!" Jill gasped. "Can you believe those Tiffany windows?"

Monday, November 19, 2001.

Judy caught up to me in the hall after English.

"The sample is viable," she said, eyes alight. "A DNA sample. From someone with a mutation. My dad's friend started running the genome map in his lab ten days ago and it's working. We should be able to see the results in the next week." I slowed to walk with her.

"What kind of mutation?" DNA was super cool to look at under a microscope, and to see a mutation first hand? That pulled my nerd strings in a very alluring way.

"It's a university lab. There's a Nuclear Magnetic Resonance Imaging machine."

Nuclear MRI? Now she was speaking my language. But I really needed, like maybe life-depends-on-it needed, to know how vampires worked. I couldn't just roll over and give Judy this win.

"My apoptosis idea can be run with drosophila and Sister said she could get them for us," I said.

"What's drosophila?"

"Fruit flies."

"Eww. They're disgusting." Meredith's accusation about me judging Judy echoed like a rock hitting my chest. "We have two weeks to commit to a hypothesis," Judy said. "How about I call you when the sample is done, and if you don't like it or think it's boring, we'll do your dead bug one."

Well, when she put it like that, what was I gonna say?

When I went upstairs after dinner, an email was waiting for me.

Dude,

I think I'm in the five stages of grief. Denial, anger, bargaining, depression and acceptance. I feel like an awful person. But I don't feel wrong. I can go to the phone booth tomorrow after school. You know what time. ~Mer

Tuesday, November 20, 2001.

I sat on my bathroom floor, on my donut, my phone plugged into the socket with the hairdryer. I looked at the toilet. It would be a more comfortable sitting place, but it felt wrong to have this conversation there.

My phone rang at exactly 4:55.

"So here's what I have to say," she said before I even said hello. "I'm struggling without you. I feel lost and sad and I haven't wanted to admit it because you seem totally fine, *everyone* seems totally fine, and I feel like I'm the only one who is miserable. So yes, I'm feeling very sorry for myself because I am grieving that my best friend is gone and I'm spending my days trying to turn Sorrel or Isaac into you and surprise, it's not working. They miss you, too, of course, but it's not the same. And my stupid math grade has dropped twenty points because I don't have you explaining it to me in a way that actually makes sense while I ply you with coffee and sushi.

"So I'm sorry if I was a big, fat B the other day, but I'm not over it. I can't fake like I'm okay, and I am totally serious when I say I'm in the five stages of grief. I'm stuck between the rock of denial and the hard place of anger. I've started asking for when I can visit you, so I think that's the 'bargaining' stage. Depression is next so get your tissues ready, Woman. You do not want me calling you depressed. Especially because you get real vampires and all I get are drills of what to do if another airplane hits a building."

I sat still, processing what she'd said. I knew I had missed her, but I hadn't realized how much my leaving had left her empty-handed. She took a long pause.

"Do you have more?" I said.

"You can go. I think I mostly said it."

"Okay. So. It's just as hard for me to be without you as it is you to be without me. I've tried not to be whiny about it, but being here has not been a picnic. Finder and Tully are awesome, but, like you said about Isaac and Sorrel, they are *not you*. No one will ever *be* you. Finder and Tully have each other. It's like I'm a peripheral friend sometimes. It's better than it was since we had a little fight-to-the-death bonding, but they are *not you*. I miss *you*. Every single minute. And you know, I didn't ask for this. Vampires, or Hidden City, or Goth boys, or any of this."

"I know!" Mer cried on the other end of the line. "*I* asked for it! I ask for it *every stinkin' day* and poof! *You*, ungrateful and cranky and boring, no offense, walk into what should be *my life*! It's so not fair!" She heaved a massive sigh. "All that to say, *you* didn't make me feel bad, you were just being you. I made myself feel bad. I'm jealous in a way that makes my freakin' bones ache, I want to be you so bad. But I can't, and that sucks, and I have to deal with it."

This was a first. Never before had Meredith expressed any desire to be like me, much less be me. It took me aback.

"One. I'm not boring. Ungrateful, maybe. Cranky, absolutely, but not boring."

"Fine, I take back boring."

"Thank you. Two. Would they let you come to Richmond for Thanksgiving? You need to see how terrifying and not glamorous this is for yourself."

"Terrifying *is* glamorous to me, my pet," Mer said, sounding almost like herself. "But since you guys won't be at our house for Thanksgiving, where you *belong*, and I am still grounded from you for my very innocent brownie eating error, my dad invited his cousin from Long Island to come."

"Eww. The one with the- "

"Serious halitosis and little biter dogs that pee on the floor when they hear sirens? Yes."

"Oh, gross. I'm so sorry."

"Not as sorry as me, Woman. Not as sorry as me."

"So, are we okay again, now?"

"I guess so. But be forewarned, you might get some sloppy, sad-sack emails and I expect you to be kind and tolerant since you have stolen my dream life, albeit unintentionally."

"I'm here for you, Mer. And trust me, if I could trade you lives, I totally would."

"You would not. You've needed a good, solid, solo adventure for a long time. And I need to put my big girl pants on and suck up some maturity. But I hate it, and I'm dying here in Debris City without you, and that is all I have to say. So have a safe trip getting up off that bathroom floor and I will email you when I get my own self back to my apartment so you know I didn't get crushed by falling buildings on my way home."

"Please do. I live for your email." I paused. "I love you, Mer. And I am sorry, for real."

"I love you, too, Stac-a-licious. And I'm not sorry yet, but I will be. Gimme some time. And if you want to learn more about vampires, seriously, you don't need to play Hidden City. You need to go to the library."

Wednesday, November 21, 2001.

"You're saying I need therapy," Finder scowled as she carried my backpack and a tall stack of Meredith's recommended vampire books for me out the main doors of the Richmond Public Library.

"I'm saying that it's good to have someone uninvolved in your life to talk to about things. I mean, it's no surprise you hate her smug, perfect exterior self. Your dad is basically trying to kill you."

"I talk to Tully. I talk to you."

"Look. If you're going to have the physically restrain yourself every time you and Michelle work on your project, you might want to get help. That's all. For your own sanity."

"Michelle is possibly the worst science fair partner in the history of earth. She's not dumb, she just does not care. Would I want her on my volleyball team? Heck, yeah. But an academic competition? Girl's a righteous mess. And for the first time ever, I have real competition this year."

I grinned like a model selling something on TV.

"I am the *master* of the science fair," I said. "The only way you'll beat me is if I don't show up."

"I see that gauntlet," she said. "And this is me picking it up."

Mama pulled up just as Finder and I got to the bottom of the steps. Jill was already parked. She waved for me to hurry up.

I deposited my own ladder of books in the trunk and the stack from Finder. She plunked in my backpack, then took two books off the top of the stack.

"I'll do these."

"Only two?"

"Are you teaching four classes a week?"

"Oh fine, be that way."

Finder said hi to Jill and I waved to Mama who pulled her car up beside ours.

Jill rolled down the passenger window.

"Are you Stacy's mom?" Mama said.

"Step-mom, yes!" A fresh, new foam donut sat on my seat. Uh, sweet and thoughtful or tremendously embarrassing? Both. "Jill Goldman. You must be Finder's mom." And they did that little dance of how great each other's kid was while Finder and I got in the cars.

"Mama, we gotta go. Class starts in a half hour."

"Wow," Jill said as we drove off. "That BMW's a classic."

"Is that your way of saying it's old?"

"It's my way of saying that there's money in that family somewhere. Either that or they keep cars for a long time."

"I think it's the latter. Finder's on scholarship. And she teaches four classes a week."

"That's so healthy. Building a solid work ethic right from the start. I babysat for years before I got my first job. I was a lifeguard at my community pool." Sometimes I forgot Jill wasn't from New York. "Maybe you could get a job. I think you can volunteer as a fifteen-year-old."

"I had a job," I said. "At home." Yes, I'd forgiven them for yanking me out of my life, but some things I'd lost still left a bitter flavor on my tongue. My income was one of them.

"What job?"

She said it as if I was wrong.

"Mrs. Frankenfeld's dog?"

"Oh yeah! Sorry. I forgot you walked that little sausage dog."

"Weiner dog. And yes. Dusty. Every day in fact. While you were with Steve. Or still asleep."

"You could walk dogs in Wilton," she said as if this was a great new idea. "We could put up signs and post a notice in the community newsletter."

"No, thanks. I have a lot more homework here than at JDS." And I'm currently being stalked by vampires so I'd rather not be walking outside at night or in the early morning before sun up, I thought. "If you're worried about me having money though, I'm open to an allowance."

"You have one. Your dad pays you to watch Steve when we go to the club."

"No, he doesn't."

"Of course he does!"

"No. He doesn't. Or if he does, I've never seen any of it. Is he like, calling himself my employer and sneaking it into a Roth IRA? 'Cuz he sure hasn't put any money in my hand."

"Are you kidding me? He told me he was paying you."

And thus, the pieces of the 'Jill looking annoyed when I said I couldn't watch Steve the other day' puzzle fell into place. She thought I was gainfully employed (I was not) and it made her mad that I'd walked away from legit paying work, especially a job she needed me to do. Ah ha.

"I could swear he told me he paid you."

I shook my head as we turned onto Boulevard. "Nope. One, he's cheap, sorry, thrifty, and two, he views babysitting as my familial duty. I'm a kept person who doesn't pay bills."

"That's ridiculous."

"That's Dad."

Half a block later, traffic was stopped. Jill pulled out her lip balm since we had several cars to wait for before we could move. A cop directed one vehicle at a time around a row of limousines parked in front of bright event lights shining on a big building. A building I knew.

Richmond's Museum of Modern Art was lit up like Rockefeller Center. A line of cars extended around the block to their parking lot. A bona fide red carpet lay over the steps, and winter coat armored paparazzi lined the walkway.

"It's the Museum Gala!" Jill exclaimed. "They hold it the night before Thanksgiving because all the old money is home for the holiday. Look at that gown! Sheesh!" She leaned forward to ogle the glitterati as we crawled forward one car length. A rotund lady in gold sequins and fur ascended the wide museum stairs waving to the photographers. "It's a big deal here," Jill went on. "Like the Met Gala at home. The paper's been covering it for days. Two thousand dollars a person and you can have a table." A flash of familiarity pulled my gaze. My heart raced in astonishment.

"Wait! Can you pull over?"

6.

November 21, continued.

Lucky for me, the traffic cop waved the guy in front of us to stop so a line of cars dropping off could clear out. I craned my neck and got a clear view of the street in front of the museum.

I stared in utter bewilderment as Darcy Jackson opened a limousine door. Another man, who I only saw from behind offered his hand and out came Matilda. Her gown was lavender satin, her hair wound into an updo. A cap like an old movie star crowned her ensemble. Flashes went off like clicking fireworks. Matilda walked up the carpet, turned, smiled at the rapt reporters, posed on all four sides for photos and then took the arm of the man who'd helped her out of the car. My jaw literally dropped as he turned toward me.

Luke? What was he doing here? What was he doing with *her?* Looked like he'd gotten a haircut, but the smiling man now walking Matilda up the red carpet to the museum entrance was definitely Luke stinkin' Whitehall.

The traffic cop waved us on. A zillion thoughts rushed through my mind. Matilda, *Matilda* was waving to the press and getting her picture taken. That went completely against my theory that she thrived on secrecy. She'd said the night of the kidnapping that she only came out of hiding every fifty years or so pretending to be her own great-granddaughter or whatever. Was this that generation?

And what in the name of tattoos and broken knees was Luke doing with her? I had to get home and call Nick.

Another matter of urgency pressed my mind. We could never know where Matilda was for sure and right now, I knew. A lexicon of chess tactics waterfalled through my mind. Fork? Pin? Skewer? How upset would she be if garlic packets and holy symbols showed up inside her house? It would get her nervous about who had the power and knowledge to do that. It might make her suspect her own people. That could be good.

Matilda was out as a member of society. She would be in the paper tomorrow for sure. Clearly, she could be photographed, so that killed the 'vampires don't reflect' myth. What would the paper reveal about her? And could I get Tully to come over right now and go with me to Maymont? Maybe Jill would have an eyeliner I could borrow.

"I have a spray bottle of holy water, a box of chalk, a stake, a crucifix, a washcloth and a Sharpie," I said, answering Nick's question as I loaded my messenger bag. "And my mezuzah." I tucked the little Jewish home protection rod into the front pocket of my bag. "And a flashlight. But what is up with Matilda and Luke? Have you talked to him? Has he mentioned going to this thing with her? Are they, like, *dating*?" I fastened my jerry-rigged Star of David necklace, now held together with a safety pin, then pulled my hair back into a pony tail.

Nick had no good answers. He sounded as alarmed as I was, but said he would call me after he talked to Luke and got the story.

The doorbell rang. Drat. Tully was early. I was hoping to put a little something in my stomach before we went. I flung my pack over my shoulder and trotted down the stairs.

"Stacy, get the door," Jill called from the kitchen. Duh. Of course, Tully was coming for me.

I unlocked the deadbolt and pulled open the door, but didn't even look at my friend. I still needed to grab my coat and when I turned around -

"Bubbe!"

I flung myself forward into my grandmother's round, forceful embrace. Ow. Tailbone. "What are you doing here?" Tears sprung to my eyes. Bubbe.

"Surprise!" Jill said behind me. "Good grief, Stacy, let the woman get in the door before you crush her to death."

I wiped away hot tears as I moved aside so my dad's mom could step up into the house. Once she passed me, I grabbed her suitcase and dragged it in. We looked each other in the eyes. She was teary, too. Her smile was so wide I saw her gold tooth.

"Shayna, honey," Bubbe said, calling me by my Yiddish nickname. "You got taller," she said between kisses on my wet cheeks.

"I did? Are you sure? That's awesome!" She pulled me back into another hug then held me at arms-length for the once over.

"Your hair's longer, too. What's this outfit, though? Funeral sportswear?" I had put on black sweatpants and a matching sweatshirt mailed-me-down from Meredith.

"Why didn't you tell me?" I said to Jill whose satisfied smile was broad enough to crack her face. I had to call Tully and let him know not to come.

Bubbe hugged me again, a hard squeeze. I clutched onto the back of her coat breathing in her frankincense and dusting powder smell. I knew I'd missed her, but I hadn't realized how much. I sighed, heart full.

"Steven! She's here!" Jill hollered over her shoulder.

"Hurry up so I can squeeze you!" Bubbe said, so loud in my ear. Bubbe let go of me, looked into my face for a long minute and winked. My turn was over. We'd talk later. "Hello sweetheart," she said, hugging Jill. "You look so relaxed and beautiful here. This country air has done you good."

"It's not really the country," Jill said, but Bubbe's eyes had already passed her, searching the living room.

"Where's Ernie?"

"Not home yet," Jill said heading for the phone.

Steve landed at the bottom of the stairs with a whoop and a slide into home plate. The slippery wood floors and his socks had just the right amount of friction for him to get a good slide if he leaped the last three stairs.

"Come here you scoundrel!"

Steve jumped up into Bubbe's arms clinging to her like a monkey. My grandmother kissed his face with big loud smooches. "Oh you rascal! What's the matter with this place? Doesn't anybody cut their hair?"

Steve got down shaking long bangs out of his eyes and started dragging her bag from the doorway toward the stairs.

"Wait! I have a present for your mother in there. Turn it on its side." Bubbe unzipped her suitcase with Steve crouched beside it. She pulled out a Chico's bag full of wrapped gifts.

"It's not Hanukkah yet, Bubbe!" Steve said.

"What's your point? I bring presents when I want to bring presents." She placed the bag just out of his reach. She handed Jill a second bag. "May you never go hungry and may your life be full of flavor," she said with a smile.

She crouched down and held her arms open for another Steve hug. She squeezed him then took hold of his shoulders. "Let me see, how big did you get? Look at those eyes. Your father's eyes. You look just like your daddy when he was a boy. Except your hair is light and straight. Spitting image, I tell you. Except for the hair." I held out my arm for her coat as she stood.

"Did you know she was coming?" I asked Steve.

"Of course," he said tapping his head with one delicate finger. "I know everything."

"And you didn't tell me?"

"Why ruin a perfectly good secret? Your squeal when you opened the door? Super worth it."

"I did not squeal."

"Oh. You did. Loud and clear."

"And you didn't come running?"

"It was a squeal of joy, duh," he said. "And you guys needed a moment. You already look happier and she's been here five minutes."

I brewed coffee for Bubbe after putting the bagels and salt she'd brought us on the dining room table next to the little pile of presents. Jill started Bubbe's house tour. I followed them around for the upstairs half, saying nothing amidst the ooohs and ahhs, just wanting to be near my grandma. Jill's mom, who preferred to be called Gram, would arrive tomorrow. Gram wore a poofy red wig and left chaos in her wake. She thought of me as Ernie's daughter and kinda ignored me and Dad in favor of Jill and Steve. I didn't blame her, except maybe about the wig. Her natural hair was totally fine, she just liked the wig better.

"I'm doing a surprise party for Ernie this year," Jill said, "the night of his actual birthday. I'd love it if you would be here."

"A New Year's Eve surprise party?" Bubbe let Steve drag her toward his room. "You know he is not a fan of his birthday and he hates surprise parties."

"With a burning passion," I added. "He hates going to them, he hates the people who plan them. He hates how embarrassing they are."

"Well, he's bringing it on himself," Jill said. "He's absolutely forbidden me to throw him a party at all which is ridiculous. Decade birthdays deserve a special something. I got him to give me permission to invite his boss over for New Year's Eve dinner, so that will be the ruse."

Bubbe stopped in Steve's doorway and looked at Jill.

"I'll tell you once and then I'll be a good mother-in-law and mind my business. A surprise party, especially for a decade birthday, especially on a major holiday, sounds terrible. It's a mistake. A big mistake. Take him out for dinner, just the family, or just the two of you. Buy some nice lingerie, but really Jill. Trust me on this. A party will be a disaster. He will feel embarrassed and put on the spot and he will never forgive you for it. Never ever as long as he lives. There, now I've said my bit. You heard every word, right?"

"I did."

"You understand he holds grudges?"

"I do."

"Very good. Then you understand why I will not even cross the state line out of New York to be part of it. Invite some of Stacy's friends from home if you need guests. He won't punish them for coming. I would never hear the end of it."

Jill leaned on the doorway as Bubbe followed Steve into his domain.

"He's not really that against surprise parties, is he?"

"Oh, he is," I said.

Jill sighed a big sigh. "There's no stopping it now. I've already sent save the date cards. Plus, Aunt Marlena and Uncle Ira will be in D.C. and said they could come down for the night. It's going to be fun. I think Ernie will enjoy it if I do it right. We won't ask him to make a speech or anything like that. He can just enjoy his friends and family. Maybe you can talk Bubbe into coming?"

I almost said, were you listening to the woman? No! Instead, I hedged.

"Can you send *change* the date cards? If you really won't cancel, which you should, maybe at least reschedule to a night with less, um, pressure? I mean, New Year's Eve parties can be kind of a thing to host." And I might be out getting eaten by vampires and saving your lives, I thought. Ugh.

Shoot! Vampires! I hadn't called Tully to tell him not to come. I guess I'd send him home and owe him a coffee. Or a smoothie. Or something. My stomach sank. Shame to miss this chance to search Maymont. I would likely not get it again.

Jill's eyes looked suddenly dark, as if bags were forming just from her thoughts.

"Are you sure you can't cancel?"

Jill crossed her arms and her brow drew in. "I'll j-j-just be quiet about it. He secretly l-l-loves attention. Why else would he w-want to do comedy?"

"Don't be upset," I said. "Take Bubbe's advice. She loves you and is trying to help. Cancel the party. Or at the least pick a different day. I'll help you figure out what to say." I had no idea why I said that. I had no clue what to say in a formal invite situation. "Maybe people could write cards and you could collect them for him in a big box?" I said. Jill's gaze fell to the floor. Her mouth tightened. I recognized her anxiety resistance face and scrambled for something comforting to say. "He'd probably be very touched by that. He likes reading."

The doorbell rang.

Crap.

Tully stood in the doorway, truck running in the driveway.

"I can't go," I said. "Jill didn't tell me but my Bubbe, my grandmother, is here to visit and she just arrived."

"Who is this handsome creature?" Bubbe said, following Steve down the stairs. "And why are you making him stand in the cold?"

Tully stepped in. Steve ran past him and shut the door before squeezing him hello around the legs.

"Bubbe, this is my friend Tully," I said.

"He's my friend, too," Steve said.

"Nice to meet you, Mrs. Goldman," Tully said, stepping forward with Steve still clutching his leg. "I'm Teularen McCleery. I go to school with Stacy."

Bubbe shook his hand with a firm, city handshake.

"Ooo, good grip," Bubbe said. "I approve."

"Thanks," Tully gave Bubbe a warm smile. "Stacy has a little PT to do this evening. Is it okay if I take her for an hour or so? I promise I'll get her back quick."

"Of course, of course."

"No, Bubbe. I can totally skip tonight. Right, Tully?" I looked at my grandmother. "I would have rescheduled if I knew you were coming. I don't want to miss any time with you."

"Don't be ridiculous. Healing your body is the priority. You kids go do your thing and I'll be right here when you get back. Jill and I'll get all the house-talk you don't care about out of the way. Curtains and rugs and appliances. So boring, right? You won't miss a thing."

I buried my first garlic packet in the dirt under the shrub outside the gate.

"They leave this one open?" I whispered to Tully as we went through.

"Servants' entrance? She can't expect them to jump the fence."

The gate had been hard to find. Tully couldn't remember which side of the formal entrance gate it was on. I knew it was on the left, but still had to search it out. I found it by running my fingers along the iron posts and bonking up against the gate latch. I hadn't seen it until I touched it.

The mansion porch lights glowed up ahead and the night lamps along the main paths flickered with gas light. The only awake spot in the house visible from outside was a light on in the men's parlor. What if there were security cameras at the doors or Bat

Suits lying in wait? I hated not knowing. That's what I should've asked when I was on the house tour. But you can't really ask that, can you? Excuse me, but is this historic landmark monitored by closed circuit TV?

"Maybe she gave them all the night off because of the gala," I said. "I wish your girlfriend was here."

"Or your brother. Totally unrelated, but why do you call your gramma 'BUH-bee'?"

"It's Yiddish for 'grandmother'." I turned to face him. "Is this a terrible idea? I don't think I have a fight-to-the-death in me tonight."

"What are we here to find out, and how badly do we need to know it?" Sensible Tully. "Here," he said. "Let's do a blessing."

We crouched under the sweeping evergreen boughs just off the path. Tully held out his hands. I took them.

"Now close your eyes." The top of my head, my crown chakra, started to tingle as our breath synched up. Tully had taught me about chakras, the energy centers in the body, when we were burying garlic packets to protect my house from vampires before I knew they were real. "Universal intelligence be with us," Tully said low and hushed.

Do not giggle, I told myself. Do. Not. Giggle.

"Show us what we need to know, guide our steps and actions toward the highest good for all involved. May we cause no harm, may we receive no harm. May our presence go unnoticed and may we be safe. May all sentient beings in this world find peace."

The top of my head buzzed as hot energy moved between Tully and me. My feet anchored strong into the earth. I opened my eyes. Tully was looking at me. He took his hands back.

"You did good not giggling."

"You're very generous to creatures who want to eat us."

"We don't really know that's what they want," he said.

"Who are you? Luke?" I thought back to Matilda's fangs in my throat at Third Rock Pancake House. I knew.

"Does it feel like a good idea to go in," asked Tully, "or should we call it?"

I felt the tingle in the top of my head. Fear had slowed and courage had filled in the gap.

"Let's go in."

I pulled my Star of David and made sure it hung on the outside of my sweatshirt. Tully was kitted out with stakes in his boots and his Dragon Slicer strapped to his back. I wondered if a smaller version would be a good weapon for me. I did not want to be Finder and fight hand to hand. At least a sword gave you a little distance from the monster you killed.

Sneaking around the back of the mansion, we left chalk crosses on the pavement and every few light posts. Our breath puffed out ahead of us. We circled the stately house checking for lights on in the windows, bats in the trees or any other signs that we were not the only ones here. Moonlight filtered down, glowing behind silvering clouds.

Moving shadow to shadow, tree to tree until we passed the side door steps, I led the way. We ducked through the shrubbery. Tully gave me a boost and I hauled myself over the porch rail wanting to avoid walking right up the steps. Pain shot down my legs. I stood for a moment on the other side waiting for the shock of fire to subside. The Southern Scotsman pulled himself up and over the rail like he did it every day.

"You okay?" he said.

I nodded. Pressing ourselves against the building to stay as out of the porch light as possible, we slid up to the mansion's side door. Inside, the gentleman's parlor would be on our far left and the welcome desk for tourists on our immediate right, by the stairs. I put my hand on the knob, took a breath and gave it a turn.

The door swung open.

"Is it a trap?" I whispered to Tully backing away from the opening. I flattened myself against the stone wall. "I expected it to be locked."

Tully gestured for me to stay. He slid past me and ducked inside the door.

"I think we're alone," he said.

"But why was the door unlocked?"

He shrugged. "Maybe they don't lock it. We didn't lock our house until a couple years ago."

That felt incomprehensible to me. Not locking your house? My entire childhood revolved around the string with my apartment key tied on it like a necklace.

Tully gestured for me to follow. I ran the step across the threshold and slid the door shut behind us. One globe light glowed on an antique sideboard, keeping the main hall visible. The only other light on was inside the men's parlor where the chess table was.

Up the stairs, small lamps were lit on either side of the Tiffany windows. I took out my flashlight.

We made quick work of hiding garlic packets under carpets, behind paintings, under furniture and anywhere else we could squirrel one away.

"Let's find where she keeps her blood," I said.

"We searched the kitchen before," he said, referring to the night of the kidnapping.

"But it was staged. And we never saw the ice room or wine cellar."

We made our way across the main hall and, lighting our way with flashlights, down the servant's stair and into the kitchen. The fridge held a paper bag with a sandwich in it, a few iced teas and some fruit. No blood. We shined our lights into the cabinets. Empty, like before.

The whole house felt sleepy and quiet, like what it was on the outside. An old house that had been turned into a museum.

We slipped down the hall to the ice room. That door had a padlock on it.

"I can try to pick it," Tully said.

"The fact that it's locked tells me enough," I said, unsure of how knowing where blood might be kept could help us. "I don't want to leave anything accidentally broken. Let's figure out if she actually lives here."

Tully followed me back upstairs. I passed the first floor and headed straight for the room I hoped would reveal the truth about where Matilda spent her days. The swan bedroom.

There were no lights on this level except the main stairwell lights illuminating the sides of the Tiffany windows at each landing. The swan bedroom lay on the left beside the bedroom given to Matilda's female companion. Her husband slept across the hall in his own manly chamber.

I peeked around the doorframe. The swan bedroom lay awash in shadows. Tully and I held very still, listening, just in case. Silence. Following the beam of my flashlight, I stepped fully into the room, then ducked under the valet ropes and stepped onto a deep blue rug. My eye went straight to the room's centerpiece. A full bed with a headboard the height of a person in the shape of a wall of feathers curving protectively over the head of the sleeper. The footboard, in the rounded shape of the swan's breast, came to a center point extending upward, neck and head floating gracefully above. Lying in the bed, it would look like you were sleeping on the back of the swan.

On my left stood a beautiful, antique armoire, all clean lines and art deco polish. I opened it. Empty. Crossing to the other side of the fireplace, I paused at a small dresser, each side of which had a carved swan to match the bed. Hoping for truths, I opened the dresser drawers. Also empty. Passing a standing mirror floating between two genuine narwhal tusks taller than me, I went to the bed. I ran my flashlight over the beautiful carving wishing I had the nerve to get in and lie down.

My flashlight caught a glint of metal at the far edge of the swan tail. I took a closer look. A bit of unpainted wood peeked out at the top.

"It's a fake," Tully whispered beside me. He tapped on it and the board moved enough to clearly show us the screws holding it to a fake, foam, swan headboard.

So if this was a facsimile of the swan bed, where was the original? No one could tell this was a fake because the room was blocked off in a way that only let you see it from one angle, like a set for a play. It looked real enough. Jill had gasped when she saw it. I had seen all of her fairy tale princess dreams flash before her eyes as she imagined herself crawling into that bed and floating away for a snooze.

Interesting as it was to explore Maymont's disallowed areas, I wasn't learning anything new here.

I turned off my flashlight and took one last look around the staged bedroom. Something caught my eye I hadn't noticed before. Inside the armoire door, a line of light crept up its wooden back. I nudged Tully. His eyes got wide.

We moved across the floor quiet as we could. The light from the hall lit the white swan furniture well enough that we didn't crash into it. But why was there a light behind the wall in the armoire? And why hadn't we noticed it before? Was it our eyes adjusting to the dim light? Or maybe, someone had just turned it on.

I stepped toward the closet and Tully caught my arm. He shook his head.

"It wouldn't be secret if she wasn't hiding something," I whispered, no small dose of urgency in my voice. "We may never get this chance again."

He touched his finger to his lips to shush me. He drew his blade and nodded toward the back of the armoire. He was ready. I traded my flashlight for one of the dinner plate-sized crosses I'd definitely not stolen from the garbage at St. Ig's the night of the kidnapping. I leaned into the armoire, putting my knee on the base. I ran my fingers along the smooth, polished back until they hit an object.

This wasn't the back of a closet. It was a door.

7.

November 21, continued.

I pulled the handle. The door opened. A narrow staircase wound around a wooden pole. Servant's stair? Over my shoulder to Tully, I raised my eyebrows. Ready? Tully nodded, yes. I turned my ear toward the staircase and listened so hard my heartbeat echoed in my head. I listened for bat wings, conversation, the movement of cloth, the scratch of a pen on paper, the turning of a page. Silence. I took a deep breath and climbed fully into the armoire. I placed one foot tentatively on the stairs. Not even a creak. These stairs were used and used often. There were no dips in the wood from decades of use, no give or shivers or weaknesses in any way. These stairs were . . . new. And carpeted with one little square on each step.

Dear God, please don't let us get caught now. And with that little prayer, I started down the steps. One story and I could tell we were behind the front hall. The second story we were at the kitchen level. One more and we were underground. The air was fresh and clean, a warm light illuminating the next stair. I stopped, listening with the intensity of my life depending on what I heard. I heard nothing. No paper, no cloth, no breathing. There was no door here. I could see a dark blue rug at the bottom of the stairs, but the next step would bring me into view of whomever or whatever occupied this room.

I leaned down and peeped around the stairwell wall into an exact replica of the bedroom we'd left upstairs. No one was here. I crept down the last few steps.

"This is the real bed!" I whispered. We stepped into the room. Light glowed from a Tiffany lamp on the bedside table that was probably worth as much as my dad's fancy new car. Heavy wood furniture glowed in polished, lived-in perfection. The house may be a museum, but this room was alive with use.

I blinked at a window overlooking daylight-infused Maymont. I caught Tully's arm.

"It's a painting," he breathed. We looked into the Maymont gardens in Spring, bright and welcoming, full of green and lush beds of early flowers. We stood together caught in the art's magic. Spring wasn't the only one. Four paintings, each occupying one of the four walls looked so realistic they could have been photographs. Summer had sun beating down on a carriage with horses, sun I could almost feel blazing onto my skin. Fall gave us the leaves around the mansion turning exquisite shades of russet and gold starting to carpet the ground. The last painting depicted a winter sunrise glowing over a canopy of snow. Each artwork was framed under paned glass to look like windows.

Over the dresser hung a paining of a beautiful gray horse, also realistic enough to be a photograph. Was this Matilda's horse? She had grown up before the era of cars. The dresser itself was a gallery of early black and white photographs. Frames of all shapes and sizes held the secret history of the Maymont family. One photograph caught my eye. It was of a teenaged girl on a swing, arms wrapped around another girl. One had blonde straight hair. The other, all curls with an infectious grin, had to be Matilda. Human Matilda, child Matilda. I smiled a little looking at it. It could be me and Meredith on the swings in Central Park.

I reached to open a dresser drawer.

"Don't touch anything!" Tully stopped my hand mid-reach. "What if she can smell you or sense your touch on things?"

"We've already touched a zillion things upstairs," I said. I was dying to open a drawer.

"But this is her bedroom."

I sighed. He had a point. Lots of people probably touched things upstairs, cleaners, tour guides, delivery people, sneaky tourists. But this was different. This, as far as we could tell, was Matilda's private space. Suddenly, I felt like an invader, like I was disturbing the peace in some kind of shrine. A shrine to the lady of blood. There was nothing crass or imperfect about it.

A large dressing room stood off to the left. I peeked in. Lavender, lavender everywhere. Dresses, gowns, shoes. Some white, some blue, no black. Mostly lavender and slightly darker violet. Interesting. I did not see one pair of pants, but maybe I wasn't looking in the right place. A floral scent floated in the air.

This room held nothing I'd expect, no wine glass rimmed with bloody lipstick, not even a laundry basket with bloody clothes. It was maybe the cleanest place I'd ever been.

"We should go," Tully whispered. "My spidey sense in tingling."

I followed him back up the stairs, the glitter of Matilda's private space dancing before my eyes.

"It was pretty uneventful," I told Steve later as I tucked him in. "We hid a lot of garlic and found what I think is- "

Footsteps behind us. Dad paused in the doorway to evaluate the path through Steve's variously assembled toy projects to get to the bed.

I climbed over to the other side of Steve as Dad sat down on the bed. My muppet brother snuggled under my arm as I leaned against the headboard.

"Teeth brushed?" Dad asked.

"Check," said Steve.

"Final potty break?"

"Check."

"No monsters under the bed?"

Steve looked at me. I leaned over to look under the bed.

"Check," I said.

It was the same routine Dad had done with me until Disaster Number One had pushed my mom over the edge. I was glad to know he did it with Steve. Dad picked up the copy of Treasure Island he and Steve were almost done with.

"Chapter twenty-one," he began.

I poured hot water though the French press, relaxed and cozy feeling from listening to Dad read to Steve. Bubbe sat at the table with her feet up on one of the chairs.

"Those are some special slippers," I said eyeing the pale grey fluff on her feet.

"Jill got them for me, along with this spectacular bathrobe," Bubbe said. "She wants me to feel at home here so she left more amenities than the Ritz Carlton in my room. Slippers, robe, shampoo, that decaf you're brewing, some fancy soap from a shop in Lennytown."

"Carytown," I said.

"Carytown, Lennytown, whatever. She's smart. She knows luring me out of the City is a project. But don't worry. I'll be back when the pool is open and she can do my nails, too."

I laughed out loud. The coffee sluiced as I pressed. The thought of Jill ever doing her own nails, much less someone else's struck me as both impossible and hilarious.

Bubbe's smile filled my heart like coffee was about to fill my cup. To the brim. She set her glasses and murder mystery down on the table and rubbed her eyes.

"How are you doing here, Shayna?" she said. "Really. I've been worried this place isn't working out for you so well."

I brought the press full of coffee to the table and set it down. I moved my donut from my usual seat to a chair closer to Bubbe. Considering how to answer, I reached for her mug and brought it next to mine.

"It was hard at first. Lonely. I missed you and Meredith. I kind of obsessed about getting home. I hatched this plan to emancipate and come live with you or Mer's family."

Obviously, I couldn't tell her the big events of the story. But there was one colossal, bizarre fact I could share.

"Oh my god! I didn't tell you this! Do you know who goes to my school? This is crazy!"

"Albert Einstein? Rock Hudson? I don't know, who?"

"Do you remember the kid who pushed us in the elevator at Nationals last year!"

"That creep? What is *he* doing in Virginia?" Her face puckered in distaste.

"He's from here!" I pressed and poured her coffee while telling her the whole story about him surprising me in the hallway and how I met Finder, and by the end she was laughing. "She was totally ready to pummel him," I said. "I guess I should be grateful he goes to St. Ig's because otherwise I might never have gotten to know Finder and Tully who have become bona fide friends. Knowing them has," I paused. "Been an education."

"I hope in a good way," Bubbe said.

"An eye-opening way, I guess." I wanted so bad to tell her, but like Jill, she'd be like, vampires are real? How about some therapy, honey. You miss the city more than you think.

Bubbe sipped her decaf and gave me her 'go on and tell me everything' look. How to describe being friends with Finder? It hadn't been the easiest start.

"Finder had something happen with her dad," I said. "Kind of the way I had something happen with mom. It's not easy for her to talk about and it left her with trust issues. She trusts me now, but it took some stuff happening to get there. She's very independent, you know? She nicknamed me Chess Team." I said.

"I approve," Bubbe said. "Speaking of which do you need me to move the pieces for your warm-ups? The thing is Friday, right?"

"You're staying to take me to my tournament?"

"Why do you think I came? Besides Jill's turkey which is the best on any planet anywhere. I certainly didn't come to spend time with *her* mother. Your first tournament as a National Master." She smiled and waved her jazz hands at me. "Wouldn't miss it for the world."

Thursday, November 22, 2001.

I was carrying the still heavy turkey pan into the kitchen when the phone rang.

"Stacy, it's for you," my dad called over the TV football game. Every Thanksgiving, he put the game on then sat in front of it and read a book, unless Meredith's dad was there.

Speaking of Meredith, who else would call me on Thanksgiving? Bubbe was already here. I set the pan on the counter by a pile of serving dishes I'd already cleared. Had her dad relented and let her end her grounding a few days early so we could talk today? Finder and Tully were each with their families so it wasn't likely to be one of them. It had to be Meredith! A smile crept onto my face. I stepped carefully over Steve and his empire-in-progress, so as not to jar my tailbone.

"No pre-dessert martini?" I asked Dad, eyeing his empty coaster.

"Only with Saul," he said. I raised my eyebrow. "It's a man thing." My jaw nearly dropped. He missed them. It was our first Thanksgiving without each other since I could remember and my dad was sitting in front of the TV missing his friend, too. I can't explain it, but I felt the tingle of a win.

My dad handed me the phone over his book.

"Did he let you off the hook early?" I said without even saying hello.

"What? Um, what?"

Oh. My god. Was she *kidding?*

"I was hoping you'd have some time to talk about our project," Judy said on the other end of the line. "Since there's no school."

"Judy, it's *Thanksgiving*. My whole family is here. I can't talk today."

In her background, a dog barked. A man shouted. Someone cursed and called Judy's name. She spoke quickly. "Our sample is back. I'd tell you the results over the phone but you need to, you know, *see* them. For yourself."

I was curious about the sample. Hmm. I said nothing.

"I'm at my mom's right now, but my dad is coming to get me. We could meet at his place maybe around 5:00?"

I said nothing.

Judy caved a little. Her voice got so quiet I strained to hear. "Maybe tomorrow, if you're busy today?"

"I have a tournament tomorrow."

The shouting behind Judy got louder, a man and a woman, arguing. Poor Judy. That was no way to spend a holiday. She was still talking. My name got my attention.

"Are you there, Stacy?"

"Yeah, I'm here."

"So you'll meet me at my dad's at five?"

No, I thought. No, I would not. Bubbe was here.

But *what had Judy found?* What was important enough in the sample that made her invite me over on Thanksgiving? In the background of Judy's call, something made of glass shattered.

"Gotta go," she said. A woman shrieked in rage.

"Judy, are you okay? It doesn't sound like you're safe." Why are you asking this? I thought. Why do you always have to help?

Judy told me her dad's address and directions in a hurry. "Just come after five," she said. "When you see these results, you'll understand why my idea can work. And win." The argument got louder. Another glass thing smashed.

"Judy, I can't- "

Judy hung up.

"What's wrong, Shayna?" Bubbe said as I walked into the kitchen. She had a glass in one hand, headed for the dishwasher. She turned off the sink faucet. "You lost all your color. Did you hit your butt? What do you need?"

I reached for a pad of paper and wrote down what Judy had told me. Then, I just stood for a second and leaned my hip against the counter. "Where're Jill and Gram?"

"Pool house. Getting the pies. What's going on?" She loaded the glass and dried her hands on a dishtowel.

"I think my science fair partner is . . . in trouble."

"She's pregnant?!"

"What? No!"

I explained what I heard on the phone and told Bubbe about Judy. How thin she was, how she didn't really eat, how she'd passed out in gym.

"I don't want to miss any of my time with you, so I told her no. But, should I go? I mean, who calls a school project partner on Thanksgiving?"

Someone who has something earth shattering to tell them, I thought.

"Am I ignoring a cry for help? I don't even think this girl wants to be my friend for real. She's all about the project. I don't owe her anything. Why do I feel like I should help her?"

"Oh sweetie," Bubbe said. "Because you're a good person. Because you do the right thing. Because you don't like to see other people suffer." She came over and wrapped her arms around me in a hug. "You have a big heart, Shayna. There is nothing wrong with wanting to help." She pulled back and looked into my face. "Do you want to go?"

"No." I had one precious weekend with Bubbe and I did not want to give any of it away to weird, whispering, won't-eat-anything Judy. "I mean, no I don't *want* to, but *should* I?"

"You have to go with your gut, Shayna. If your gut says do it, that's God asking you."

Gram entered carrying a stack of three pie boxes. "God asking her what?" she said. "Which pie is best?" A glittery headband topped Gram's wig. She gave me a big smile as Jill came up behind her with the other pies. "Ready for an amazing dessert?"

I sat on the toilet this time to rest my achey tailbone. I was using my serious inside voice. I didn't want Meredith to get caught sneaking a call because one of my parents heard us talking.

"Look, Woman, this girl is a freak. And don't let Bubbe goad you into doing what you don't want to do. We love her dearly, and, she was married to a rabbi. Of course she's gonna take the God road. What I want to know is what in the name of all that is holy was Luke stinkin' Whitehall doing with Matilda at a gala? That seems insane. And it makes my gut feel kinda wobbly, like something is wrong with a capital 'W'. Didn't she, like, try to eat him before?"

"She did. I have no idea. Nick said he would try to find out."

"Hmm. And I'm totally going on the internet to see if I can find pictures of the swan bedroom. That blows my mind. What are you going to do with that little secret?"

I didn't know yet. Data collection mode, on.

"New Year's is stressing me out," Mer said. "Don't take this the wrong way, and don't answer this right now, but if you step back and look at the offer objectively, why shouldn't Finder accept?"

I flashed right back to being pressed against the counter by a hungry Matilda at Third Rock. There were so many reasons. It wasn't something I was willing to explain over the phone.

"Maybe I should come visit for New Year's," Mer said. I started to interrupt her to tell her that was *not* a good idea, but she steamrollered me. "Listen, I gotta head home in a sec. My dad might give in and let me call you for real later."

"He might? Yay!" I was glad to drop the subject of vampires. "Where did you tell them you were going?"

"I didn't tell them anything! Mom sent me to deliver her cookies to the Mitzvah Corps doing the food pantry."

"Why are *you* not running the food pantry? That's your big hurrah."

"It was until the head of the philanthropy group moved away and *somebody* had to take over her spot so the little kids wouldn't try to raise money for candy!"

"Oh." Ouch. "Okay, well, tell me if you need help and I'll do what I can."

"Good grief! Just be where you are. I got this no prob. And totally changing the subject: Kiss? You would have told me already if he kissed you, right?"

"He's been gone all week!"

I could hear her shaking her head. "Okay, fine. I'll be patient, but seriously, I. Can. Not. Wait forever! If you get to sixteen without even a tiny snog, I'm going to have a crisis."

"I've been fifteen for two weeks. Gimme a chance!"

"I'll give you a chance if you give me a break. I need news of romance fulfilled! And I'll never speak to you again if he kisses you and you tell Finder first. As the person who pulled rocks out of your nostrils in kindergarten and personally fed you glue, Best

Friend is mine, mine, mine. My right and title for ever and ever. Make sure she knows that."

I laughed. I couldn't help it. "As you wish."

"Okay, good. 'Bye, Woman. Hopefully, I'll call you with permission later and we can toast our reunion with pie and Shirley Temples."

"Only if you can tie the stem into a knot with your tongue."

She sighed. "Okay, for real now. 'Bye."

Meredith had been trying for years to tie the Shirley Temple cherry stem into a knot with her tongue. It was the one thing, maybe the only weird personal thing, that I had done first besides the obvious (vampires). She had kissed already, worn a bikini already, broken up with a boyfriend already. I had done none of those things. If Matilda got her way, it was possible I never would do any of those things. I could however, tie the stem of a Shirley Temple cherry into a knot with my tongue. Not that that would help fight vampires. But you never know.

Thanksgiving, still.

Tully's truck rattled along the dirt road as the sunset glowed on the horizon. Dark, leafless tress silhouetted against pale pink and orange as we headed toward Judy's.

"I'm so full. I feel like I may never eat again," Finder said.

"Am I crazy," I said turning the newspaper page again in the falling dark, "or is she seriously not in this?"

"I'm not looking again," Finder said. "I know you said she was all over that red carpet, but like you asked, I read every word in the article this morning and neither her nor Luke are pictured or mentioned in any of the gala coverage."

"I looked, too," Tully said, "right after you called. My mom was about to use the paper for turkey drippings so I got it just in time."

"Are you absolutely sure it was him you saw?" Finder said, looking over her shoulder at me, squished into my usual jump seat.

"I would be shocked if it wasn't him," I said. "Twin brother maybe?"

"I'm not saying you're wrong. I just can't wrap my head around why, of all the righteous humans she could choose from, she would have Luke Whitehall as her plus one at a formal event. That makes zero sense."

"Agreed," Tully said. "It's so strange." The Southern Scotsman groaned and shifted in his seat. "Don't think there's any way I'm fitting in dessert when we get back."

My own belly bulged from multiple slices of pie.

"You have at least an hour to digest," Finder said to her boyfriend. "I'm sure you'll make room."

"Yeah," he sighed. "Fencing coach be damned. Besides, can't miss my annual chocolate bomb."

"What's a chocolate bomb?" Whatever it was, I wanted one.

"It's technically called a pot de creme," said Tully. "It's a chocolate custard thing baked in a little oven dish."

"Ramekin, you philistine," Finder said. "And it's not baked. It's steamed. You put all the filled ramekins in a tray of boiling water and put the whole thing in the oven." She looked over her shoulder at me. "You would die."

"That is how I want to go," I said, using the folded newspaper to shade my eyes from the sunset glare. "Drowned in chocolate. Like Veruca Salt or whichever one of them drowns in the chocolate river."

"I think it's Augustus Gloop," Tully said.

"Never read it," Finder said. "I'm more of a James and the Giant Peach girl myself."

"Do your families always do Thanksgiving together?" I asked, a smear of envy on my lips.

"Only dessert," Tully said. "Every family does dinner with their main people during the day, and then my mom indulges herself in making all these deserts that are too fancy for the rest of the year. Including the chocolate bombs. We'll invite your family next time. She does a serious spread."

"I bring cookies," Finder said, "but no one eats them."

"I eat them," Tully said. "All week after. Those jam print ones are my favorite cookies on earth."

"You make jam cookies?"

"Don't let her fool you," Tully said. "This woman can bake."

It's not like I was surprised Finder was good at something other than fighting, but jam cookies? They seemed kind of . . . delicate.

"After my dad vanished, people were like whoa, is he a drug dealer? Did somebody shoot your dad and hide his body? I was like, no he's a brilliant financial manager stolen by vampires, but, nobody's gonna listen to that. So, I stuck it out through the end of the school year since taking me out would've made the rumors worse. To get my mind off it, everyday after school my mom and I baked."

"What about her job? I thought she worked."

"She changed her hours. I was in public school and my cousin Christopher lived with us. He went to the high school. Mama was afraid I'd get snatched, too, this was before we knew about the vampire part, so she made Christopher drive me and wait until he saw me go inside the building. He picked me up at three, took me home and then went back to his school for football. Why am I talking about this again?"

"'Cuz I asked. But what about your dojo?"

"Where do you think I took all the stuff I baked? My class didn't start until 6:00, so it was a perfect way to dispose of it all."

"And she saved some for me."

"Yes, yes I did." Finder reached over and patted Tully's thigh. "Tully came to my dojo way back when," she said. "He was a sweet little tub of Scottish jam. All squishy around the middle." She poked his stomach with her finger.

"Hey." He batted her hand away.

"I fixed that for him, of course," she said.

"Your dad fixed it," Tully corrected. "You fed me snickerdoodles and pound cake. Mr. Jackson was on a quest to get me into competitions, especially jiu-jitsu, because I was big and could wrestle."

"But soft-hearted Teularen just didn't have the wee mean streak it takes to compete in jiu-jitsu." Finder touched his cheek. "He was too kind."

"I'm not kind," he said.

"You are the most kind," I said from the back.

"See?" Finder said. "Listen to Chess Team. She knows what's up." This was fascinating. I waited for the story to continue.

"Tully's family lived in the Fan, which as you know is far from Flying Eagle, so he came home with me after class and we'd do homework and play until his dad picked him up. Tully's dad was the one who got me started on the path to St. Ig's."

"And failing miserably at Flying Eagle is how I got started fencing. Martial arts weren't so much for me."

"So how does all this relate to the cookies?"

"It was a long three hours between school and practice. Tully had already moved on to fencing by the time my dad disappeared. Practice made me depressed because martial arts was always what I did with my dad. He was an original partner in Flying Eagle. He and my mom met learning martial arts when they both lived in Japan."

"She was a fighter, too? What were they doing in Japan?" I was sitting forward now, leaning between the front seats.

"Is this the turn?" Tully asked, glare from the last strip of sun in his eyes. He slowed the truck as we approached what looked like a national park sign.

Finder looked at the directions.

"Mattaponi Indian Reservation?" I read off the sign. "This can't be it."

"Right at red sign," Finder said, reading my notes. "Maybe rez sign?"

"Has to be," Tully said. "Approximate drive time, 45 minutes, and that's about how long we've been going."

"Looks like a whole lotta nothing up ahead," Finder added.

"But why would Judy live on an Indian Reservation?" I asked.

"Are you kidding?" Finder said as Tully turned right onto a small paved road. "Stacy, duh!"

"Duh what?" I asked. "Judy isn't Native American."

Finder face palmed. "Do you seriously have no human observation skills whatsoever? No wonder you thought Nick was a vampire."

Could there be albino Native Americans? I had never thought about it. And her last name was Forest, not Eagle Feather or something that screamed Native American. Sitting back in my seat, I pictured Judy in my head, coloring in her white-blonde hair, eyebrows and skin in various shades of tea and black. Holy cow. How had I never seen it? No wonder she didn't care about Thanksgiving.

"First right should be Cloud Walker Way," Finder said, referring again to my written directions. "If it's not, we're in the wrong place." She scrunched up her face. "What does this say?"

I leaned up and peered over her shoulder. She pointed to the last line on my directions. Riv, 2 fr.

"It means if we get to the river, we've gone too far."

"Remind me not to borrow your notes," Finder said. "I'd fail a test if I studied from you."

"Ah ha! Cloud Walker Way," I said, pointing up ahead. Tully turned right, left and right again onto a one lane road lined with tall, coniferous trees. They grew close together, tight to the road in a way that made my skin prickle.

"I just want to say out loud that if we come to a white or gray house with wind chimes and a pickup truck parked outside, I am *not* going in. I am not dying a horror movie death out here in the middle of nowhere."

"Relax. It's just forest," Finder said.

"It looks like a horror movie."

"It looks like a *forest*," Finder said. We drove for a few minutes in silence, trees so thick on either side of the road I couldn't see ten feet in. Another small, park-looking sign came up on our right.

Mattaponi Burial Ground .8 mi.

"See?" I said, a little too loud. "Horror movie!"

"It's a reservation, Stacy. That sign's as normal as a 'gift shop' sign at a museum."

Five minutes later, a white mailbox marked a single driveway leading back into the trees. Judy lived here?

This was maybe the most remote place I had ever been. After about ten more blocks worth of gravel drive, we saw the house. A new-looking gray house sat at the rear of a clearing. Two raised boxes, each the size of a full city parking space, sat inside a tall, mesh fence. Wind chimes hung from the porch and a blue pickup sat in the driveway. Through the trees behind the house, a river ran fast and wide.

"I'm not getting out," I said.

Finder rolled her eyes. The front door opened and Judy, looking almost colored in against the neutral house siding, waved for us to come in.

The inside of the house was clean and very modern. Sitting at the kitchen island with a bottle of wine, a pair of glasses, and an uncut pie between them, were two clean-cut men in jeans and flannels. The one on the left with dark hair, broad, open features and skin the color of strong iced tea stood and welcomed us.

"I'm Judy's dad," he said, "John Forest Stalker and this is my partner," he said indicating the other man, "Dr. Julian Windworth."

Judy shortened her last name! Native American after all. Looking at her next to her dad, I totally saw it.

"First names here, please," Julian said, shaking hands with us. "Julian and John is good with us." Julian smiled at Tully, who had turned an odd shade of pink. "And yes," Julian said, running thin fingers through short, light hair. "So you don't have to wonder, we are that kind of partners."

Tully actually sputtered. "I um — I wasn't — um. It's none of my — um. I wasn't going to ask."

"Of course you weren't," Julian said. "You're a well brought up, Catholic school student with genuinely straight parents and probably a boatload of siblings, correct?"

Tully shifted his weight. "Yes, sir."

"So you'd never ask, but your eyes went the size of saucers when you walked in here and I bet it wasn't because you know the age of my grandmother's rocking chair."

A slender antique rocker sat inside the corner entrance of the living room. The recessed lights were dimmed, a cheerful fire burned in the wood stove and the TV glowed with crossfading scenes of natural landmarks.

Julian poured himself a glass of wine. He let it sit on the counter as he picked up a file folder. "Which one of you is the science fair partner?"

I held up my hand.

Julian pulled out a chair at a round kitchen table tucked into a bay window overlooking the parking-space boxes in the front yard. He gestured for us to sit.

"It's our garden," Julian said following my gaze. "That green patch is winter kale, the last of our produce for this year. Those vines," he pointed to a dirt pile with some vines growing out of it, "gave us the pumpkin in John's pie, plus the one on the front porch."

"You grew pumpkins?" I said. "In your own garden? That's amazing." I knew of course that somebody had to grow pumpkins, but the thought of a person I knew doing it boggled my mind. Plant lovers at home grew micro greens, not squashes bigger than their heads.

Julian opened the file folder as Judy's dad set a tray with dessert plates, forks and napkins in the center of the table.

"We don't celebrate Thanksgiving," he said, "but any excuse to share a pie is a good enough reason to make one." He placed his homemade pie, cut into six equal wedges, on the table and began serving. Oh no. More food.

I watched Judy out of the corner of my eye as I ate the best pumpkin pie I'd ever put in my mouth, sweet yet robust. The crust melted in my mouth.

Judy regarded her pie with determination. She put a cautious forkful into her mouth. She chewed and swallowed, but it looked painful, like it took effort. Tully nudged me under the table. Julian was asking me a question.

"Sorry, what?" I said.

Julian moved his plate aside and pointed to a chart in the lab results. I looked at the first sheet of tables and numbers. I'd seen charts like this in my science camp last summer. I let my mind reach back for how to interpret what stared up at me from the page.

"This DNA sample comes from a person who- "

"It's mine," Judy interrupted. "The DNA swab is mine."

Julian stared at her in astonishment. She got up and came to stand between us. She pointed at the first chart of results.

"Do you see how these lines dip down? That's the dominant gene of my albinism. This here," she pointed to a blip in the line, "is an abnormality. It indicates an incorrect nucleotide binding to a healthy DNA strand. It's why my eyes are so light sensitive. It's that specific nucleotide."

I started to see how to read the charts. Judy turned the page.

"This one here," she pointed to a line graph, "shows the number of incorrect nucleotides in a specific strand."

"It's over a thousand," I said. "That can't be correct."

Judy pinned me with her gaze. "It is."

She sat back down in her spot. Her food was untouched except for the one tiny bite.

"I have an unusual . . . condition," she said, "besides albinism."

An unreasonable fear grabbed me. I'd been skimming the Meredith vampire library stack. Some could go out in daylight. They didn't eat, they were horribly thin and pale. I gripped my thighs under the table. Breath stuck in my throat.

8.

Thanksgiving, continued.

"It's a . . . very painful condition," Judy went on, "and the only way I can repress it is to keep my body weight very low. So I try not to eat. I know everyone at school thinks I'm anorexic, and I guess I am, but it's not what anyone thinks. Look at the next page."

I tuned the page. Judy pressed her lips together and closed her eyes. When she opened them, her eyes were wet.

Julian came to the rescue.

"This column indicates which observed strands are active and functioning. That's what the yellow dots mean." Every item had a yellow dot. "This column is the nucleotide monitor. Green dots mean healthy. Red dots mean incorrect nucleotides are attached."

Every strand had a red dot. Every. Single. One.

"Holy righteous Moly," Finder said. "What's the condition?"

John and Julian exchanged a look.

"I'd rather not say," Judy said. "It's rare, it's genetic, it's painful. And it can . . . shorten your life."

Hmm. Not a vampire. Interesting.

"The average life span of a person with it is only fifty years."

"There's been no research done on the condition because it's so rare," said Judy's dad. "Judy was so grateful to get you as her partner, Stacy, because she thinks if anyone can figure out how to reverse the nucleotide attachment Julian thinks is the cause, it's you."

I sat stunned. Me? Were they kidding?

"My initial hypothesis," said Julian, "was that too many incorrect nucleotides were bonding to a single strand and causing the genes to shift or mutate. I tested this with seven affected subjects and had almost identical results each time. All seven, all with the condition, had the same misplaced chemical bonds on their DNA."

"What were the results?" I asked.

"No change."

Everyone was looking at me. I sat, said nothing. Processing what I'd heard. Finally, I spoke.

"And you think I can solve this? In the context of a high school science fair project?"

"Why not?" said Julian. "I've been trying, but I can't get the right combination of conditions. You might be able to think about it in a new way and unlock the secret."

"If it's even possible," said John. "Which I suspect it's not."

"I can give you access to the lab at VCU," said Julian. "We have a nuclear MRI for separating and viewing strands."

"That I could use?" I asked.

"That you could use."

"Told you," said Judy.

I admit, I salivated. Free rein in a University lab? Yum.

"You said it was genetic," I said to Judy's dad. "Do you have it, too?"

John paused. He swirled the wine in his glass. Deciding. Deciding to tell me? Or deciding to tell me the truth?

"Yes," he said.

But he was the physical opposite of his daughter, healthy and vibrant. And he wasn't albino.

"So I could compare your DNA?"

"I suppose."

I looked at Julian. "At your lab?"

"Yes."

"Is the condition painful for you?" I asked John.

"When I was young," he said, "but not now. I've learned to manage it. I've . . . surrendered to it in some ways."

I turned back to Judy. "So then is the research really necessary or do you just need whatever pain management techniques your dad uses?"

Judy's eyes were full of tears. "It doesn't work for me the way it works for him. Please, Stacy. I want this to go away. I want to live a normal life. I need your help." A single tear trickled down her tissue paper cheek. Blue veins stood out beneath.

Say no, I told myself. These people need professionals. Do it. Say no.

"A map would have to be made of each of your DNA to separate out obvious differences like gender and albinism."

I was not doing this, was I?

"Then the incorrect nucleotides' placement would need to be analyzed for commonalities."

What about my vampire project? What about beating Matilda?

"After that, we'd wing it until we have a hypothesis that seems feasible."

Ugh. Why me? *Why* did I always have to *help*? I looked at Finder. "Maybe you and Michelle could do the apoptosis project? Those dead cells won't come back to life on their own."

Friday, November 23, 2001.

I lay on my back, staring at the banquet hall ceiling. Flowers on the trim, or ladies dancing? My head rested on Bubbe's thigh as she knitted some fuzzy thing piled onto her other leg. I'd pushed a row of chairs together to make my makeshift couch. Not super comfy, but better than one more minute on my donut where I'd sat, off and on, mostly on, for the last six-and-a-half hours. I was four for four so far and the fifth and final pairings hadn't been announced. I closed my eyes and took a long breath. The magic thing about chess is that when you're playing, there's no room in your mind for anything else. It's like trying not to slip when you're walking on ice. Your body and brain are both so busy concentrating that if you start thinking about what kind of coffee you're risking your life on the ice to go get, you will fall right on your butt. I was anxious to get back to the board.

I hadn't slept well last night, maybe because I ate so much, but maybe because Judy was relying on me to solve a life-or-death health problem for her with a science fair project I stupidly let her and her parents rope me into. The Matilda confrontation was one day closer, I had zero ideas about what to do, and I had no confidence whatsoever that Matilda or Darcy Jackson were going to leave us alone until then. There was also a constant buzz in the back of my mind that sooner or later the Man with No Face might resurface.

And not gonna lie, Jill's mom was also kind of a lot. Gram forced Jill's hand a lot; dictating when we ate, when we went out, what we did when we went out, even down to which toys she wanted Steve to play with. She was sweet in her heart and meant well, but it was hard to have her stay with us because she had to control everything down to the most minute detail. She had insisted I wear dress shoes today, for example. She thought they looked chess-ier. Bubbe had stuck my sneakers in her bag and I changed in the car. And yesterday, every one of us had to try every single pie she bought at this swanky bakery in Richmond (three) plus the one she spent Thanksgiving morning making and the two she brought from her favorite bakery in Florida. Six pies. That's one. Entire pie. Per person. Can you say digestive distress? At least the toilet was the one place I could comfortably sit.

Behind me, Joseph Thornton's over zealous laughter polluted the din of chatting. One of his cronies had probably farted. I hated

Joseph Thornton as much as I hated waiting for vampires to show up unexpectedly and jump me. I think every person on the island of Manhattan on 9/11 got a PTSD bully trigger installed in their brain that day, and I was no exception. Joseph Thornton pushed that trigger for me big time. When someone tried to step in and destroy or take control of something I perceived as mine or ours in a collective way, literal hairs rose on my arms. Joseph's laugh gave me this same reaction. My arm hairs prickled. And then, as if his foul laugh had summoned her, Mrs. Bason entered the skittles room like a cold breeze.

Bubbe must've felt me tense, because her needles stopped clicking and she said low enough so only I heard, "Shayna? You okay?" Everyone else in the room hushed.

"Will all the members of the St. Ignatius College Preparatory Academy Team come to me, please?" Mrs. Bason (pronounced Bay-SAW) drawled in her thick Virginia accent. I rolled onto my side and swung my legs over my chairs.

I gave Bubbe a little smile, fighting off an odd dread in my belly. I stood, stretched, and went to stand with the ancient crone. Her shriveled face floated above the pale scarf she always wore tied in a knot at her throat. Joseph came and stood right next to me.

"Hello, *friend,*" he said smiling down at me. Ugh.

"Not your friend."

"What if I want to be your friend?" he said. Those tiny, tiny teeth. As if the neck beard wasn't enough.

"Eat dirt, Thornton."

"Mmm. I *love* dirt. Especially if it gets me *dirty.*"

Mrs. Bason cleared her throat. Her gaze landed squarely, darkly on me. Anger twittered on the edge of my mouth as I ignored Joseph. I would not let her blame me for him being out of line.

Stockings loose around her ankles, Mrs. Bason led the twelve of us out of the skittles room where everyone played Blitz or Bughouse and ate snacks between games.

"Ms. Goldman, Mr. Thornton," she said, closing the door to our team's tiny closet of a prep room. "You are currently stacked as the two players to beat in this final round. You are matched against the two top rated seniors from East Richmond High School. Neither you nor your opponents have lost or drawn a game today. You will be the four top placers in the tournament, but that does not guarantee a team win. The rest of you need to win or draw your games. You each have at least one or more losses. You will be playing other students with similar ratings and loss streaks. Please do your best. We can only win as a team if the rest of you stop relying on Mr. Thornton to collect your wins. Get this last one for yourselves."

Mr. Thornton to collect the wins? Mr. Thornton? Bah. She had left me out on purpose. The fact was, I had won each of my games with more points than Joseph and as a 2200 rated National Master, only one other player at this tournament could match me. Daniel Lee Williams, known to the chess community as Hank. He was my height, my age, Asian, had the guts to have nicknamed himself because Dan means something in Chinese he didn't like. He was also a National Master. He was graduating high school early to go to MIT for engineering. We'd played each other lots of times at Nationals. The outcome was a toss-up every time and the most fun I'd have all day.

Bradly Joe Rifkin came up beside me after Mrs. Bason released us. I checked my watch. Ten minutes until the ballroom doors opened.

"Looks like you get to play Hank, Stay-cee," he said. "You know he's homeschooled."

"I know."

I started walking toward the ladies' room. I turned, paranoid, to make sure Joseph wasn't following me. He was not. Rifkin was on my heels.

Jill had told me Bradley's mother had paid for all our team's new clocks and boards at the beginning of the school year to make sure Mrs. Bason didn't kick him out. It was hard for me to imagine the skulking old howler indebted to anyone, but whatever. Mrs. Rifkin wanted her baby to have a chess credit for his college applications, and a chess credit he would have.

We arrived at the bathroom.

"Good luck with your game," I said. I started to push open the door, but then I had a thought. "Just use the Lawn Mower," I said over my shoulder. He blinked at me. "Keep your rooks and queen from getting captured and use them to bulldoze the King at the end, like I showed you. You might just win."

After washing my hands, I headed down the hall and back toward the ballroom.

"Stacy!" A cheerful voice behind me. Hank, whose hair had grown long enough to touch his shoulders, came bopping up beside me. He hugged me and I hugged him back.

"We get to play! I'm so excited!" he said, blowing a foof of hair out of his eyes.

"Me too! You're the only person today who is going to give me a real game."

"Thank you oh honored National Master," he said faking an Asian accent he did not really have.

I giggled. "I should say the same to you!"

"You gotta come to my chess camp next summer," he said. "All the coaches are IMs or GMs and they just wipe the floor with me every time. Now, how are you here? Did you move or something?"

We spent the next few minutes catching up and then went to our table. He would play white. That meant he'd gotten more points than I had over the tournament today. I wondered how many.

"One," he said like he was reading my mind. "I'm one point ahead of you." He pressed his lips together. "I feel like I should offer you white to be polite," he said. "As a welcome gift to my sweet city, but I think I'd get in trouble."

I smiled. "You would. And it's not like this tournament matters except to our personal ratings."

"Oh but the schools are so happy when they win," he said. I followed his gaze to Joseph. "What's Thug Cheater Thornton doing here?"

I filled Hank in on Joseph having moved back to Richmond over the summer to play for St.Ig's. As we sat, Hank whispered to me, "I registered a complaint against him at last Nationals." My ears perked up. Oh, had he now? Perhaps for the same reason as me? "He tried to bribe me to throw the game. He threatened to beat me up." My jaw dropped. Hank put his fake Asian accent back on. "But you know we Asian have special martial arts skill and I tell him fork off or I squash his nuts like berries." I laughed out loud.

The proctor called for quiet. I unbuckled my watch and pocketed it, breathing slow to stop my fit of giggles. I composed myself enough to look up, see my friend's wry, trickster grin and snort out one final giggle as I hit his clock to start our game.

"Sneaky and vicious, Stacy Goldman! That's my girl!" Hank said as we shook hands.

"You're amazing!" I said. That had been a major workout. I pulled my shirt from where it stuck damply to my back and armpits.

"Look at this whole section!" Hank came around the table and stood next to me as we waited for the proctor to come and finalize our mate. My mate. At move twenty-two, Hank had started this brilliant bishop attack, and I mean brilliant. He'd used his knights and pawn to control the center and then slipped his bishops out to pin both my rooks and make it difficult for me to capture any material. There was not one capture until move twenty-six! It was a tight game, claustrophobic and unbelievably hard to maneuver.

"You hate to capture early in the game," he said, "I remembered that from before, so I looked for an attack that would trap you in ways that made it impossible for you to capture so I could force you to use your own pieces to hang yourself."

"It was amazing," I said. "You really should have won after that."

"Except I got greedy here." He pointed to move forty-three. RxBg3. I had lost a Bishop, but by capturing, Hank inadvertently opened the lines for my queen three moves later. He raced to recover his position, but once I'd gotten the advantage, I kept it and carried it through to a win. I wished I could get an advantage with vampires as easily as I could in chess.

The proctor okayed our mate and we sat back down, setting up the board as it had been for move 43. Hank worked from his notes and me from mine.

"What I should have done was this." He moved his queen two squares instead.

"Yes! That would have forced my move here," I moved my own queen back a space to defend the rook Hank's queen attacked.

"Right! Because without that defense, I could come right though here and have mate in," he paused, counting how may moves until he'd have checkmate, "eight."

I stared for a minute going through the next several move options in my head. "I don't see it."

We played out the next three moves which we both agreed on and then I saw it. Yes, he would absolutely have beaten me. A nice, clean, smothered mate, like he'd set up earlier in the game.

"Wow," I said as we got up. "If that's what you got from chess camp, I'm totally coming next year."

"You really should. When was the last time you lost?"

"You mean other than one second ago in the replay that should have been our game?"

"Yeah. When was your last real bona fide loss?"

"Not to the computer?"

"Not to the computer. To a person."

I had to think about that. Hank opened the ballroom door and held it for me.

"I don't remember. Probably in chess club at home."

"Do you want to know how many games I won at camp?"

We stopped at the water fountain. "Sure."

"Two."

I pursed my lips. "How many days?"

"Ten."

"How many games per day?"

"Five or six."

"And you only won *two*? That's impossible."

"Nope. I won my first game against the other ranked kid in the camp and after that, they only let me play the instructors. Two weeks of IMs and GMs! I fell asleep every night with all their moves swirling in this mess of oblivion in my mind. It was like I couldn't even make sense of the strategy it was so advanced. I only won one other game, and it was when the IM played the whole camp in a simul."

IM in chess stands for International Master. IM rating is over 3500 which means you're not just really good, you're really super mega good.

"Do you want to be an IM?" I asked.

Hank thought for a minute. "Dunno," he said sticking his hands in his jeans pockets. "They seem kinda obsessed. I think I want a life outside of chess. Not that I want to stop playing."

"Me, too," I said. "I'm tempted to go for it though just to make the girls-can-be-IMs point though, you know? It makes me mad that people always refer to any IM whose name they don't know as 'he'."

"Totally grok," Hank said.

"Grok?"

Hank took my shoulders in his hands and turned me to face him. "What?? Are you kidding? You haven't read *Stranger in A Strange Land?* It's Heinlien. You. Must. Read. It." He let go of my shoulders and tucked his hair behind his ears. "Grok is a word Heinlien made up that means understand, but, like, on a deep level. Like deep in your bones understanding. You can grok a thing, like chess or you can grok a person, meaning that you really *get* each other. I think you and I grok each other."

"Grokking," I said. "When your hand moves to touch a piece before you've even quite decided it's the one?"

"Kind of. It's a little more otherworldly. Like when you understand something before you intellectually know you understand it."

"You have to grok to play a simul."

"Yes! At least if you want to win. Have you ever done one? They're so fun."

I'd only played a simul once. Rabbi Berman had set up our classroom tables in a square and put out eight boards. I stood on the inside of the square and played white in every game. I walked around from board to board while my teammates sat at their boards on the outside. Nobody spoke. They all tried to beat me. One of them did. Still, I felt good about it. Seven wins at once! It was like my body didn't even exist. There was only my mind, my thoughts and chess. Glorious.

"I didn't want to be rude before, but what's that?" The donut. I gave him the regular person's explanation.

A balding man with a thick, grey beard announced the winners. I placed first, Hank placed second, Joseph placed fourth and the other kid from East Richmond High placed third. Joseph lost his final round despite Mrs. Bason's warnings. St. Ig's placed third in team wins because our lower ranked players won fewer games with fewer points that East Richmond. We needed two out of three tournaments to go on to teams at state level then a state win to go to nationals.

I needed to up my game. I might not get lucky and beat Hank twice.

He and his mom caught up with Bubbe and me as we were leaving. The adults introduced and Hank handed me a piece of paper. "It's my phone number and email," he said. "If you email. Maybe we could, you know. Meet up. And play."

"Yes!" I said before thinking about it. A real chess friend!

His face lit up. "Great! I can't next weekend, but maybe one afternoon when you're done with school. I have a flexible schedule being all independently educated." He said the last bit with flourish.

"That boy likes you, Shayna," Bubbe said with a twinkle as we headed into the elevator. I checked my back before we got in, but we were the only ones waiting.

"I like him, too. We've played each other at Nationals for years. Sometimes he wins, sometimes I do. We're very evenly matched."

"Oh, I think he's interested in more than chess. His mother said he grinned ear to ear the minute he saw you. But you know. He's not really someone you could date for very long."

"Date? No. That's not how I like him, Bubbe. Not at all."

"Good," she said, unlocking the car.

"We just wanna play chess. We're chess friends."

She loaded her knitting bag into the back seat. "Make sure he knows that. He seems very sweet and you don't want to hurt his feelings. But he wouldn't be a good boyfriend."

What was she talking about? Hank was sweet and considerate and polite and a freaking genius. And he was cute. He'd make a great boyfriend. If I liked him that way, which I didn't.

"It's too bad I don't like him that way," I said, thinking of Nick. "I think Hank would make a great boyfriend." We got in and she shut her door.

"Absolutely not. What if you fell in love and wanted to marry him? It's not possible."

"Why? Because he's Asian? Because he's adopted?" She started the car, shaking her head. She looked at me and said dead serious, "Because he's not Jewish."

November 23, continued.

"Ow!"

Steve's fingernails dug into the back of my hand.

"Sorry," he said, but didn't let go.

"What's the matter?"

Steve clutched Monster with one small fist and me with the other, looking left across the street and right into the trees as we walked across the parking lot.

"Nothing." He shivered inside his forest green puffy coat.

"Are you scared to meet a bunch of new people?" Steve got jittery when it came to that sometimes. Cold wind whipped my skirt around my thighs. Why did Meredith's hand-me-downs have to be so short? Didn't she know it got cold in Virginia?

Ahead of me and Steve, dressed up for Friday night Shabbat, walked Bubbe, Gram, Jill and my dad. We came around the corner and stepped onto the Temple sidewalk. The Temple Beth Shamar was brightly lit with blue and white spotlights on a new-looking, sandstone colored building. It had wide glass doors in front, and a bunch of Hebrew words I couldn't read engraved into the side of the building and like a banner around the top. In front of the doors stood two armed guys in security guard uniforms.

"What the hell is this?" said Gram, eyeing the security guards. "Are we criminals now for going to temple?"

"They're to protect you, not arrest you, Sharon. Everyone has them after what happened," Bubbe said referring to 9/11. "Leo Oppenheim, remember him Jill, the tall guy with eight kids? He owns a security company and donated two pairs of his guys to us. They rotate weekends."

"You make it sound like you own them," Gram said to Bubbe, tucking her bright red lipstick back in her purse. "I hope you pay them, at least."

Steve squeezed my hand. I raised my eyebrows in reply. Right? I thought. Ouch. But Steve was looking elsewhere.

I followed his gaze to a black sedan parked across the street. I froze, gripping Steve's hand too tight.

"Ow. Leggo. Let go, Stacy!" I released a little. I did not let go. I pushed Steve slightly behind me, so that I stood between my family and the vampire leaning against the shiny car.

9.

November 23, continued.

Darcy Jackson waggled his fingers at me. Hello. Then he made a V with his first two fingers and pointed them at his eyes, then at me. I see you.

You see me, I thought. What does that mean? You see me what? What did Darcy Jackson expect? Me to just pop over for a chat?

He raised his eyebrows and put up one finger waggling it back and forth. No-no. He shook his head. You've been naughty.

Did he know about the holy water? Had he seen us?

Darcy Jackson pointed to the sign on the corner, feet from where he was parked. A big, red, octagon. STOP.

I almost rolled my eyes at the obviousness of it.

Good grief. Message received.

I must've been squeezing harder than I thought.

Steve wriggled to get me to let go.

"Quit it!" I said under my breath. I had to make a decision, tell Steve or not. Tell or not. Crap. "Steve," I said, turning my back to Finder's dad, still pointing at the stop sign. "There is a- "

"I smell it," he said. He wrinkled his nose and stopped struggling. He bit his lip. "Is it that man staring at you? Will he follow us inside?"

"Yes. And no." I hoped I wasn't lying.

"Does it know you?"

I nodded again.

"Never ever look them in the eyes," I said. "Wherever they are."

"How did it know we'd be here?"

"Shayna? Everything okay?" Bubbe eyed me with her darn grandmother perception.

I smiled. "Yup. Fine."

She raised an eyebrow. Doubtful.

On the one hand, having a smart gramma is a great thing. On the other hand, not so much. I took a breath, thought about what a great Bubbe she was, and met her gaze. I thought, I am alive, I am safe. Nothing bad is happening.

She held my look and then relaxed. She reached out a hand to help Gram onto the curb.

"I'm fine," said Gram, refusing the help.

"I just thought I'd help in case those heels put you off balance," Bubbe said. "They're so high."

Gram shot Bubbe a look that echoed the one I wanted to shoot at Darcy Jackson, hard and pointy.

I took one more look over my shoulder at the car. The windows were tinted. Was Matilda inside? I did not like Darcy Jackson scoping out my family. We were going out to dinner after this. Would he follow us? Would he attack? Were there other Bat Suits around? Was Finder okay? Why, why, had I left my phone at home?

Steve's question hung in his eyes. How did Darcy Jackson know to find us here? I shrugged, a tiny shoulder lift. I didn't know how he knew. A swirl of questions went round in my own mind. Questions about being followed, or having our phones tapped, or bats spying on us. Clutching my little brother's hand like a stake, I followed my family inside. Gripping my hand just as tight, Steve turned more than once to peek over his shoulder.

I would like to report that we had a peaceful service, that I was able to listen and enjoy the music, the happy shabbat vibe, and just the warm, spicy smell of the synagogue sanctuary, but that would be untrue. I worried as I looked up and saw the sanctuary roof was partly upright glass. It was like a solid octagon lid with glass sides that sat on the roof of the temple. It was beautiful. It was not secure. Bats could sit on that roof and look through the sides to see us inside. I sat on my donut between Bubbe and Steve. Gram sat on Steve's other side. Dad and Jill were bookends, each sitting next to their mom. I resisted a thousand urges to look over my shoulder and to stare up. Could Darcy Jackson come in here? What about Matilda? What did they want with me now, tonight? Had Matilda changed the rules again? Had they gone against her promise and kidnapped Finder? Was she safe? Were we? The front of my mind registered a few things, the service seemed very liberal, some people wore jeans and sweaters. The rabbi was a woman with short dark hair and there were banners hung around the sanctuary welcoming people of all diversities.

Steve was not as good at impulse control as I was. He looked over his shoulder and up multiple times during the service and leaned up to whisper in my ear.

"It smells bad, Stacy. Really bad. Like *bad* bad. Are they going to eat us? What do they want?" Jill reached a hand over to shush him. I made my face look as reassuring as possible while doing my best to catch a whiff of what he smelled. Frankincense, myrrh. Nothing bad, and definitely nothing *bad* bad. We were alive, we were safe. Nothing bad was happening.

Something thumped against the glass lid. I looked up. A couple other members of the congregation also looked up. Nothing.

You are so paranoid, Goldman, I told myself. He probably just smells the lady behind us's cologne. And then again, thump. Small, like a ball of socks hitting the glass. Then two. Thump, thump. And then a rain: thump thump thump thump thump.

Even the cantor had started staring at the roof. The rabbi and she exchanged a look. What was going on?

Oh no. This wasn't a message for them. It was a message for me. A big, public message.

But what was she trying to say? We got to one of the standing portions of the service. As we followed the leaders, moving in a way that looked suspiciously like the hokey-pokey, I whispered to Steve.

"Be right back." I was so quiet even Jill missed it. Steve gripped my hand. I pulled his fingers off one by one. I was tempted to lie, to tell him I was just going to the bathroom, but Steve was one of us now. He deserved the truth. "It's okay," I whispered. "I'm armed." Not a lie. I had my Star of David necklace on. It wasn't much, but it had saved my life last Thursday. It would have to do. I scooted past Bubbe and my dad, mouthing the word "bathroom" as the tiny gold star weighed just beneath my collar. I hoped I wouldn't need it.

Thump, thump, thump, thump, thump against the stained glass roof. One of the security guards, after a look to the rabbi, turned and left the sanctuary, closing the door without a sound. I slipped out behind him.

"Stay in the sanctuary, Miss," said a guard as I emerged into the hallway.

"I have to go to the bathroom," I did my best to shrink into myself, to make him think I was eleven or twelve rather than fifteen.

Both guards at the doors stood inside against the cold. And the rain pelting the glass doors. The rain of flying creatures.

I squinted to get a better look. Bats, pigeons, cardinals, crows, starlings and sparrows. Slamming themselves over and over into the doors. They began to hit the sidewalk outside. Just lying there, unmoving.

The guards didn't say anything, as they stood, hands on hips, staring out the doors. It was an act of nature, not terrorism. There were hundreds, maybe even thousands of birds and bats flinging themselves against the temple building. Flinging? Or being flung?

Blood streaked down the glass as a small gray bird hit too hard. I ran closer to get a better look. Another fell. And another. The birds lay motionless on the sidewalk outside the doors.

"Miss, please go back into the sanctuary," said one guard holding out his arm to block me. Across the street, Darcy Jackson's car was gone.

The onslaught of birds was the talk of coffee hour. Even people who normally didn't stay to schmooze, stayed tonight. I heard all kinds of theories from the scientific to the divine.

"A change in air current temperature can make birds of multiple species swarm like that," said some guy with glasses.

"It was an angelic message," said a lady in yellow.

You're both wrong, I wanted to say. I don't know how she did it, but there's a very angry vampire in Richmond with powers I don't even know the scope of. Summoning swarms of animals had not been on my list.

I needed to call Finder. We'd established that there was a lot she didn't know either, but this was going to blow her mind. The swarm had stopped as abruptly as it had begun, leaving a hurricane-level mess outside and a panicking temple staff on the phone to the groundskeepers.

Steve had left my side after two cups of cocoa to play with a group of other little kids. Jill stood chatting with her new friends from the Maymont tour, and the grandmothers had found their way into what I named 'the circle of grandmothers' back home. I stood with Dad near the cookie bar, trying to look occupied and go unnoticed by the youth group leaders.

"How's the coffee?" he said, holding a chocolate chip cookie on a napkin.

"Not bad," I said. "How was work?"

"Ridiculous. I'd never get this kind of case in New York." We called this 'the talk trick'. Dad and I had figured it out in grief support after my mom left. One of us held a drink and the other held food while we talked to each other. When we did that, a lot fewer people tried to interact with us than if we both just had drinks or both food.

"This Native tribe claims a chunk of land on their reservation is sacred land. Ancient burial ground, whatever. Our client is suing for the land because they say their ancestor, some Civil War muckety-muck, is buried, of course, on the same little hill."

"Mattaponi?"

"Sorry?"

"The Mattaponi Tribe?"

"Yeah. Heard of them?"

"Judy? My science fair partner? She's Mattaponi. I think her dad's the tribe spokesperson for the lawsuit."

"You gotta be kidding me."

"And the tribe is right. It is their land."

"Of course it's their land. White people got here in 1600 when? My client's all B.S. if you ask me, but somebody's gotta pay the bills. And she's a partner. Suing people is kind of a perk."

"Is it Mrs. Macy?" I asked. Dad raised an eyebrow. I never remembered anyone's name, but here I was knowing his lawyers. Super weird.

"No," he said. "It's Ms. Lee, but Macy found the ancestor and got her started on the case. Now, Lee's convinced that it's her family land. Honestly, unless we start digging up bones to see who's actually buried where, the whole suit is pointless."

"Hey, Dad?"

"Yes, honey?"

"The old ladies are starting to eye us. Wanna see if the Judaica shop is open? I need a sweatshirt and I think Jill would like it if I bought one here."

"Good idea," he said. "Maybe I'll get one for her, too. I can use it for Hanukkah."

Close to an hour later, an announcement was made that people could get to their cars.

Outside the temple, it looked like wreckage from a bad storm. Tree branches were down, leaves were plastered to the cars like it had rained them. Black trash bags stood full by the sidewalks as a groundskeeper hosed down the cement. Momentarily overcome by morbid curiosity, I toed one of the bags. Soft. Feathers stuck out of the top where the ties hadn't been pulled all the way shut. I counted ten bags. Ten massive garbage bags. That had to be hundreds of birds.

How could Matilda do this? How could she compel what looked like half the winged population of Richmond to crash into a building? Darcy had come. He told me to stop setting booby traps at Maymont.

Did she think she had to reinforce that message? A fury lit in my belly. Regardless of her annoyance with me, she had no right to destroy like this. All these lives made no difference to her whatsoever. This wasn't just revenge or bullying. This was destruction for the sake of destruction. This was evil. And evil made me angry.

Steve stayed curled into me the whole way home. "Will they bury them?" he asked, pressing tighter to my side. The bag with my new temple sweatshirt, hat, and a couple stickers, crinkled between my feet. The baseball cap I'd picked for Steve was already on his head. Big ol' Star of David logo on the front.

"Of course, honey," Bubbe said from the front seat. "They died at a temple. It's sacred ground. The groundskeeper will find a place and the rabbi will bless them and bury them. That was the weirdest thing, wasn't it? And multiple kinds of birds, too, so it wasn't a migration mistake or something."

Maybe it *was* a bizarre natural phenomenon, I told myself, looking out the windows at the sleepy Richmond streets. By the time we got home, I had almost convinced myself that was true.

Bedtime arrived after two rounds of Rummy, half a bottle of something Gram had brought from Florida that I was not allowed to try, and most of Steve's current favorite movie. The chess tournament had started at seven a.m. so I'd been up at five-thirty. I said good night to Gram and Jill then followed Bubbe and Steve upstairs. Dad had turned in an hour ago, unable to keep his eyes open after the card game turned into family gossip and catch-up chat.

"Jammies on, Muppet," I said. "Your mom will come tuck you in."

"Can you tuck me in?" His eyes were wide. Ah. He was signaling me that he had questions.

"What am I? Chopped liver?"

Steve wrapped his arms around Bubbe's legs and squeezed. "Story?"

She winked at me and followed him in. "I'll come give you a bonus tuck, how's that?" I said, turning to head toward my own jammies.

"Don't leave," he said. "Please." Ugh. Why? I was tired, too.

Okay. Fine. I sat on his floor in my temple clothes and closed my eyes while Bubbe read to him. First one book. Then another. Then a third.

"Do you never fall asleep, child?"

Steve shook his head. "Not during story time. I'm going to be a famous author someday so I stay on high alert during story time."

"Oh. Well. Good for you. Now go to sleep. I love you like meat loves salt," Bubbe said, quoting the story.

"I love you like meat loves salt, too."

"Of course you do. Now, sleep." She kissed his forehead and got up to go.

"I'll come say goodnight in a minute," I said to Bubbe as she waited for me to follow her. I pulled Steve's covers up to his chin and leaned down close.

"What?"

"I smell something. But it's not, like super strong. I wanted to tell you so you'll be safe. They can't get in the house right?"

"No. Of course not." I had no idea if that was true.

"Okay. I love you, Stacy."

"I love you, too, Muppet. Sleep tight." I took Monster the monkey and tucked him in beside Steve on his pillow. I checked the garlic packets at the window and gave a little thought energy to them.

By the power of three by three, this house is made safe by me. To cause no harm nor return on me. As I will, so mote it be.

It occurred to me I could teach that to Steve in the morning.

Stopping by Bubbe's room, I made sure she had everything she needed then hugged her good night.

"I'm very proud of you, Shayna," she said. "That was a good win today. Your win. Remember that. Whatever happens here, you are the absolute soul of that chess team, and all of that horrible woman's wins are because of you."

"Thanks, Bubbe."

"And no dating the little Asian boy. He's cute, but not for you."

"I'm not going to date him." I paused and considered. "I like someone else."

"You do? Wonderful! Is he Jewish?"

"Bubbe, I'm fifteen. I'm not getting married to him, I just like him." She scowled at me, but her eyes twinkled.

"I met your grandfather when I was fifteen. You never know."

"You're right," I said. "You never know."

"But he's not Jewish," Bubbe said, catching my evasion.

"No."

"It's not really my preference, but he could convert. Does he go to your school?"

"No."

"That's a plus. Did I meet him at the tournament?"

"No. He doesn't play."

"Good. Men don't like to lose all the time. You should never try to lose when you can win. Always win. It's very important not to change who you are for a man, Shayna. Any man. No matter how much you love him. Be yourself and let him love you for that."

"Thanks, Bubbe. I will."

"Okay, good. I love you, Shayna. But, please. I can't let you use my chuppah if you marry someone not Jewish. Your grandfather would die."

I did not remind her that he was already dead.

"Got it. Marry Jewish. The chuppah is waiting. Good night, Bubbe. See you in the morning."

I turned on the light in my bedroom and shut the door behind me. Something felt . . . *off*. I stood on my cushy carpet and tried to place it. What is it? What is different? I checked my windows, all normal. All garlic packets in place.

I flipped on the light switch in my bathroom.

My hand flew to my mouth, repressing a scream. I stepped back involuntarily.

10.

November 23, continued.

A bloody heap of dead birds lay in the center of my bathroom rug. I stared at the corpses, unable to look away. Twenty-odd delicate bodies were mangled as if they had been held in someone's fist and literally *crushed.*

A thousand thoughts at once: a vampire had been *in my house?* In my bathroom? Which one? How had it come in? Was it still here? How powerful were these creatures? Was Steve ok? Was everyone ok? What was this message meant to say? Heart slamming into my ribs, I ripped my gaze away and backed out of my bathroom. I yanked my stake out from under the bed covers. My limbs felt cold and stony as I pulled my Star on its broken chain from under my collar.

Holding the stake low and tucked between my ribs and my arm, I ran down the hall to Steve's bedroom and cracked open the door. He was in bed, asleep. I knocked on Bubbe's door.

I heard her shower running. I peeked into Dad and Jill's room. He was in bed, also asleep, light left on for his late night wife. Leaning over the balcony, Jill and Gram's voices floated up as the clinking of glasses and woosh of running water told me they were cleaning up from cards. But they were together. And they were safe.

This message was for *me.*

Back in my bedroom, I turned on every light, looked behind the curtains, under the bed and yanked back the shower curtain. I flung open my closet door ready to slam the stake forward. Nothing. I was alone.

I shut my bedroom door.

"This is UNACCEPTABLE," I said out loud. "You may NOT come in my house. You may NOT be near my people. I don't care what you think I did, but this is IT. I am done being scared of you and I am done being nice. I am COMING."

I picked up the phone to call Finder.

"Tomorrow morning," I said, after telling her what had happened, "tomorrow morning we start my training."

It was time to put some blood on the floor.

Saturday, November 24, 2001.

Regret was an understatement. My lungs ached like ice cubes were trying to explode out of my chest.

"Why didn't you call the angel?" Finder said, not even breaking a sweat beside me. "I think if this happens again, that's what you should do." I had to stop for a sec. I leaned forward, pressing my hands on tight, crampy thighs. It hadn't even occurred to me to call on the angel for help.

Are you callable? I asked in my head. No answer. Finder jogged in place. Alongside us, the flowing James River reminded me of the uptown stretch of Fifth Avenue that floods in winter rain.

"No staying still, Chess Team. You can do it. Heart rate's gotta stay up to build stamina."

"Think of it like this," Tully said, from my other side, "it's your body experiencing math."

"Don't be a freak, Teularen. Listen to me, sis. I got you."

I stood upright with a ragged breath. It had taken an hour to get the dead birds out of my bedroom and into the forest behind my house in a way that didn't attract attention.

Fear and fury make interesting companions. A vampire had been in my *bedroom*. As much as that scared me, if I were Finder and could fight with a stake reliably, I'd sneak down that secret staircase tonight. Threatening me was one thing, but breaking into my home? That threatened my family. And threatening my family was not okay.

Bandaging me up the night of the kidnapping, Mama'd said, "You're a fighter now, baby, whether you like it or not."

I did not like it. Fighting scared me.

"Thirty-seven days," I gasped out, meaning between now and New Year's Eve, "isn't enough time."

"You'd be surprised what I can do with somebody in a month," Finder said. She jogged backwards ahead of me, eyes bright and encouraging. I let out a small groan as I forced myself to jog a few steps. "Have faith, Chess Team. You're scrawny, but scrappy. I won't let you down. Right, Tully? You've seen me work my magic." Walk, walk, jog two steps. Walk, walk, jog two steps. I was not cut out for this athlete gig.

Leafless trees arched toward the sky over our heads like the arms of Nutcracker ballerinas at Rockefeller Center. Finder ran ahead of me and Tully who had slowed to walk beside my jog, then turned around and ran back, her expression happy and free.

Think of the birds, I told myself. Think of Steve. I ran five steps inside two of Tully's. My lungs and legs ached from exertion.

"I think let's just kill Matilda," she said when she reached us. Finder jogged, knees up, in front of us. "That would be the easiest thing. Might have to burn the mansion to the ground, but really, let's just whack the B and get it done. I think we can run the rest off if she's gone." Finder grinned at her boyfriend.

"Uh oh, Tul. I just talked about killing and Chess Team didn't even blink. Come on, girl! Catch me." Finder turned and ran off down the trail, disappearing around a curve.

"She wants you to run," said Tully, smiling down at me. Oh. Joking about the killing. I get it. Trying to goad me into running.

This was not exercise for pleasure, this was training a life-or-death skill I needed yesterday. I took a breath and ran. I had to succeed.

Yes, that determination to succeed outside of your comfort zone. Now you're thinking like a wielder, said the archangel, voice in my head, but not in my head.

What's a wielder? I thought back. *And how do I call you or whatever? Is that allowed? I could've used help last night.*

No response.

At the end of the bike path, Finder stared into a pile of leaves.

"Check this out."

A set of clean white sticks and an oval shaped stone looking thing lay nestled in the decomposing leaves.

"Deer," Finder said. "Sometimes you'll see 'em off the trail but hardly ever this many bones." Tully paused to do a set of chin-ups on the park sign. I took long, slow breaths, grateful to be standing still. I started to crouch down to look closer. Pain shot down my legs. Stupid tailbone.

"That's an actual deer skull?"

"Right! You've probably never seen one, have you?"

"Have you ever seen a halal cart turned upside down with its wheels in the air?"

"What's a halal cart?" Finder asked.

"Exactly."

Finder leaned down and picked up the skull, shaking damp leaves from its base. She handed it to me.

It was weird, holding the skull of a dead animal. I handed it back to her. The only bones I'd touched that weren't food related had been in science class or at the Museum of Natural History. I'd never seen bones in nature where the animal had actually died.

Finder pointed to two rough holes on the top of the skull. "Looks like somebody broke out the antlers. Seems dumb to me, but whatever. If I found a full skull with antlers, I'd take the whole thing."

"No thanks," I said. "I don't need to touch skulls, even if I do find them where they die."

1:37 p.m.

"Ready for my plan?"

We all jumped, startled. Steve stood in our home gym doorway holding Monster and wearing his backpack.

"Back upstairs, Superboy," Finder said pausing in her punishment of the punching bag. "We're doing stuff down here."

"But it's the strategy session and I have a plan. Stacy said I could come." He shook the paper bag in his other hand. "Gummy worms or Swedish Fish? She told me you'd be more chill if I brought snacks."

I laid on my back on a gym mat that barely squeezed between the stair machine and the treadmill feeling Finder's querying gaze like heat on my face.

"I'll explain," I said. I wanted to sit up, but sitting hurt and lying on my back did not. So I stayed where I was. Finder mopped her face with a towel. Tully took my ankles in his hands.

"Hold onto the bar," he said. I reached my arms over my head and grabbed the base of the weight bench behind me. Tully pulled my legs. All the pressure immediately lifted off my tailbone.

"That's amazing," I murmured. My body softened as Tully held the pull. "Don't stop. Ever." I closed my eyes and took some deep breaths. After what felt like not long enough Tully set me down.

"Traction," Finder said, nodding approval. "One of his many talents. Roll onto your side. Slow. Superboy, go get your sister's donut."

"Aye aye, Captain."

"Explain," Finder whispered when Steve was gone.

"He's like you."

"Tall, Black and brilliant? I don't see it."

I rolled to my hands and knees.

"Like you sense vampires, Steve smells them," I said.

"That's cool," said Tully.

"You probably wouldn't think so if you smelled them," Steve said, coming back in with my donut.

"Reach for the bench," Finder said. I did. "Good. Now get up, one knee at a time."

I knelt like I was proposing marriage to the weight bench. I started to stand. Pain shot from my butt to my feet.

"Did I say twist?" Finder scolded.

I tried to make words but all that came out was a groan.

"Do it again," Finder said. "You have to do it so it doesn't hurt. You have to do it right."

I hesitated. I didn't want to risk another agony spasm.

"Back to all fours, Goldman."

Steve closed the door behind him. "Meanie."

"Hush up, Superkid," Finder said, reaching for my hand to help me back down. "Without me, your sister would be soup right now."

"Without her, you'd be a vampire right now. If I were you, I'd be nicer."

We all paused in astonishment.

"How do you know that?" I asked.

"I have sources."

"No, seriously, Steven. This is not time to play comic book detective. *How do you know that?*"

"My *friend*," he said, giving me a look, "said there was a ruckus at Maymont last Thursday night. A mouse named Wendell saw the whole thing and told my friend what happened. She came to see if you made it home, but you were at Finder's." He put one hand on his hip, just like his mom. "And it's a good thing she told me you were okay or I would have been worried sick all day at school.

Luckily, we were only doing alphabetical order which is easy so it didn't matter that I was distracted."

Finder and Tully's jaws had both gone slack.

My little brother was a total freak.

Finder broke the silence. "Your friend can talk to animals?"

Steve sighed. "No. Talking to animals isn't real. My friend turns *into* an animal and when she turns back human she talks to me."

"Because *that's* more realistic," Finder said with her signature eye roll.

"Oh, how the tables have turned," I said.

Tully snorted.

As if learning about kids turning into animals was normal, Finder crossed the room to a rack of round weights with handles. "Kettlebells," she said coming back with a softball sized weight in each hand. "You're already warm and we don't want to start over, so welcome to talking and working out at the same time." Finder gripped the kettlebell with both hands and held it over her head. She squatted, dipping the weight behind her head, then lifting it back up as she stood.

"I'm not doing that," I said. Peek-a-boo with heavy objects near my head seemed kinda un-smart to me.

"You asked me to train you, right? I did hear that correctly?"

"Yeah." Stupid bird death hurricane.

"You don't have to be Mr. Miyagi," Finder said to me, "but you won't be able to defend yourself with zero muscle tone."

"Who's Mr. Miyagi?"

Finder's jaw dropped. She looked at Steve. "You know who Mr. Miyagi is, right?"

"Totally," he said. Then he giggled. "No idea. Who's Mr. Miyagi?"

Finder stared at us, blinked, then turned to her boyfriend. "We have to show them. Do you have it on DVD?"

"Probably VHS."

"We don't have a VHS player," I said. "Nobody has those anymore."

"We do," Tully said. "Works, too. My dad throws nothing away. Basement's filled with all kinds of stuff."

Finder handed me the littlest kettlebell and demonstrated an arm curl. "Ten on each side," she said. "Slow. You tear more muscle fiber and build up faster if you do your reps slow."

Ripping muscle fiber sounds attractive, I thought, imitating her arm curl. I had not liked the feeling of being weak in my body fighting the vampires. After last night, I wanted to be as strong and fast as my scrawny body could get.

Steve lay sprawled under the weight bench at work with paper and crayons.

"My friend said before the angel saved you, you guys were getting wiped. She says Wendell is willing to feed you information about what's happening in the mansion if you feed him seeds. Winter's coming you know."

"Did she suggest how we can get an advantage?" I asked.

Steve sighed his mother's are-we-really-having-this-discussion-again sigh.

"Wendell. Is willing. To feed you. Information," he said. "How much bigger an advantage do you want? Let's analyze what we have."

Steve dropped a crayon into the cookie tin and held up his drawing. "This is you," he said to Finder. He pointed to a stick figure with purple eyes. "Has finding magic, can fight. Doesn't want to be turned into a vampire. This one," he nodded at Tully, "is you. Also fights, also doesn't want to go vamp. Your magic isn't like her magic, but it's not video game magic throwing fireballs and stuff. Yours is more cleric healing magic."

"You know about clerics?" Tully asked.

"My mom plays Dungeons & Dragons."

"She *does*?" I paused in my curls. Jill playing D&D was flabbergasting.

"Mmm-hmm," he said. "At least at home she did. With some other nerds from her psychology program. They used to play at her office after work once a month."

"*That's* what she was doing the nights she stayed late?" My head spun in disbelief. "She can't play D&D. She wears designer shoes!"

"Not mutually exclusive," Steve said, tapping the green crayon against his cheek. "My mother is very creative," he said with not a little pride. "And she's brave. She climbed a ladder to hang a swing for me yesterday in the yard. She grew up in Ohio and said her mom hung a swing for her when she was little so she was gonna hang one for me, and she climbed right up that ladder and did it."

He pointed to a small turtle in the corner of his picture. "This is Stacy. She doesn't fight."

"Yet," Finder said.

"She has a thick shell, but can still be stepped on and killed."

He tapped below a little red 'm' bird with his finger. "This is me," he said. "I'm only marginally involved, so I can see lots of stuff and gather information from a wider perspective."

I did not appreciate how the kettlebells got heavier with every rep.

"I've been thinking," Steve said. "Our best approach with Matilda is to be like Tommy Johnson. Everyone in my class runs faster after snack now because Tommy Johnson always gets to the fort bricks first. The fort bricks are everyone's favorite but anyone who wants them has to play the way he says because he gets to them first."

"You want us to hog Matilda's toys?" Finder said.

"If you take the toys Matilda wants before she gets them, she's gonna have to run faster."

"You're talking about forcing her moves," I said.

Steve face palmed. "That analogy was so transparent, Stacy! Do I have to spell it out for you?"

We all stared at him.

"You have to control her access to blood!"

We looked at each other, then back at him.

"Matilda wants blood," Steve said. "And more importantly, she *has* to have it. It's not negotiable. So the way to get her to do what you say is to be in charge of her blood."

"It's impossible, Steve," I said. I'd thought interfering with her blood was the answer the night she threatened us at Third Rock, but had put it out of my mind as too risky.

"It's not. What is impossible is you allowing her to maintain a consistent threat with uncertain consequences you're stuck reacting to."

"Child, your vocabulary is making my head explode," said Finder.

"Mom's a shrink, Dad's a lawyer, and my sister's a National Chess Master. Vocabulary's the only way I keep up."

"Even if we completely ruin her typical hunt, she has that locked ice room," I said. "You don't drink blood for decades without keeping some kind of stash."

"What if you block her regular hunt and force her to use up her stash?" Steve said.

We worked out for thirty more minutes, hashing out different ideas which all ended the same way. Badly. At minute twenty-four, Steve stuck a gummy worm in each nostril and pretended to sneeze all over Finder. The worms hit her shirt and then fell on the floor. Steve picked one up, waggled it in the air then slurped it into his mouth.

"I was starting to think you were secretly forty," Finder said. "Thanks for clearing that up."

I knew I should be thinking important strategizing thoughts, but I was exhausted. As I dismounted the treadmill, the only thought that came to mind was, *we have a ladder?*

11.

Monday, November 26, 2001.

"Do you have to go home?" I asked. I lounged on Bubbe's freshly made bed as she folded her clothes into a neat stack for packing.

"Maybe your dad will let you come to the City for New Year's, hmm? Get you out of the line of fire for this ridiculous surprise party. Oh! I'd have been so mad if I'd gotten home with this still in my bag!"

Bubbe handed me a black velvet box that fit in my palm. "Jill told me your chain got broken at school. Take it off and I'll walk it over to Jerry to repair. In the meantime, you can wear this."

A beautiful, slightly less delicate, gold chain hung over a display card.

"Bubbe, this is gorgeous! Thank you!"

"You're welcome. Twenty-four carat and a bigger link. Should be stronger. Turn around."

Bubbe unhooked my safety pinned together chain that Matilda had broken at the diner. She slid the pendant off while I gently maneuvered the new chain out of its pretty bed.

"Much better," Bubbe said, doing up the fastener as I held my hair. "It's been driving me crazy seeing you wearing the broken one, but every time I started to give you the new one something happened and I forgot." She dropped my damaged chain into the box from the new one and packed it back in her suitcase. The new chain was shorter, more like a choker. I went to Bubbe's mirror to admire its perfect vampire repellant placement.

"If you come for New Year's, we'll have champagne cupcakes and stand on the roof for the ball drop."

Champagne cupcakes from Barstops Bakery were my favorite of anything that wasn't chocolate. They were tiny cupcakes made from cake so light it felt like it should float and slathered in frosting that sparkled in your mouth. It was like they carbonated it somehow even though that was impossible. I have no idea how they made them, but they were everywhere in the city, weddings, mitzvahs, and of course, anyone who was anyone ate them on New Year's Eve. The rest of us did, too. You had to order them six months in advance and they were not cheap.

"I wish I could," it made my teeth ache to say the rest. "I already have plans."

"Plans? With who?"

A vampire. Her minions. My life.

"Finder and Tully and I have . . . a thing we're going to," I said. "We already promised we'd be there otherwise believe me, I'd ditch it. I could come the following weekend maybe?" If I'm still alive. "Listen, Bubbe, I need some advice."

"I see," she said with a little smile. "What's his name?"

"Oh, it's nothing like that," I said, embarrassed. "This isn't romantic advice."

"That's too bad. I didn't get to be this old without learning a few things. I give very good romantic advice."

Jill popped around the corner bundled in her bathrobe. Fresh from the shower, she had her hair in a towel and an armload of laundry in her arms.

"Who's getting romantic advice?" Jill asked. Face floating in a sea of fluffy terry cloth, my father's wife didn't look much older than me. Sometimes that creeped me out a little. Now was one of those times.

"Jill honey, get dressed. You look twelve in that get up. Gives me the shivers because you're married to my son who turns fifty in a month."

Sometimes, I think Bubbe and I are the same person split into two bodies. Though personally, I might not choose to marry a rabbi.

Jill giggled and stepped fully into the guest room shutting the door behind her.

"The giggling makes it worse, right?" Bubbe said to me.

"Yes," I said, "it does. It makes her look thirteen."

"And nobody likes thirteen-year-olds." Bubbe eyed me as she laid the pile of clothes in the case. "Even you were a little insufferable at that age."

"I sent out a possible date change for the party!" Jill said, all secret-y, voice soft as her bathrobe. "Close enough to still be festive, but out of the holidays enough that it shouldn't be stressful. I'm hoping for positive RSVPs. I did good, right? Please tell me I did good."

Bubbe reached out and hugged her. "Ya did good," she said. "Even though I normally don't hug thirty-year-old teenagers in bathrobes—"

"Thirty-five."

"Fine, thirty-five-year-old teenagers in bathrobes. I think you made a very wise decision. Better for you, better for him, better for everyone. Nicely done, honey." Bubbe let her go. Jill's smile was broad and victorious.

"Make sure you have all your stuff for school," Jill said to me. "I'll drop you right after we get Bubbe to the train."

"I knew I liked her for a reason," Bubbe said to me as she patted Jill on the shoulder. "She lets you miss a morning of school because your Bubbe can't bear to be parted from you. And when it comes to taking my advice, she has at least one full ounce of sense."

"I can be taught!" Jill said. "Have fun with the romantic advice!" She opened the door and headed back down the hall to do, I hoped, something that would make her look her age, even if she wasn't going to act it.

"So." Bubbe sat down in the comfy chair opposite her bed. She propped her stocking feet on the bed and sighed. "How can I help?"

"I don't know, Bubbe," I said, rolling onto my side. "It's been such a whirlwind since I got here. New school, new friends, I still feel guilty for leaving when I should've been helping. I know Meredith has my philanthropy group, but I worry. Every day, no matter what other things are on my mind, I wake up with guilt for leaving. I think I've forgiven Dad for moving us here, I kind of had a come to Jesus about that- "

"An epiphany, Shayna. Jews don't have come to Jesus moments. We have epiphanies. Moments of clarity where you see the truth that's been staring you in the face all along?"

I nodded.

"Epiphany. Not to be confused with the Christian festival 'Epiphany' celebrating the coming of the wise men."

"Right. Okay, so I had an epiphany." I sighed long and deep. Maybe for the first time since arriving in Richmond I felt truly whole. Confused yes, but like pieces of me weren't scattered all over the floor like Steve's disassembled train tracks.

I rolled onto my belly and looked at Bubbe. "Do you believe in angels?"

"Of course."

"I mean seriously. Like one could walk up to you or whisper in your ear and you'd be like, yup that's an angel. Absolutely for sure no question?"

"Yes."

I pushed myself to sitting up. "Tell me why."

Bubbe folded her hands on her belly and closed her eyes for a moment. She was deciding.

"I am going to be seventy-five years old next year and that is a miracle, as you know. The summer I was fourteen, the same age as you when you left the City, it was very ugly for us in Poland. You know that, too. It was the week before school let out and it was unusually hot for so early in the season. My father owned a bakery. Every morning before school, my day was already half over. I got up at 2:30 in the morning to help him get the dough started and roll the danish he'd put up the day before.

"On this day, I woke up early, close to midnight and a voice was so loud in my head I thought it was a person. It said Get up. Get a change of clothes. Wake your family. I can't tell you Shayna, how I knew, or what I knew, but it was not from my brain. And I can not tell you why I did what it said. We knew there was a family at the end of our road who was hiding people and helping them escape, but my father was so stubborn. He kept saying it was all going to pass. But I got up and I woke him up and your great-grandmother and your great-aunt Millie and I told them what I'd heard. My father refused to come with us, but he said we could go hide and then come home that afternoon. I begged him to come with us, Shayna. I begged him. I remember being on my knees in his bedroom holding his clothes and crying and the voice in my head said Get up now. Go. Now. And you know what? I did. I kissed my father on his scratchy cheek and I went. The three of us went to the people at the end of the road and not one hour later, not one full hour, the house was searched. We laid on our backs utterly still in almost unbearable heat all day as every building on our block was searched and my father was arrested and taken. My school was emptied that day, too. All my friends gone, just like that. My mother and sister and I were packed into barrels and trays of pickles and fish were fitted in over our heads to cover the smell of sweating bodies in case the truck was searched and we were driven to the next town where we joined a group of 11 others and well, that's a story for another time. But we made it to Sweden. It took months, sometimes only going the distance of a block to change hiding places or break us up into smaller groups easier to disguise. The whole time we travelled and even after we made it here to New York, I kept asking if I was doing, if I had done, the right thing. But one night in Sweden as I lay on the ground under a cart to stay out of the snow, that voice came to me so loud I felt heat radiate around my body like a hug. It said, You are going to live. I am Michael and I am with you. I knew it was no lie, Shayna, but I can't tell you how I knew.

"That Archangel saved me, tried to save my whole family. Maybe he spoke to every family, every person in danger. Maybe some were too scared to hear, or like my father, were in denial about what was happening. Even we didn't know the extent of the genocide until we got here. I've wondered about that moment many times in my life since. I made up lots of stories, I was so cold I was hallucinating. I made it up like an imaginary friend. It was just my intuition."

Bubbe sighed and her fingers lay interlaced over her belly. "I understand feeling guilty for leaving, Shayna. I still feel it. Not a day goes by where I don't think about your great-grandfather. About the sound of his voice, the flour on his apron and in what was left of his hair. About the determination in his eyes, the disbelief when I begged him to come with us. Not a single day goes by where I don't apologize for leaving him. But if I hadn't listened to that voice, to the Archangel Michael I am absolutely sure, I wouldn't be seventy-five. I wouldn't have met your grandfather. His smile lit up every sandwich he made. He worked in the deli next to the laundry where I had my first job. He gave me extra pickles. Until I told him I didn't like pickles. He asked me if I liked tomatoes and I said I did and he gave me extra tomatoes on anything I ordered. Sometimes he would wrap them for me separate so I could eat them as a snack later. Do you know where he took me on our first date? To the temple. His father was the rabbi, but you knew that. He'd been a rabbi in Poland too, very involved in politics and when the first oppressions started, he saw what was coming. He had to make some very difficult decisions. He had to decide to run or to fight. He very quietly shut down his synagogue, and started doing everything he could to get his congregation out of Poland. And you know what? He did. Every single man, woman and child from his synagogue got out. And many more, too. He got out with his Torah which is almost inconceivable. And that Torah, as you know, is our Torah. He was a brilliant thinker, your great grandfather on grandpa's side. But if I hadn't listened to that angel, Shayna, and come here to meet that adorable boy at the deli, your father, you, Steven, none of you would exist. And my purpose on this earth may only have been to make sure you all got here. I certainly don't feel like I have lived to accomplish great things, but I can be kind. I can help where I can. I can hold your grandfather's vision of Beth Israel and his community so that it gets passed down to the next generation. Or, maybe I'm only on this earth because you needed to be here. Maybe you or Steve is going to do something incredible in your lifetimes long after I'm gone. I don't know. I don't need to know.

"I was angry at my father for many years for throwing away his life for a bakery when we should have been his priority, but I think that's why he needed to save it, to fight for it. Because without it he'd have no way to take care of us. Nobody knows if they are making the right decisions when they make them, Shayna. We all just do the best we can. We do what seems right at the time and if you are very lucky, or a very good listener, you maybe can hear the angels speaking to you, guiding you. I believe they are here for anyone who asks and that they will answer. We have to be open enough to hear them. We have to be quiet enough to listen. We have to have faith and trust. It's hard more than it's not, I'll tell you that. But when Michael woke me up at midnight and told me go now, I knew in my very bones that it was life or death and that I absolutely had to obey. So yes, I believe in angels."

We sat for minutes without saying anything. I had never seen this side of Bubbe. The young woman who had fought for her life, for the lives of her family. A girl in love, a girl betrayed, a girl who had no choice but to become a woman in a country that wasn't her own knowing she had left someone behind who had done everything for her and died in what could only have been an unthinkable way.

"Did you ever forgive your father?"

"Forgive him? For making a decision that cost him his life? No. And yes." Her eyes filled again with tears. "I prayed about this a lot over the course of my life. To become peaceful with his decision. I pray he fought them and was killed quickly and soon so he didn't suffer. But I would never, ever, abandon my family. Family is everything. If you're lucky enough to have one. I know if he'd had a crystal ball, he would've come with us. He made the best decision could at the time. Protect the two things he'd built his life around, the bakery and us. But I don't know God's mind, Shayna. Maybe my father would have sneezed at the wrong moment and we'd all have gotten caught. I have to trust that even though I disagree with his choice, it's not for me to judge. I've come to believe that in whatever way, he was also working under God's will. But true forgiveness, that may be a project for another day."

"You'll feel better," I said. "If you really forgive him."

"I will, huh? And how do you know?"

"Like I said. I had an epiphany. I wasn't like, trying to. But," I thought back to the moment I realized what I had to do. "My life kinda depended on it."

Bubbe smiled and I caught the gleam of her gold tooth. "Such drama," she said. "Did Meredith give you that as a going away present? Not that I don't love her, but she has a flare for the melodramatic. Trust me, Shayna. When your life does depend on something, and I hope it never does, but if it happens, you'll know."

Oh Bubbe, I thought. I know. Believe me, I know.

Jill and Steve stayed in the car with the blinkers on while I walked Bubbe to her train gate. "Do you still hear from Michael?" I asked as if it were such a normal question.

"Which Michael? Oh the uh-?" She looked up at the sky. I nodded. "Yes. Whenever I ask for him to speak to me, he does. In my head. I don't, you know, hear a voice speaking to me like a radio."

"What do you ask him?"

"Whatever I need to know. How to handle things that make me afraid. Michael is a warrior angel. He helps most when you need to not be afraid."

Hmm. That made sense.

It was hard for me to imagine Bubbe as I knew her being afraid of anything. Even the story she told me earlier convinced me of her bravery. She was hardcore, my Bubbe.

I hugged her hard and kissed her rumpled cheek goodbye. "I love you, Bubbe. I'm so glad you came. It wouldn't have been Thanksgiving without you. Are you coming back for Hanukkah?"

"I don't know, honey. Maybe. It's a long ride for me. Think about cancelling your New Year's plans and coming to visit me instead. Besides, I already ordered the cupcakes."

Wednesday, November 28, 2001.

I felt Mrs. Bason's eyes on me as I stalked out of her classroom, three more wins against Jospeh Thornton under my belt. My face flushed with rage. How dare she suggest that he was letting me win? How dare she suggest that I resign from the team because I was a distraction to her most valuable player?

She's angry because you won the meet and not him, said the voice.

"That's clear," I muttered out loud. "Why would she suggest I leave the team? That doesn't even make sense." I stopped at my locker to ditch the books from my morning classes and pick up the ones for the afternoon.

Anger is born of fear. Figure out what she's afraid of and you'll know why she's so upset.

Are you really Michael the Archangel? I asked in my head. After the convo with Bubbe, I wondered if maybe I could just ask.

I am.

Am I really hearing you or am I making you up?

You are. You are not.

Why didn't you just introduce yourself? I thought/said as I stacked my books in my locker, ordered for the next day.

I did. In the gym. You were very tired. I touched you with my wings.

That was real?

The Archangel sighed. *Do you know the definition of insanity?*

Doing the same thing over and over and expecting a different result?

Correct. You keep asking the same question over and over. Is this real? Yes. Still yes. Again yes. It's all real. Vampires, shifters, the Famelicus, myself. What you need to be asking yourself now is how and why you are involved.

"I don't understand," I said out loud.

Evidently.

A familiar voice drew my attention.

"Ahh-m just sayin' I'm afraid you're gonna break yourself. You need to eat. It's just an apple and half a sandwich. I'm not tryin' to force you to eat a steak."

I peeked around my locker door. Standing in the doorway of Sister Elizabeth Religion's classroom, Bradley Joe Rifkin held out a paper lunch bag. To Judy.

12.

November 28, continued.

"Please?" His voice was sweet and sincere. "I'm worried about you. We all are."

I'd never even seen them together before and now he was talking to her like she was his girlfriend.

A pause. I couldn't hear her too soft reply.

"But what if that happens?" he said. "What would we do?"

Judy pushed past the hefty boy, leaving him standing in the doorframe holding the bag.

"What was that?" I whispered into my locker.

A call to action, said Michael.

"What action? What am I supposed to do?"

Go to your friend. Offer to help.

I could practically hear the angel shaking his head at my ignorance.

I caught up with Judy at the end of the hall, going the opposite way from my next class.

"Hey," I said. I started to ask a question but stopped when I saw her face. Her skin was almost blue with pallor, her eyes had purple bags beneath them, sinking almost to her cheekbones. Thanksgiving had only been a few days ago and she'd looked almost her normal self then.

"This is what it does to me," she said. "My condition. And I won't eat, so don't bother asking."

"Are you . . . in pain?"

"No. I'm fine."

Except for starving yourself, I thought.

Judy put a hand out and steadied herself on the wall. "Can you work after school today?"

"Yes," I said. "Lab or library?"

"Lab. If Julian can meet us there. He doesn't go to campus every day. If he can't get us in, it'll have to be the library. I'll leave a note in your locker by sixth period."

Judy did not leave me a note. Sister Mary Medical said she'd gotten picked up early after passing out in fourth period.

November 28, continued.

"It's for a project," I said, finishing my list as Jill pulled into the craft store parking lot.

"I'm getting air dry clay," Steve said. "Not for a project. It's for meeeeeeee!"

Walking through the automatic glass doors, Steve dancing in excitement ahead of me, my jaw dropped. As a city dweller who rarely left Manhattan, retail space of this volume felt unreal. The sheer number of aisles and amount of empty space over my head made me dizzy. It was like shopping in an airplane hangar. An older lady with a cart full of yarn and a bundled up mom with a cart spewing little kids passed me on either side with room to spare.

Just find your supplies, I thought. Get in, get out. Too. Much. Room.

Jill looked over my shoulder as I put my stash down at the register. A blue nose ring decorated one of the cashier's nostrils and pink hair stuck out in odd clumps, maybe punk, maybe lazy overslept. I couldn't tell.

"Oh! I have a coupon," Jill said and dug in her purse. "Just a sec." She put Steve's air dry clay next to my fabric, thread, needles, scissors, markers, velcro, and assorted jewelry makings.

The cashier looked bored. "I have one here," she said and pulled a newspaper clipping from under her register. She scanned it and took Jill's credit card. Crap. I needed one more thing.

"Hey Jill? Can we please run into the grocery store? I need birdseed."

Jill looked at me like I'd grown a second head.

"Birdseed? Why?" Think quick, Goldman.

"For the cardinals. In the yard."

"And the squirrels!" Steve said.

Jill hedged. "Um, I guess?"

"Come on, aren't you impressed that I even know what cardinals are? It's not like we saw so many of them flying around Manhattan. Dad would be totally impressed."

"I'm impressed," said Steve. "Can we get birdseed, Mommy? Please, please, please?"

Steve gave my hand a squeeze. To the grocery store we went. Having a six-year-old was handy.

"Thanks for buying my stuff," I said, on our way to the car. "Let me see the receipts and I'll give you my part."

"I got it," Jill said with a smile. "Save your money for going out with your friends. If your father starts paying you to babysit, we can renegotiate. Besides, I got forty percent off with that coupon. Richmond has its bonuses."

"Yeah," I said, thinking about why I needed the supplies in the first place. "Richmond sure does have some . . . bonuses."

Thursday, November 29, 2001.

The list of DNA strands blurred in front of my eyes. I'd been staring at them too long, notebook open on the treadmill shelf. Finder had made me swear I'd go in the gym every day and do something, even if it was only two minutes and ten kettlebell lifts.

Today I had promised myself nine slow, walking minutes on the treadmill, but when I looked at my watch, I'd been here for nearly thirty trying to make a connection between the DNA strands I stared at. Judy hadn't come to school today. I thought about calling but figured if she wasn't well enough to be at school, she probably didn't want to talk about the project.

I was just starting a three minute jog when the doorbell rang. Steve jumped off the rec room couch to answer it.

"I smell something sweet!"

I grabbed a towel to mop my face and followed my little brother upstairs.

A skinny teenager in a baggy T-shirt and jeans with a massive foof of curly orange hair hanging in his face stood at our door.

"Um, is Stacy here?" he said.

"I'm Stacy," I said. Steve hopped from foot to foot.

"You have my seeds?"

Steve opened the door wide so the boy could come in. He entered the foyer, sniffing like a dog, his nose visibly twitching. "I haven't used this shape in months," he said. He knit his hands together and rubbed his fingers back and forth. "I feel very awkward. Very tall. Too tall. May I please have my seeds so I can go?"

I had expected another little kid.

"Are you Wendell?"

"Wendell. Yes. I'm Wendell."

Wendell squatted down. He examined the shoes on our shoe rack.

"I recognize your shoes," he said. "You are the right person. The holy water was very clever, but it made her upset. And the chalk was funny. You should have seen them all cringe when they saw the marks. Cringing."

"Would you like something to eat?" I said, remembering Evia's reminder that woodland creatures were always hungry in winter. "Do you mind leaving your sneakers here?"

Wendell dropped to his butt and untied mud-crusted high tops. He smelled dusty and faintly like gym class. Boy needed a shower.

In the kitchen, Steve knelt on a counter stool peeling a carrot into the sink. Next to him on the chopping block sat more carrots, a celery, a cucumber, and a block of cheese.

I pulled out a knife.

After a few minutes we were seated around the table with crackers, peanut butter, cheese and cut up veggies which Wendell inhaled. He took tiny, speedy bites, holding each snack with both hands to his lips.

"Have you seen them feed?" I asked, eager to get some answers.

Wendell nodded, speed nibbling a cracker into nothing. "Only she feeds on humans. The men aren't allowed." I snorted. They were certainly allowed the night we were there. I had the mental scars to prove it.

"Are those seeds for me?" Wendell said, nose twitching toward the birdseed. He picked up another piece of cheese with both hands.

"Both bags," I said. Steve got up and dragged the shopping bag with the seeds into the foyer.

"Put it with his shoes," I said.

A trickle of delight and anticipation lit him up. "My mouse body is very efficient. I'm sad for you that you can't shift. Though you do, you know, have to die first."

"How did you die?" Steve stared at Wendell in fascination as he climbed back up into his seat.

"I jumped off a bridge."

"Why?"

Wendell shrugged. "Of all my options, it seemed to make the most sense."

"Why?"

"Steve!" I said. "Not your business. Sorry, Wendell."

"I kind of like being asked," Wendell said. "It makes me feel. Y'know. Seen."

Oh. Okay. Steve sat forward, chin on his hands. Story time.

"When my mom got cancer, I dropped out of high school to get a job and help with bills, figuring that would maybe save her life or something. It didn't, and after she died, my dad lost it. Do you, um, know what drugs are?"

"Kind of," Steve said.

"Well, they're bad for you and you should stay away from them," Wendell said. "They make you mean and ugly and a monster to people who love you. So that happened and I got sad and lonely and decided I wanted a do-over. New body, maybe not so ugly, and a new family, also maybe not so ugly. So I jumped off the bridge over the highway and four cars hit me. One of them was an ambulance. I had a bunch of broken bones and was dead for close to six minutes. The ambulance driver made them keep trying to revive me and on the very last attempt to restart my heart, it worked. Well. Obviously. The last attempt." Wendell reached for another carrot.

"Six months in the hospital 'til I could walk and when I finally went home, my dad got high and decided to help me succeed where I'd failed." Wendell looked at me. I got it.

"I don't know how it happened, but suddenly I was in a mouse body and escaped. I've always loved Maymont so I stayed in my mouse body and moved in. I didn't know what the deal was then, and at first I didn't believe what I saw. But then I was like, Dude, you can *turn into a mouse*. Why can't there be vampires?" He shrugged, a small movement, lifting bony shoulders. Steve stared, rapt.

"Tell me everything," I said, greedy now for information. "Start with how they feed. I mean not the biting part, but when and on whom? And is blood stashed in the ice room?"

"There's no blood stashed anywhere. She only drinks fresh. Every Friday night, the bald one goes out and brings home a man, sometimes two, always just for her."

"Does she . . . kill them?"

"Oh no. She just drinks from them and sends them home. Sometimes, if they really like it, she'll like, get their numbers or something."

Get their numbers? Hmm. Did she have a secret list somewhere of people she fed on? Could that be something I could use to beat her at New Year's? I filed that little detail away.

"She can go longer without, if the bald guy doesn't bring home someone she likes. But once she's full, the rest of them feed. On her."

He gave me a surreptitious little look.

"She . . . likes it quite a lot."

Oh. Uh, yuck. I gave Wendell the TMI glance and he left that topic alone. But the sneaky smile on his face told me Wendell watched maybe more Vampire HBO than he should. That part at least, was none of my business.

"It's why her guys are so loyal to her," he went on. "Something about the blood sharing makes them all do-whatever-you-say-ish. And it's why the bald guy usually brings home two. One for before she feeds her men, and another one for after.

"Once she caught one of her guys sneaking a feed on his own and she killed him. Yeah," Wendell said, reacting to the surprise on my face. "I know! Right? Killed him dead. I think it was kind of an accident? She was reaming the snot out of him when dawn hit and they all collapsed on the floor. He was in front of the window and when that sun came through, poof. Ashes in minutes."

"Why didn't the rest of them die?" asked Steve.

"They weren't in the sunlight. Matilda's morning girl had to vacuum the dusted guy up and get the rest moved into the ice room. She opens the mansion before the regular employees show up in case something weird happens. Like Matilda being collapsed on the stairs with a collection of her men asleep all over the floor."

"And what keeps her loyal?" I asked. "Does she drink the blood, too?"

"I think so. All her servants do. I don't know much about them other than they seem to love her. In a with all-their-hearts kind of way. I mean, they don't drag her body into the sunlight even though they know where she sleeps. And they could do that. When vampires are out, they're *out*."

I leaned forward, fascinated, like when I first understood why opening with a side ranked pawn is a terrible idea. This space where beginner ignorance lived got brushed away and a new container opened. A container for functional knowledge.

"So they can't be out in daylight at all?" I said.

"No ma'am. Sunshine hits 'em, they turn to ash."

"Have you seen it again?"

"Just the once."

This was incredible. Wendell knew everything I needed to know. Best bag of birdseed I'd ever bought.

"So, just making sure I'm clear," I said, "she doesn't kill her victims."

"Nope."

"And they don't become vampires after getting bitten?"

"None I've seen."

"Have you ever seen her make a new vampire?"

"No, but she's the only one that can do it. Her guys grumble about that a lot."

"That can't be right. Darcy Jackson wants to turn his daughter into vampire and Matilda's all for it."

What if Wendell's information was wrong? Maybe his mouse mind had twisted the facts.

"Her blood is the only blood strong enough to change someone. So if one of them wants to change someone, Matilda has to be involved. Sharing blood with the victim or something like that. Honestly, I kinda hope I never really know how it works."

"And the feeding victims? She wipes their memories so they don't recall what happened?"

"I've never followed one home and asked, but nobody calls the police on her or anything after they have a nice evening of screaming and being drained of blood."

"Who knows about the secret underground bedroom?" Wendell's eyes got round.

"Matilda has a secret underground bedroom?" Steve shouted smacking his hands on the table. "That's awesome!"

"Who has a secret underground bedroom?" Jill said coming around the corner, groceries in her arms. A breeze blew in behind me. I almost jumped out of my chair. How did she come in without us hearing her?

"Momeeeeee!" Steve leaped up and went to hug her. A pile of dirty Wendell clothes settled under the table.

"You're home early," I said, scooping the laundry into a ball. The stove clock read 5:13. She was way early.

"Cancellation. And I forgot to buy bay leaf for the roast- " suddenly Jill screamed. "Mouse! Oh my god is that a *mouse* in here?"

Wendell vanished down the back stairs. I shot Steve a look and he bolted down the stairs to let our new friend out.

"Steven! Don't chase it!"

"I'll get the broom," I said. Instead, I ducked into the foyer and grabbed Wendell's shoes. I stuffed them and his clothes into the bag with the birdseed. I ducked out the front door and ran to the back of the pool house where I stashed the bag out of sight from the main house windows.

"Your stuff is back here, Wendell," I said loud enough that I hoped he heard. He's a smart mouse, I thought. And his clothes are ripe. He'll figure it out.

Friday, November 30, 2001.

"We have to catch one hunting," I whispered outside Mrs. Bason's classroom.

"Girl, you are crazy. There is no freakin' way," Finder said.

"I don't know," Tully said. "Maybe we could."

"Catch one hunting? And then what? Stake it and chain it up for a month in my dojo basement until New Year's Eve? Most unrighteous."

I headed into chess as my friends headed to the cafeteria. I wasn't in the mood to eat my packed lunch so I said hello to my ancient, scowling coach and went to set up my board. I needed this practice today. I needed a few solid games to invent and process our new plan.

"You seem distracted today, Miss Goldman," said Mrs. Bason halfway through my first game. I played a freshman whose name I couldn't remember. Mrs. Bason peered over our game. She spoke to my opponent.

"Miss Goldman rarely makes mistakes in the middle game, but she has left you an opening if you can figure out how to take advantage of it," Mrs. Bason said. "And you," she said to me, "mate in four if he misses your mistake. You really shouldn't use this opening. It doesn't suit your style of play."

I found my shortcoming, doubled pawns on the edge, and made notes. I must be distracted, I thought. I never double pawns. The other kid saw it, too, but couldn't figure out what to do about it. I beat him, mate in five. I lost a tempo replying to his useless reaction to my pawns.

"Hi Stay-cee," Bradley Joe said, snagging the seat across from me for the next game. I didn't have this in me today.

"Shave the neck beard," I said, opening with pawn to d4. "And please use your rooks. Please. Can you get Mrs. Bason to give you, I don't know, extra lessons or something?"

"I know my play was pretty sorry at the tournament," he said.

"It was. Abysmal. Do you even like chess?" It sounded harsh, but my tone was kind. I felt bad for Bradley Joe.

"I think I'd like it if I understood it more. I don't really get the point to be honest. And thinking ahead moves is impossible."

"Why do you play if you don't like it?"

"My mom thinks I can get a scholarship to college if I play chess," he said. "She thinks it'll balance out my IEP."

I raised an eyebrow.

"Individualized Education Plan," he said. "I have some . . . stuff going on with the way I learn."

Right. This was the other side of academia, the side I knew exactly nothing about.

"Don't move that!" I said. His thick hand floated over his bishop. "Do you want me to beat you in one move?" Bradley Joe stared at the board. I glared at Mrs. Bason. She should be teaching him, not me.

"Look here," I said, and proceeded to explain to him a series of basic opening mistakes called the Fool's Mate. It was unthinkable that she hadn't taught him this, drilled him in it until the pattern was embedded in his brain. But maybe she hadn't. Or maybe he just forgot. I looked up and caught Mrs. Bason watching me over her thick glasses. She wore her usual brown tweed skirt suit today. Her pantyhose bagged around her ankles above comfortable shoes.

I couldn't tell if her glance was approving or not, but good grief. Someone had to teach this poor kid how to play. Quick glance at my watch. Ten minutes before we could change partners, so I set up mate puzzles for him to solve using the rook-queen or double-rook mate I'd reminded him about at the tournament.

"You use your two rooks or your rook and queen to slice the board. Then, you alternate pieces to push your opponent's king onto his back rank and block him in with an attack he can't avoid. Voila. The Lawn Mower. Basic but effective."

If Bradley Joe could avoid the Fool's Mate and have one mate he knew how to use, maybe he could win.

As we were getting up from our game, he reached out to shake my hand.

"I still would really like for you to come out on a date with me sometime, Stay-cee," he said, not letting go of my hand.

"Nope," I said, pulling my hand out of his massive paw. "Pick another girl."

"Pick another girl for what?" snarled my least favorite human at St. Ig's. Perhaps my least favorite human on earth.

"None of your business, dirtface," I said. "Let's get this over with. I have homework to finish." That last bit was a lie. I had done my homework. But even standing near Joseph Thornton made me want to crawl out of my skin and start pummeling someone. I hated him with a burning passion.

"Bye, Stay-cee," Bradley Joe said as he left for his last rotation. "Thanks for the lesson."

"Anytime," I said out of habit. "Didn't mean that," I tossed over my shoulder to him. "Not anytime. Maybe not again. Not ever." I said, not smiling. He smiled back.

"Totally grok," he said and winked.

It was harder than usual to control myself around Joseph today. My urges to say rude things were frequent and my desires to leap across the table and punch him in the face were getting harder and harder to resist. Every comment out of his mouth, every sigh, every snorting breath made me angrier than the one before. I admit, my game was not as tight as usual, (how do you catch a vampire?) but Joseph still could not beat me. Even when Mrs. Bason came over and gave him a broad hint about the best move for him to use, I overcame it and won in six.

"You're never going to beat me, you disgusting, ignorant sloth," I said, pushing my chair back and grabbing up my backpack. "Not ever."

"Oh, yes I am," he said with a vicious smile. And I swear his eyes flashed just a little bit red. Hands balled into fists, it took all my willpower to turn and walk away.

Saturday, December 1, 2001.

"Why isn't Jill picking up?" said Gram. "She said to call you if I was ever worried. Why is it so loud behind you?" There was something surreal about talking on a phone not tethered to a wall or phone booth while standing in the middle of a mall. I stretched my shoulders, sore from this afternoon's workout, while clutching the bag with my dad's birthday present under my arm. Finder glanced at her watch for the hundredth time, restless, shifting her weight. Couples and other teenagers hustled past us like rats in a maze.

Jill's mom didn't pause for me to reply. "She swore they'd be in tonight, but I've rung three times and no one's answering. What's going on?"

"They might've gone out to dinner since I'm out and Steve's sleeping over at a friend's. Did you leave a message?"

I watched for Nick's trench-coated shape. The mall entrance music played a little too loud, as if the huge display of reindeer and elves didn't make the season clear. I did like the garlands overhead.

They reminded me of Macy's Santa's Shop where parents stood outside and let their kids pick out gifts with tiny fistfuls of five dollar bills; bath puffs or aftershave or tchotchkes claiming Best Mom Ever.

Cold air rustled my coat every time the glass doors slid open. Tully kept his arms around Finder as she leaned her back against him, keeping warm. A man in a dark suit came through the doors. The hairs prickled on the back of my arms.

"I thought you watched Steven on Saturdays," Gram said.

"In the afternoons while they golf." I nudged Finder with my elbow and looked toward the Suit Man. Finder followed my gaze and shrugged. I ran through the catalog of Bat Suit faces I remembered from Maymont, and this guy did not fit. That was a good thing, right? Not that I was panicking, but nowadays men in suits walking toward me after dark triggered my alarms. I felt the weight of my teeny Star of David necklace and worried. My hand went to my messenger bag. Though I had misted my clothes in holy water before I left and had my now usual collection of unpleasant vampire surprises, I still felt weaponless. Finder was probably the best one, and soon she and Tully would be in their movie. I did have freshly made craft project presents for everyone. If this guy was a Bat Suit, my gifts would, I hoped, stave him off. The labor intensive part of my new project lay in process on my bedroom floor awaiting final instructions from my creative other half.

"Why aren't they picking up?" Gram demanded, voice gravelly from the cigarettes of the fifties. What did she want me to say?

Suit Man brushed by us without a glance. How paranoid was healthy under the circumstances? If Finder wasn't worried, I shouldn't be worried, right? She'd sense one if it were here, wouldn't she?

"Stacy? Are you there?"

"I'm here, Gram." The movie line grew.

"Is he going to show?" Finder asked as if I wasn't on the phone, as if Suit Man wasn't one of Matilda's's Bat Suits. He moved off into the crowd.

"Listen, Stacy, do you have a pen?" I didn't. "I need to leave my emergency information for my Paris trip. I just booked my ticket because Charlie finally said he can be here for Degas and Leonardo. Jill said call the minute I got everything squared away and now she can't even answer the phone?"

"I'm not at home, Gram. Maybe they . . . can't get the phone."

"What are they doing that's so important? Playing Scrabble?"

My panic kicked in. Were they okay? Matilda wouldn't go after my family early, would she?

Calm down, Goldman, I told myself. They are adults. They're allowed to engage in activities that keep them from the phone. Both kids out and the house to themselves, what would my parents be doing?

I tried not to think about it.

"Okay, well, Stacy, can you remember my flights?"

"Probably." And then I saw Nick.

He bounced across the parking lot, trench coat billowing in the cold Richmond night. A smile came unbidden to my face.

Jill's mom rattled off a stream of numbers. Though I felt cold, my palms broke out in sweats. I glanced at Finder, she'd seen him, too.

Nick burst through the doors wearing a smile as wide as his Hulk. Tully waved him over.

"Can you say that back to me?" Gram asked.

Nick bounded up and threw his arms around me. He picked me up off the floor and set me back down.

"Happy to see her much?" Finder said.

Nick smelled wonderful, like incense and coffee with a note of leather jacket. I smiled back at him as he looked down at me, slowly releasing his embrace.

Gram was asking me again to repeat her flight numbers. Somehow, I did.

Nick let go of me and backed up a foot, mouthing 'sorry!' I guess he hadn't noticed I was on the phone.

"Our movie starts in five," Finder said. "See you righteous slayers after." Finder started to drag Tully into the sea of humanity that was the theatre.

"Wait!" I called, feeling for their presents in my pocket. Suit Man had made me nervous. "Hang on just a sec, please, Gram," I said. I pressed a small thing into each of their hands. "Just in case."

"Wow, Stacy!" Tully said. "Thank you! This is beautiful. Did you make these?"

I nodded. Tully slid his bracelet onto his wrist. I'd chosen dark and bright blue lapis lazuli beads for Tully. They alternated every fifth one with a stone bead stamped with a cross. Finder rolled a red jasper version in her fingers before sliding it on. She looked at me for a sec, an unreadable expression on her face. Then she opened her arms wide, and scooped me in for a hug. The whole world got slow. *Finder* was hugging me. Astonished, I hugged her back.

"Thank you," she said. Then, she let me go. "Yeah. This is cool. Thanks."

"What about the suit?" I called after them, still stunned from Finder's hug.

"Gone. Don't worry about it."

Sometimes, I hated how cavalier she could be. Worry, excitement and first date jitters clashed together across my spine. I smiled at Nick, digging for his present in my pocket.

"Sorry, Gram," I said, returning to my phone call. "Tell me that last bit one more time."

"Is there a boy there?"

"Huh?"

"A boy. Do your parents know you're with a boy? Jill says she's never had to tell you a number twice."

My cheeks got so hot. I could see Gram's brassy red hair shaking as she sipped and swallowed.

"How's the smoothie?"

"Fine. Reminds me I'm supposed to be grateful to be alive. The worst part about trading one addiction for another is I was never fat when I smoked."

"No one cares what size you are, Gram. We're just happy to have you around."

"Keyword, a-round. Have Jill call me tomorrow. And tell my good-for-nothing daughter and her husband that they missed my call."

They're fine, I told myself as I pushed the end call button. They just aren't answering the phone.

"Hi," I said, looking up into Nick's pine green eyes. I stuffed the heavy brick of a phone into my messenger bag.

"Cold tonight," Nick said rubbing his hands together. His face broke open into the warmest smile I'd seen in forever. "It is so good to see you," he said. I felt ridiculously happy to see him, too.

"How was your trip?"

A kid in a Harley-Davidson T-shirt and no jacket bumped me in the back. A jolt of pain went through my tailbone. I sucked in a breath.

"Excuse you," Nick said.

"Sorry," the kid muttered and turned back to his friends. Nick moved between the kid and me, sighed and shook his head.

I'd asked Meredith what I was supposed to do now. Try to pay? Buy popcorn if he pays? Offer to pay next time if the date goes well? Formal dating confused me. At home, when I'd gone to movies with Isaac, we paid for ourselves. Then again, we'd never gone on a date.

"Two for Anime 61," Nick said before I could jump in.

"Here," I said, holding out a ten as we walked toward the doors.

"Oh no." He stepped back and smiled that luscious Goth boy smile. "Maybe Yankee boys let y'all pay," he said, putting on a high class Southern drawl. "But you're in Vuh-*gin*-yuh now, dah'lin." He opened the door for me, handing our tickets to an usher.

Nick reached for my hand. He still wore his half-fingerless leather gloves.

"Oh, here," I said, digging in my pocket. "This is for you." I put his bracelet into his open palm. I'd picked onyx for Nick, polished black beads with the alternating cross symbol beads. "I dunked it in holy water," I said. "I hope it works."

"I hope we don't have to find out. Thank you. This is awesome." He slid it on his wrist. Mine was a pale yellow citrine and featured Star of David beads as the alternates. I'd been astonished the craft store had them.

Turns out we both liked middle-back seats. One point for compatibility.

As he pulled off his trench coat/leather jacket combo, Bach's Fugue in G Minor came muffled from its folds.

"I got a phone!" he said, giving me a rather embarrassed look as he dug it out and answered. "Hey man, what's going on?" He winked at me and plunked down in his seat. I took off my coat and arranged it in my chair creating a kind of mini-donut for my tailbone. I sat *very* gently. Nick's face grew somber, listening. His expression flashed me back to the first time I saw him; an Adorable Goth Boy, talking over the counter at Third Rock Pancake House. I don't think I'd ever been so happy to see another Goth in my life.

I shouldn't say 'another Goth', because my compulsion to wear black had nothing to do with actual Goth-ness, either in style nor philosophy. It did have to do with twenty-one hundred and one people who died six blocks from my apartment two months ago on

September eleventh, and the massive boxes of all black, mostly Goth mail-me-downs Meredith insisted on sending.

Nick's face fell.

"Dude, I'm so sorry. What I can do?" There was a long pause. "Uh-no, it hasn't started yet. We just got our tickets," Nick sighed, looking concerned. "No. No, that's totally fine, don't even worry about it." He slumped over in his seat, clearly torn about something. "Let me call you back." Nick hung up and turned to me. "They think one of Luke's dogs got hit by a car."

"That's awful! Is he okay?"

"She. They don't know. Luke wants me to come look at her."

"Why you? What about their vet?" I said, puzzled.

"Out of town. Luke's wife's a little obsessive about the dogs. She doesn't trust any of the emergency clinics so Luke says I'm the next best thing. Their other dog is missing."

Disappointment washed over me in a wave that threatened to pull me under. As long as I didn't cry in front of him, everything would be recoverable. "I guess we'll talk later?"

"No!" he said, looking horrified. "No! Come with me. We can get something to eat after. Whatever you want. I can take you home no problem."

"Finder and Tully expect us back here. And they don't have phones."

And my dad will ground me until I'm thirty if he catches me coming home in the car of a boy he's never met. I'd taken that chance once and gotten lucky. Best not to push it.

We put on our coats as the previews started. I did have my own reason for wanting to see Luke, though. Wendell's new information had left the flavor of curiosity on my tongue.

"Luke lives close. We can get back before Finder and Tully's movie ends."

Following him out of the theatre, I hoped against hope I wasn't walking into a disaster.

13.

December 1, continued.

Bitsy the Basset Hound lay motionless on her side. Luke had arranged her on the kitchen rug, covered in a blanket in front of the oven, warm and open. Kneeling by the dog and stroking her head, he wore the same uniform he'd worn at the diner; jeans, black T-shirt, thin pony tail. His lips were dry with worry.

His wife (I assume his wife), the absolute opposite of Matilda, earthy in cargo pants and a messy bun, cried into the phone, hiccoughing sobs between answers to somebody's questions. A sheet of paper shook in her hands.

I stood back as Nick dropped his coats on the floor and knelt down to the chubby, long eared dog. I held the medical kit he'd pulled from his trunk in my hands.

"Hi Bitsy. Hey girl. Hello sweet dogness," he said, pulling back her blanket. He stroked her all over, pressing now and then around her ribs, her stomach, her head. He gestured for his kit.

Luke looked up, noticing me for the first time.

"Are you kidding me?" Luke's wife cursed into the phone then held it away from her face. "I am on hold again!" Luke's wife let loose a longer, more impressive stream of cursing. Bubbe's disapproving scold the one time I cursed in front of her came to me: You kiss your mother with that mouth? Coming from Bubbe, that otherwise mild comment had shamed me enough to cure me of adult curse word use in public forever.

"Are you sure you don't want me to do this part?" Luke asked.

"You don't *know* everything, Luke! Only *I* know everything!"

Hmm. Maybe not so different from Matilda after all, I thought. Her glare was palpable.

"Nina, this is Nick's friend, Stacy," Luke said. Nina glanced at me and maybe said hi, or maybe grunted. I couldn't quite tell.

Nick held his stethoscope to Bitsy's chest, then her back, then her belly. He ran his hands over her again, squeezing each limb, moving it, double checking his work.

"Could she be drugged?" Nick asked. "The only symptoms she has are of an animal who's been tranquilized. Her vitals are perfect."

"She's not hurt anywhere?"

"Doesn't seem to be."

"Nothing broken?"

"Ribs and legs feel good. Even a tranq-ed dog will react if you squeeze a broken bone." He squeezed her legs again, then pushed her ribs to demonstrate. Bitsy slept peacefully; not a wince, not a flutter.

"No symptoms of trauma in her pulses, her eyes. Nothing blood shot, nothing irregular. No swelling and every joint moves fine. No signs of dehydration. I think she's been dosed. Probably Ketamine if they're professionals."

"Professionals? Professional whats?" said Nina from across the room. She wound and unwound the yellow phone cord around her arm.

"Dog thieves," said Nick.

"What about cardiac arrest?"

Nick shook his head. "They'd have had to use something unusual to drug her, and that gets expensive. People who steal dogs are usually in it to make money, not spend it."

Nina's attention went back to the phone.

"Hello? Finally! Wolfdog. A breeding male. Alaskan Grey Wolf/Husky Hybrid Wolfdog."

"Should we search?" Nick said.

"Already done."

"Want to go around again? Different eyes see different things."

"I didn't miss anything," Luke said. The shadow of his role-playing game character flashed across his face, a wisp of arrogance, the leader not enjoying being questioned.

"I'm sure you didn't. I'll just take a quick look in case I see anything. Satisfy my own curiosity." Nick smiled. Again, the role-playing relationship stacking up in reality. Nick playing the charming, harmless, don't-mind-me subordinate. Weird.

Nick grabbed his coats. "Are you good?" he said to me. "I'll be right back."

"Okay," I would have gone with him, but he'd dog search a lot faster on his own. This tailbone thing was a super drag. Four weeks until Dr. K. said I should be not feeling it much anymore. Three months to fully heal.

Luke and I stared at each other for a minute, then both looked away. He sat down beside his dog and stroked her fur.

"How was the Museum Gala?" I asked. Luke leaped to his feet blocking my view of his wife and putting a finger to his lips.

Question number one, answered. He motioned me out of the room.

"The bathroom is just over here," he said a little too loud. Down the hall, Luke spoke again, sotto voce. "Nina knows I play live-actions, but she doesn't know about Maymont. Or Matilda. How'd you know I was at the Gala?"

I told him. My gaze fell on the still healing red words ripped into his arm. *Ich bin eine falschüng.* I am a false thing.

"How did you explain the tattoo?"

He looked at me like I was super dumb. "How does anyone explain a tattoo?"

"I have no idea. You got drunk and your fraternity brothers did it as a joke?"

"Listen, Stacy. How do I explain this?" He looked around as if the answer would come to him from one of the landscapes on the hallway wall.

"Nina doesn't game."

"Neither do I," I said.

"Right, but you have some . . . special friends you trust about this kind of stuff."

"Sort of." Where was he going with this?

"She gets very jealous of the time I spend in what she considers my fantasy life."

"It is your fantasy life."

"I know, but it's very important to me. If she thought that something happened in that world that meant more to me than she does, she'd make it very hard for me to keep gaming."

"But that wouldn't happen. She's your wife."

Luke looked at me with a strange expression. "You're young, Stacy," he said and tousled my hair. "Sorry about hijacking your date with Nick. It's not your *first* date is it?" He smiled. I scowled. Jerk.

"Are you dating Matilda?" I whispered. His eyes got wide. "Are you . . . feeding her?" Luke's lips drew tight.

I went on. "I know she feeds on men and I know she has . . . regulars. Are you one of them?"

"I don't see how any of this is your business," Luke said, arms crossed over his chest.

"Because in case you missed the point of that little visit at the diner, my friends' lives are coming up on the chopping block in four weeks," I said. "If you aren't on my side, I need to know. Please, Luke. Be honest. I won't tell Nick anything you don't want him to know. I won't tell anyone. But I have to know if I can count on you. I can't have a weak link. Not this time. Not on New Year's."

"I can't talk about it."

"You mean you won't talk about it." I struggled with what to say next. Finally, the thing I was desperate to know burst out. "Are you going to betray us, Luke?"

He looked like I'd just punched him in the gut. "No!" he said. "No. I would never. I'm not having an affair with her and she's not feeding on me."

"Are you drinking her blood?"

"No!"

"But you would if she offered," I said, seeing something in his eyes I didn't like.

"No. I'd never do that either."

"I don't believe you," I said, not sure where this boldness came from in me. "I think you're lying to me and I don't like it."

"Luke!" Nina shrieked from the kitchen. He turned and actually ran.

Drat. This conversation was over.

"Wolfdog? Like a wolf/dog hybrid?" Finder asked over her banana split.

Nick nodded. "I'm pretty sure that dog was stolen. I found a syringe in their driveway. Luke says they locked the house when they left to go eat and the dogs were inside. The door was unlocked when they came home. I think it has to be a neighbor. Someone who knows their patterns and which rock hides the key. Luke's wife is all flipped out."

I felt a pang of pity for Nina.

"She probably has a reason," I said.

"Yeah, those dogs are expensive," Tully said, dipping his spoon in lemon sorbet. "She probably paid two grand for him."

"How do you people know this stuff?" I asked.

"My parents bred Scotties," Tully said. "When Bronwyn and I were little. After the girls were born that was that, but they did it for a long time."

"Thousands of shelter dogs put down every year and people still breed dogs," I said, scooping up a melty bite of chocolate and nuts. "I don't get it."

"Can't show mutts," Tully said, scraping his dish. "It's a good business, if you love dogs." I did a double take. That dish had been full a moment ago.

"It's still wrong," I said. I glanced out the restaurant window into the rest of the mall.

Across the way, the Suit Man I'd noticed earlier leaned on a bank of phones, arms crossed. Suit Man saw me see him. He waved. An ice cream bite paused midway to my mouth.

"Stacy, what's the matter?" said Tully.

"Behind you out the window. Suit. Just waved at me."

Tully turned like he was passing something to Nick and glanced sidelong out the window.

"That guy was outside the theatre when we came out."

Finder closed her eyes.

She took a breath, put down her spoon. On the other side of the window, Suit Man fingered his tie then took out a cell phone.

"I have a stake. And holy water in my bag," I said, reaching to open it. "We can catch him."

"He's a Bat Suit?" Nick said, sliding into his leather. I passed Tully the stake.

Finder opened her eyes. "I don't think so."

"Could you be wrong?" I asked. I did not want another vampires-in-the-diner experience. But if we could catch him somehow . . .

"My skin's not crawling guys," Finder said. "I think he's just a dude."

"Then why is he waving at us and heading this way?"

"Vamp or not, today is not the day," Finder said. "I'm not dealing with this. Time to go."

Suit Man tailed us out of the mall.

"We should not be running!" I said. "If he wants to talk to us, we should let him! I'm telling you, we have to catch one! It's the only way she'll leave us alone!"

I glanced over my shoulder as Tully dipped and wove us through the parked cars. My tailbone ached with the effort pace. Suit Man jogged to catch up. I started to slow down. "Guys! He's outnumbered. Let's catch him!" Finder and Nick each grabbed one of my arms, popped them over their shoulders and ran me behind Tully. Another over shoulder peek. Crap. Where'd he go?

"Catching him means leverage!" I cried. "I'm the strategy guy! Why is no one listening to me?"

"Because you've lost your freakin' mind," Finder said. "Nobody listens to lunatics."

Tully's pickup was parked at the far edge of the lot under the mall sign, a good sprint closer than the Hulk. The full moon lit the parking lot as much as the lights did. I searched the sky for bats. Nothing. I scanned the lot for our assailant. Drat. Looked like we'd lost him.

"If he's alone, it's the perfect time to grab him!"

"I don't think he's a vampire," Finder said, "but I'm not in the mood to find out." Nick and Finder lifted me in and plunked me down on my donut, (Geez, that girl was strong) then leaped into their own seats. Tully turned the engine on. Pealed out.

"We'll follow you home," Tully said.

A convertible, top down, pulled into our parking aisle going the wrong way. Tully threw the truck into reverse, but someone pulled into the aisle behind us. Trapped.

Suit Man stopped head to head with Tully's truck. He got out.

Adrenaline pushed panic into my stomach. I grabbed my cross from inside the messenger bag. I held it up to the window. Suit Man did not react at all. He held up an envelope and pointed to Finder. He knocked on the window.

"Layla Jackson?" A bit muffled through the closed window.

"No, thanks," said Finder.

"He won't be pleased if I return still carrying it."

"Stake him!" I said. "Tully! Stake him!" I thought holy words at my cross.

"Go away," said Finder.

"Jump out! Stake him!" I urged again.

Bat Suit stuck the envelope into the crevice between window and door then turned abruptly away. Revving his engine, off he went.

"All that for that?" Tully sighed in relief.

"Huge opportunity," I said, "totally lost." I absolutely had to be able to fight on my own. Being dependent on Finder and Tully was not going to cut it. "Aren't you at least going to open it?" I said.

"If we drive fast enough, it'll blow away."

I rolled down my window, and snagged the envelope. I slid a finger under the flap.

The front of the card had a photo of a bulldog in a party hat holding a bunch of balloons. The inside read:

Happy 17th, Layla!
Love, Dad.

Sunday, December 2, 2001.

"Stacy! Phone!"

Jill's voice. Reality. Me all over sweating, nearly choked with sheet balled up in my mouth. Daylight. No Matilda. I sucked in a breath of relief. My chest ached, sore as if someone sat on me. I crawled out of bed and reached toward my desk.

Please be Meredith. Please be Mer.

"Hello?" I croaked, licking parched lips.

"Stace, it's Tul. How 'bout some yoga? I'll come get you. By the way, I'm sure Finder will never tell you, but we both really like Nick. How *old* is he?"

"We have a Don't Ask, Don't Tell age policy right now," I said, yawning.

"Ah. Old, then. I'll pick you up in forty-five minutes."

"Wait. No. I don't wanna go to yoga. I wanna sleep. And was it really Finder's birthday?"

"You're coming. And yes. Yesterday."

"Why didn't we have a party?"

"She doesn't celebrate." That seemed depressing. Who doesn't want to do at least something fun on their birthday?

"Why not?" I said. Tully paused.

"Never mind. I'll ask her myself."

"Be ready at quarter of," he said.

"Don't wanna. Not gonna."

He hung up. Darn him.

I was going to stupid yoga.

A dog barked outside. I jumped. Ugh. Nothing like paranoia of vampires in the morning.

Five minutes and my coziest sweatpants later, the kitchen smelled warm and buttery. My dad shook the newspaper out in front of him as Jill put a plate down next to his cup of tea.

"You got danishes?" I said, looking at the stove for pancakes or the possible source of the mouthwatering smell. "From where?" I got a plate from the cabinet and eyed the golden pastries sitting on the counter.

"I didn't *get* danishes. I *made* danishes!"

I paused reaching for the tea kettle. Flour dusted the counters and every mixing bowl and measuring cup we owned lay piled in the sink. "You *made* danishes?"

"You were barely here yesterday. You didn't notice my major mess making the dough? These two have cheese." She made a face. Right. Gross. "And these four have raspberry jam." I went for a raspberry one. Only my dad ate cheese danishes. The rest of us knew the truth. Cheese did not belong in a danish. Danishes, however, were the most perfect vehicle for raspberry jam. Like pasta is the vehicle for meatballs and bagels for whitefish or lox.

I put down my tea then scooted the cheese pastries onto my dad's plate so the others wouldn't get contaminated.

"This may be the most explicitly gory photograph I've ever seen in a newspaper," said Dad. "Here. Look."

"Why do people do that?" I asked Jill. "Here, this is so gross, you try some. Makes no sense. I'm eating, Dad. Why would I look at your disgusting graphic photo while I'm eating?"

"It's an amazing piece of photo journalism. Look."

"No. It's breakfast. On a weekend. I do not want to see something gross. It's like when there was that subway accident and you bought me a pretzel then dragged me into the station to look."

"I did not drag you in to look. It was our station. It was raining and the next closest stop was ten blocks away. And you were hungry. I was doing you a favor."

"You nearly got me stampeded to death."

"You have to admit, seeing the train all crushed like that was impressive."

"Tully is coming to get me. He's making me go to yoga." I bit into my breakfast. It was not what I expected. Toothy and tender, warm and sweet, it was the best blinkin' danish I had ever put between my lips. I closed my eyes and chewed. When I opened my eyes Jill was looking at me with a worried expression.

"Is it okay?"

Speechless, I nodded and ate another bite. Flaky pastry melted in my mouth with the tart raspberry jam popping in citrusy glory all over my tongue.

"You made this? No lie?" I mumbled. Jill nodded, relief flooding her face.

"This is absolutely unbelievable," said Dad. "You guys, really. Look at these pictures." He started to spread out the paper but the table was full. He flipped it around and held up the full page article. I caught a glimpse. No, thank you. I looked at my plate.

"Some jogger in King William found the remains of a man they think was attacked and eaten by a mountain lion. Could also have been a bear. I shoulda been a journalist." He shook his head. "Amazing. The animal actually ate the guy. Like tore apart and *ate*. They found a bunch of his bones licked clean. But you know what's really nuts?"

I ate another bite of glorious, perfect, unfathomably divine danish, not looking at the paper.

"Stacy going to yoga is pretty nuts," Jill said. "Almost as nuts as where she'll be Monday and Wednesdays after school starting next week with me and Steve."

Oh no. What was this? Jill twinkled with mischief.

"What's really nuts," my dad went on, "is that this can be in a physical newspaper within hours of it happening. The jogger says his dog ran off the path before dawn this morning and wouldn't come when called. When the guy caught up, his dog was standing in the pile of remains."

"You and Steve and I," Jill said, holding her hands together in excitement, are starting martial arts classes! And guess who is going to be our teacher?"

My stomach dropped into my socks.

"You're joking," I said, the danish frozen in my hand.

"Nope." Her smile was so big. "Isn't it exciting? Finder had a session with Joanne at the counseling center and when I saw her there, she mentioned that you specifically had said you wanted to start working out! I've always wanted to try martial arts and Steven, well. Isn't it perfect? We're supporting your friend's business and we get to learn some great new skills as a family and work out at the same time!"

"Is Dad going? If he's not going, it's not really going as a family," I said. I knew my dad would die before going to martial arts class. If he could get out of it, I should be able to, too. I know I had vowed just last night to become my own fighter, but faced with taking Finder's class, I was like, nope. I knew I had to work out and get stronger, but in public? And taught by my classmate and friend? That seemed cruel and unusual. I was thinking more like shooting bows and arrows. Distance fighting seemed nice.

"Finder said she thought it would be good for you, Stacy."

I was going to kill that girl. Kill until truly dead.

"And within minutes," said Dad as if Jill hadn't just dropped a major bomb on me, "cops and reporters were on the scene, the guy was interviewed, and poof, here it is in the paper."

"Maybe the dog ate the guy," I said. Maybe if I ignored Jill, her new plan would go away. My dad put the paper back in his lap.

"That's ridiculous," Dad said. "Dogs don't eat people."

"Really hungry ones?" I said.

Jill turned on the radio. "Are you people trying to put me back on my Azirapan?"

"What? This isn't going to happen to you. You don't jog." Dad reached for his tea. "I'm just saying, it's amazing. Something you don't see in New York." He looked over his danish at me. "Sure you don't want to take a look?" He was not going to let this go.

"Fine." I got up and stood behind him. A tiny bald spot was starting on the very top of his head.

"Hey, Dad! There's a- " I paused. Maybe telling a middle-aged man he was starting to go bald was not the best course of action. I might need him to help convince his wife that martial arts was not a good activity for me. If he hadn't noticed the bald spot yet, I didn't have to be the one to tell him. "Nevermind." Besides, why distract a man from his gory news photos?

"I love you, Daddy," I said. I leaned over to kiss his cheek.

"That's very nice," he said. "Whadda ya want?" I glanced at my pastry, making sure Steve was not about to sneak up and shark it. Steve wasn't even downstairs yet. Good. He had enough to think about this week without adding hungry mountain lions.

"Will you please tell Jill I don't need martial arts classes?"

"I think it's a good idea. Steve will love having his big sister in class with him."

"What? You can't be serious."

"After the whole fall on your tailbone, and your reluctance to ride the bike- "

"I'm not reluctant," I said, indignant. "Dr. K. said I *can't* ride the bike until my tailbone's healed."

"I think some exercise in coordination will be good for you."

"I'm leaving for *yoga* with Tully in half an hour." Dad sipped his tea and stayed glued to his news. "Traitor," I said. "We have the home gym, which I use more than anyone else. I don't need more exercise." He ignored me.

"Looks like a chicken bone only with a hand on the end." Caving, I looked down at the paper.

Sure enough, the photos documented a gory pile of body parts. My stomach did an uncomfortable flip. I had seen some gore myself recently, but not like this. At least vampires didn't bleed. I looked away. Going back to my seat, I wondered. Could Matilda do something like this? Would she? The situation seemed uncanny to me. Would a wild animal be discriminating enough or hungry enough to eat an entire person leaving behind the hands and feet and head? I looked again at the picture and yep, sinew showed. Ripped was right. Made a subway accident seem positively civilized.

Hmm. I'd have to ask Finder what she thought. After I killed her. Meanwhile, I had a danish to finish, a parent scheme to circumvent, my first yoga class to attend and a vampire to trap. My plate was full.

14.

December 2, continued.

Tully unrolled a thin, blue mat onto the chilly studio floor, then unrolled a purple one for me. It was a soft, rubbery thing imprinted with a woven texture. He staggered it beside and a little behind his, aligning its edges with the floorboards.

Following his lead, I sat down. Brr. Zipping up my sweatshirt, I looked on in awe as other students, including Tully, stripped down to tank tops and shorts.

"You have to at least take your socks off," Tully said. "So you don't slip."

I did not like the idea of parting with my warm, cozy socks, much less letting my bare feet touch this weird bumpy mat that who-knows-who had sweat on in the past, but, I'd come this far. Off came the socks.

Ten more people filed in gradually, each laid out a mat. Some stretched out on them, some sat, eyes closed, one man sat on his heels then bent forward touching his forehead to the floor. One of the ladies out-aged Bubbe, the rest were peers to my parents. One man exchanged greetings with Tully, asking first about fencing, then school. Funny, he didn't ask about vampire slaying. I suppose Tully kept that to himself.

The soft-voiced teacher began. "Does anyone have any injuries or is new to yoga?"

Should I say anything? Tully nodded like 'yeah, go', so I raised my hand.

"I have a broken tailbone. And I've never done yoga before."

Teacher lady went to the closet.

"I'm Saanvi," she said. "Lift up." Smiling, she scooted a cushion wide as a bleacher seat and six inches thick under each cheek, replicating my donut in a much more dignified way. "Use these for the seated poses." Thin and vibrant, she sat down cross-legged on a mat matching mine, addressing us all with a smile.

"Allow your sit bones to melt into the floor."

That meant my butt, right?

"With your body now present on the mat, allow your mind to arrive fully. Release any worries or events leftover from the week."

As if.

"Close your eyes. Take in a full, deep breath, expanding the lower ribs and letting the side and back body expand. The front of our bodies represents consciousness, our back-bodies the subconscious. Allow your breath to deepen, filling all unused space in the back body."

I sat up straighter, filled up my lungs.

"Let go of the corners of your eyes. Release your jaw."

Following her instructions, my skin actually moved. Relaxing my eyes and jaw made my face feel like it dropped an inch. Talk about weird! I hadn't even known I'd been squeezing my eyes closed or that my teeth gripped together like magnets. Saanvi kept talking. I found myself incredibly busy for someone sitting still with her eyes closed.

"We'll open our practice with three oms. Om is three separate sounds," she said, "'Ah', resonating at the base of the spine at the seat of *kundalini*," (what?) "'ooo', rising energy up through the heart chakra, (yay, I knew what that was!) and 'mmm' vibrating the third eye and pouring out through the crown of the skull." She took in an audible breath. The whole class started together.

"Aaahhhoooooommmmmm."

Repressing a giggle, I snorted, playing it off as a sneeze.

"Aaahhhoooooommmmmm."

I pinched my tongue with my teeth. I didn't want to embarrass Tully, but it was sooo hard not to laugh.

"Aaahhhoooooommmmm."

Thank goodness it ended fast.

"Come onto all fours," Saanvi coached, doing it herself. "Breathe deep in your belly. Allow your spine to lengthen, pull the heart forward as you raise your eyes toward the ceiling."

Saanvi warned us that we were going to push back into something called downward facing dog.

Rear ends in the air, palms and feet on the mat, the class resembled a small mountain range.

"Spread your fingers. Press into the mat."

My arms started to shake.

"Release your breath," Saanvi coached. I hadn't realized I'd been holding it. "May I give you an assist?" she asked.

"Okay," I said. She put her hands on my hip bones and pulled. It was like a standing version of when Tully did traction on me. It felt amazing. My arms shook harder, though. I tried to breathe, squeezing my eyes shut in concentration.

"Come back to this pose to rest any time during the vinyasa sequence."

Rest? This pose? My legs trembled with effort as she let go. Next, she led us into a front knee bent, ninety degree lunge, arms straight up. My left thigh graduated from tremble to full on shake and burn. Sweat dripped into my bra.

Saanvi came and put her hands again on my hips.

"You want them square to the front of the room," she said giving me a little twist.

I was going to die! Matilda or no Matilda, this yoga woman intended to crush me. I'd heard yoga relaxed you. Ha! I glanced under my arm at Tully. Sweat dripped off his face onto his mat. Eyes closed, even he looked like this was hard. Saanvi clicked a button on her cd player. Chanting filled the room.

"Soften your face. Place your hands on the mat. Step back to plank, the base of a push-up position. Bend your elbows, lower perpendicular to the floor into *chaturanga*." (Chat-er-UN-gah.)

What?

As we went on through 'the practice' as she called it, I found muscles I didn't know I had. I struggled to hold each pose for a full ten breaths. I pushed hard. My muscles burned and shook. My breath came in rough bursts, as if I'd been running.

We took a real rest in the forehead touching the floor pose I'd seen before class started. I took a few big breaths. Before I could stop them, silent tears dropped loud as pennies on my mat.

What is going on today? Come on, Goldman. Get it together.

Your body is releasing trauma, said Michael. *It's a good thing.*

I don't understand.

You moved your muscles deeply. Where do you think your memories are stored, your experiences? Your body. This is exactly what you need.

I wasn't sure I agreed. Yoga was hard.

Class almost over, Saanvi had us all lie on our backs. I couldn't because my tailbone ached after all the movement, so she showed me how to lie on my side with one leg over the cushion thing from the start of class. Then, she covered my sweaty self with a (was she crazy?) wool blanket.

"Let go of any places in your body or mind where you're still holding on," she said to the group. "Close your eyes, let the asanas settle. Allow yourself to reap the benefits of the practice. Take rest."

We lay still for a long time. Quiet in the near dark, resting after the intensity. Slow regular breathing. A slow tingle in my crown chakra. It was familiar now, that opening. The new part was the sensation in my chest, as if it had a soft, comfy weight in the center. I took a big breath and the weight hummed, then stopped. Each breath brought the hum and then let it go. A clear, bright, bell tone resonated from the front of the room. A second ring and a third, clear and energizing. Silence again.

My body still tingling and humming, Saanvi led us to a seated pose, palms pressed together at our hearts.

"Thank yourself for practicing today, and I thank you for sharing your yoga with me. Tomorrow evening's practice will be gentle and include more pranayama. And please remember there is a discussion of the eight limbs of yoga and incorporating the principals into our daily life on Thursday after practice. I hope to see you all there. Have a beautiful week."

She said a word I didn't understand and everyone repeated it.

I didn't speak again until we were just about home. I felt like putty. Tully looked at me and smiled.

"Want a yogurt?"

I took one and opened the other, handing it to him at a red light. I didn't even like yogurt, but somehow this tasted so delicious I wanted more when I'd finished. After a bit, we pulled into my driveway.

"What was that word?" I said. "At the end."

"Namaste?" He said it, nah-mah-STAY.

"What does it mean?"

"It's cheesy. Sure you wanna know?"

"Yeah. I mean, if I'm gonna say it I should probably know what it means."

"The literal translation is 'I bow to you' and it was used to greet elders. So, in India it's basically 'Hello'. But Saanvi says so many American yogis expect it at the end of class, she uses it as a blessing. She said words can mean anything if the intention is right."

"So what's her intention?"

"The divine in me beholds the divine in you."

We held each other's gaze for a long time.

"Oh."

Monday, December 3, 2001.

The phone rang while I was pouring the water for Dad's tea.

"It's 6:04 in the morning," he said. "Who the hell is calling right now?"

Oh my god really? Six? A.M.? Ugh. It had to be Judy. Who else would call me at a ridiculous hour on a school day? I picked up the phone. "Hello?"

"It's MEEEEEEEE!" Meredith said, way too loud into the phone "I'M UNGROUNDED!!!!! I'm FREEEEEEEEEEE!"

I squealed and jumped up and down, just for a second. My father gave me a glare.

"I feel like a brick just rolled off my back, for real," I said.

"Me too! I am so happy! Look, I know you have the bus in like six minutes, but I couldn't wait to call you."

"I'm glad you didn't. This is a glorious day! Call me after school. I'm home at- "

"4:30. I know."

"I have so MUCH to tell you."

"Okay. I'm just so relieved we can talk again," without sneaking around, she didn't say, but I heard it in her tone.

"Me too. Call me, later."

"Don't worry, Woman. Tell Finder move over! BFF Meredith is back in the house!"

December 3, continued.

I caught my breath as Finder, Tully and I scanned the Maymont gate. It gleamed in the cold winter sunshine. Sweat soaked my shirts under my fleece vest. We had just done my first 'long' outdoor run-walk, four and a half miles from school to Maymont.

"I think daytime is more dangerous than night," Finder said. "Security cameras, human watchers we don't know about. Park police. Spies. I feel like we should come back at twilight, once it's closed, but before the Bat Suits show up for work."

"We're just refreshing some of the big signs," I said, stretching my arms overhead. 'Signs' meaning the booby traps we'd set with holy symbols, water and garlic. "No one will notice."

"Unless they do," said Tully. He and Finder had chalk, I had a spray bottle and cloth. "Is keeping her annoyed really such a good idea?"

"It's about maintaining pressure," I said. "Right now, we have no way to affect her, but she has a zillion ways to affect us. If we have no way to make her uncomfortable in the way she makes us uncomfortable, then we lose every exchange. That will not land us a win at New Year's. I've said it a zillion times. We need to catch one of her Bat Suits."

"And do what with it?" said Finder. "Set it like a trophy on the side of the board? Catching a vampire and capturing a chess piece are not the same thing."

"When did you become Miss Passive?" I said. "You've advocated staking from the very beginning! And I owe you one very painful friend death, by the way. What were you thinking telling Jill I want dojo classses? She signed us up!"

"Martial arts is gonna make all your workouts so practical. You'll see." Finder zipped up her sweatshirt. "And I'm not being passive. I'm redirecting. Miss Joanne says my unresolved anger issues from when my dad left are affecting my relationships," she glanced at Tully. "That I'm not vulnerable or trusting enough so I keep people who I want close to me at a distance."

Not now, therapy. Please, not now.

"She and I created an action plan where I slow down on the aggression and stand in responsibility for my own emotions. Instead of taking them out on others."

An *action plan*? Seriously? The only action plan we needed now was the one that put Matilda under our shoes. Ugh. This was my own fault! Why, why had I suggested therapy? I needed Finder's grr, not her open stinkin' heart.

"Is the best time to heal old wounds when your life is in danger?" I said.

"Healing is always a priority," Tully said, taking Finder's hand.

"No! Guys! Not now! Until we figure out how to maintain the advantage, we have got to stay focused!"

Locked in each other's eyes, they were having a moment.

"Oh good grief," I said. "There's a bench over there. Go. Talk. Heal. Whatever. Give me the chalk."

"You're on a separate journey right now, is all," Meredith said. "Relax. Everything's gonna be fine."

"Whose side are you on?" Despite my sore feet and legs, I paced my room, pausing at my window. The moon hung fat and bright reflecting in ripples on the river. "I had to refresh all the booby traps myself. I was totally paranoid the whole time, like flying monkeys were everywhere, ready to report me to the Wicked Witch of the West."

"Take a bath. Do some calculus. Read some freaky science book."

"My body feels like toothpaste, but I can't stop thinking. It'd be best if I could work in the lab, but it's closed and I don't have keys."

"Call the hot college boyfriend and make him take you out for coffee. I bet he can help you figure out what to do with that restless energy." I could hear her smiling on the other end of the line.

"Meredith, you're impossible."

"Yes. Yes, I am. And tired of waiting for news of kissing. Get on your game, Woman! Let's go!"

Two hours later, my phone rang again.

"Stacy," Finder said, voice quiet and uncertain. "Can I tell you something?"

Finder never sounded quiet and uncertain. I went straight to emergency mode.

"Are there bats? Did they follow us? Is Matilda or your dad there?"

"Stacy," she said again. "For real. Tully and I had sex."

15.

December 3, continued.

That sentence hung in the air. Finder spoke again.

"Did you hear what I said?"

I had heard her. I just didn't know what to say.

"You did? Tonight? Like, just now?"

"Uh huh."

"Wow. I mean . . . wow. Was your mom home?"

"Book club. They eat a ton of appetizers, have wine and then discuss the book or whatever. She has to stay long enough to sober up before she drives home, so she's always home late. Tully just left."

"Do you think she'll know?"

"My mom?"

"Yeah."

"When I tell her she'll know."

"You're going to tell her?"

"Probably. I mean maybe not like tomorrow, but probably soon. Why? Is that weird?"

I had no idea. Was it weird? Would I tell Jill if Nick and I . . . ? No. Definitely not. At least not for a long, long time.

"She'll probably be relieved," Finder said. "She thinks Tully's gay and will dump me any minute. This might make her feel, I don't know, like I'm not spending every day getting closer to having my heart broken."

I could not imagine Finder heartbroken. Then again, I had seen her look at her dad.

"Thanks for picking up," Finder said sounding a little more confident. "Tully isn't home yet and he was kind of, you know, involved in the events. So that left you."

Me? I thought about it. I was the friend to call? I didn't see Finder with a whole lot of people at school, and at the dojo she was a teacher. Surely she had other friends?

"Don't be shocked, Chess Team. After the thing with my dad, there weren't too many people I could talk to. Right? Hi, I'm Layla Jackson and my father is a vampire. Nice to meet you. What's your bizarre family secret?"

I got it. We bizarre family secret keepers had to stick together.

"So can I ask you a question?" I asked.

"You mean *the* question? Go ahead."

"Did it hurt or did it feel good?"

"Both. Tully, well. Let's just say he has big feet."

"Oh my god!" I blushed. "Is that a real correlation?"

"In my limited experience, yes."

I giggled. "Sorry, it's not funny."

"It kinda is. The condom didn't help. But it did what it was supposed to do so that's what counts."

"You had a condom? Like, in the house?"

"Stacy. My cousin Christopher used to *live* here. And you know my mama. She has one of everything in this house."

"I'm glad you, you know, didn't take a chance."

"Yeah, that part was stressful. But for real, Tully might be traumatized."

"Why?"

"I dunno, but Stacy. He cried."

"He *cried?*"

"Yeah. Maybe I pushed him too fast or something, but I feel . . . weird. Like he was only doing it for me. I mean, he was sweet and willing and I know it felt good on some level, because well. Because. But he seemed really sad when he left. And he wouldn't talk about it. So, can you, like, check on him tomorrow or the next day? Be subtle, don't say hey I know you and Finder did it and she's scared she traumatized you, but you know. Something. Better phrased."

"Of course I will. I'll tell you what he says."

"Nah, don't. He can tell me what he wants or not. I just wanna know he's okay. He pretends to be okay around me sometimes and thinks I don't know. But I know." She paused and let out a big breath. "I'm kind of afraid he was pretending tonight."

Tuesday, December 4, 2001.

I sat with Judy, in St. Ig's library going over the attachments one more time. The vaulted ceiling gave off serious Ivy-League vibes.

"If DNA is a wall," I said, "nucleotides are the bricks."

"Okay."

"So, a brick is a mix of clay, sand and water. A nucleotide is a mix of nitrogen, phosphorus and deoxyribose which is a sugar. Every nucleotide, every 'brick', is made of those same three base materials." I adjusted my glasses on my nose. I hadn't thought I'd have to explain it in this detail, but this morning in class, I realized that Judy, though good in the lab, had no idea what the basics of our project were.

"I'm with you," Judy said. "Each brick, which in DNA is called a nucleotide, is made of nitrogen, sugar and phosphorus."

"Correct."

I looked up and saw Tully walking across the library. I waved, but he didn't see me. Drat. I had to do my Finder-promised duty and check in. He looked like he was heading for the gym. "So we're building a wall. Each brick is a color, but there are only four color options; adenine, guanine, cytosine and thymine. Are you following?"

"Yeah."

"So here," I pointed to the picture in our text book. "We're calling adenine red, guanine green, cytosine blue and thymine yellow. So we want only one color in our wall, and that color is orange. So which two nucleotide bases should bond?"

"Adenine and thymine?"

"Bingo!"

"But a lot of my bonds aren't orange."

"Right," I said. The door shut behind Tully. "Yours are either transitions, which are when adenine binds to guanine, adding a third hydrogen bond, or when thymine binds to cytosine. If we reverse those dance partners we get something called a transversion or mispairing. That's what your DNA does too much of. Here, read this part one more time, I'll be right back."

I got up and jogged across the library to push open the door Tully disappeared through.

"Did she ask you to check on me?"

My hand flew to my chest. "Oh my god, you startled me! I was expecting to chase you." Tully stooped in the low arched hall. "And yes, she did," I said.

"Did she tell you why?"

I thought about lying. I decided against it.

"She was worried she pushed you too fast and upset you." I didn't want to say, yeah she told me you cried in bed.

"Tell her I'm fine."

"Are you fine?"

"I'm fine." Tully was a terrible liar.

"I told her I'd tell her what you said, and she said not to. She said, 'Check on him and find out if he's for real ok. You don't have to tell me what he says.'"

Tully gave a little half smile. "Finder is amazing like that." He sighed and looked at the end of the hall. "Then no, I'm not fine, but I will be. There's nothing to worry about. It was kind of a surprise and I was worried about hurting her. If she's good, I'll be good, too."

"Okay," I nodded. "I'm no expert, but if you need anything, I'm here." I held out my fist. He bumped it with his.

"Thanks."

"Sure. And wish me luck. My first class at Flying Eagle is tonight."

"Some new faces," Finder said, pausing for a brief moment of eye contact with each person on the mat. I had never seen Finder so at ease. She smiled in her whole body, completely in her comfort zone. I shifted my weight, awkward in the new uniform. The pants fit loose, open at the ankles like flannel pajamas, but not comfy like that. I expected the uniform to be soft, but it felt like a cotton version of my St. Ig's uniform. Stiff and awkward. But maybe that was just me. I'd worked out here with Finder and Tully before, and part of me wanted to be here. My goal was to be able to stake a vampire, not be a vampire's steak. But being forced into it on Jill's agenda had sucked the fun right out.

Finder, who introduced herself as Sensei (SEN-say) Layla, had us run around the mats to get our blood pumping and alternate with sets of push-ups. I made it around four laps without my lungs feeling like frozen, asthmatic icicles. Could all the home workouts be making a difference? Was being able to breathe a sign of progress? I made it through four push-ups and faked my way through the rest. Finder came and stood next to me.

"Pretend I'm holding you like a suitcase," she said. "You have muscles on the sides of your ribs that help hold you up if you squeeze your abs. Squeeze!" I did and pushed back up. Once.

"Good," she said. "More like that one."

My arms shook and burned. I tried one more push-up squeezing the daylights out of my abs and fell right on my belly. I rolled onto my back for a break. An enormous dude joined Finder on the mat. He had broad features, a chest the size of a public mailbox and a sparkly, big energy. He spotted me and smiled, then came over. He offered a hand to help me up.

"Hey, Year of the Tiger! How you doin'? Welcome to our home away from home."

"You remember Bolo, right?" Finder said. I did. The bouncer from the all-ages dance club who'd figured out how old I was by identifying my Chinese astrological year. That night seemed a hundred years ago even though it was only a month.

"Bolo, this is Stacy." Finder lowered her voice so only we could hear. "Sis needs to get in gear for some righteous bite fights. That's her step-mom, Jill and her little brother Steve, over there. Stacy *knows*, and the little sprout knows, but mom is in the blank. They're new tonight, so work your magic."

"Roger that, boss lady." I stood as high as the top of Bolo's ribcage.

Sensei Bolo called Steve over and helped us as Finder led the class through a slow series of partner movements. Bolo explained how each one worked. Punching wasn't just throwing your fist, it was a contraction of the shoulder that twisted from your body to protect your thumb when you eventually struck something other than air. He taught us to always aim to the right, so as to land your stake in the heart.

A half hour later, I laid on the mat sweating like I have never sweat before. Except when fighting vampires.

Bolo went to help someone else and partnered me and Steve with a potato-shaped kid whose head barely reached my shoulder.

"I have diabetes," said the kid.

"I have Jewish guilt," I said mopping my forehead with my sleeve.

"I have a stuffed monkey named Monster. I'm Steve," said Steve, smiling at his new friend. "What's your name?"

"Xavier." He looked Steve in the eyes. "Did you know you have a pancreas in your belly?" His face was serious, waiting for an answer. This was not a rhetorical question.

"Nope," said Steve. "I have dinner in my belly."

"The pancreas is an organ, like your stomach or your heart. It turns the sugar from your food into energy. If your body can't turn sugar into energy, you die."

"That's weird," said Steve.

"I'm in this class to stimulate my adrenaline. That's what my mom says. She's over there." He waved at a sweet-looking lady. The baby in her arms tugged on her long, black braid.

"She says if I raise my adrenaline I won't need so much insulin in my shots. Karate class is way cheaper than insulin. I turn twelve next week. How old are you?"

Steve and Xavier traded air punches as Xavier gave Steve a detailed explanation of what he expected to happen at his birthday party and a lecture on how diabetes works. I stopped listening and focused instead on practicing the footwork Bolo had shown me.

Not content with only one captive audience member, after a few minutes Xavier tugged on my sleeve. "Excuse me," he said. "Excuse me. I want to tell you something. If glucose builds up in your pancreas without insulin it's like stacking bricks on a cupcake. And then you die."

"How many times have you died?" I asked.

The kid rolled his eyes at me like I was sooooo dumb.

"I didn't die," he said. "I *almost* died. On Halloween. I went into a haunted house after eating too much candy and I got really scared and my mom says my adrenaline got too high and too much glucose stuck in my pancreas so I went to the hospital."

"Did you die and come back?" This seemed to be a running theme these days.

"No. But I did black out."

"Tell me about the piñata again," Steve said to the older boy. "Stacy, remind me to tell Mommy. I want a piñata for my next birthday, too!"

"My mom says my body was a shook up soda can," said Xavier, not tracking that Steve had changed the subject. "Having no insulin was like shaking the soda can until," he opened his hands, wiggling his fingers in a horseshoe shape in front of his chest, "boom!"

Welcome to life, kiddo, I thought.

Boom.

Sunday, December 9, 2001.

My dad flipped another latke onto my plate. A plastic arrow whizzed past my head.

"Steve! Cut it out! Can we not let him shoot those things in the kitchen?" I said. "It nearly landed in my food."

"Sorry!" Steve ran past the table and pulled all six arrows off the suction-cup dart board he had hung on the pantry cabinet knob.

"It's the right height for him to hit the target," Dad said, flipping the last potato latke in his frying pan. "And there's nothing he can break in here. In the family room there're lamps and photos and glass things he could knock over."

"Who are you, and what have you done with my father?" I asked. Truly. "Do you remember when you freaked out at the scarves?"

"Oh yeah. That was the circus thing right?"

Yes, I thought. A circus came to Battery Park so Meredith and I tried learning to juggle scarves so we could run away and join.

"You'd have thought we were throwing bowling balls in the tea cup section of the Met, the way you reacted," I said. "But this little cub gets to shoot darts in the kitchen? Not fair at all."

"It's a bow and arrows," Steve said. Whiz. My hair blew in the breeze.

"You get the hot latkes," Dad said. True that. And hot latkes were my favorite thing on the planet next to chocolate and coffee so I guess I shouldn't complain. Jill sat at the other side of the table with only a bite left in her salad bowl and an entire latke getting cold on her plate. Barbarian. She flipped though a catalog that had come in the mail.

"Should I order us outdoor furniture for this summer?" she said.

"You ask this in December?" Dad said. "The dreidels are by the menorah and you want to talk about life poolside?"

"Never too early to plan ahead," she said, looking smug. "I found something you will love."

"Oh really?" He did not look convinced. She flipped the catalog and held up the magazine, wide open. In the center of the page was a gigantic grill.

"I thought this house came with a grill."

"Not one like this." Jill started the run down of all the fancy features as I smeared half of my latke with apple sauce and the other half with sour cream. Steve moved from corner to corner of the room to shoot his plastic projectiles from all sides of his target.

In the middle of the table sat a wide candle holder that would, by the end of this week, hold nine narrow taper candles. Our menorah. Tonight, it had the center one called the shamash lit and the one on the far right. Jill had opened a pair of fuzzy handmade socks, I had opened a copy of a chess-based thriller novel, and Dad had opened a chain for his glasses so he'd quit losing/leaving them everywhere. Steve had opened the bow and arrows set. Tomorrow's gift would be fairly anti-climactic as it was homemade gift night. Since none of us were huge crafty people, we all kind of failed. I was going to come home from school and make brownies to give since I didn't think anyone would like a beautifully written math equation or chess puzzle to admire. Bubbe insisted that one night always be homemade gifts to remember our ancestors who traded in sand and camels, but I think it was really because she loved giving homemade stuff. I wished she was here.

The phone rang and I jumped to answer it.

"Look outside your windows," Finder said. "Do you see bats?"

I took the phone and walked over to the kitchen bay window.

"No. Why?"

"Look again." I squinted, making it so my indoor evening vision could adjust to seeing more details in the dark outside.

"No, I don't see anyth- " I said. And then, I froze.

16.

December 9, continued.

Three little bats sat in the tree outside my kitchen window. When one of them saw me see it, it flapped its wings.

Why did we have no kitchen curtains?

I headed downstairs into the rec room. I went to the sliding glass doors and locked them. "What's going on?" I hissed hoping no one upstairs would hear.

"How many can you see?"

"Three."

"Same here and same at Tully's."

"Why? Are they trying for another birthday card delivery?"

"That guy who followed us at the mall wasn't a vampire," Finder said. "Mama said it was Phil, my dad's assistant. He's human. It's why my spidey sense didn't tingle. These are definitely vampires."

Steve came hurtling down the stairs.

"Hang on," I said and set down the phone. I opened my arms and he rushed in, grabbing my shoulders and jumping into my arms. I shifted him onto my hip like a Koala bear. "I smell them," he whispered near my ear. "Strong. Like more than one."

"There's three," I said, fear fluttering up my spine. I shivered. I hated being pinned. Forks, annoying but okay, Skewered, same thing, but pinned? Ugh.

"Recharge your garlic packets," Finder said. "And keep weapons nearby. I don't know what this is about, but I don't like it."

"Recharge? What does that mean?"

"Go around to every room we put garlic in and stoke up the energy. Do the blessing again. You remember it, right?"

"Yeah, but, we're like right in the middle of doing Hanukkah. If I go wandering the house they're going to want to know why."

"I'd find an excuse. Make the little sprout help you. Nobody cares where the little kids go on holidays. And it'll only take a few minutes. Just do like Tully and make the energy buzz. I'll call you if anything happens here. You do the same."

And what if we're in pieces by the time I can use the phone? I thought as I hung up.

"Hold my hand," I said to Steve as I set him down. "Finder doesn't know what's going on, but we have to work together. I need you to learn a poem, then go upstairs and say it in every room. Got it?"

"What poem?"

"By the power of three by three, this house is made safe by me, to cause no harm nor return on me, as I will, so mote it be."

Steve rolled his eyes. "That's an incantation. Not a poem. And I already know it."

"What? You do?"

"You and Finder said it like a zillion times the night she slept over." He popped one hand on his hip and gave me a look I was starting to recognize. "I told you, Chess Team, I know everything."

"Do you know why bats are watching our house?" It was weird to hear Steve call me by Finder's nickname. I wasn't sure I liked it coming from him.

"I can guess. Holy water isn't very subtle."

"What? You know about that?"

Steve opened his hands, raised his eyebrows and gave me the look.

"You know everything. Right." I led him back up the kitchen stairs, whispering as we went. "So, right now there are three vampires watching our house and we have to- "

"Two," he said. "Two vampires watching our house." He was looking out the window past my shoulder.

I turned around and sure enough, one of the bats was gone.

The front doorbell rang. Steve sniffed the air like a dog. His face bloomed in a mask of panic.

"Who is that?" Jill said.

"I'll get it." Fear spilled over me. I could not let Jill near the vampires. I grabbed a bulb of garlic out of the onion basket. The doorbell rang again.

"Coming," I called. I squeezed Steve's hand too tight, then let go. "Stay here or go hide," I whispered in his ear.

"By the power of three by three, this house is made safe by me, to cause no harm nor return on me, as I will so mote it be," I said under my breath as I left the kitchen and entered the foyer.

Ding-dong.

I went to the door, never so glad as I was now to be wearing a sweatshirt that had come from a synagogue gift shop.

I peeped out the peep hole. Saw nothing. I put my hand on the door handle and pulled. Nothing happened. It was dead bolted, of course. I undid the bolt.

Ding-dong.

"Stacy are you getting the door?" I had better open it before she came out to see who it was or why I was stalling.

"Yes, I got it! Sorry!"

I took a breath. I let it out long and slow.

Please don't be my last breath ever, I thought. And I opened the door.

No one was there. On the mat in front of me lay an envelope.

My name danced across it in fancy cursive script. Red Goatee Suit sat on the wide porch swing under the big tree and waved. He winced when he saw my sweatshirt.

"Who is it?" Jill came around the corner. I grabbed the card and shut the door.

"Nobody," I said. "Just a card delivered. For me."

"How thoughtful for someone to remember Hanukkah, but who was it? Why didn't they stay to come in?"

I shrugged, tailing her back to the kitchen.

"Three little battys sitting in a tree," Steve sang, aiming another arrow. He glanced at me and out the window, the third bat had retuned.

"Didn't you order curtains for that window?" I asked.

"Blinds, yes. Don't you remember? They were the wrong size so I had to return them. They're shipping me new ones but it could be weeks before they get here. Thank goodness for the trees. Other than squirrels, no one can see in from the road or behind the house."

No one but vampires, I thought.

"Who's the card from?" Jill asked.

I slid my finger under the flap and felt the paper give. Inside was a cream colored linen card with a raised ink outline of Maymont on it. I opened it, half expecting it to explode or puff poisoned dust in my face.

"Who's it from?" Jill asked again.

Inside the card just read:

Annoying, isn't it?

STOP.

The phone rang. I jumped.

Jill got up to answer it. "It's for you," she said.

Tully said, "Did you get your note?"

"Mmm-hmm."

"I told my mom it was an inside joke from one of the fencing team captains. Maybe you should do the same."

"That's brilliant," I said. And realizing I should try to make this conversation sound normal, I said, "And I'm already sore from stupid yoga this morning. Do we have to do this now every Sunday?"

Tully chuckled on the other end of the line. "Nice cover. You'll thank me someday. Are yours gone yet?" I looked out the bay window. No bats.

"Mmm-hmm. At least I hope so."

"See you in the morning. Call me if anything gets weird and you need backup."

"Thanks, Tully," I said. "That's very thoughtful. Happy Hanukkah to you, too."

I caught a glimpse of myself in the stove backsplash as I put my plate in the dishwasher. This sweatshirt might be my new favorite item of clothing. The Beth Shamar logo had a big, and I mean *ginormous*, Star of David on it. And right now, no Star could be too huge.

Monday, December 10, 2001.

Finder and Tully had never done anything Hanukkah before so after our workout, they stayed for latkes and candle lighting. My dad, of course, thought he was sooooo funny. Every time you got another latke, you had to endure a joke. "This one's for Stacy," he said when I got my final piece of fried potato pancake bliss.

"What did Thor need when he broke his behind?"

"Dad, no. Please."

"An As-gard!"

Finder, Jill and I exchanged a look. Tully and Steve busted out laughing. And kept laughing. My dad joined them. Finder shook her head. Jill smiled with pity. I sat there. Males. This joke. Was. Not. Funny.

Jill, being Jill, had a little present for Finder and Tully each to open during present time.

"Tonight is homemade gift night," Jill said, "but I didn't want to subject you to bad craft projects, so I got you each a real present." A pair of fluffy wool socks.

Tully lit up when he opened his. "I love this brand of socks!"

"You've heard of them?" Jill's eyes went wide in surprise.

"Oh yeah, they're the best. I had a pair but wore them out. It's the organic wool and recycled poly blend that makes the magic."

"It does!" And off she and Tully went chatting on about the gloriousness of socks.

Finder rubbed hers between her fingers. "Really soft. For wool socks," she said, approving.

"There's a joke in there somewhere," my father said.

"Well if there is, keep it to yourself," I said, handing him my gift. It was a dessert plate, with a thick fudge brownie made by me, a teeny cup of espresso, also made by me and a chocolate cherry dreidel from the box Bubbe brought at Thanksgiving. I have a weakness for chocolate cherry anything and these were the most perfect cherry cordials on earth. This one candy shop on the West Side only made them in November and December.

Finder bit into her dreidel. She closed her eyes, and, like a true chocolate lover, savored.

I walked Finder and Tully outside to Tully's truck after we had turned on every outside light we had. We all stood on my porch scanning the trees for bats. Tully trotted down the steps and stood in the driveway facing the house. He gave a thumbs up. We seemed to be alone. Over dinner I had done some processing.

"The rule in chess is to control the center of the board. Blood is the center of Matilda's board. Does that make sense?"

They nodded.

"It's why it's been so easy for her to treat us like a game, because until now, we've had zero center board control. That's how she sees this. Even though our booby traps annoyed her, they were not an actual problem. Which is why she sent her guys to watch us and leave the notes. Annoying- "

"And scary," Tully said.

"And scary," I repeated, "but not an actual problem. We know empowered holy symbols work against them on some level and we know she hunts on Friday nights."

"Nice sweatshirt, by the way," Finder said, eyeing the massive star.

"Thanks, I love this thing. Might buy another one. Now, if we can control her center board, meaning her blood supply, we can maybe win this round, meaning get you off the hook, and get me and Tully out of the Bat Suit supply chain."

"If she finds out we're causing the problem . . ." Tully didn't have to finish that sentence.

"Right," I said. "We just have to make sure she doesn't find out."

Saturday, December 15, 2001.
10:13 a.m.

Judy looked less weird in regular clothes. Standing on my doorstep in a gray parka and jeans, she resembled a black and white line drawing of anyone else. She waved goodbye to a mousy-haired woman driving a beat-up burgundy hatchback.

"Does she want to come in?" I said, stepping aside to invite Judy inside. "I mean you're staying over and she's like, never even met my parents." I picked up her backpack and set it inside the door.

"She has an appointment," Judy said, stepping into the foyer. "Wow. This is a . . . big house."

"Too big. Can I take your coat?"

She stuck her notebook between her knees and took off the parka, carefully edging its worn cuff over a gauze bandaged hand.

"What happened?"

"Dog bite," she said, resentment and disgust coloring her voice. "Dogs hate me," Judy went on. "Still, my mom couldn't get this one into the crate, so I helped her. It bit me."

"Your mom has a dog that hates you?"

"Her boyfriend does. Sometimes we babysit it."

"I dog sat for my neighbor's dachshund at home," I said leading her back toward the kitchen. "He bit me once, but it was my own fault."

"This wasn't my fault."

"Oh no, I didn't mean *you* were at fault. I just meant *I* was stupid. That's all."

Time to find some chocolate.

Judy's tee, worn over a long johns shirt, had a pretty good hand painted picture of a bonfire and said 'Girl Scout Troop 1010 Halloween BBQ'.

"Make that shirt?"

Judy nodded.

"I stopped after Brownies," I said.

"Stacy, please make sure your room's ready for Whirlene to come and clean tomorrow," Jill said, kneeling in front of the open fridge, flanked by a small wall of half empty plastic containers, take out Chinese boxes and one elderly celery. "She has to set up both guest rooms and," she looked around the open fridge door, about to give me another set of instructions by the business-like look on her face.

"Oh! Hello!" Jill shot me a why-didn't-you-stop-me look and then paused, taking in the absence of color and mass that was Judy.

Jill wasn't much for recovering once she got off balance. And when Jill got off balance, she got anxious and when she got anxious she—

"Y-y-you're J-Judy, is that r-right?"

Stuttered.

"Yes ma'am," Judy said, barely audible.

This was my first time seeing Judy meet a stranger other than me. She visibly shrank. Fascinated, I squinted to see if my eyes were playing tricks on me, but Judy did seem to get smaller. Her shoulders bunched together as if she could make herself vanish, or pull a Wendell and dash under the floorboards. Jill collected the containers and stood, closing the fridge door with her heel.

"I'm s-s-sorry, I didn't say hello right away. I d-didn't realize you'd ar-r-ived. I'm Jill. I'm S-S-Stacy's s-stepmom." Judy kept her eyes down and nodded the smallest of nods. Jill looked at me as if I was somehow supposed to jump in and save the situation. Smoothing out awkward introductions was not my specialty. Jill was the one with small talk skills. "Are you a," she took a long deep breath. "A n-native," she took another long breath. "A native Richmonder, Judy?" Jill asked, her voice suddenly very quiet, too.

"Yes, ma'am."

"Why are you wearing sunglasses inside?" said Steve from under the dining room table. He knelt on the rug, plastic lines of track in hand. Around him splayed an elaborate roundhouse train set up. Track, buildings, obstacles and train cars extended from where he was to the far kitchen door leading outside to the balcony style deck. I'd warned him not to stare. Who knew whether or not he'd listen.

"Light hurts my eyes. If I wear the glasses, it hurts less."

"Why does light hurt your eyes?"

Jill stepped past me and dumped the leftover containers into the sink.

"Would you g-girls like a snack? Or is it too early? There's a v-veggie tray from Ukrops in the pool house fridge. And I have all kinds of sandwich makings for lunch when the time comes." Jill turned on the sink and began emptying the contents of the containers into the disposal. Judy crossed back to the kitchen entryway.

"Are you okay with seafood for dinner, Judy?" Jill asked over her shoulder. "I'm sautéing some halibut, steaming some asparagus and broccoli, and maybe doing a shrimp cocktail?"

Judy went even paler, her face going almost gray for a few seconds. "I'm fine with anything," she said. "I'm not a big eater."

"Stacy, before you disappear downstairs, can you please prep the garlic? I'm going to bake it before I go to the market for the halibut."

I would eat literally any savory food if warm garlic was spread on it.

"Jill, dinner is hours away."

"But if you prep it now before you girls get started then I don't have to interrupt you and it's already done. Otherwise, I might forget."

"It'll just take a second," I said to my guest, "and then we'll get started." I grabbed a bundle of bulbs from the bowl Jill kept on the counter and pulled them apart, quick and expert. I sliced the end of each bulb. The room filled with the luscious pungency of raw garlic. Judy sneezed.

"Bless you."

Skins still on, I stuck the bulbs, cut side down, in the garlic baking dish. I poured olive oil over them and rubbed it over all the skins. After baking, I'd squash each bulb with a rolling pin, mash out all the baked garlic and scrape it into a serving bowl. I would then proceed to consume ninety percent of it while pretending to share with the rest of my family. Judy sneezed again.

"You must be the science fair partner," my father said, walking into the room. "I'm so sorry. This one is a competitive beast when it comes to the science fair. She'll hold your feet to the fire. You go to St. Ignatius, you must like Catholic jokes. What do you call the nun that lives upstairs?" He paused. Judy stared at him. "None of the above!"

"I'm sorry to introduce you," I said, "but this is my dad, Ernie Goldman. He thinks he's hilarious."

"I am hilarious," he said sticking out his hand. Judy took it. I caught a glimpse. Oh no, a dead fish handshake. Dad gave me the side eye, but kept talking. "You can call me Mr. Hilarious, by the way. Or Mr. Lord of the Universe. Emperor of All Things. I've been trying to train Stacy to call me that for years. If she thought it would help her win the science fair, she would do it."

"Hello Lord of the Universe," said Steve, crawling out from his under-the-table train world. "Emperor of All Things!" He went to Dad and stuck his arms in the air. My dad scooped him up and let him hang like a monkey on his hip.

"See? He understands me." Dad looked to Jill. "Do you want to run over to the club and meet one of my partners for drinks and apps while the girls work and can watch Steve? There's a case that's been in the works since before I got here and it's about to get serious. I kinda have to go with or without you, but I'd rather go with you."

"Drinks and apps? It's not even noon."

"Mimosas and late brunch then, whatever. The point is, I gotta go."

Steve wriggled and Dad put him down. He stood in front of Judy and sniffed. "Why does light hurt your eyes?"

Judy shifted her weight, looking a little cornered.

"Steven," Jill said, "don't be rude."

Judy shrugged.

"He's not being rude, ma'am," she said. "He's just curious. My retinas are very thin. Recessive F1 gene. It typically accompanies the dominant gene that makes me albino."

"Oh." He went to the pantry cabinet.

He pulled a box of cheese crackers off a shelf and set it on the counter. "Mommy, can I have jellybeans?"

"Nope. Daddy finished them."

He stuck his nose in the cabinet. "No. We have some still."

"I told you, they got eaten," she said.

Steve stuck his head back inside the cabinet. "There are definitely jellybeans in here somewhere."

"Sorry. You can have the yogurt covered raisins."

Steve scowled and closed the cabinet. Nobody but Jill ever ate the yogurt covered raisins. Steve regarded me, now standing by Judy near the door. I hefted my backpack.

"Do *you* have the jellybeans?"

"Sorry, Muppet."

He looked at Judy. "You?"

She shook her head.

Dark blue jeans floated above his ankles showing the stripes on his socks as he resumed his post under the table. Had he grown that much since we moved here? Six weeks ago, those jeans were brand new, like all our stuff. Everything we owned with the exception of some jewelry and coins that couldn't be ruined by smoke and chemical debris had been lost on 9/11.

I led Judy toward the stairs to the rec room, stopping by the pantry Steve had just closed. I selected a box of organic shortbread cookies and the Nutella.

"I got you a veggie tray," Jill said.

Downstairs, Judy took in the room. "It goes on forever."

"The couch or the whole place?" I said. "And sorry about Jill. She stutters when she gets anxious."

"I didn't mean to upset her. Is she shy, too?"

"No, she's a therapist. Nobody becomes a therapist who doesn't, you know. Need therapy."

Judy smiled at that. I gave her the rec room tour, pointing out the iced tea stocked mini-fridge, the home gym and my chess table.

"Wanna see the pool house?"

Going quick because it was cold in just our socks, we padded across the stone pool deck to the little cottage. Judy paused, taking a long look at the river. I looked around the corner of the pool house to see if the secret rock had been turned. It had. That meant news from Maymont.

Her back to me, Judy stood enthralled by the river. I picked up the fake rock and quickly harvested the note from the little chamber inside. I replaced the rock as Judy turned around. Whew. Timing.

I snagged the pool house key from under the mat.

"You lock it?" Judy said. "In your own backyard?"

"There's a public path right below the property." I pointed. "You can see it from that gate. Anybody could walk up here."

"And do what?" Judy gave a half laugh. "Go for a swim?" The pool was covered in a big, green rubber thing that looked like a trampoline, though we had to assure Steve daily it was not.

"Someone could break in."

"They'd have to be stupid," Judy said, following me inside. "Houses like this always have alarms, or big dogs, or owners with guns or something. I don't even have keys to where I live. My mom's or my dad's."

"Are you kidding?"

"Nope. We never lock the doors. We don't lock our cars either. My mom leaves the key in it so she doesn't lose it."

I turned to face her. "And it's never been stolen?"

Judy sputtered a laugh. "You saw it! A 1986 Honda Civic? With a broken bumper and dents all over it? No."

I stared in amazement. "Where I'm from, you can lock a terrible car five different ways, then nail it to the street and still find it gone in the morning. Or at least missing the radio."

Judy shrugged, a movement like sharp mountain peaks rubbing against each other. She was so thin it made me want to eat a sandwich for her. She peeked in the tiny bathroom and changing room. "This changing room is bigger than my bedroom."

"Mine too," I said, "at home." My mind's eye filled with my cozy bedroom six blocks from the World Trade Center, before the Towers went down. I could feel the presence of my little bed tucked between tall bookshelves and the steam radiator that took up so much space from the wall I had to go sideways to get into my closet.

"I'm from the land of tiny apartments," I said. "If there was heat out here, I'd have moved in as soon as we arrived."

"A private house," Judy said, her voice full of longing. "Wouldn't that be just the thing?"

I got the veggie tray out of the fridge. "Jill will bug me if we don't eat some of this," I said, making a face at the food. "Sorry it's so boring. Finder keeps telling me to eat more vegetables, so I guess I can make some of it go away." Judy didn't reply. I turned around to see if she had heard me, but she was gone.

I found her a moment later, outside the pool house, staring at the river. I hadn't heard her leave.

"My dad's house is by a river, too," Judy said. "The Mattaponi tho, not the James." She looked up at the house, then nodded toward a curved bay window in the upper left corner. "That your room?"

"Yeah."

"I like seeing the river from my bed. Can you see it from yours?"

"No. Just from the window."

She looked at the river like a friend. I thought about telling her all the nature here creeped me out and I would much rather be surrounded by nice, solid concrete and walls.

"We're close to the mountains, too, so there's good hiking and nature stuff." It sounded like an invitation. "If you're into that?"

No, thank you. I was not.

December 15, continued.
11:41 a.m.

Judy read out loud. "Purpose Statement: The purpose of this project is to reverse incorrect nucleotide attachments in DNA. The goal of this research is to develop a DNA flaw reversal method in order to achieve a healthier population by minimizing frequency of DNA-based disease vulnerability."

"I think it's too general." I sipped my iced tea. "Try this: The purpose of this project is to use cell-generated repair enzymes to reverse incorrect nucleotide mispairings in specific hereditary DNA strands. Benefits could include minimization of genetic disease vulnerability and/or minimization or reversal of genetic mutations caused by DNA nucleotide malfunctions."

Judy wrote down what I said and read it back to me. I nodded. Rough, but it was a start. We'd spent a little time in the lab, mostly looking at previously run DNA, not figuring out how to fix it. That's what January was for. We had the month to figure it out, then the first two weeks of February to get the project board ready.

I laid the page Julian had given us at Thanksgiving next to the new DNA results we'd run from Judy's parents.

"This doesn't make sense," I said. "You've got some common genetics with your mom, but zero with your dad. This DNA has to have gotten mixed up. Mitochondrial DNA only runs from the mother, so maybe it's that? Can we get a new sample and rerun it ourselves? It'll take two weeks to get a fully mapped genome if we can get it in right away. I mean, I appreciate Julian helping, but this DNA couldn't belong to your parent. Makes no sense at all."

"Maybe he ran his by mistake?"

Or maybe he didn't want me to figure out what was wrong with Judy. That was ridiculous. What could be in it for him for her to stay sick?

"Are you sure you can't tell me the name or the type of your illness?" I said. "If I knew what I was looking for it would make things easier."

Judy looked hard at her notebook and shrank into herself. Ugh.

"I'm not dying," she said. "If that's what you're worried about."

Okay. Not dying was good.

"Since you won't tell me anything, I have no idea what to expect," I said. "You're not going to like, get super sick on a competition day, are you? Because if that's the case, we have to talk to Sister Mary Chemistry. I'm not doing all this work just to be disqualified for a missing partner."

Judy glanced up.

"I'm kidding," I said. (Was I?) "The point is, if- "

"Sister Mary Chemistry?" she said. "Do you mean Sister Maria Alberta?"

I hedged. "Is that our chemistry teacher?"

Judy giggled. "Do you seriously not know the Sisters' names?" Something thumped outside.

"They all kind of look the same in their outfits, so I get them confused."

"Habits. Not outfits. You can remember random sequences of DNA pairings, but you can't remember your teacher's name?"

I reached to open the veggie tray. Judy didn't touch it. Another thump against the glass doors. I got up and went to the glass, a chill of fear sliding up my spine. Please, I thought, please do not be birds.

"Stacy?"

Steve stood at the bottom of the stairs. "Something's wrong with Evia." His voice shook.

Thump.

A squirrel smacked into the glass.

Thump. Thump.

Steve ran to the door and was about to open it, when Judy, who I hadn't even heard get up, clapped her hand over the handle.

"Don't open the door."

17.

December 15, continued.

Steve grabbed my shirt and tugged. "We have to let her in! What if she's trying to," he paused, deciding what he could say in front of someone who didn't know about shapeshifters. "Trying to *tell me something* and I'm not listening? What if she needs help?"

I went right to the worst case. What if it's going to be *all* the squirrels slamming into the windows?

"See how her eyes are rolling back like that?" Judy said, pointing. Thump. Sure enough, the squirrel's eyes were unfocused and cockeyed. "That means she is sick."

Steve looked near tears. "I have to make her well!" He slipped his hand into mine. "It's just her," he said. "It's not all of them like at the temple." He looked at me hard. "I don't smell anything yucky."

It was mid-morning. Yucky didn't start until dark.

"What's wrong with her?" I asked. Judy shrugged.

"Dunno. But I know a sick animal when I see one. And that animal is definitely sick."

We had nothing to keep a sick squirrel in. I agreed with Steve, though. Evia was a friend. We couldn't just leave her if she was asking for help.

"Let's call Tully," I said. "He has sisters. There must be a gerbil or rabbit cage somewhere in that house. He said his dad never throws anything away."

Steve ran ahead of me and Judy up the stairs, then hoisted himself, belly first, across the kitchen counter to snatch the telephone handset off its cradle and hand it to me. Judy paced back and forth in front of the windows, arms crossed tight over her chest.

"Mrs. McCleery? Hi. This is Stacy Goldman calling. May I please speak to Tully?"

Thump from downstairs. It was as if Evia had gotten stronger in the short time we'd taken to climb the stairs. Tully came on the line.

"We have a squirrel problem."

Downstairs the thumping stopped. The alarm beeped. Someone was opening a door. I looked for Steve.

Oh no.

"Steven!" I shouted, heading for the stairs. I handed the phone to Judy when I got to the end of the cord. "You put that squirrel right back out- " But there he stood at the bottom of the stairs with his little friend curled and trembling against his chest.

Judy sneezed.

Steve backed up as I went down the stairs toward him.

"It feels like she's trying to shift," he whispered.

The little squirrel's muscles rippled tight, thinning her fur as the skin stretched. It looked like thunderclouds roiling, ready to burst out from inside her. Her tiny paws clutched at Steve's shirt, seizing the fabric in tiny squirrel fists.

"Please don't shift," I whispered. Not while Judy is here, I thought. Please don't-

"We can try castor oil." I nearly jumped out of my skin. Judy had come down the stairs so quietly I hadn't even felt the air stir. "If it's something she ate, castor oil will make her vomit. And Tully says we can come borrow a cage."

I'd heard of castor oil. It was some old fashioned thing Bubbe had mentioned with distaste. There was no chance at all we had it.

"I think my mommy has that," Steve said. Evia's tail flicked in his face. And then she spasmed, a hard convulsion that almost made Steve drop her. This squirrel could not shift in front of innocent, normal Judy. I did not want to spend my afternoon explaining unimaginables to someone who would never, ever believe it.

Jill's cell number was posted on the refrigerator whiteboard. She picked up on the first ring.

"Yes, castor oil," I said, kinda shouting over the restaurant noise behind her. "It's . . . for our project."

Well, who knew? I gave Team Squirrel the thumbs up, then put the phone on the counter. In Steve's arms, the squirrel convulsed again, strong and hard.

"I think she's having a seizure," Judy said. Upstairs, in Jill and Dad's bedroom, I grabbed the cordless off the cradle and put Jill on speaker. Steve sat on the bed cradling Evia over the mattress in case she convulsed again and fell out of his hands.

"Where, again?" I strained to hear Jill above the ambient noise.

Leave it to Jill. Under her sink was a lidded tub filled with bottles. The one labeled Organic Castor Oil still had the plastic seal around the lid.

"I'm not even sure why I replaced it when we moved," she said.

"My mom uses it," Judy said. "when the babies are late and she needs to induce labor."

"That's so progressive! Is your mom an OB-GYN?"

"A midwife," Judy said.

A midwife? I thought. For real? I struggled with the plastic on the castor oil bottle.

"I almost had a midwife," Jill said. The people noise in her background faded and the outdoor wind noise picked up. "But Stacy's dad wasn't on board. And Steven was born with the cord tight around his neck and the caul over his face so a hospital birth ended up okay. He needed resuscitation right away."

"My mom has to resuscitate sometimes," Judy said. "Her hardest births are when a big one breeches and she has to turn it around."

I finally got the plastic off the castor oil bottle.

"Steve was born with a cord around his neck? What kind of cord? And a call over his face? I don't understand."

"Not *a* cord, Stacy," Jill said. "*The* cord. His umbilical cord. It's not uncommon. Sometimes when babies move into position, they get tangled up. When he came out it was also around one ankle. He was a monkey even then."

"I'm a monkey!" Steve said from the bedroom.

"How did I not know this?"

"You were nine. I don't think we gave you the details of the birth." She laughed. I did not.

"So he nearly died and nobody thought to tell me?"

"He was fine. Lots of babies have close calls at the beginning. No reason to freak you out. Bubbe knew."

A piece of the unimaginables puzzle I hadn't seen fell, click, into place. Steve had had a near death experience. He could smell unimaginables. Finder had had a near death experience. She could find unimaginables. Evia had, in fact, died and come back. Wendell, too. They *were* unimaginables. The now obvious pattern rose to the surface of my mind.

"So did Steve die and they brought him back?"

"Oh no," Jill said. "I probably would have died myself if that had happened! He never died, just couldn't start breathing right away because the cord was too tight and his mouth and nose were covered by the caul. It was nearly a minute before they got him breathing. Poor little monkey was purple for days."

"Stacy, hurry! She's having another seizure!" Steve called from the bedroom. We hung up with Jill.

"Have *you* had a near death experience?" I asked as I filled an eye dropper with sticky castor oil.

"No. Have you?"

I shook my head. Whew. Judy was normal, like me.

"Will one dropper be enough?"

"If she doesn't vomit, we can do another," Judy said. I called to Steve. He paused at the entrance to the bathroom and looked from Evia to Judy. "Are you sure you don't have jelly beans?"

"I don't eat candy."

"Come closer," I said. "Is the seizure over? If we give her the oil while she's in one, she might choke." Judy coughed as Steve brushed past her.

"Ugh," she said, blowing air into her nose to clear it. "That squirrel stinks."

I sniffed, I didn't smell it.

"Sorry," Judy said backing away. "My sense of smell is kind of on overdrive. It's . . . part of my package." Her senses *were* on overdrive. Judy's eyes were watering.

Steve smiled down at the squirrel trying to mash herself up under his chin.

"Sorry, Evia," I said. I handed the dropper to Judy who took it at arm's length. I accepted the little squirrel from Steve. Her body shook like a 9th Avenue subway grate in rush hour. Under warm skin, her muscles still roiled.

Please, please do not shift.

"You should probably use a towel," Judy said, holding one hand over her nose and the dropper over the sink.

Steve took a towel and laid it over my chest. Evia let me wrap her in it.

Judy said, "Who is going to open her mouth?"

"Evia," Steve said, "I'm sorry this oil is nasty but," he leaned forward and whispered in the tiny animal's ear.

"Okay," he said. "You can give her the medicine now."

"She won't just take it. You'll have to force- " Judy's sentence caught in her mouth as the squirrel opened her tiny jaws wide, two sets of excruciatingly long teeth parting to make room for the dropper. Holding Evia in one arm, I took the dropper from Judy, then squeezed the oil into Evia's waiting itty bitty maw. The squirrel swallowed once, twice, then shook her head. A spray of castor oil droplets flew into my face. My eyes shut in defense. Evia struggled for a second, then, stronger than I thought she should be, broke from my grasp.

The towel fell. I reached up to wipe my eyes. When I opened them, Evia clung to Judy's sleeve. The pale girl froze as Evia ran up her arm. Evia paused on Judy's shoulder. Judy sneezed, then gagged and convulsed.

"Get it off me!"

The squirrel hopped across Judy's shoulders and scrambled down her back and leg like it was a tree trunk. Judy kicked out to get Evia off her and the squirrel launched back up toward Judy's head. Judy's textured long johns shirt got stuck in Evia's teeny claws. Judy shook herself.

"Let go! Let go!"

Evia ran up Judy's back, shirts still caught. The shirts slid up her back, revealing inches of—

I forgot the squirrel entirely.

Amazed, dumbfounded even, I stared.

18.

December 15, continued.

"Judy! Do you have a *tattoo*?"

"No!" She turned sharply, yanking her shirt over the swirly black lines. She held the edges tight to her hips as Steve reached to disentangle Evia. Judy's eyes were wide and panicked.

"Do your parents not know?" I asked.

The secret Judy! Her cool points suddenly tripled.

"I don't have a tattoo!" She pressed her back to the towel rack.

"It's okay," I said. "I won't tell, I promise! Let me see the whole thing."

"I don't know what you think you saw, but it wasn't real. You made it up."

Uh, no. I definitely did not make up a massive tattoo that covered every inch I saw of her back.

Judy sneezed into her elbow. She recoiled from where Evia had clung to her sleeve.

"Does it cover your whole back?" I said. "And do you have a job or something? Ink like that is super expensive, at least in New York."

Judy had stopped listening to me.

"Oh no," she said, blowing hard out of her nose to clear it again. "Oh. No."

"What?"

Panic filled her eyes. "You can't smell that? At all?"

Steve buried his nose in his friend's fur. He shrugged. I couldn't smell it, either. Maybe albinism did give Judy a more critical sense of smell. But I knew when to ask questions and now was not the time. Evia had something wrong with her and I hoped we could fix it before she shifted in front of Judy.

"Her smell is not what's wrong," I said.

Judy pressed her lips together, then opened her mouth to speak, then decided something, and again, pressed her lips. Ugh! New Yorkers did not do this. We are a direct people. Meredith would never hold back if she knew something. Ne-ver.

I had to stay focused. The squirrel was having seizures. What would cause seizures? And . . .

I was dying, *dying,* to know the story behind the tattoo! This was no 'I heart mom' doodle. This was serious, artist action, *ink.* Why on earth did she not want to talk about it? Never had I met someone with tattoos who wouldn't readily strip off almost any article of clothing to show off their art.

Evia gagged and gasped suddenly, drawing all of our attention. She gagged a second time, like she meant business. Judy and I both stepped back. The squirrel convulsed, then, with a hock that shook her whole body, hurled whatever nuts she'd had for lunch all over my little brother's shirt.

I held Evia in my lap in the hall outside Steve's room while he changed. Judy had gone to do the same because of the 'smell.' Evia's skin had started roiling again, and she'd had one full-on seizure. So much for the castor oil helping.

"Can you give me any hints?" I said, lifting her close to my face. "You came to us to help you, but I don't know what's wrong." When she didn't respond, I lowered her to my lap. I petted her back and she settled down, lying like a silky squirrel pillow on my thigh. "I guess it wasn't something you ate." Evia's skin moved over her back like another animal was under there, crawling and trying to get out. Or maybe swimming. I pushed on the roiling lump. Soft and liquid, it squished and flattened under my fingers.

"Eww," I said, stopping. She dug her claws into my pants.

"Ow. What is it? Does it hurt? Do you know what it is?" The squirrel laid her head back on my thigh. Then, Evia squeezed and released her tiny squirrel shoulders as if the thing under her skin itched. A tremor went through her. She shivered. "Poor squirrel girl," I said. "What's wrong with you?" She dug her teensy, needle sharp claws again into my jeans.

"Ow! Stop poking me!"

Evia dug again, harder this time.

"Ow!" I pulled her off my leg and held her where she couldn't claw me. Her eyes went cockeyed again, then fluttered shut. I prayed she wouldn't shift.

Steve, clad in a clean shirt, came out of his room, ignored my attempt to hand him the squirrel, ran past me and came back carrying the cordless from Jill and Dad's bedroom. He handed it to me like I knew what he was thinking.

"Nick?" he said.

Duh. Of course.

Evia started chittering as soon as she climbed into Steve's arms.

"I think it means she's hungry," he said. She'd just emptied her stomach, so no surprise there. Steve took Evia downstairs. I followed.

The future doctor picked up on the third ring. I explained to him, very quietly in case Judy came downstairs, what was going on and the steps we'd already taken. Steve sat on the couch and fed his little friend bites from the veggie tray.

"I'm kind of thinking she's been in contact with some kind of neurotoxin," I said. Nick and I walked down the list of symptoms, then a list of possible causes.

"Stroke, head injury, meningitis," Nick said. "Epilepsy. There's so many reasons for seizures."

"She was throwing herself against our back doors. Could she have hurt her head then, and the seizures are from that? The sickness is something else?"

"Not impossible. The root cause for any seizure is too much electrical activity in the brain. We'd need more diagnostic information. Maybe run a couple tests? It's gonna take time."

"Nick, there is something *moving* under her skin. I don't have time. Or if I do, I don't know how much. I can't tell if it's a thing, like a parasite, or a tumor, or some weird shifter disease no one's heard of." I looked at Evia to see if her skin was moving. The little squirrel was chowing down. Was it good news that the problem wasn't something she ate? Or bad news?

"Loss of appetite is not a problem," I added.

Nick took a breath on the other end of the line. "Okay, lemme think."

I thought about the advanced placement science program I'd done all last summer. Surprise surprise, shapeshifters hadn't come up. Still, we'd gotten to play around in all kinds of subjects way beyond what high schoolers typically get to do. In the unit on genetics, we'd even run processes with our own DNA. In the unit designed to lure us into being doctors, or, for the less ambitious, lab techs, we'd tested each other for all kinds of diseases using polymerase chain reaction tests. We'd even tested each other for point mutations using ligase chain reaction tests. It was one reason I wasn't majorly stoked about Judy's project idea. I'd already kinda done it. But now? Hmm.

"Hey," I said, "what about doing a PCR?"

We could swab Evia and take her samples to Julian's lab. We could run a PCR test and in six hours, maybe less because squirrels had fewer pairings to examine, maybe see what kind of causality we were dealing with.

"If you graduate med school before I do, I'm gonna need therapy," Nick said.

"Nah." I smiled. "You can just buy me coffees in exchange for tutoring." We hung up.

"We need to go to the lab," I said, when Judy came downstairs.

"But we don't understand what's wrong with her," Judy said, looking at the floor.

"Hopefully this will help us figure that out." I wasn't sure if Judy had noticed Evia's skin, because she'd been staying so far away to spare her nose. I hoped she hadn't.

Judy called Julian to make the arrangements. While she was talking, I knelt beside the couch.

"I don't think we can let your mom see her . . . like this," I whispered to Steve as the squirrel's skin roiled again. "You'll probably have to keep a blanket over the cage."

"He's there working all afternoon," Judy said, hanging up. "Are we close enough to walk?"

We were not.

"You totally owe that squirrel, Judy," I said. "She just ate your portion of the veggie tray."

1:37 p.m.

By the time Jill and Dad got home, Steve had Evia settled in a cardboard box I'd cut holes in and Judy and I were ready to go.

"Do you think she'll be okay by herself?" Steve said. "I want to come help get the cage."

1:46 p.m.

Two rockers decorated the porch of Tully's family's narrow row house. Up and down his Fan District street, other porches were similarly furnished, some with potted plants and little holiday flags sticking out of yards too small to park a hotdog cart.

Tully's mom, round, but not round, opened the front door.

"This part of the Fan is so historic! I love the houses. And thanks so much for helping us out with the cage," Jill said, shaking hands with Tully's folks. Jill had drawn the proverbial short straw and gotten to schlep the teenagers. Luckily, both the lab and Tully's house were close.

Steve slid out from under his mom's arm, squeezed Tully around the legs in greeting, then vanished into the clutches of two cherubic McCleerys.

"Be nice to the laddie, girls!" Tully's dad called after them in a lilt that made me feel like I was in a BBC movie.

"So glad we could help with his pet," said Tully's mom. "Come in, come in. It's hard to move and not have all your old things. Coming to the US was impossible like that. Took me a near decade to settle in."

We did the rest of the pleasantries, including introducing Judy who could barely speak in such a large crowd.

"They could be there for an hour," I whispered to Tully. "Jill's a professional at asking questions."

"And my folks'll keep answering," Tully said, leading me and Judy up a narrow set of clean wooden stairs.

"We don't have an hour," Judy said. "We have to get to the lab."

"Can we keep it quick, Tul?"

"Yup. That's my Gramma Addie's room," he indicated a tidy bedroom done in green and white. "Formerly shared with my older sister Bronwyn before she moved in with her college friends. My parents' room," he said tapping the closed door, "and that's the twins' and Grainne's (GRAHN-yah's) room," he nodded toward a bedroom fitted with a bigger mattress on the bottom bunk and a smaller on the top.

The last door separated us from squeaking springs punctuated by shrieks of glee. Tully opened the door into a pile of shoes on the floor. Three of his sisters, Steve, and a pair of identical, pint-sized Tully clones were jumping on the beds. Sheesh. I had thought the girls looked like him.

"Down, pirates!" Tully said. "One more year of me, then you can destroy my mattress however you like."

This bedroom, a creamy, lemon pie color where it wasn't peppered with stickers and posters, was the biggest so far. Two full-sized beds were squashed to walls separated by a dresser barely bigger than a nightstand. The ceiling sloped down on either side of an old fashioned dormer window. The kids bounced from bed to bed like jumping a pit of alligators.

"Steve, stop! Get down!" I said.

Tully scooped up a twin in each arm and set them on the floor. "Go jump on your own bed," he told them.

"It's shocking how much you look alike," I said.

"Creepy, yeah?" said one of the girls, jumping one last jump to land in the middle of the mattress on her butt. I'm Sinead," she said. "I'm nine. I'm in fourth grade and I'm going to be an archaeologist when I grow up."

"Nice to meet you, Sinead," I said.

"Shin-AID," she corrected. "Not SHIN-aid. And this is Grainne," (GRAHN-yah), "Ailsa," (EL-sa), "Angus," (Ang rhymes with hang) "and Sean" (Sh-ahn).

"Mom's Scottish, Dad's Irish," Tully said. "Half of us are named Irish. The lucky half are named Scottish." This prompted a rush of smaller McCleerys to shout like banshees and attack Tully. He pulled each sibling burr off himself one at a time, tickled that sibling until they surrendered, then tossed them back onto his bouncy mattress.

"Do you always make your bed?" I asked, "or did you have trampoline anticipation?"

"I make it. Accomplishment first thing in the morning makes the rest of the day less daunting."

I noticed his shoes, huge shoes, lined up on the floor at the foot of his bed, and his closet, doorless, but neatly arranged.

"All the posters are Tully's," Sinead said, seeing my inspection. "Except those." She waved her hand overhead at the cartoon pony posters on the wall by the messy other bed.

Tully's wall had variety. Old movie posters from It's a Wonderful Life and Casablanca butted up to Madonna, Sinead O'Connor, the Chelsea soccer team, David Beckham, Madonna again. Alice in Chains, and Rusted Root had spots on the wall overlapped by rugby player trading cards and magazine pages of Olympic fencers. On the far side, a whole section of wall was devoted to knights. There was very little lemon pie visible on Tully's side of the room.

"Where's Gidget's old cage?" he asked the tallest cherub: Grainne. Maybe the oldest of this crew?

"In my closet. Why?"

A hundred questions about the squirrel later, Tully, Judy, who had made herself basically invisible amidst the herd of noisy children, and I were on our way downstairs carrying the rabbit cage we'd emptied of stuffed animals, ballet shoes and other closet buried inhabitants.

"May I use your bathroom?" Judy said. Tully pointed it out and we went the rest of the way downstairs.

"Judy is the strangest person," I whispered, as we rounded the landing. "Did you know she has a *tattoo*? I think it covers her whole back! I don't think she's who I expected her to be. At all."

2:16 p.m.

"We're going to the market for the halibut. I thought I'd pick up a chocolate babka for dessert at the bakery while we're out. Judy have you ever done anything Hanukkah? It's our Festival of Lights. I know everyone thinks it's Jewish Christmas, but it's actually a very minor holiday. It's a great excuse for chocolate babka, though, unless you prefer jelly donuts? Maybe I'll get both."

In the back seat, Steve stuck his arms in the air.

"Both! Both! Both! Both!"

"Stop that! No chanting!" Jill scolded with a smile. "Is there anything I can pick up that you would especially like to have at dinner, Judy?"

"No, ma'am. Thank you. That's very thoughtful of you to ask."

"Are you sure? If you think of anything, Stacy can call me." She patted the black, plastic brick sticking out of her purse. "I love this thing! Okay girls, you have a little under an hour."

"Can I go with Stacy, Mommy?"

"No," Jill and I said at the same time.

"Jinx," I said, climbing out. "Another time, Muppet. I promise I'll bring you to the lab when it's not a time crunch." And when I'm not trying to only say half of everything because I'm with someone who doesn't *know*.

Julian's lab assistant waited for us, machines running. He showed us what was where and within thirty-five minutes we had set the polymerase chain reaction test to run, prepped and set a swab in the system to run a full DNA scan that would take over a week to complete, and were on our way back downstairs to wait for Jill and Steve. They pulled up just as we came down. Julian's project needed checking at 7:30 so it would work perfectly for us to come back and get our own results at 8:00. The only thing I didn't like was that 8:00 was after dark.

7:57 p.m.

"The lighting of the candles was beautiful," Judy said as we climbed the steps to the lab. "Your dad's voice sounded cool when he said the prayers, too. Thanks for letting me come over. I didn't know it was a holiday."

"Yup. You're an honorary Jew now," I said. "Anyone who can beat Steve at dreidel deserves at least that."

"Do you need me to be here, or can I run out?" said Julian as we threw our coats into the closet. I turned on the sink to wash my hands.

"You can go," Judy said. "We're just doing results."

Fifteen minutes later, Judy and I stood shoulder-to-shoulder looking at Evia's samples.

"These are somatic, right? Mutations that occurred during her lifetime?"

"Right," I said. Makes sense, I thought. Since Evia wasn't born a shifter.

"So not like me."

"Nope. Not like you. Yours are all hereditary." Because you're a typical albino, I thought, not a shapeshifter.

Judy's expression was both hopeful and lost. Guilt poked me in the belly.

"If you really want me to help you, you have got to tell me what condition you have," I said. "I need a place to start."

"Something's wrong with my DNA," she said. "That's all we know."

"But being albino isn't having something wrong with your DNA," I said. "It's having something different. Nothing in your sample indicates malfunction. You may not like being albino, but your body thinks it's fine."

Judy scowled down at the scope.

"This isn't about being albino," she said.

"Well, I can't go much further without knowing what it is about," I said. "I mean, we could run your sample again since the ones Julian ran were such a mess. But seriously, Judy. Even though it looks kinda wackadoodle, your DNA looks and behaves totally normally. For what it is."

I pointed to a series of lines on Evia's DNA map.

"This is so freakin' fascinating," I said. "Evia's nucleotide bonds are 100% transitions. All A to G. Yours," I said, pulling her map over to compare, "are 100% transversions, A to T. How weird is it that every single one of her wrong attachments is Adenine to Guanine? Why are there no Cytosine to Thymine transitions? And why are yours all transversions?"

Judy put her eye again to the microscope. "Stacy!" she said. "Look!"

Under the microscope one of the helixes thrashed. It looked like a worm trying to escape a pan of water. My heart almost stopped beating. Had I done it? Had my enzyme mixture fixed the bond? The helix calmed for one pulse and then pop! A burst of deoxyribose spilled out of several nucleotides. My hand trembled as I went to adjust the magnifier. Could we see any closer? We watched in awe as the helix rolled, shuddered once then turned itself inside out. Then, as if by magic, one spot in the ladder pulsed and sucked all the spilled deoxyribose right back in, like a nucleotide vacuum cleaner.

"What's happening?" Judy said.

"The helix is changing shape," I said, my voice a lot softer than I meant it to be. "It's . . . shifting."

"Make it stop," Judy said.

"It's amazing," I said. Was this what happened to Evia's cells when she shifted from human to squirrel?

"Make it stop, Stacy! What do you need? More enzyme?" Judy bolted across the lab to the fridge.

Nothing, I thought. I'm not touching it. It's miraculous. It's beautiful. The helix rolled in its new form. Eye pressed to the scope, I watched it pulse and gently enlarge. It pulsed again, again grew bigger. Then, as if suddenly too full of fluid, the helix bulged and exploded.

"Crap."

"Did it explode?" Judy said.

"Yeah. How did you guess?"

"I just figured."

I worried. Was this going to happen to Evia if she shifted while whatever was making her sick was in her system?

Judy paced the lab as I sat for the next ten minutes taking apart the pieces.

"It needs an enzyme binder to the deoxyribose," I said. "If we can separate the transitioned pairs and get them to re-bind purine to pyrimidine like they are supposed to, I think we could stop the cells from inverting. Maybe? I could be totally wrong."

"You're not wrong. You're Stacy."

Less than a half hour left in the lab before we invoked parental fury, so I mixed two different enzyme batches and Judy separated two more helixes.

The first one did nothing. The helix turned inside out, squirted sugar, vacuumed it up, and burst. Drat.

The second attempt got twice the amount of enzyme and a tiny bit of another protein I though might help anchor the binding. I needed to stop the expulsion of the deoxyribose sugar and its re-assimilation. That was the most likely key to halting the explosion. Judy and I both leaned in, pressing our eyes to the scope. The helix inverted. It pulsed and roiled. It expressed its cloud of sugar fluid. Drat. Fail.

Next, it would burst. I stepped away and went to my notebook to mark this option as failed. I looked at my notes. What else could I change to make this work?

"Stacy," Judy said. "Come back."

"Should I add more protein, do you think?" I said. "Did it even slow the explosion?"

"Just look."

I put my eye to my half of the scope. The nitrogen atoms were sucking the deoxyribose back in, the vacuum cleaner effect. But the helix wasn't behaving the same way. It wasn't enlarging. It wasn't shuddering. It was gently moving side to side in its fluid.

Judy reached over and grabbed my hand. She squeezed it tight. Neither of us dared to breathe. And then, the helix reverted.

It took three full minutes to complete its cycle, but in the end, the helix stood correct as before. Still mutated, of course, but no longer inside out.

"Oh my god, Stacy! You did it!" Judy threw her arms around me.

"Did what?" said Julian, walking back in. His coffee smelled amazing. If he had told me he was getting coffees, I would've given him money for one for me.

Judy insisted we make four times what we would need to dose Evia, and beating Jill's clock by the hair of our chinny-chin-chins, we left Julian locking the lab, and us bolting down three flights of stairs with a handful of paper lab results, a vial of potential antidote and two syringes in the baggie that had contained our swabs.

Saturday, December 16, 2001.
12:02 a.m.

Sleep did not come.

The note from Wendell lay unfurled on my nightstand. *Feeding on each other. No hunt.*

What did that mean for me? Had she given up hunting? Would she send a different Bat Suit to do it? One who I hadn't blackmailed?

I laid in my comfy, too big bed, lights out, a bright half moon having risen in my window. Every time I closed my eyes they popped open, my mind filled with worries and images of the evening. As soon as we gave Evia her shot, her seizures halted. After a couple hours, when she showed no more weird symptoms of shifting, we'd opened the cage into the backyard, but she hadn't gone out. So tonight Evia stayed with Steve. Waves of victory and guilt took turns overcoming me. What if I had trapped her in her squirrel body forever? Had I confined a human child to a squirrel's life for good? Steve, happy she seemed better but also worried, had spent the evening playing beside her cage. I still didn't know what had made Evia's body react so violently, trying to turn her DNA and maybe her whole body inside out.

It did not look comfortable.

Judy, knowing none of the bigger picture, saw the entire play as a win. I had never seen her smile so much. Even at dinner of which she ate a small portion and later threw up in her bathroom, which she probably didn't know I heard, she seemed happy.

I spent the next hour trying every trick I knew to relax enough to fall asleep. Reading, chess puzzles, I even took a shower. I imagined kissing Nick and wished I could have him here now. If he made it back in time and my plan worked, meaning we all lived, there would be a serious New Year's Eve kiss-fest happening. I thought about calling him, but it was after midnight. I doubted his family would appreciate having the phone ring at this hour.

Wrapping myself in Meredith's outgrown black terry bathrobe, I padded out of my room.

As I waked past the hallway window, the curtains moved.

I jumped, my heart missing a beat. Not the curtains. Judy. She stood by the hall window gazing out at the moon.

"Sorry," she said. "Didn't mean to startle you." I let my hand down from my chest where it had flown. "I couldn't sleep," she said. "I think I'm too excited."

It was weird how she blended into the curtains and I didn't see her when I first came out.

Downstairs in the kitchen, I turned on just the stove light. Judy leaned on the counter, staring out the big bay window..

"Moon's pretty," I said.

"It always seems brighter when it's waxing," she said, wrapping herself in a tight, bony hug.

"Are you cold?" I asked. "Do you want a sweatshirt or something?" I washed out my teapot and opened a cabinet for the kettle.

"I'm not cold. He added to my ink this week and it feels better to stretch it." I looked at her in the dim light and yes, she was standing so that the skin across her shoulders would stretch.

"Can I see it? Your tattoo?"

"No."

"Please?"

"No. And please don't tell anyone about it either. Not even your friends. I don't want anyone to know."

Oops. I'd have to tell Tully not to mention it.

I understood having a secret, but printing one on your body? It didn't make sense.

"I've never known anyone with ink who didn't want people to see it," I said.

"Now you do."

Harsh. Okay.

"How did you know the helixes might explode?" I asked. "I never would have thought of that."

"It was a guess." She studied the table surface, tracing the woodgrain with her finger tip.

"I don't think it was. You seemed pretty sure about what was going on."

"You were the one that figured it out."

"But it's science, Judy. You can figure anything out if you ask the right question."

"I got lucky."

Ugh. Finder all over again. What was with these Richmond girls and their secrets? The difference was Judy at least asked for help.

"What kind of tea? Black or green?" I asked. "Or I have this raspberry one."

"Never tried green tea."

I set up our cups. Next stop, the freezer. I'd worked out for forty-five minutes before Judy came over. I could afford some calories. I asked Judy, even though I knew the answer.

"Fudgecicle?"

"No, thanks."

"Mind if I do?"

"G'head."

We sat forty-five degrees from each other at the round kitchen table. In the moonlight, Judy's pallor vanished, smoothed into shades of gray. Hair glimmering, her whole self glowed as if she belonged to the night somehow, to the shadows and the moon. Her expression shifted from peaceful to sad. We were quiet for a long time.

The kettle wobbled on the burner, the sign of hitting a boil.

I snagged it before it whistled. As I carried brim-full mugs back to the table, I caught a look of apprehension on Judy's face, but locked in on her eyes.

"This is kind of a personal question," I said.

Judy met my gaze, curious.

"I was kind of worried after our phone call at Thanksgiving. I'm not sure, you know, what was happening at your mom's place but it didn't sound okay. Or, I mean, safe. I know this is none of my business, but is your mom's boyfriend, or someone else . . . a problem?"

Judy's shoulders fell into a slump.

Her forehead scrunched for a second. Deciding. Deciding if she could trust me and how far.

"I know it couldn't work out between her and my dad for, you know, obvious reasons, but Ed is . . ." She took a deep, uneven breath. "He's poison."

"Poison, how?" I said. I had to be careful here. I wanted her to keep talking but I didn't want her to feel like I was prying. Steel filled her gaze when she looked up at me. A layer of determination I'd only seen once, when we butted heads about what to do for our project. This time, it was much harder.

She tilted her head up, took a long breath in. I wanted to blurt out, if vampires are involved you can just tell me, but I didn't. I had learned this much from Jill, when you wanted someone else to talk, stay quiet and wait.

"Ed, my mom's boyfriend, has something wrong with him," she said. "It affects his body and his brain. Eventually, it'll kill him. I know it sounds awful, but I don't have a problem with that. But," her eyes filled with tears, "I'm afraid he's passed it to my mom.

"Being with my dad is stressful, too, because of his lawsuit. This private trust is trying to take Mattaponi land that belongs to the tribe."

Oh no. A land lawsuit? Crap.

"Are they arguing that their historically significant ancestors are buried there?"

"Yeah, how'd you know?"

I hated to say this.

"I think my father's firm is handling it. The person suing is one of his partners. The great-great-granddaughter of- "

"Robert E. Lee."

I nodded.

"We can't give up that land. Ed and his cronies want to move onto it. I don't know why they want it so bad. Nobody does. But in the last month it's been like their lives are at stake, the way they're fighting. I think that whatever condition he has is affecting his brain."

Condition? Condition. Why that word? Hmmm.

She sipped her tea.

"Eww." She looked into the cup like she could find something better in there. "Sorry, it's not bad," she covered.

"Green tea *is* kinda gross," I said. "Here, let me make you a chai." I took her cup and dumped it. I got the milk out of the fridge. I felt very clever. Chai had so much milk and honey in it, I might actually get Judy to consume calories she might not barf back up.

Upstairs, I rolled over and over in bed, my body still refusing to relax. Ugh. Fine. Desperate times called for desperate measures. I got out of bed and went to my hands and knees on my carpet. I went from down-dog to plank, then back to down-dog. I needed to control Matilda's access to blood. But how?

I stood and did a sun salutation, then another and another until I settled into the facing Mecca pose I'd learned was called child's pose. Distracted by worry for Evia even though she now seemed fine, the same unrelated thought kept coming into my mind.

Fine, I said to myself, but this is ridiculous. You're going to be wrong.

I turned on my desk light and pulled out the lab results. I laid Judy's DNA map next to Evia's DNA map. I studied every chain, comparing each nucleotide bond. They had nothing in common. Except one thing. Every mutation was in the exact same place in the chain.

19.

Monday, December 18, 2001.

Steve stood next to the tree Evia had run up. He looked sad.

Jill had put her foot down about the squirrel staying in the house any longer than absolutely necessary to make sure she was okay. I'd given Evia the antidote Saturday night when we got home from the lab and her seizures had stopped within the hour. Steve had gotten to 'keep' her an extra day, but Jill was adamant. Wild animals belonged in the wild, no matter how much you loved them and how 'tame' they had become.

"I'm worried about her still," he said. I stood beside him, squinting up into the branches. Steve said, "I don't think what happened to her was an accident."

"I don't either, but I can't imagine what it was."

We waited until Evia scampered from our tree to the next and then the next after that. She climbed so high we could no longer see anything but branches moving in her wake. And then, she was gone.

"She knows what she's doing, Steve. She's a smart girl. You'll see her again soon."

Friday, December 21, 2001.

The gas fireplace burned on high. Steve sat at the coffee table gluing paper chain links, glancing up at the holiday movie he had playing on TV and eating the popcorn I'd made him. He sneezed.

"Bless you." I stood in the powder room analyzing the high ponytail Meredith advised me would be right for the 1950's St. Ignatius Winter Dance sock hop theme. My hair would be both period and off my neck when I got sweaty dancing. I tied Jill's scarf around the pony tail, then applied her bright red lipstick. It matched my poodle skirt.

Jill had made some NYC transplant friends at Beth Shamar and dragged my dad to early services figuring they could get home before Tully came to get me. Steve sneezed, again.

"Stacy!" He held his hand under his nose, the universal signal for 'I am now holding a massive glob of snot in my palm and need help.'

"I just can't figure it out," I said, taking the powder room tissue box out to him. He waved his other hand for me to hurry. "How can we take control of her blood supply? How? I know I should be able to do this. I've been declared the strategy guy, but I feel trapped." Steve blew his nose and wiped his hand. He held the dirty tissues out to me.

"Gross, dude! I don't want your kinder-cold. Throw those away yourself." I picked up my hot chocolate and sipped. "I feel like I'm looking at an empty board trying to find a move with pieces that don't exist, and someone's behind me shouting win, win, win!"

"Do like Rabbi Berman taught you. Make a plan, stick to the plan, be ready to change the plan. Keep your mind on the mate." Steve picked up a pencil with his tiny, now snot free, hand. "Let's start at the beginning."

I put down my drink and went back into the bathroom.

"Okay, I'm ready. Coach away. Hey, does this scarf make me look like an actual poodle?"

"No non-sequiturs while strategizing!" he said. "But no."

"You didn't even look!"

He looked. "You do not look like a poodle." He looked back at his construction paper. "You look like a Dalmatian."

"I do not."

I did. Darn polka dots.

"Can we work, please?" said Steve. "Who's playing white?"

In other words, who, as of now, had the advantage?

"Matilda."

"Type of game?"

"Aggressive."

"So how do we play to win?"

"Strong and risky to break her capture pattern. Move pieces out to control the center so she can't run me over."

"Okay, good. What's the middle game?" Steve sneezed again. I took the bathroom trash bin and plunked it down next to him.

"For Matilda to make Darcy Jackson swear to not turn Finder into a vampire, acknowledge that her guys attacked us first, and agree we were acting in self defense and don't owe her new guys- "

"You're solving variables out of order. You're skipping to the end."

I paused and thought. Was I?

Dang. I was.

Like algebra, I had to simplify the equation to make sense of it. I was focused on solving the end before simplifying the beginning. Okay, I felt a little calmer. It's just math, Stace, I told myself. Easy, orderly, predictable math.

Appearance managed, I went to sit beside Steve on the couch. I closed my eyes and brought my mug again to my lips. As chocolate swooshed around in my mouth, I let my head clear. What's the middle game?

"She needs to recognize the strength of our pieces," I said, visualizing a chess board with a solid opening. "Or, I need to force her moves." I sighed, my body relaxed. That was the answer, wasn't it? "I need to force her moves," I said out loud again.

Steve nodded. "And if you do that, what's the mate?"

I visualized a clean endgame in progress. "It's a queen mate with back up. A rook, a bishop. King gets pinned by the bishop who moves aside to reveal a rook skewer keeping the king immobilized and offering a queen checkmate in the next move."

"Analogy," Steve said. "Good. Now, translate that. What's the real world mate?"

"I have to pin her," I said. "I have to make it so she has no choice but to leave us alone," I said. Clear goal, simple to focus on. But how could we get it to happen? I opened my eyes. Steve sat crosslegged with a straight spine. His eyes were closed, too. Hands open on his knees.

"What're you doing?" I said.

"I'm listening."

"You're listening?" He looked like Saanvi at the end of yoga class.

"This is what Mommy does when she gets stuck on a client. She sits like this and closes her eyes while they talk. Deep listening, she says. Close your eyes again. We need to listen."

"How do you know my eyes aren't closed?" I asked. They weren't.

"I can feel it. Close. Your eyes. Please."

Good grief. I closed my eyes.

"What are we listening for?"

"You'll know it when you hear it," Steve said.

"What are you, the Dalai Lama?"

He ignored me. My snide remarks were apparently not what he was waiting for.

I set my cup down and leaned more deeply into the couch. Next time I closed my eyes to listen, I wanted to have music on. They Might be Giants would be a good band, maybe. Something that would make me giggle.

"Can you try to be quieter, please?" Steve said.

"I'm just siting here!" I opened my eyes again.

"Your thoughts are very loud. You're thinking, not listening."

Good grief. Really? Fine. I said nothing, closed my eyes again and sighed. I tried to think more quietly.

We had to get Finder's dad to not want her to be a vampire with him anymore. How could we do that? Could we reason with him, convince him somehow, or did we have to get nasty? I didn't think we could win a physical fight but-

"Stop thinking!" Steve shouted. "I can't listen with you filling up all the space!"

"What?" My eyes flew open. "This is ridiculous. You can not hear me thinking! It's thinking! It's in my head!"

"What you're thinking doesn't matter! What matters is that you're not listening! That's the point, you have to put your mind on listening!" His face got red under the gentle waves falling in his face. He looked like he looked when the adults were ignoring him. A knot of guilt tightened in my belly.

"I can't listen any quieter," I said. "I'm trying. I truly am." That was kind of a lie. I'm not sure I had been trying. But the guilt I felt at Steve feeling like I hadn't heard him hurt. It was how my mom made me feel. How my dad had made me feel after my mom left, totally without his knowing it. I would not do that to Steve. He needed to have someone in his life who he knew . . . well, who he knew was listening.

"Tell me what to do."

"Close your eyes."

Done.

"When you start thinking thoughts, tell them to wait a minute. Like, oh hi thoughts. Glad you could make it. I have to listen to something else for a minute and I'll get right back to you."

I felt my thoughts start to tell me all about how silly this was. Just a second, thoughts, I thought. I have to listen to this other thing for a sec and I'll be right back.

"Change your focus to something else. Like your heartbeat, or the fireplace crackle or my breathing or Mommy's clock ticking or something you can listen to on purpose."

The gas fireplace didn't crackle so much as hum. And I had turned on the dishwasher when we finished dinner, so that kinda hummed and swished too. I listened as hard as I could. Fireplace, dishwasher. Dishwasher, fireplace. Chill out thoughts, I'll be right back.

"That's way better," Steve said. "Keep doing it. When your thoughts jump back in or you forget you're listening, just talk to your thoughts. You might forget to listen a lot, but every time you notice you've stopped listening, and are thinking again, stop and start over."

"What am I listening for besides the dishwasher?" I said.

"You'll know it when you hear it."

"And how do you know how to do all this again?"

"I keep telling you, Stacy," he said. "I know everything."

"Do you know the mate?"

"Duh," he said. "I know everything *I'm* supposed to know. That's something *you're* supposed to know. Shh and keep listening. I think you're getting close."

December 21, continued.

The St. Ig's Winter Dance was a 'sock hop'. None of us had any idea what a sock hop was until the school Christmas party when the Sisters showed the whole school this old movie from the 1980's about going back in time. The movie was supposed to teach us all everything we needed to know about sock hops, so much so that we would all be inclined to go home, dress up and rush back to school for a shoe-less, teenaged dance party, i.e. sock hop, of our own. The nuns had boxes of poodle skirts to loan out, one skirt of which I wore now. Poodle skirts have, no joke, poodles (yes, the dogs) stitched on them. They're made for partner and swing dancing, which of course, none of us knew how to do. We danced like regular teenagers, bouncing and swaying to the beat in an attempt to have fun and not wipe out dancing in just our socks.

Finder and Tully had significant public dance experience from many nights spent at The Station, the underage dance club where Bolo worked. I danced between them content and convinced that not one soul would notice me.

I was wrong.

"Beggin' your pardon, Stay-cee. May I have this dance?"

Finder turned into Tully's shoulder, her face protected by his bulk. Meredith would not laugh. Meredith would save me.

Seconds ticked by. Bradley Joe stood there smiling in that hopeful way, still holding his hand out, like we were at a cotillion. His socks were red and blue striped.

"Cool socks, Bradley Joe," Tully said as he wrapped his arms around Finder whose shoulders were now shaking with laughter.

"I'm not really dance partner material," I said. Oh, so lame.

"Sure you are, Stay-cee," he said as if I just needed a little encouragement. "If you can walk, you can dance. Here, I'll lead. You'll be fine."

The way he said 'fine' sounded like he said 'faaahn'. Tully turned, dancing Finder away from me and Bradley Joe. His shoulders were shaking, too. Disloyal rat.

I put my hand in Bradley Joe's and said, "Faahn. If you can make me look like I know what I'm doing, I'm all for it."

He smiled a wide smile that lit him up from the inside out. "You almost sounded Southern there for a minute, Stay-cee," he said, completely missing my point. "There's hope for you Yankees, yet."

Bradley Joe held out his other hand, asking for mine. I felt like a Chihuahua standing next to a Great Dane.

Finder snapped a picture. The 'gift' we each got for coming to the dance was a disposable camera to take pictures of our friends in their doofy poodle skirts. We could label our cameras and leave them in the basket by the door at the end of the dance, and the photography club would develop the film to see if we got any shots good enough to go in the school newspaper. I shot her a glare to end all glares, but she just smiled sweet as could be and whispered something in Tully's ear that made him laugh out loud. Jerks.

Bradley Joe led me into an emptier space and scooted my hands so they lay on top of his palms. He brought me toward him and then pushed me out a few times until I got the hang of it.

"Step in ball change. Step out ball change," he said, over the music. "Relax! Let me lead!" I had no earthly clue what that meant, but I made a decision I had only made once before, earlier that afternoon. I decided to quit thinking and listen.

Dancing is not my comfort zone. I enjoy bopping along to music, but this was not like any dancing I had ever done before. Bradley Joe was like, a *professional*. He showed me a couple steps with me mirroring his feet, then he sped them up a little. My worry about doing it wrong fell away as I surrendered to someone else making the decisions. The lumbering good ol' boy vanished and a clear and decisive, kind leader emerged. The way he held my hands, closing and opening his fingers like I was a set of venetian blinds, made it obvious when to step and when to let go. A smile spread across my face as Bradley Joe pushed me into my first whirl. He put his hand on my shoulder to spin me out and pulled on my hand to reel me in. I'm not sure how my feet found their way, but they did. He moved my arms over my head so they crossed in front of me then he spun me out again. It was fast and dizzying and fun.

I was sweating and giggling when the umpteenth song ended and Bradley Joe and I took a break at the refreshment table. I gulped down a cup of punch and regretted it, too sweet and syrupy.

I tossed the cup and went for a water. I did a double take. Hank, my chess friend, stood a table down, piling cookies into a napkin.

"Hank! What're you doing here?"

"Oh Stacy! Yay! I was hoping you'd be here. My friend Junior invited me. She's over there." He pointed to a bench near the door. The only person on it was Judy, sitting in a bubble gum pink poodle skirt.

"You mean Judy?" I said, surprised. "How do you know each other?"

"S'up, Beej?" said Hank as Bradley Joe came up beside me. He and Bradley Joe knocked fists. Knocked fists? Wait. They knew each other well enough to do a complicated multi-step fist bump?

"I met Judy in homeschool Hike Club when we were like, ten. She was homeschooled before high school. You didn't know that?"

I did not. I guess I never asked.

"I was, too," Bradley Joe said. "But just for a year."

"Beej here used to compete in ballroom," Hank said. "Won dance competitions like we win chess. Got him outta school for a whole year before he got too tall and his mom retired him."

"That's not why she retired me," he said. "It got too expensive after Aunt June closed the studio."

"It makes me feel better to think being tall could be a flaw, that's all," said Hank with a grin. "Hey, Judy's dad wants to make sure you dance with her. He thinks she'll like dancing if *you* do it with her. I'm kind of offended." He gave Bradly Joe another big smile. "Nah. Not really. You may be the dance boss, but you know. She *likes me*." Hank gave the much larger kid a friendly punch in the shoulder.

"You and Judy are a couple? Like boyfriend-girlfriend?" Shut up, Goldman! I told myself. What was I, twelve?

"She's the only girl I've ever met who doesn't mind that I'm shorter than her." That had never occurred to me.

"But yes," he said. "We're official, finally. We've been making out since we were like eleven, though. In secret of course." He waggled his eyebrows. "Hike Club."

Too much information.

Bradley Joe nodded, arms crossed over his bulky chest. "And Big J approves?"

"Yup. He's in like Flynn."

Big J? Was that Judy's dad? And why would Bradley Joe refer to him so familiarly?

"You better treat her right," Bradley Joe said. "I don't wanna have to come find you."

My reality shook. Judy was at the dance. And two boys, weird and nerdy, but highly nice boys, were kind of fighting over her.

"Gotta catch me first, hot stuff," Hank said and headed back to Judy with a napkin full of cookies he would have to eat himself. He looked over his shoulder. "Remember to dance with her! She's got the solstice blues."

Near where Judy sat, John Forest Stalker stood chatting with Sister Elizabeth Religion, my favorite nun at St. Ig's. Ah ha. I got it. Dad volunteers to chaperone, daughter must go to dance and pretend to be social. Hank was one of the most outgoing people I knew. It seemed an odd match.

A slow song started. Relief flooded me that Bradley Joe didn't ask me to dance this one with him, too.

"If you ever want to go on a date with me, Stay-cee, we could go dancin'."

Oh no. Why did he have to bring it up? I felt bad rejecting him after that wonderful dance.

"I have a boyfriend now, Bradley," I said.

"Oh," he said, eyes downcast in disappointment. "Who? Does he go here?"

"He goes to VCU. He has a fraternity thing tonight so he couldn't come."

Finder and Tully, now over their snarky giggle fest, rolled up beside us looking astonished and impressed.

"Me next, please," Finder said to my dance partner. Incredulity brightened his face.

"Then me," Tully said. "Just kidding. But seriously dude, you can *dance*."

"Gee, thanks. My aunt taught me. I sure do enjoy it. Do *you* really want to dance with *me*?" Bradley Joe asked Finder. "You're not gonna like, go all Kung Fu if I squeeze your hand wrong, right?" He looked dead serious.

"If you can make me dance like you made her dance, I promise no Kung Fu."

"Is it okay?" he asked Tully.

Tully smiled. "Why are you asking me? This woman does what she wants."

"May I have your leave, Stay-cee?"

"What?"

"He's asking if you mind if he dances with another girl," said Tully.

"Oh. Of course. I mean yes, my leave. Yes. Go. Leave. Dance. Have fun. Whatever." I smiled at them both. Tully popped a mini-cupcake into his mouth and handed one to Finder.

"Here!" Finder tossed me her disposable camera and handed me the cupcake. "Take something righteous! Let's go, Bradley Joe," she said. "Show me whatcha got!" Finder and Bradley Joe pealed off to the gym floor.

"That dude is unbelievable," Tully said as I snapped a pic on Finder's camera. "It looked like you really knew what you were doing."

"I had no clue what I was doing," I said. "I was just along for the ride."

"Looked like a good ride," he said. "How's Nick going to feel about this?"

"Considering he couldn't be here, he'd better feel just fine about it." I looked at Tully. "I don't *like* Bradley Joe," I said.

"He *likes* you."

"I've been very clear since the first time he asked me out that I'm a no."

"He asked you out?"

"Asks. Yeah. Like every time he sees me."

"Hmm. Interesting."

"Why is it interesting?"

"It just is," Tully paused and snagged another pair of cupcakes. He handed the chocolate one to me. "I think someone on my fencing team likes him. I thought the feeling was mutual."

"Isn't the fencing team only guys?"

"No, it's coed. I tried to get Finder to try out. She'd be an amazing fencer." He looked wistful. I imagined Finder with swords.

"Would I be a good fencer?"

The question popped out of my mouth before I could judge it and keep it in. Who was I? Forty-five minutes of swing dancing and now I wanted to be a fencer? Come back, Goldman, I said to myself. Math-letes, not athletes. Don't be who you're not.

But what if you are?

"What?" I asked.

Tully's eyes went wide as he watched Bradley Joe swing dance with his girlfriend. "Wow! I didn't know she could do that."

"It's him," I said. "I didn't think I could do any of what he showed me. He just leads and if you follow, then magic happens."

"I was thinking about your question," Tully said, after a pause. "You could try fencing. Your size would limit your reach, but if you were fast you'd be hard to hit."

"It's okay," I said. "Despite working out, I'm not really the fighter type."

Unless you are.

My hand froze midair reaching for a frosted sugar cookie.

Michael?

Yes?

You're talking to me at a dance?

You asked an important question.

If I could be a fencer?

No. You asked, 'who am I?'

I meant I was surprised I thought the dancing was fun.

No. You meant who am I? The dancing being fun was a catalyst, but when you asked 'who am I?' instead of becoming open and curious, you denied a possibility.

I did?

Yes. It's a habit. You've decided what is true about yourself and you are not open to change.

What? I believe vampires are real now! Shapeshifters are real. I've agreed to live in Richmond. I am so open to change.

That's adapting. Not changing.

What?

You are adapting your current behaviors and habits to accommodate a new reality. You are not changing.

Adapting and changing are the same thing.

Are they?

"Are adapting and changing the same thing?" I said nudging Tully in the arm.

"In regards to what?"

"Anything," I said.

"Adapting is a kind of changing, maybe? Like modifying a yoga pose. She adapts the pose to suit the student and it does change it kind of, but wait. No. Even if you alter it, it's essentially still the same pose, so, no. I guess not."

"But you can't change who you are."

"You can. I don't think you should have to, but you can."

"Isn't that just pretending? You can't like, suddenly become someone you aren't, right? I can't change my love for chess. I can't change— "

I'm not suggesting you change who you already are, I'm suggesting you change to become who you are meant to be. Evolution. And maybe the person you are evolving into has a streak of fighter.

You think I'm in fighter denial?

Are you?

"What you're saying is that if you deny a part of yourself by refusing to explore it, you might be shutting down something important about who you're meant to be."

"What?" said Tully.

I looked up at him. "I didn't say anything."

"Yes, you did."

Crap, had I said all that out loud? Oops.

"It sounded important," Tully said. "Do you want to go outside and talk?"

"No." I crossed my arms over my chest.

Denial isn't healthy, said Michael.

I thought angels were supposed to be nice?

"Yes. Okay. Fine," I said.

"We don't have to, I just thought if you needed- "

"Yes. Fine. I need to talk. Because I am *not in denial.*"

I grabbed a frosted snowman cookie and stalked out of the gymnasium. I pushed my way out the main gymnasium doors and plopped down on a bench. Tully stretched to touch the center stone of the Gothic arch above us.

"Apparently," I said, letting the cool night air wash over me, "I have a . . . a friend who thinks I need to change."

"Is this Nick?"

"No."

"Are you sure?"

"Yes."

"'Cuz it's okay to be honest. I won't tell anyone."

"Except Finder."

"That was a vampire thing," he said, referring to when I had told him a secret and he had taken it straight to Finder the night we saved Nick and Luke at Maymont.

I bit the head off my cookie.

"This . . . friend, thinks I am denying my fighter nature."

I didn't say that.

I sighed a heavy, annoyed sigh.

"That I am denying aspects of myself, like perhaps physical fighting, that may or may not be inhibiting me from becoming who I am meant to be. In the world."

Tully nodded and leaned against the arch. "I'd agree with that."

"You would!?"

"Yeah."

"Why?"

Tully stuffed his hands into his pockets. A corner of his pale yellow button down had come out from being tucked in and hung over his jeans. He shook his hair back from his face. "Has anyone besides me seen you fight?"

"Tully, until Maymont, I'd never fought anything stronger than a sneeze."

"See, that's what I mean. You can downplay it all you want, but you *did* fight. You didn't cower and you didn't cry and you didn't run. And you could have. But you *fought*. And you won. And when it came down to it, you dove back in to fight again. We could have left Nick and Luke, you know. It was you who insisted we go back. You."

I took little bites of my snowman, savoring the frosting as the cookie melted in my mouth. I did not see myself the way Tully saw me. I had insisted we save Nick and Luke, but not because I wanted to fight.

"No one should have to be a victim of someone else's ignorance and rage." My face suddenly felt hot. Victim. The word made my insides cringe.

"You're right. Finder knows you fought, but she never saw you. Nick neither. Your family's certainly never seen you fight. I feel like, like I've seen a part of you that no one else has. I feel like I imagine I'm a fighter, but it's all in my head. Like I'm faking it somehow. But when you told me you were going to meet Nicolai and the vampires, I know I turned my back on you in that moment, but I went home and got my weapons ready. I knew I'd come help you even before Finder called me."

"He would have killed me if you hadn't come."

"No doubt. This is weird to say out loud, but I feel like I can trust you, Stacy. You had my back in that fight. I saved your life. You saved my life. I think twice. You saved Finder's life. And to be brutally honest, the second we stepped off Maymont's grass, you shoved that 'I'm the guy that saves my friends and brawls like a wicked banshee' part of you away. You are a fighter, Stacy. Do you think it's an accident Finder and I are the friends you found here?" His blue eyes caught the light. "Deny it all you want, but you are a fighter."

"I don't want to fight. I don't like it. I've been training for what, a month now? I am determined to beat Matilda but every time I walk into my little gym, or the dojo or even into yoga I feel anxious and scared. Like it just isn't me."

"I don't think you have a choice. Your 'no fighter' option ended when you came to Richmond. Before Hidden City turned into something real. In New York you could live only in your head. But not here."

I broke what was left of the snowman and handed Tully half. He sat beside me. We chewed in silence.

"I did cry when he bit me, by the way," I said. "It really hurt."

"Truth?" he said. "I cried when he bit me, too." I looked over into Tully's face. Vulnerable blue eyes with a sparkle of humor met mine. A breeze blew the trees into a whisper. Finder had had sex with this man. That was so weird to know.

"Did you already scan for bats?" I asked.

"As soon as we came out."

"Did you look for Mr. Jackson's car?"

"Yes."

"Me too," I licked a bit of sticky frosting off my fingers.

"That's what I mean, Stacy. You may not want to change, but you are. You have. And Finder says you are doing great in class." He leaned forward and put his elbows on his knees. I scooted deeper on the bench, leaning my back against the rough cut stone.

"She does? She never tells me I'm doing great." I took a breath. Could Michael be right?

"I don't like pain," I said.

"Who does?"

"No, I mean obviously no one likes pain, but Finder has . . . tolerance. The ability to take a punch. You have it, too. I don't have that. Pain scares me. Getting physically hurt scares me. It shuts me down. I have no idea how I made it through those fights other than the terror of death being more powerful than my fear of getting hurt. Maybe it helped that I didn't know what was coming."

"That's how I got through those fights." Tully's hair hung over his shoulder leaving part of his face in shadow.

"But you and Finder like fighting."

"No, Finder and I like competing. Fencing is a parlor sport, clean, strategic. And usually, fair."

"But history. Duels and blood and knifing people. That's not clean. That's not fair."

"I don't fight duels. I poke people in the chest to make a buzzer go off and give me points. Not to say that we don't get bruises and we aren't risking breaking a finger or toe at some point, and there isn't a part of my brain that's living a fantasy novel slaying dragons, but fencing's about endurance. It's about being strong and fast, not brutal. That's what I mean when I say I imagine I'm a fighter. My competition skills barely translated at Maymont. I have fast reflexes and I know an attack when I see it, but what we fought? I've never done anything like that in my life. Bloody terrifying, my father would say. I'm in no hurry to do it again."

"Finder is."

"Maybe. She's got a warrior's spirit."

"She told me once that white people have a cultural assumption that Black people are impervious to pain. Do you think that's true?"

Tully shrugged and thought.

"I don't think it's conscious, if we do. If I do. But maybe I do assume she's tougher than she is."

"She likes being tough, though," I said.

"She likes being strong. She's a very delicate person actually. So's her mom. When Mr. Jackson disappeared, Mrs. Jackson wouldn't leave the house for fear her husband would come back hurt and find no one there to care for him. She had a lot of support from her church and her siblings, but when bad things like that happen, the support only lasts so long before people wander off, or worse, start wondering how, or if, you caused it.

"Mrs. Jackson didn't want Layla to see how distressed she was, so she had her spend a lot of nights at my house. She'd curl up in bed with my sisters, all of them asleep on each other like a pile of puppies. I think Mama felt like Layla was safer with my family, too, maybe because we were white. And there's so many of us, she was always in a group. Layla clung, just clung to my family."

"My cling friend is Meredith."

"Cling friend?"

"You said Finder clung to your family. When my mom left, my dad and I clung to my friend Meredith's family. And my Bubbe, who you met. When the Towers came down, again. All of us. We had Jill and Steve by then, too, so like you said. Safety in numbers." A dense cloud filtered over the moon and a shadow fell across our alcove. "I still feel guilty. For leaving so soon after. Even though it wasn't my choice or my idea. You can't imagine Tully. The city, it was like what I imagine a war zone would be. The Lower East Side was . . . indescribable. People were opening their doors and inviting strangers in to take showers and call their families. I've never seen New Yorkers behave like that, but if you were on that island that day, you were family. More people were ready to help than could be safely put to work. Once I got my little kids uptown to the other JDS, I was ready to go right back downtown. Meredith and I argued so hard to be allowed to go back out. Later that night, once we knew fully what had happened, Bubbe and our Rabbi opened our temple as a shelter for other families that were displaced and people who couldn't get home. Nobody knew if Jews were going to be targeted in some way so it was pretty tense. I ran the youth philanthropy group and I know we would've done more if I'd been there longer. If I'd stayed."

"See?" Tully said. "Survivor. Fighter."

An idea slid into my mind. I felt my face brighten. "We should make a pact."

"A pact?"

"We promise that we'll do whatever is necessary to keep each other out of denial and moving toward being the people we're meant to be."

"No way." Tully got up like I'd pinched him.

"Why not?"

"Just, no."

"Great! It's a deal. We'll be denial buddies."

"Are you even listening to me say no?" He ran his fingers through his thick hair. It caught the lamp light in golden strands.

"Of course. But I'm a fighter, remember?" I stood up and did a little imitation of Finder striking a pose at her dojo. "Right?"

He cracked a small smile.

"So here I go. This is me. Right now. Fighting. For my friend. And our Be Our Full and True Selves pact. BOFTS. We're BOFTS now. Like BFFs only different. I saw that!" I said as he smiled a little more. "I saw that almost laugh. See? You're with me. You know you are. I'm a survivor. And so are you." I smiled at him. "Grr."

"Okay, but we're not calling it BOFTS. That's ugly and too complicated." He thought for a moment then said, "How about SBS? The Self Betterment Society?"

"I love it."

"Good. Maybe we'll drop the first S and nickname it what it really is. B.S."

"Ha ha." I stuck out my hand to shake. "Welcome to the first meeting of the Self Betterment Society," I said.

"Why do I think I'm going to regret this?"

"Jill says new commitments come with a healthy compliment of fear. It's how you know you're doing the right thing."

"Like you being a fighter,"

"Yup," I said. "Like that."

"Seems counterintuitive."

"It totally is."

"Finder's gotta be wondering where we've gone off to." Tully said as we started back toward the door to the gym.

"You wish," I said. "Your girlfriend is dancing with the best dance partner in the history of earth, and is probably feeling goddess-like right now." Both my camera and Finder's dangled from my wrist on little paper straps. Oops. I was supposed to have been taking pictures. "I have never felt more like a proper lady in my life. Don't ask me how he did it."

"He led."

"That was a rhetorical question."

"Oh. Okay. But the way he did it was by leading. Just so you don't feel, you know, like it's a big mystery or anything. Bradley Joe evidently knows how to dance and does it well. It's not like. You know. Magic."

"Shh. No more reality. I want some magic. Dear God, please bring me a boyfriend with magic. Do you think Nick has magic?"

Tully smiled. "Bring him to the next dance and we'll see."

"Hey. Before we go back in," I said, "can I ask you one more thing?" Tully stopped walking and stood. I paused, a bigger question weighing on my mind. "I still haven't figured out how we can beat Matilda at New Year's," I said, voice low. "Have you . . . had any ideas?"

Tully shook his head.

"I know we need to control her blood supply," I said. "Just need a miracle to figure out how."

Tully reached for the tip of the arch. "Today's December twenty-first. Eleven days left."

A pigeon flew under the arch and landed with a flutter, almost crashing into my foot. I yelped and stepped out of its way.

"Weird," Tully said as we walked away. "Pigeons aren't night flyers."

A sharp poke in my ankle made me kick out. "Ow! Dude!"

The pigeon pecked me again, this time on the shoe.

"Are you kidding, pigeon?"

You asked for a miracle. Please don't kick my pigeon.

The pigeon hopped up on my shoe and stood there, staring up at me with dark, glassy eyes. I put my hand on Tully's arm. Wait.

"Okay," I said. "I get it. You want me to stand here."

The pigeon jumped off my foot and flew up into the low branches of the evergreens lining the sidewalk in front of St. Ig's. "Hold your breath," I said.

I turned toward Tully and braced myself on his arm. A breeze blew, heavier then normal but with my feet anchored and my lungs filled, I came through without even a cough. A girl, maybe ten years old, maybe twelve, climbed down from the pine tree and dropped to the ground like a cat burglar.

"I'm Pia." She had caramel skin and fine features with the most luscious curtain of wavy hair I'd ever seen outside of the movies or TV. "Wendell says to tell you the bald one left to hunt."

I grabbed her up in a hug.

"Thank you!" I said. "I don't know why I'm so happy about this because I have no idea what I'm doing, but this. This is amazing." Pia breathed rough, like I was squashing her. "Sorry," I said letting her go. "I'm not usually a hugger."

"Do you know where he went?" Go Tully with the presence of mind to ask a sensible question.

"I don't know if he'll still be there because I went to your house first trying to find you. It's called Bar 8:30. 830 East Andover Street in Shockoe Slip."

"We're on our way," I said. "Tell Wendell thank you!" I was already unzipping my skirt as we ran inside to get Finder.

20.

December 21, continued.

"Hold still," Finder said, moving the eye pencil away from my face. "Quit blinking."

She leaned one hip on her locker as I stood in front of her trying to be still while tucking my sock hop blouse into the emergency sweatpants I kept stashed for PE class. Poodle skirts and vampire hunting didn't really mesh. Finder had changed back into the jeans she had worn to the dance before borrowing her skirt. She hadn't gone home after school. Knowing she was going to Tully's before the dance, she'd packed spare clothes. Nerves tickled my spine.

"If you want this star to actually have six points," Finder said, "you gotta be still."

I did my best to quit fidgeting. Half of me thought for sure this exercise was pointless. The other half was like, buck up, Fighter Girl. Make a plan. Stick to the plan. Be ready to change the plan. Keep your mind on the mate.

Mate was making sure Bald Suit didn't take a victim back to Matilda. The plan? Show up and figure it out. Find a way to get to mate. A way. Any way. I had a list of options to discuss on the ride over. Whatever was about to happen depended less on my plan and more on what we found when we got to Bar 8:30.

Finder looked toward the bathroom where Tully was finishing his own costume change.

"Do you know what's up with my man?" she asked. "I know you guys went outside to talk while Bradley Joe was giving me the dance of my freakin' life- whoo! That boy has some moves!"

"I was shocked," I said, relieved at her change in subject. "I could've danced with him all night long. Somehow he . . ."

"Made you feel like a beamin' princess. I know it. Took the curl right outta my hair."

I giggled.

"I have a whole new respect for that boy, let me tell you what. But seriously, did the Tul give you any clues about what's up?" Her forehead crinkled with worry. "He's been super jumpy since we . . . any insight?"

"We mostly talked about me. About me being a fighter. Or not."

"Of course you're a fighter, duh. You play chess. The war game to end all war games. But for real, if the lightbulb goes on and you figure out Tully's deal, I need to know. That boy and his moods are gonna make me grey before my time."

"His moods?" I laughed out loud. "What about your moods?"

"I'm not moody," Finder said. "I'm sensitive."

I snorted.

"What? Stop moving," she said, taking the pencil off my skin. "My father's evil, my mother lost a leg, and now I'm supposed to just live and let live? You shoulda seen me before I started therapy." Her eyes twinkled.

"I'm the one who made you get therapy!"

"Oh, yeah. Well, still. I have some unresolved anger issues you can't even crack open."

"I feel ridiculous," Tully said, coming out of the boys bathroom. Jeans rolled up over his knees, he struggled to belt Finder's poodle skirt around his waist. "Do these things only come in microscopic sizes?"

"You just need a tinier waistline," Finder said. "It fit me fine."

Tully's hair cascaded to his shoulders as he turned his attention to arranging his girlfriend's headscarf around his skull like a babushka. Tully was one big lady.

Finder took my chin in her hand and surveyed her work. "Done. I pronounce you ready for battle."

"Wow," Tully said. "That looks great."

Finder capped her eyeliner, helped Tully arrange his belt around the top of the skirt, then dug again in her bag.

"Can't risk them recognizing us," Finder said with a smirk, swiping eye shadow over his lids.

"You just want to torture me," he said, scowling.

"You have sisters," she said. "You've lived through worse."

"Yeah, but not in public."

"Quit complaining and warm up. If tonight goes well, you'll need to be stretched out." She crossed her arms over her chest and stood with her back to him. "Can you crack my back?"

We parked on a busy street, miraculously scoring a spot in front of a brick front, three-story townhouse with a trendy font painted on the window. Our destination, *Bar 8:30* glowed in neon orange over the door.

I scanned the street for any signs of Bat Suits, meaning cars I recognized, or bats haunting the spindly, leafless trees. I searched the rooftops one more time, but saw nothing out of the ordinary.

"Should we call Nick?" I asked. "I don't know if he's twenty-one, but maybe . . ."

"No. We're conspicuous enough without a flamboyantly memorable Goth coming along. Have some faith, Chess Team. There is definitely a vampire in there." Finder warmed up, fists held up, dancing back and forth from foot-to-foot like she did before whaling on my punching bag.

I left my coat in the truck. With a mugger cap pulled over my hair and sunglasses on, I hoped Bald Suit wouldn't recognize me. Finder tucked a stake into each boot from the stash we now kept in Tully's truck. I had my new 'weapons' which, as of the day I finished them, lived in the messenger bag I no longer left home without.

"Embrace the fighter?" Tully held out his fist. I knocked his fist with mine.

"Embrace the fighter," I said.

Finder bonked his fist, then mine, too. "This," she said with a grin, "this is gonna be fun."

Loud, crowded and smoky, Bar 8:30 embodied everything I disliked about adult nightlife; crowds, booze, volume and smoke. High-backed booths occupied most of the dining room. The bar on the right ran the length of the place front to back. People sat and stood, packing the bar as we squeezed in the door. I looked for Bald Suit's shiny skull. I noticed a hostess stand at the far back next to doors that probably led to the kitchen. Weird to have it there instead of at the front, but I was not a bar aficionado, and if this place was typical, I never would be. The smoke and crush of bodies made me want to turn right back around and leave.

I noticed a sign over the bar crowning a display of news articles written about the place. It read: Owned by Richmond's most Famous Family. And then I spotted Bald Suit passing some cash to the bartender. Short, stocky and fit, he wore a black turtleneck shirt, a zip front sweater, also black, and black pants and shoes.

"Hamlet, spotted on the right," Finder said in my ear.

"I see him," I said. Looked like we were just in time. Bald Suit offered his hand to a woman in blue. She tossed a mane of long hair over her shoulder.

I started to press my way through the bodies. Bald Suit hadn't seemed to notice us, which was exactly what we wanted. He spoke to the man sitting on the woman's other side. I stopped walking forward. Finder bumped into my back.

Bald Suit led the couple back to the hostess stand. She checked something on a clipboard and nodded. He followed her through the doors and disappeared from view.

"Hey," I heard from my right. "Hey, excuse me, Miss?" I turned. Drat, I was hoping to look enough like a boy that I'd go unnoticed. But the bartender wasn't looking at me. The bartender was talking to Tully.

"You can't bring your kids in here," he said. "Twenty-one and over."

Behind his scarf, what I could see of Tully's face was beet red.

Finder spoke up. "She just brought us in to use the bathroom. She comes here all the time."

He glanced at me, then squinted at Tully. "If anyone knows the regulars, it's me. I'm here six nights a week."

"Oh, not *that* kind of all the time," Finder said. "I mean like birthdays, anniversaries, all the time like, whenever they go out, which is kind of never."

The bartender did a double take trying to match his assumption that Finder was Tully's kid with the new information that they didn't match.

"I'm sorry, I can't let you guys in- "

"Got it, no problem. Just let her pee. Meet you back at the car," Finder said. She turned around and pushed Tully toward the front door ignoring the protest from the bartender as I beelined for the restroom signs. What were the chances of him coming back here to snag me from the bathroom? I needed to stay in here long enough for him to forget about me and get back to his job. We'd made a contingency for getting separated. I'd sneak out the back, and they would meet me.

I took advantage of my location to do what it was meant for, then check my cheek stars when I washed my hands. There were oh so many ways this plan could go south. Do not think of those, I told myself. Time to charge up my holy symbols. I imagined my little Stars being filled with divine white light.

"Baruch atah Adonai," I began, focusing my intention; Bald Suit would not want to touch me. Or bite me. Or kidnap me and take me back to Maymont. I sang the rest quietly, letting my intention fill me the way Saanvi had us do in yoga. "Eloheinu melech ha'olam," I struggled for more words. I repeated the beginning. What was the rest of this prayer? It was the one for safety, but the only ones that came to mind where the Hanukkah ones I'd just heard two weeks ago. I fell back on the Shema. "Shema Yisrael, Adonai Elohenu Adonai echad."

I stuffed my mugger cap into the messenger bag, loosened my hair, then velcro-ed one homemade arm band around each forearm. The holy symbols faced inside, so if I held my arms up in defense, they'd show. I tied my Beth Shamar sweatshirt around my waist, so the Star of David faced out, protecting me, in theory, from behind. My overall strategy was that when the bartender looked for my white shirt, hat, and sunglasses, he'd see my long hair and sweatshirt and maybe not realize it was me. I peeped out the bathroom door and ducked my head waiting for the hostess to step away from her station. Within a minute, another couple approached the stand. She checked her clipboard and walked them through the swinging doors. I noticed a sign I hadn't seen before: Private Dining Rooms.

I waited until the bartender's back was turned, then walked out of the bathroom with confidence, like I hadn't just finagled something. I pushed through the swinging, leather-coated, Private Dining Rooms doors.

The narrow hallway was lined with numbered doors. A few stood open. A velvet bench curved around a half-moon shaped table set for four. An oblong, Tiffany glass style lamp hung low over the table. Sconces glowed on the velvet wallpapered walls. The vibe was dark and smouldery, kind of 1920's speakeasy.

I counted eight dining rooms. I heard the hostess finish seating her couple. I flattened myself behind the door of the nearest open dining room. Sweat broke out under my armpits. The hostess passed me, then a server knocked and opened the door to the room directly across from mine. The food smelled delicious, steak and onions and garlic. I'd had cupcakes and cookies, but smelling real food made me realize I was hungry. A chorus of happy, admiring noises came from the room. I guessed that was not where my quarry was dining.

I needed Finder. She would know exactly which door to open. I waited until I heard the door click closed across the hall and the kitchen door swing shut. All but one door on the opposite side of the hall were shut. Three doors to choose from. Happy steak people were behind door number one. Was Bald Suit behind door number two or door number three? I went to the farthest end of the hall. I stood still, heart thumping so loud I feared Bald Suit could hear it.

There were no other ways in or out of this hall. The kitchen was one, and the main restaurant the other. I guess they didn't want people sneaking out and not paying their bills. I couldn't just stand here hoping Finder and Tully would figure out a way in. I paused. What was I going to do when I opened that door? What if they were just eating dinner? Above the door, a red light flashed on. Do Not Disturb. I glanced down the hall and sure enough, every door had a little light over it. None of them were on.

Crap. A bolt of panic ran through me. I was losing a tempo. I had to make a move or I was going to get caught standing like an underage dope in this hallway and get thrown out before I could even play. Mate was stopping Bald Suit from taking anyone home to Matilda. Why was he in this room instead of leaving and taking them back to Maymont?

Wait. Them. *Them.* Matilda didn't allow *thems.* She only allowed *hims.* The woman wouldn't be fed on. She was safe. Except that she was in a room with a vampire who wasn't allowed to touch her. And whose boss wasn't looking.

I reached into my messenger bag and pulled out the one thing I had with me that wasn't for hunting vampires.

Am I doing the right thing? Michael?

Nothing.

Of course. Ask and ye shall receive, bah humbug.

My massive holy symbol necklace bonked against my belly as I hoped to heck I was making the right decision.

I pushed open the dining room door.

21.

December 21, continued.

Bald Suit's face was buried in the throat of the woman in the blue dress. Her face was contorted in pain and terror. Her boyfriend, or whoever he was, slumped in the booth beside her. Dead or asleep?

I lifted my sock hop gift camera to my eye and snapped, snapped and snapped. Bald Suit was so involved in what he was doing, he didn't notice me. A few seconds stretched into several. Snap, turn, snap, turn, snap. The room was dim enough to be a photo ruiner so I kept clicking the button and rolling the film to the next frame.

After what seemed like an anti-climactically long time, the woman gasped, "Help!"

It was then that Bald Suit realized something was up. He let go of her throat, whipped round and saw me. Click. She shoved against him, but he had her pinned to the booth. Click. I kicked shut the door behind me.

The woman was bleeding down into a black towel he held to her shoulder. Click.

"Help!" she cried, hand going to her bleeding wound. Click. Blood was all over his face. Click. As Bald Suit started to lunge for me, I stuffed the camera down my shirt. I bent my elbows and brandished my arm bands sewn with holy symbols. He winced. He hissed as he backed away.

What?? This was *working?*

"Get out," I said to the woman. Still holding one wrist up, I unclipped my holy water spray bottle from my belt.

She sobbed, shaking the collapsed man.

"Wake him up," I said to Bald Suit. "WAKE HIM UP!" He stared at me, as if he wasn't quite sure what was going on. I did not have time for him to figure it out. I sprayed holy water in his face. He shrieked. Liquid sizzled on his skin.

"Wake up!" said Bald Suit. And snap, the man was awake, like he'd never been asleep.

The door at my back swung open. Finder burst in, Tully on her heels. One glance to assess, then she shoved me aside. She pressed her stake into Bald Suit's chest.

"One move and it's over."

Tully, still dressed in his lady costume, gestured for the humans to come out.

"No!" Bald Suit shrieked, wiping at his face. "They can't leave! I haven't washed them!" Finder's eyes flicked to the couple and lightning fast, the vampire threw a punch at Finder's face. She blocked as if she'd expected it, then leaned hard into the stake. He grunted as it punctured his chest.

"Want me to drive it home?" she said. "Swing again, and I will." The vampire twitched, moving his head side-to-side like he was searching for eye contact. The couple looked torn between running and fighting. Tully shut the door.

"He needs to wipe their minds," Tully said, the voice of fierce reason. "It's better for all of us if they don't remember this."

"But her neck wound?" I said.

"Take this toothpick out and I'll heal it," said Bald Suit.

"Don't come near me!" the woman sobbed.

"You're safe now," I said. "This is all a terrible, uh . . . . imaginary moment."

The woman turned on her date. "Did you put Blue Star in my drink?" She pushed him in the chest. "Did you drug me?"

"No! I'd never!"

"This isn't real!" she cried. She slapped herself in the face. "Wake up, Sarah! Wake up!"

"Fix this," Tully said to Bald Suit, but looking at me. It was hard, so hard to avoid looking Bald Suit in the eyes. I pulled out my sunglasses and put them on.

"Can you heal her?" Finder demanded.

"Gotta lick it," the vampire said.

Gross. But wait, he could heal his bite wounds by licking them?

"Do you want to wake up?" Tully asked the woman. "To wake up, you have to be still. You have to stay in the dream another minute so he can heal you."

It took Tully another few words to convince her. He went behind Bald Suit and held his arms, absolutely useless against his superior strength and speed, but she didn't know that. It made her willing to step near him.

Bald Suit didn't lean toward her. "It's the stake," he said. "If you want me to move, you gotta take out the stake."

"Not a chance," Finder said. Tully tipped Bald Suit forward so he could reach the woman's neck. When she moved the napkin away, ragged skin hung from where he'd torn her throat.

The vampire coughed once, twice and then made a wet gargling sound like he was hocking up a loogie. He closed his lips and sloshed something around in his mouth. He jerked his head, indicating for her to come closer.

Reluctance all over her face, she did.

Bald Suit spat a wad of greenish phlegm onto her throat.

"It stings!" Little tears squirted out the corners of her eyes as she squeezed them shut. Bat Suit used his tongue to spread his mouth slime over the wound. She moaned in pain as the skin scabbed back together. He spat another layer and the wound healed, fading to a dark purple bruise. One more hack, spit and spread and her neck looked like it had never been touched.

"Look at me," said Bald Suit. I did, the power of persuasion in his voice snagging my attention. When my eyes went to meet his, he was looking at her. I caught myself and looked instead at the woman.

That was close.

"What a wonderful dinner," he said.

"What a wonderful dinner," she repeated.

"Can't wait to go home, have a cookie and go to sleep."

"Can't wait to go home, have a cookie and go to sleep."

"That's right," he said. "You will remember your coat from the coat check, walk out of the restaurant and go home safely. You will not remember me or any of these people in the room with us except your boyfriend,"

"I'm not her boyfriend."

"Shut up. You will remember only that man. Point her to the man," he said.

I got her to look at me and then aim her shoulders to the man who wasn't Bald Suit or Tully.

"Let her out," said Bald Suit.

"Don't forget your purse," said the man, handing it to her.

I opened the door and let her out. I watched her steady walk down the hall and through the doors back into the main restaurant.

The kitchen door started to swing open and I shut mine in a hurry, grateful for the flashing light. Do Not Disturb.

"I let the nice innocent human go, so can you take this thing out of my chest?"

"No," I said. "What about him?"

"I need him," Bald Suit said.

"Sorry," I said. "This restaurant doesn't do take out."

"I can't show up empty handed."

"He's not going with you," Tully said. He also had a stake in hand now.

"You want to come with me, though, don't you?" Bald Suit said to the man.

"Yes, I do," said the man, looking a little glazed in his eyes.

Finder leaned on the stake. "Let him go."

"Ow!"

"Wipe his mind." Tully poked him with the other stake.

Bald Suit snarled, "I am going to kill you all so hard when this is over." He got less scary as he whined.

After a few more pokes and threats, the same process happened. The man left looking calm and happy.

"This where you usually hunt?" I asked.

"I'm not telling you anything," Bald Suit said.

"Okay," I said. "Stake him."

Finder took a breath to prepare.

"Matilda owns this place," he said. "She wants us to hunt only here so if we ever need to track a problem victim, or find someone for any reason, we know where they came from. No more. Done talking."

I shook my spray bottle.

A wind swirled in the room and Bald Suit shut his eyes. Then the wind stopped. His eyes shot open, surprised.

"Can't go to bat with a stake in your chest, hmm?" Finder said.

"No pun intended," said Bald Suit. Finder leaned a little more and he yelped in pain.

"Now relax. Like my friend said, we just want to talk."

"I'm told Matilda doesn't allow you to feed on women," I said.

"How do you know that?" Bald Suit was the poster child for righteous indignation at that moment.

"I know lots of things," I said. "Including having an entire camera filled with photographs of you feeding on that woman, photographs I assume you'd rather Matilda not be aware of."

"Blackmail? Are you kidding?"

"The way I see it, you have two choices. One, we can push that stake through your heart and return your body to Matilda. Two, we can let you live, hold on to your little secret and you can do what we ask when we ask it."

"You want me to be a double agent?"

"I want you to fail to bring home the bacon."

"The puns never end with you," said Bald Suit. Finder pushed a smidge. Bald Suit grunted. "She'll just send someone else."

"In that case, you can tell us who they are, where they're going, and any extra information that might be useful."

"No way."

"Who usually hunts?"

"I'm not telling. Did Darcy Jackson rat me out?"

"Please let me stake him," Finder said.

I scrunched my face. "No. He's going to agree. Aren't you? You're going to agree to fail to hunt. You're also going to agree to tell me who else hunts if it isn't you, and when, and where.

"You are not going to share this conversation because if you do, I will know. Just like I knew where to find you tonight and I knew that Matilda doesn't allow girls. Do you want to know what else I know? You aren't allowed to feed *except* on Matilda. And she hates hunting for herself. Does she let you have a little taste as your hunting reward? How will she react if she receives an envelope of photographs of you buried deep in that woman's neck? Make the wrong choice now, and you'll find out."

"Torture before killing?" Finder asked.

"What about feeding him to the other butlers," Tully said.

"Too easy," I said. "She'd feed him to *him.*"

I paused, still keeping my eyes focused on Bald Suit's shoes. It was so hard not to look up, to stare into his evil face and make my threats. I could not, would not let him mesmerize me. I would not meet his eyes.

"I hate you," Bald Suit wriggled, trying to get a grip on his partially paralyzed body. "I am going to hunt you down and kill you myself."

"Do you agree to my terms or should Finder push that stake in the rest of the way? She's dying to do it."

"I might do it anyway. Just for fun," she said and leaned on the wood. The vampire groaned.

I racked my brain for anything else I could say or do to get Bald Suit to keep our secret. I sorted through the possibilities, trying to see moves ahead. Just how afraid of Matilda was he? And then I got an idea.

It arrived as a full blown plan, like when I'm deep in the middle game and scrambling for advantage. My brain sorts through patterns I know, patterns I can imagine coming from what I see in front of me and then, whoosh! The idea of how to get to mate arrives.

"Hold his arm," I said to Tully. He came around from behind the vampire and picked up his limp arm. Bald Suit tried to resist, arm twitching, but to no use.

The table knives at each place setting were too dull.

"Do either of you have a knife?"

"Left front," Finder said. Tully was holding Bald Suit's arm and blocking where I needed to reach. He tucked his hand into Finder's pocket then handed me her pocket knife.

I picked up a wine glass half full of water, and dumped its contents.

Bald Suit had just fed. Did that mean he could bleed?

I looked at the stake jammed into his flesh. A tiny ring of red showed around its edge. The night we fought them, there was no gore. Staking Stinky Suit and the vampire Sloan had resembled staking bags of rotting street garbage. They stank to high heaven when punctured, but no blood had come out.

I grabbed Bat Suit's hand and anchored it, palm up, to the table.

"What the- ?"

I looked away so I wouldn't lose my nerve. Think of it as a piece of cheese, I told myself. I stabbed down with all my might.

Bald Suit shrieked. I yanked the knife back out and tossed it on the table. A tiny well of blood oozed up out of his hand.

I held his hand over the glass and squeezed. Drip. Drip. Drip.

"What are you doing?" Tully said, voice soft. Finder stared at me in astonishment.

"This blood is insurance," I said, hoping that this utter fiction would sound real. "Insurance that you keep this secret and do what we say." I pushed from Bald Suit's wrist to his palm to squeeze out more blood. It started to flow a little faster. Drip, drip, drip.

"This blood is your essence," I said. "And now, I own it. If I want to find where you sleep during the day, three little drops of your blood will tell me. Three drops and I can see what you're doing and where you are at any moment." I glanced up and saw his eyes were wide. Finder's mouth was agape. I looked away. Don't lose it, Goldman, I coached myself. Just pretend. Just be Meredith.

"I will know when you feed. I will know how much and on whom. And the best part is, you don't even know the half of what I can do with your blood. Tracking you is easy stuff. You're mine now. Do you understand?"

Silence.

"Speak!" I was surprised and how threatening I sounded.

"Yes," he said, trembling.

"Yes what?"

"Yes, I understand."

"So what are you going to do?"

"I'm going to fail to hunt."

"And?" I picked Finder's knife up off the table. His cut was already healing. I nodded at Finder. She pushed the stake a little further into his chest.

"And I'll tell you if she sends someone other than me.

"A little more."

"I'll tell you when and where they go."

"Correct. Most importantly you will make sure that she gets how much blood?"

"None?"

"Good. I see you understand me now. What's your name?"

"I'm not tell- " Finder pushed on the stake. The vampire groaned.

"Terrence."

"How many people can you mind wipe at once, Terrence?"

"I've only tried one at a time."

That wasn't good enough.

"We'll have to leave through the kitchen," I said. "Tully can you reach his wallet?"

"What? All this and you're mugging me, too?"

Tully reached into Terrence's inside coat pocket and handed me the wallet. I found his cash and took out a twenty. I put it on the table. I took the opportunity to rifle through. Cash, credit cards, all in his name except one which bore his name and Maymont Investments, Inc. I put that one in my pocket. He had two business cards which I also took out.

"Are either of these your businesses?"

He looked at me like I was an idiot. "No."

"Are they places you do business?" I asked, pocketing them.

"Call them and find out."

"Nice," I said. "Still acting like you're the one winning." I handed Tully the wallet who took it between two fingers and dropped it back into the vampire's coat pocket. Metal clinked against metal.

"Pull those out," I said. This was going even better than I'd hoped.

I held out my hand and Tully tossed me four keys on an I heart my Pug key ring. I almost missed but caught them against my chest. I put them in my pocket.

"We're going to walk through the kitchen," I said, "and you're going to make anyone who looks at us forget they saw us. Especially you. You look terrible. If you scream or resist, Finder will stake you where you stand."

"Please scream," Finder said. "Please resist. Please."

I took the glass of blood and put a cloth napkin over the top. "Ready?"

Finder and Tully nodded.

I opened the door to our private dining room right in the face of a server.

I gave her a big smile. "Live-action role playing game," I said. "Doesn't his costume look great? Tip's on the table. Thank you!" She stepped out of the way as I pushed through the kitchen door. Behind me I heard Terrence mutter, "Sorry, Lisa. Forget."

It hadn't occurred to me that this was a regular spot for him. Oh no. These people knew him. Did they know what he was? Had I made a big mistake? I rounded a long stainless steel serving counter with little papers stuck to the top.

"Hey!" someone shouted. "You can't go through here!"

"Sorry!" I said pushing past him. Surprised, he didn't resist.

"Forget," hissed Bald Suit Terrence.

I heard the guy grunt.

"Left," Tully said. I saw our destination.

Two more kitchen staff tried to tell us we couldn't use that door, but Terrence met their eyes and we were outside and away before anyone could try to chase us. Tully had moved the truck into the alley. It took him and Finder both to move the vampire since his knees didn't seem to be doing their job with a stake in his chest. We loaded Terrence into the back seat. Finder got into the squished little compartment with him, my usual spot, because she could push the stake in whereas I could not.

I set the wine glass, about a quarter filled with the vampire's blood, into the cup holder. I saw a hair tie on the console and snagged it, using it to anchor the napkin covering the cup.

"So tell me, Terrence," Finder said in a conversational tone, "Where did you get the abysmal fighter training you displayed fighting me in the ring last month? Surely not my father. Oh, and is my father sleeping with Matilda?"

"They'll come looking for me soon," Terrence was saying as I got back in the truck. The guy at the hardware store key counter had given me an annoyed glare as I asked him to make copies of four keys just as the store was closing. But my pocket was full of jingle and I was ready for phase two. We couldn't talk about anything significant with Terrence in the car, nor could we trust that his super hearing wouldn't pick up on anything we said far away outside the truck either.

"I have an idea," Finder said. "Why don't we take him home, sit him in front of open windows and leave the stake in so he can't move? Then whatever happens happens. We did not technically kill him if asked, and we all get home on time?"

"No leaving anything to chance," I said, yawning already. "Matilda can't get him back until it's too close to sunrise for her to retaliate."

"She is going to freak out," Terrence said from his prone position in the backseat. "I'm her best hunter. You have no idea how hard it is to get humans to go somewhere alone with a single man. Everyone assumes you're an axe murderer."

"You *are* an axe murderer, Terrence," Finder said, rolling another stake between her hands.

"I am part of a long lineage of night-stalking predators who terrorize innocent people for the sheer joy of it."

Finder rolled her eyes. "Did you memorize that speech? It sounds so fake."

"We all memorize the speech," Terrence said. "Matilda can't have humans knowing the truth about us."

"You mean the soul sucking?" I asked. Tully pulled the truck up in view of the Hollywood Cemetery front gate. There was a guard posted twenty-four hours on the weekends, so we decided it would be a safe enough place to wait out the night before dropping Terrence off at the mansion.

"Sorry to interrupt," Tully said, "but do you want to call home? Finder and I both took turns at the pay phone by the hardware store."

Oh. Yeah. Guess that was a thing.

"You're going to let me call home?" Terrence said. "Like a ransom call? That's exciting."

"Be quiet or I'll try out my new toy," Finder said. She'd asked me to buy her a mallet at the hardware store, so I had. Now she was holding it, bouncing the hard rubber head back and forth from knee to knee. She was in a rare good mood. I think hunting vampires suited her.

"Tell me more about my father," she said.

"He's rich."

"Is that the best you can do? I could tap the stake every time you give me a stupid answer."

I dug in my bag for my cell phone. Hmm. How could I tell my parents the truth without telling the *truth?*

"He reminds Matilda of Mr. Dillworth, her butler when she was alive," said Terrence.

"Okay, that's better. What else? And no bedroom details. It's bad enough to know that's happening."

"It's all blood related. Once you're dead, your body doesn't do human bedroom business anymore."

"Top ten reasons not to become a vampire," she said.

The phone rang at my house.

"Shh," I said, wanting quiet for my call.

"Hi, honey. We were just starting to worry," said Dad. A late night host cracked a joke to audience applause in the background. "Do you need a ride?"

"Nope. I'm with Tully and Finder. They got permission to be out a little later. We have a friend we have to drop off, but not for a little bit yet. Is it okay if I come home late?"

"Let me speak to Teularen."

"Um. Okay. Why?"

"Just let me speak to him."

Good grief.

"My dad wants to talk to you."

"Hello, Mr Goldman," Tully said. He paused. "Yes, full tank. Mmm-hmm. Four of us, myself, Layla, Stacy and our friend Terrence. We're dropping him off and then I'll bring her home. I can bring her home first if you- Oh. Okay. Very good, sir. Thank you. Here she is."

Tully handed me back the phone.

"Why are you giving him the third degree?" I said.

"I do not need to answer that. I was a teenager once. I know how things are. Try not to be out too late. And who's Terrence?"

"He's old. And gross. Don't worry, Dad, I'm not doing anything I'm not supposed to do."

"Except kidnapping," Terrence said, way too loud.

"What was that?" said Dad.

"They're holding me pris- " Finder tapped the stake with her mallet. Terrence gasped and shut up.

"He thinks he so funny. Okay Dad, gonna let you go. See you later."

"About what time?"

"Don't know yet. No school tomorrow and I don't have anything planned other than babysitting Steve while you golf so I think I'll be fine whatever time I get home." Like dawn, I thought. "Okay, Dad, my battery's dying. I gotta go. Love you." And I hung up.

"Okay Dad my battery is dying and the man we kidnapped is dreaming about ripping our throats out and telling his mistress everything we did. Yeah, like um. Like yeah. Dad." Terrence's voice was weak from the last stake pound, but he laughed a little at his own performance.

"Can we *not* wait until sunrise to drop this off?" said Finder. "He's grating on my nerves. And I do like the feel of this mallet a little too much."

"Do not kill him," I said. "We need him."

It was quiet in the truck for a while. Tully turned off the engine and we sat in tense silence waiting for Terrence to remember some secret power he had that he could use to attack us. Tully had a stake in his lap, like Finder, but also a fencing foil sharpened to be useful within reach. I had my arm bands on and my spray bottle of holy water. Finder had herself, a stake and her fancy new mallet. I dug in my bag for my tiny notebook and a pen.

I began a shopping list.

Because doesn't everyone parked in a truck outside a graveyard with a half-staked vampire in the backseat think about shopping?

Saturday, December 22, 2001.
3:26 a.m.

I woke with a start. My head snapped up from where I leaned on the truck window. Tully snored in the seat next to me. Finder was limp in the backseat and Terrence was staring into space. His eyes flicked to me and our gazes met.

"Let me go," he said. I looked away from him, but his suggestion felt like a good idea. Yeah. Poor guy. We'd had him trapped for a long time, he must be uncomfortable. If I just pulled out the stake for a few minutes, he could move around. I got on my knees and turned around to lean over my seat. I reached for the stake.

Finder's arm shot out like a viper striking.

"Ow!" Her karate chop hurt. She gripped my arm as I started to pull it away. Terrence's influence evaporated.

"It's a monster, Chess Team. It wants to drink your blood and suck your soul until you die. Don't forget that." She let go. She pushed up her sunglasses so I could see her eyes. "And don't look him in the eyes."

I knew that, of course. How had I been so careless?

Human shaped. Not human. Formerly human. Now demonic. Or something else not nice. And soul sucking *hurt*. I was not in the market to ever feel that kind of pain again. I wanted to pry for more information, but at this point anything he told us would likely be lies, so silence was probably best. I also didn't want to give information away by accident that Matilda could use against us.

"It's 3:30," Finder said. "Can we ditch this thing, please?"

Tully started the engine.

On the one hand, I was exhausted, too. On the other hand, if we let Terrence get found too early, Matilda would have time to retaliate. If he arrived all torn up, were they less likely to suspect him of being a double agent? Would they smell us on him? Maybe a spritz of holy water all over would clear our scent? How did Jill deodorize things? I remembered her using a spray cleaner that smelled like salad dressing. What was in salad dressing that made things not stink?

We sat parked a block from Maymont for nearly an hour trying to figure out a safe place to leave Terrence. We wanted him to be found, but we didn't want to get caught. Leaving him on the steps of the mansion was ideal for presentation and theatricality, but impractical. We couldn't risk him getting turned to ash by sunlight. We needed Terrence to foul the next couple hunts. We needed Matilda blood-free until New Year's Eve.

We went through a list of possible places to leave Terrence at Maymont. The nature center, outbuildings, shrubbery, middle of the lawn, parking lot, Darcy Jackson's car (which was right over there) but none of them were locations where we could be sure we wouldn't be seen.

"It'll be scarier for Matilda if they find him here," Tully said as we drove by the lower Maymont parking lot. "They won't want to think about vampire hunters knowing their headquarters."

"Just search little known facts about Richmond on the internet," I said. "If there were vampire hunters other than us, this and Hollywood would be the first places they would hunt."

"She's not wrong," Finder sat with her legs stretched out over her prone seat-mate. Terrence had been very quiet since Finder had tapped the stake with her mallet. I think he'd realized that his un-life was in our hands.

She had wrapped her headscarf around his eyes to make sure we didn't have another accident. Her hair was so high unbound, even with her slumped it touched the roof of the truck. "I know where to leave him!" she said. "And if we go now, we might still get there while the others are here."

Almost an hour later we found the single twenty-four hour market in Richmond that was more than a gas station.

Tully held the funnel as I transferred my holy water into an empty drink bottle and then poured straight white vinegar into the spray bottle. I had looked for a new spray bottle, but there were none to be found. I guess you had to shop at normal hours for that.

When we got to Terrence's apartment, the sky glowed with a gray purple pre-dawn.

Armed to the teeth and smelling like the salad in an Italian restaurant minus the parm, I used Terrence's fob to open the sliding glass doors, then access the elevator. No one was at the desk. I hoped there wasn't video surveillance.

Finder and Tully heaved the stocky, pale vampire inside his apartment door. They laid him on the floor. I crouched down beside him.

"I am going to repeat this one time," I said. "I have your blood. If you betray me, I will use it to boil the dead meat you're made of and rot you from the inside out. You are going to fail in every hunt. Every time she sends you out to get her a victim, something is going to go wrong. Every hunt, you will fail. I will know when you are hunting because I can track you with your blood. I will know if you slip up and feed yourself. You will not bring blood back here unless it is dead animal blood you buy at a butcher."

Terrence's eyes narrowed.

"Can't eat that," he said voice slurring from paralysis. "S' like rotten milk."

Interesting.

"Just so we're clear," I said, "I will know if you bring back a victim for her, and I swear on my grandfather's grave that if you do it, you will be dead by nightfall. If I give her my photographs, you know she'll make an example of you. Your death will not be quick. Or painless. Do you understand everything I have said to you?"

"Yes, master," he slurred in a nasty, nasty way.

"While you're failing to hunt, if you figure out a way to get Matilda to leave us alone forever, as in for the rest of our lives and the lives of our offspring and so on and so forth, I'll help you take her down and grab control of Richmond for yourself."

Sunrise came and with it, rigor mortis. I poked Terrence's leg with my shoe. It felt like toeing furniture.

Finder took off his blindfold.

"Unstake him or leave it?" she said.

Tough decision. Did we want the vampires on alert that someone was hunting them? No. I think we did not. A staked vampire and a problem getting blood would be too easy to connect. And far too easy to connect to us, the obvious threats.

"Take it out," I said.

I sprayed him again with vinegar. We spritzed his keys and the doorknobs after we touched them. Who knew if it would work, but it was worth a shot.

Finder chucked the stake that had occupied Terrence's chest into the truck bed. She regarded me with a smile of pride. "I didn't know you had that in you, Chess Team. Let no one ever say you are not righteously badass."

22.

December 22, continued.

I opened the front door as quietly as I could, but the alarm system beeped anyway. Behind me, a gray winter dawn spread over the sky.

I shut the door and turned the beep off within my 30 second window. I wiped my feet, dirty from the quick walk to the pool house to stash my glass of blood, and made straight for the stairs. Awake enough after my truck nap, I had some research to do before I showered and slept.

"Stacy. Rachel. Goldman."

Dad's voice from the kitchen. Crap. Why was he up so early? I was doomed.

"Good morning," I said as if everything was normal and fine. "How was your night?"

"You said you'd be home late, not that you'd be home *tomorrow*. I have been sitting here trying to decide if I should call the police or not."

His voice was quiet and calm. That, for my dad, was bad. Very bad. He wasn't angry. He was *livid*.

"You could've called my phone."

"I did. Several times." His gaze hardened. "No answer."

I stood in the kitchen doorway. Very still. If this came out wrong, even one tiny bit wrong, I could get myself grounded from now until summer vacation. It had to be honest and sincere. And missing several important details.

"I'm sorry, Dad. I didn't mean to scare you. I wasn't doing anything bad, no sex, no drugs, no drinking. I went to a restaurant with Tully and Finder and we ran into Terrence. He had been . . . drinking . . . and by the time we left, he couldn't drive home by himself. He's like a brother to Finder's dad, so we took him home. We were afraid he might hurt himself, he was so messed up. He lives alone, so we decided to stay with him for a little while. He fell asleep and we did too."

My dad's expression was blank, but for slight accusation in his eyes and tightness around his mouth and brow. The litigation stare.

I'm not guilty of anything, I told myself. I took a breath. I am alive, I am safe. Nothing bad is happening. All true. But I knew my dad. And it was time to grovel.

"My phone battery died right after I called you the first time," I set down my messenger bag and came fully into the kitchen. "The charger is here, upstairs. I should have called you from Terrence's." I pulled out the chair across from him and started to sit down. A thump against the front door froze me. I looked toward the door. "I'll get it," I said. It was daylight, it wasn't a vampire, that I knew. I did know that, right? Heart thudding in my chest, I went to the front door and peeped through the peep hole. Nobody. I opened the door and saw the culprit lying where it had bounced just off the doormat. The Sunday paper. I sighed in embarrassed relief. I reached down, picked up the thick roll and took it in. I set it on the table in front of him. A peace offering. I sat down across from him.

"I've never been around someone who was in the kind of condition Terrence was in, especially an adult. Not even you after mom went to prison. It was pretty terrible."

"You know I'm not proud of that time," he said. "Once I realized I was going down a road that was, well, that was what it was, I went to my mother and she got me some help. You know that's how I met Jill, right? She was training at the clinic I went to for therapy."

"What? Therapy? I thought you met her at the theatre!" I said. "You told me you met her at work. She was an actress."

"I did meet her at work and she was an actress. At night. I just didn't clarify that I met her during the day."

Mind blown.

"So, that's how you did your 180? Jill gave you therapy?"

"No. I got therapy at the clinic where she worked. It's why I'm a one martini man."

This was news to me. I was nine when my mom went off the deep end and my dad had followed in quick succession. "A reaction," Bubbe had said when I would stay with her or stay a week at Meredith's. "He's having a reaction. He loves you and he's going to be fine, we just have to give him a little space." Remembering, I was back in her apartment, her holding me snug on her lap. She would kiss my hair and say, "Just like we are having a reaction to all of them going crazy. So we are going to bake cookies, get lunch at Frank's, and spend our afternoon at The Met."

"I had no idea," I said.

"Sometimes life is on a need to know basis," he said.

Well, wasn't that the damn truth.

We sat looking at each other. Dad's stare had broken, vulnerability crept in around the corners of his eyes. He had been through more than most divorcing my mom, and for the first time it occurred to me that she maybe broke his heart. She had definitely broken mine, but it was a slow break, a chip from a china cup every time she knocked it against the counter or the side of the sink. I hadn't even known it was broken until the night she went for Dad and I defended him.

"If Tully and Finder weren't both tall and strong, there's no way Terrence would have gotten inside his apartment," I went on. "When we got him out of the truck, he couldn't walk by himself."

Not one lie. Attorney's daughter points for me.

"I'm so sorry, Dad. I wasn't thinking about you or how you would feel with me coming home so much later than you thought. I did think about calling again, from Terrence's house but it was three in the morning and I figured you'd be asleep. I'm really so, so sorry. I didn't mean for you to worry."

He sighed. "I forgive you. But Stacy, if you ever do that to me again, I swear I'm going to have heart failure and die and it will be all your fault. There you'll be, calling Bubbe and telling her my cause of death was you being out too late, and think about how you'll feel then."

"The guilt," I said. "One word to her and I'll be dead right beside you."

"Like Romeo and Juliet," he said.

"No, Dad. Not even a little like them. Think more . . . Macbeth."

"I was just thinking they both die in the end."

"The Macbeths die, too. And speaking of guilt that could kill you, don't forget Christmas. Did Santa get something for Steve?" I asked.

Dad sighed and slid the rubber band from around his paper. "Can't we end the charade? I feel like it's wrong to lie to him. It's not like we're Christians."

Unrelated: I was suddenly starving.

"Dad! Santa isn't about religion. Santa's about magic." I got a bowl from the cabinet. After my narrow miss from being grounded for life, my appetite had reawakened. I turned the heat on under the kettle, poured myself some cereal and set up my tea. English breakfast. The kettle whistled. "Get the kid a present," I said. "Do you really want him to go to school with all the other little kids talking about Santa and what they got and he's like Santa doesn't come to my house because I'm Jewish?"

"We're a truthful people, Stacy. Want the honey?"

I nodded and he handed it to me. I spooned some into my tea and drizzled more over my cereal. Dad continued, "Santa is a bald faced lie."

"St. Nicholas was a historical figure," I argued. "And Santa is real if a kid believes in him. Do presents appear as if my magic? Yes? Then voila. Poof. Santa." I chewed and swallowed.

"If we come at it that way," Dad said, "Santa is upstairs snoring in my bed."

"See?" I said. "Actual elf identity is irrelevant."

"Elf? Santa isn't an elf. Santa has elves."

"Santa is the biggest, most important elf, Dad. Duh. How do you think the whole chimney thing works? Plus apartments." He stared at me over the edge of his paper. "Elf or no, Santa is absolutely real," I said, then slurped the last of my milk from the bowl. "We *are* a truthful people."

"Any interest in interning at my firm?"

"Not even an ounce."

"Too bad. You have potential."

"I can see it now," I said. "On the front page of the paper. Headline: The Santa Suit, Wilton Elementary sues family of child who reveals truth about Santa Claus."

I got up to go upstairs. I was tired. I kissed my dad on the head.

"There are more things in heaven and earth, Horatio," I said, "than are dreamt of in your philosophies. Don't be the magic police, Dad."

"Julius Caesar?"

I rolled my eyes. Horatio. Ugh.

"Hamlet. Maybe you need to play more Jeopardy."

"Maybe you need to go to a less fancy high school."

"Oh, the Shakespeare isn't from high school," I said. "It's from Meredith. She read the comics in sixth grade, then quoted them until I threatened to make her eat them. Sayings are catchy, though.

Stuck in my head." I stooped and collected my bag of vampire fighting tools, super glad I had sneaked the blood into the pool house fridge before coming inside. That would have been fun to explain. Dad shook out his front page and settled in for the news.

"Take a nap," he said. "I think you're getting delirious."

I did not take a nap. I turned on my computer and jumped on the internet. I looked up the New York Prisoner Advocacy Group and three mental health non-profits, one of which worked exclusively with teens and gave all services for free. I also found a charity that advocated for foster kids stuck in the court system and finally a scholarship program specifically for suicide attempt survivors. As the former head of the Beth Israel Youth Philanthropy Group I enjoyed making donations. Especially big ones. It made any day Christmas in my book. Last but not least, I did some magical Santa shopping of my own.

December 22, continued.

I sneaked the glass of blood from where I'd hidden it in the way back behind the party drinks in the pool house fridge. I tucked it into a plastic bag then slid the whole thing into a brown paper lunch bag. I stashed it in the side pocket of my backpack, where, in theory, I could keep it upright.

Jill was waiting in the garage to drive me to the lab at VCU.

"You're sure they'll be there?" Jill said. "A university lab on the weekend?"

"Science doesn't wait," I said, yawning. "Think about all the Ph.D. candidates or master's students who have experiments and things to check on." Jill still looked skeptical. "He's a professor," I said. "He has a key."

That seemed to convince her because she hit a little button and the garage door opened behind us.

"I'm not sure this makes sense," Julian said. I practically bounced with anticipation. Judy stood over our science fair project samples scooping just enough out of each petri dish to scrape across a microscope slide. At the big microscope, Julian was looking at Terrence's blood.

"Two highly unusual characteristics," Julian stepped aside so I could look through the lens. The blood cells were oddly formed, uneven and blobular like misshapen light bulbs. And, they were moving. "I don't understand the shape," he said. "It's like they once had a healthy normal shape, but now are deformed. Like they died and then reshaped themselves when they came back to life. But since that's impossible, they must be diseased in some way."

Do not correct him, do *not* correct him, I coached myself.

"And the other thing, look how they move. Healthy cells float around, moving under the tiny electrical impulses that come from electrons interacting, but these," he took off his glasses and rubbed his face. "These are *aggressive*." Julian was not wrong. The little cells looked like they were in a mosh pit- they slammed against each other as if they were trying to break each other apart with impact. Then, one did. I gasped. The cell impacted another cell hard enough to shatter it. Like a plate hitting the floor, the victim cell broke into several pieces of uneven sizes. Each one in turn, started hammering against the sides of other cells but not to split them, to enter them. Once a cell got big enough, it bullied the other cells until one broke and started the cycle over again.

"Amazing," I whispered. "Is this what you saw?" I asked, almost reverent. I turned the lens back to Julian who swore in astonishment.

"Unbelievable," he said. "Who's blood is this again?" Crap. I'd been so involved in watching the vicious little cells do their thing I forgot to a) hide it from him and b) have a handy dandy lie ready to go. I grasped for an answer.

"Just . . . a guy," I said.

Julian looked up from the microscope and narrowed his eyes. He and Judy exchanged a glance. Then Julian went still. "What *kind* of guy?"

He could not possibly know. Unless he did. He took a breath and said in a casual way, "We have some odd animals in Richmond. I thought maybe this was animal blood. Are you sure it's from a . . . guy?"

Wait, did he know about the shifters? Shifter blood might be unusual, but wouldn't be anything like this. Would it? Would it have the dead first characteristics? I suddenly realized that yes, it could. The shifters were all humans who had died and then come back. Well, been *brought* back. And vampires also first dead, could shift into bats.

"If it's from a unusual source, you can tell me," Julian said. "We're scientists. We discover life. We treasure it. Every cell has the breath of perfection in it somewhere, right?"

Judy had come over to look at the cells under the microscope while I'd been staring like a cornered rabbit.

"Julian," Judy said in her super quiet voice. "I think I know what this is."

23.

December 22, continued.

Predator blood, she'd said. The phrase rolled over and over in my mind as I hoofed it from the lab to Chapter & Mercy. I walked like I walked at home, a fast lope that breathed with the streets and lights and traffic. Not like we really had traffic in the Fan District, but there were enough cars that I could pretend. The sky glowed orange as the sunset took hold, gripping the buildings with tendrils of light through the bare tree limbs.

Richmond has a lot of trees, I thought, my body relaxing into the rhythm of walking on concrete. I walked a little faster. Dark was coming.

Predator blood. But no vampire talk. No mention of shifters. A tingle of nerves spread across my back. I scanned over my shoulder, no Bat Suits, and up into the trees. No bats. It was still too light for vampires as the sun hadn't quite dropped below the horizon, but paranoia or self preservation made me look anyway. It felt good to walk fast. It felt bad to be doing it scared. I am alive, I am safe. Nothing bad is happening.

As I turned left onto West Main Street, it occurred to me I was getting to know my way around this weird city. Sleepy on the outside, but alert and hungry on the inside. Who'd a thunk I'd leave New York only to realize it was the more peaceful of the two?

Predator blood. I recognized the way to the VCU library and the turn toward Hollywood Cemetery.

Predator blood. I pushed through the Chapter & Mercy door on the caffeine side, not the bookstore side. I breathed in the roasted bean and sugar scent of the store, letting it ground me from my walking worry. I am alive, I am safe. Nothing bad is happening.

I reminded myself to keep my eyes open for Pia. She would bring me information about who was going hunting and where they were headed or arrived. If we had to hunt another one tonight to keep Matilda from getting blood, what would I do? We'd been in the lab for four hours. I'd had precious little sleep. I searched the couches, comfy chairs and my favorite nook, the two seater table nestled atop some stairs in the back corner near the restrooms. No Nick.

I went up the steps and put my stuff on 'my' chair. I went to the bussing station and grabbed a rag to wipe up the mess some imbecile had left on my table. Rude. Then, I went to the counter.

"Hi Jeanette," I said to the cute, crop-haired barista.

"Oh, hi Stacy, where's Nicky?"

"On his way."

"Cool. What can I getcha? The usual?"

"Please. Double shot tonight."

"Double espresso, double mocha," she said to the new guy at the register. She started making my coffee. "And you do real dairy, right?"

"Only," I said. "The other stuff is when Tully comes with me."

"He's the hottie who dates whatshername? With the big hair?"

"Finder, yes."

"He's adorable. You can tell him I said so. If they ever un-couple or there's trouble in paradise, Scotland can look my way."

"How did you know he was Scottish?" I asked.

"Kilt?" She waggled her eyebrows at me. She set my cup on its saucer, then used tongs to snag me the biggest chocolate chip biscotti. I stuck a dollar in her tip jar.

I stood at the register to pay and the new barista scrunched his eyebrows. Wait. I recognized him. At least I thought I did. Handsome, Latino, 20s. So familiar. Why?

"Do I know you?" His accent melted over me like warm butter on toast. His white T-shirt clung to his chest. I wasn't sure why Jeanette was thinking about Tully when she had *this* to admire. Tully was adorable, but this guy was hot. I almost said it out loud as the realization of who he was hit me. Hot Calculus Guy!

"Did you used to work at Starbucks on Cary Street?" I said.

Recognition dawned on his face. "You're the midnight calculus girl!"

"If I ever write a memoir, I'm totally calling it that. The Life and Times of Midnight Calculus Girl."

"I sign the rights to my creation right over," he said.

"Why did you come work here?"

"Closer to home. Closer to school." We chatted for a few minutes about nothing in particular. Being so close to him made me a little nervous. Finder and Tully were gorgeous, but they were my age and I was used to them now. But Hot Calculus Guy, now Roberto (please remember, please remember, please remember) was not just beautiful, he was a trigger warning for anyone who has ever thought a naughty thought and liked boys even a little. And with that calculus in his pocket, he was elevated to a whole 'nother level in my book of dreamy guys.

"Roberto, are you stealing my girlfriend?" I started and turned around, right into Nick's warm pine smell and leather jacket. He wrapped his arms around me and gave me a hug.

"Hi," he said, smiling down at me. "How was the dance?" With his other hand he did the fist bump thing over the counter with Hot Calculus Guy. Roberto. I reminded myself. Roberto.

"This is *Stacy*?" Roberto said.

"This is *my* Stacy you horny pedophile," Nick said teasing. "She's fifteen and she is *not for you*. Go find a Stacy of your own, closer to your old-man age. Happy Birthday, by the way. Sorry I wasn't at the house for the big par-tay."

"You missed a good one," he said. "Twenty four different kinds of booze, twenty-four candles on the cake, twenty-four Phi Kappa's from Tech came to keep us company. It was a great time."

"I'll do my best to miss the next one, too, I mean, I'll be there for sure. Wouldn't miss it."

"We're having a dinner party at my apartment next weekend. You can bring your Stacy and she and I will retire to my salon and talk math while you and Carla and the rest of the doctors get skunked."

I felt like I was outside my body, this was so foreign. Discomfort tensed my arms and squeezed my chest. Maybe it's just that they were older, or both guys, or both in college, but I felt deeply out of place. A nice, safe coffee back in my alcove was plenty for now, thanks. Maybe I didn't know how to handle this windfall of hot guys. Maybe I was nervous about being obvious I was out of my league.

"You guys feel free to flirt as long as you like," I said channeling Meredith. "I have a coffee begging for my attention." I took my cup and headed for my nook.

Nick came up and sat down across from me once he'd gotten his muffin and coffee. He put a cookie on my saucer. Double chocolate with glaze.

"I hope Roberto and I didn't make you uncomfortable," he said, shluffing off his jackets then tossing them over the back of his chair. "We've been friends since I was a freshman. He was my next door dorm neighbor and now we have a couple classes in common. His fiancé is in my program so we see each other a lot."

I sipped my coffee.

"'Berto's a smart guy. He's a double major. Econ and Physical Therapy. Wants to be rich, hence the Econ and buff, hence the PT.

Rich and gorgeous. Family owns an entire business empire in Guatemala. Rich and gorgeous is how they fly."

"If his family is rich, why is he working in a coffee shop?"

Nick shrugged. "Ask him. He does throw a rockin' dinner party. So. Tell me about the dance last night. And the lab today. To be honest, you look a little spooked."

I closed my eyes and took a deep breath. When I opened them, Nick rested his forearms on the table, hands cupping his steaming mug. His involuntary tattoo had healed over the weeks, gleaming in black off his fair skin. I stared at it a second too long.

"Wanna go with me after coffee?" he asked. "I don't need to look at this every day for the rest of my life." Nick opened and closed his hand, scar still fresh from the knife that had impaled his palm.

"Are you getting it removed tonight?"

"Nah. Gonna meet the guy and get his opinion. Can't give me a price without seeing it. Luke is keeping his, I think. He's a lot more of a masochist than me." Nick rolled his arm over and we both looked at the thin line of German words inked into the flesh on the outside of the bone. *Ich bin eine falschüng.* I am a false thing.

Dear Dad. Stop. Going with college-age boyfriend to tattoo shop. Stop. Home later. Stop. Love, teenaged daughter. Stop.

Good thing telegrams were no longer a thing.

"Masochist is the one where you inflict pain on yourself?"

"Yup. Sadist is inflicting pain on others. The guy that did this."

"Or the evil vampire queen who ordered it."

"Wasn't her idea," Nick said. "Her minion was very chatty while he was torturing us. Half of it was in German so I couldn't understand, but he made sure we knew exactly how much he was enjoying himself. He didn't stake our hands to the table until Luke threw up."

"Luke threw up?"

"Soon as he saw the tattoo stuff. I love game vampires, but I sincerely hate real ones. Like. A lot."

I completely understood. I bit into my cookie. Chocolate burst in my mouth, a glorious explosion of flavor depth over my coffee. "This is amazing," I said. "Thank you."

Nick smiled. "You're welcome. Tell me about the sock hop and the lab. I'm so sorry I couldn't make it."

I told him everything. Quietly. It took my entire coffee to do it.

Nick sat back in his chair, an expression of astonishment.

"Would you feel safer at home? Or with Finder and Tully?"

"Finder has a tournament coming up so she's at her dojo. She's safe enough there, I think. Tully is home with his family, also safe enough. In theory, no one but Terrence knows what happened and he should be motivated to keep it to himself."

Nick shook his head. "It's a dangerous game, Stacy. I think you're gonna need a better strategy."

"Nope. This one is working," I said. "Make a plan. Stick to the plan. We control her blood supply for eight more days. On New Year's Eve, we use that leverage to convince her to replace her own Bat Suits, make Darcy stop tormenting his daughter, and leave us alone for good."

Nick emptied the last dregs from his cup. "What's the long term mate? You're clear about this round. What about the next? How do you make it so she won't ask to play you again?"

"That is part of the 'leave us alone' portion."

"She's immortal, Stacy. She is going to live long after you and you need to solve this problem for good. She might agree to leave you alone, but then she gets a little itch for revenge and goes after your children or grandchildren or three generations from now."

"We'll all be back in New York by then," I said, suddenly uncertain. Nick was right. I hadn't thought about the eternity part of her mindset.

Ugh. I hated vampires so much.

"Living in Richmond now doesn't mean she won't get bored and expand. She could send a group of minions to any city she likes to set up a household for her. I think we need to strategize about this in a much more wholistic way."

We tossed around a few ideas and then, my brain still spinning with the fact that I was depending on an enemy move to successfully construct my win, I put on my coat and let Nick lead me toward the tattoo shop.

Leaving Chapter & Mercy, Nick had thrown my backpack over his shoulder and scooped my hand into his. It was warm and his half-glove enveloped my hand. He shortened his stride to match mine. At our first Don't Walk sign, he took off the glove, bare palm intimate after holding hands with the glove on.

A wooden sign swung in the evening wind. It had the word Tattoo in ornate, gold trimmed, red lettering with carved white, feathery wings coming out of either side of the word.

The phone was ringing as we entered the tattoo shop. A young, olive-skinned, white woman with dreadlocks flowing to her behind answered. "Tattooed Angel, this is Daja." She said it DAH-ja, but the j was soft, like the French j in deja vu. She gave us a little wave hello as she spun away from us on her seat. Behind the counter, a sketchbook sat open in front of her. Her back now to us, I noticed that some of her dreads had objects in them; beads, bells, tiny sea shells.

"Jeff's available Thursday at eleven if you can do that," she said. "Yes, p.m." Noise came from behind a closed door in the back. A loud whoop of victory followed laughter and the cheerful competition of multiple voices.

My immediate vibe was of a West Village apartment packed with art. Every inch of space on the walls was taken up by drawings or paintings of designs, and images of tattooed people;

some framed, some pinned to various bulletin boards and some taped right to the wall.

One pinned picture caught my eye. It was a smallish, black and white photograph of a woman's inked back. Fair hair wrapped around her bare shoulder like a scarf framing a massive full back ink of a fox, or maybe a wolf. It felt like that animal was staring right at me. I found it hard to look away.

There were three small work areas crammed with funky furniture, a lit glass case full of designs and drawings, and a tight row of theatre chairs tucked up against the wall, I guess for people waiting, or deciding, or whatever.

"What can I do for you guys?" Daja said, unwinding the phone cord from her arm and hanging up. "And we don't do kids," she said to me with an apologetic smile. "Eighteen and up only."

"We're here for me. I have one I'd like to get rid of," Nick said.

"Oh, you talked to me," said a guy sitting in the way back at a computer. He spun around on his chair. He was somewhere in his forties with an orange beard and bright blue eyes. His head was stubbly. He stood up. Built like a tank, small and compact, I was amazed to see we were eye-to-eye. He and Nick shook hands. "I'm Jeff. Let's see the boo-boo."

Daja's open sketchbook drawing was beautiful, I couldn't help noticing. A wolf in absolutely photographic detail. I scanned the counter for the photo she was copying, but nope. She was drawing free hand. Or maybe it was tucked in the sketchbook somewhere?

"That's gorgeous," I said.

"Thank you. Getting bored with tribal. I'm ready for a more fine art addition." Her arms, sleeves rolled up, were covered with ink. Vines and flowers peeked out from one arm and tribal symbols, bold and crisp, came out the other.

Jeff examined Nick's arm, then squinted into his face. "Sorry. Can't help you."

"Why not? You seemed confident on the phone that this wouldn't be a big deal."

"Sorry, dude."

"What's the matter?" Daja's dreads clicked against the counter as she leaned over to inspect Nick's arm. The friendliness in her face evaporated. "We don't erase gang tats," she said. "Sorry. You should leave."

"No," Nick said, a sniff of desperation creeping into his voice. "This isn't a- " he reached for her phrase and missed. "It's not a, whatever you said it was."

Jeff and Daja exchanged a look. A how-do-we-get-them-out-of-here look. Nick saw it.

"It's not. Seriously. It's just a mistake."

Jeff crossed his arms. "I can't remove gang tats," he said. "They'll shut me down."

"It's not a gang tat," Nick said. Jeff scrutinized his arm again.

"It's definitely home done," Jeff said. "It's unevenly placed," he pointed to, but didn't touch Nick's arm, "and the color is too thick here and here, see, almost all the way in. The lines aren't consistent around the edges of the lettering and this here," a slight sweat broke out on his head, "is a scar. Gang tat guys do that on purpose so you can't ever fully get rid of it." He looked at Nick with an apologetic wince. "Plus, dude. It's in German. Sorry. You're gonna have to find someone else."

Nick's face blanched.

"We don't do business with white supremacists." Daja was standing now, behind the counter with her hands out of sight. A shiver ran up my spine.

"He's not a white supremacist," I said not quite believing what she said. "I'm proof." I pulled my scarf aside revealing my necklace. "Stacy *Goldman*, Bat Mitzvahed in 1999, nice to meet you," I said, sticking my hand out to shake. Neither of them went for it. "My grandfather was a rabbi." I took Nick's hand. "This tattoo was inflicted on him by a total sadist when he was unconscious. No gangs. I promise."

The back room door opened. I hadn't noticed how quiet it had gotten in the shop until now. "Everything okay out here?" said a familiar southern drawl.

I almost didn't recognize Bradley Joe out of his school uniform. He had on a cartoon character tee with a flannel, jeans and work boots.

"Well, how 'bout that? It's St. Ignatius day at the Tattooed Angel! Junior, come on out and see who's here! What're you doing here, Stay-cee? I didn't know you liked tattoos."

"Lock the door," said Daja to Jeff. "You know these folks, Beej?"

"May I?" said Jeff, gesturing to step past us in the tight quarters. I stepped aside.

"Heck, yeah! Stay-cee goes to St. Ig's with us. She's on my chess team."

"From what I hear she kind of *is* your chess team," Nick said.

Bradley Joe smiled. "That's not far from the truth, let me tell you what. Junior, come say hi. Stay-cee Goldman is here!" Someone behind Bradly Joe shut the door to the back room. I heard voices, but couldn't make out words.

What was going on here?

"You don't have a tattoo, do you?" I asked Bradley Joe.

"Aw nah. Tonight's game night. We do it every solstice. It's a party kinda. Daja hosts it 'cuz she likes to bake and we all come 'cuz we like to eat. Tonight, especially. Longest night of the year. Makes a man hungry. Can I get y'all a snack? We got all kinds of stuff in the back. Zucchini muffins, vegan cinnamon rolls, sourdough peanut butter and jelly sandwiches. Oh, and what do you call them cookies, Daja? The ones with the swirls?"

Nick slid his hand into mine. Bradley Joe saw it. A look of disappointment crossed his face.

"Well, shoot," said Bradley Joe. "I was kinda hopin' you made that story up about having a boyfriend. Guess not?"

Nick introduced himself and shook Bradley Joe's hand.

"I hear you're an amazing dancer. Sorry I wasn't there to see it."

"Don't take this the wrong way, but I'm glad you weren't! She might not a danced with me if you'd been there."

"As awkward and fun as this is," I said, trying to act more flip than I felt, "we really need to figure out what's going to happen with Nick's tattoo."

Jeff clicked the deadbolt and turned around.

"What's going on? Why are you locking us in here?"

"Aw, he's not locking y'all in," said Bradley Joe. "He's locking eavesdroppers out."

Jeff eyed Bradley Joe and cleared his throat.

"Oh, heh. I guess that means I should buzz off, too. Okay. I'm gonna go kick these kids' butts at Uno. See you when school starts again, Stay-cee. Happy Holidays there, Nick. Sure nice to meet you." Bradley Joe vanished into the back room.

Both Jeff and Daja wore expressions I recognized from my mirror. Scared ones. More specifically, scared but trying not to look scared. The question was, why? I didn't feel especially threatened.

"There are a lot of unusual people in Richmond," Jeff said. "This business is our livelihood and we can't afford to lose it because someone gets upset we took off a tattoo they used to mark someone." Jeff gestured for Nick's arm. "Would you mind coming where I can put the light on you?" Jeff took a magnifying glass and looked very closely under much brighter light. Seconds ticked by. And more seconds. Finally a minute.

He looked up at Daja who had come to lean on the back of the couch.

"There's no signature," he said. "That's good."

"Very good," she agreed. "Most gang artists sign their work," she said. "Marking their property. It's revolting."

"Do they . . . retaliate when you refuse to work on them?" I asked.

"Some get cranky," said Daja. "But they respect Jeff's decision." They exchanged another look. "At least they do now."

"We had to explain it once in a not so nice way," Jeff said, "but they respect us as long as we refuse work on all of them. No doing, no undoing. Non-negotiable. Policy across the board and we stay out of the crosshairs. I'm sure now you understand why I can't touch you unless you can convince me absolutely that this is not a gang mark of any kind."

Nick opened and closed his hand, eyes lingering on the inch long knife scar in his palm from where he'd been skewered. He pulled his arm back out of the light.

"I know it's not a gang mark," Nick said, "but I don't know how to explain it to you. What happened to me . . ." his eyes met mine, pools of green that suddenly weren't so grown up. "Doesn't really make sense. Thanks for looking at it. You think it can be removed, though, right?"

Jeff nodded. "Give it six months to fully heal. It's healed on the surface, but you want all the layers of skin healed and then you want to give it some time to fade in the sun before I take a laser to it. The scar's permanent unless you do plastic surgery."

Nick nodded. He slid his jacket back on.

Jeff paused by the counter as we headed back up front. He handed Nick a business card.

"I know you think whatever it is, whoever did that to you, I won't understand, but if you ever need someone to talk to, Richmond's shown me some pretty wild stuff. I'd never pry, but if you want, you can come to me."

"Or me," said Daja who had come up so quietly it was like she just appeared in her spot behind the counter. "I hang out at a lot of open mics, so you maybe can find me there if I'm not here. I don't have a phone except the one here. I hate 'em."

Nick's eyes begged the questions I was asking, too. Did they *know*? How could we find out without giving away what we knew?

Jeff unlocked the door.

Nick took hold of my hand as we exited the shop and took our first block in silence. Who in the world had we just met? My eyes were everywhere, alert for bats, Bat Suits, Darcy Jacksons's car and one specific pigeon. I kept my other hand in my messenger bag, clutching my holy water spray bottle like other girls carry mace. I must've looked over my shoulder twenty times.

"Do you think the Tattooed Angel people know about Matilda?" Nick asked.

"He was definitely not spilling anything without you spilling first."

We arrived at the Hulk, parked in front of a dilapidated row house. Nick opened the door for me and I got in.

"Are you okay?" he asked once he got in the driver's side and shut the door.

"What's the joke? Just because you're paranoid doesn't mean someone isn't following you?"

Nick collected me into a hug, pulling me across the seat.

"You're safe with me, Stacy. Do you know that?"

I sighed, breathing in the pine and leather smell of him. I wanted what he said to be true. We sat together, me tucked under Nick's arm, waiting as the car blew first cold, then warmer and finally hot air on us from the massive dashboard vents. I closed my eyes. Nick's scent, mixed with the comforting antique car smells, transported me home, like I was leaning on a bench in Central Park.

When I opened my eyes, Nick was looking down at me. Our faces were close enough that with just a very small lean in on either of our parts we would be touching noses. Or something else. His eyes travelled from my eyes to my lips and back again. Should I do it? Should I lean in? Was he waiting for me? Waiting for some signal that I wanted him to kiss me? The answer was yes. Yes please, kiss me. I was fifteen, a perfectly reasonable age for a first kiss. Old maybe, even. Why was he hesitating? Meredith hadn't prepared me for this. She had told me to file away every detail of the first kiss so I could tell her, but she hadn't told me what I was supposed to do. Who was supposed to move first? Me or him? If he was really old, like eighteen, would he be scared to kiss me? Was I supposed to make a permission speech or something? First kiss, here we come. I looked at Nick. I looked at the lovely curve of his lower lip. I imagined how his mouth would feel on mine. I waited. I hoped. I froze.

Nick's forehead rumpled as he looked at me. He pressed his lips together and put the car in gear. He maneuvered it out from the parking space.

"I'm uncomfortable leaving you like this," he said, after some minutes went by.

Like what? I thought to myself. Dying for you to kiss me?

"I should be here this week, even just as back up." Drat. Vampire talk. "You wouldn't be in this situation if it wasn't for me."

Not a lie.

"I wish you could stay, too," I said. Also not a lie. Kissing, please.

"I promised I'd be home for Christmas," he said. "I'm leaving tomorrow morning so I can be there for Christmas Eve. I should take you with me." He smiled that smile as he turned the corner. "That would keep you safe."

"Yeah," I said. "If only it was that simple."

"If I can stay with Ashlyn again, it'll work to come back early."

"Ashlyn?"

"My roommate's cousin. She lives in the house where I was parked. The dorm closed at nine Friday night and she let me sleep on her couch so I could be here for the weekend. So I could see you."

"But if you stayed the weekend for me, why didn't you come to the dance?"

Moment of silence.

Calculating silence.

Nick was deciding what to tell me. I wasn't sure I liked that.

24.

December 22, continued.

"I belong to a fraternity," he said. "Two, actually. One's here at VCU. A future doctor social thing. The other one is more . . . interest driven."

"So, gaming?"

"No. Not gaming. But we all have a lot in common and we had an important thing last night and I needed to be there. It was out of town."

Was I supposed to say something other than, oh okay? So I said nothing.

"You're not upset are you? I know I don't fit the typical frat boy profile."

Confusion bubbled in my mind. After everything we'd been through, why was I on a need to know basis about a fraternity event?

"So Ashlyn's loaning you her couch?"

"She is."

Ha. I remembered *her* name. Don't be jealous, Stacy, I told myself. Nick is a grown person. A trustworthy grown person. Nothing's going on you need to know about that he hasn't told you.

"I want you to kiss me," I blurted.

The words hung in the air between us.

"What?" Streetlight slid in the car window, brightening Nick's face for just a flash. "I mean, oh. You do. You do?"

"Yes," I said. "I do."

We turned into Wilton, trees thickening on either side of the road.

"I'm not sure that's a good idea," he said. "I mean it's a great idea, an amazing idea, one I'm all for in many ways. But. Um," Nick turned onto my street. There weren't any other cars, so he slowed.

"There's a playground three blocks over," I said. I gave directions as we drove past my house, down the hill and turned right. Two more blocks and there, on the other side of the road from the river, sat swings and a wooden play ship 'docked' on rubber chips. Nick pulled into the gravel parking lot. It was teensy, only about three cars could fit. It was usually all strollers and bikes. The playground itself was gated so that little kids couldn't run across the street and slip on the muddy banks or drown themselves in the shallows.

My watch read 8:14. Still super early. Still super dark. I opened my door and got out. I scanned for bats. Clear. I opened the playground gate and crossed to the swings.

"Is there a reason why you haven't tried to kiss me, yet?" I said as Nick got on the swing beside me and pushed off. "I'm pretty surprised I'm even asking because it's entirely possible I don't want to know. Like maybe you're gay, or maybe you've realized that you only like me as a friend, or- "

"Or maybe I'm afraid that as soon as I start kissing you, I'll want more. And then you won't want to make me upset and you'll do things that you aren't ready for to make me happy and then . . . it's a slippery slope, you know?"

I did not know.

"It's different if you're both virgins," he said. "When it's like that, you can take it slow together, or fumble along, or try to figure it out as you go. But when one person isn't a virgin, it's, well. It's different."

"If you've never tried chocolate, you don't know what you're missing, so you don't crave chocolate," I said. "But once you've tried chocolate, you want more. And sometimes a bit or a taste is worse than not having it at all?"

"Exactly."

"I totally disagree. Even a taste of Godiva is better than never having tried it. The complexity in flavor you then have as your standard of excellence, the standard by which you judge all other chocolate, doesn't make you enjoy the other chocolate less, it makes you appreciate the more sophisticated chocolate even more."

"Do you know what your IQ is?"

"Are you asking because I can make analogies of chocolate to kissing? I don't think that's very original."

"I'm asking because you catch on to everything so fast. You identify the answer formula before the equation is fully copied out."

"I really don't."

"You really do. It's kind of a problem for me."

"What? Why?"

"It's sexy as hell."

Well. That shut me up.

Boys called Meredith sexy. I heard comments at school and knew that a lot of people called Finder sexy, had evaluated her sexiness myself even. She was a *ten*. I had even heard my dad tell Jill *she* was sexy which was kind of awesome and kind of gross all the same time. Glad they're in love and all, but, TMI.

Never had anyone ever referred to me using that word. Smart, yes. Determined, yes. Responsible, always. Independent, sure, and every now and then, if it was someone in my family, pretty. But the S word? No. Nope. Never once. No one had ever told me I, or anything about me at all, was sexy. And it left me speechless.

"Did I . . . say something wrong?" Nick asked. I scanned the treetops for bats again. None. I had absolutely no words to explain how I felt or what was happening inside of me at that moment. There was a part of me that wanted to be offended. I shouldn't have to be sexy to be loved or respected. Another part of me was just astonished that he had even said it. Another part of me felt like I had just been crowned Princess of the Whole Entire World.

Nick giggled. "Have I rendered you speechless?"

I quit pumping my legs and my swing started to slow. When my feet finally scraped the dirt, I came to a stop. I sat, the half moon spilling light through the trees and onto my boots. The light was beautiful on his pale skin, bringing out the glistening black shine of his hair.

"How old are you?" I said.

He said nothing for a long time. I had shocked him into silence as well.

"Can I plead the fifth?" he said after an even longer while.

"You're going to have to tell me sometime."

"So you think," he said. "Maybe we'll fall in love and live together and our ages will be irrelevant."

"If we live together I'll have to know your birthday," I said. "For tax purposes, and ID. And . . . stuff."

"Good point," he said. "Even the fact that your brain skipped right to estate planning or taxes or whatever is sexy to me," he said.

"You have a messed up idea of what's sexy," I said. "Taxes?"

"I didn't say taxes were sexy. Taxes are evil. Evil like Matilda's shoes," he said. And a different smile flashed across his face, a wicked smile that reminded me of his role-playing character, Nicolai. "But I want you to understand where I'm coming from. Let's skip ahead to the day when we're at your house, making out on your couch when no one is home and we miss all possible exterior cues, like the car door shutting or the key in the lock and your dad walks in on us. It's hopefully never going to happen, because that would be . . . embarrassing. But say that it does. Then what?"

"I don't understand what this *horrendous* suggestion has to do with anything."

"Go with me here. We get walked in on and your dad freaks out. Which he would, right?"

"Right."

"And then you're grounded or he has grabbed his secret shotgun and run me off forbidding us to see each other."

I giggled. My father. A shotgun.

"My father is a lawyer born and bred in Queens," I said. "He doesn't have a shotgun."

"South could change that. Either way, my point is, what if the price for kissing you was not being able to see you at all?"

"So you're making up stories about something that may never happen to avoid kissing me?" I said. "You are totally lying about thinking I'm- " I said, unable to push the 's word' out of my own mouth. "You can't be wanting to kiss me and putting up this much of a fight. Meredith had a boyfriend like that. Planning for seminary now."

Nick's jaw dropped. "You're kidding?"

"Cross my heart and hope to die. Wants to make wine and cheese upstate. Says he's asexual. It's a thing."

"It is? Holy moly."

"Yes," I replied. Exactly.

"Why do you think I'm always holding your hand?"

"Because you like me?"

"Because you're a magnet. If I'm touching you, I'm okay. We're connected and I feel secure. But when we're not connected, when I'm not touching you, it's impossible to concentrate on anything other than wanting to be touching you. Then I start thinking about touching you, and my mind fast forwards to doing more than touching you, which, as you may imagine, is not helpful. Once I have your hand in mine, it's easier somehow. It's like my body settles down."

"You just described Steve's baby relationship with his pacifier."

This was not what romance novels were made of.

"It's not unlike that," he said. "Not very manly." He reached out and took my hand. We pushed back together on our swings. "The worst part is that I have found you deeply distracting since the moment you chased me out of the alley as Nicolai. I went to every single Hidden City event after that looking for you. I even made up a human hunter character so I could scope out the other side of the game hoping I'd find you. When Ethan called and told me you'd been looking for me at Third Rock, I couldn't wait until it was dark out so I could reply to your message."

"Really?"

"Would I make this up? The night you cried on my shoulder at Hollywood, it was everything I could do to not kiss those tears off your face. I wanted to scoop you up, take you back to my room, lock the door and make love to you until you felt like you were safe and whole and loved forever. And not just Nicolai wanted you. I did. Me. Nick O'Malley, mathlete, ping pong champion and future MD. That night with you changed my life. And to be clear, I thought you were in college, so I wasn't, like, being a pedophile."

"Like you are now," I said. I giggled.

"Why aren't we kissing, she asks. I want to be very clear that I am employing all of my personal physical restraint around you, Stacy Goldman, every time I see you. But the idea of being parted from you is such that I have agreed to control myself in that way until such a time as it is reasonable."

Until such a time as it is reasonable? Um. When would that be exactly?

"So, no kissing," I said.

"Long term investment," he said.

"What if I volunteer? What if I insist I want kissing?"

"It doesn't change what's real Stacy. It doesn't change me being able to look into your parents' faces and be completely honest when I tell them nothing has happened."

"What if I get to define 'nothing'? What if kissing is still under the definition?" One of Meredith's warnings came unbidden to my mind. "You aren't a no-sex-before-marriage person, are you?" I blurted.

"I thought I'd made it clear that one of us *is* a virgin and one of us is *not*."

"How do you know I am? Is it just my age?"

"Can we change the subject, please? I have a long drive tomorrow and I need to be thinking about something besides your virginity. Or not."

I smiled. A gorgeous boy was thinking about my virginity. A zap of energy flowed through me, a familiar feeling that was somehow brand new. Where had I felt this before? Not with my family or my friends or my school. I closed my eyes and tried to place it, a cross between giddy excitement and utter conviction and confidence. Where had I felt it? Why did I know it so well?

Chess. This feeling, whatever it was, had fueled my relationship with chess. The first time I played and lost, this feeling ran through me. It shook me, showed me that more existed than what was in front of me. I could do more than I had. I could be more than I presently was. I could win.

Chess woke me up to myself, broke open something in me waiting to be discovered, waiting to be . . . unleashed. It was this feeling I wanted when I played, this unnamed sensation rattling me to the depths of my core. And right now, that feeling electrified every part of me. The Nick board was mine. The choice to play or not play. The ability to own the outcome of this situation, whatever situation I chose for it to be, was completely in my hands. I could win. Suddenly clear, I recognized the feeling and its name crawled into my mind.

Power.

I had power.

Tears burned behind my eyes. Swinging in and out of the moonlight shine, one rolled down my face. How did this boy crack me open so easily? Why was I even crying?

Because you need it, said Michael. *Because you hold everything in.*

"I don't," I said softly.

"Don't what?" said Nick.

You do. Because you are brave. You feel release right now because you are safe.

I was safe. I looked at Nick across our hands, still linked between the swings. He glanced from our hands to my face and back again. Like an opponent looking at his queen, I realized he was looking at something of value to him. And that something was me.

And then, like a bolt of lightning striking the rod, I understood. This power I was feeling wasn't new and it wasn't from chess. Not originally. Chess was a substitute for the original source. My mother deciding I wasn't worth her time stole the only power I had as a little kid. The power I should have spent my childhood developing and growing. The power to be loved beyond reason. I thought about Steve clinging to Jill's clothes and leaping into my dad's arms when he had barely put down his briefcase. Steve had undiluted power, but not because he took it, because they gave it to him and he cultivated it.

Having no value in the eyes of someone for whom I should have been priceless was . . . I struggled for a definition.

"It has two solutions," I said out loud. "One is rational and one is irrational."

"Not sure I follow."

"My response," I said. "Rational, but also wrong. Steve's is irrational, but completely correct."

"Are you talking about quadratic equations?" Nick asked.

I'd been powerless. Powerless to stop her, powerless to heal her mental illness or my father's broken heart. So I reached for the rational. I reached for control. I walked my neighbor's dog. I did well in school, I proved my worthiness by controlling myself and becoming responsible, reliable, dutiful even. Yet not powerful. Power, this feeling I had right now, felt different. It felt like choice, it felt like life. It felt like wind in my hair with a storm blowing in. Power.

No wonder Matilda didn't want to lose it. It was what kept her going. I saw that now. Why would you give up absolute confidence that things will be as you wish?

And someone was challenging her. That someone was me.

I sniffed and pulled a little bit of my sleeve out from under my jacket. I mopped my face.

"Matilda is so going to kill me," I said. The top of my head felt buzzy and hot. Crown chakra, open for business. "And I am so . . . happy right now," I said, snuffling. "I just had an epiphany."

"About quadratic equations?" he said. I shook my head. "Tell me." Nick slowed our swing to a slight rock. My feet touched down in the rubber playground 'dirt'.

"Don't know if I can. Articulate it."

Nick let go of my hand so I could unwrap it from behind the swing chain anchored in the crook of my elbow.

"Sit by the river?" he said.

We crossed the empty road and found a large, flat-ish rock with room for both of us if we sat close. We sat close, thighs pressed together. My tears had stopped, but I wiped my face one more time. I had no idea how to put into words what I was feeling, the vast breath it felt like I could, at long last, take.

"I'm not a victim."

"Of course you're not," Nick brought my hand to his lips. His very warm, very distracting lips. He let them linger a long time, breathing me in. His breath warmed the back of my hand. The top of my head almost stung it was so tingly.

"My mom has some problems," I said, "and they made her into kind of a bully. She said whatever she had to make sure she was big and I was small, if that makes any sense." I looked at our intertwined fingers resting in my lap. Silver laced in the moonlight. Nick's longer than mine, graceful for a man's hands. "And then there was this kid who plays chess and tried to get me to throw my game at Nationals which was crazy in itself but then he shoved me in the elevator and sprained my grandmother's wrist. I'd say it was normal bully stuff, but it turns out he lives here and is on my chess team now and I won't lie, every time I'm in his presence I am filled with this wackadoodle desire to punch him in the face. It's like I'm not even me for a minute, you know?"

Nick nodded.

"Have you ever punched anybody? In the face?" I asked.

"Only once and it was by accident. I'm not much of a fighter," Nick said. "I'm more the squishy wizard of the party."

"What?"

"Never mind," he said. "Gamer talk. I'll explain if you ever want to play."

"I probably won't," I said. "But you could tell my best friend Meredith if she ever comes to visit. She's into all that stuff. Anyway, I put Sociopathic Joseph Thornton in his place but, you know, I shouldn't have to. So circling back to Nationals, then 9/11 happened, talk about feeling helpless, and there's the whole culture of being Jewish. I mean, do you have any idea how many other peoples of the earth have tried to extinguish us? Like we all know World War II, but there were like a gazillion different attempts to squash Jews out of existence before that and I'm like seriously, what did we do? Anyway, now there's Matilda and her Bat Suits and Darcy Jackson trying to steal Finder.

"Any one single piece of that is enough to bind a person to victimhood for life, you know? So you can be a victim or, you can be a survivor. The thing about survivors or survivor-ness or whatever, is that in order to survive, you have to have been a victim. I hate that. I hate it, Nick, so much." The tears burned my eyes again, but I didn't try to stop them. "Sitting on the swings, I realized that I don't have to participate in any of that ever again. I can decide different. I can't explain how it happened but you were talking and we were holding hands and then it hit me. That I'm not a victim. Or I can choose not to be one.

"I'm fifteen, I know, but I'm not a child, Nick. I'm a person. A person who has lived through things, and who is going to live through a lot more."

Silver moonlight lit the green in Nick's eyes as he looked at me. A streak of fury thrilled up my spine.

"I killed for you," I said. I reached over and grabbed the lapel of his jacket. "I yanked a *knife* out of your hand when it was pinned to a table. I risked my own life and the lives of my friends to *save* you. And you have the nerve to tell me I'm not old enough to kiss?" I leaned in and pressed my mouth to his.

25.

December 22, continued.

The entire universe ground to a screeching halt.

A tiny, two person supernova.

It was several minutes before we came apart. Nick tipped his chin down and pressed his forehead against mine. Breath ragged, we clung to each other, sounds of the water running beside us. I leaned in for more.

He reached one finger up to touch my lip. A bolt of electricity ran through me.

"You've never done that before?" he said, voice rough.

"Never." My lips felt swollen as my breath puffed out in ribbons. I have never wanted to melt my entire body into someone else, but I wanted to now.

"Seriously, never?"

"Nope." I pulled back and met his eyes. "But can I tell you something?"

"Always."

"It's better than chess."

He smiled. I slid my hands up behind his neck. His hair was so soft, fine and feathery. I drew his head toward mine and he didn't stop me. This time I felt a little more like I knew what I was doing. I opened my mouth on his soft lips and relished the feeling of him.

In the first kiss there was a weird moment where I thought, dude, I'm touching someone else's tongue, but that evaporated into a thirst for him as we forged a rhythm for our kissing. I planned to scold Meredith for some serious oversights in her descriptive education. She had not, for example, explained that you have to choose between mouth breathing and nose breathing, with the latter being way better. She also had not told me about swallowing. Kissing makes saliva build up in your mouth and yes, you're going to share some of that with your partner, but the rest has to go somewhere. (Swallow, please.) Once she told me about kissing some boy who basically spent the whole time spitting into her mouth (totally gross) and I swore that whenever I did start kissing, that that would never be a story someone could tell about me. Nick did not seem disappointed in my newness in any way.

Now, I gave all my attention to devouring him, one kiss at a time. He pulled back, just enough to touch the corner of my mouth with his tongue. He traced a thin line down to my throat. He buried his face in my hair. Then his breath was on the pulse right under my jaw. He kissed and kissed a line down to my collar and breathed in a deep draught of me.

"Stacy," he said almost so quietly I couldn't hear him over my own breathing and my heart pounding in my ears.

He raised his head and the look in his eyes was not the playful boy Nick I was used to. It was man Nick. A man who had tasted what he wanted and had hunger for more in his eyes. I had no intention of denying him.

He took my head in his hands. The kiss was soft, elegant almost as he nudged my mouth open and caressed it one lip at a time. He drank me in and said "Forgive me." He pulled gently away, brushing my hair back from my face with his hand.

"I have to stop before . . . Do you understand?" I did. I nodded. "You are the most desirable woman I have ever known," he said and tears glittered in his eyes. "How did this happen to me?" His voice was filled with awe. "How did I get so lucky to have found you and for you . . . to like me?"

His eyes were the most beautiful things I had ever seen. Green with moonlight glow. My heart felt wide, uncontainable, yet full.

Once again, I was speechless. I turned around to sit in front of him, leaning back against his chest. He wrapped his arms around me and we sat for a long time in the quiet aftermath.

The river in front of us burbled. Moonlight sparkled across its rippling surface, lapping against our rock with such ease. We sat, held together, saying nothing for many, many minutes.

Go me, I thought. Appreciating some nature.

When we finally stood up to get back in the car, it was almost 9:30. Two yellow-green eyes glowed out of the shadows. I started, and Nick grabbed me to shove me behind him. I put my hand on his arm. I shifted my weight and crouched, focusing. The fox got up from where it was sitting, probably having been watching us.

"Don't go near it," Nick said. "It might be rabid. They usually won't come close to people."

"It's not rabid," I said. "Just be still."

The fox approached and that's when I saw it had something in its mouth. A stick. It tossed its head and the stick flew toward me. I reached out to catch it and missed. It landed neatly in Nick's hand.

"Hands of a juggler," he said with that smile.

"You don't juggle," I said.

"Four summers at circus camp," he whispered. "I juggle."

Of course you do, I thought. Of course. But I can talk to animals.

The fox pawed the ground. It looked like she was pointing to me. Nick handed me the stick.

The part I touched was wet from having been in the fox's mouth. A piece of paper was wrapped around the dry end. I unwrapped it. The fox sat, watching me.

T back out to hunt. ~W

"Can you take a note back to Wendell for me?" I asked the fox. She licked her chops. I took that for a yes.

I dug in my pocket for a pen and found a nub of pencil. I ripped Wendell's half of the note off and stuck it in my pocket. I wrote:

Thank you. Will go see.

Heading home after.

Please t.m. what happens.

U R the best!

I wrapped the note back around the stick and squashed it tight so it wouldn't come off. The fox reached over and took it in her delicate jaw. Then off she ran into the woods, headed for Maymont.

We didn't do any more kissing, even as we sat in the car across from Bar 8:30 holding hands and watching. I had to explain about the shifter kids three times. Nick had seen the Bat Suits change, so he wasn't as hard to convince as he could have been.

At around 10:30, Terrence came out escorting a clean-cut man in a leather jacket. They got in Terrence's car and drove to an historic, brick apartment building where the man got out. He stood there for a minute after Terrence drove off, staring into space. Then as if he was waking up, he shook his body like a wet dog, dug for his keys, and went inside.

We found Terrence's little red car parked in the Maymont lot.

"Do you want to see if we can see what the reaction is?" Nick asked.

"Definitely not," I said. "Wendell will tell me what I need to know." Nick slowed the Hulk as we passed the main gate. "Don't stop," I said. "Keep driving." If Matilda got wind that I was the culprit behind her lack of dinner, things would go badly.

Nick turned into Wilton for the second time that night.

Not even 11:00 yet, and I was home. Nick came around and opened the heavy car door for me. Standing in the driveway of this ridiculous huge house, under a bright more than half-full moon, I wanted to get right back in the car. I wanted to go right back to that rock by the river and see what would have happened next had we kept going.

"I probably shouldn't hug you or anything since your parents haven't met me yet," Nick said. "Who knows who might be peeking out the windows."

Oh dear lord, that rock star smile.

"You can totally hug me," I said. He opened his arms and I stepped in, wrapping my arms around his waist. I laid my cheek on his chest and breathed him in. Leather, trees. "Have a safe drive in the morning." He gave me an extra squeeze and we separated.

He took my hand in his and brought it to his lips. "Merry Christmas," he said. I sighed and my entire body vibrated with a sensation I now could name. Desire.

"Oh wait!" He let go of my hand and trotted over to his trunk. He shuffled some things around, unearthing a wrapped gift the size of a shoe box. "I almost forgot!"

I gasped. Christmas presents! In the thunder of events, I'd forgotten completely except for Steve and Santa.

"Oh! No! Don't give me anything." I said. "I don't have a present for you!"

Nick came close, pressing the box into my hands. Leaning down he said "I already got my present," into my ear. Being this close and not kissing him almost hurt. He stepped back and rubbed his hands together. "That is for Christmas morning, I don't know how your family does things, Christmas present-y or not, but I wanted you to have one."

I almost made an excuse about why I couldn't take it, but I felt power tingle inside me. Power to make him smile, to offer him something he could get nowhere else. My delight. I smiled at him. Here is what I intended to say: You are the most adorable human I have ever encountered. Thank you. What came out of my mouth was:

"Please come back early."

He pressed his lips to the center of my forehead and lingered there. And pop, chakras open, the top of my head tingling as strong as it ever had.

I went a little off balance in surprise and Nick caught me.

"Oops," he said. "Sorry about that. A little chakra opening right in my face there. You okay?"

"I didn't know you knew about chakras," I said. "I thought that was all Tully stuff."

"Tully is into the occult?" Nick said, a look on his face I hadn't seen before. Maybe it was the shadows from the moon behind the clouds.

"I don't know if you'd call it occult," I said, "but he does yoga and taught me about chakras and stuff. Finder's mom taught him, I think."

"Interesting."

I glanced at the house. I would definitely get the third degree, literally, if I stood out here with him much longer.

"Thank you," I said, indicating the box. "I'll open it on Christmas." Satisfied, my Adorable Goth Boy gave my hand a final squeeze then went to close his trunk. "Drive safe," I said as he moved to the driver's door.

"I'll be back before you know it." The look of concern and longing on his face shifted to his rock star smile, this time with a wicked gleam in his eyes. "I've definitely been inspired to shorten my trip."

26.

Tuesday, December 25, 2001.

The phone rang on Christmas morning. I leapt to answer it.

"Merry Christmas, beautiful," Nick said. I blushed.

"Merry Christmas. How's Florida?"

"Humid. And all my aunts are here so it's also very loud. Sorry to call so early, but I wanted to make sure I talked to you before the rest of the day carries me off into gossip and food and yelling at the TV screen."

"Why do you yell at the TV?"

"My aunts play drinking games with their favorite TV shows. They get completed sauced by dinner, then fall asleep on the furniture before dessert."

"That sounds, um."

"Like not a lot of fun? It's funny for the first few shows and then I go downstairs to play Monopoly with all the little cousins. We used to play Operation but no one could beat me and you know me. I just can't throw a game."

"Totally grok," I said, smiling. "Not even for a draw."

There was a pause and quiet filled the line.

"I miss you," Nick's voice was soft and warm like a hug. "Wish I could see you today. Be with you. I'd rather be with you than here. Does that make me a bad person?"

"Does not," I said. "Was that even a serious question?"

"Kinda. I feel bad, like I should want to be here and be with my family. The cousins are really cute."

"See? You're fine. Your heart is in the right place."

"True that. Your pocket."

I blushed again. Pause. Silence.

"When are you coming back?"

"The plan's Saturday, but I want to be in Richmond for New Year's."

"Mistletoe?" I asked.

"Matilda. How's everything going?"

I answered with silence.

"Oh, duh, your family's there."

"Right."

"Can I call you back later?" Nick asked. "I just wanted you to know that you were the first thing I thought about when I woke up this morning. I miss you."

"I miss you, too," I said, tucking my head so no one who wandered in would hear me. "I wish you were here."

"Mmm." I could almost hear him closing his eyes and relishing what I said. "Oh! Did you open your present?"

"No! Should I do it now?" I looked out the doorway at Jill and Dad sprawled over the couches. Steve sang to himself, firing dart after dart at the fridge.

"It's your present. Open it when you want."

I carried the phone upstairs to my room. Nick's box sat on my night table.

I tore off the paper with as much gusto as I could so he could hear it over the phone.

"Gosh, thanks!" I said. "I love crinkle confetti! What a thoughtful gift."

"Ha ha," he said. "Keep digging."

Under the thick layer of rainbow confetti lay a dark purple book with an odd looking ladder on the front, its rungs linked by circles containing Hebrew letters.

"What's this?"

"Kaballah," Nick said, voice taking on an almost reverent tone. "I thought it might pique your interest. Have you heard of it?"

"No."

"It's Jewish mysticism. And it's kind of math-y."

"Well, I do like math-y."

"Keep digging."

Underneath the purple book lay a second book, thick and shiny with chess pieces on the front.

"The Amateur's Mind! Thank you! I've been meaning to pick this up!"

"The guy at Chapter & Mercy said it's great. I hope he's right. There's a gift receipt inside the cover in case you already have it."

"I don't. Thank you. This is so sweet, Nick. I'm sorry I didn't have anything for you. I've been so obsessed- "

"No excuses necessary. I am fine with what I got."

And then silence.

"When can you give me the Maymont update?" he said.

"Two hours? I'll charge my phone and make sure I'm outside."

"What else are you guys up to today?"

I sighed. "Going to a movie this afternoon. Take out for dinner. Until then, reading my fancy new books. And I'm gonna work out. This is so weird, but I think I'm getting my homework done faster on days where I'm on the treadmill. It's like it clears my head. Oh, and I'll do some chess. Steve is enthralled with his new Santa loot."

Nick laughed, not a giggle, but not a guffaw.

"What's so funny?"

"The casualness with which you deliver the stereotype tickles me, that's all."

"What stereotype?"

"Movies and Chinese food on Christmas."

"I didn't say Chinese food. I said take out."

"And what will you be taking out?"

I smiled. "Chinese food," I said, "or maybe Thai." I could almost hear his smile. "You gotta admit, a blockbuster action movie plus Mu Shu pancakes does equal perfection."

"I love your idea of perfect," Nick said. "I'll call you in two hours."

"I'll be freezing in the yard."

Steve crouched next to a pile of seeds and apple slices when I arrived outside with my phone in hand.

"What're you doing?" I asked. "You're not supposed to be outside by yourself."

"Mommy said I could. I have to stay where I can see the windows." I squatted down to look at what he was looking at. It felt so good to squat without my tailbone hurting.

"Evia hasn't touched her seeds in two days," he said. The wilted apple slices were browning around the edges. "I have a Christmas present for her but she isn't here."

He cupped a pinecone spread with peanut butter and covered in dried cranberries, raisins, cashews, walnuts and pistachios.

"Is that your mom's gourmet trail mix?"

He nodded. "Don't tell."

"I won't. She'd kill me for not stopping you."

"Evia eats her seeds and apples everyday," he said. "She taps on my window to say thank you. I'm worried."

"It's Christmas," I said. "Maybe she found someone to spend the holiday with and is in her human form. Maybe she and Wendell and Pia and all the shifter kids hang out together and celebrate."

"None of them have houses," he said like I was the dumbest person on earth. "They live in the woods."

"How do you know? Wendell lives at Maymont."

"In the *barn* at Maymont, and he has a small nest in the house behind some bricks in the pantry. No place he could have human company."

"I'm just trying to help you figure it out," I said. "If you don't want my help, it's fine."

Just then my phone rang. I walked away from Steve toward the bench behind the pool house overlooking the river.

"Are we alone now?" came Nick's rockstar voice on the phone. "Because I have to tell you that all I thought about the whole drive to Florida was sitting with you on that rock."

I smiled. "I've thought about little else. Except, you know." I caught Nick up on all the vampire goings on as Steve circled the yard and walked the edge of the woods. He went a lot farther than he was allowed to go outside by himself. Here on the bench I could see through the leafless trees far into the woods and all the way down the hill to the walking path and the river.

I watched as Steve wandered into the woods. He turned around and waved to me and I gave him the thumbs up. He walked away looking every bit like a lumberjack, but with a plastic bow and arrows and a pom pom on top of his hat.

"Between Pia and Wendell, I'm getting information every day. Wendell watches the house and tells Pia when Terrence, the bald headed Bat Suit, leaves the mansion to hunt. So far, he has gone to the same place where he usually hunts, because that's where Matilda expects him to go, snags some dude into the back room like usual, buys him a drink and then leaves with him so that whoever is spying for her there can see him do it. Just like what we saw. After he loses the guy on his way back to Maymont, he makes up a story to tell her about why he's home empty handed. The problem is that he's having to get more and more creative every time he hunts and fails. Wendell said she is sending out a different Bat Suit tonight. I'm pushing for us to eat early enough that I can be home in time to go out with Finder and Tully to spy."

"That sounds complicated," Nick said, a strain of worry in his voice.

"It is, but what choice do we have? If I lose one advantage, I could lose the whole game."

"It's not really a game if people could die," Nick said. "Is there anything you can feed the victims so they aren't drinkable? If we could supply him with something he could use . . ."

"Feed them? Like what?"

Nick was quiet, thinking. "Like medications that won't hurt the person who takes them but will have stinky body odor side effects. Maybe they could make blood taste bad, too."

Steve became a tiny flicker of blue in the trees beyond.

"Far enough, Steve!" I yelled. He stopped walking for a second, so I knew he heard me. But then he kept going.

"Steve! Steven!" I got up and walked to the edge of the woods, covering the end of my phone and holding it away from my face. "Far! Enough!"

He kept going.

"We gotta follow Steve," I said. "He's looking for Evia. Or more pine cones or something. Not that we have any pine trees in our yard."

Nick stayed with me. I heard the pages of a book flipping.

"Luckily for you," he said, "I am such an amazing student I brought two of my text books with me and one of them is a book about surgical procedures that includes a fair bit of drug information. Oh!"

"What?"

"My cheat sheet on initial cut and suture technique. I've been looking for this! Thought I'd lost it."

"You have *cheat sheets* on how to cut people open and sew them up? That is *not* encouraging."

"Med school, lady. Not always a pretty picture. Memorizing these techniques will help me make it less ugly on every patient I have."

Ugh.

"So you say spike her drinks. Give the victims something that won't harm them or cause any negative reaction for *them*, but will taste terrible or make *her* not feel well."

"Yes."

Not starving Matilda, but feeding her. Genius. I needed to talk to Mama.

Wednesday, December 26, 2001.

I rang Finder's doorbell the day after Christmas with a plateful of cookies in my hand.

Finder opened the door, wearing a onesie with reindeer on it. A onesie with feet. A Santa hat was pinned to Finder's hair.

I laughed. "What is *this?*"

"Merry Christmas to you, too," she said. "Family tradition." I stepped in as she let the door shut behind us.

"Hello, Stacy!" Mama said coming forward to envelop me in a hug. She also wore pajamas and a Santa hat. "Did Jill bring you? Does she want to come in?"

"I told her it had to be a quick stop. I still have a lot to do. How was the shelter yesterday?"

"Oh everyone appreciates the volunteers on Christmas," Mama said. "I've been Mrs. Claus for maybe five years running, right, Layla? Handing out gifts to the adults is fun, but it's the kids. Seeing their little faces light up when they get gifts is all the Christmas I need." I looked at Finder.

"It is pretty sweet," she said. "I run the crafts table usually, but this year another dude ran it, so I was in the kitchen, and I gotta say, the kitchen volunteers were hardcore. We fed four hundred and fifty people full Christmas dinner in five hours."

"Our reward is that today we do nothing but eat leftovers in our pajamas, exchange gifts and watch movies," Mama said. "And receive our favorite visitors, of course."

Mama disappeared into the kitchen and came back out with something in her hand.

"Put this in your pocket. Call me later if you have questions. I wrote some instructions." I shoved the small paper bag into my coat pocket.

"Thank you so much for this, Mama," I said. "Especially on short notice. Were you able to get the . . . other thing we talked about?"

"You're welcome, baby. And yes. I have it safe and sound. I had to call in a favor, but we got it."

A thrill of excitement tickled my spine. We had a secret weapon. The first glimmer of hope for a New Year's win blossomed in my mind.

"You're the best!"

"It's true, I am. And we'll see you back here tomorrow for practice, right? Christopher has come a long way since Darcy and has a lot to share." Her look was pointed. I got it. I'd be here. "Oh! Take this to your step-mama," she handed me a paper plate of cookies covered in plastic wrap from the dining room table.

"Are these the jam ones Tully loves?"

Finder smiled. "They are."

I couldn't wait.

December 26, continued.

According to Tully, a fifty degree, snow-less Christmas week in Richmond was not uncommon. Loading myself and my backpack onto my bicycle an hour before sunset, I was grateful Virginia weather was weird. My first real ride since the tailbone incident, I did not feel at all certain this was going to go well, but at least it wasn't cold. I had gotten on the stationary bike and rode/read my new chess book for fifteen minutes this morning and that had gone fine, but this was real world riding, with curbs and bumps and hills.

Tully had family day-after-Christmas stuff, Nick was still in Florida, Finder lived far and didn't have her own car, and I was absolutely not going to ask Dad or Jill to please drive me to the local vampire nest so I could drop off a bag of drugs. If I wanted this done, I was gonna have to do it myself. My bike was my option.

I double-checked all my freaky reflectors and safety gear and climbed aboard. No pain. Nice. After a few miles, I felt pretty good. Maybe this treadmill habit was making a difference.

I rode to the apartment building with its pristine exterior and polished chrome doorway. I checked my messenger bag making sure everything important was within reach. My holy water spray bottle attached to my belt on a stretchy dog lead, I had on my temple sweatshirt, I had velcroed on my arm bands turned so they would show if I raised my arms to block a strike, my hair was back in a low ponytail to make it difficult to grab, and I adjusted my St. Ignatius mugger cap to reveal the slightly crooked Star of David I'd drawn in eyeliner on my forehead. I wore the new running shoes I'd gotten at Hanukkah.

I touched the thigh-warm mezuzah nestled in my pocket. It had been a hard decision to let Jill think the mezuzah she'd specially picked for this house was stolen and not put it back, but it would have been weirder to explain that I had taken it. What would I have said? I'm so sorry Jill, but I took it off the door frame to fight vampires and it did a really good job, so I'm gonna hang onto it for a while? As soon as I master the stake, I'll give it back. Promise.

Yeah. Not so much.

My messenger bag held my two big crosses and, speaking of, a sharp stake. I spritzed holy water over my clothes and the top of my head, doing my best to get as much of the mist on me as I could. I donned my mirrored sunglasses. Then, I dug in my bag, and extracted a tiny bottle I'd bought at the grocery store. The final touch. I dabbed the garlic infused olive oil onto my wrists and behind my ears.

Smelling like a pizza, I entered the lobby.

27.

December 26, continued.

The desk girl recognized me.

"Are you here to see- ?"

"Terrence," I said. "Is he awake?"

She narrowed her eyes at me for a split second. Like I'd said the name of the tactic she was about to spring in the middle game.

She picked up her phone and pressed a button.

"Mr. Delmonico? Good evening. You have a visitor in the lobby. Shall I send her down?"

"I'm not going down. He needs to come up," I said. "By himself. No friends. Tell him it's Stacy Goldman."

She repeated my message and then hung up. "He'll be right up."

He really must not want Matilda to see those pictures.

I braced myself when the elevator door opened. I had the brown paper bag of pills in one hand and my spray bottle in the other, tucked into my messenger bag like a holster.

Terrence looked like I looked in the morning before a shower, disheveled in sweatpants. He winced at the stars on my forehead and sweatshirt. Like they were too bright to look at.

"What do you want?" he said, looking away from me.

"I think this will help," I said. I held out the bag.

"Just put it down," he said. I set the bag on the floor and backed up. Terrence stepped in. The brown paper crinkled as he poked it. Why? Was it gonna shock him? Satisfied, he picked it up and peeked inside. I had included Mama's sheet of paper with instructions.

Mama had assured me that all of these pills were garbage returns from a nursing home, and wouldn't be missed. They were most likely miscounts by inattentive nurses; no opiates or controlled substances. Those she sent back to the pharma companies. She also assured me none of the medications would harm the takers if they only took one dose, and were the most likely to have a bad personal stench as a side effect. We could only hope it made their blood taste terrible as well.

"For flavor," I said. "If you have to quit failing."

He kept his gaze averted as if I were too bright to look directly at. A glimmer of something, maybe relief, crossed his face. I backed up toward the doors, unwilling to give my enemy my back. I couldn't have been more surprised when I heard him speak again.

"Thank you."

Thursday, December 27, 2001.

This time when I knocked on Finder's door, there was no answer. Tully said, "They're probably around back."

Sure enough, in Finder's back yard, Mama stood by their picnic table, heads together with a man. I gasped when the man looked up. I looked into the tiger-golden eyes of the most drop dead gorgeous twenty-something I had ever laid eyes on. Finder introduced me to her cousin, Christopher. Hel-lo! I tried not to ogle as we shook hands. Tully gave Christopher an awkward hug. Nick was super yummy, don't get me wrong, but this man was *beautiful* in a put-his-picture-on-your-wall kind of way. I wondered about being that gorgeous. Did it affect your relationships? Did people avoid you because you made them so self conscious they couldn't speak?

"You've stunned her into silence," Finder said, kicking her cousin playfully in the rear. He arched a flawless eyebrow.

"Children!" Mama said. "Focus! Hello, Stacy. Come give us a hug." I obeyed. Mama hugs were now my favorite Richmond hugs; not quite as recalibrating as Bubbe's, but warm and grounding and safe feeling, nonetheless. "Christy, are you gonna light these things or are we just gonna admire them?" Mama said to him over my shoulder.

A pair of stakes with marshmallow-shaped ends lay on the table. Oh, not stakes, I thought, as he lit the first one. Torches.

"It's not gonna 'throw' flames, per se," he said, voice soft and delicate, "but the way I was taught, I can make the fire go quite a distance. Step back, please." Tully and I stepped back. Christopher tipped a small yellow flask into his mouth. He did a spit-take into the head of the torch. A thick tongue of flame lit up the air several feet in front of him. I felt the heat from where I stood.

"Christy works for the circus," said Mama with pride.

Christopher swirled the torch and licked his hand. He touched the torch to it and for a moment a tiny lick of flame came off his palm.

"I'm an aerialist primarily," he said, "and a hand balancer, but I asked the fire guy to teach me some basics and now it's kind of an obsession."

"And you do that pole thing," Finder said.

"Chinese pole, yeah."

Whatever that was. But, ah ha. I now understood his physique.

"Blowing fire isn't practical for serious combat," Christopher went on, "but I want everything available. The only thing I know for sure is she always shows up with an army. We should anticipate being outnumbered."

"Have you . . . fought her before?" Why had we not taken him with us on the kidnapping night? Where had they been hiding him if he knew what he was doing?

Those tiger eyes met mine. Oh dear. Tully nudged me. Staring. Sorry. I swallowed.

"When Uncle Darcy got taken, I tried to get him back. I was only in high school, though. A guy on my football team said he thought he knew what had taken him and he turned out to be right. I didn't believe at first, of course, but then Uncle Darcy came and hurt Aunt Lettie. We thought their leader was a male vampire named Glen Bacon, and that we had made a deal with him to leave us alone, but Matilda was using one of her men as a decoy. It's a long story," he said. "The only thing that's relevant now is that Matilda is no longer in hiding. No one knows why." He waved the torch in front of him. It whooshed in the air, much louder than I would have thought as he waved it in a circle. He offered the torch to us. Tully took a turn swiping it like a sword in front of him.

"It's hotter than it looks," Tully said.

"Wear your hair back," said Christopher. "I'm the only one who will blow fire for this fight, but you should know how it works in case of emergency."

Mama and Christopher showed us the rest of their arsenal, including two old paint sprayers we could use for holy water, and the secret weapon I had thought of.

We practiced drills swiping the fire, throwing lit torches to Christopher and covering him while he fought with fire. We practiced positions we could get in to protect each other and getting the hang of the pump action on the water sprayer. Mama practiced 'blowing' fire by lighting puffs of cooking spray with a kitchen torch. It didn't do what Christopher had done, but could help in a pinch.

Finder had us practice falls and rolls on the bare ground since it would feel different than on the mats at the dojo. Last but not least, we threw and caught stakes, then tennis balls representing small objects of whatever variety, and finally, a mock up of the secret weapon itself.

Inside, after all the physical work was done, Mama poured us all lemonades, and passed around a bottle of garlic tablets.

"Four each," she said, "every day from now until Monday. I want us taking every possible precaution." Her idea was that the garlic tablets would take a couple days to build up and hopefully make us less appetizing.

She put a deck of cards on the table. We all sat. Finder shuffled. Mama believed that all physical exercise should be followed by something easy and restful to let your body process what it had learned. For her, that was cards. Mama dealt.

"The only way she will leave any of us alone, guaranteed, is if she's dead," said Christopher, picking up his cards. "I think an opportunity to kill her is unlikely, but you never know."

"I'm worried about zombies," said Mama. "If the vampires don't get enough soul to fuel their consciousness, it could get ugly. I'm not as worried about them not having fed on blood in two weeks- "

"Seven days," I corrected, organizing my hand. Crap. My cards were terrible.

"No baby, two weeks. You gotta assume since you snagged her man on the twenty first, she hadn't eaten seven days prior to that. That's two weeks."

Duh, right.

"No blood will make them hopefully weaker, and for sure physically edgy, which we are prepared for," said Mama, "but I'm worried about them being mentally rough, too, since they haven't had soul."

A disconnect poked at me.

"Wendell says the Bat Suits don't feed on humans. They feed on Matilda. And if she's a vampire without a soul, how can that work? They drink her blood, that I get, but does she pass the soul food to them the same way?"

Finder snorted as she put the deck in the middle. "Sorry," she said. "Soul food." She and Christopher smiled.

Mama tapped her fingers on the table.

"That is an excellent question."

We stood in a collective moment of theoretical head scratching. Mama broke the uncertainly with the opening play of the game.

"Well, children, we just have to be alert. If we do get a zombie, remember, they are vicious, starving and will stop at nothing to eat. They don't care how old you are, or what shoes you wear. If you're meat, they'll eat you."

Friday, December 28, 2001.

Tully and I met Finder and her cousin at the dojo for a fireless practice, working with dry torches, our formations, rolls, tossing and catching the torches and lighters and partner combat moves. Tully brought out his dragon slicer, a massive broad sword. We did some practice with it, but Finder and Christopher both thought it would limit his agility too much with the stronger, faster vampires. Out back in the alley, we did a wet run with the sprayers. Tully had found a second one in his dad's basement collection of everything so we cleaned it and got it up and running, too. I named it my weapon of choice.

Finder and Christopher sparred with each other as Tully and I stretched to cool down. Finder pretended to be each of the Bat Suits she had fought in the arena on the kidnapping night.

"He's short," she said about Red Goatee Suit, "a good street fighter. He did lots of this." She demonstrated some punches that made Christopher nod knowingly and reply with moves I didn't recognize.

"Stop drooling," Tully whispered.

"It's like looking at a work of art. I don't want to *do* anything with the art, I just can't look away."

Saturday, December 29, 2001.

"I raise you three." Finder pushed three more pieces of Hanukkah geld into the center of the mat.

"What does that mean again?" I eyed my dwindling stack of candy coins.

"Stop with the questions," Finder said. She looked over her hand at her boyfriend. "She does this to torture me."

"And why not?" I said. "You bring me here to torture me."

Flying Eagle was done up for the holidays with shiny tinsel garlands in the windows and multicolored lights strung from the ceiling. A Christmas tree stood in one corner away from the mat. It was decorated with cute little karate-themed ornaments. I'd sneaked my pile of presents under it when we arrived. With all the stuff we schlepped for practice now, torches, sprayers, stakes, shoes, holsters, my messenger bag, coats, hats, sunglasses and so on, neither Tully nor Finder had noticed the extra boxes nor where I had put them.

I pushed six of my chocolates into the center. I hoped Tully took my bet. Finder would have to add three more to stay in. Bubbe had sent the fake coins from one of the best chocolateries in Manhattan and I wanted to win at least some of them back. I held my cards close to my chest.

"Fold." Tully laid down his cards and pushed them toward the middle. He stretched out on the mat letting his eyes rest on the dojo ceiling.

Finder put in three more to meet my bet. She bet one more.

I did the same. "Call," I said.

I smiled as she smugly laid down her cards, three aces and two kings. I pretended to look impressed. "Nice hand, Sensei," I said. "What do you call it again?"

"Gah!" Finder shook her hands by her face.

"It's my strategy," I said, grinning. "I ask basic questions so you underestimate me and then I play my," I waited until she and Tully were both looking at me, "royal flush to win."

"What?" Finder leapt up to a crouch. She got on all fours and leaned over to get a better view. "You're kidding?"

"Nope!" I said. "The best hand I've ever, ever had!"

"That's amazing. Did I deal that? The only person to ever beat me with a royal flush was my dad," Finder said. "Two nights before he disappeared. Do you even know the probability of that hand?"

"One in 649,739," I said. "Maybe the same odds as being recruited as the investment banker for a vampire. Maybe less in Richmond."

Finder stared for a minute at the Christmas tree, expression uncertain.

"What's the chance I'm going to still be human at this time next week?"

My body tensed at the question, even as hers went slack. We were all very quiet.

"Is it about the same as a royal flush?" she said.

"We've been practicing every day," said Tully. "We're ready, Layla."

"Are we?" she asked.

"I won't let them take you," Tully said.

"You will if they kill you," Finder said.

Crap. This was not a tongue-in-cheek conversation. Finder did not believe she was going to make it through New Year's Eve.

"I've been thinking about bolting. Packing up my mom and getting the hell out of Richmond. Maybe we could go to Florida or Canada, somewhere too far for her to let him hunt me."

"You can't leave," Tully said.

"I can," she said. "I don't want to, but I can't let him turn me into a monster. And kill all of you in the process. I," she fought to keep herself together. "I don't want to die. And then," she paused for a long breath. "Be like that. Forever."

It was time.

"I'm not trying to change the subject," I said, "but do I see presents under that tree?" Nobody moved. "Take a look."

Tully exchanged a glance with Finder, then walked over. He crouched in front of the tiny tree. "Are these from you?"

I shook my head. "They're from Santa."

"Santa." Finder stood and popped a hand onto her hip. "Mmm hmm." She and I joined Tully at the edge of the mat. I reached under the tree and handed the first gift to Tully.

He unwrapped the small box. Excitement built in my belly. I had tried hard to pick out something I thought he would like and that would suit his fighting style. He stared down into the tissue. "Are these . . . stakes?"

"You may have to sharpen them some. I think the guy who makes them thinks of them more as props, but they should work. Solid hardwood with the handles all wrapped."

He pulled them out and hefted them in both hands. "The leather is soft," he said. "It fits my hand perfect." Each round stake was about a foot long with a six-inch handle wrapped in deer skin leather. Polished and hard, the tip was surprisingly pointy.

"Thank you, Stacy," he said. "These are beautiful."

"You're welcome," I said, excitement for the next round of opening.

"This one's for you," I handed Finder a similar small box. "I couldn't give you your presents before today because they hadn't arrived yet. Last night I got home from the dojo and there they were! I hope you like them."

"Holy hand grenades, Batman," Finder whispered, reaching into the box. She withdrew a pair of antique solid silver fighting blades, each a little shorter than a sheet of paper.

"They're German werewolf fighting blades from the 1800's," I said. "Solid silver." Finder's mouth hung open. "I got them from an antique dealer who said that there was this town in Germany where everyone believed in werewolves. They believed so much that they made weapons to defeat them. I know we aren't fighting werewolves, but vampires are close enough, right? The guy said they've never been used."

Tully reached for one and Finder laid it in his hands. He closed his eyes.

"That guy was wrong."

"They do have a vibe kinda, right?" I said. Finder and Tully traded weapons, each testing out the other guy's stuff.

"You can share during real fights," I said, "but I thought the pairs should stay together in an ownership sense." They both stared at me. "And here are the big ones."

I handed them each a long heavy box.

Finder opened hers first.

"You're kidding me, right? How could you afford this? I know what this is and what it's worth." She lifted the hand-forged steel katana out of its velvet box and stood.

"I had some help," I said. "A drop in the bucket."

Tully caught on first. "Terrence's credit card?"

"Not exactly *Terrence's*," I repressed a sly grin.

"You are *wicked*, Stacy Goldman," Finder said.

Tully opened his big box. He gasped. He looked at me, then back into the box.

"Those are from the same antique dealer as the werewolf blades," I said. "Said he got them at an auction after two museums rejected them because they'd seen too much combat to be beautiful."

Tully pulled out the first sabre and turned it over in his hands. It was delicate, refined looking in his hands. The blade curved ever so slightly upwards at the tip and had a basket around the handle intricate as a spider's web. He stood and swung. The sword cut through the air with a sound like a switch. When he turned back to me, his cheeks were wet.

"They're French dueling sabres from the late 18th century," he said. "They stopped making this shaped basket about twenty years before dueling was outlawed in Paris."

I didn't know about any of that. "I just thought they felt like you."

Finder took her stance in the middle of the floor and held her new, untried blade in front of her. Then she carried it over to the altar and laid it on the mat. She got down on her knees and sat with her hands in her lap. Then she touched her forehead to the floor. Child's pose. Go me, remembering my yoga.

"I was thinking your dragon slicer isn't very helpful indoors and fencing foils aren't gonna behead anything, if you know what I mean," I said.

Finder got up and took two steps into the center of the mat. She lifted her new blade overhead and began a familiar kata.

Down cut, diagonal right, diagonal left. She stepped forward and back, breathing and moving with each strike. Side cut right, side cut left. Each cut small and efficient, stopping at the center line of her imaginary target. Upward cut turning the blade, her imaginary opponent sliced from hip to shoulder. A penultimate cut straight up into the groin. And lastly straight on, a blade through the heart, or the eye.

We had tomorrow left. Then, it was show time. Tomorrow day, and Monday day remained to work the new toys into what we'd practiced. We still didn't know if Nick would be back from Florida in time or if Luke would show, though Nick said they were both planning to be there. We pulled some extra weapons for them, but decided to rely on each other.

The plan for Monday was for all of us to lie low, eat a lot of carbs, meet for a final practice in the afternoon, then pretend like it was any ordinary New Year's Eve.

I was nervous, but watching Tully and Finder spar with their new toys made me feel better. When Tully asked if I wanted to go over the drills one more time, I did not. But I said yes and spent the next ten minutes ducking, dodging and working up a whole new sweat as he and Finder leaped past me with new stakes and blades.

Sunday, December 30, 2001.

I shut the front door behind me.

"Be right back," I said to Tully as I put my water bottle on the passenger seat of his pickup. I ran beside the house and down to the pool house. I went around it, out of view of the living room windows, and stopped beside the rock pile that housed the secret rock. It was exactly as I had left it. I opened it anyway. Drat. No note from Maymont.

"I don't think no news is good news," I said as I got in and fastened my seatbelt. We speculated about what could be happening all the way to class.

I tripped though the practice as if I'd never done it before. Every time I tried to get present on the mat, listen to my breath, even count my breaths in Down Dog, I got lost in nerves. What was happening at Maymont? How were we going to arrange the meeting? Had Matilda figured out my strategy and chosen a reply? Would everything/anything we had practiced work? Was Terrence still secret or had he been found out? Maybe it was brain overdrive, but every part of my body felt itchy for no reason.

"The full moon might be making you feel extra tired today," Yoga Saanvi said, "or extra energized. Just be easy with yourself and let the practice flow."

Calm down, Goldman, I told myself. You've practiced and practiced. It's going to work. You're all going to walk away alive and fine. Everything is going to work.

At the end, I laid on my back in sivasana, corpse pose, and sighed a deep sigh. I looked for the chakra opening I'd grown used to, starting at the crown, but the top of my head didn't tingle. It felt like a hand was pressing down on my forehead and keeping everything in place. When Saanvi came over and pulled my legs like Tully had in traction, my whole body softened. Glorious.

"This is the last practice of the year," she said in her soothing end of class voice. "Allow yourself to take a moment and let go of what 2001 brought you, to release yourself to a new phase of life in 2002. And as you rest, open your heart in thanks for all of your gifts. No matter what form they came in."

I had lost my home, watched a handful of people dive to their deaths, and fought for my life against real vampires. I had earned my first title in chess, kissed a boy for the first time, made three real friends, figured out how to navigate a city without a subway and learned that forgiveness was a living power. I'd made friends with an archangel who knew my grandmother and was real. And I'd gone from falling on my belly in chaturanga dandasana to being able to hover for one whole breath. It had been the hardest year of my life. And, there had been highlights.

Lying on my mat, the invisible pressure lifted off my forehead. In the next breath, my belly got hot, my crown chakra buzzy at last. My chest softened as I followed Saanvi's weird, kinda yucky instructions to let my muscles fall off the bones. I let my body 'sink into the earth'. In that weird moment, something unfamiliar washed over me. Gratitude. Gratitude for a truly rotten apple. Thank you, Joseph Thornton, for being such an evil jerk. Because if you hadn't threatened me at Nationals, then been ready to jump me in the hallway my first day at St. Ig's, Finder might never have noticed me. And without Finder, who would I be? Some normal girl leading a normal life without vampires, shapeshifting woodland animals, and who knew what else?

I'd be Stacy Goldman, National Master. Now, I was Stacy Goldman, National Master, For Real Vampire Hunter and Girlfriend of Adorable Goth/Hot College Boy who was an amazing kisser. I let all of that soak into my body. Please Universe, I thought in Saanvi-speak, please let us all live through tomorrow night. Please, please, please help us win.

28.

December 30, continued.

After yoga, Tully and I drove first to St. Ignatius. Mass was letting out as we slipped in through the side gate of the school and went around to the vestry entrance of the church.

"Most people fill, like, perfume sized bottles," Tully said as we entered the back of the sanctuary. "Not pints and quarts."

"It is what it is, dude. Unless we can get one of the Sisters to bless a few gallons for us, this is the only way."

"Sister Elizabeth has a good sense of humor. I bet she'd do it. If she could."

We arrived at the holy water urn. I guess you call it an urn? Holy water bowl? It looked like a stone birdbath.

"You mean she can't?"

"Nope. Has to be an ordained priest."

"Why?" I pulled our jars from my messenger bag. I handed one to Tully.

"It just does."

"But the Sisters are holy people."

"They're not ordained."

Tully crossed himself and dipped the first jar carefully into the water.

"What does 'ordained' even mean?" I said. Tully handed me the jar and I screwed on a lid. I traded him the other jars.

"When you receive a vocational calling to become a priest, it's supposed to be a message from God." He dipped the second jar. "When you get ordained, you get blessed in a certain way that makes you, the priest, like, an embodiment of Jesus. It's why priests can forgive sins and bless people and do the mass."

"Father Jacob is an embodiment of Jesus," I said, as Tully dipped the remaining jar. I was incredulous that this was even a conversation we could have.

"Yes. Or. That's how it's supposed to be."

I put the lids on the filled jam-sized jars as Tully handed them to me. Tully crossed himself again. "It's a very serious undertaking, becoming a priest," Tully said as we trailed the lagging mass-goers out of the sanctuary.

"And why can't women get ordained?" I asked.

"Tully shrugged. "Jesus was a man. His apostles were men and priests are descended from the apostles. Spiritually speaking."

"That's ridiculous. What do the Sisters get if they aren't ordained, too?"

"They get confirmed. Nuns *and* Sisters."

"I'm so confused."

"Ask Sister Elizabeth. She can explain it better than me."

"So what's she? A nun or a Sister?"

Tully shrugged.

I shook my head. "Lots of women are rabbis," I said.

"Catholic is Catholic," Tully said, "and if you want to be ordained you gotta be a guy. That's just the way it is."

"Well, I think it's ridiculous."

"You should be grateful," Tully said. "You didn't have to take an entire semester of Religion for the Modern Man. The entire point of the class is to sell us on being priests. We spent ten minutes of each class in silent prayer waiting for our vocations to show up."

"Did one show up for you? You have a pretty strong spiritual mojo."

"No. I don't have a vocation."

"Did *anything* show up? I feel like you're the kind of person who would have something show up."

Tully opened my side of the truck and helped me load the jars from my messenger bag into a box.

"Self Betterment Society," I said.

"Fine. Yes," he said, "something showed up."

"Ooo, cool." We replaced the full jars with a new round of empty ones. Two gallons of holy water was gonna take more than one church.

"What was it?"

"That's all you get. Now be a good SBS and mind your business."

Monday, December 31, 2001.

Nick called my cell at three minutes after five. Despite the stress of the night coming, I was excited and happy to hear his voice.

"You're back?" I said. Tully gently rolled his truck over speed bumps at the entrance to Wilton.

"Just got off the plane. I'm at a pay phone. Wanna meet at Chapter & Mercy?"

"I just got home from the dojo and I'm gross," I said, disappointed.

"What's the plan for tonight? I could come over early."

The prospect both thrilled and terrified me. I stared into an imaginary boxing ring, not sure I felt prepared for: Adorable Goth Boyfriend vs. Protective Attorney Father.

"Everyone is home," I said before I realized what I was saying. Tully pulled into my driveway.

"Are you afraid for me to meet your dad?"

"No. Of course I'm not."

"Great! See you in about forty minutes." We hung up.

"Good thing he couldn't see your face," Tully said, pulling into my driveway. As I got out, he said, "Thank you again for the presents. They are amazing to fight with. I kinda don't know what to say."

"Bring all of it," I said. "We're gonna win." I held his clear, blue gaze. "It's a good plan," I said. "We're not going to let them take her. Or any of us."

"Right."

"Right." I held out my fist. I was not a National Master because I was afraid to play hard. Matilda had challenged the wrong girl. "And if things go wrong, we'll kill 'em with fire." I smiled at the Southern Scotsman. He smiled back.

"Embrace the fighter," I said.

"Damn straight, SBS." We bonked fists.

When I pushed open the front door, Jill, wearing a gold-sequined sheath dress, shoved a plastic grocery bag into my arms.

"Oh my god! Finally! Where have you been? Make those look pretty on the banister." She slid across the marble in her stocking feet. Behind her, the living room was edged by cloth covered buffet tables. "Hurry, Stacy! Why are you so late? I told you, be home by four! They'll be here in half an hour!" The phone rang. She reached for it with one hand, twisting in an earring with the other. "The cake guy," she said as she answered.

I stood frozen. Dad's birthday. I'd completely forgotten.

"I thought we rescheduled this!" Dropping my backpack and the grocery bag, I grabbed my phone and dialed.

"I tried! Nobody could make it, remember?"

I did not.

"This is Nick. Leave a message."

Oh no. I left a message, then dialed his land line.

"Hi, it's Nick and Dave. The positions advertised are still available. Please leave your name, number and which position

you're applying for: missionary, doggie, lampshade, etc! Thanks!"
Beeeep.

How embarrassing. What was I supposed to say after that?

"Nick, it's Stacy. Call me if you get this before you come over."

I pulled a roll of tape out of the bag Jill handed me, then started twisting streamers up the long stairway banister.

At the top of the stairs, I hollered for Steve.

Stiff and frowning in dress pants and a gold bow tie, he rounded the corner from his room, clutching Monster in one arm and his Superhero cape in the other.

"I don't want the scary lawyers to come over," he said.

"Who does?"

"Mommy."

"Steven!" A shout from the kitchen. He looked at me as if maybe I could stop this whole thing, then padded off. The doorbell rang.

"Stacy! It's the caterer!" Translation: Stacy, answer the door! For a shrink, Jill needed to learn to say what she meant.

A college-age kid with a buzz cut and big white bags stood in our doorway. I pointed him toward the kitchen, grabbed my pack, ditched the décor bag, and hurtled upstairs.

I shot a longing glance at my shower, but, no time. I leaped out of my workout sweats into Meredith's antique pencil skirt and a snug black long-sleeved tee, then pulled the present I'd bought for Dad the night Luke's dog was stolen out of my closet. Maybe Steve could come up and wrap it for me?

No one would see my socks under the skirt and combat boots so I launched back downstairs, yanking out my ponytail holder and popping it over the round banister top. I shook out my hair and wiped the smudges off my glasses. Boots on and, ta-da.

The kitchen buzzed with activity: food and warming trays covered every available surface. Four guys prepped, running back and forth, food soldiers with laden arms.

Jill hesitated when she saw me, gaze settling on my outfit. "Would you like to borrow my new jade necklace?" She stepped into gold pumps.

"No, thanks."

"I think your father would like it on you."

"You look like an Oscar," I said. She gave me a look. "It's a compliment," I said. The irritation did not vanish from her face. "Would you rather look like an Emmy? If you hold your arms up, you could be an Emmy."

Steve entered through the archway from the living room carrying a hand wrapped present so big I could only see his legs.

"I told you to use the small box, Steven! Oh for crying out loud, p-p-put it d-d-down! You'll b-break it!" Steve carefully set the box on the floor. He'd managed to fix his cape on so the strings didn't show beneath his bowtie. Holding Monster in his teeth, he eyed the caterers with outright suspicion.

"Monster goes back in your room," Jill said. "And I asked you to put away that cape."

"I need them," he said, panic rising in his voice.

"You are too old for this now, Steven!" she said in exasperation. "How many times do I have to tell you, you are perfectly safe and perfectly capable in the world just as you are! Now put them away."

Steve backed out of the kitchen. I followed.

"I have an idea," I whispered when he got to the stairs. "Go get your backpack."

When he came back, we untied his cape, folded it and placed it in the backpack, then, in went Monster, comfortably seated, head sticking out. I'd hear about it later, but Steve needed that monkey. Four months ago his whole world had been turned upside down. And now his best friend was a missing squirrel shapeshifter and his big sister was hunted by vampires. Sometimes, I think Jill forgot he's only six.

The doorbell rang.

"Should I get it?" I shouted back toward the kitchen. Behind me, the caterer guys had made the buffet go from blank to fully draped with appetizers, utensils, napkins, etc. Chatting and smiling as they worked, they hustled back and forth from food central.

Looking through the peephole, I didn't recognize anyone, but they had that law firm look about them. I took a breath and opened the door.

"You must be Staaay-cee," drawled a rotund woman engulfed by a shiny fur coat.

"Ah'm Mae Anne Lee," she said with pride, leaning heavily on the last name and extending her hand for a very limp fishy handshake. "Great-great-granddaughter to Gen'ral Lee. I'm a senior partner at Sweete, Lee & Whitesmith. I hired your father."

"May I take your coat?" I said.

Jill came rushing in from the kitchen. Ms. Granddaughter Lee clicked over to her.

"Jill, I presume?" she said, embracing. "Such a delight to finally meet you! Ernie just can't stop goin' on about how wonderful you are!" She said it like *won*-dah-full. This from a woman in four-inch stilettos who barely capped five feet. I'd hate to face her in a courtroom. The shorter the attorney, the meaner he or she tends to be.

"What a beautiful job you've done with this home," she purred. "My, my."

I hung up the coats from my dad's other co-workers. They bee-lined for the appetizers. I answered two more door loads of attorneys, secretaries, etc. while Grandaught-ah Lee monopolized my stepmother.

Jill's cell phone rang.

"That was Joe, everyone," she said as if speaking to crowd of fifty, not fifteen. "They finished the golf game and will be here in ten!"

Steve and I hung some more of the shiny Happy Birthday signs, especially ones with 50 on them. My dad thought he was bringing one of the partners and his wife home for New Year's Eve dinner after a nice game of golf. Surprise.

Jill thought she'd been terribly clever. I had blocked it out, knowing how Dad felt about surprises.

The doorbell rang.

Aunt Marlena and Uncle Ira burst in. Behind them, Dad's money mobile turned the corner.

"Hurry!" I said, slamming the door behind them. "What're you doing here?" I said as we hugged.

"What are you? In mourning? We just spent a few days in D.C., honey. We saw Ira's Uncle Butch who's about to die any minute and his Aunt Lulu who's got Alzheimer's and had no idea who we were. It was a very nice trip."

Car doors shut outside.

"He's here!" I called to Jill.

Everyone got very quiet. The doorknob turned.

"Hello," Dad called, not looking in as he ushered a short, fattish man and his matching wife through the door. Another fur coat. Fur for golf? Really? They reminded me of a pair of pugs, cute, in a mashed face kind of way. My father stepped inside.

"Surprise!" everyone yelled. Dad froze, expression changing from normal to horror to what I, and maybe only I, knew was the 'cover my fury' face.

"Happy Birthday!" Jill rushed to him followed immediately by Marlena, black crepe pants rustling in her wake.

"My baby brother is fifty," Marlena exclaimed. "How old does that make me?"

I reached up to hug my dad.

"Tried to stop her," I whispered in his ear.

"Not hard enough," he whispered back, smiling for his public. "Thanks, honey," he said out loud, like I'd said happy birthday.

Again, the doorbell.

Nick in torn jeans, trench coat and boots, hair spiked, backpack flung over one shoulder, stood in the doorway, a coffee in each hand and a single red rose in his teeth.

29.

December 31, continued.

"Uh-oh," Nick said around the rose.

"I . . . forgot something," I said.

"Uh-huh." He leaned forward. I took the rose.

"Dad," I said, "this is my friend. Nick."

"Hello, sir," Nick said, quickly assessing the situation. I took a coffee so they could shake hands.

"Nice to meet you. Nick." Dad gave me the We'll Be Talking About This Later, Young Lady look.

"This can't be *your* birthday," Nick said, stepping inside. "The signs all say happy fifty." He smiled at my dad.

Smooth, college boy. Very smooth.

"Flattery gets you everywhere," Dad said, aware he was both on stage and surrounded. Facing away from the crowd, I mouthed 'I'm sorry! I forgot!' to Nick. He smiled, I sniffed my beverage. Chocolate. Espresso. Yum.

"Stacy," Jill said. I had forgotten about her, standing as Dad's arm candy. Oops.

I made a hurried introduction, hoping to whisk Nick out of the fray. Jill shot me a look in the same vein as Dad's, but slightly more personal since we had not discussed me inviting friends to the party.

"Pleasure to meet you, Mrs. Goldman," Nick said with the sincerest of smiles. "Stacy's told me how hard you've been working to put this all together." He took an appreciative look around. "It's a beautiful party. Wow! Who made that cake?"

The crowd went back to birthday congratulations as the doorbell rang and my father greeted another contingent from his office. Wow, Nick was flawless. Jill's face relaxed as my Adorable Goth Boyfriend led her on a merry chat about surprise party planning. I couldn't believe she was laughing! Her real, regular, fun Jill laugh.

"How did you do that?" I asked, leading Nick to the side of the chaos as Jill went to greet more of Dad's work guests.

"I apologized for crashing the party, told her I thought it was later and I could catch you before everything started. She accepted my apology and then I just asked questions. She's sweet. Now, do you need to catch me up on anything or should I clear out and meet you later? At the, you know?"

"No! Stay. Please." I lowered my voice. "Once I put in the obligatory nice to meet you appearance they'll be just as happy to see me vanish." Nick nodded, looking skeptical.

Speaking of which, I caught Dad's eye and knew I'd better go shake with the newcomers. I handed Nick our plate and told him how to get downstairs.

A few minutes later, I found him setting up the chess table.

"Pretty fancy digs, Miss Stacy."

"I'm getting used to it." I opened the door to our overstuffed gym. "This is Finder's favorite room." I walked in and pointed out all the stuff I'd been learning to use.

When I turned around, Nick was leaning on the doorframe. Not looking at the gym. Looking at me.

"So that's kind of everything," I said.

Nick didn't budge as I stepped toward the doorway. My heart pounded loud and fast in my ears. I stopped a few feet from him. He closed the gap. My ribcage shook, my heart beat so hard. He put his hands on my face. They felt warm under the fabric of his fingerless gloves; rough on my cheeks as he tilted my face up toward his.

He drank me in, eyes lingering on each of my features like taking sips from something delicious. Then, he leaned over, closed his eyes and with focused intention, took complete possession of my mouth.

My chakras popped open like I'd touched something electric and the switch flipped on. This time, more than my crown chakra buzzed. There was no way adults could come down here without us hearing them, right? I started to reach my arms up around his neck, but he caught them in his.

"Stopping," he breathed. "We're stopping. Slippery slope," he said, drawing me to him.

"We could go for a walk," I said as he held me. "The stairs out back lead to the river. We could find a rock."

"Nice try, temptress." He stepped out of the embrace. "I missed you in Florida. I have to say I fantasized about kissing you all the way home."

"That's a long time," I said.

"It is. That was . . . a very worthwhile kiss, however."

"I kinda don't remember it," I said. "Maybe we should do it again."

"Stop," he said pointing at me. "I'm trying to be good." He turned to my chess table. "Care for a warm up?" He gave me his rock star smile.

I wanted a warm up all right.

"This is a first," I said. "Never in my life have I been disappointed to have someone offer me chess."

Sixteen moves in, I snagged the mate. Nick and I both started when the kitchen door slammed. Steve almost fell down the stairs he ran so fast. Small tears crept down his face.

"W-w-werewolf!" he choked. "Upstairs!"

30.

December 31, continued.

"Start over. Go slow," I said.

"Mrs. Macy is a *werewolf?*" Steve blurted.

Who was Mrs. Macy? I scooted my chair and made room in my lap.

"No!" he said. "No sitting! You have to come!"

Nick and I got up to follow Steve back upstairs.

"Mommy sent me to put my backpack away. I smelled this stinky sweet smell like the time we found the dead mouse under the kitchen trash can. Remember that?" I did. "It smelled like that, only rottener, and coming from my room. I looked inside and Mrs. Macy was standing by Evia's cage. When she saw me, she growled! Like, with teeth, growled. So I ran away. Stacy, what if Evia's in danger? I haven't seen her since we let her go! She always comes when I leave the seeds."

"Could she maybe be hibernating?" said Nick.

Steve stopped in the middle of the kitchen, pulled out of his panic for a moment. He gave Nick a look of disdain. "Squirrels do not hibernate," Steve said. "I see why she had to save you." He looked at me. "New boyfriend fails to impress," he said.

"Steve! So rude!"

He stood as tall as he got. "I'm your brother," he said, sniffling. "It's my job to evaluate the people you date."

"You're six!"

"He's not wrong," Nick said. "And he won't always be six."

"I don't think we were officially introduced," Nick said, offering Steve his hand. "I'm Nicholas O'Malley."

Steve wrapped his tiny paw around two of Nick's fingers. "Steven Goldman." They shook.

When we emerged into the living room, Steve pointed to the buffet table where a puffy looking Asian woman with dyed blonde hair stood alone, picking what she wanted out of the shrimp salad.

"That's Mrs. Macy," he whispered.

She wore a too small designer blazer over a black skirt. I guess I imagined a werewolf in human form would appear more, I don't know, healthy? Outdoorsy maybe?

I bucked the crowd around the buffet and stepped in next to her.

"Hi," I said, unleashing my achievement smile. Adults usually loooove the achievement smile. Mrs. Macy glared. I held her eye contact for a moment, but I didn't want to seem like a freak so I looked away. What was I hunting for, anyway? A name tag reading Hello My Name is Werewolf? What would I say? Why were you snooping in my little brother's bedroom? The doorbell rang again.

I wedged my way toward the food, searching for my next move. The alarm beeped as Jill opened the door for the next round of guests. Beside me, Mrs. Macy let out a loud breath of annoyance as we reached for the same dessert. A familiar voice said,

"Surprise!"

Dr. Saul Karzinsky, Meredith's dad, stood in the doorway wearing a gold party hat. His wife, Helen, stood next to him in an über classy coat. Behind them bobbed a bouquet of dorky Happy Birthday/Happy New Year balloons. I missed a breath looking for the curly headed, midnight Goth who must, *must* be anchoring those balloons.

Plate abandoned to the buffet, I almost mowed down a line of guests running for the door. Screaming like a major girl, I threw myself into Meredith's arms.

We jumped up and down hugging each other so hard. And squealing. A lot. When we finally let go of each other, both of our faces were sopping with tears.

Dad and Meredith's dad did that half handshake, half hug thing men do. We were close enough to hear my dad say oh so quietly, "How about you pronounce me suddenly ill or dead or something? We can clear this place out and have a martini?"

A few minutes later, the families had completed the extensive hellos and Nick had vanished from the doorway. I led Meredith through the kitchen and to the back stairs.

"You look great in my clothes," Meredith said, approval sparkling in her wet eyes. Halfway down the stairs, she stopped dead.

"Yum," she said.

I nudged her in the back.

"Oh, sorry. You must be Nick?"

"I am," he smiled. She returned it.

She extended her hand and bopped the rest of the way down the stairs. "I'm Meredith, the fiercely protective best friend from New York. Break her heart and I'll come for you."

"Meredith!"

"I just wanted to be clear straight form the start," she said.

She let go of Nick's hand, but not before turning it over in her own and noticing his chippy black nail polish.

"Mmmm. Double earrings. Not every boy can pull that off." She let go of his hand, then looked at me. "I approve." Back to him. "How's your chess game? You are aware you don't have a chance, right?"

Nick looked back and forth between the two of us.

"I understand so much more about you right now," he said to me, beautiful eyes twinkling. He looked back at Mer. She melted just a little.

"Is that the new Morpheus shirt?" he asked.

"Fresh off the press. I wish they'd make them in girly cut shirts. These boxy, man-tees are not awesome."

"I didn't start collecting until issue twenty-six, but better late than never, right?"

Meredith stared. "What, you started collecting when you were seven? Issue twenty-six came out in like nineteen ninety two."

Nick flashed my friend his classic rock star smile. "Ahead of my time."

Or, you're a whole lot older than you want me to know.

Mer raised an eyebrow at me. Brilliant Goth Boy Nick asked her another fan question and they were off and running. Nick winked at me. He had this under control.

"I'll be right back," I said. Steve would never forgive me if I left him hanging. Time to finish my Mrs. Macy/Werewolf investigation. Then, I would tell Mer all about it.

Upstairs, I didn't see her. Granddaughter Lee stood at the bar waiting for a cocktail.

"Did Mrs. Macy leave?" I asked.

"If she's not at the buffet, I'd assume yes. That woman's appetite is insatiable. I don't know how she fits in her clothes. And always the early go-homer," she said. "When she isn't sick. That woman misses so much work I'd fire her, except she speaks five languages. And she's my only Asian." The bartender handed her a full glass rimmed in white crystals. Sugar or salt? Hmm. Hard to guess.

"You have a good night now, sweetheart. I hope your Daddy's havin' a wonderful birthday. Don't drink anything naughty! But definitely get something. I'd let that boy shake my cocktail if I were your age." She winked at me. Ewww.

I looked out the front windows. No sign of Mrs. Macy. I guess I wasn't adding 'werewolf hunter' to my list of new occupations tonight. A phone rang behind me. It was coming from the front hall powder room.

A string of curses caught my attention. A woman's voice, pausing and talking in conversation. I went to the hall closet and opened the door, like I was looking for something. It got me closest to the bathroom without standing at the door obviously eavesdropping.

"I don't know, you dolt! The mother says he let it go."

She paused, listening.

"What, do you think I have? A crystal ball? The cage wasn't clean. Yes, the scent was true. Yes! I am sure. It was the right squirrel, stop hounding me. You have to quit experimenting and get this done. I am not gonna die with my meat stripped off my bones like Max and now April. You have a month to figure it out. And don't think I don't know about your extracurricular activities. Cathy's stench was all over you last night. That stops now, or I'll put Theo in your place. Then we'll just put you out for dinner."

Seconds of silence passed. Had she hung up? I closed the closet door and took a few steps away. Mrs. Macy came out of the bathroom, phone still in hand. She barely looked at me. She walked right to the front door and let herself out without even a goodbye. I looked out the side window after her. She got into a shiny black Mercedes and pealed out of the driveway.

"Happy Birthday to you, happy birthday to you, happy birthday dear Ernie, happy birthday to you!" Dad took a deep breath and blew out the candles on his cake.

Meredith, Nick and I stood with Steve on the far side of the adults, questions tight on our lips. I had filled them in on what I'd heard and we were trying to put the pieces together. Now, Mer and I held hands like we'd never let go. My eyes filled again with tears.

"Cut it out," she said. "You're gonna make me cry, too."

Nick held Steve on his hip so he was high enough to see the cake cutting. I leaned forward to accept a plate and handed it to Mer.

Jill had spared no expense. The dinner spread had been extensive, all my dad's favorites.

"Hows that tailbone feeling, Miss?" Meredith's dad asked as I crammed another mouthful of cake. The fancy bakery frosting melted on my tongue. I chewed and swallowed before answering.

"Good," I said. "I do forty-five of cardio on the treadmill every afternoon, forty-five of light weights three days a week for PT and yoga on Sundays with my friend Tully who is totally not the sort of person you'd look at and think went to yoga. Oh, and sometimes my friend Finder makes me run. And Jill bought me a bike, so I cycle some, too."

"Wow," he said. "Who are you and what have you done with Stacy Goldman? My daughter's best friend is the sort of person who would only run if the zombies were chasing her."

And so they are, I thought. More or less.

The conversation quickly turned to typical stuff, the house, the car, the schools, who we'd found as friends, how much we missed the City and so on.

"Has there been more kissing?" Meredith demanded in a whisper as Nick preceded us down the stairs. We carried more cake.

"Tell you later."

"I hate you so much right now," she said no longer soto voce.

"Stacy, stop," Nick said. His voice, suddenly serious, held warning.

I stopped, mid-staircase. Darcy Jackson stood at my back door. And he was smiling.

I'd have grabbed Meredith by the shoulders and turned her right around, if my hands hadn't been full of cake. "No eye contact!" I said, "Go!"

"What's going on?" she said as I hustled her back upstairs. "Who's that guy?"

"Finder's father," Nick said. Steve barreled into Meredith as we came around the corner into the kitchen. His face had gone white. I put our plates of extra cake on the counter.

"Finder's father the *vampire?*" Meredith squealed. "Wait! I wanna see!" I caught and held her arm.

My watch said 6:43. I'd thought we'd have more time. I'd been wondering how to arrange the meeting.

Matilda would be so angry if Darcy Jackson killed me without her, I hoped I'd be safe. I had to go out and meet him, but not unarmed. I took the stairs two at a time to my room. Meredith and Steve followed me. Nick exerted some major self-control and stayed downstairs. He wanted no questions raised about boys being in girls' bedrooms.

I grabbed my temple sweatshirt and my loaded messenger bag. I dug through my weapons for the mezuzah and slid it into my pocket.

"Stay here," I said. "You'll be safe here." Meredith started to ignore me and follow. "No," I said. She stepped back, surprised. It may have been the most forceful thing I'd ever said to her. "Stay with Steve."

I looked at him. *Do not let her out of this room.* He nodded, comprehending. "There's a stake under the pillow if anything goes wrong," I said, "and one under the sink in the bathroom. You have to hit them in the heart to kill. Anywhere else, it's just paralysis." I grabbed the stake I kept by my door and put it in my messenger bag. "I'll be right back. If I'm not back in ten minutes, find Nick. If you don't find him either, draw holy symbols on yourselves where they can be seen. Finder and Tully's numbers are in my phone on speed dial. It's right there." I nodded to where my phone sat on its charger base on my desk.

I grabbed mirrored sunglasses from beside the phone and bolted out the door. The party was in full force as I crossed the landing. Our living room was crowded with lawyers, Jill's temple friends, and neighbors invited over, all talking, drinking and eating cake. Music played from the stereo Jill bought the family as a holiday present. Dad and Jill stood by the big windows, facing inside, talking with their guests.

Nick waited for me at the bottom of the stairs. "I'm coming with you."

"You are not."

He started to protest.

"If something goes wrong, I need you to manage Steve and Meredith. And cover me."

I knew the alarm would beep the door opening. "Stepping outside for a sec!" I called in my most cheerful voice. I don't think anyone heard me.

Beep beep beep.

I stepped outside and pulled on my Beth Shamar sweatshirt. I velcroed on my arm bands and loosened my spray bottle on its stretchy dog lead. I walked around the windowless garage side of the house.

Darcy Jackson occupied a lounge chair by the closed pool, feet up, hands tucked behind his head.

"You could've sent a note," I said. I scanned the tree tops. No bats.

"What fun would that be when I can come visit and sit by the pool?" Darcy Jackson's eyes seemed deeper set than usual, his skin pale and ashy. His feet twitched as he sat.

"Mansion at 9:00," he said. "My mistress is eager to get tonights' events underway."

"She demanded the meeting and the date. Diplomatic rule says I set the terms. We'll be behind the Carillon at 11:30. The side furthest from Dogwood Dell."

The grassy knoll behind the Carillon was the most private spot in the park, bordered on the rear side by trees. As Tully and I scouted meeting spots after our holy water acquisition adventure, we chose a mixture of privacy and public access, hoping the combination would keep us safer. With houses and a street the length of a football field away on one side, it wasn't so private that she could shred us and not expect to draw attention.

"My Lady doesn't like to be told what to do."

"I don't either," I said. "And you can remind her that *she* attacked *us* at the museum. If she hadn't kidnapped Nick and Luke and set her minions on us— "

"We are not minions," he said. His foot twitched.

"You are totally minions," I said. "Especially you."

Darcy's gaze made me flinch, like mosquitos on my skin, his will tickled the back of my neck. *Look at me.*

"Stop that." I stood firm, eyes on his shoulder.

"Interesting," he said, "hardly anyone notices that." He cocked his head, sniffing the air like he could smell me. He licked his lips. "I'll deliver your message," he said. "She'll probably send us to interrupt the party and bring you back to the mansion. You might want to be prepared for that."

"I am *not going* to the mansion. She might want to be prepared for that."

I angled my arms to flash my arm bands. Darcy winced as the moonlight caught the stars painted on them.

"If she declines to meet my terms, I win by default," I said. "Whatever you have to do to keep your boss in check tonight, do it. If anyone threatens my family, I will set fire to her secret underground bedroom with her in it. Don't think I won't."

Darcy went still. His face drew tight.

"How do you know about that?"

"I know a lot of things," I said. "Just like you." I started to walk away, but paused. "I just dealt you a good card," I said as a false wind picked up. "Might want to hold it close to your chest."

Sweat ran in a slick rivulet down my back. Nick waited for me at the front door.

"Remind me not to get on your bad side," he said breath coming quick. "I heard everything. From downstairs. Right behind the glass."

Meredith was beside herself.

"He turned into a *bat*! I *saw it*! It's not like I didn't believe you. I totally did. But, whoa." She sat down on my bed. "Oh. My god." Steve and Meredith had watched the whole conversation from my window, but hadn't heard what was said.

I called Finder and Tully on the phone in that order. I warned them to be prepared in case Matilda got cranky and anyone else received an early visitor.

I went into my bathroom and took stock. I pulled off my temple sweatshirt. My hair had frizzed out around my head, my face was tight and stressed.

I touched a group of crumpled and opened notes on my vanity, looking through them one more time.

M stalking around, hungry, upset. That one was Thursday. *M in a rage about rotten fruit.* Friday.

And on Saturday, *M threatening to hunt for herself.*

Sunday's note read: *Another sour one arrived. Feeding on each other, but not enough to go around.*

Today's note made me nervous: *Getting ugly. Watch yourself.*

I laid the notes in a row on the shiny vanity top. Meredith came up behind me and looked over my shoulder.

"You're staying with Steve tonight," I said.

"As if!" she said with a snort, looking at me in the mirror.

"You saw one. Check the box," I said. "You can't come. You could die."

"I could get hit by a bus on my way downtown to school. I could get crushed when an airplane crashes into a building. Life is full of hazards, Woman. Doesn't mean I'm not going to live it."

Maybe this made me a bad person, but I half wanted her with me. I needed someone in my corner who wasn't part of weird, supernatural Richmond. Someone to double check my decisions and keep my perspective. If Meredith saw a serious interaction with Matilda, she might be more equipped to help me in the future. Go me and optimism.

I hoped for a violence-free outcome tonight, maybe that's why I'd armed my friends with all the weapons I could procure. I glanced back at the notes.

Getting ugly. Watch yourself.

"I can't let you risk your life," I said.

Meredith leaned on the vanity then hopped up to sit on it. "She's manipulating you," she said. "We know this. What we don't know is why. We don't know what she gets out of keeping her fist in your mouth other than a power trip, but there has to be something. She has to want something more than baring her fangs and showing off what an evil vampire she is. Tonight you need to find out what she wants so you can react like yourself and not like some newbie who thinks black is a worse position. Did you have the advantage from the start? No. When has that stopped you before? Never."

What was wrong with me?

She was right. I had been playing like a beginner, and I'd been playing like I was losing.

"So it's not as as complicated as I think," I said.

"No. Duh. We're going to show up and find out what she wants and how crushing you serves that goal. Then we're gonna squash it." Mer smiled at me in the mirror. "She wouldn't be meeting you if there wasn't a pay off. We have to make it more advantageous to her to leave Finder human than turn her. Or change her, whatever they call it. We want her to see the plus side of letting you live." Meredith wrapped her arms around my shoulders and gave me a squeeze. "Wouldn't it be so awesome," she said, "if you had vampires as friends?"

Matilda had made it clear what being her 'friend' would entail the night she jumped us at Third Rock.

"No," I said. "I do not want vampires as friends. I have friends. And my best one is staying with Steve tonight. Safe and far from conflict. And that's final."

31.

December 31, continued. 11:16 p.m.

The moon hung fat and full over the Carillon, a five story stone and brick war memorial at the center of Byrd Park, next door to Maymont.

Meredith let go of my hand as Finder and Mama walked up. "You won't regret this," she whispered. "I'm a total asset. You'll see."

Finder and Meredith locked eyes for a long moment, giving each other a silent, alley cat once over.

"I'm Meredith," Mer said, by way of introduction.

"Right. The friend from New York," Finder said.

"Best," Mer added. "*Best* friend from New York. Since Kindergarten."

"Righteous." Finder knocked fists with Tully, the first of us to have arrived, then pulled him toward her for a quick and efficient PDA of the kissing variety. I'd never seen Finder mark her territory so clearly. Nick came up behind me, his presence warming my back.

Christopher, fully kitted out like a fictional vampire hunter crossed the street from where he'd parked. Black coat, hat, sunglasses, and a tool belt with many things including a mallet, all contrasted with his cappuccino delicate features.

"You have a gorget?" Finder said as she reached out and touched the newcomer's metal throat collar. "I want a gorget!"

"It's kind of uncomfortable," he said in his soft voice. "We'll see how it works tonight. Hi Aunt Lettie," he said, going around to give Mama a hug. His coat clacked a little as he embraced her. When it fell open, the inside was lined with stakes and torches.

Another figured jogged toward us from across the park. I handed Nick my spray bottle of holy water and he spritzed me all over. My jitters were growing with every new arrival. How would I make sure none of them got hurt?

"Not late am I? 11:20, right?" Luke had trimmed his hair. Tonight, it floated just above his shoulders.

"Is that your Aegisthus costume?" I asked, surveying his floofy, not-fight-practical wardrobe.

"Matilda picked it out," he said. "Was thinking she'd feel kinder toward us if she sees that I like her choices."

Finder rolled her eyes. "We're not here to make friends, Luke."

"How'd you get the blood out of the shirt?" Nick cocked a suspicious eyebrow as I spritzed him with the holy water.

"This is a new one," Luke said. "I threw the dirty one away."

Luke's blousy white sleeves were rolled up so his tattoo showed. The new addition to the costume was a belt with stakes tucked into loops.

"This everybody?"

"I invited Bolo," Finder said, "but he had plans out of town. I told him this was gonna be way more happening, but what can you do?"

By some miracle, the park was empty except for us. Finder and I walked to the Carillon side by side, her in the king position to my right, katana shining across her back, stakes in her boots. She was the one they wanted to capture. I took the queen position as the strategy boss. Meredith and Luke flanked us, bishops. They were armed with crosses and the paint sprayers filled with holy water. Nick walked on Meredith's outside positioned as her knight, and Mama, who did not limp at all even with her prosthetic leg, kept up as knight to her daughter. Tully held ground as my rook and strongest fighter, while Christopher stood as Finder's castle, on the end.

Everyone had been briefed. If it came to violence, let the fighters do the fighting. Stay away from the fire. And for Nick, Luke and Meredith who hadn't been practicing with us this week, when in doubt, run away and hide in the shrubbery until it's over.

Matilda arrived in a cloud of flapping.

11:30 exactly.

My body tightened as a colony of bats circled us, silhouetted against silver, full moon clouds. They landed in a circumference around us, as we'd predicted they would. We formed up. Nick was to stick by Tully, Mer by me and Luke by Christopher. Everyone was to pretend Mama, the holder of the secret weapon, wasn't even there.

"Hold your breath," I said to Meredith, going back-to-back to steady her. I exhaled, anchoring my feet. The vampires all changed at once in a furious gust. If any one of us went down, it'd be dominoes. We stayed standing.

Matilda, Darcy Jackson and Mr. Lorne (Terminator Suit) unfolded from their tiny bat bodies across from me. The beaded fringe on Matilda's glittery New Year's Eve dress clicked as she settled. How did she plan to fight in those shoes?

Those shoes . . . Matilda didn't plan to fight. She planned to win. I also planned to win, even without cute, strappy shoes.

I let go of my spray bottle. It bounced on a tether against my thigh. I loosed my arms to my sides and centered myself across from her. Keep the center. Press the Queen. Get mate. I'd played with worse odds.

"Kiss your little friends good-bye," Matilda said to Finder. "Party's in full force at my house and it's not the same without the guest of honor." She adjusted a wide, blingy bracelet on her wrist. Fidgeting.

A hum, a vibration to the vampires I hadn't seen before thrummed through them. Even Darcy Jackson, normally smooth as a glass of water, shifted his weight foot to foot. Finder and Tully noticed it, too. Their hands went tight on their weapons.

"Last month— " I began.

"Cut to the chase," Matilda snarled. I jumped. Meredith put out a hand to steady me. Matilda's usual veneer of humanity slipped. Her eyes, bright in moonlight, had a reddish tinge. I looked away before getting caught in her gaze. Her pale skin had lost its luster, cheeks dull and sunken.

She was controlling herself. That was clear. Why?

Terrence, bald skull reflecting the moonlight, bounced a little in his knees to the right of Mr. Lorne. I ignored him. If Matilda could read thoughts, one thought about our recent history with Terrence could ruin my entire plan. Red Goatee Suit, hovering too close to Tully, snarled past him at Finder. The remaining Bat Suit army fanned out behind me. Tully and Christopher shifted to face them, the way we'd practiced. Luke stayed between the vampires and Mama, his entire job to keep their attention away from her, to keep what she kept inside her coat away from their awareness until we needed it. If we needed it.

Out-numbered. Surrounded. Not ideal, but my army occupied the key position, the center. Now, we had to hold it. Starving the vampires before the big negotiation? Maybe not such a smart idea.

Matilda drew down on Finder. She extended her hand. "Time to go."

Finder did not move. She did not speak. She held a stake in her hands and waited.

"Layla, be reasonable," said her dad. "People beg for what Matilda's offering you. They stay and serve long after their contracts are up. Hoping."

"Hoping, hoping, sad, little hoping," Matilda said. "I would have done for one or two of them, too, if they hadn't been such good servants. Do you have any idea how hard it is to find a ladies' maid that knows what she's doing? Georgia Anderson was the legacy to follow." Matilda's curls bounced against her cheeks.

"Finder is no one's maid," Meredith said New Yorker loud from beside me. I stomped on the steel toe of her combat boot. This was *not the time* to stand up for social justice.

"Oh for heaven's sake!" said Matilda. "I AM AWARE. It was a comparison!" Matilda refocused on her target. Finder stood still, breath steady. Fighter mode. The calm before the storm. Matilda didn't seem to notice.

"I don't understand your refusal," the vampire continued. "You'd have health, wealth, eternal beauty, and all the . . . punching bags you could damage. People would do your bidding with a glance. You'd have speed and strength. Did I mention eternal life? As in zero death? And you'd be very rich. Very. Rich. Compounding interest over generations is not to be scoffed at, Miss. I have found ways to give my most loyal servants some longevity of course, but not what I'm offering you." She tapped her lip with one finger, gaze landing on Mama. Oh no, did she smell it?

"I could maybe take your mother into the household if that would make you more willing," she said.

Mama made a comment I will not repeat.

"Oh, ha! Maybe not, then," Matilda said. "Hello Letitia." She waved with a little simper. "Sorry for stealing your husband. Oh wait, no, I'm not. He is adorable. But that's how these things happen, you know?"

Across the grass, Mama seethed. She gripped her torch like setting Matilda on fire would really make her happy.

"I'm offering you the real deal, Miss Jackson," Matilda said, a little wobbly on her feet. Her body lacked its usual slithery grace. "Power. So much power. Power greater, even, than your father's over time."

"What's that?" Darcy Jackson said.

"Never mind, dear."

It was time to make my big move. Tell her I controlled her blood. I took a breath to speak.

"*I'll* take it," Meredith stepped out from behind me. "I'll take your offer." Finder, Tully and I stood stunned.

"No!" I said. "I've got this under control!" I grabbed her arm. She pinched me so hard I yiped.

"Ow!"

Oh. No. What was she doing? Mer shot me a split second eyebrow raise I knew too well. Much too well. She had concocted a scheme without me and this was act one.

"Meredith!" I said, panic flooding through me. "Stop!"

"And who is this lovely bud of womanhood?" Matilda asked.

"None of your business," I said, stepping in front of Mer. "Are you brainwashing her?"

Meredith cleared her throat. Our old signal for me to let her work. But Matilda was not a typical adult Mer was trying to snow or charm into something. Matilda was dangerous. And this time, *I* was the one with the plan.

"You are so strong and powerful," Meredith purred, her gaze low on Matilda's bosom. "Why do you care about these pathetic humans? What can they possibly offer you that you don't already have?"

Matilda took a long sniff, as if Meredith wore the finest perfume.

"Oh, you are delightful," Matilda said. "At last, someone who has also attended 'seduction school'. But, it's a holiday, sweeting, and I never reveal my secret motivations on holidays." Matilda put her hand over her heart. "Ripe for plucking though you are, whoever you are, this isn't an open offer. I am the queen on this chess board and the only reason I'd accept another woman standing by me is because my sweet Darcy so desperately wants her." Matilda looked Meredith up and down, too slowly. Meredith saw it, and did this thing where she moved her hips so the cut of her shirt immediately became more alluring. She'd tried to teach me to do it but it was incomprehensible in my scrawny body. She did it a second time and Matilda licked her chops.

I gripped my cross in one hand and holy water spray in the other.

"Why bother with someone so resistant?" Mer asked, voice soft. "She'll never respect you. She'll always hate you for forcing her into something she doesn't want and then one day she'll betray you to your death. She's a terrible investment. The worst." Meredith made a face. "I, on the other hand, I'm ready. Willing. My blood is hot under my skin . . ." Meredith ran her hand along her neck. Tully and Mama both looked at me. This was not part of the plan. I gave them our hand signal for 'wait'. I'd give her five more seconds to do whatever she was doing, then it was back to the back rank for her.

Matilda reached out to stroke Meredith's face.

"No!" I said. I yanked Meredith's arm and shoved her behind me.

"No!" the vampire mocked. She turned on me. I felt her energy move like she'd shoved me. "I convinced the wrong girl. I'm too stupid to convince the right one. I *told* you to bring Layla Jackson *willing!*"

Matilda lunged forward, fast, too fast. Finder jumped aside. Matilda's fingers just missed grasping the front of her shirt. Finder drew her katana and stepped in to swing. Darcy and Mr. Lorne grabbed Matilda's arms, jerking her back out of Finder's range. The katana whizzed by the vampire boss' nose.

Snarling, Matilda pulled against their straining arms. Straining. Those two big fighter guys were *straining* to hold tiny Matilda back. Oh dear.

Darcy shouted, "Terrence! Now!" A flash of horror crossed the bald vampire's face. Terrence shot me a look, a look filled with hate and blame.

"Do it!" shouted Darcy. Terrence looked back and forth between me and Darcy Jackson calling his shots. "Hurry!" The bald vampire narrowed his eyes as if this was all my fault. He shoved up his sleeve.

Wait. Was Darcy Jackson blackmailing Terrence, too? Finder's dad grinned at me. A grin showing fang. He knew. He knew I had manipulated Terrence. Somehow, he had figured out how to use that as leverage to his own ends. What ends those were, I did not know.

Terrence, still glaring hatred at me, brought his arm to his mouth. Fangs gleaming in the moonlight, the vampire ripped open his own wrist. The meat was like undercooked chicken, damp and slightly bloody. Matilda closed on the gash like a viper.

Meredith gasped as I pulled her back and away. Terrence groaned as Matilda sucked what little moisture he had. She bit and spat out a hunk of grey meat. It looked like every pop of moisture had been sucked out. Arms still anchored by her henchmen, she stripped the flesh from Terrence's arm with her bite alone, spitting out chunk after bloodless chunk as she scavenged for drink. Her teeth clicked against something hard. Bone. Terrence grunted and fell to his knees, out of Matilda's reach. His face was turned away from where she'd savaged his arm.

Matilda shrieked, yanking her arms out of her captors' grips. She flung herself on Terrence knocking him to the ground. Her claw-like hands dug into his flesh as her mouth closed on his throat. Darcy Jackson grabbed for her, but her fist shot out and slammed into his knee. He staggered back.

A ligament audibly snapped in Matilda's teeth. Terrence cried out. Desperation rose on Darcy's face.

"Who has blood, boys?" Darcy shouted, limping. "Who has anything left?" No vampire responded.

Red Goatee Suit's gaze fell on us. "We could get some."

This was not going as I had planned.

Behind me, Meredith clutched my sweatshirt.

Matilda growled, stockings now ripped as she lay half on the ground, ruining Terrence's throat and shoulder.

Red Goatee Suit squared off with Finder on my left. Again, the click of fang on bone from Matilda and Terrence. Matilda dug deeper looking for blood that wasn't there. Nick shuddered, gripping one of Finder's new silver knives. Tully drew stakes on my right. Matilda spat out another mouthful of dead flesh. Terrence's face was a mask of pain. I hated stupid Terrence, but this happening to him was bad. And somehow, I was certain it was my fault, my responsibility.

"Matilda!" I shouted. No response. I had to get her off him. "Matilda!"

"Move, Stacy," Nick said, trying to block me from danger. We cleared Finder room to fight as Red Goatee Suit braced himself to pounce.

"Stay by me!" I said to Meredith. "Prep your sprayer!" What I meant was, prep *my* sprayer. I had given her my one big weapon. Mama and Christopher moved into position to cover Finder. Once Finder was 'safe', I ran toward where Matilda ripped deeper into Terrence. Meredith pumped the action and aimed her sprayer nozzle over my shoulder.

"Go!" I said. Meredith sprayed, soaking the vampires. Their exposed skin sizzled. Terrence screamed. But Matilda didn't stop trying to feed.

Mr. Lorne grabbed for me. I ducked, and when his hand brushed my shirt, a spark flew.

"Ow!"

Thank you, holy water! I thought. Meredith sprayed the huge vampire from over my shoulder. He hissed and backed away.

Red Goatee Suit and Finder circled each other to my left. I had to do something. This was about to become a major melee disaster. All the vampires centered on us. It was time.

"Hey! Hey, Matilda! Hungry?" I said, opening my arms to Mama in the signal we'd planned.

Mama pulled out the football-sized secret weapon. She threw it to Tully. He tossed it to me. It sloshed as I caught it.

I gripped and shook the bag of blood drive blood. Matilda's movement came to a complete stop.

A car length away, Finder and Red Goatee Suit traded blows.

A look of terror crossed Darcy Jackson's face. "No!" he cried. "It's dead! She can't drink it dead!" I shook the bag again. Matilda dove for it. I screamed and threw the bag toward her.

She snapped the bag out of the air like a frog catching a fly.

"Stop her!" Darcy shouted, but even her own Bat Suits backed away to give her space. Strange how suddenly neat she was as she guzzled her proper food, the end of the bag in her mouth, not a drop spilling.

We all stood still, watching as she drank, except Red Goatee Suit bent on settling his score with Finder. He swung, she blocked. He swung again. She kicked him in the chest. As he rebounded, a stake appeared in her hand. The next minute, it protruded from the vampire's chest. He twitched, and fell. Finder yanked her katana out of its sheath. Her cut was clean and fast. Red Goatee Suit's bloodless head rolled away from his body. His eyes blinked once, twice, then went still. Finder stood panting. She had slain her first vampire.

32.

December 31, continued.

A Bat Suit I didn't recognize squared off against Finder who held her blade at the ready. She must've anticipated his inhuman acceleration, because she swung just as he started toward her. Finder beheaded the monster as if it were the easiest thing in the world. His bloodless head rolled to a stop in the short winter grass.

"Two," she shouted, stepping over his body. "Who's three?" Behind her mirrored sunglasses, she faced Mr. Lorne, easily thrice her size. Mr. Lorne stared at the heads on the ground in disbelief. She swung her blade up by her shoulder, ready to strike the much larger monster. She flashed Mr. Lorne her father's smile. The vampire roared.

"Lorne!" Darcy shouted. Was he the general here? "Help Matilda!" Not a request. A command. The boss vampire fed with a focus so intense, she didn't seem aware of Finder's destruction.

Christopher, taking advantage of Mr. Lorne's inaction, ran at him with a stake. Lorne swatted him away with an arm like a baseball bat. Christopher fell back.

Darcy clambered to his feet and launched for Matilda. She raised a hand. Darcy slammed into an invisible barrier.

"Stop her, you fools!" Darcy shouted. "Get the bag away from her!" Not one Bat Suit moved.

Heads lay in the grass. Finder, in full-on warrior mode, stood over them, vigilant as she waited for her next opponent. Darcy Jackson slammed again and again into Matilda's invisible barrier, a bird flying into a window.

"She *feeds* us!" he cried. "If she goes, we all go!" Something crunched as Darcy tried again to break through the unseen wall. When he went for his next leap, one arm hung limp at his side.

"Help!" Darcy shrieked at the Bat Suits. "What's wrong with you?" Darcy shouted. Desperate he turned to his daughter.

"Layla! Help me!" He launched again. Matilda flicked her wrist. Darcy's feet left the ground as he flew backward. He slammed into the stone Carillon.

"Dad!" Finder shouted. She ran toward him. I started to scream 'Stop! What are you doing?' at her but the thick, blond Bat Suit stepped in her way. She swung her katana, but not fast enough. He ducked. Moving in a blur of speed he grabbed her wrists. She rammed her knee up into his groin. The vampire's eyes went wide as he crumpled and let go. She threw her blade to Tully, just like we'd practiced in the drills, then yanked her other stake from her boot. She slammed it two-handed into the blond Bat Suit's back. He collapsed.

Darcy lay in a heap on the steps at the back of the monument. Finder ran for him.

"Layla, stop!" shouted Mama. Finder did not stop.

In front of us, Matilda tossed the empty blood bag to the ground. She stood up, licked her lips, and kicked the wounded Terrence aside.

Something was wrong. Behind my graying sunglasses, her eyes looked darker, her snarl curled back from long silver fangs and her skin, already pale, had gone chalk white. The blood had not calmed her. She closed her eyes as if listening, then sniffed the air like an animal. The air around her snapped with electricity. Static prickled across my skin.

"What's happening?" Meredith said, almost a whisper in my ear. I shook my head. I didn't know.

Matilda's skin began darkening from white to gray. Luster faded from her shiny hair. Her reddening eyes were losing their intelligence by the second and gaining . . . ferocity. She met my gaze, but made no attempt to mesmerize me. What I saw was worse. A vicious, animal thirst. Matilda shook her head like an animal, a dead animal. And she was hungry.

"Matilda!" Luke cried from the far edge of our perimeter. Ignoring him, she stalked toward Tully, Nick, and I. Skin flaked like ash off her face.

Tully leapt forward and thrust his stake into Matilda's chest. Luke screamed, "No!"

Annoyance fluttered across Matilda's face. She reached down and yanked the stake out. She flung it away with a casual toss. Meredith gasped as it embedded itself into a tree trunk.

Mama shouted from the other perimeter. "Zombie!"

Everything started moving very fast. Before I knew it, Christopher was on his feet running toward us with fire. Luke was running from the other side. Tully raised Finder's katana. He was aiming a killing blow for Matilda's throat when Luke jumped in front of him.

Luke flung himself toward Matilda.

Before Tully could react, Matilda dove. She sank her fangs into Luke's throat.

Tully ran behind the vampire and slammed a second stake into her back. Luke moaned as Matilda dropped to her knees, dragging him with her. She shrugged her shoulders to dislodge the stake, but when it stuck, she just kept going, chewing into Luke's neck.

Blood. So much blood.

Matilda did not eat neatly this time. And it was no dead thing she fed on. Luke let out a shriek, a heart-rending cry that made my skin want to shred off my body. I knew that sound. I'd made it myself when a vampire had sucked my soul.

I wrapped my fist around the strongest weapon I had. My mezuzah.

Michael! I shouted in my mind. *What do I do?*

One breath. No reply.

Christopher reached the feeding vampire, torch lit, but it was too late. If we attacked with violent weapons we'd injure or kill Luke. Around us, eight Bat Suits thrummed with desire as the coppery tang of blood filled the air. I didn't have time to wait.

"Tully, move!" I mashed the tiny rod into the back of her neck, the one spot I could reach with the stake sticking out of her back. A thread of smoke rose from pearlescent skin. Her arm shot out and grabbed my ankle. The next second I was on my back in the grass, breath slammed out of my body. The mezuzah had flown. I rolled, like Finder had drilled into me at the dojo. Tully held out his hand. Gasping, I grabbed it, and with one tug, he had me on my feet.

Christopher threw Tully his mallet and Tully swung, pounding the stake deeper. Luke screamed as it exited Matilda's chest and punctured his.

Luke's face was splashed with his own blood. Crushed in Matilda's killing embrace, he met my gaze, blue eyes bright and blind with pain. He had knocked over his king.

"Luke!" I screamed. "Fight!"

He did not fight. He had thrown himself to her on purpose.

I reached for my dinner plate sized crucifix. Finder ran up beside us. "Killing her now?!"

"Yes!" I shouted, slamming my big cross into the back of her head. My arm rang with the shock as the crucifix cracked. It was like hitting a stone. Darcy Jackson hobbled toward us.

"Get her off him!" he screamed. Finder put her hands in the air and Tully threw her blade. In one smooth motion, Finder caught it, then swung the katana down on the back of Matilda's neck with all her might. It sliced through the flesh but bounced, *bounced*, off the bones.

"Ahhgh!" Finder cried staggering back, surprised.

"Again, Layla! Don't let her kill him!"

"Tully!" Finder shouted. As if he could read her mind, Tully ran toward Darcy Jackson. And helped him up. He slid one arm under the vampire, supporting him as he limped toward us from the Carillon.

"Layla!" Darcy screamed again. "Don't let her kill him! If he dies, we all die!"

Did he mean vampires 'we' or all of us 'we'?

She slammed the katana down again. The blade cut through desiccating flesh, but rang as it ricocheted off the bone. Finder's arms quivered with impact.

"She's like steel!" Finder shouted to her dad.

"Strike her head! Make her let go! Strike!"

Finder roundhouse kicked Matilda in the side of the head. The vampire's arm shot out. She grabbed Finder's leg and flipped the girl onto her back, just like she had me. The katana landed in the grass. Finder rolled backwards over her shoulder and came to her feet, landing in a crouch. She grabbed up her weapon.

What was Darcy doing? Was he setting Finder up to get killed, too? Mama waved fire at the Bat Suits near her as Christopher slammed a stake backward into the belly of a Bat Suit who had broken free of his mental paralysis and run up behind him. Christopher turned and drove the stake home.

I was out of weapons. Luke's full sprayer sat on the ground a truck length from the fight. I ran and picked it up. I pumped the action, getting ready. Meredith ran toward Nick.

"Duck!" she cried. He did and she sprayed the Bat Suit about to surprise him. The Bat Suit shrieked and backed up, steam sizzling off his exposed skin.

"I'm almost out!" Mer cried, pumping the action to no avail. Nick snagged the sprayer out of her hands. Christopher pulled a torch out of his coat, lit it, and threw it to Meredith. She missed catching it, but grabbed it up off the ground still lit.

"Cover Mama!" he shouted. Meredith ran toward her.

 J.S. Furlong

Christopher ran forward with his torch. He burned a line across Matilda's shoulders. She screamed and let go of Luke. The second she let go, Nick dove in and dragged the damaged Luke out of the fray.

"Back up, children!" Mama said, coming toward us with more fire. I ran past her and sprayed the Bat Suit coming at her back. Meredith screamed and ran toward it. She shoved her fire into its face, forcing it away from me. The Bat Suit screamed. The pungency of burning hair filled my nose.

Terrence, crawling on the ground, grabbed my ankle.

I sprayed him without thinking.

He screamed as holy water burned him a second time. He shrieked at me, "I'm gonna kill you!"

"Strike, Layla!" Darcy shouted and Finder again leaped into action. She kicked Matilda in the face and this time something was different.

Matilda's forehead had something on it, something small and glowing. The vampire did not retaliate to Finder's blow. She threw herself to the ground and rolled to put out the fire on her back as the mark grew bigger. The stake in her back cracked and broke, splintering into her chest. The mark spread and turned into something geometric. A symbol I didn't recognize flamed bright on Matilda's forehead.

"Back up! Back up!" Darcy shouted. We all stood in a moment of bewilderment as Matilda's forehead seemed to burn with the symbol. She writhed, putting out the last of the fire on her back. Then she let out an ear ripping scream. Her body went limp. The symbol, as if it had never been there, blazed out.

"What in righteous hell was that?" said Finder.

Darcy shouted orders. Four Bat Suits snapped out of their stupor staggering toward their unmoving mistress. Mama faced them with fire. I pumped the action on my sprayer again, holding the nozzle in front of me like a pistol.

"Let them through," said Darcy. "Unless you want her free when she comes to."

Each Bat Suit was tight as a wire, looking longingly, hungrily at Luke, sprawled, bloodied and torn as they held their mistress to the ground. Darcy scowled down at Matilda, whose hair was returning to its normal luster. He yanked the slivers of stake out of her bloody back.

Nick crouched over Luke, pressing his hands to the brutal wound. "He needs an ambulance," Nick said, looking at me. "He's going to bleed to death."

"You can't take this boy to the hospital," Mama said.

"She has to heal him," I gasped, breath coming hard. "Mr. Jackson, make her heal him!"

Matilda's voice rang in the air.

Let me up. I wasn't finished.

"Are you 'you' again, sweeting?" he said.

"Sweeting?" Disdain dripped off Mama's lips. "Disgusting."

Darcy shrugged.

"Make her heal him!" I pointed at Luke.

"Of course," Darcy Jackson said, "for a price." His gaze rested on his daughter.

"No," Finder and I said.

I aimed my holy water at him.

Darcy moved too fast. Tully was on the ground, Darcy's face hovering over his throat before we even knew what happened.

"Then I'll make a better trade."

I didn't think, I sprayed. Mr. Lorne who I hadn't seen get up, grabbed me by the shirt, yanking me off my feet and threw me into the air, away from where father and daughter faced off. Meredith screamed. The sprayer flew out of my hands. I hit the ground with a painful thud. Mama hit Mr. Lorne with a cloud of fire that engulfed his jacket. He flung himself to the ground to put the fire out.

"Let him go, Dad."

"Come and get him."

33.

December 31, continued.

I crawled to my feet, ignoring the bruising from the fall. I got up and picked up my sprayer. I ran as best I could to my friend.

"Back off, Stacy," Finder said quietly. "I got this." She'd just killed her first two vampires. Was her dad next? I didn't have time to wonder. I had to act; help get Darcy Jackson off Tully. Without sacrificing Finder. I stood still. I'd attacked and failed. Time to analyze the board.

Mama and Christopher stood with Meredith, holding their own and facing off with the remaining three Bat Suits. The vampires trembled with tension, ready to strike, but wary of the fire the three humans held. Four Bat Suits anchored the now writhing and moaning Matilda. Terrence lay in grass littered with pieces of his arm. Two Bat Suits were dead, two more lay staked, unmoving on the ground. Mr. Lorne was putting out the fire— wait. Where was Mr. Lorne? Crap. Mr. Lorne was gone. A chill of worry ran up my spine. Gone for reinforcements? There weren't *more* Bat Suits somewhere, were there? My eyes flew frantically around.

Luke was down, Tully was captured. Finder was pinned. Nick was out of direct fire, crouched by Luke.

"I'm not going with you, Dad," Finder said. "And you can't have Tully either."

"Oh, I think I can."

He dipped his head down and bit. Finder charged forward. And there was Mr. Lorne, huge and tank-like, burnt face crusted with black, stepping out from behind Darcy where he had been,

 J.S. Furlong

where? Crouching? He knocked the stake out of Finder's hand. They fought blow for blow for seconds, Finder staying one step ahead of the monster with each strike. Tully moaned and Finder lost a split second of focus. Mr. Lorne grabbed her wrist and spun behind her. He dropped her to her knees with an aikido move she'd tried to show me. One that would break her wrist if she struggled. Finder slammed her head backwards into the Bat Suit's groin. Mr. Lorne howled in rage, then kicked her in the spine. Finder fell forward onto her face, Lorne hunched over her, knee in her back, still gripping her captured wrist.

"Let him go, Dad," Finder said, face pressed into dirt. Darcy continued to feed. He made a satisfied noise of pleasure. Finder shouted, "Let him go, Dad!"

Darcy Jackson was not the eater Matilda was. Tully's blood covered his chin and designer shirt.

"It's been weeks," Darcy slurred, "since we've had a . . . real meal. You have no idea how good this moment is."

Tully panted in the monster's grasp, blood from his torn throat dripping too quickly into the grass.

"Come with me, Layla," said Darcy.

Mama said, "Touch one hair on that child's head, Darcy Jackson and I'll- "

"Quiet," said Darcy. Mama hushed. She must've been looking at his eyes.

"You are my world, Layla. You are the only thing missing from my forever life. Would you deprive your father of his greatest love?"

"He's lying!" Meredith shouted. "If he loved you, he would never ask you for this."

Finder's jaw clenched. Her dad disappeared when she was nine. My guess was Finder had waited years to hear Darcy Jackson tell her he loved her. Could this be the tipping point?

Darcy leaned down and drank another long draught. Tully moaned.

"Tell her to say yes," Darcy said to Tully. "You know she'll do anything for you. Then, your blood, your soul can be her first. Kind of fitting, don't you thi- ?"

Darcy looked up in astonishment as Mama and Meredith let out battle cries. They lunged, swinging fire at the Bat Suits closest to them. The monsters shrieked and backed away. While Darcy had been talking, Mama, Christopher and Meredith had angled themselves between Finder and the last of the standing vampires. Now, Christopher bolted toward his uncle with stakes in his hands. Mama covered him with bursts of fire. Meredith waved her torch to discourage any Bat Suits from going near Mama.

Mr. Lorne leapt off Finder, a blur of speed. He slammed his arm down on Meredith's wrist and she dropped her torch. He snatched her off the ground, but weakened from his own lack of fuel, stumbled and fell. Dragging her with him, he tore into her throat.

"No!" I screamed and ran toward them. Meredith fought, screaming and kicking as hard as she could. I heard something crunch in his face as she backhanded him with her fist.

As if Mr. Lorne's feeding unleashed a wave, the other Bat Suits lunged.

The next sixty seconds were a melee blur. A Bat Suit grabbed Mama from behind. She flung her torch at him but missed. Finder got up and bolted to save her mom.

I slammed my remaining cross into Mr. Lorne's head until his hair started to smoke from being touched by the holy symbol. I snatched up Meredith's torch from the ground. Out of the corner of my eye, I saw Nick lunge with his stake, but too late. One of the monsters holding down Matilda leaped forward and body slammed him to the ground. The monster bit, then shrieked and let go, shaking his head to get Nick's blood out of his mouth. Nick grabbed his stake and rammed it into the Bat Suit's chest.

I lit Mr. Lorne's hair on fire. He dropped Meredith and beat the flames out with his hands. I helped her up and pushed her toward Mama, who, rescued by her daughter, thrust a stake into Meredith's hands. I backed away from the massive vampire waving my fire. Finder had run back to Tully and was helping him to his feet.

Christopher fought Darcy Jackson, trained fighters, strong and vicious. Darcy dove to bite, but the metal gorget around Christopher's throat prevented him. A Bat Suit ran up behind Christopher. Christopher slammed a stake backward into its thigh. He spun and drove a second spike into its chest. The vampire folded and fell. Christopher grabbed another stake out of his coat.

Darcy looked up and met Christopher's eyes.

"Stop."

Christopher did. But not before he let that stake fly.

Finder caught it. She slammed the stake into her father's back.

Matilda made a snarling, angry sound. The last two Bat Suits anchoring her let go and backed off.

The vampire boss, glittery dress ruined, hair a mess, skin growing slowly back, crawled to her hands and knees.

This was not at all how I'd thought tonight would go down.

I stood over the bedraggled Matilda.

"I'll make you a deal," I said, catching my breath. I held the torch defensively between us. I spoke slowly. "You leave us alone, and by us, I mean every single person here, and their families and friends for all foreseeable generations, and I will let you have your blood back. How does that sound?"

Matilda, glittery, bloody and filthy knelt in the grass. Suddenly, she got very, very still. I said nothing as the vampire put the pieces together in her mind.

"This starvation diet we've been on? This is *your* doing?"

"Mine," I said. "Yes."

Her voice floated in the air like it had that night at Maymont.

I am going to kill you until you are truly dead.

"You are going to instruct all of your butlers to heal who they bit. *You* are going to heal who you bit." My glance shot to Tully, standing again beside Finder, pressing his hand to his wound. "You are going to inform your chief butler and minion, Mr. Darcy Jackson, that his daughter and all of her friends, family members and the generations that follow them are, from this moment forward, completely and entirely off limits. No spying, no attacking and no," I thought of Darcy sitting at my pool earlier tonight, "*visiting.* You are going to admit that your butlers dying two months ago was your own fault. You started that fight and nobody owes you replacements for what got ruined." I took a big breath.

"I am going to kill you," Matilda said out loud.

"Maybe," I said, "but not before you sign this. In blood." I pulled a folded page out of my pocket and read it to her. In its entirety.

"Or what? You'll sue me? Little lawyer's daughter?"

"No. A law suit won't hurt you at all. I plan to make absolutely certain that, Not. One. Drop of clean blood finds its way between your lips ever again. And if you come near my home, or my family, or my bedroom a second time, I will do so much worse than leave a pile of dead birds in your bathroom."

Matilda snorted in derision.

"A second time? As if there's been a first. Believe me, dear, if Mother Matilda had been in your *bedroom*, you would know."

"Did you have one of your butlers deliver the birds?"

"What birds?"

"The ones you killed and left on my bathroom rug."

Matilda's face wrinkled in disgust.

"I don't kill *birds*. And alive or dead, I would never allow them in the house. They have parasites."

"The thousand birds at my temple? And the ones you left at my home? Those weren't dead? If they killed themselves at your bidding, it's still you killing them!"

"That's disgusting. And beneath me. If I'm going to terrorize you, precious pumpkin, you will know." She leaned forward and whispered, "Because you will be screaming for me to keep going."

I shivered.

"Liar."

Matilda slapped me so hard I almost fell.

My ears rang. A drip of blood went into my mouth from where my teeth split the inside of my cheek. I got my balance back and looked Matilda dead in the face.

"I am many things," Matilda said, "but a *liar* is *not* one of them."

"The birds weren't you?"

"I don't answer the same question twice."

"Good. Then you agree to the terms of this contract? You agree to leave the people I mentioned alone and I agree not to interfere with your blood supply?"

"I don't think you can keep me from clean blood for very long," she said, tapping a not fully fleshed finger against her lips.

Meredith's voice came strong from behind me. "Do you want to find out? Is giving your butler a pet he will love more than you, *worth* finding out?"

"Where did you find her?" Matilda asked. "I kind of want one. And, how *did* you work your pestilence with my blood supply, by the way? I'm curious."

"I never reveal my secrets on holidays," I said.

Luke's blood must have made Matilda feel better. She gave me a bona fide eye roll.

I rattled the paper I held in my hands.

Matilda bit her finger and put her blood on the contract.

"Now you," she said. I dipped my finger in the blood from my split cheek. I put out my hand. I felt her raw bones as we shook.

"I believe you," I said. "I believe you didn't send the birds." I took a big breath. "I believe you wouldn't invade my private space, because you would never want me to invade yours." I paused. "The paintings that look like windows around the swan bed are so beautiful."

Tuesday, January 1, 2002.
1:16 a.m.

Finder's living room was a mess of weapons, sleeping bags and first-aid supplies. Seven vampires were dead. Matilda had signed my contract and Finder was free. We had won.

Tully and Finder sat on the couch cleaning the blades, Meredith funneled the remaining holy water from the sprayers into smaller bottles for 'individual' use. Christopher was taking the last turn in the bathroom to clean up and change while I stood in the kitchen scrubbing off all the stakes that had made it home. Mama answered the phone when it rang. Everyone looked up. We all stayed quiet through the long pause of her listening.

"I can't, baby, I am sorry. I had to call in all my favors to get the one. No. Of course they won't look for low blood with no wound." She paused. "Do you want to talk to her?" She handed the phone to me.

Nick sounded as weary as I'd ever heard him.

"He's unconscious," he said. "Not a coma, but pretty bad. They aren't admitting him until they can find cause. The ER is full of people with alcohol poisoning and drunk people with injuries so since he has pretty regular vitals they aren't making him a priority. I couldn't force them to give him a transfusion. My handy medical student credentials don't weigh much in a real hospital." He sighed in frustration. "What was that stunt tonight? Does he value his life at all?" Nick's voice had a dark timbre I'd never heard before. "And why, after that obvious stupidity, do I feel compelled to save him? I hate having friends that make bad decisions. And now I have to find a way to convince the doctors that Luke needs blood. A lot of blood. And then have them not ask questions."

We were quiet for a long time.

I looked at Finder after Nick hung up. She must've seen the loss in my eyes.

"We'll go with you," she said. "Weapons are clean and ready. Right, Tul?"

34.

January 1, continued.

I pushed my key into Terrence's apartment's lock.

"Did we know she had that?" Nick said.

"She didn't tell us," Tully said. I jiggled the key. It didn't want to turn.

"Want me to try?" Nick said.

"She made it at the hardware store the night we kidnapped him," Finder said. "On my advice."

"It wasn't kidnapping," I said still struggling with the key. "It was negotiating." Meredith pushed me out of the way. She leaned into the door and pulled the key out just a bit like my finicky apartment key at home. Pop. The lock turned.

"I let you leave and now you can't even turn a key? Oy."

"Terrence?" I said as I opened the door. A whiff of dirty toilet brushed my nose. "Are you home?"

"Somebody with fangs is home," Finder said. She shook her shoulders like a spider crawled between them.

"And is intentionally not answering the door," Terrence said. He sat on his couch, back to us, in a sweatshirt watching silent TV with subtitles in the dark. "Maybe I was ignoring you or hoping you'd get caught by my neighbors or spontaneously combust from my outright hatred. Or would maybe just go away."

"We need your help."

"Drop dead."

His bandaged arm laid over the back of the couch like a chicken bone wrapped in tin foil, not a whole piece of meat.

Matilda must have given him some blood at least. He seemed much calmer than before.

"One of our friends is- "

"I don't care. I hate your guts. Go away."

"He's at the hos- "

"Eat dirt and die. I am never helping you again."

"I'll give you the camera with the photos on it."

Terrence turned to look at us over his shoulder.

"I can smell when you're lying, you know. You plan to give me a fake camera and keep the real one."

Crap. True.

"Now get out of my apartment before I call my friends over."

I glanced at Finder. She closed her eyes and took a breath, *finding.*

"Sorry son," she said. "You're the only one home."

"You're bad for security, Miss *Finder.* Your father got his way because putting you in the blender lets Matilda plug the security leak, and keep her secret."

"The blender?"

"It's how it feels when we get made. Like your insides and outsides are getting all blendered up together."

"I would not expect that," Meredith said, tapping her chin like she was considering. "Does it hurt when you're hungry?"

"Not a good time for research," Finder said.

"Listen, Terrence," I began again.

"Stop using my name like I'm your friend!" he shouted. "I *hate* you! Is it not clear that the minute she gives permission to kill you, I am first in line?" He turned off the TV throwing us into pitch black. Someone hit the switch on the wall and blue light shone into the apartment's tiny foyer. I jumped. The vampire was on his feet a foot in front of my face. I stepped back without thinking. We all did. I held up my holy water spray in front of me. Terrence knocked it out of my hand. It bounced against my thigh on its elastic tether. Finder and Tully had stakes in their hands. Blue light gleamed off Terrence's skull.

"You'll get a lot of blood if you help us. Fresh blood. Enough to heal that arm."

"You're lying."

"She's not," Finder said. "I swear on my dad's bank account."

"I need you to brainwash the people at the hospital so we can get the guy who saved your life some blood."

"And how does this help me?"

"I told you! You'll get to feed. Heal your arm."

He stuck his nose in the air, like an animal sniffing.

"Do I get to drink from you?"

"No," Nick said fast. "Luke is my friend. You can drink from me."

In the blue light, something on the couch caught my eye. A shoe. A woman's shoe. I grabbed my spray bottle and sprayed Terrence's bad arm and he backed up. "Ow! What the — ?" I shoved past him.

Sprawled across his couch lay the desk attendant. Her eyes were open and unseeing, her throat pristine.

"I clean up after myself," he said. I wanted to scream, to call the police, to do something. But this must be how it was here. Someone had to be the emergency food source.

My friends saw what I saw just a moment later. Meredith stifled a scream. Nick gasped. The others were still. The toilet smell was stronger over here. A puppy puddle pad lay on his couch under his victim. I'd never seen a dead body before, but this, I was certain, was it.

"Stake him," I said. But Terrence leaped up, clinging to his ceiling just out of our reach.

"Oh no!" he said. "No more staking. If you want me to help you, you have to treat me nice."

"How about we treat you like you treated her?" Finder said, looking like she wished she could leap right up onto that ceiling beside him.

"I'm not arguing ethics with you, human," he said. "I am what I am which is why you are here, asking for my help. Your little friend is going to die unless I come help you. And I say no. Unless I get to drink from her." He looked at me.

How had I gotten into this? Luke wasn't really even my friend.

"You get to drink from me," Nick said.

"No."

"I'll give you your credit card back."

"Already cancelled it. Don't care."

"And your keys."

"Also easy to fix."

"You can call on me whenever you want," Nick said. "I'll feed you willingly. Whenever you call. Our little secret."

"Getting warmer," Terrence said.

"You'll never hear from us or see us again," I said.

"That is tempting," he said, "but no."

"I'll feed you," I said. "Blood only. No soul."

"Warmer," he said.

I didn't want Nick's friend to die. Even if he had tried to save Matilda.

"Whenever you want," I said, voice low.

"Sold!"

Terrence jumped down from the ceiling. Finder gripped her stake. "Do it," he said opening his arms. "G'head. I dare you. Stake me and see just how fast she comes for you after that little paper signing business. You'll be in Daddy's arms within the hour."

Luke Stupid Whitehall. He was gonna owe me for this.

4:12 a.m.

"Does it hurt when you volunteer or is it different?" Meredith said as I turned on my shower.

"Did it look like it hurt?" I had used every ounce of will power I had not to cry. The second his fangs sank into my wrist, I thought I was gonna throw up. Tully practically had to hold Nick down, he was so freaked out having Terrence bite me. The nausea was overwhelming, the pain of the cuts and, the shock of blood flowing out of my body just stinking *hurt*. But we'd been in a hospital. Nobody thought twice about a sprinkle of blood on the floor. Plus, if something had gone badly wrong, we would have pulled a Luke, and given me a transfusion, too.

Everyone had objected to me being the snack pack, but Terrence wouldn't help us any other way. I seriously thought about letting Luke die. But what would happen to his dog if we ever found him? He couldn't be left with Luke's horrible wife. Still, I wasn't happy about this. I didn't feel noble or helpful or like saving his vampire-loving life was worth it. I just felt mad. But I couldn't not save him, either.

Ugh. I hated stupid saving.

"Can we talk after my shower?" I said.

"I'm going downstairs for snacks," she said.

"Will you check on Steve when you come back up? He's worried because he hasn't seen Evia since we let her go before Christmas and Mrs. Macy got him all upset about it again at the party. I want to make sure he finally fell asleep."

"He can come sleep with us."

"I told him that, but he wants to be at his own window in case Evia shows up."

Ten minutes later, I had scrubbed the green crust off my arm, washed my hair, and made it so I no longer smelled like blood, death and hospitals. I put on my comfiest pajamas.

Meredith was propped on my bed with a bowl of ice cream in her lap talking on the phone. As one does at four in the morning.

"Oh no, they didn't even notice," she said. "We had permission to be out and we were together, they knew where we were, or so they thought and they didn't expect us back 'til super late anywho. All the 'rents were sound as- oh, here. She's out of the shower now." She handed me the phone.

"Are you okay? Do you want me to come over?" Nick's warm voice came over the line. He sounded so concerned, so comforting. I wanted nothing more than for him to come over.

"Yes, but it's the middle of the night. Mer's with me. I'm okay. Not happy about how it all went down, but we did win. Luke is okay?"

"Yep. I just got him home and all tucked in. You'd never know anything other than a solid New Year's Eve party had happened to him."

"That's unfair."

"I'm pretty upset that this vampire has access to you now, Stacy. It was a bad deal to make. You should've let me take it."

"None of us should have to take it. I made a bad aggressive move, I know. But it was the only one he would accept."

"We'll figure a way out of it. I don't have a good idea yet, but it'll come. We can't let this cost you, cost us, the game."

The game, meaning my life.

Meredith, I would totally die for and not think twice about it. Steve, absolutely. Nick, Tully and Finder, I'd think for a second, but I'd still do it. But Luke? I barely knew Luke. And after tonight, what I knew of him, I didn't really like. I had made a bad deal. And it *was* going to cost me.

An hour later, despite being exhausted, and dawn being right around the corner, we still couldn't relax enough to sleep. Meredith rolled over in my bed and propped her head up on her arm.

"Can I tell you something secret?"

"And I never shall repeat it."

This was a ritual we'd used since fourth grade. It was our equivalent of a secret telling pinky promise. Meredith sighed and pressed her lips together.

"I think I maybe hate Finder. Is that okay? I mean I don't *hate* her hate her. I just feel intimidated. Like, she's a badass fighter and oh my god have you ever seen a woman so bloody gorgeous? And she has psychic super powers that let her find vampires because her dad is one and she has the second cutest boyfriend in the history of earth, yours being first. Feel free to loan Nick to me, by the way." Meredith was curled up, her feet poking the side of my thigh like when we were little. "I will tell you he has a major character flaw that could cause problems. Are you aware?"

"I don't know. What do you mean?"

"I mean his rescuer complex. It's super common. They mean well, don't get me wrong, but rescuers are a hard sell at the end of the day. Their success is dependent on you being helpless. Or on somebody being helpless. I'm just sayin'. I still want to scoop him up and roll him around in a very naughty way, mind you. Is it wrong to have a crush on your best friend's hot Goth boyfriend? And Finder's cousin? Whoo-hoo! Too bad he plays for the other team because that man is *pie on a plate.* Smokin' HOT. What's with Richmond being full of scrumptious guys? You totally lucked out coming here for your prime dating years. I mean for *real.*"

She sat up and reached for her bottle of water.

"Anyway, I feel super flat and plain and boring. And like over time you might decide to love Miss Cool Nickname Finder more than me and so. I hate her. Did I mention how I feel lame and boring?" I took a breath to speak. "And don't tell me I'm not lame and boring in comparison because it will not make me feel better."

"Meredith. I love you more than any other human on earth, maybe even more than the ones I am related to, so shut up."

"You don't love me more than Steve."

"I've known you longer. We've known him the exact same amount of time because you were with me when I went to the hospital to meet him. You love the little muppet as much as I do."

"Oh, you're probably right." She sighed. "Steve is my little Brain Nugget."

The candlelight flickered on the walls. Outside my window, a thin film of grey had begun to filter the darkness.

"I'm totally breaking down without you at home," she said. "Just so you know, being with you now, it's partly like heaven and partly like hell because I know that when I leave, that hole of missing you is going to open back up in my chest. Just like when Matilda yanked the stake out of herself. I can't believe . . . It's totally out of this world. And seeing it for myself? Whoa. You living here without me is totally unfair. Maybe I can come live with you next year. Do you think we could talk my dad into it? My mom would be like, boarding school? Yay! But Dad would take some convincing." She took the final swig of her water and recapped the bottle. "Without me, no one would eat his challah."

I rolled to face her. "Are you serious? You would leave home and come here? To BFE Virginia?"

"It's like a horror movie or seeing sex on TV. You can't unsee that stuff once it's in your eye. Books you filter; like your imagination only translates the words into images it can handle, but seeing something for yourself with your actual eyes? It's a whole 'nother ball game. Besides, you need me."

She wasn't wrong. I needed Meredith like I needed food and water. I'd been starving without her and for the first time since we came to Virginia, I felt full. We were quiet for a few minutes.

"I'm not sure how to feel about my vacation home not even having the spa open during my visit," she said sighing and leaning back against the headboard. She stretched her legs out in front of her. "And no fireplaces in the bedrooms."

"You liked the Jacuzzi tub," I said.

"Yeah. That and the contents of the industrial-sized freezer are the only things keeping me sane right now. I'm losing my mind trying to figure out a way to get you out of being Terrance's snack shop. I can't believe you agreed to that. You don't even like Luke!"

"I can't let him die for no reason."

"Yes. Yes, you can. He threw himself at her of his own accord." She tossed her water bottle toward the desk trash. She missed. We each had a candle lit on our bedside tables. Shadows played across our faces.

She turned to look at me. "Vampires are real," she said as if this was the first time she said it out loud and believed it.

"Yup." I remembered that moment of initial belief for me. I had been bleeding at Finder's kitchen table with a gash the size of a credit card in my throat.

"You're a vampire fighter now," she said.

"Yup."

"That's incredible."

"It's something to do," I said.

My victory didn't feel like a win. I hadn't given in to the bully, I *was* the bully, forcing Terrence to help us. And he'd forced me right back. Could I blame him? When Terrence bit me tonight, I'd felt helpless. I had agreed to be his victim. *Agreed* to it. And it felt awful. It felt like I'd surrendered to Joseph Thornton when he bullied me at Nationals. My not-a-victim epiphany the night I kissed Nick on the rock by the river had evaporated and tonight's events shoved me right back where I'd been before. Only worse.

I snuggled up next to Mer like I had the night the Towers fell. She wrapped her arms around me and poked the ticklish spot in my ribs. But it didn't tickle. It made me sad. I felt like I'd thrown the game.

35.

January 1, continued.

Our dads huddled over the newspaper, my dad in his chair, Saul, a.k.a. Dr. K., standing behind him reading over his shoulder, cup of coffee in hand.

"Good morning, girls," said Meredith's mom. "How was the teenager New Year's Eve Party? Did you have fun?"

She sat across from Jill, delicate and thin, like you'd imagine an editor at a high fashion magazine would be. She'd pulled her mahogany hair back in a graceful twist.

"It was exhausting," Meredith said. "We went to the Carillon park and partied with the local vampires. Finder's mom carried a flame thrower. It was a lot more than I expected."

I froze in shock. What was she doing? Her mother sighed and fanned herself with a napkin.

"Can you even imagine what it's like living with this child?" she said to Jill. "Imagination everything. Honestly, Meredith. Why can't you give me a straight answer about your night?"

Mer draped an arm around her dad's shoulders. "I tell them the truth about everything," she said to me. "Is it my fault they don't believe me?"

"I like your outfit, Mrs. K.," I said.

"Thank you, Stacy," she said. "Halston."

"Impressive," I said, no idea what Halston was.

"It's from the '98 collection, but it's so comfortable I can't resist it. Especially when I'm going to be in a car for six hours."

"Totally understand," I said. "I feel the same way about sweatpants."

Helen rolled her eyes and turned to Jill. "Will we never get through to them?" she said. "Just teenagers in ratty black, black, black. Like a vagabond funeral." The last of the bagels and whitefish Meredith's family had brought from the City were spread out on the counter next to a pile of clean plates and utensils. The lox were long gone. A tray of cut up fruit sat in the table's center.

I beelined for the coffee.

"No ma'am," said Saul as I reached for the carafe. "It'll stunt your growth."

"Too late," Meredith said.

"No, Stacy. Seriously. Caffeine is an addictive drug," he said and sipped. "It's bad for you in a whole host of ways. Do you want me to put my doctor hat on and get started?"

"No thanks," I said, moving away from the pot.

"Hot chocolate?" I asked Mer. Yes, there was still caffeine in chocolate, but not nearly so much.

Jill made good coffee, but not great, so I wasn't missing much. Her water temperature was wrong to steep the beans without over triggering the ph to make the coffee bitter.

Steve barreled around the corner, practically skidding on one heel like a cartoon.

"She's here!" he said. "Evia! She's on the back deck eating seeds!"

He ran past us down the stars to the rec room.

"You should see this," Jill said to Helen. "He's tamed this little squirrel into a pet . . ." Jill led Helen downstairs behind Steve to show off her son's newfound connection to nature.

Meredith and I prepped our bagels and sat down to eat.

"It's unbelievable, right?" my dad said. "Bones stripped completely clean."

Meredith's bagel froze in her hand. I shoved back my chair and went to look over Dad's shoulder. A grisly murder, twin to the one from last month, had made the front page.

The photos matched what Matilda had done to Terrence except so much worse. A whole body had been stripped. Mer raised her eyebrows. Yes, Captain Obvious, I thought. I see the similarity.

"What do they think's doing it?"

"Bear's the best guess so far. What else would be strong enough? A pack of wildcats maybe."

My BFF put down her bagel and came over.

"Same exact thing last month. They were talking about it at work. The boss said wolves, but everyone said Richmond doesn't have them. Coyotes maybe."

Mer scrunched her lips together and raised both eyebrows.

Right. I know.

I read over Dad's shoulder. The first murder had been a retired Navy captain in his sixties, Maxwell Haltrop, and this one was a young marketing exec in her twenties, April Martinez. Max and April. Where had I heard those names recently? Had we been introduced last night?

Meredith came back to our spot and bumped my arm, more aggressively this time, eyes wide. I gave her a look that kept her mouth shut.

"Does it give an estimated time of death?" I asked. Would Matilda have done this before or after she'd gotten dressed for her party? Before or after she'd seen us?

"Says here, the remains were found yesterday morning on a trail near the river. Like last time. And they were fresh, so the attack was probably late Sunday or in the early hours of Monday morning."

If Terrence had passed out from pain, a vampire who had tolerated having a stake buried in his chest for hours, this seemed like a horrible end. I had the sinking, awful feeling this death was my fault.

Heavy northbound traffic on Interstate 95 bought Mer and I another hour of time together. We peeked in on Steve and Evia sitting together on the back deck, him feeding her seeds out of his hands. Then we went up to my room and closed the door.

Meredith grabbed my notebook.

"Max and April are the names Mrs. Macy used on the phone," she said, finding the page where she had written down everything I had told them from the call.

"If Matilda's killing werewolves, it's none of my business."

"But Mrs. Macy said 'he', like she knew who was doing it," said Mer.

"Bat Suits are all male. Could be any one of them."

Could the murderer be a vampire? Was this the result of me having poisoned their blood? But what would that have to do with Mrs. Macy and werewolves? Ugh. TMI. It was like when your hypothesis was too vague, and you could insert any circumstances to have the experiment turn out right. So, so frustrating.

At least when the vampires fed normally, meaning when they hadn't been starved, they left their victims alive, minds wiped of any memories. Except the ones they enslaved. But then I thought about the soul sucking. The soul sucking was brutal. And it really, really hurt.

I hadn't told Meredith much about the soul sucking part. To be honest it was hard to explain. And I didn't want her to know that the part of me that had been sucked away was her part. And I'm not sure it had all been returned. There were memories, things about her that I used to know that I had to reach for now. Images like dishrags worn too thin. The saturation was gone, they were delicate and fragile as if I could rip them or shred them with a touch and then they would dissolve for good. So I didn't reach.

I held out my hand for the notebook.

Meredith passed it over.

"These murders are not your problem," she said. "Are you listening to me? You are not the vampire police. You're a math nerd from Battery Park City who can let Finder and her hot cousin and big, brawny boyfriend be the vampire police. But not you. I am not willing to risk you getting eaten by one of these things. It's not just about you, woman. It's about me. What would I do if you died? Seriously. What would I do?" Meredith finished her performance by flinging herself onto my bed. Not that every word wasn't sincere, it totally was. It was also hard-boiled melodrama in true Mer style.

"Do you trust Darcy Jackson to leave her alone for real?" she said after a few minutes.

I shrugged. "No, but I think he'll back off if Matilda makes him."

"What's he doing with her, anyway?" Meredith said. "He's clearly still in love with his wife."

"He is?"

"Woman, do you not have eyes? The way he looked at her! Her and Finder. He is completely devoted to them. I'd love to know how her royal fangness got her claws sunk in him so deep."

"He ripped Mrs. Jackson's leg off at the knee," I said. "That's not love."

"He was *starving*. After what we saw, that is obvious. Bat Witch was probably doing blood deprivation to torture him or get him to swear his loyalty to her or something."

"How do you see these things?" I asked. I had seen none of that.

"I am an actress," she said in a theatrical voice. "I observe, translate and interpret human behavior." She lay sprawled, gazing at the ceiling.

I was a scientist. I selected, evaluated and interpreted data. These were two entirely different things. No wonder I had to tell Nick to kiss me.

"What do you think about Nick?" I asked.

"Super adorable," she said. "Smart, considerate, good vibe for sure. And the eyelashes? To die for. Just beware. He totally wants to get in your pants."

"He does not!"

"Oh, he does. Who is the master of human motivation? You or me? Very good, you're right, it's me and I say he wants to play hide the mousey with you for sure. He'll restrain himself, that's clear. I'm just saying, stay alert. That boy, no not really boy, that man, but not really man either, guy? We'll use guy, that guy wants you so bad. It's cute. Seems like he respects you though so that's good. He hasn't tried to grab your boob yet, right?"

"Oh my god, Mer! No!"

"Just checking. If he made it through the long kiss-fest without trying to cop a feel, I think he's worth keeping. For now. We'll see how this goes. For the time being, I give you my blessing and approval."

I picked up the clothes she was supposed to be packing, tossing them at her one garment at a time.

"Thank you oh so much your royal observerness," I said. "Your opinion means everything," I bowed and threw a sock on her chest.

"Well it should," she said. "And I reiterate, I am the best friend. Me, me, me. Not Finder. Forgot thou not the true identity of thy BFF."

"What?"

"Woman. You are so pedestrian."

"Girls! Come here, please!" Meredith's dad called up from downstairs.

"Come on, Dad!" Meredith shouted. "Another hour? Please? I'm not done packing!"

We went into the hall and leaned over the balcony rail.

"How's another night?"

We squealed and leaped into each other's arms.

"I heard," Nick said, leading Mer and I up the cemetery hill. "Tractor trailer overturned, toxic spillage across all lanes. Whole interstate shut both ways. Traffic from Delaware to North Carolina is a mess."

I took a big breath and let out a long sigh. On my left, I held hands with Nick, on my right Mer had my other paw in her grip, squeezing as we rounded every corner.

"I feel like I should intervene," I said. "Like if Matilda is responsible somehow for these people being murdered, I should- "

"Look at that one!" Meredith let go of my hand and ran for a tombstone in the shape of a small girl angel. I had never been to Hollywood Cemetery in daylight. The Goths flanking me were not wrong. It was magic.

"Is this really your favorite place in Richmond?" I said, eyes wandering over the landscape of carved stones and winter brown grass, "or was that just your character?"

"It's in my top three," Nick said. "There are a lot of cool places here, but this one's pretty special. Always something more to notice even when I think I've learned every path."

"It's beautiful." My thoughts were hard to keep on track. "I feel so responsible," I said. "What if those two people died because I was starving the vampires? What if Mrs. Macy dies the same way and it's my fault?"

"Well, you and Matilda made a deal. If the murders were your fault for starving her, and I think they were not because the first one happened long before you blackmailed Terrence, then there won't be any more of them. If she or her Bat Suits are killing for fun, that has nothing to do with you."

"Exactly what I told her," Meredith said, skipping back to join us and scooping up my hand again. "She needs to learn to mind her own business. And if she ever dumps you," Mer made a little angel statue pose, "may I recommend New York City as a great place to look for a replacement."

Nick smiled. "Thanks. I'll file that away."

"He'll put it in the *circular* file, you rotten hussy," I said to Mer.

"What? If you're done with him what's the harm?" She winked at Nick. "I love giving her a hard time. No sense of humor, this one." She poked me in the ribs.

"Seriously guys," I said. "I can't just let her slaughter people. I mean Mrs. Macy knew the name of a victim who hadn't been publicized yet, and expected she'd be next."

Meredith looked past me and her eyes lit up. "Look at that stone!" She bolted past us back down the path to a towering megalith with gargoyles carved on the sides. She put her hands on the name and leaned in to hug the stone. "I love this so much! Dude, please if I die early you have to make sure my parents put gargoyles like this on mine!"

"I am so sorry," I said to Nick. "Duct tape should come with her operating instructions."

Nick stopped and took both my hands. "She loves and misses you. She's your soul sister. You're lucky to have a friend like that. I wish I did."

"'Kay," said Mer, jumping back onto the path with us. "Thanks for hitting pause on that for me. These stones are beyond the beyond. I am in heaven right now, by the way. Now, back to the mystery solving. Why would Mrs. Macy be next?"

"Dunno. It's confusing. All the other shifters we know are kids, and they're all really nice. Mrs. Macy is definitely neither of those. And Steve says the shifter kids smell all, nature-ey."

"Not Mrs. Macy," said Mer. "Steve said she smells like a pile of sh- "

"Rotten fruit and dead things," Nick ran his fingers though his hair, thinking. "That's what he said." Sunlight dappled down from the trees catching the green in his eyes. Sigh.

Mer's black lace fingerless gloves rubbed across my palm. I wore an outfit from her latest delivery of hand me downs.

"It's possible you should just let this one go, Stace," Mer said. "Leave that notebook closed. I mean, what can you do? If it happens again and Matilda is responsible, you've already played the poisoned blood card."

"Meredith has a point," Nick said. "Why don't you just let this lie for now? We have enough trouble with Terrence to manage."

"How do we get her out of that?" Mer said over my head to Nick. "That has me very nervous. What if he drains her all the way?"

"He's not going to drain me," I said. "Why would he? I'm a hunt-free food source available any time. Independent of and potentially endorsable by his hideous boss lady."

"What if you play the poisoned blood card on yourself?" Mer said. "Maybe eat more garlic." I stopped walking.

"Ha!" said Mer. "See that? I got her! Every now and then, right?"

Nick stood at the sink rinsing dishes. I washed down three garlic tablets with a glass of water. Not sure why it hadn't occurred to me to do it all the time, not just for New Year's. Beside Nick, Jill loaded the dishwasher.

"It's just how it was in our house," he continued. "With a single mom, if you ate, you cleaned up."

"It's different now?" Jill asked, taking another dripping salad bowl.

"What do you mean?"

"You used the past tense. Made it sound like you don't live at home anymore."

"Ready for more?" I said, setting another load of plates by the sink.

"Always," Nick said with that smile.

"Does your family live near here?" Jill asked. Ugh. A dog with a bone, she'd worry it until it broke. Nick glanced at me for his cue, I opened my eyes wide and shook my head no very, very slightly.

"This is a beautiful house," Nick said. "You're only the third family to live in it?" Jill shook her head.

"Fourth, I think. The Brentwoods built it in 1925, but only stayed six months before the husband got transferred to Rome for his job."

"Boy, that's too bad!"

"No kidding. I keep asking Mr. Goldman why he can't get a job in Rome. Or Paris. I'd even take Brussels in a pinch. Now where again did you say you live?"

"Well," Nick looked at me, an apology behind his eyes.

Oh doom.

"I live in the Fan."

"Just you and mom?"

He offered her a handful of silverware. She took it. Knives. Terrific.

"No. My mom's home in Florida. I have a roommate." Jill dumped the knives in the utensil basket then wiped her hands on a dishtowel. One hand on the counter and the other on her hip, she looked directly at me.

"I thought you went to school with Stacy."

"We study a lot of the same subjects," he said.

I shot a desperate glance to Mer, theoretically clearing the table, but watching Nick and Jill with interest. I willed her to drop a glass or knock over the centerpiece or something. Help distract Jill!

My BFF missed my cue.

"What school do you go to?" Again, right to me. Slowly, she turned to Nick.

36.

January 1, continued, and very stressful.

My Adorable Goth Boyfriend looked Jill straight in the face and said, as if it might not change everything:

"I go to VCU."

"Virginia Commonwealth *University*? Ernie," Jill said, interrupting a conversation between my father and Meredith's dad, "Did you know Nick is in *college*?"

Shock and anger look pretty much the same on my dad. Furrowed brow, tight jaw, narrowed eyes. Hand it to the attorney, though, he didn't miss a beat. Just sipped his water and said, "A freshman, I presume."

"No, sir." Nick did not even look at me. He was on his own now with, gulp, my father. "I'm in my second year of med school."

Dad barely moved. He nailed Nick with his scary don't-lie-to-your-counsellor stare.

"You mean pre-med?"

"No, sir. I've finished my pre-med. Two more years and I'll be Dr. Nick." He flashed his super Nick rock star smile.

"Pre-med is a regular four-year degree," said Saul. The two dads exchanged a look. Mine sat up straight, set down his glass and put his feet flat on the floor, just like in court. Oh dear.

"I graduated high-school early and finished my first degree in an accelerated two-and-a-half-year program."

Saul laughed out loud. "Good grief, son, what's your I.Q.?"

Nick fingered the dishtowel he'd thrown over one shoulder. "Do you really want to know?"

"If you know it? Absolutely." Saul's bald patch had a pink flush to it. Wearing a somewhat wolfish grin, the doctor looked entirely amused.

"One seventy," Nick said. My jaw dropped. One seventy? *Seventy?*

I might have gasped out loud. One *forty* was MENSA genius level. No wonder Nick didn't talk about his age. He was way ahead of where he should be.

"How old are you, exactly?"

Nick tried to look casual under my father's scrutiny, but I saw him take a steadying breath. The kitchen went very, very quiet.

"I'm twenty, sir."

"Twenty!" Meredith clapped her hand over her mouth.

My jaw fell open just for a second. Holy crap. *Twenty?* Years old? I guessed maybe eighteen. Oh, this was not going to be good.

"Sorry," Mer said, looking at me. "I'm so sorry."

My father sat still absorbing. Jill stood frozen, eyes wide in astonishment. A cold, salty bead ran down my back.

"So you're a twenty-year-old genius, basically," my father said in an accusatory tone, "Yet my *fifteen*-year-old daughter refers to you as her 'boyfriend'."

"I hope so, sir." Absolute deadpan, just the facts from future Dr. Nick.

Meredith's dad covered his mouth with his hand. Under his glowering brow, his shoulders shook. I glared at him. This was not funny!

"And why, precisely, are you interested in Stacy?"

"She's a very unique person, sir, as you know. She's smart, intelligent, personable. Not to mention brave, interesting, and," he paused, "a little bossy."

Dr. K. couldn't take it anymore. He burst out laughing.

"Shut up, Saul," said Dad.

Meredith's dad only laughed harder. Her mom just sat across from her husband looking scandalized.

"I'm going to have to think about whether or not this is okay with me," Dad said.

"I appreciate that, sir. I value how important your approval is to your daughter," Nick folded his hands low in front of him, "but my main concern is that 'this' is okay with Stacy."

My father's turn for a jaw drop.

"She's responsible, she's very considerate of how you feel about what she does, and she makes great decisions. She's also mature enough to make her own choices regarding her friends and, if I do say so myself, I don't think she'll disappoint you."

Never in my life had someone defended me like that, especially to my father.

"Are you implying I don't trust my daughter?" My father shot back. Nick let a slow rock star smile spread from his mouth to his eyes. He liked my dad.

"Not at all, sir. I'm acknowledging what a special and trustworthy person you've raised. I hope you can respect her choices and feelings as much as she respects yours."

My father sat silent. I stared. I had never seen anyone disarm him so entirely. Jill looked from one to the other of them. Her gaze landed on Helen, who gave the tiniest of tiny "glad it's not my daughter," looks. Three long seconds turned into five, six and finally seven. Meredith looked like she was about to speak. I shot her my hardest Don't You Dare look.

"I hope I haven't offended you," Nick said. "Would you like to have a more private conversation?"

"Can I come?" Steve said.

"No," Dad and Jill said at the same time. "Whatever you have to say, you can say in front of everyone," said Dad.

"Very well. It's important to me that Stacy's treated with the utmost respect. I promise you'll never have to come find me for using drugs or alcohol." He paused and looked right into my dad's eyes, "Or anything *else* against the law."

What? Oh no! Did that mean no kissing? A knot of nerves I didn't know had been growing took root in my stomach. I was not okay with no kissing!

Nick smiled at Dad, a small, more private version of his rock star smile. "I'm not interested in keeping secrets from you, sir. I truly enjoy your daughter's company and I trust that nothing I've said or done tonight will harm the progression of our friendship." A question and statement in one.

My father sat for a long minute. He squinted at Nick.

"Ever considered a career in law?"

"No, sir. But I'll take that as a compliment."

"I wouldn't if I were you," Saul said. "They're a dreadful lot."

"Not compared to some people I know." Nick glanced over his shoulder at me and Mer. How true.

On one hand, we now knew his age. That load of bricks crumbled off my legs. On the other hand, had he just promised my father he wouldn't kiss me? That would be horrible. I was okay with some limits beyond kissing, at least for now. But no kissing? Please, please no.

Now, I only hid some other facts from Dad: Shapeshifters and vampires were not fiction. I had vampire hunters as friends. I was becoming one myself. I wondered if Nick could break those tiny little facts to him, too. Okay 2002, I thought. Here we go.

Nick and Meredith and I sat in the rec room sifting through DVDs for a movie to watch.

"If Hollywood Cemetery is number three, what's your number one place?" Mer said. "If it's half as good, we should go there."

"Already arrived," he said gazing down at me. She paused her sorting, drinking us in.

"Aww! Okay, now I'm jealous." She flopped back on the couch. "Cute and sweet. Could you, like, develop a tragic flaw in the next twelve hours so I can go home feeling less inferior about my previous choices in men?"

"I'm a gamer," he said. He ducked behind the bar and opened the mini-fridge.

"Nope. For me that's a plus."

"Peach or Raspberry?" he asked us.

"Peach," said Mer. I gave a thumbs up. The peach was definitely better.

"I have a picture of kittens on my credit card." He set out three iced teas.

"That's adorable. Doesn't count."

He looked at me. "What's my tragic flaw?" I had to think. We'd gotten around his age and the fact that he wasn't Jewish. I looked at his lips and felt longing. I knew exactly what the flaw was.

"I've got it!" Meredith said. "It's the no kissing thing you just promised her dad."

How had she read my mind? Ugh! I felt my face turn hot and red. I shoved a throw pillow at her. "Meredith!"

"No really. We have to talk about this." Behind her, the moon glowed through the glass patio doors like a deep orange pumpkin hanging in the sky. "I have had many boyfriends with many flaws, okay only four boyfriends, and Sam Rittenbacher doesn't count because it was like, less than a week and there was no kissing, but not wanting to kiss me has never been one of their flaws. Dude, you gotta get over that crapola right now. So like I was saying, I'm Stacy's BFF and official fairy godmother and- "

"Guys, look," Nick interrupted, staring past where Meredith sat on the couch. "Seriously. Look." I pushed myself out of the teenager-eating cushions. A massive black animal stood between the woods and the pool house.

"Holy wildlife, Batman! Is that a dog or a coyote?" Meredith went to the doors. "It's like a pony!"

A second later, a white dog, smaller but still probably taller than my hip, emerged from the hill by the river. It moved to stand beside the black dog and stared straight at us.

"Staaaaaaaayceeee!" Steve came tumbling down the stairs in a flurry of cape and slippers. He almost smacked into the glass. The dogs turned and padded off into the woods.

"Werewolves, werewolves, werewolves!" Steve danced back and forth, hopping from one foot to the other.

"Do they smell like Mrs. Macy?" I said.

"No! These ones smell like fire pits and pine trees."

"How do you know you aren't just smelling the fireplace and the pine trees?" Meredith said. Steve gave her a withering look.

"Our fire place is gas. It smells like nothing. And those," he pointed into the yard, "are deciduous hardwoods flanked by cedar trees which smell entirely different from pine."

"This morning when you sat on my lap, I thought maybe I missed you," Meredith said. "I was wrong."

Steve stuck his tongue out at her.

"Well, they're gone now. Should we be concerned or go look for them or anything?" said Mer.

"Yes!" said Steve.

"No," I said. "We have enough weird Richmond problems as it is. There might be nothing unusual about those dogs."

"Could there be good werewolves and bad werewolves?" said Nick. "Hence the scent difference?"

"Whose side are you on? That seems excessive and complicated," I said, searching the dark behind the glass for green glowing eyes. "Nature tends to keep things simple."

"Are these things natural, though?" said Mer.

"Let's let it go for now," Nick said. "At the moment we have no reason to assume anything. Even though I'm pretty sure those were the same dogs I saw at the Carillon last night."

"There were dogs at the Carillon?" I asked. This was news to me.

"Yeah. They watched the whole fight from the shrub line."

"I saw them too," said Mer. "You were busy fighting and feeding blood to Matilda."

"At one point I thought they were going to jump into the fray," said Nick, "but they just left."

"Why didn't you guys say anything?"

"Oh by the way, stray dogs were watching the fight?" Mer said. "Who cares? I mean, now we maybe do, but at the time it didn't seem important."

"I have a better view from my room," Steve said. "I'm going to go keep watch."

"Let us know if you see them again," said Nick. Steve saluted and ran back up the stairs.

"Pick a movie," I said. "My head is going to explode." Nick came and sat beside me on the couch. He opened my tea and handed it to me.

"About the kissing thing," said Mer, fussing with the DVD player. "Let me repeat, I am the fairy godmother and BFF and I give you full permission for kissing. Forget her dad. He's fifty, I'm sixteen. I'm going to live with her longer, and I do not plan to listen to her whine about how when she was just a girl she couldn't get any kissing from her, excuse me, *twenty*-year-old boyfriend. Seriously. My permission is the important one. Next to hers, of course."

"Thank you," Nick said, eyes twinkling. "I accept your permission." He put his arm around me and tapped a small, polite kiss on my cheek. Nick made eye contact with Meredith. "And just so you feel sure, I am fully capable of," he paused, gaze instantly very grown up, "*kissing* . . . your friend." I pressed my lips together, the echo of his touch stirring in me the craving for more.

Meredith stood with her mouth slightly open. "You guys are actually gorgeous together. Like utterly stunning. I can't take it. We're picking a movie now so I can think about something other than kissing."

I squeezed Nick's hand. I was thinking the exact same thing.

"What you said to my dad," I said as I walked Nick to the Hulk. "It doesn't mean we can't *ever* . . . ?"

"I saw in his face what he worried about. Your dad's smart, Stacy. He'd see through me if I danced around it so, I addressed it directly."

I shivered in my coat.

"But now you've promised. Meredith is right. What about if we want to?" I looked up into his eyes catching the moonlight as he turned and leaned against his car.

"It's a little early in the relationship to be negotiating about this."

"We're not negotiating. We're just talking about kissing. I don't think it should be that big a deal."

"I think your dad was talking about more than kissing. Things happen when it's the right time. Hopefully, by whenever that is for us, your father will trust me and we won't have to always look over our shoulders because he thinks I'm a jerk."

I sighed. No argument for that. All the 'right time' talk grated on my nerves. You were a virgin or you weren't and according to all two people I knew who had lost it, the first time was rough no matter whom you were with. I'd prefer it happen with someone I loved and trusted, like Finder and Tully had with each other.

Nick reached down and brushed a stray strand of hair out of my face. His fingers lingered on my cheek.

"Don't get me wrong, Stacy. I want to." He laughed a little. "I'm a guy, I'm twenty, I've wanted to from the start. But that doesn't mean I have to. I think it's too soon. Let's shelve it for now and we'll see what happens later."

37.

The entire rest of uneventful January.

If my life were a movie, this would be the montage, a series of action shots backed by an upbeat sound track condensing a period of growth and development. There would be shots of me building a snowman with Steve, me checking the secret rock for Maymont news and coming up empty. Shots of me and Hank meeting at Chapter & Mercy for chess. Me doing homework on the outdoor bench as Steve pushed human Evia on the swing. Nick and I hanging "Have You Seen This Dog?" signs with Luke, Finder and Tully and I passing notes in class, working out in my home gym and at Flying Eagle. Bolo and Steve becoming friends as big dude helped little dude learn to throw a punch. Tully and I at yoga, Finder and I having post-workout sleepovers and baking. Finder, Tully and I, sometimes with Nick and Luke, sharing meals at Third Rock and coffees at Chapter & Mercy. Me in the lab trying to figure out how to get Judy's hereditary DNA misprints to unpair, one painstaking failure at a time. Fun, but sadly kiss-less dates with Nick, mostly to the movies, long walks at Hollywood, some dinners at a cool Mongolian barbecue near VCU and more often than not, doing homework together at Chapter & Mercy.

Michael the Archangel was absent, Terrence the Archnemesis was uncomfortably present. I read all the vampire books I'd checked out, at least partially, and talked for hours with Meredith on the phone. Someone should invent video calls!

No further updates on Finder and Tully's bedroom life, either. It was a freakishly busy yet uneventful month. Oh, except for the murder. Another human shredded by the mystery critter. I still think it's Matilda, but I can't prove it.

Montage over, it's February 2002, on the first day where hopefully something of interest will happen. The St. Ignatius Preparatory Academy Schoolwide Science Fair.

Wednesday, February 13, 2002.

"I wish they'd do it in rounds. Like in chess," I said.

"Martial arts, too," Finder said. We stood together at the water fountain as the judges deliberated.

"Right? So you could see who got eliminated first and who you're competing with at the end."

"Yeah, sis. I hear that."

"It has to be one of us," I said.

"It does," she said. Sister Mary Chemistry gesticulated in frustration. One of the judges shrugged and they kept talking.

"It's definitely us," Finder said. We sat down together in a cafeteria booth hiding from our partners.

"Have you figured out what Judy's deal is, yet? What her illness is?"

I shook my head. "You and Steve can do what you do 'cuz of your near-death experiences. From what other clues we have, unimaginables have died and come back with extra. That's definitely not her. I'm trying to find a disease that matches the DNA in her body. The only thing that comes close is cancer, but she doesn't have that."

"How do you know?"

"I guess I don't. I've straight up asked her and she won't say yes or no."

"So maybe that's it." Finder touched the silver cross necklace she'd started wearing. "She looks horrible, she won't eat and she misses tons of school. Maybe because of treatment?"

"You'd think she would have told me if she had cancer."

Finder looked toward the judges. They were shuffling the medals and tapping the mic and the lectern.

"Wanna place your bet?"

"No. I might be wrong."

"You're first, I'm second, Ling is third. Five bucks." She stuck our her hand to shake.

"I will not take that bet."

Thursday, February 14, 2002.

Nick rang the doorbell at 6:45. He'd told me to dress up and be sure to have long sleeves. I was wearing another set of Meredith's Goth cast-offs, but tried to make them more upscale looking. Still, this was Nick. He wasn't showing up in a suit.

I opened the door, and there stood Nick, in a suit. It was black, with a black button-down shirt and a red satin tie. He wore tiny silver hoop earrings and had gotten his hair trimmed. He wore no eyeliner and his cheeks were pink from the icy February wind. He gave me a broad, appreciative smile.

"I am here for the St. Ignatius Preparatory Academy First Place Science Fair winner, please," he said and held out his hand. On it rested a wax bag bearing my favorite cookie from Chapter & Mercy, the massive double chocolate with icing.

A freezing gust blew leaves in behind him. "Sorry, come in." I shut the door. "Thank you," I said taking the cookie. My whole family filed out of the kitchen to get a look at the Valentine's couple.

"Hello, Nick," said Dad. "You look very nice."

Understatement. Nick looked amazing.

"Thank you, sir. May I borrow you for a moment in the kitchen?"

"I really like this dress on you Stacy," Jill said, touching my sleeve.

"Thanks," I had my hair down with the sides pulled back out of my face. I had my vampire mini-kit in a chunky black handbag I'd borrowed from Jill along with my wallet, phone, and lip balm.

Steve pulled my skirt. "Is Nick coming over when you baby-sit me tomorrow night? I want to play him."

I shrugged. "Invite him," I said. Of course, I wanted Nick to come over, but I couldn't invite him to be alone with me in the house. That would not go over well. Steve on the other hand, could get away with it. Especially in the name of chess.

"Mommy, can Nick come over when you and Daddy go out to your Valentine's Day tomorrow night? Please please please please please?" He hopped up and down, then butted his head gently in her belly. He hugged her around the waist. "Please please pretty please. I want to play him at chess. Stacy won't let me win and Hank won't let me win and I want to see if I really know how to play or not."

Jill thought about it for a second. I was careful not to make eye contact, instead shrugging into my black wool pea coat.

"Do you want Nick to come over, Stacy?"

"Sure. We can watch movies with Steve after chess."

"He has to go home when Steve goes to bed," she said.

"That's fine," I said.

"Chess and arrows!" Steve said in triumph. The bow and arrow set Steve got for Hanukkah had not worn off as his toy obsession. He pulled my hand to get me to lean down. He whispered in my ear, "Can I please invite Evia?"

"That's a good idea," I said. It would be nice for him to be able to play with her inside the house like real kids for once. And we could catch up on the Maymont news at the same time.

Nick came out of the kitchen with my dad. They both looked like they'd won the exchange.

"Shall we?" Nick said. I smiled and picked up my handbag.

"Home work done?" Dad asked.

"Dad," I said. "Duh."

"Phone charged?"

I opened my bag and pulled it out. He looked at it. Battery full, ringer on.

"Okay," he said. "Have fun, kids." He looked at Nick. "Home by ten, please. It's a school night."

Nick gave him a conspiratorial smile. "Absolutely. See you then."

"Why does my dad look so smug?" I asked, wind whipping under my skirt. Brr. Nick opened the Hulk passenger door for me. A puff of heat came out.

"He's just pleased with himself is all," Nick said. A dozen long stemmed roses sat in my spot. I slid in beside them. Nick had left the car running so it was warm when I got in. The roses made the cab smell like summer. A little wrapped box sat next to them on the wide bench seat. A thrill of excitement ran through me. Was that for me, too?

Nick slid in behind the wheel. He rubbed his hands together.

"Are these for me?" I asked.

Nick smiled. "Do you like them?"

No one had ever given me flowers before, much less a dozen red roses.

"I love them. Thank you," I brought the bouquet to my nose and inhaled. I closed my eyes, breathing in the sweet aroma as we pulled out of my driveway. My first real Valentine's Day date ever.

"Where are we going?"

He turned on Alan Parson's Project. "You'll see."

A half-hour later, we pulled into a driveway that went between a tiny country house and a brick warehouse with a sign: Virginia Archery Center. The parking lot was full of cars. Nick pulled past the main lot and into a smaller, emptier lot around the side of the building. The sign over the door said VCU Archery.

"What's going on?" I had thought we were going out to dinner or maybe to a show or something.

"Just wait," Nick said. "I've got everything covered. Bring your little box." He opened the door for me. My boots crunched on gravel as he led me around to the front doors of the building.

The warehouse was divided into different sections, all filled with people of all ages, shooting bows at targets. Some were in class, some practicing on their own. Nick walked up to the counter. He beckoned to me and I stepped up.

"Sign this," said the guy.

"I have this already for her," Nick handed over a sheet of paper. The guy inspected it and seemed satisfied. "It's your liability waiver," Nick said. "I had to get your dad to sign it."

My dad knew about this? I felt a deep disappointment dragging down my delight in the roses, being dressed up and the secret-destination Valentine's date. Nick's idea of romance was bringing me to archery class? In fancy clothes? Some people turned to stare at us. Self-conscious, I tried to ignore them. I am alive, I am safe. Nothing bad is happening.

A compact woman greeted Nick warmly and shook my hand.

"You look stunning," she said to me with a genuine smile. "Is this your first Valentine's Day together?"

"It is," Nick said, taking my arm and twining it with his. We walked across the archery club to a white door. The woman opened it and Nick stepped aside so I could walk in first. The room was some kind of archery practice room. Right now, it was lit with candles. A table for two was set toward the back. Something smelled fantastic.

"Enjoy your meal," she said with a twinkle in her eye. "I'll come for your lesson after dinner."

The woman shut the door behind us.

"Welcome to Chez Ar-cherie," Nick said with a fake French accent, "My name is Nicholas and I'll be your server this evening."

I still felt a little confused. Rose petals littered the floor around the table. "May I take your coat, madame?" I gave it to him. Nick stepped in and pulled out a chair for me to sit. It was obviously a folding chair, but it had been covered in a velvet cloth on top of cushions to make it comfy. Nick tucked me in. A moment later, I heard a small pop. Nick came back to the table with two glasses of something pink fizzing in champagne flutes.

"Sparkling raspberry cider," he said, setting down the glasses, one in front of me and opposite me, in his spot. "Musical selection?" he said and offered me a tray of CDs.

"How did you come up with this?" I asked. I selected Peter Gabriel because of a kissing song on the cd. Hopefully Nick would take the hint. Although this was not what I'd expected, a smile spread across my face. Nick had obviously gone to great lengths to prepare this for me. He'd thought it through enough to even get my dad to sign the permission slip.

Nick opened a warming tray and brought over a plate of small dumplings with tooth picks stuck in them. There were two dippers of sauce and two small appetizer plates. I unrolled my cloth napkin into my lap. Nick sat across from me.

His eyes glittered in the firelight.

He picked up his flute and held it up. "To a beautiful woman and a beautiful night," he said. We gently clinked glasses. The raspberry cider burst in my mouth, it was so sweet and good.

"Dim sum dumplings," Nick said. "From the place you like near your house." The dumplings were amazing. I wanted to ask

Nick more about why we were here, but I decided to just eat and enjoy. A little later, Nick brought me a plate with glazed chicken, roasted asparagus, and mashed potatoes. There was a small pile of bright orange mash I couldn't identify, but it was so delicious I had to ask.

"Honey glazed carrots and baked sweet potatoes mashed together," he said. "Family specialty."

"Wait. You cooked all this?"

"I did," he said. "I love cooking. How is it? I tried to include all your favorites."

"It's incredible."

He took his time between bites, sometimes just sitting back and watching me eat.

"I wanted to have you all to myself," he said. "Just you and me all alone. No server, no friends, no vampires." He smiled. "Just us. My dorm room was too small, so I had to improvise. I couldn't very well take you to a hotel room, as enjoyable an evening as that might provide," he said with a wicked gleam in his eye. "One of my fraternity brothers works here. They already had the warming dishes and such for when they rent this out for parties and as long as I bought a lesson, the owner was fine with us having the room."

"So we're doing archery after this?"

He took a bite, "Mmm hmm."

I used my bread to mop up the last bit of sauce from the chicken.

"You need a way to fight from a distance," he said. "I thought maybe archery."

It was true. There was no way I was ever going to force a stake through a vampire's chest. I had holy water and symbols for close range.

"Plus," he said, "it's best to learn a new skill when you're not in an emergency. That way you have time to get good at it before, you know, your life depends on it."

"What have you been doing?" I asked.

"Two things," he said, setting down his fork. "I'm now an official VCU gym rat. I go twice a week in the mornings before class. And, I come here. I've 'gator shot my whole life, but since Richmond isn't rife with alligators for hunting, archery club seemed like as good a bet as any. I figured I'd try it and see if I liked it. And I do. But mostly every time I practice, I think about you and how this is so your sport."

He reached over and took my hand in his. A jolt of electricity went through my body distracting me from asking him questions about alligator hunting.

"Your size is no obstacle in archery," he said. "It's all about balance and aim. Arm and shoulder strength does play a role, but you've been working on that in yoga and with Finder."

His pine forest eyes reflected the candle flames. There was a heat in them I'm sure was not candle related. He'd been looking at me more and more like that over the last few weeks and I was sure, absolutely sure, tonight was going to be the night. The night we would spend a good, long time kissing. I was curious about what else could come after. He wouldn't let me go through Valentine's Day without kissing, right? That would just be wrong. Here we were, roses, a private dinner, archery, okay maybe not the archery, but surely this was a lead up to something even better, right? Right? Like kissing. Kissing absolutely had to be on his agenda. Had. To. Be. It was definitely on mine.

"Where's your little box?" I told him and he got it from my coat pocket. Inside, a small silver disc on a chain lay on a square of velvet. The disc was covered in intricate, tiny engravings. They almost looked like equations except I didn't recognize the symbols. "It's for protection," he said. "And strength. I thought it would suit you."

"Thank you," I said. It was beautiful. Not sure what to say, I held it out. Nick took it and came behind me. He fastened it around my neck. It felt warm to the touch as he tucked it into the neck of my dress.

"It's inside jewelry," he whispered under my ear. "Wear it next to your skin."

After we finished eating, Nick stepped out for a minute, I assume to let the lady know that we were lesson ready. My dress felt a little snugger around my belly from having eaten, but as long as my stomach didn't bulge out, I thought the dress still looked good. It was snug to my body like a sheath with a turtleneck top. The sleeves had artsy little torn and frayed places where a silky mesh showed though. This was ex-Meredith-wear after all. It wasn't like she would send me something that didn't have a little grunge somewhere. I wore my spiked wrist cuff, just because it went with the boots and made me look a little Goth-ier, which made me feel more like I matched Nick. I had a silver Star of David on a black, silky string around my neck. A little bigger than my gold bat mitzvah star, it looked like it was floating in a sea of black. Now, I rubbed the fabric of my dress over the silver disc hiding under it.

My hair came down over my shoulders in a thick fall. Meredith had tried to convince me that fishnet stockings were the way to fly for leg coverings, but Dad and Jill would never in a million years let me out of the house in fishnet stockings, especially with a boy. Forget it. I wore thick black tights that did nothing against the cold even though they were described as 'warm'. They kind of matched the mesh under the frayed parts of the sleeves so I thought they looked good.

I got up from my chair and wandered over to the rack of bows. The door clicked open, and Nick came back in with our instructor.

"I'm Linda," she said. Linda was maybe fifty with shoulder-length blonde turning gray hair and a puffy gray vest. She looked like and ad from a camping catalog. She eyed me up and down, then measured my arm.

"If the bow doesn't fit you," she said, "you won't be able to draw it, much less propel an arrow into a target."

Linda measured Nick for his bow, and then, handed each of us a metal contraption. A modern sports bow has almost no resemblance to what I imagined a bow would be like. For one, there was no wood on it at all. Second, it was heavy. Like textbook times two heavy. In my obviously primitive imagination, a bow was a wooden arch that you pulled the string back from, stuck an arrow in the string, and then let it go. The thing I held could not be farther from that idea. It was black and technical and the "string" was a wire. Linda showed us how to "nock" an arrow, and draw our bows back by using our first two fingers like a claw to grip the wire and pull it back by our faces. The string got tightened to a certain number of pounds to create enough tension to launch the arrow. Drawing the bow was awkward and when it was my turn to shoot, my arrow skittered across the floor. Nick's struck the big square bag of stuffing, but didn't penetrate. That was good. As least I wasn't the only klutz who couldn't do this easily.

"You learn best when you immediately teach the thing you just got the hang of," Linda said, "so, Nick, please teach Stacy what you just learned about getting your bow situated for a shot."

Nick came and stood, very close behind/beside me. I could feel the warmth of him through my dress. He had taken off his suit jacket for the archery lesson. Reaching around me, he put his hand over mine. He stood so close I almost lost my balance leaning into him. Standing together like this was deeply distracting. He drew back the string with me and together we let go a shot that struck the target.

"Oh, that makes sense now," I said. I had not been using enough force. Using force in a physical way was not my go-to action. Before Finder took charge of me, I'd never pulled anything stronger than the leash of a determined dachshund.

Many exercises later, we took turns shooting and 'teaching'. Teaching could have quickly evolved into snuggling had Linda not been present. I deeply wished Linda were not present. But chaperoned we were, so snuggle we did not.

As I became aware of how hard I needed to pull on the bow string, I also became aware of a more Nick-related message from my body. What if, right now, Linda left? Would he brush my hair aside and kiss the back of my neck? And if he did, when would I turn around? Would he take the bow out of my hands and set it aside, pulling me into his arms for an embrace? Or, would we stay locked in each others' eyes and then, bodies so close, he could scoop me tight into him. At long last, we would both lean in and-

"Stacy?"

"Sorry. What?" Yanked out of my fantasy, Nick nudged me. Linda was asking me a question. Again.

" . . . interested in coming out for more lessons? We have group classes for beginners on Tuesdays, Thursdays and Saturday mornings."

"Yes," I said. "Thank you." I could see how archery could be a very advantageous skill for me to have. Nick stepped back from me and slid into his jacket. It struck me again how absolutely gorgeous he looked in that suit. Linda gave me a few more pointers about holding my bow and aiming, then wrote down all the details about classes, my bow size, and what kind of gear I would eventually need to buy. Behind us, Nick bussed our table into a cardboard box and packed up our candles, etc.

Thanking Linda for the lesson and all the info again, and for letting us have the room for the evening, we headed out.

A thread of disappointment wound around my heart. I wanted this night to keep going.

"Home?" I asked as we pulled out the gravel drive.

"Home? It's only 8:30. We have another stop. Unless you're too tired and want me to take you home? Are you feeling done?"

Another stop? Was it to a nice, private place where we could get to work with the kissing part? Had to be. Had to be. Right?

I smiled. I was not feeling done at all.

38.

February 14, continued.

When Nick parked in front of the supper club where we'd
captured Terrence, my skin prickled.

"Why are we here?"

Nick smiled. "You'll see." I wasn't sure I wanted to see. I did
not want anything to do with Matilda's weirdo hunting ground. I
did not want to ruin my Valentine's Day with any vampires, be they
minions or no. And I was not even old enough to be a customer at
Bar 8:30. Confusion rippled through me as Nick came around and
opened my door. I took his hand and got out. Nick led me not to
yucky vampire-ville, but to a small Italian restaurant three doors
down. We walked into a packed dining room. Nick gave his name
to the hostess and she told us our reservation would be ready in ten
minutes. Nick started to lead me back outside. "Let's stay in here," I
said. Outside was cold and, well, vampires.

The Italian place was loud in a crammed-with-bodies kind of
way, but we found a spot near the full bench packed with people
waiting for tables. Nick slid his arm around my waist, snugging me
into him as we stood. He leaned against a glass wall divider and
pulled me even closer as another couple squeezed into the sardine
can alcove. His thigh slid between mine.

Oh. Um. That was informative.

"We can go outside if it's too tight in here," he said.

"No thanks," I said. I looked him straight in the eye and
pressed in even closer. "I'm good here." Take the hint, boy, I
thought to myself. Take the hint. I smiled a closed lip smile.

"I made this reservation in December," he said. "It's the only way to get in. Those people will be waiting for hours. I tried to get us a dinner reservation, but you have to make those before Thanksgiving. I could only get us in for dessert."

Nick was rambling. Adorable! I slid my arm around his waist under his jacket. Another party came in, squashing us even more. I had nothing to fear. Kissing was coming after dessert. I was sure of it.

"O'Malley? For two?" called the hostess.

I followed the hostess to our table, a tiny half-booth set with a table cloth, candle in a hurricane glass, two upside-down wine glasses and cloth napkins. This was gonna be some dessert! She handed us each a small book-like menu with desserts embossed on the cover then turned over our glasses.

The menu was stunning, cheesecakes, cannoli, tiramisu, cakes, tarts and an Italian cookie and pastry list that made my mouth water. There were two pages of liqueurs and aperitifs and ports, but those were obviously out. Our server took one look at me and retracted the wine list she had been about to hand Nick. She filled our wine glasses with ice water. Nick offered me to order my coffee first. He then asked for his own coffee and a cookie assortment as an appetizer. We'd place our full dessert order when the coffees arrived.

"Do you want to get a few and share, or just choose your own?" he asked.

I imagined him feeding me cake on a fork. "Let's share."

That was the answer he wanted, I guess, because his eyes lit up. He suggested we order the flourless chocolate cake with raspberry mousse, two cannoli, (they were small) a slice of the fruit tart and a slice of New York cheesecake.

"Does the fruit tart have that shiny gel stuff on it?" I asked. "I hate that stuff."

"Me too," he said as if I'd told him something incredible. "This tart is not like that. You'll see."

When our server came back with our coffees and a plate of eight tiny cookies, Nick gave her a list. I wondered how our tiny table would fit all the plates.

"You look amazing," I said. "If I haven't already told you. The suit, the earrings. You look . . . stunning."

"Thank you," he said reaching his hand across the table. I put my hand in it. He took my fingers to his lips and laid them on the backs of my knuckles. He flicked his tongue over the back of one knuckle.

The tongue flick echoed across my whole body. I caught my breath. He must've seen the effect the touch had on me because he got a mischievous look in his eye.

"Are your ears pierced?" He reached over and pushed aside my hair, twining a strand of it around his finger.

I, in fact, did not have my ears pierced. I had thought about it, but never done it. I went along as moral support for Meredith who got another ear piercing every time her mother made her really angry. She had several holes in each ear.

"Do you want them pierced?" he said. "Are you not allowed?"

"I'm allowed," I said, "I just never did it. It's kinda the same reason I don't love martial arts. I know I should be all 'yeah, let's fight' under the circumstances, but I don't like pain. I don't like getting hit."

"It's why I love Hidden City," he said. "In your head, you're in this mega battle, and in real life it's cards and dice and acting out the parts. I love that. Try one of these." He nudged a white cookie about the size of a quarter toward me. I popped the tiny cookie into my mouth. It was like eating a fairy. Delicate and robust with almonds, the pastry was so fine it dissolved as soon as it hit my tongue. "Holy wow," I said.

"Yeah. Just wait for the next course."

February 14, continued.

"What do you mean he didn't kiss you?" Meredith shrieked into the phone. "I'm going to kill him! Are you serious? All that and no kissing? Weird romantic archery dinner, dessert at fancy schmancy's restaurant and all you got was his lips on your hand? Oh my stupid, stinkin' god, Woman!" She took a breath. I started to agree but she went on. "And what about you? What's the matter with you? Didn't *you* try to kiss *him?*"

I kinda had. I'd hinted several times in the car on the way home that maybe we could stop and look at the river, or park somewhere and talk for a while. We could go for a walk on campus, or at Hollywood, but he said they kept a heavier security team on Valentine's Day since so many couple tried to sneak in to make out.

"He's gay," Meredith said. "He has to be gay. This is totally insane."

"He's not gay. He's . . . lawful."

"What?"

"He was explaining something he called alignment- it's a role-playing game thing. He says that Finder and I are chaotic good and Tully and he are lawful good. They don't like breaking the rules or something and he promised my father that he wouldn't touch me until I was sixteen and- "

"Are you kidding me? Your *Goth* boyfriend who graduated *early* and is dating a *fifteen*-year-old and who sneaks into graveyards to play vampire LARPs and who can pick locks thinks his alignment is *lawful?* That's ridiculous. Tully may be lawful, but Nick? Oh no. Definitely not." I heard her fridge open in the background. "I cannot handle this at all. I'm getting ice cream. I have to soothe my nerves."

I would have gone to my own freezer with her, but I was so full from dessert I felt like even one spoonful would burst me at the seams. I lay on my bed staring at the ceiling.

"You wore my scratch and sniff dress, right?" she said.

"Right."

"Hair down and boots?"

"I did it just how you said."

"I don't understand. That combo worked for me every time. You didn't like, wear a puffer coat over it or anything right?"

"I wore my coat. It's thirty degrees."

"But your peacoat, right? Not some dumb sports looking thing."

"Yes, the peacoat. Classic double-breasted wool. Not some dumb sports looking thing."

"I don't get it," she said. "He should have been hard as a rock all night. He should have been dying for you."

"We stood pretty close a couple times," I said. "Once at archery and once in the restaurant. Unless I have zero anatomical knowledge whatsoever, his body says he's into me. I think he just promised my father, and I'm done for until sixteen. His eyes when he kisses my hand, Mer- they're like, on fire."

"And the night you did kiss, like what? Months ago now, he was into it?"

"*So into it.*"

"Okay. Well, this is a three scoop problem." She closed the freezer. I heard the drawer slide open to get a spoon.

"We either have to make you so irresistible that he breaks his stupid vow of chastity or whatever he told your dad, or he just gets weak and changes his mind. Or, you just have to gird your loins my dear, put his hand where you want it and kiss him first."

"I'm not kissing him first."

"Why? Why, woman, why?"

"I kissed him first the night on the rock and he hasn't come near me since!"

"Are you falling in love with him?" Tone serious, all business. "Because if you're seriously falling in love, we have got to do something about this immediately. If you fall in love and it turns out that he's like a sloppy spit kisser, or has a really tiny penis or something, then you're gonna be so screwed. Or not, as the case my be."

"Mer! That's an awful thing to say!"

"Well it's true! Why do you think so many of the no-sex-before-marriage people get divorced? They get married so they can finally do it and then they realize that as much as they, like, love their spouse, the sex is rancid and they are going to spend their whole lives miserable. So, back to the courthouse they go. For real, Stac-a-licious. This no kissing thing is absolutely not okay. I'll talk to him. Give me his number."

"No. I do not need you to talk to him. And he's not a sloppy spit kisser. I told you. That kissing was freakin' sublime."

"Maybe Nick needs me to talk to Nick. Seriously, I cannot handle the stress." Her spoon clinked against her bowl. "Kissing must take place again soon," clink, "or at the very least I will die of disappointment."

"You will not die of disappointment," I said.

"Watch me." Clink. "And there you will be at my funeral, ridden with guilt because all you had to do for me to live was kiss a dreamy boy. Are you coming home for the summer by the way? 'Cuz if you're not, my mom and Jill were talking about me getting a summer job in Richmond and coming to stay with you."

I sat straight up. "What? You might come here for the whole summer? Yes, yes, yes!"

"Only if you don't come home," Mer said. "I'd rather you come here."

Summer in New York? But what about Steve? I couldn't leave him here alone in monster world. It would probably be better if Mer came to me.

"I have a swimming pool. And a hot tub." I said. "And maybe Nick has a friend."

My best friend snorted. "Nick's friends will do me no good. I want a boy with some action in him."

Nick has action, I thought to myself, remembering our thighs entangled at the restaurant. My no kissing disappointment mitigated by the thought of having Meredith here for the entire summer, I sighed and let her off the phone.

Now, I could sleep.

Friday February 15, 2002.

"Have fun!" Steve called as our parents walked out the front door. He watched out the window until the car vanished down the driveway, then he ran to the kitchen. Nick leaned down and hugged me hello. There was a definite awkward moment where the kiss should have been. We followed Steve into the kitchen. When we got there he was standing on the counter pressing buttons on the oven timer. Beep beep beep.

"If she forgets something, it'll be soon," he said. "Otherwise they won't be back for hours, hours, hours!" He held out his arms and Nick lifted him down from the counter.

Steve ran to his pile of Legos strewn between the dining room table and the kitchen proper. Nick stood over him surveying the mess, then crouched down. I put coffee on and took a log of cookie dough Jill had made for us out of the fridge. As I sliced and they assembled, the timer went off. Steve bolted to the front door.

"Clear!" he shouted and ran down the back stairs. In moments we heard the joyful hellos of Steve and Evia greeting each other in the rec room.

She froze when she saw Nick.

"It's okay," Steve said grabbing her hand. "He's our friend and he knows everything. "He's the one that Matilda kidnapped." Evia still didn't move.

"Hi," Nick said, voice soft, like he was approaching a shy stray. "Wanna see my scars as proof?" He held out his hand and pushed up his sleeve so she could see the thick white scar in the center of his palm and the dark words inked on his forearm.

"You have angel magick," Evia said, eyes narrowed.

"I hear you turn into a squirrel," Nick said, completely ignoring her comment.

"I don't like angel magick. My daddy had angel magick, but it didn't save him."

"What's angel magick?" I said, wondering if the Michael voice I kept hearing was what she was talking about.

"It's when people try to harness the angels and make them do what the people want. It's bad."

Nick shrugged. "No idea. Do you guys wanna play Legos?"

Evia looked at me with her big, blue eyes. "You should make him leave. Angel magick is dangerous."

"I've never seen Nick do anything magical or dangerous," I said, "so I think it's okay."

She narrowed her eyes at me and Nick and whispered something to Steve. They started to bolt out of the room. "Wait, wait!" I said. "Before you guys run off, Evia, can you tell me what's been going on at Maymont? Do you want some seeds?"

"Steve said there'd be cookies." She looked hopeful.

"Much better option," I said. Nick stood beside me at the counter as I finished cutting and laying chocolate chip slices on a baking sheet. I felt him near me like I felt the subway rattle under my feet at home. Comforting but also aware- like my body ran the timing of the trains. Now, my body felt more alive just having Nick in the room.

Evia jumped up and sat on the counter. Must be the squirrel in her, I thought. That kid could jump.

"The biggest news is the party. She's planning a big party for Spring and it's got everybody busy. There's an old lady Wendell thinks lives with Matilda. She goes away every morning and comes home every night, but sometimes it's days before they see her and only the young woman comes and goes. Maybe they are related, since Wendell says they have a very similar smell. Grandmother and granddaughter, he thinks. So far nobody has seen," she whispered this next part, "the Man with No Face, but his smell has been detected. The woodland creatures are scared of him because his scent is so strong at the full moon and no one can tell where it's coming from. And speaking of the full moon, no one has seen what's eating the people, but after the first two, when we saw it was only killing on the full moon, we all hide on those nights."

Wait. The murders were happening on the full moon? This was a huge and obvious clue. How had I missed it?

"Because, city girl," Nick said as if reading my mind, "when have you ever followed the phases of the moon? Or even given them a second thought?"

True that. Evia kept talking.

"Darcy Jackson has been very busy. Working on all the money takes him away from the mansion and keeps him in his office, says Wendell. This makes Matilda sad and happy. The vampire you broke is still mad and wants revenge but Matilda won't let him. He thinks you have something of his that he wants back, but only Darcy Jackson knows. Darcy seems to know more than any of the others. Matilda gets nervous when the murders happen since she doesn't know what or who is doing it."

"So she's not doing the murders?" I asked. "It's not vampires?"

"Doesn't smell like vampires. Nobody hides in the woods when vampires come. They don't bother us because eating us does them no good. I already told you what it does smell like and I don't want to say you-know-what out loud again. That's everything, I think. She is still mad you won your argument but she hates you-know-what so much that she would rather lie low if it means he might never come back. That is what she hopes. She thinks if she starts making more vampires it will call him to her somehow. So I think part of her is glad you won and got her off the hook. Oh, and Pia says hello and thank you for the seeds. Let's play!"

Evia, still eyeing Nick with outright suspicion, followed Steve out of the kitchen.

"That's impressive," Nick said. "How fast she can talk."

I pulled a cooling rack out of the cabinet. "Can you grab my notebook out of my backpack, please?" I said. I nodded toward where it sat on the garage entryway bench. "There's no way I'll remember all that."

"The important thing," he said, doing as I asked, "is that bothering you and hunting Finder are off the agenda."

I nodded. The timer went off and I took the first tray of cookies out of the oven. There's nothing like the smell of hot, fresh cookies. Nick got a spatula and moved them to the rack. I began laying out the next batch. Some of the chocolate chips started melting as soon as they hit the hot metal.

"Oh!" I said, suddenly remembering for no good reason whatsoever, "What are you doing Friday, April twenty-sixth?"

Nick smiled and shrugged. "Whatever you want me to be doing." The look in his eye stopped me still for a moment. I knew exactly what I wanted him to be doing and my face flushed.

What I planned to say was would you like to go to the spring formal with me. What came out of my mouth was:

"I want you to kiss me."

A slow smile spread across Nick's face. He came over to me.

"Maybe put that pan in the oven?"

I did and set the timer. Nick stood so close to me our bodies pressed together front to front. He put his hands on my face stroking gently back from my cheeks. He rubbed one thumb across my lips. I thought I was going to disintegrate. He slid his thigh between mine like he had at the dessert place, only more intentional. He brought his lips next to my cheek. Our lips were so close. His breath fell into my collar.

"I want to kiss you so bad it physically hurts," he whispered. "But I promised your dad I wouldn't touch you."

"I don't think he meant just kissing," I said.

"It's a risk I can't take," he said. "I am going to be a doctor and I have to think about what any kind of stain on my reputation could mean for me in the long run." He leaned his chin on my head and pulled me into him. I could smell his clean T-shirt over his warm pine and books scent.

He laid his cheek on the top of my head.

"I think about you all the time," he said, voice very quiet. "I daydream about you, about things we can do, like, in life things, about what we could be to each other, about what it will feel like to lay my lips on more than your hand. I night-dream about doing things with you that I can't even put into words. But if you truly are for me, Stacy, then I can wait." He drew back and looked in my eyes. "I want you to have everything. Everything of me, from me." He put his forehead against mine. "Everything you want from me, I want to give you. I even want to not give you certain things if you don't want them. But we have to wait."

"I don't want to wait. It's just a kiss."

"And this coming November when you turn sixteen, and we will have been waiting nearly a year to kiss each other, what a kiss it will be."

He took my hand and brought it to his mouth. He kissed each finger, each knuckle. He turned my hand over and kissed my palm. He looked up into my eyes. Something behind his held an intensity I'd never seen. It was more than desire, it was power. He was holding back something very deep, something very integral to who he was and whatever that was, he wanted me, me to receive it.

"Please," I whispered tears coming for no good reason to my eyes. "Can we, once? So I know you mean it."

"No," he whispered. "It's a hard price, a year for a lifetime. But it's worth paying."

A lifetime? What?

Steve and Evia barreled through the kitchen door.

"Cookies!"

I jumped to separate but the counter was at my back. Nick squeezed me to him even tighter.

"What do you think, Steve?" he asked. "Do you think I'm a good boyfriend for your sister?" He looked at me with a sly side eye.

"I think she should make Tully her boyfriend," Steve said. This was not what Nick had expected to hear. "She needs someone who can protect her," he said. "You're nice and I like you," he said with utter sincerity to Nick's face, "but you aren't strong like he is and you don't use a sword. I think Stacy needs a man who can use his sword."

I snorted. Sorry. Couldn't help it.

Nick caught my snort and looked back and forth between my little brother and me.

"Did you ask him to say that?" he said.

"I did not," I snorted again, louder this time, and then I laughed. Loud.

"What's so funny?" Steve asked popping one hand onto his little hip. "What did I miss?"

"Nothing," I said.

"Liar, liar, pants on fire." The timer beeped. I slid my arms out from Nick's embrace and he stepped back so I could pull the next batch of cookies out of the oven. Evia bounced on her toes and hopped into a chair as Steve got the milk out of the fridge. Nick looked to me and I nodded toward a cabinet. He got out four glasses.

"Evia," I asked, sliding three cookies onto her plate, "careful those are hot, did you say that Matilda is upset about the murders that have been happening?"

"Mmhmm."

"Can you be absolutely sure she isn't somehow involved with them?"

"What does 'absolutely' mean?"

"It means you are super-duper really, really sure."

"Wendell says she pitches a fit every time one happens."

"Are you sure she isn't pitching a fit because she got caught?"

Evia shrugged. "Maybe. I hadn't thought about that."

Nick and I joined the littles at the table. We all dunked hot cookies and ate for a few minutes in silence.

Matilda had been my only idea. If it wasn't her, who else could our killer be?

Nick and I sat on the couch not nearly close enough. He'd spent the rest of the evening not touching me in a very deliberate kind of way. Evia and Steve built train tracks across the living room, periodically jumping up to dance to a song they loved on the *Steve and Stacy Are Siblings* cd I burned last year for Steve's birthday. Nick had played Steve at chess while I showed Evia how the pieces moved, and now my beautiful, unkissable Goth boyfriend sat with a notebook in his lap watching the train track extravaganza grow. Every few minutes, he wrote another line in the notebook. I sipped my coffee.

"Game?" I said, nodding toward the chess board. An awkward energy had slid over us since I'd asked him to kiss me in the kitchen and I wasn't happy about it.

"Sure," he said and took another note. "Is this everything we know about the murders?"

"Read me the list," I said as I moved the portable chess board onto the couch and drew my legs up under me. First, he read off the dates and locations of each murder. The first one was November thirtieth, exactly two weeks after we saved Nick and Luke at Maymont. The next one was Sunday, December thirtieth, then Monday, January twenty-eighth. So it wasn't a weekend thing. I set the board, white corner on the right and aligned our armies.

"Write down- look up full moons," I said.

"Already noted."

All the murders happened in the woods, all at night, all victims found in the mornings, all stripped clean of their body meat. We hadn't messed with Matilda's blood sources until mid-December, so that didn't line up. Mrs. Macy had known the names of the victims, the second one before the murder was even in the paper. She had seemed to think she was next, but the January victim had been another man.

"Why would Mrs. Macy think she was vulnerable?" I said. "Why would she think this murderer targets specific victims? Seems like random people on a trail."

I reset my favorite analog timer to a neutral twelve o'clock.

"Maybe she knows who's doing it."

Evia looked up from the trains and swore a very adult swear word.

The front door burst open and a massive gust of false wind from inside the house met a real one from outside as my parents burst into the house. "It's not like that, Lea!" Dad was saying into his phone in his second martini voice.

"Hi kids," Jill said as she shut the door. "Sorry we're early. Hit a bit of a snag at the restaurant."

My dad stuffed his coat onto a hanger in the front closet, holding the phone against his shoulder.

"Listen, I know this is a pain in the ass, but we cannot keep going like this. I am not going to argue cases in a restaurant on a date with my wife outside of business hours! If you want to argue, then you go down there and have your own damn conversation. I am done with this until Monday, is that clear? I only called you because it's *your* case and I don't want to get in trouble for talking to *your* opposition!" Pause. "Yes, I know she is. And yes, I know that too. I'm sorry Lea, I'm off tonight and I'm going to hang up now. Good night." He sighed and dropped his phone behind me on the couch. "She's a crazy person right now," he said. "She's like a rabid animal about this case and there is no possible way she can lose. It's ridiculous. She's arguing as if her life depended on it. I'm like, sheesh woman, take a valium and go to bed."

"What happened?" I asked as he flopped into his favorite chair.

"The lawyer for the defense happened to be having dinner at Tito's too, and once he saw me, it was like game on. The bastard wouldn't leave me alone."

"He was really rude and awful," Jill said. "I would have thought his wife could have called him off, but it was like she didn't exist. He was crazy, truly. It was kind of scary."

"Why didn't you pick anther restaurant?" I said.

"On Friday night the day after Valentine's Day?" said my father. "There isn't a table for two available anywhere you'd actually want to eat in all of Richmond."

"Not where *you'd* actually want to eat," Jill clarified. "I could have found something."

"I'm not eating at Tango Ralph's or China Gourmet on a night where I'm ready for a steak and a glass of wine," said Dad, laying his head back and taking off his glasses. "This guy would not leave us alone. He even had the hostess reseat them to the table next to us saying we were friends. I said to him it's not even my case! Truly. Horrible."

"I'm so sorry," said Nick. "What a waste of an evening."

"Looks like things went well here. Do I still smell cookies?"

"You do," I said. "Want me to get you some?"

Dad looked at Nick. "How many times has she beaten you?"

Steve came down stairs carrying his backpack. I hadn't noticed him go up to get it. Jill toed off her strappy heels and sighed in relief.

"We warned you," Jill said to Nick. "She's a menace with a queen in her hand."

Jill went into the kitchen and came out chewing and holding half a cookie. She handed it to Dad.

"Glad you didn't eat all of these," she said. "Anybody want some tea?"

Dad shook his head. No thanks from me and Nick.

"Okay then," she said, "Just me." Dad closed his eyes and rubbed his face. Steve ducked behind the couch. I watched the space behind the couch over Nick's shoulder as Steve opened his backpack just out of Dad's line of sight. Evia, now in squirrel form, jumped in. Steve bundled her clothes in on top of her. Nick turned and looked over his shoulder. His eyes went wide. Steve zipped his pack shut, blinked a bunch of times at Nick, his attempt at winking, and headed for the rec room stairs.

"Stay in school forever, son," Dad said. "The real world isn't worth it."

"Which case was it?"

"The land suit," he said. "The Mattaponi tribe isn't going to win. They are right as the ethics go, their burial ground is what it is, but this is Virginia and a descendant of *Gen'ral Lee*, namely my partner, is too influential. She has too many contacts and too much history here. She's going to win even though it's wrong and there is nothing Jesus, Satan or Santa Claus can do about it." Dad got up and stretched.

"I thought you were the only person who said that," Nick said to me.

"The apple lies beneath the tree," said Dad leaning over to kiss the top of my head. "I'm cranky and exhausted. I didn't even give Jill her present. Can you baby-sit tomorrow? I think she's gonna need a do-over of tonight or I'll be going to court for reasons of my own." He smiled at Nick. "Women are a project. Always want something you maybe can't deliver."

He scrubbed my hair with his hand. "Except maybe this one," he said. "She's pretty low maintenance. You're welcome." He smiled and headed into the kitchen where we heard him kiss Jill and say something apologetic. He walked back through the living room to the stairs.

"Good cookies, honey," he said. And with that, he was gone, thunking up the steps to his bathtub and his bed.

My dad was a simple creature if he wasn't arguing your case.

Steve came back up, backpack open and dropped it, climbing into Nick's lap.

"Let's win," Steve said, rubbing his hands together.

"I'm ready if you are."

Thursday, February 21, 2002.

I had a new plan for Nick this evening. Meredith was right. I'd been passive on this front for too long. Dad or no dad, it was time to take matters into my own hands. Literally. I had gone to the library and found a book explaining what points on the hands were connected to the deep pleasure centers of your brain. I wanted to know why Nick's hand kissing melted me into a puddle every time it happened. Now I knew. And, I had learned some things.

Nick shrugged out of his jacket. He wore a white T-shirt. His ink was fully visible, scarring his forearm in its hatefulness. Nick's arms and shoulders had gotten bulkier, more defined over the winter. The clean, white cotton fell across newly defined pectoral muscles. His biceps had shadows on the outside now, where the muscles had gone from wiry to noticeable. He wore a silver ring on his left hand that I hadn't noticed before.

Nick brushed his hair back out of his face. Auburn roots gleamed from under the black dye. I reached for his hand and he took mine, starting to bring it to his lips.

"No," I said.

"No?" He started to raise it again.

"You don't get to kiss my hands again until after."

"After?"

I held his eyes. He shifted in his chair. I turned his hand over in mine.

"I like your ring," I said, stroking the center line of his palm with one finger. "What do the symbols stand for?"

"So I can't kiss your hand again until . . ."

I was not budging.

"Until after you elect to follow my will instead of the will of my father."

"Your *will*," he said. "That's new language for you."

I took his hand and brought it to my mouth. I kissed the tip of each finger and kissed each knuckle, letting my tongue tap and circle each one. Nick closed his eyes. His breath was slow and, to my satisfaction, a little unsteady.

I set his hand back down on the table. He took a few more slow breaths and then opened his eyes. He devoured my face with his gaze and then took his time looking at the rest of me, drinking me in.

"Your body shape has changed since you started working out," he said. I blushed.

"Yours, too."

He smiled. "Thanks. I've upped my workouts. I'm not ready to be told again by a six-year-old that I'm not good boyfriend material because I'm too scrawny."

"Steve takes his brother role very seriously." I sipped my coffee. "We can sit together and do homework," I said, "or we can take a walk and maybe you can earn your hand kissing privileges back."

"Did it work?" Meredith asked on the phone as I fast-walked my physical frustration out on the treadmill.

"He didn't kiss me yet, but I think it was a step in the right direction. I missed my hand kissing."

"You'll live. And you're going to thank, thank, thank me! He has to give in sooner or later."

"I feel bad manipulating him to kiss me if he feels like it's wrong," I said.

"This is not manipulation, Woman! This is survival. It's just kissing for crying out loud. You're not asking him to give you the heir to the throne. And I'm glad he's getting rid of that filthy tattoo. Now, last thing. Are you coming home for Spring Break?"

39.

Friday, March 15, 2002.

Hotels were for winning.

Finder beelined for me as the Mid-Virginia Regional Science Fair judges and photographer cleared her project. The silver, second-place medal lay against her chest.

"That's right, Chess Team," she said holding up her hand for a high five. "We smoked those righteous Bs." Grinning, I agreed, my own first-place gold around my neck. "And I will mention that you only beat me by four points," she said. "Four!"

"I am the point master," I said. "We'd better find our moms before they bulldoze us. Oh, there's Judy's dad."

John Forest Stalker was on the other side of the hotel ballroom hugging his daughter and talking to her and Julian. He took a picture of them together with her gold medal. Judy's mom stood nearby, arms wrapped around herself like she was cold.

"States next month," I said to Finder. "I want my asteroid. MIT's Lincoln Lab named an asteroid after last year's National winner for the first time and this year they're doing it again. I want that asteroid to be me."

"As long as you make your name Stacy Rachel Layla Jackson Goldman, I agree to be excited for you."

"Rather than punishing me with a thousand push-ups in class?" I said.

"I can do that, too," she said. "Why are you rubbing you arm like that?"

"Mosquito bite," I said. It was our new code word for when Terrence showed up to claim his privilege. "It's been over a month. I think she was on to him and he stayed away so she wouldn't find out. But last night he was starving and he ripped the daylights out of my upper arm. It's super sore today. And it itches."

"That's why you looked so nauseated this morning? I thought maybe it was nerves."

"Nope. Blood loss. I vomited right before we left. Jill was all upset because she thought I was having a panic attack. Oh, there's Nick!"

"We need to stake that mosquito," Finder said. "Or make him go feed on Luke."

"I'd happily hand him over, but he hates me so bad he won't agree to anyone else. Nick has tried and tried."

"Congratulations!" Nick picked me up and swung me around. Ow. Arm. I grinned at him anyway. He set me down and hugged Finder, too.

"You ladies are the talk of the house! DNA mutation reversal in hereditary mispairings, and apoptosis leading to immortal cells. You're amazing!"

"New project," Finder said, all business. "We gotta take care of Terrence."

"Agreed. I'm getting much better with my archery," said Nick. "Can we target him from a distance?"

I jumped in. "We signed in blood to leave each other alone."

"Then she can't know it's us," Finder said. "Seriously, Stacy. How long do we let this go on? He's *immortal.* Are you gonna be eighty-two and still have disgusting Terrence knocking on your window?"

I really hated being Terrence's local Chapter & Mercy.

"Archery and distance," Nick agreed.

"I have half a vial of his blood in the lab fridge at VCU," I said. "As long as I have his blood, he'll behave. I threatened to use it to burn him where he slept if he sucked any soul, and he believes me. The no soul sucking is my only advantage right now."

"It's dangerous when your advantage is someone else's ignorance," said Finder.

"You have his blood?" said Nick.

"Yeah." Had we never told him the whole story of the night we kidnapped Terrence? Finder gave Nick the ten second version of me drawing Terrence's blood and making up this wackadoodle story about what I could do with it. The vampire had believed me.

Nick looked at me in a way I couldn't translate. "You just made up that you could do that?"

"Yup."

"And you still have his blood at the lab?"

"I do."

"Crazy lady," he said and scooped up my hand. He started to bring it to his lips.

"Nope!" I said. "No hand kissing."

"Please?" he said, giving me the puppy dog look.

"Oh stop, y'all," Finder said. "Get a room."

Thursday March 28, 2002.

I let my arrow fly. Shooting wasn't getting easier as fast as I'd hoped, but I could draw the bow by myself without feeling like my shoulder was about to snap. Of course, I didn't really need Nick to know I could do it without him, did I?

On this unseasonably bright afternoon, his arms were around mine as I leaned against his chest. Together we steadied the bow for the next shot. I pressed into him. He pressed back. I could think of worse ways to spend my spring break.

My Adorable Goth Boy leaned forward over my shoulder. The warmth of his cheek so close beside mine drew me like a magnet. I turned to look at him. Just a little closer and-

"Wanna give it a try, Mr. Goldman?" Nick said, stepping away from me as my father slid open the sliding glass door.

Rats.

Cool air rushed across my back where I'd been leaning against Nick's warm chest. It had been thirty-five days since my no hand kissing ultimatum. *Thirty-five.* Much to my disappointment, Nick was the willpower master of delayed gratification.

Dad stepped outside in his slippers, taking a long breath of the humid March air.

"Sure, I'll give it a go," Dad said. "I need to get the news outta my head. Did you guys hear? Suicide bomber at a hotel in Israel killed thirty innocent people yesterday, wounded a hundred and forty more. Went in during their seder. Been all over the news today." I handed him my bow.

"Happy Passover, right?" I said. Dad shook his head.

"Land and religion," he said. "Two things that make people crazy."

Nick explained how to load a dart into the sliding chamber beneath the main mechanism, hold the bow in the left hand and draw the string back toward the center of your chest. "It's a little small for you, but it'll work. Aim directly at the target."

Nick went to stand behind him. "A little more to the left, there. That's better." He moved Dad's arm a touch toward me. "I grew up on the edge of the bayou. Learned to shoot as soon as I was big enough to hold a gun."

"I've never shot a gun," my father said. "No desire whatsoever. That kid who blew himself up in Israel, he was just a few years older than you. Part of a group where they teach five and six-year-olds that suicide bombing is a desirable death. Guns are like pacifiers in their hands. I can't make sense of it. Hate as standard issue philosophy."

My father hit the target two out of three shots.

"Not bad first shots, sir."

Not even my father could resist that rock star smile.

"Let's see, honey," Dad said, handing the compound bow back to me. "Let's see how you do."

Without Nick to steady me, my shot went wide. The second one hit the target, but landed too close to the edge. Nick looked at my father, maybe for permission. Dad gave a little nod and Nick stepped in close to me again. His pine wood smell and the touch of his bare arm skin on my bare arm skin distracted me. What was I doing again? Oh yeah. Aiming.

"What are you kids gonna do while we're at the club tonight?" he asked.

Nick is going to finally surrender to my ultimatum and we are going to make out like bandits on the couch. As if.

"We might take Steve out for ice cream," I said. "But don't tell him. In case we change our minds." I tipped the bow down toward the ground, slid another arrow into the channel and drew back my bowstring. It locked in place. Convinced everything looked set, I lifted the bow shoulder height, parallel to the ground.

This time, I hit the target.

"Nice shot, honey. Who knew living in the South would awaken such a warrior?" Dad brushed his hands on his golf pants.

Nick smiled at me as if to say, 'See?'

"Any more, sir?" Nick asked.

"No, thanks. Jill just wanted me to come down and let you guys know we were leaving. It was fun, though."

While Steve was getting his pjs on and picking out his stories, I walked Nick out. He leaned against the Hulk.

"I'm always nervous leaving you and Steve alone."

"Then don't leave," I said. I rested my head against his chest. His arms encircled me in safety.

"April 26 is still on your calendar, right?" I said, breathing him in. "The St. Ig's Spring Formal? It's a Bloomin' Spring theme."

"Do I get to wear my suit?"

I shifted to look up at him. His gaze flickered from my eyes to my mouth. I reached up and touched his cheek with my fingers. Then I let them trail over his lips. His breath was warm as he closed his eyes.

I pressed my body into his. No escaping until you kiss me, I thought. I stood on my tip toes and ran the end of my nose along his neck.

"Just one?" I said. He pulled me into a tighter hug. His silent 'no'. I ran my tongue up his neck to the back of his ear. He tasted slightly salty. He pulled back but I hung on, layering kisses from his ear to his shoulder. He tightened in my embrace.

Oh, fine. I sighed and gave up.

40.

Friday, April 26, 2002.

I gasped. Emerging from the petal pink archway into the full experience of the St. Ignatius' Spring Formal, I thought a florist shop had exploded in the gym. Garlands of flowers both real and paper hung everywhere. Fluffy tissue blossoms sprouted from the gym walls in taped and scalloped strands like old-fashioned paper dolls linked at the hands. Long silky drapes billowed from the metal roof beams. It smelled like the gardens at the Metropolitan Museum of Art in June. Huge bouquets of fresh roses and spring lilies adorned each table along the gym side.

I turned around and looked at the archway I had walked through. A mix of fresh branches, blossoms of some small, sweet-smelling pink flower we don't have in New York and some tiny yellow bloom I recognized from shrubs all over Wilton front yards were woven together. Mouth slack, I stood for a second and took it all in. I had to admit, I was impressed. Michelle Longwarder might be a rotten science fair partner and a total wench in gym, but boy. That girl could organize a formal.

Finder and Tully stood on the far side of the gym, talking as usual, to each other. Two guys from one of Tully's teams hovered chatting. As I got closer I could see that they were only half paying attention to the conversation, eyeballs drifting every few seconds to Finder.

"That's one way to do it," Jill said coming up beside me.

Finder was an exotic, night petalled flower in this garden of blonde and pastel. Her shiny crimson dress looked, how should I say it? Poured on? I was impressed Mama'd let her out of the house.

"Tully looks great in that kilt," Jill said. "Not everyone could pull that off."

"He looks . . . manly in it," I said. "I thought kilts would look, you know, girly somehow, but on him it looks like . . ."

"Like warrior garb."

"Yes," I said. "Like. Warrior garb."

Jill raised an eyebrow as two more guys came over to drool on Finder. "Good thing," she said. "By the end of the night, warrior garb might be required. Speaking of which— "

"He'll be here soon," I said.

"I wasn't talking about Nick." She gave me a sterner look.

"My alarm is already set for 6:45." I said. "It's my competition, I'll get up. Honestly, it'll be a miracle if I sleep at all."

Jill was obsessed with being early for everything. She said in the theatre if you were on time, you were late. The stage manager could legit fire an actor if he or she arrived exactly at or one minute after call time more than three times in a row. Not that I gave one hoot about theatre rules, but Jill lived by them out of 'habit'. Although, let it be said, in the seven years I had known her, she had done not one single play.

A swirl of black Goth formalwear drew my eye from under the flowery arch, bumping my heart into my throat. My breath actually stuck a little in my chest. Nick wore a black silk tailcoat buttoned in front. He was clean shaven and had styled his hair to flip just so under a vintage top hat. The flower in his button hole matched the corsage in his hand. When he saw me, his eyes lit up. He spoke to Jill first.

"Mrs. Goldman," he said with a polite half bow, "formal wear suits you."

"Thank you, Nick," she said. "Chaperoning has its benefits. I so rarely get to dress up." Taller than she had been in front of the mirror, Jill now sported her full-length gown with its champagne-colored glitterati and pretty beige heels.

"Miss Goldman," he said, offering to tie on my dress matching corsage.

"How did you know what color my dress would be?" I gave him my hand. Nick and Jill exchanged sneaky smiles as he tied on the corsage.

Flower successfully attached to my wrist, Nick turned back to his partner in crime. "May I take your charge to the dance floor?"

Jill let out a short chuckle.

"My charge?" she said. "What is this, a shopping spree?" But she nodded, and Nick sailed me right into the crowd of dancing high schoolers.

"You look," he paused and took in the expanse of my throat and shoulders, open in my strapless dress. He leaned close to my ear. "You look astonishing."

The music made dance floor conversation impossible, so I did my best to keep the beat and Nick did his best to keep my hand. At the end of a few up-tempo songs, a slow song came on. Would Nick want to dance to the slow song or would he bolt for the snacks? I watched as some of the dance floor cleared. Finder caught my eye. She and Tully made their way toward me and Nick.

Nick kept my one hand in his and used his open arm to pull my body right up close. His warm palm settled in the middle of my back above my waist. He leaned down and inhaled right under my ear, breath warm on my bare skin. Meredith had been right about the choker.

"If my lips were to accidentally connect with your neck right now, do you think Jill would be mad?"

Words froze in my mouth. I wanted nothing more in this very moment with his arm around my waist than for him to kiss my neck. This is the night! I thought. A thrill of satisfaction made me smile. My no-hand-kissing resolution was working! Real kissing was definitely happening tonight.

"She's chaperoning because after the last dance, we spent the evening catching Terrence and I was out all night. Dad was not about to let that happen again."

"I'm surprised he's not here himself, knowing I'd be here."

"He's at a work party. Jill's gonna go meet him if we're done early enough. It's why she looks extra fancy." The slow song played on. Finder and Tully danced over. Her arms were around his neck, and he held her close, both arms around her waist. She rested her head on his chest.

"Nice kilt, laddie," Nick said.

"Thank you," Tully replied.

"You look stunning, Ms. Jackson," Nick said. "What time does the band take the stage?" Cut at the knee, her dress did look like something a 1960's singing star would have worn.

"What time does your tap routine start?" she replied, framing him with a wide smile. Between his tails and my poofy crinoline skirt, we did give off a kinda old movie musical vibe.

The slow song ended and in a minute the dance floor was packed. We switched up partners and spent most of the songs dancing together as a group. We slid into partners; me with Tully, Nick with Finder, then came back around. At one point Nick and Tully broke into step on some popular dance they both knew and danced together. Finder smiled at me, a broad, happy smile. She looked at Nick, then raised an eyebrow at me and winked. Tonight? Yes, I smiled back, I think so. Even though we didn't say any words, the conversations was clear.

During the next dance, the purse I wore on a delicate chain across my body vibrated. Buzz. Pause. Buzz. Pause. Who was calling me? Jill was here. Maybe her phone was in the car and there was an emergency at home? Was the house being raided by Bat Suits? I reached for my bag.

"Hello? Dad? Is everything okay?"

"Stacy, it's Judy."

Whew. Not Dad. Everything was fine.

"Are you still at home?" I asked. "Do you want me to tell Hank you're running late? I haven't seen him, yet, or Bradley Joe either if you want in line for a dance."

"I'm sorry, Stacy," she said stilted, sniffing. A dog barked loud in her background. She kept talking. I struggled to hear.

"Hang on," I said weaving my way through the throng of bouncing formal wear to the propped open side door of the gym. Between the barking and over-the-top loud music, I couldn't even get every other word.

I waved to Sister Elizabeth Religion, doing door monitor duty with her usual generous smile. She wrote something on a clipboard and waved back. I ducked out. The cool air felt clammy on my skin.

"Judy?" I said. "Aren't you coming? We can talk when you get here."

"Stacy," she choked over the barking. "I'm sorry, I really am. I thought it would work, but the last three months, even after the adjustments we made, it's not. My DNA is still the same!" Her sob was wet and desperate.

"Wait. I thought we were talking about the dance. What do you mean your DNA is still the same?"

"I mean, I needed the DNA reversal to work and it doesn't! It worked on all the samples and it worked on the squirrel but it's not working on me," she gulped. "I'm so sorry. I tried every month and still nothing. I'm not coming tonight. And . . ." she took a big breath and sobbed. "I can't come to States tomorrow."

My heart skipped a beat.

"How can you *not come to States?*" I paused. I paced. I stopped.

"You knew it was about me, Stacy. About my condition. I've been so happy for you that we've been winning, I didn't have the heart to tell you it's working on the lab samples but not on me."

"But, it's not designed to work on you. We made the serums specifically for the samples," I said.

"My DNA is the sample! I switched it right at the start so you wouldn't notice a difference. I told you at Thanksgiving it was me we were experimenting on."

"You told me *one* sample was yours. One! Not all! You said everything else Julian got through his lab."

"He did. We took the samples *from me* at the lab. I thought you knew!"

"You lied to me!"

"I didn't. Not once. I thought you understood what was going on."

I paused. I didn't know what to say.

"Stacy? Are you stupid? All these months? I've given you a thousand clues! Do you really not see it? With vampires following you everywhere you go? Your brother playing with a shape shifting squirrel? You've been staring at my DNA since Thanksgiving. I can't go to States, Stacy, and I can't come to the dance because tonight starts the full moon!"

My blood gummed up in my veins. What did the full moon have to do with the science fair?

"Judy, YOU HAVE to be there! We can't place without both of us. I don't understand what's going on, but just come and we'll figure it out."

Desperation had its grip around my throat. I would say anything, anything she wanted to make sure she showed up tomorrow.

"We won't figure it out!" she cried. "I've tried everything! The mispairings are too many and too locked. They don't stop the change. I've tried a couple variations on my own, but something's still missing. I can't get it to work."

"I don't understand," I said. "What do you need the serums to do? What result are we missing? And I don't understand why the serums not working on you means you can't be there tomorrow. What's the correlation?"

I stood there, struggling to figure out what was going on, totally confused. A woman's voice in the background called Judy's name.

"The project disc with the media on it is in my locker. I'm 245. The combination is 13-24-7. I didn't expect you to, like, come out and tell me you knew, but how could *you* not figure this out?"

And, still sobbing, she hung up.

Finder came up beside me. "I just watched all the color drain from your already pasty body." Then, she whispered, "Is it Maltilda? Is Steve okay?"

"Judy isn't coming to States tomorrow. She says it's the full moon."

"What?"

I whispered so we wouldn't be overheard. "She knows about vampires. And that Evia is a shifter. I think she's known the whole time."

"That's impossible. *Judy? Knows?*"

"I've missed something really big, Finder. Something she thought I knew." I looked at my friend, tears of fury welling in my eyes. "She's been using the serums on herself! She called me sobbing and says she can't come tomorrow and the disc is in her locker. Months of work. Months!"

Do not cry, Goldman, I told myself. Do. Not. Cry.

Finder took hold of my shoulders and made me look at her.

"We'll go get her. We'll go out to the reservation and pick her up and have her tell us everything. She'll spend the night at your house so we'll already have her with us in the morning. We'll figure this out. It's gonna be okay."

But I knew, I just knew in my body that this was not, not, not going to be okay at all. I felt loose in my joints, weak in the knees. "I need to sit down."

Finder led me back into the warm, noisy gym, my body moving as if through mud. I wondered if I was about to pull a Judy and pass out. Finder found a bench near the snack table. As I sat, she took the phone from my hand and hit redial. She stood. She paced. No answer.

I sifted through information, hunting for what I may have missed. Judy showing me her DNA on Thanksgiving, her knowing Evia was sick, all the commonalities we found I thought were only coincidences. None of this meant she was herself an unimaginable though, right? Judy had never had a near death experience. And Steve hadn't smelled anything weird about her.

Judy had been the one to identify the vampire blood I'd put under the microscope as predator blood. How and why had she figured that out? And why the word 'predator'? I felt like I was looking at a jigsaw puzzle with a massive missing piece, the one that made the whole picture fall into place.

"Stay here. I'll be right back." Finder disappeared into the crowd.

And what did the full moon have to do with any of this?

And then, I saw it.

Judy at my house in the moonlight looking so at home. Judy starving herself nearly to death before three day stretches where she'd be absent from school. Three day stretches when somebody died. Judy looking full and content when she came back. Like she'd *eaten*. I thought when she said condition, she meant something threatening *her* life. Wrong. So wrong. Judy was-

Jill sat down beside me on the bench.

"What happened? Finder said something's wrong with Judy? Or her parents can't drive her tomorrow? We can go get her, whatever we need to do." She wrapped her arms around me. "How can I help?"

"Does the full moon last more than one night?"

"I think technically it's three, but maybe peaks on the one in the middle? Why?"

"Didn't Dad say the last bear attack happened on the full moon?"

"I think so," Jill said. "The paper noted it last time that all the deaths have coincidentally been on the full moon."

"So," I paused, "there's going to be another one. Tomorrow."

No wonder Judy was desperate. She was going to kill someone and had been using our project to try to make it stop.

Finder arrived a second later carrying hot chocolate and a cookie. She shoved them into my hands.

Finder dialed Judy five more times. On try number six, she traded me cocoa for phone. The answering machine had picked up, "—Reached Cathy and Judy. Leave a message after the tone. If you're looking for money or are a bill collector, piss off. You can't get blood from a stone."

"Hi Mrs. Forest, Hi Judy, this is Stacy. Judy, I think I understand what you were trying to tell me before. About the moon. I can help. There has to be a way to control . . .um . . . what you need to *not* do. We're going to come out tonight to pick you up. Please call me back. We're gonna work this out." I left my number and my dad's number and Jill's number and my house telephone number and my email. She had to call me back. She had to show up.

"I feel nauseated," I said out loud.

"Eat," Finder said imitating her mother. "You just need some sugar in your brain to make you think."

"I'm not sure I can. I might be sick."

"Eat it. I'm going to go ask Sister Maria Alberta if she'll be at States tomorrow and if she can figure out a way for Judy to be absent and you still qualify. Where in righteous dance-land is Tully?"

"It's a guaranteed win for you if she doesn't show up." My voice was weaker than I wanted it to be.

"Winning is no fun against an unskilled opponent." Finder leaned over and put her hands on my knees. "Don't worry, Chess Team. We're gonna solve this. Right, Mrs. Goldman? We'll get that girl to the fair whatever we have to do. Eat. That. Cookie."

I did. It would have been delicious if I'd had an ounce of appreciation left in my body. Finder smiled. She winked. She was trying to cheer me up. Or cover for me. And with that she left, melting into the crowd of dancers to go find a nun.

Jill sat with me, running over practical options and assuring me that whatever was needed, sleepover, early pick up on the reservation, whatever, we could make it work. I stared into the dancers. Colorful dresses swirled like helixes.

Had Judy really told me what I thought she was telling me? Was it connected to her tattoo? What if we went to the reservation and Judy didn't want to be found?

"I'm going to go get our media disc from Judy's locker," I said to Jill. "I'm not sure how much longer I want to stay."

Torn between anger, guilt and worry, I looked around for my friends. I didn't see Nick or Tully or Finder. I would go get the disc and come back before anyone noticed I was gone.

Locker number 245. 13-24-7. That's what was running through my mind as I crossed the hall outside the gym. 245 would be on the second floor on the opposite side of the building. The quickest way to get there cut through the sanctuary. Maybe a walk through St. Ignatius' safe, quiet place would make me feel better or help me figure out some kind of solution.

Pushing open the heavy wooden doors, I took a breath of frankincense-tinged air. Electric sconces on the walls held the ideal dimness to let real candlelight flicker on the ceiling, candlelight from the little votive altar at the front of the sanctuary. I should light a candle. I would light a candle. Yes. Good idea.

"Michael?" I said so quietly I barely heard myself. "I need you now. Please talk to me." I waited. No response. "Okay. I know you might be busy in, like, war torn countries, but I could use some advice. I think Judy is going to kill somebody. Please help me. I'm going to light a candle for you."

At home in New York, I'd watched Wall Street types come in to St. Peter's Basilica, drop a dollar in the donation box, then stand, pray and light a candle. Six blocks from my apartment, St. Peter's was the one place a kid could sit uninterrupted for as long as the doors were open.

I stood for a second now, brow furrowed. I had a massive problem. The last time I had a massive problem I'd summoned an angel and blown away the Man with No Face. Maybe by forgiving my father, I'd lit a candle on a gigantic scale.

I sighed, my toes touching the tips of my fancy formal shoes. Lighting a candle might not help, but it might. I took the left aisle toward the votive altar.

Closer ahead of me, something scuffled. I stopped and listened. Was somebody else in here? I scrutinized the rows of pews. Nobody. Again a scuffing sound. Like curtains rustling. It was coming from the little sheltered alcove housing the St. Michael statue. Had he manifested again in physical form to help me? I had to pass that alcove to get to the candles and the door leading to Judy's locker. I decided to find out. Then, I paused.

What if it was Matilda? Or Terrence hoping for a snack? I opened my tiny purse and palmed the only anti-vampire weapon it fit. My mezuzah. I could be strangled with the purse chain, so I unclipped it and tucked it into the purse. Then, I wedged the whole thing into the waistband of my dress in case I had to run. I wished I was Finder or Steve, wished I had some way of knowing if whatever was rustling was human or not.

Calm down, Goldman, I told myself. There are no vampires here. It's a *church*. It's probably a custodian, or somebody praying at the St. Michael.

Unless it's not. This was Richmond, after all.

The shuffling came again and this time, a whisper. A whisper? Michael wouldn't whisper if he was alone, would he? Was there *more than one* person/vampire/who knows what hiding? Decision time. Run, don't run? Sneak away hoping I'd gone unnoticed? Stand and fight? Scare the daylights out of some innocent person praying to St. Michael out loud? Crap.

I stepped out of my fancy formal shoes. If I had to run, the heels would slow me down. If I had to sneak, they might make noise. Girls always slid pumps off after a couple hours of dancing anyway. No one would think it was weird. I picked them up and gripped them around the middle in one hand, heels forward, like weapons.

I heard Meredith's voice in my head. Woman, you're totally overreacting. Just go light your damn candle and pretend like things are normal. No one at the St. Ignatius Spring Formal is out to get you.

Right. I am alive, I am safe. Nothing bad is happening. I had as much right to be in this sanctuary as anyone else. I took a breath and stepped out.

I padded down the side aisle. The shuffling sound came again, this time with a whisper and an odd breathy noise. I kept my eyes straight ahead as I walked forward to pass the chapel alcove. My dress brushed against a pew and the crinoline under it made a thick shushing sound. I froze and so did everything else. I stood for a second in the silence, waiting. Nothing. The breathy shuffling resumed. Go light your candle.

I walked forward. As I passed the chapel, behind me, a thump and a gasp. Something touched my leg.

I turned, and attacked, thrusting my mezuzah forward. It made hard contact with something in the shadows.

"Ow!"

A curtain of blond hair shook back, the eyes facing me startled.

"Tully?"

I had my shoes, heels raised, in the other hand ready to clobber . . . Tully? I gasped and stepped back. It wasn't Tully I'd whacked with the mezuzah. I'd hit the back of someone's skull. Tully was not alone.

41.

April 26, continued.

Nick's head snapped around. Tully's kilt was hitched up around his thigh. Nick pulled his hand back from beneath it.

I staggered back as if I'd been punched. I couldn't get a breath.

"It's not what you think," Nick said fast. "Let me explain." My body felt thunderstruck with disbelief, charged and painful as if I'd gotten a shock from a broken electric cord. Tully wiped a hand across his mouth and looked at the floor. Nick stepped toward me, lips swollen from hard kissing. I stepped away.

I have solved a lot of puzzles in my life. I make it a policy to figure out people's moves before they make them. Even creepy Mrs. Bason says I am very good at it. I felt like the board had been thrown in the air and the pieces were falling toward me. I knew they were going to whack me on the way to the ground and it was going to hurt. I hadn't in a million years seen this coming.

"Your sweet, homosexual friend here was very obviously checking out other guys," Nick went on. "I teased him. Told him to ask one to dance. Which I probably shouldn't have done, I'm sorry," he said to Tully, then back to me. "But I did and Tully did his whole I'm not gay thing. I disagreed and he started getting upset so we left the gym and I pulled him in here. I dared him. I'm sorry. It was a bad idea."

My head swam. Nick and Tully. Tully and Nick. My Adorable Goth Boy had his hand under Tully's kilt. And had been kissing him. *Kissing. Him.* It felt like my body was on fire. My vocabulary was completely gone.

"It was stupid, Stacy. I just wanted him to have a chance to be himself, you know? To have someone safe to test the water with? Just once. We're not together or anything. I thought it would help him. It sounds so dumb saying it out loud, but that's all it was."

The image of Nick's hand coming out from under Tully's kilt played over in my mind.

"He's telling the truth," Tully said. "This wasn't anything real. Nick was . . . proving a point." He moved his hip and the kilt fell back into place.

We all stood in silence as they waited for me to react.

"Is *this* why you won't kiss me?" I said to Nick. My eyes got hot and wet. The reality of him wanting to be with boys crushed me. Had he been lying to me this whole time? Why would he do that? What about the chemistry between us? Was that all a lie?

"Oh my god Stacy, NO! Look you know I've mentioned that I like everybody, right? Boys and girls."

"No," I said. "You have *not* mentioned that you like *everybody*. You've mentioned that you like *me*."

"And I happen to like you above all other humans on earth. I may even be falling in actual love with you, but you are fifteen and I am not. I am hyperaware of rushing you which not only do I not want to do, I promised your father I wouldn't."

I glared at him. Who was he dating? My father or me?

"Tully's my friend, too, now," Nick said. "Have you seen how he looks at other boys? I told him it was okay and he could tell me and when he kept saying no, I made a mistake. I'd been dancing with you in that dress and smelling your skin and I was . . ." he gave me a look. "I'm sorry. It was stupid. I know. But in the moment, it felt like a good opportunity for Tully to un-closet, at least to himself. And," he looked at the floor. Was that shame I saw? Good. Good. "I admit it was also an outlet for me."

Long seconds ticked by. Then the faucet opened.

"So you wanted me, but instead of talking to me to see what I wanted, or kissing ME which I am dying for you to do, you rotten moron, you grab Tully? You dare *him* to kiss you? You make out with him, HIM to work off the feelings you got from dancing with ME? And you tell yourself that you are helping HIM?" I literally saw red. Fury filled me. I aimed at Tully next.

"And you selfish, thoughtless jerk, made out with my boyfriend!" A burst of shame coated me. Did I say that? Was I so petty and selfish?

"It wasn't about you at *all*, Stacy," Nick said. "It was about Tully. He's been in an existential crisis for months! How much support do you think a young gay man from a sincere and devout Irish Catholic family has here at *St. Ignatius*? How many people can he be honest with? Would you have me NOT help him? Would you rather he killed himself because of guilt that God can't change him?

"What if he turned to drugs or booze? What if he marries Finder, hates having sex with her, and they start hating each other? What if they cheat on each other to experience even small moments of satisfaction or joy?

"You aren't thinking about this the right way, Stacy. People *die* staying in the closet. Did you know that? In your sheltered little world do you know how many suicides happen because people think they can't come out?"

I had never seen Nick this angry. Not even when Luke threw himself to Matilda. Part of my brain watched with interest. Another part realized he was right. The hurt part was angry at him anyway.

"I saw a chance to help, Stacy. Help a person I care about, who my very special, beautiful, sexually desirable and tragically young girlfriend cares about. My intention was to keep him safe. To give him an experience he's never had and desperately wanted so he can figure out his stuff, and make healthy decisions. I'm not *dating* him.

We didn't have sex! I *kissed* him so he could see what it was like to kiss a real boy and go find a boyfriend of his own. Is that so terrible? Am I such a bad person? And who is always telling me that kissing counts as 'doing nothing'?"

Ouch. Standing on the other side of that, my tables had turned. Nick didn't wait for me to reply.

"I'm going to take a vow in the not so far future to do no harm. Doesn't that also mean try to do good? To me, it does. I don't want to only save people's lives. I want to improve them. I want my patients to feel strong and good, not just not sick anymore. Why shouldn't I help Tully if I can? He's an awesome person. And he's not in love with me. We're never going to touch each other again. He just needed a little push out the closet door."

Nick shifted his weight and settled onto both feet.

"Look. Boy-girl rules are one way," he said. "Boy-boy rules are different. Sometimes. Kissing doesn't have to be a commitment. Sometimes it's just a way to feel comfort, to connect with another person and know you're alive and okay. It's that thing *you* say when you think no one notices. I am alive, I am safe, nothing bad is happening." Nick turned to Tully and brushed his hair out of his face, tucking a thick lock behind his ear.

The tenderness in the gesture made me ache.

"After that speech I actually am kind of in love with you," Tully said. Wait. Were his eyes . . . wet? The corner of Nick's mouth turned up and he kicked him gently in the shin.

"I am trying to save my future marriage here," he said. "So you should probably shut up."

WHAT DID HE JUST SAY? Future WHAT?

Nick turned back to me. "Are you really that surprised?" Nick asked, energy suddenly much lighter. "Didn't your gay-dar go off at all the last few months?" Wait, now they were joking about this? I was so confused. Not to mention furious.

"My gay-dar? My GAY-DAR?" My shout filled the sanctuary with echoing anger. "No, Nick! My gay-dar did not go off. Tully," I pointed at him with my whole arm stuck out "is devoted to Finder!" I pointed back to the gym. Tully looked away.

"I love Finder," Tully said. "She's my best friend. I don't want to hurt her. But I don't want to have sex with her again, either. Her," he paused, looking at Nick. "Or any girl." An admission. His face reddened. He struggled for words, but the pressure to explain himself was too much. "And I don't know how to talk about it, okay? Vaginas are scary!" he blurted. "Every time I think about actual sex with a girl, I feel . . . panic! And like nope. Just not for me."

Nope. Just not for me. Those words echoed in my fire-filled brain. I knew it wasn't a choice he was making to deliberately hurt her, but in that moment all I saw were two selfish children who had managed to break the hearts and crush the expectations of two people they claimed to love.

Speaking of childish, "You're both rotten liars and I hate you!" I shouted. "Sorry to interrupt the make-out session." I glared at Nick. "That hand under his kilt? Was that a dare, too?" I flashed back to the first time I met Nick and had walked in on him necking with a girl in an alley. I guess some people never change.

He opened his mouth to say something else. I turned and walked away. They did not follow me. Smart. Curse words of all varieties filled my mouth and I muttered them in a long, vicious stream as I walked past the candle altar and pushed open the heavy wooden door. So much for devotions.

Tully was gay. Tully had Nick's beautiful eyes staring into his. He had Nick's perfectly curved lip in his mouth. Tully's arms had been wrapped around that narrow waist. Tully had been pressed up against my Adorable Goth Boy in a way that made the encounter very intimate indeed and I was wearing a fancy, off the shoulder party dress for nothing. I had planned to be the one pressed up against that wall with that perfect lip pressed to my mouth. Not only was I angry, and disappointed, I was jealous. Jealous of stupid, stinking Tully. Who Nick had dared to kiss him.

I realized I was still holding my shoes. I stopped and put them on. My face was wet. I needed to pee. And I had to get to Judy's locker.

I went into the girls' bathroom and mopped my face with tp. I will thank Jill someday for the waterproof mascara, I thought. Small miracles. I looked not as bad as when I sometimes cried, maybe because I was repressing and had refused to ugly cry. I looked tired and kind of rained on. Some tears had left little drops on the top of my dress. Good thing I'd taken Mer's advice and worn the push-up bra, otherwise the tears would have fallen straight to the skirt and I'd look like I walked through a sprinkler.

"I hate men," I said out loud. Untrue, but it made me feel better to say it. "Stupid, stupid Y chromosome." I should become a lesbian. It would serve Nick right. Meredith and Finder and I should be lesbians together and live happily ever after, I thought.

But the truth? Vaginas scared me, too. I looked into my own eyes in the mirror and gave serious consideration to having sex with another girl. For about five seconds.

Nope, not for me.

Darn it. I understood Tully's point.

All the way up the stairs and to Judy's locker, I seethed. Meredith had a zero cheating policy so she was going to tell me dumping Nick was the only answer. And what, what, what was I going to tell Finder? I had to tell her, right? Would she even speak to me again if she ever found out I knew and didn't tell her?

I arrived at locker 245. 13-24-7. Left, right, left. Nothing. My hands shook. I took a deep breath and tried again. The lock didn't budge. I pulled the locker door, shaking it on its hinges. One more try. It. Did. Not. Open. I backed up and kicked the locker hard with the flat of my foot.

"Open!" I shouted, kicking the locker harder this time. "Open you stupid, ignorant, hateful, freakin' locker!" I slammed it with my hands.

The locker sat. It did not hear me. It did not care.

You have to calm down, Goldman, I told myself. I turned from the locker and walked halfway down the hall. No one is dying. You are alive, you are safe. Nothing bad is happening. This was all true. I walked slowly back to Judy's locker. I double-checked to be sure I'd been beating up the right one. I had. I put my hands on the cool metal and tried to settle my churning emotions.

"Hello friendly locker," I said out loud. "I need to get something from inside you. Please let your lock open."

Left, 13. Breathe. Right, 24. Breathe. Left, 7. Inhale, and the door popped open.

"Ohmygod, thank you."

Short stack of textbooks on the bottom, St. Ig's blazer and sweater on the hooks, dog-eared novel from English on the top shelf. No jewel case. No disc. I took out the novel and riffled the pages, looked under it and behind. I stood on my tiptoes and felt all the way to the back of the top shelf. No disc. I crouched and took out every text book, most identical to my own. AP Chem, AP Calc, AP English and Religion. I shook each heavy book so the pages fluttered open. No disc between the texts, no disc stuck in the pages.

A pocket-sized wolf calendar hung taped inside the locker door. I flipped back to January. The 27th, 28th and 29th were marked with yellow highlighter. February 26, 27, 28. March 27, 28, 29 all the same. If I noted those dates, and looked up the full moon and the murders, would they coincide? I bet they would.

Because Judy was the murderer.

I searched her blazer and sweater pockets for our project disc. Nothing. Anxiety grew in my belly. I emptied the locker onto the hallway floor, frantic to find the disc. I shook out every object twice. Someone approached from the other end of the hall.

"Ransacking lockers now?" Nick said. He and Tully walked side by side, spaced apart as if to say- look we're not touching.

I kept searching. They stood watching.

"Judy isn't coming tomorrow. Left our disc in her locker."

"What?" they said in unison. "What happened? Why won't she be there? Is she sick?" The thought of telling them the whole story spurred a feeling of panic in me so strong I thought I might scream.

Here is what I did not say:

Something's wrong with her DNA that makes her eat people. Or turn into something that eats people. She asked me to help her make it stop and I failed. Six innocent people are dead and *it's my fault.*

I said, "It's the full moon." I stood and kicked the chem book out of the way. "But I can't find our stupid disc!" The boys launched into action, searching and researching as I had just done. In the end it was unanimous. There was no disc in the locker.

Nick came close, but not too close. He waited for me to look at him. "Just tell me what you need."

I hugged Jill goodbye and told her I'd be home as soon as we got the disc. It could only be at one of two places, Judy's mom's or her dad's, but they were almost an hour away on the reservation and we didn't know the mom's address. Jill gave me permission to be home late and we both left the formal early.

Finder and Tully were coming with us so we'd all have chaperones. Each other. Ha, I thought, dripping with irony. Finder and I were the only ones who didn't need one.

I sat huddled in my matching shawl in the corner of the car. Finder and Tully occupied the back seat, snuggled together behind

Nick. Finder, Tully and I had all grabbed our gym sneakers out of our lockers and put our good shoes in Nick's trunk next to his bizarre collection of trunk stuff. Jack, tire, sleeping bag, medical field kit, water.

"What's that?" Finder had asked about a small leather bag tucked into the front.

"It's my overnight kit," he said. "Toothbrush, toothpaste. That kinda stuff. I'm a complete travel set." He smiled at us. He carried an *overnight* kit? I did not smile back.

Nick turned the heat to high and offered me his coat to wrap up in. The last thing I wanted, the thing I wanted more than anything, was to be wrapped in his comforting, pine tree scent. Jerk. Betrayer. Stupid boy. No thanks for the coat. Keep your stupid, yummy scent to yourself.

I replayed walking in on them over and over again in my mind. Their rustling had been loud enough that if I hadn't been distracted thinking about how to stop Judy, I might have recognized what I was hearing. It didn't even occur to me that someone might sneak into the chapel for privacy. Thanks to Terrence jumping me for blood freakin' whenever, of course I hear a noise and my head goes straight to vampires. Even though I KNOW that holy stuff repels them.

You're so self-centered, Goldman, I scolded. Why would Terrence care about you the night after he fed? Matilda doesn't care about you either. You're just a road to Finder.

I rolled my mezuzah over and over in my hands, fidgeting. Thinking. Rain started falling with little tick tack sounds on the windshield.

How little must I, as an individual, mean to Matilda? You'd think if you were going to ruin someone's life, you'd at least hate that person for a good reason. But Matilda didn't hate me. She didn't care about me at all. She cared about herself.

I faced a hard truth. No one in Richmond cared about me like they said they did. Nick treated himself to a smooch-fest in the name of 'helping' Tully, Tully was thinking about himself, trying to figure out who he was or whatever. *I* had not factored into *either* of their decisions. Nick had even said so. *It's not about you at all*, he'd said. Finder cared about me, but I was useful to her. She got to teach me about pummeling which I'm sure made her feel superior and I was largely responsible for her still being human, something I paid for every time Terrence knocked on my door. Judy had straight up used me. She had never pretended to be my friend, though. I had thought maybe it was happening anyway, friendship, but obviously not. If she was my friend, she would have told me what was going on. Explained it in no uncertain terms. I would have known she was using the serums for herself. I'd have known she wasn't getting the results she wanted and that she needed results or someone else would die. If she cared about me even a little bit, she would have let me know that if I failed to do what she needed, i.e. what I *didn't know* I was supposed to be doing, it could make her *miss the Statewide Science Fair* competition.

"She probably hoped that the serum would work, whatever that means," Nick said gently. "Maybe she didn't tell you because she was hoping she'd be there."

"How do you freakin' DO THAT?" I said. "Can you read my mind?"

"No. I feel your thought trails kind of. It felt like you're trying to make sense of why Judy isn't coming tomorrow and maybe hadn't thought of it from her point of view."

I had not one word to say to that.

I'd thought I was making real friends. Meredith had even approved of my now maybe not real friends. I put my hands under the shawl and against my belly. I felt sick, or maybe hungry. My face was hard with anger, but my heart pulsed with hurt. Every breath I pulled in landed in a lake of betrayal leaving me lonelier than when I'd arrived in Richmond months ago. The people who'd said they cared about me had lied.

We drove at least a mile in the vibrating silence. Finder had her eyes closed, head resting on Tully's shoulder. I watched Nick out of the corner of my eye. Restrategizing. His lips clung tight at the corners as he squinted into the rainy windshield. Two glaring points of light came toward us on the other side of the road. It was the first car we'd seen since getting on highway 1.5. Behind us, an engine revved. Nick sped up a little. A bright glare filled our cab as a car rode up and drove right on our behind.

"Just pass us, dude," Tully said, looking over his shoulder out the window.

"Pass me," Nick said. "What's your freakin' rush?" He kept pace, going a little faster. The oncoming car was close enough to see. A dark minivan. Nick pulled a little to the right. The road had double yellow lines. The tailgater swerved left over the lines into the other lane, right into the lights of the oncoming car. It laid on its horn. Nick hit the brakes. The tan SUV cut us off, speeding back into our lane.

"What the hell, dude!" Nick shouted swerving onto the narrow shoulder to avoid getting hit. Suddenly, a screeching scrape and a monstrous Bang! as the Hulk's right front tire hit something big. I slammed forward into my seat belt. The car scraped, jerked forward then screeched metal on pavement. Nick slammed on the brakes.

"Ohmygod. You guys okay? Is everyone okay?"

My heart slammed in my chest.

Hands still on the wheel, Nick turned to me. "Are you okay? What was wrong with that guy? I'm so sorry." The Hulk was still running.

I turned around and looked at Finder and Tully. We were all okay. After a minute, Tully and Finder got out to survey the damage.

"That scared the bejesus out of me," Nick said, still in the cab with me. "Was that guy drunk? But you're sure? You're really fine?"

"I'm sure."

"You're sure you're sure?"

"I'm sure. You?"

"Yeah. Okay. Freaked out, but not hurt or anything," he said. Both our chests rose and fell with adrenaline. That had been close. Too close. What had we hit when Nick swerved?

Nick took a long breath, focusing on me, giving me his Dr. Nick once over. "Is there any pain in your back, your neck?"

I shook my head. "No. I'm not hurt."

The highway was dark, quiet except for the rain. His pine eyes searched my face, his own shadowy in the dark cab. Was he truly clueless about how badly I had wanted to kiss him? Something in his gaze shifted and I realized what I was thinking must have shown in my eyes because his lips parted for a second. Then, he pressed them together, gave me a final appraisal, and got out of the car.

An hour later, we were all wet. We were dirty. It had taken all four of us to change that tire. Mother nature gave us one mercy. The rain had stopped.

A black Mercedes sped by us driving down the center of the empty road to give us the lane. Grit and sandy dirt spat onto us as it whizzed by. Finder caught my arm as the boys finished packing the tools back in the truck.

"Did something happen at the dance? Besides Judy freaking out?" she said. "There is some major tension in this car and I'm not sure if it's me and Tully or you and Nick or both." The trunk shut behind us.

"Later," I said. "Later."

Judy's dad's house was, ironically, less creepy in the dark. The whole place was lit up, lights on in every window, a little landing strip of garden lights lighting the walkway from the driveway to the house. Strings of white fairy lights clung to the edge of the porch giving a welcoming cottage air to what during the day looked lonesome. Tonight, it felt like a party.

Julian opened the door as we came up the porch steps. Inside, a cozy fire burned in the wood stove. A bottle of wine sat corked on the counter, the glass on the table empty, but used. The sink was full of dirty bowls and glasses and the stove had a big pot with the lid off. Had they had friends over for dinner? Propped by the door, something stood that hadn't been there at Thanksgiving. A really big gun.

"Can I ask you a personal question?" I asked after searching Judy's cute, magazine perfect bedroom and not finding the disk.

"I suppose."

"Did you know Judy injected herself with our project serums to resolve whatever her condition is that she won't tell me about?"

"She what?"

I told him what she told me. "She said she couldn't come to the Statewide Science Fair tomorrow because the serum hadn't worked and it was the full moon. We can't qualify without both partners present. Does any of this serum, full moon stuff make sense to you?"

The scientist took a long, familiar pause. An annoying pause that screamed I'm hiding something. Now, I named it.

The Richmond Pause.

Julian squinted at me. I was bad, truly terrible, at playing dumb. I knew more than I was saying and was sure he knew it. Oh, for crying out loud, I thought. Enough with the secrets. Just go ahead and tell me.

"Judy didn't come home after school today," Julian said. "She said she was with you. Going to the dance."

"What? No. She was at her mom's. A woman's voice was in the background. Her dog was barking."

"Judy's mom doesn't have a dog."

42.

April 26, continued.

"Is this the right address?" Nick said, pulling into the square of dirt next to the beat-up, burgundy hatchback.

"Why would he give us a fake one?" said Finder.

"Why didn't he come with us if he's worried?" said Tully.

"Because everyone in Richmond is a dirt stomping *liar!*" I said, too loud. "Everyone has a secret, nobody tells you anything until your life is freakin' in danger from not knowing, people sneak up on you and drink your blood and everywhere you turn someone is doing something they shouldn't!"

"Right on, Chess Team," Finder said. "Tell us how you really feel."

I huffed a big, frustrated breath and got out of the car.

Drum music from a neighbor's party echoed from the dense woods behind the house. Must be houses behind, I thought. I hadn't noticed any others close by on this road. The walkway to the tiny, run down home was made of beachy, half-circle paver blocks, but the house, a perfect rectangle mounted on blocks, couldn't have been farther from beachy. The bulb at the front door was yellowed and strung with cobwebs. Moths and bugs flew against it with little taps and buzzes. The cracked step was made of stacked bricks. I didn't see a doorbell, so I knocked. No response. No dog barking. I knocked again.

"Judy?" I called. Stepping over a pot of dead plants, I looked into the window. One light on.

Nick brought his flashlight over and handed it to me.

"Need me to help with that?" he said eyeing the door lock.

I don't even have a key to my house, Judy had said standing in my backyard at Christmas. I turned the knob and the door opened.

The smoke and sour stench overwhelmed me before I even stepped in.

"Judy?" I called. "Mrs. Forest?" Silence.

I avoided a layer of wet newspapers just inside the door. They bore a smell any dog walker would recognize. Cigarette butts overflowed ashtrays and beer bottles stuffed the recycling bin by the back door. The kitchen light was on, a single fluorescent bulb dangling over the sink.

"First time in a trailer?" Nick asked, wiping his feet before coming inside. A sunken plaid couch sat in front of a new-looking TV.

I turned left out of the living room and shone the flashlight into the first bedroom. Full-sized mattress on the floor, mirror propped against the wall, laundry everywhere. A plastic laundry basket overflowed at the end of the room, but those clothes didn't match the wadded-up lace underwear, bras, skinny jeans and scrubs scattered and piled on the linoleum floor. The contents of that laundry basket belonged to a man.

The next room had to be Judy's. I knocked, then opened the door. I flipped on the light switch. Except for tape marks and torn paint spots, the walls were completely bare. It looked like the walls had once been covered in pictures and posters, but they'd been ripped down. The ceiling was painted sky blue. A twin bed on a child-like white bed frame stood made and tidy. Next to the bed, on the nightstand, stood a small lamp, and a book. The window was open.

Judy's school backpack leaned against her desk, a tiny 'secretary' style writing table that looked older than the house. The single drawer was half open. A framed photograph peeked out. I pulled the drawer open. The photo was of a beautiful white wolf sitting next to a large gray wolf. The glass in the frame was cracked. I closed the drawer. I unzipped the backpack and there, right in the front, was our disc.

Nick stood in the kitchen, arms crossed.

"Are these from your lab?"

I went over and there on the counter stood a lab rack labeled Forest/Goldman with one vial on it. A full vial. I uncorked the vial and sniffed.

My serum all right. But it should be refrigerated. I opened the fridge and regretted it. The smell of rotten milk wafted out. Some vegetables had disintegrated into a moldy soup on the bottom shelf, but the top shelf held another rack of serum. I shut the door in disgust. I hope it rotted in her lying belly.

"Let's go," I said, still clutching the vial of serum from the counter. If Judy was our culprit, we had to find her and trap her before whatever turned her into a people killer did its job.

Nick said nothing and followed me out.

Finder and Tully were not in the car. The moon hung a distant, bright orb as the clouds parted. I looked around for my friends.

"Where'd they go?" I said, looking toward the dark woods. Light flickered in the distance.

"Stacy," Nick said, "I owe you an apology."

I stopped and looked at him. Regret showed in every line of his face.

"I am so sorry. You're right. I had no business doing what I did. You guys are younger than me and it's not my job to show you, or Tully, or anyone what you haven't already figured out on your own. It was selfish of me, trying to save the day, and I'm sorry. I don't know how I can make this right with you. Will you let me try?"

"Why do you respect Tully more than me?" I said. "You said you were helping him get his needs met or whatever. What about my needs? I'm upset that you'll," I made air quotes, "'help' him but ignore me when I tell you what I need in the exact same category." I crossed my arms over my chest. "It doesn't make sense and it's not fair." I paused. "These are not rhetorical questions."

Nick was quiet as the moonlight lit his face.

"I hadn't thought of it that way. Unconscious double standard?" he said, with a shrug.

"That is a deeply unsatisfactory answer."

"Guys!" Finder waved at us from the tree line. She gestured for us to come.

"I want to know why boy-boy and boy-girl rules are different," I said before we were close enough to be overheard. "What about girl-girl rules? Shouldn't it just be human-human rules? And who makes up these stupid rules anyway?"

"You're not going to believe this," Finder said, tugging her sweatshirt down toward her hips.

The heady smell of early spring forest permeated the damp night air. Tully and Finder led us back toward the music and firelight.

Why was she leading us down here? This party wasn't our business. Finder put out her arm and stopped us when we got close enough to see the blaze, a bright bonfire burning as tall as the people dancing around it. The music wasn't recorded, like I'd assumed. There were three drummers on the far side of the fire, all dressed in ratty pants or shorts. The dancers were dressed similarly, one, a thin man, wore a loincloth and nothing else. One woman, blonde and Asian looking in the firelight, wore a loincloth style bikini.

Good grief, I thought. Weren't they cold?

Tully crouched down and crept to the left off the trail. I could see where he was headed, a massive tree trunk lay on its side, a perfect place to stay hidden and watch. Finder pulled me behind a tree and squeezed close to me. She pointed to a table set up by the fire.

"Look," she whispered. "Look at the table." A table holding a rack with a vial of serum.

"What is this?" I whispered back. Pressed against my back, I felt her shrug. I was a Stacy sandwich, tree in front, me in the middle and Finder behind. If we stood side by side, the tree wouldn't shelter us from view.

"Dunno, but is that you and Judy's serum?"

It had to be.

The dancers whooped and shouted going round and round the fire. I searched for Judy in their midst. Not that I could ever picture her dancing half-naked around a fire.

I counted eight people including the drummers. No Judy. A smallish woman sat by a tree, thin, familiar. Judy's mom? I'd only met her once close up.

Two of the biggest plastic dog crates I'd ever seen sat behind the fire by the drummers. Sides toward me, I couldn't see inside them. A tan SUV was parked behind them and further yet, another row of cars. No trash cans, no picnic benches. This was no park or official campsite. This party felt secret. A cold breeze blew, like a giant refrigerator opened and quickly shut. Something here was wrong.

"We should go," I said.

"Agreed," Finder whispered close in my ear. I grabbed her hand.

Not yet. Set your fear aside. Judy needs you.

"Just a sec," I said to Finder. And the drums stopped.

There you are! I said in my head to Michael. *Where were you earlier?*

Busy. Sorry. I didn't reply because you weren't in any danger. Judy is.

Judy isn't here, I said.

Loincloth Man spoke deep in his gut, a dark sounding set of words I didn't understand. He raised his hands, then shook sweat out of his cropped hair.

Another man opened one crate. A big Husky dog shot out. The man grabbed the leash and the dog choked as it fell over backward trying to run away.

"It's okay," the man soothed. "You're okay, dog." The dog calmed down as it got further from the crate, still turning and looking over its shoulder, winding its leash around the man's legs as it turned this way and that trying to find an escape. Loincloth Man went to the table. He filled a syringe with serum.

What was he doing with *my science*? Did he even know what that was? What it could do? Should I stop him?

Nick slid to our tree behind Finder. "That's Luke's dog!" he whispered.

"That's my serum!" I whispered back. "And how could it be Luke's dog? Didn't they find them?"

"No. It's Grendel. Has to be. See the one white paw? Super rare marking in wolf hybrids."

Finder put her hands on both of our shoulders to hush us. The fire dancers were slowing. A thin, grey tentacle of smoke, darker and thicker than what blew from the bonfire, drifted low in front of the table. It wound around the dog. The dog barked like it had been stung and tried to run. The man holding the leash lost his balance and let go. He crashed into the table. Loincloth Man ran for the dog and stepped on the leash. The dog jerked and Loincloth Man fell, the syringe in his hand flying into the air. A drummer dove forward grabbing the leash and stopping the dog from bolting. The syringe hit the ground. The Asian woman snatched it up. She jammed it into the dog's neck.

"Tie it!" she said. "Tie it! This had better work this time, Ed!"

The two men yanked and pulled the frightened dog to a tree where they used a carabiner to hook the leash to itself. The heavy smoke swirled around the dog.

"I don't think that's smoke," said Nick.

The dog began to writhe.

43.

April 26, continued.

Muscle moved under the fur as the dog howled, a deep, wolflike howl. Maybe it was the firelight, but it looked like another animal ran under the dog's skin. I had seen this before. The dog convulsed in a seizure. Yes. I'd seen this months ago when Evia had gotten sick. The dog shook itself, and convulsed again, but this time, something was different. Its legs elongated, its teeth grew to below its jaw. On the fourth shake, the dog was barely recognizable as itself. No longer a regular dog, a monster stood before us. What had been in that syringe?

The smoke drifted closer. The Asian woman started a chant. All the fire dancers fell to their hands and knees like marionettes jerked on strings. Dissonant and rough sounding, the dancers joined the chant. I tried to make out words, but couldn't. The chant wasn't English, or any language I recognized. The sound was unearthly and strange, like it came from underneath the ground. Loincloth Man raised one hand and the chanting ceased.

He spoke, also in the weird resonant language, vibrating the difficult words deep in his chest. He raised his hands, bent and touched the earth, then took a handful of ash and sprinkled it from the fire to the dog monster's tree. The smoke followed the path of the ash. The dog monster snarled, baring its fangs as the smoke got closer. The smoke touched its nose. The dog shrieked in pain, jerking back from the smoke. The shock of searing pain echoed through my body. In a flash of certainty, I knew. I had been touched by that creature. The icy smoke was, like Nick said, not smoke at all. Bodiless, incorporeal, but no less itself, that smoke was the Man with No Face. The struggling dog's restraint snapped. The smoke slid toward the dog monster's ear. Terrified, the creature bolted into the forest.

"Catch it!" cried the Asian woman. Three of the fire dancers ran off in chase.

And then, from the other dog crate came a hollow, frightened scream. A scream like someone waking up from a nightmare. The crate shook. Pale fingers wrapped around the crate's door bars. Human fingers.

The Man with No Face slid like a snake back along the ash path through the fire toward Loincloth Man. It swirled up to the ash on his fingers, sniffing, if it could sniff. Loincloth Man didn't move. He gasped and crushed his eyes shut. The smoke slithered around his neck. Loincloth man winced. The smoke slid down his chest and leg leaving a scalding red burn in its wake. It disturbed the wet dirt around the fire, swirling in the soft earth making what looked like an intentional pattern. Then with a hiss, or maybe a sizzle, it slithered off into the forest following the direction the dog monster had gone. Finder, Nick and I held each other behind the tree hardly daring to breathe.

The Asian woman and Loincloth Man crawled to the spot where the smoke had been.

She cursed loud and long.

She said something to Loincloth Man I was too far away to hear. She shoved him hard and he fell on his butt in the dirt. She grabbed him by the hair and slapped his face.

"How could you bungle this?" she shouted. "If it doesn't work, we are dead!" Another scream, long and sharp, and the second crate rocked on its edge. A thump and the crate rocked to the other side. And with one kick of a small, too pale foot, the door burst off the crate.

Judy slid out.

I blinked, stunned.

"Did you drug me, Ed, you filth?" she said louder than I had ever heard her speak. A wave of relief grabbed me. Judy was here and she was human! We could catch her. Finder grabbed my hands. She was thinking what I was thinking. We were gonna make this okay. We just didn't know how.

Judy leaped to her feet, graceful, strong and half-naked in ratty short shorts and tank. She turned to face Loincloth Man, back to us. Her tank top, tied around her back and neck with strings, contrasted with the heavy chain that bound her wrists. Behind me, Finder gasped.

Beautiful and detailed neck to thigh, Judy's tattoo was fully visible except the slivers blocked by her bound arms and covered by her shorts. A wolf, almost photographic in detail, looked over its shoulder, painted in this moment by orange and gold brushstrokes of firelight behind her.

"I did more than drug you," Ed hissed. "Look at your arm."

A dark pattern of bruising encircled half moons. Bite marks.

"You think it'll come for me instead of you if you poison me with your venom? I'm not anything like you." She flexed her fists and pulled once, twice. The thick chain cracked. It snapped off her wrists, falling to the dirt. "Do whatever you want to me, you pig. The Famelicus only eats- " Her sentence was cut off by her scream. Hair fell over Judy's face as she contorted forward, hands curling into fists.

Judy's cry turned mute. An ear-splitting tearing sound cracked the air. Fur broke out above the ridge of her spine. Along her ribs, the wolf tattoo rolled across her skin. More fur erupted in a spray mist of blood. Beside the crackle of the fire, a new sound split the air; the sharp snap of bone cracking as Judy's body pushed its way through a brutal change.

A snow-white wolf emerged as she transformed from the core out. Her grasping hands changed last. Fully in wolf form, Judy, the most stunningly gorgeous animal I'd ever seen outside of a zoo, took two slow steps backward and crouched. She threw herself forward at Ed/Loincloth Man. As a wolf, Judy almost matched his size. She slammed into him. He hit the ground. He shrieked when she bit him.

I shivered. Was she going to eat him? I squeezed my eyes shut. Think Goldman, think. None of the other victims were on the reservation. They were all in Richmond City proper. In a moment of quiet, I opened my eyes. The blonde Asian woman had run to the knocked over table and was kneeling, searching. She found what she was looking for.

Sticking her arms straight out in front of her like a trained shooter, she aimed the gun at Judy. Before I could even shout no, she pulled the trigger. Pop.

"Ow!" Ed cursed as a dart struck his arm. Judy rounded for another attack. "What the hell, Lea?"

"I thought it was a real gun! And I was aiming for her!" She dropped the tranquilizer pistol.

Lea? I'd heard that name, but not at school. It hit me why she was familiar. Mrs. Macy from Dad's law firm! The woman I eavesdropped on at our party.

But how had Steve been wrong? Judy was the werewolf, not Mrs. Macy.

"Get the other syringe! The first shot wasn't enough!"

"Ed! No!" shrieked Judy's mom still sitting by the tree. "Don't poison her again!"

Mrs. Macy searched fast. Judy snarled and leapt. Ed raised his arm to fend her off, but not fast enough. She bit him in the face.

"Lea, stop!" The woman's voice was a sobbing surge of desperation. Mrs. Macy ignored her, ran up behind Judy and jammed down with the syringe. The wolf whirled on the older woman, lips curling back. Wolf Judy rammed her head into Mrs. Macy knocking her down. Then Judy's whole body spasmed. She leapt in the air twisting as if she could shake off what hurt her. Her fur began to roil.

Wolf Judy landed feet on the ground. Her head dropped low to the dirt. A lump moved like a wave beneath her fur. Like it had with the dog before it became a monster. Like it had with Evia before I made her cure. Everyone went still. Wolf Judy sniffed the air and looked straight through the trees. At us. She barked once.

Help.

Fur still roiling, Judy bounded off into the woods.

"Catch her!" Ed cried, bleeding on the ground. The remaining dancers took off after the wolf.

"As long as *he* catches her, it's fine," Mrs. Macy said. "He's hungry."

"He doesn't want *her*," Ed said, pointing to the dirt in front of the fire.

My insides felt like a shaken pickle jar, bits and pieces of sediment churning. I needed to get the ripping sound of fur and bones breaking out of my head.

We stayed hidden while Ed and Mrs. Macy cleaned his bloody face and bite wounds with a towel.

Judy's mom struggled against the tree. Not sitting by choice, I now saw. Sitting because she was bound.

"Please let me go, Ed. Please, Lea! He can't eat my baby! Please! Please let me go find her!" Mrs. Macy walked over to her.

"Be quiet, Cathy, or I'll break your jaw."

"Please Lea, she's a child. She can't- " Mrs. Macy kicked Judy's mom in the face.

"And the next time Ed comes to your bed," she said, "keep your filthy legs shut. I'm alpha here, not you." Ed stumbled from the ketamine shot as he and Mrs. Macy loaded the crates into the back of a tan SUV. I bet the one that almost creamed us on the highway. They drove off on a road little more than a trail of tire tracks.

I bolted forward to free Judy's mom. Tully got there first, and started working on the knots.

"Stacy!" Cathy Forest cried. "What are you doing here?"

"What did he inject her with?" I grabbed her shoulders. "What did he have in that shot?" She stared at me. There was a bad smell on her breath. A sour, boozy smell. I made her look at me. I repeated my question.

"Don't know," she said. "Venom is mixed in. He thought it might not be enough to force her to change when she was already a wolf, so he bit her, too." Tears mixed with the snot running down her face.

"Is it our project serum?" I said, ready to shake her. "What is in the vials in your house?"

"Whatever Julian gave him," she said.

Whatever *Julian* gave him? I opened my mouth to speak, but no words came out. He doesn't want *her*, Ed/Loincloth Man said.

I ran to the fire. It blazed hot and high as my chest. The dirt was disturbed with fancy cursive script.

You must honor me.

Finder came up beside me. "Is Judy in danger?"

I was about to say I didn't know. But maybe I did.

I held up my hand, just a sec. I looked into the fire. Judy said she had told me everything and I hadn't seen the clues. I hadn't been looking for them. In other words, I hadn't been listening.

Steve would listen.

I closed my eyes, heat from the fire strong on my face. Hang on thoughts, I said. I'll be right back. I listened to the fire crackling, my friends' voices soft behind me. I listened to my breath move in and out of my body. The moment I got quiet, the information came loud in my mind.

Ask Julian.

"We have to go right now," I said. "Back to Judy's dad's."

Tully got the ropes loose enough to free Cathy. He and Nick helped her stand.

"Will she shift like the dog? Into a monster? Where would she run?" Finder was asking. "Where does that road lead?"

"Like the dog, yes. And she'll run to the river. She'll go to her dad. They hunt together."

"He's a wolf, too?"

"It's a hereditary condition," she said.

Hereditary. Condition. Click. A puzzle piece fell into place. Judy's mutations were in the same spot as Evia's because they both changed shape. Evia's had come from a near death experience, Judy's were hereditary. One's DNA changed with transitions, the other transversions. Click. None of my serums worked on Judy because her DNA recognized her mutations as correct and normal, so the repair enzymes registered as useless.

Judy's mom was still talking. " . . . one parent can pass the gene. I don't have it."

"The full moon triggers it?" asked Nick.

She looked at him like I used to look at Bradley Joe in chess. "Okay," he said. "The full moon triggers it."

"Ed and Lea think if Judy is gone, John will give over the land battle. Did you see it tonight? In the smoke? He's eaten six and barely built himself a row of teeth! He's going to eat us all if we don't find an answer. I don't want him to eat my baby!" Tears leaked again down her face.

Finder grabbed Cathy's shoulders. "He who? Who is eating you?!"

She started to tremble. "I can't say his name or he might come back. Ed thinks he'll eat the hybrid dogs and John's pack instead of us if they have the venom in them. The only flesh that feeds him has to have his venom in it." She wiped her snotty nose on her arm.

"So it's not Judy doing the killing?" I said. "The full moon murders aren't her?"

Cathy shook her head. "No." A sob burst from her. "Ed wants her to be one of the ones it eats!"

"That's why they stabbed Judy with venom?"

She nodded. "And Julian's serum. So she'll become a monster."

"Where do they hunt?" Finder asked. "How can we find them before they catch her again?"

"Ed and Lea will take this track to the river and follow the road that runs beside it. They'll get to the bridge and cross the river where it's low and thin. Probably drive back up the other side."

She wove unsteadily back down the path back toward the trailer. Nick kept her from falling twice.

"Not that this is any of my business," I said, before running for the car. "But throw him out. And clean your house. Your daughter deserves better."

"What did you do to my serum!" I said as loud as I'd ever spoken to an adult. Julian stared as we pushed past him into the cottage. I threw the syringes and vials I'd collected at the fire site into the now clean sink. "When your science fair partner is a werewolf, somebody should TELL YOU! And, THIS IS NOT my serum! It's venom! *What did you do to it?*" I shook the vial from Judy's mom's counter in his face.

"I don't know what you're talking about."

"She went wolf in front of us, Julian. At a bonfire behind her mother's house. And right before they injected her, they injected this dog and it became a monster."

Julian stood, not saying or doing anything. Anything except calculating how much he still could avoid telling me. The Richmond Pause.

"When the squirrel got sick, she wasn't sick, was she? She'd been injected with whatever this is, a clinical trial, right? Mrs. Macy knew she was on the list of people to be eaten by this thing and wanted to create a substitute. The question is why does it want to eat her? For dancing around a fire and chanting? I don't know, but you do, don't you, Julian?"

He said nothing.

"Tonight, the venom or whatever *you made for them* wasn't strong enough. It didn't turn Judy all monster-y, like it did the dog. But she ran off. So maybe it did work and we don't know. When this happened to the squirrel, I caught the mutant proteins and made a repair enzyme that worked. When we looked at her DNA again it was as regular as it got for her. Right?" I moved away from the sink toward him. "I'm right, right? TALK TO ME!"

"Yes," he said. "Yes, you're right."

"And you used my serum, not my Evia serum, but my save-Judy-from-certain-doom-from-whatever-her-condition-is serum to make the monster brew that is now maybe turning her into whatever that dog turned into? Right?"

"Yes."

"And her *condition* is that she's a *werewolf!*"

I cussed. I think for the first time ever in front of an adult, I cussed full scale, adult curse words.

Stunned silence filled the room.

I eyed the rifle in the corner. Julian would never use that on people, would he?

"Ed wants the land to keep his people safe and John is in his way," Julian said, voice Judy quiet. "He threatened to kill him if I didn't cooperate."

My body got tense, tense like someone grabbed me and told me to stop asking questions.

I fought the urge. I opened my mouth again to tell him the rest.

Stop, Stacy. Loud and clear in my mind.

Why?

He is not going to tell you any more truth tonight.

Did you grab my arm?

No. That was your body. See how you are leaning away from him? How your muscles feel like stones?

Yes.

That's your body wisdom helping you. Telling you no. Look at the door.

I looked at the door.

Feel that pull? Feel your body moving toward it ever so slightly?

Weird, I did.

Listen to that. Please.

"Give me the keys to the lab," I said.

"I can't do that."

"You can. And you will. Unless you happen to have that antidote handy."

"He'll murder John!"

"Not if your serum works! Not if she turns into a monster and kills John herself because she has no mind left to know friend from enemy! And what will John do if he finds out you used his daughter's very own science project to get her killed?"

44.

April 26, continued.

My body felt locked, like a bowstring taut with an arrow.

"What are the chances that's really the lab key and not, like, a classroom?" Finder leaned over the center of the front seat. She tossed a fun size chocolate into each of our laps. "Stress relief," she said.

"I cannot think that way right now," I said. "If he gave us the wrong key, Nick will pick the lock."

"I need you to teach me to do that, by the way," Tully said.

I snorted. As if Nick hadn't taught him enough.

Part of me wanted to talk about what we had seen, part of me was processing. Route 1.5 was dark and still as we barreled down it. I knew we were driving past fields on one side, woods on the other but it felt like driving through Steve's deep ocean TV shows, black as far as you can conceive and filled with creatures. Creatures you couldn't imagine. Creatures you might be the only living person to have seen. Creatures who, if they saw you, would eat you because you were meat and they were hungry.

The lights of the interstate came into view in the distance. Nick felt a mile away on the wide bench seat. Just where my dad would want him. Far away.

"I'm not sure- "

"Do you think- " we said at once.

"You go," we both said again. I paused, waiting for him. He paused, waiting for me.

"Go," I said.

"I was going to say that I know we saw what we saw and that Richmond is, you know, what it is, but how was that possible? Like . . . medically? It's explainable," Nick said, "I get that. But how is it *possible*?"

"Are werewolves harder to accept than vampires?" Finder asked.

"No," Nick said, "and yes." Nick reached closer to me on the seat, an offer to hold hands.

I wasn't sure I wanted to hold Nick's hand right now. I mean, I desperately wanted to hold Nick's hand. But Before Nick, not Now Nick. It's not that what I'd walked in on was wrong or even weird, it was just that it was Nick. My Nick. First boyfriend not a jerk Nick who was supposed to have eyes only for me.

My fury had faded in the overwhelm of everything else. Faded to the dull thud of angry disappointment. In Nick, in Tully. In me. Wasn't I enough? And maybe it was like he said. Boys have different rules. Boys couldn't get each other pregnant. Boys don't tend to tell their parents they are playing with other boys so an age difference isn't such a big deal because the whole situation is secret. I started to rub my face with my hands, but they smelled like dirt.

"Why didn't Steve smell Judy if she's a werewolf?" Finder asked. I shook my head.

"He smelled Mrs. Macy. He caught her sniffing Evia's cage in his room and said she smelled like rotten things. I don't remember him smelling anything when Judy was around. It's one reason why I assumed she was normal."

We turned onto the highway, worry and decisions pressing me into my corner of the wide cab. I tried to thrust away images of the blood flying from Judy's skin as fur broke through. And worse, the sounds of her screaming, screaming as her skin stretched and bones cracked. I couldn't get the echo of it out of my ears.

As if he was reading my mind, Nick popped a tape into the player. Alan Parson's Project. He turned it up.

"Do we catch her to keep her safe?" said Finder.

I was no expert animal trapper. I had no idea how to catch a werewolf.

Who, besides Julian who wasn't 'fessing up, would know about werewolves? There was something big, very big that Julian wasn't telling us. Something bigger than werewolves, bigger than serums, bigger than trying to save one life by sacrificing another. Who would know the bigger picture?

A shiver ran up my spine. I knew where we had to go. My hand shook.

"Do you think she's the only option?" Nick said as if I'd said my awful, inevitable idea out loud.

"You're creeping me out with all the replying to what I'm thinking," I said. "Could you stop?"

"I thought you liked me being smart."

"I do, but does smart have to mean psychic?"

"It's critical thinking," he said. "You asked Julian for the lab key. That means that your first thought is to go to the lab and drum up some of the antidote for Judy you used on Evia. But Evia was a squirrel and cooperative. Judy is a werewolf and may or may not be cooperative, plus we have no way to track her or catch her other than saying, 'Here, Judy, Judy, Judy'. So you are realizing your original plan has a flaw. Though you still want to go make the antidote, we need the missing piece of information Julian refuses to tell us. He may be playing both sides for reasons beyond protecting his lover and so we are stuck. That's all."

"Who are you, Sherlock Holmes?" said Finder.

Nick pulled into the DQ parking lot. "Cherry or chocolate dips for the backseat?" he said. "And then we'll go arm up."

Maymont Mansion glittered. Moonlight shone through parting silver clouds and reflected off a path rife with puddles from the earlier rain. The back gate stood open as if Matilda expected us.

Did she? Or worse, was she expecting someone else and we were about to interrupt? Was the Man with No Face here? No door need be open for *him*, all smoke and teeth. I stopped at the top of the hill in front of the carriage house.

"Is this a trap?" I said.

No one replied.

The lawn sponged beneath our feet as we left the path. Each step released the fresh green scent of mowed grass and damp earth. It was so opposite New York, where the patina leaned to the tang of metal and the oily musk of asphalt and cars. Maymont's smells were deceptive. The simple, clear olfactory reminders of spring hid blood and soul thievery, dusty, dry flesh, and musty lies. They disguised the tang of hairspray and old lady lavender soap, the scents of Matilda.

Finder stood on my right, the post ice-cream stop at Flying Eagle giving her a change of clothes and her full arsenal of weapons. Nick had two stakes hidden in the folds of his coat. Tully had stakes, too, the ones with handles I'd given him and a deal with Finder that she would throw him a blade if needed.

"I'm just gonna say this once so I can say I said it," Nick said, "I do not like it here." He held up his hand and sure enough, it trembled. "I am going to make every effort not to wet myself, but if I fail, please don't tell anyone. Especially my roommate. Lastly, if I die, I want you all to know," his green eyes locked on me, "that I am sorry. For stuff."

I rolled my eyes. "You aren't going to die, Nick. This cannot possibly be scarier than meeting her at the Carillon and if she wanted to kill you, you'd already be dead."

"Maybe, to the second point," he said, "but to the first, this is definitely scarier. The last time I was in this house, things did not go well."

"They went great," Finder said. "We got your sorry behind out alive."

Nick shrugged. That was true.

"We could try to catch a werewolf for information if you'd prefer," Finder said.

Oh for heaven's sake.

"Stop thinking about the ways we can lose," I said. "We have a plan. If there's any bargaining to do, *I'll* do it." Emphasis on the *'I'll'*. With the level of guilt flowing out of his pores, I didn't want Nick volunteering himself for something stupid to save me like he had with Luke. And we all know where that got us. Us, meaning me.

"Full information, lowest possible price. Leave alive and undamaged. Mate."

I stood as tall as I could in my dirty, crushed, formal wear and sneakers. Matilda would notice. She would comment. I could not let her belittling throw me. She would do whatever she could to lord her superiority over me and scare me. A bully like any other. Like Joseph Thornton. Like my mom. The only difference was Matilda had superpowers, minions and a special thirst for my blood.

I had a mezuzah in my purse, a Star of David around my throat and a spray bottle of holy water hidden in my skirt.

I closed my eyes and unclenched my fists. Breathe, Goldman. Saanvi's voice spoke in my head. Accept this moment. Let your body lead. You are enough.

Was I enough? Was I really? Could I get this information and figure out how to stop the next night's murder? Could I get Judy safe from whatever was poisoning her? Could I figure out what Julian wasn't telling us?

What if Matilda didn't know? What if she did know but wouldn't tell? What if she didn't know the right information? What if she ate us? STOP. Do *not* think about the ways you can lose.

"This part's easy," I said. "It's just vampires. It's not like, you know. Finals."

The wide porch gables stood like the columns of a Roman court as we approached the mansion. Light glimmered from every window.

"Is that music?"

Finder and I exchanged a look. Vampires needed something to do, too, on a Saturday night? They couldn't be strutting about biting people *all* the time, could they? I shivered. I kinda thought they could.

Tully and Finder split off to keep watch from a distance and see if they could get a view into the windows. If we didn't come out in half an hour, they'd come in after us.

Nick and I went across the path, up the steps. One last breath. I rang the mansion doorbell.

Voices, many voices, and music definitely now, dance music. But not like the spring formal. This was old fashioned dance music, waltz maybe? Like in the movies.

"Should I ring again?" I asked Nick. A Bat Suit I recognized flung the door open.

My mouth dropped open in a little "o".

Matilda was having a party.

45.

April 26, continued.

Over six feet tall and backlit by golden party lights, the Bat Suit loomed above me like a Goliath. Where had he been the night of New Year's? Maybe left home to guard the house? He certainly was big enough.

A rook, I said to myself. Just a big rook. Go diagonal and he can't touch you.

"Is Mrs. Bacon available?" I asked, trying to keep my voice cool and professional.

"Your gown is soiled," he said. "She won't allow you in if your gown is soiled."

"Close the door, Sturch!" called a cool, familiar voice. "Everyone is here we are expecting." Matilda sailed into view. She stopped when she saw me. Her slim fitting lavender gown fell around her like a rhinestone waterfall. It was cut above the shin in the front to keep her feet clear, for dancing, I assume, and to show her shapely calves. Behind her, it caressed the floor like a pool of gentle silk.

"Miss Goldman," she said through a light smile. "What an interesting time for you to appear. You're like a little troll, aren't you? Popping up unwanted at inconvenient times." She eyed Nick. "I'm surprised to see *you* darkening my doorstep." She turned her body toward me. I looked at her right shoulder, not at her eyes. "Have you changed your mind about our," she paused lowering her voice even more, "conversation? Come back tomorrow and dress with more . . . discretion. Now is not a good time." She started to turn away.

"It's an emergency."

"No emergencies on party nights," she said. "It's the rule. And what happened to your dress? How did you even know to come in one? My parties are invitation only affairs."

A young woman on the girl/woman cusp, came up behind Matilda and laid a familiar hand on her lower back. Clad in light green, she looked up into Matilda's face.

"Everything is fine, sweeting," Matilda replied to the girl's expression of concern. "I'm turning away an unwanted guest."

The girl turned to look at us. Without thinking I made eye contact. She gazed back at me, surprise riding behind her eyes. Something about her was familiar. I recognized her as the Young Docent who had led our Maymont tour back at Thanksgiving. Just taller than me, thin, sharp and intelligent as she assessed my appearance. She did not approve.

"Can I help?" she asked Matilda, looking back and forth between Nick and I.

"I need to talk to *you*, Mrs. Bacon," I said. "It's urgent."

"Sounds like a favor, if you ask me. My price for favors is quite," she eyed my open throat, "specific."

"No favor," I said, keeping my voice low and steady. "Unless you want to owe me one. It's about *him*."

The vampire's body weight shifted. I kept my eyes on the tiny crystal beads sewn to the shoulder of her dress.

The young woman said something to Matilda I couldn't hear. Then, louder she added, "Miss Goldman's not a time waster. I think she would only come here if she had something important for you. She might even enjoy the party if we clean her up a bit."

"I just want to talk," I said. "We're not staying." Wait. How did she know I wasn't a time waster? Did she *know me* know me? And it seemed unlikely she'd remember my name from months ago.

"Mmm," she said. "We'll see."

I did not like that one bit. What was happening at this party that this woman/girl thought I should stay? I'd read *Interview with the Vampire*. Most of it anyway. Vampire parties were not healthy for humans to attend.

She gave me an even look. I had to know her from more than the tour. I filtered through the blondes in my classes, but no match. Unless she had spoken to me, would I have even noticed her at St. Ig's? Was she a regular at Third Rock or Chapter & Mercy? No dings of recognition, but I swear I knew her.

"You have three minutes," Matilda said. "Irene, the settee."

Looks like we were going to this party after all.

Matilda turned away from the door. Lavender silk rustled across the entryway tile behind her. Nick and I exchanged a look. You don't have to come with me, my look said. He nodded, he understood. He was not leaving my side.

The proper front door of Maymont mansion opened into a narrow parquet floor foyer which, in turn, opened on the left into an elaborate man's study and on the right an even more elaborate Louis XIV style pink sitting room. Even the ceiling was painted. Heavy wood furniture with velvet cushions had been moved into attractive nooks. Thick, wood framed doors were flung open to reveal the high ceilinged, glittering center hall turned ballroom. The scents of appetizers, cake and wine wafted though the doors as we passed though.

Irene plumped a cushion as two guests cleared a small settee. It sat beside a cozy chair in a visible corner farthest from the dancing. The band stood on the landing above the stairs where we'd staked our first vampire. Graceful as an old-school movie actress, Matilda descended to her seat in a swoosh of crystal-beaded sparkles.

"Smile, idiots," she said. "At least look like you're at a party." Her teeth caught the light as she faked a perfect laugh. "No one can hear us here," she said. "Irene has certain skills that keep our conversation private." Matilda smiled and waved at someone on the other side of the room.

"Every full moon since November there has been a murder," I said. Should I tell her I'd suspected her? Probably not.

"Don't strategize," Irene said. "Get to the point."

She could read my strategy face? How did she know my strategy face? I squinted at her. Did she play chess? Not an ounce of nerdiness in her. I would have remembered her from a tournament.

Time was running out and so was Matilda's patience. I wished I had written a script of what to say because I was flustered now.

"There are werewolves in Richmond."

"I know that, dimwit. Who cares?"

"I think they are connected to the murders that have been happening every month. And I think, *he* is eating the people. Some humans summoned him."

"Humans summoned him? On purpose?" Matilda looked at Irene. "Who's stupid enough to do such a thing?"

"The Winter Coven?" Irene shrugged.

Matilda made a face. "I'd forgotten about them. Was *he* . . . fully formed?" A crease of worry set on her perfect brow.

"No. More like smoke. What's the Winter Coven?"

She shivered, ignoring my question. "It's so much worse when," she paused, skipped the word 'he', and replaced it with raised eyebrows, "is incorporeal," she said. "I've only seen it once before and it was hideous. Are you here to warn me? Is - coming here?"

"I don't know."

"Well, you should! If you're going to bother me on a party night, you should at least have some real news!"

"Can you tell me how werewolves operate?"

Her face registered disgust. "Operate? They're monsters." She shivered again. "You explain," she nodded at Irene and looked over my head toward her guests.

"They start as regular people, then - bites them and the venom triggers the change- "

Matilda interrupted. "They turn into big, fangy, and not *good* fangy like some creatures you know," she smiled at me, flashing her canines, "but over-sized, filthy fur, howling at the moon, eating people they rip into pieces, monsters. Vile."

"So it's not hereditary?"

"What's hereditary? Once - puts his venom in," she made a sound of disgust, "they change gradually, full moon to full moon. First moon, what long hair you have grandmother, the next moon, what big teeth you have. The third who knows. After a year or so, they are fully developed. And then it gets worse."

"Is it lycanthropy?"

"Eww. No. They're special creations of - . Like me. Only hairy, loathsome, gigantic and without any shred of humanity. Not like me at all."

"Do they go in and out of human form?"

"What does this have to do with me? If you don't say something pertinent in the next ten seconds I'm going back to my party." She waved and smiled over our heads at another guest.

Irene gave a short nod. "They are human until the full moon when they change."

"Did I invite you to speak?" Matilda said, a verbal slap. Irene stepped back, cowed. "I apologize, my Lady."

"They are animals," Matilda said. "Once the venom gets in their blood, their humanity degrades. At first, maybe a few years, they," she raised her hands like claws and made a face "only at the full moon, but as they age it becomes harder and harder for them to control it. It, being the monster inside them. The full moon awakens it. They deteriorate, until they are only in human form a few days a month. Eventually, they can't change back at all. They sleep in caves during the dark phase of the moon and get more and more active as the moon grows. Their humanity evaporates. It's when they're most delicious, apparently."

"Do other . . . creatures feed on them?"

Matilda's face contorted in offense. "I'm not even going to answer that." She stood. "Irene, show them out."

Matilda rose and sailed back into her sea of guests, regular people gazing in adoration as a vampire walked through them stopping to exchange a word, a gesture, a couple laughing sentences.

In my head, the edge of the jigsaw was coming together. No wonder Judy wanted to redraw her genetic mutations if they were caused by the venom. Her transformation into a wolf had hurt even to watch. That part I got. But if she was already a creature that belonged to the Man with No Face, why had Mrs. Macy and Ed the Loincloth Man injected her with serum? Maybe to advance her change to more monstrous so he would eat her first? Maybe the dog hadn't been horrible enough? Yes! Yes. That had to be it. But wait. Mrs. Macy and Ed weren't wolves at all. Why were they so sure he would come for them? And why so adamant to get the land?

Irene stepped aside, making it obvious our time was up. Nick and I stood.

A massive chunk of information was still missing. The Queens had been taken off the board. Julian had taken them. But why?

I stepped out of our nook and crashed into a man. I looked up in a hurry to apologize.

"*Dad?*"

"Stacy? What're you doing here? It's so late. Are you okay?" His hands were wet and he was holding a paper towel. That's my dad. Always forgets to throw the paper towel from the bathroom away until he gets back to the table.

"I could ask you the same thing!" I said.

"What do you mean? This is the event I told you about. All my partners are here and the hostess is that lady there in purple. Matilda Bacon," he said. A slight smile of admiration crossed his face. "Jill got here an hour ago. She was all dressed up already. Why go home when she could come to this with me?" He looked over his shoulder, probably looking for her. He turned back to me. "She said you kids left the formal early to go pick up a piece of your project at Judy's house?" He eyed my dress and my boyfriend with narrowed eyes. "What happened to your dress?"

"We got a flat tire on our way," I said. "In pouring rain. It was kind of awful."

"We did get the disc, though," Nick said with a smile.

I was processing. Matilda was having a lawyer party? What was this about? Wait, I had just seen Mrs. Macy! I searched, but sure enough, I didn't spot her in the crowd.

"Is Mrs. Macy here?"

"She called in sick today. What's the matter? Why did you need to find us?" he said.

Irene slid in. "Pure coincidence. Miss Goldman came by to pay her respects to Mrs. Bacon." She was as polished as a formal tabletop. "They met at a game tournament and Mrs. Bacon extended an open invitation to stop by for chess. Anytime. The children had availability after their excursion, so dropped by. I was just getting them desserts." Irene gave me a look, friendly on the outside, steely underneath. Oh no. I didn't even know this girl but now I owed her.

"Oh, well that makes sense."

What? It did? My dad was at a work party and I show up and this girl says one sentence to him and he's like oh yeah, no prob everything is normal? Something was happening and I couldn't see it. I did not like this at all. I searched the room again. Darcy Jackson, check, in the corner with a group of people chatting.

Terrence? Yep, standing by the fireplace with Mr. Lorne. Holding drinks to look casual, but facing away from each other and scanning the room, obviously on security detail. I didn't see Jill.

"Do you want to say hello to my partners, honey? You met some of them at my birthday. Oh, but well," he took in my dress. "Maybe your clothes . . ."

"Yeah. The tire change," I said. "Nick needed help."

"Everything okay with the car, now?"

"We got the flat fixed and stopped here to play some chess," Nick said, "on the way to drop Stacy off at your house. I thought it was better if we spent the evening in company."

My father nodded in approval. "There are some things about you I really do like, despite your age. Or maybe because of it," my father said, smiling at Nick. "You seem very together."

"Thank you, sir. I could say the same of you."

"Listen kids, I need to get back to my partners and Mrs. Bacon," he said. "There's all kinds of people here you know." He lowered his voice. "The mayor was here for a while earlier! Very much the hoi-poloi this evening. See you at home sweetheart," he said, stopping to kiss my forehead. "Mrs. Bacon's events tend to run into the wee hours of the morning, so I'm told. I don't know when we'll be home. You should be fine by yourself, though. The alarm is on. And you should have seen Steven's face when we dropped him at the Rubenstein's to sleepover. This kid has a playroom with a rope gym to climb inside the house. Speaking of which, can you believe this place? It's even more incredible open like this than for the tours."

Off he went, moving like a magnet toward Matilda.

My hands tingled with nerves. "I do not like my father fraternizing with vampires," I said under my breath to Nick.

"She won't hurt any of them in public. She's too conservative."

"But is she magnetizing them? Is she making them human servants? Is she making my dad a human servant?" A thrill of desperation crept up my spine.

Irene said, "Come with me." I wasn't sure I wanted to do that. I didn't trust her. She was as likely to tell me lies as anything else. But she had just kinda saved my bacon, no pun intended. I was almighty confused.

Irene landed that even gaze back on my face. "I'm not a vampire," she said. "I won't say you can trust me, but I mean you no ill will. Come and I'll explain a little more about your . . . problem."

Irene picked up two slices of cheesecake as we passed the dessert table, then led us down the short, wood paneled hall that opened into the museum entrance foyer, now the bar area. Oh, there was Jill, standing trapped by Ms. Grand-daughter Lee in front of the ancestor paintings. She didn't notice me in the crowd, but at least she wasn't talking to vampires.

We crossed the balconied room into the gentleman's parlor with the chess. Irene placed the desserts on a small coffee table and gestured for us to sit on the loveseat. Its springs squeaked when I sat. She leaned opposite us on a chair with carved wooden arms.

"Please. Enjoy. It's from Busters," she said, "the most famous bakery in Richmond and the oldest. The owner moved from Italy in 1846 and brought all of his family recipes with him."

"Is the owner a vampire?" Nick said, voice low.

"Oh no," she said with a wistful smile. "His great grandson owns it now. You can speak freely here," she said. "With me. Like Madame Matilda said, I have a special gift. My conversation goes widely unnoticed. It doesn't become silent per se. It's more that I have the ability to pass by most people's broad attention. I'm . . . quiet. Unnoticeable. I've learned to tune that skill to conversation. It helps Madame extensively."

"But you aren't her servant?"

"I lived here at Maymont for several years. I was a friend of the family and came here to be Mrs. Bacon's companion. She got lonely with the Major always off doing business. We became . . . friends."

"But you're young," I said.

"In a manner of speaking," she said. For the first time I noticed her accent. Soft and Southern. Maybe I was getting too used to this place. "But you need to know about the wolves."

I watched her with interest as I took a bite of cheesecake.

"Oh my glorious bejangled god," I said.

"I told you," she said. I looked at Nick's plate. He had set it down and was replacing his fork. How did these men eat so fast?

"Maybe the best you'll ever eat," she said.

I took another silky bite. "It's incredible."

She nodded.

"Wolves," Nick said.

"*He* eats them. They sustain his physical presence. Like that cake sustains yours."

The cake suddenly felt like chalk in my mouth. Nick was lucky he'd finished his.

"Last year, a few weeks before Thanksgiving, something happened to him. His physical body was destroyed. No one here seems to know how, a fact I find very interesting. Unfortunately, he is not fully dependent on a body to exist and affect the world, but I'm told it makes his job, whatever that is, easier if he has a body."

The Man with No Face had a *job?* The hairs on my arms stood straight up.

"So now, he is rebuilding his physical form. He is eating . . ." she gestured with her hand like she held the answer in it.

"People," I filled in.

"Frequently," she corrected. "Consuming his cattle every full moon when they take their monstrous forms."

"Why isn't he eating the ones in the caves? The ones that don't lose their monster forms?"

"He ate them all first. I'm told they were found with the very marrow sucked out of their bones."

"Who found them?" Nick asked.

"The witches," she said. "They use werewolf hair in spells. The Winter Coven sneaks out to the caves when they think the monsters are asleep to collect it."

There were *witches*?

Stupid Richmond. Of course there were witches. Maybe Steve had been wrong and mislabeled Mrs. Macy a werewolf when she was actually a witch.

"How many werewolves does he have to eat before he gets his body back?" I said.

She shrugged.

"How many does he eat when he is corporeal?" Nick asked.

"One, sometimes two, a year. It's considered an honor to feed him, but everyone knows that is a story. No one, not even one of those vile monsters, wants to be eaten by him. Eaten. Alive." Her face wrinkled in revulsion.

"So the full moon murderer can't be him," I said. "All the people killed are regular people."

"You said there were people summoning him?" said Irene.

"If that's what we saw," I said.

"Maybe the coven." She looked over her shoulder. "I must return to the party before I am missed," she said. "But you should know, the werewolves hate him, as does my mistress," she whispered. "It is the werewolves' only redeeming quality. His, *its*, existence is efficient," she said. "Everything he creates feeds him in some way. The werewolves feed his body, my mistress feeds his consciousness and mind, the zombies feed him emotionally with fear. The list goes on. The wolves, foul as they are, are fighting for their lives. And I warn you, do not kill one. Even one. He values them above all his other creatures, my lady included. If you kill one, he will come for you. Plan ahead, Miss Goldman. Watch your step. He always has a tempo." She rose and turned to go.

A tempo. She did play chess.

"Why are you helping us?" I asked. "Your boss hates me."

"She is not my boss," Irene said with a slight smile, "though we are deeply linked." She turned back around to face me. "And I am helping you because I wish that someone had helped me." Her face grew wistful. "That is the only reason. I have nothing to gain or lose whatever actions you take."

"Wait, Irene. What about my dad? Does she know he's my dad? Is he safe here?"

"She hasn't made the connection to my knowledge. I am uncertain how Madame will react if she discovers your relationship."

"I have to get him and Jill out of here!"

"That would be unwise," she said, placing a cool hand on my arm. "Drawing her attention to him in any way could trigger an action you will not like."

I looked at her soft round face and wide eyes. She was soooo familiar. "Have we met before? At a tournament or something? New York, maybe two years ago? Or Nationals in Tennessee, 1999?"

She looked at Nick holding his plate.

"Busters," she said. "He sells it by the slice, but the whole cake is better. Fresher. And waiting until you are married is both appropriate and wise," she said with a special look at Nick, "if difficult."

She turned and left, cocktail dress blooming softly behind her.

Nick eyed the plate I still held.

"Are you going to finish that?"

11:09 p.m.

"Julian needs to tell us what he's hiding," I said, spreading peanut butter on my bread.

My friends sat at my kitchen counter in various states of food consumption and prep. I had tossed out sandwich makings, bowls for cereal and a choice of bottled iced teas. That cheesecake had started Nick and my bellies rumbling. It was late and we were all starving. At last, the coffee was ready.

"Does this sound crazy or right to you?" I asked them.

"I think the witches are the ones who bribed Julian and want the land. They also want the Man with No Face to get his body back, who knows why, and are pumping Judy up with the venom infused serum to get her to be next on the menu."

"Steve was very sure that Mrs. Macy was a werewolf," Nick said, closing the cereal box. "But she didn't change. Judy shifted into wolf form under the moon, but Mrs. Macy didn't. And she would have, right?"

"She would," Finder said. "My dojo friend wolfs out every full moon for all three days."

"Am I the only person who just learned a full moon lasted three days?"

"Yes," said my friends.

"In yoga we take it easy on the moon days. Saanvi says the moon affects us because the body is 98% water."

"Is that why we did the weird class with all the bolsters and stuff?" I asked.

"Yup."

"Something isn't lining up," Nick said. "If Judy's dad is also a werewolf, he doesn't fit Matilda's description at all. He seems very humane and normal. Not like he's about to hole up in a cave and eat people."

"Maybe Julian created a serum to keep the effects minimized," said Finder. "Maybe that's why the witches bribed him to make a serum for them? Because they knew what he made for the werewolves worked."

My phone rang.

I did not know any living human who would call me at 11:30 at night unless someone was dead.

Finder picked up my phone and looked at the caller ID. "It's Julian," she said. A bolt of panic went through all of us. No one voiced it, but I'm sure we all thought the same thing.

I put him on speaker.

"If your drivers are awake enough to come out here again safely," he said, "There's something you should see."

"I had a three hour nap this afternoon," Nick said. "Totally good to go here."

Tully picked his head up off the table.

I went upstairs to change my clothes. Finder came with.

"Do you know what's wrong with Tully?" she said as soon as we were out of earshot of the boys. "He's barely said three words since we left the dance."

Crap. What should I do? A litany of excuses arrived.

1. I needed to focus on problem solving right now. 2. I didn't want to stir up that pot and get all emotional again myself. 3. Tully was my SBS partner. 4. It wasn't my news to tell. I could absolutely not breathe a word. On the same note, how would I feel if she knew something important like this and didn't tell me? Crap. I could't not tell her.

"Hang here for a sec," I said. I reached inside my door without stepping in. I flipped on the overhead and pulled out the stake and cross I kept in a new umbrella stand just inside my doorframe. I checked inside my closet, and my bathroom, under my bed and in the nursery nook with the desk and bookcase. "Okay, we're good," I put my weapons back under the towel that covered the stand.

"Do you do this every time you come in here?" Finder asked.

"Every time I haven't been in here since daylight."

"'Cuz you know I would have told you if we had company."

I got my black jeans and a T-shirt then stepped into my bathroom. Tell her but don't *tell* her. I told myself. I am alive. I am safe. Nothing bad is happening. Dressed, I came out and dug in my laundry for my Beth Shamar sweatshirt. "He and Nick were in the sanctuary," I said. True. "I interrupted them," I said. Also true. "I don't know what they talked about." Still true.

"Sis, you are as obviously withholding information as Julian."

Was I that transparent? Crap.

"But I get it," she went on, picking up my Manhattan snow globe and shaking it. "You overheard them talking about something and you don't want to tell me. You think he should tell me. I hear that. You're right. But damn girl. He's like an early oyster sometimes. It could be weeks before that shell pries open." She watched as the snow fell on my still standing towers. "Does he like somebody else? I keep wondering if that's what's been up. It might be Wendy Gillian. She's on the fencing team, too. Super Irish. How about this, if he doesn't tell me in the next three days, I come back to you? I hide it well, I know," she said, setting my globe back in its place. "But I worry about that boy. All the time."

I left Dad and Jill a note telling them we were going back out to the res because Nick and I had grabbed the wrong disc. I know, not true, but what was I gonna say? Werewolf problems, back soon? All I could do at this point was hope Matilda's party truly did go into the wee hours and my parents could stay awake long enough to keep dancing and not notice how late I'd be getting home.

46.

April 26, continued.

Finder plunked down in the comfy chair in John and Julian's living room and threw her leg over the arm.

"So," she said, "have you decided to quit lying to us, or do I get to encourage you?"

Julian had been crying.

"I'm not a bad person," he said. "I know you know there are things I'm not telling you. I can't. I have to keep John safe. Anything I tell you could get him killed."

He pulled on a fleece and tied his hiking boots.

"But I can show you one thing."

Ten minutes later, Julian led us up a steep hill so thick with rocks I thought I was going to wipe out. Nick held my hand and I hate to admit I clung to it out of practicality, not desire to be near him. Finder walked ahead with Julian, ready to take him out if he made a false move. Tully brought up the rear. The far behind kind of rear. A couple times we stopped to wait for him, Nick keeping an eye over his shoulder to make sure his make-out buddy didn't get lost. I know. That was mean.

I felt like I was standing at the shore with waves lapping at my feet. Some waves were of anger and disappointment, some envy and some forgiveness. They all eroded my foundation, pulling at the sand I stood on. Right now, I needed solid ground a step or two back from the where the waves flowed in. Some waves were bigger and more ferocious than others. One minute I felt bad for Tully and wanted to support him and forgive him and Nick, and the next I considered shoving them both down the side of this mountain.

Michael, I said in my mind. *How do I do this?*

I had forgiven my father for snatching me out of my life and bringing me to this monster-infested nature trail called Richmond, but *how* had I done it? In the moment where I'd forgiven him, I was desperate to not be ruled by the Man with No Face, and I just poof, did it.

How long do you want to feel awful? said the angel.

Not at all.

Then stop. Decide not to be bothered by it. Decide. How you feel is always your choice.

Was it though? Could I really help how I felt? Jill would agree with Michael. I kinda thought no, I couldn't, that the point of feelings was that they happened and you were stuck with them whatever they were.

But this was miserable. I could not concentrate on rescuing Judy with these distractions.

Acknowledge what your experience is, painful, not painful, emotional, not emotional, whatever. Feel what you feel. Feel it fully. Choose to let it go. Choose to invest your energy in yourself, in your purpose on earth, not on a random emotional experience that will not help you.

What? Oh good grief. I was about to disagree with the archangel when I slid on a stone. Nick caught me before my knees hit the rocks.

"Thanks," I said as he stabilized me. I had to step high to keep myself from tripping over some roots as we took the last bit of the steep trail. The trees opened up ahead of us.

The moon glowed bright behind silver clouds as we crested the top of the hill and emerged into a clearing. High grass brushed above my ankles as Julian led us to a rock outcropping. He turned to us and put a finger to his lips. Not that we were talking anyway. Tully, for example, had not said a word.

Julian gestured for us to approach the outcropping. The rocks were two and three times my size. Julian offered for Nick and Finder to climb up. They both did. I stayed near Julian. Tully stood back from the rocks. Julian beckoned him forward and soon he climbed up beside the others. Julian motioned for me to climb. I shook my head. Finder extended a hand down and I declined. She offered again and Julian nodded go. Fine. I grabbed her hand and half scrambled, half dragged my exhausted self up the rocks. Nick and Tully were standing very close to each other, but not touching. Not that there was much choice. The outcropping was not terribly large. Finder stood at the pinnacle overlooking the pine dusted valley below. Julian climbed up after me putting his feet exactly where he knew to climb. He raised his arm and pointed. And then, all at once, we saw them.

Light grey forms moving in the shadows four stories below us. As they came into the moonlight, their features became clear.

Wolves. Lithe bodies, strong and agile. The sight made me catch my breath. Wolves are inspiring any way you see them, in pictures, on TV, in the movies. But like this, settled in their natural habitat, unnatural wolves though they may be, lounging about and acting like wolves, they were stunning.

There was nothing monstrous about them.

"The silver crest is John," whispered Julian in my ear.

"Who are the others?"

"Not for me to say," he said. He had a look in his eye, a relaxed look on his face, the first time I'd seen his face truly at ease all night. There was his love down there sitting in the trees, his love who was also a wolf. I counted, three wolves. One, John. Two, a stocky lighter grey wolf with a red dorsal crest running from his spine to his tail. A sand colored wolf, this one with a light muzzle, or so it looked from here, loped out of the trees behind John. My heart felt big and awestruck seeing them.

John threw back his head and howled a long deep, throaty call. Movement fluttered the grass and the edges of the tree clearing around him. A wolf so black he gleamed silver in the moonlight, emerged from the trees to the left. He was by far the most massive of the wolves, out-sizing John by at least half. The giant black wolf had a smaller, more silvery wolf following close behind. Five wolves. When there should be more.

"Are the rest regular wolves?" I asked, super quiet. "Like, are they real wolves, or, not real but, wolves all the time?"

Julian shook his head. "They're all like John," he said, "and Judy."

"Do they all live here? On the reservation?"

He ignored my question. "Watch."

The wolves came together sniffing and licking each other. The thick-set grey wolf grabbed the big black wolf by the scruff and rolled him over. He stayed on his back for a minute, then twisted and leaped to his feet. They rammed into each other and then the black wolf rolled over on his own. The grey wolf and John played a similar game, with the grey one submitting to John. One by one they all let John sniff them as they lay on their backs, belly exposed. Then John turned and looked up at the rocks. Breath caught in Julian's throat.

"He knows we're here," he said.

"Can we talk to him? Can you tell him what happened to Judy?"

Julian looked at me as if we hadn't spent hours in the lab being smart together. "He's a wolf."

"I know but he's not a *wolf* wolf. Doesn't he, like, still have his regular mind somewhere? If you talked to him, told him Judy was in trouble, wouldn't he understand?"

"No."

Hmmm. That wasn't the answer I wanted. How were we going to be able to warn them of what was coming? I took a long breath.

The wolves all paused, heads glancing over shoulders to regard us. I watched them watch us from our ridge. John turned and trotted like water over rocks into the forest. His pack followed. The last wolf, the smallest, flicked his tail in our direction and did a playful half twist in the air before following his pack. It looked like he was waving goodbye.

Julian sat on a flat spot and zipped his fleece so the wind wouldn't go down his collar. It wasn't cold yet, but a breeze not as warm as when we left the house tickled my face.

"This is the sacred land," Julian said. "Beyond those trees is the ritual healing spot for the Mattaponi people. Just beyond that is where they bury their dead. Bordering that is what the tribe calls the *stolen land*. It's Mattaponi land occupied by white settlers, stolen from the Mattaponi people between 1689 and 1754. It was restored to the reservation in 1965 as part of the American Indian Land Reclamation Act. It's the stolen land the suit is contesting.

"No one's white ancestors are buried there. It's a false claim the lawyers are using to manipulate the courts. They want from this ridge to the outer border." He paused and turned to face the overlook. He pointed off to the left. "Do you see how the light changes just above what looks like a mountain line? It's not a mountain, it's trees, but that's where the land ends. And," he said, "The only thing it's good for is growing pine trees. So unless they want to start a lumber business or Christmas tree farm, the land is useless. Except that it shares a tiny corner of the sacred land, and nothing made of evil can cross its border."

I followed his finger and squinted until I could make out the spot he meant, a pale line differentiating between the navy sky and the black trees in the distance.

"So they'd be safe on this land, but not the stolen land," Finder said. "The stolen land's just the entry point for the lawsuit."

"Correct. Their enemy can't cross the boundary, from the stolen land to here or the tiny corner of sacred land they want."

Julian stood, face hard in the moonlight. "Their enemy, nor their master." We were all quiet for a moment letting that sink in. It was as Irene had told us. Their enemy. Their master.

"Does John's pack stay on sacred land?"

"On the peak full moon nights? Always."

"How do you keep these wolves from becoming monsters?" I said.

Julian stood up, but said nothing.

"Do you give them a serum to keep them from going into monster mode? Is that the problem Judy wanted me to fix?" He started climbing down. I lay on my belly and half climbed, half slid down the rocks to follow him.

"Wait. Julian. Is it why she said it was working on others but not on her? Is it why her mom's fridge had a stash of my serums she said came from you?" Julian walked away from the rock, ignoring my questions.

"Julian! You have to answer me! Did Ed and Mrs. Macy give Judy a shot to reverse the effects of your anti-monster serum? If that's it, how likely is it to work? Will she attack her own pack? Julian!"

Nick touched my arm. "He's not going to answer you. My money says you're right."

Finder jumped off a low rock, half way down the outcropping. Low meaning twice my height. She landed in a crouch with one hand touching the ground, like a superhero. "Always wanted to do that," she said. We ran to catch up to Julian.

"So John's the alpha?" Finder asked. Julian nodded.

"The alpha male."

"Who's the alpha female?" asked Nick. "Did we see her?"

"No. It's Judy."

"She can't be alpha if her father is alpha," Finder said, assuming her guardian spot again beside Julian as we made our way back up the switchback. "Wolf pack alphas are mates. Nah. That's a little too redneck, even for Richmond."

"It's different in this pack," said Julian. "John is alpha, but his mate isn't a wolf, and the only female other than Judy is too submissive for alpha. Judy's alpha by virtue of being blood kin. When she's old enough, John will allow himself to be beaten by a younger male he thinks is suitable to lead alongside Judy and be her mate."

Lead? Alongside *Judy*? The girl who could barely speak out loud? She had stood up to Ed tonight, though. Maybe being a werewolf was different.

Down the hill and through the pine forest, fallen needles soft underfoot, we walked along the river back in the direction of the house.

"Will you please answer my questions?" I pleaded as we got close.

"No. I only brought you so you could see why protecting them is so important to me. Go home, Stacy. Do the science fair tomorrow and sleep the weekend away. Stay safe and out of this. I can't explain any more." The fairy lights of the porch twinkled in the distance. "I'm sorry you'll be on your own tomorrow," he said. "If what we'd tried had worked, I bet you two would have won."

My chest ached as emotion welled up. I didn't want to go anywhere near that science fair in the morning. I wanted to figure out what Julian was leaving out of the equation.

The forest night was quiet in a way that was not my kind of quiet. My quiet had a white noise, a din of traffic, a palette of human sounds behind it. Here the quiet settled on me like a blanket of weighted hush, smelling of earth and pine, water and wind. Our footsteps were muffled by pine needles underfoot, now that we had passed the downhill slope of rocks and roots. Except for a slight whispering of wind in the trees, my breath was the loudest thing I heard. I felt each step as awkward as a sneeze during a calculus test.

Julian's face was tense in the bright moon light as we arrived at his porch. A strategy face. I asked to use the bathroom before we drove home since the res was a full forty-five minutes from Wilton.

I did what needed doing in their cute, black and white bathroom then washed my hands. The towel to dry them was soft and fluffy.

Finder and Tully were standing on the porch when I came out. Finder reached over and took Tully's hand. He didn't stop her, but his jaw tightened. He looked like he was going to cry. I couldn't take it.

"Hey Tul," I said, "I have something in my backpack for you. Come here for a sec." He let go of Finder's hand and followed me to the Hulk where I pretended to search my bag.

I spoke in almost whisper. "I was really mad before, and I'm sorry. What Nick will or won't do with me has nothing at all to do with you and I shouldn't expect you to be, I don't know, like, thinking of me when he approached you. I get it. I wouldn't say no if he wanted to kiss me like that. Anyway, I'm sorry. I still want to be your SBS partner."

"No thanks." Tully turned away, looking down the long driveway. "This is something I have to deal with by myself."

"You don't," I said. "Whatever's happening- "

"*Nothing* is happening, Stacy. Nothing has changed. I don't need your help. Thanks for the advice."

"You could talk to Jill," I said, but he was already walking away.

The car ride home was tense. Four people all occupying heavy thinking space as we struggled to unearth the missing piece.

"Judy's mom said she thought Judy would go to her dad, but she wasn't there when we saw them. We have no idea how to track or catch a wolf. Judy is safe from the Man with No Face if she's on the sacred land. But if John smells her and leads the pack to her, will she attack them because of what's in her? What is Julian not telling us? Gah!" I slammed my fists into my seat. "Something about all this still doesn't make sense! Even Richmond sense!"

We all stared out the windows as Nick drove. What was the missing factor?

47.

Saturday, April 27, 2002.

I caught up to Finder at the continental breakfast table. Her project was across the ballroom from mine and we hadn't even seen each other long enough to wave hello.

"I am officially worried about the Tul now," she said by way of greeting. "I asked him what was the matter last night when he dropped me off and he threw up in my mother's flowers."

"That's horrible," I said. "Are you sure it wasn't stress? Or a virus?"

This bomb was his to drop, not mine, right? If they were like, walking to the altar I might have to interfere, but the wake-up call was barely twelve hours ago. I needed to give him time to figure out his own plan before I went all truth teller. He loved Finder. He would tell her himself when he was ready. I just needed to give him a day or two. Finder loaded a spoonful of hummus onto her paper plate.

"When he was a little kid at the dojo he would get anxious every now and then before a competition and barf in the bathroom before his bout."

"Poor Tully," I said, feeling kind of nauseated myself.

"Every now and then he has a spell like this," Finder scooped some fruit onto her plate. "He gets depressed and shuts down for a few weeks, but this one seems different, like he's riding a bigger wave of sad. I used to think it was me, you know? Something I said, something I did. But it's just him. Part of his DNA I guess. Maybe you can figure *that* out and make *him* a serum. He pulls out of it every time but I always worry he won't. I don't get it. Oh look, is that a judge hovering by your sexy science fair project?"

"Why am I even bothering?" I said. "They won't let me place." Nonetheless, I crammed a mini-muffin into my mouth and walked fast to my project. Judging wasn't supposed to start for another fifteen minutes.

"Hi," I said as I slid my filled plate behind my project board.

"Is this your project?" said the stout woman holding a clip board.

"It is."

"Did you separate this DNA yourself?"

"Yes. The lab at VCU is very well equipped."

"Who helped you?"

"Do you mean who was our advisor?" I asked. "Sister Mary Chem- sorry, Sister Maria Alberta at St. Ignatius College Prep was our in-school advisor and Dr. Julian Windworth oversaw our work at the University."

"And which pieces of Dr. Windworth's research did you use?"

"None. His work is completely unrelated to hereditary mutations in DNA."

"Did he loan you any past experiments, results or hypotheses?"

"No ma'am. The research and ideas were all ours."

"Two high school girls?"

I wasn't sure what to say to that so I just held my ground.

"Do you even know what this is?" she said.

Werewolf sauce? I thought. But surely she couldn't mean that. I tried on a charm-the-adult smile.

"Since I spent the last six months on it, I think so." She glowered. Fine. I could play that way, too.

"It's a repair enzyme messenger capable of breaking an incorrect connection and inserting the correct one." I pointed to Judy's illustration on the board. "We watched how naturally occurring repair proteins worked. Here," I handed her our lists of observations, "you can see that we were only able to observe somatic mutations get repaired. The body only willingly repairs things it recognizes as incorrect. If you're born with a faulty DNA structure, the body doesn't recognize it as wrong, so doesn't develop the faculty to repair it. A typical repair enzyme can change a somatic mutation, but not a hereditary one. We observed the difference between somatic and hereditary mutations is only one bond per strand." I pointed to Judy's super close-up drawings of the difference. The judge's scowl deepened. What was the matter? Did she not see the connection? Was I talking too fast?

"While looking at our samples, we noticed a protein already aggressive in its capabilities." I turned to our formula page in the binder I'd handed her. "We observed this protein had a higher ratio of sugar to phosphorus than the other repair proteins we observed. That gave us our hypothesis." I pointed to it on the board and read it aloud. "When protein x receives extra deoxyribose, it will attack any DNA mutation and create an opportunity for the naturally occurring repair enzymes to work."

Why was she scowling like that? Geez. I figured I'd wrap up quick so she could move on.

"When we isolated and enhanced that particular protein with extra deoxyribose using this formula," I pointed, "it successfully attacked the previously repair-immune hereditary strand. Like a predator. Once the protein broke the bond, the body's regular repair enzymes got to work and rebuilt the correct adenine to thymine bond." I took the binder from her hands and pointed to the bond drawing Judy had done on the last panel of our board.

I tapped on the laptop computer Dad had borrowed for us from his office. The cd Judy had burned had all of our presentation materials flowing together like an animated video. I pushed play.

"We call it the Predator Protein," my voice came on in the video. "Though it may be limited in the types of mutations it will change, transitions versus transversions, also known as mispairings, adenine to guanine transitional mutations and cytosine to thymine transitional mutations have all been successfully and repeatedly corrected. See page twelve of our laboratory report."

The judge looked at me like I was stupid. And that made me angry. "It's like a predator," I said. "It eats away the mutation and kills any part of the problem DNA. It enables the repair."

The woman's jaw dropped. She turned and walked away. Startled by her rudeness, I called after her. "If you read the project report you'll see we did a very thorough job!"

She did not so much as flick a glance over her shoulder toward me. She disappeared into the crowd of teachers and judges heading for the aisle across from mine where the judging would begin.

I looked at the title of our project, Predator Proteins: Eliminating Hereditary Transitional DNA Mutations One Cell at a Time.

Wait.

I stared at my project title.

Like a deck of cards handled by a master shuffler, a piece of Judy's mystery slid into place.

I grabbed my phone and slammed my finger into the speed dial button for Nick.

"Are you ready, Stacy?" Jill said running over. I turned away from her like I hadn't even seen her.

I was almost in tears. Tears of victory, tears of terror. "Nick," I said into his answering machine. "Nick! I figured it out! I know how to save Judy! Call me as soon as you can." And I hung up.

"Are you okay?" Jill asked putting her hand to my forehead. "You're all flushed. Do you have a fever? Are you having anxiety?"

I brushed her hand away.

"I'm fine," I said. "I need a notebook. Can you please get me a notebook? And a pen? And Finder. I need Finder!"

Maybe she could stand and explain my project. I needed to get out of here right now and get moving. There was so much to do.

The next two hours were murder. My body was in hyperdrive as I wrote down everything. Everything we knew, everything that added up, everything we had to do between now and moonrise. I could only hope our lab sample was still viable. Nick called me back and I got him started on the list of things to do. First thing, what time is moonrise? He got on his computer and found it, 9:08 p.m. My watch read 11:35 a.m. Less than ten hours. The science fair ended at 3:00. I wasn't sure I could make it. Finder came running to me after her project was judged.

"What's going on, Chess Team? Your step-momma's freakin' out over there. She said you were sick or something?"

"I'm not sick." I reached, slowly so she could see me, I knew better than to surprise Finder with a grab, and took hold of my friend's shoulders. "Listen to me," I said. "Just. Listen."

48.

April 27, continued.

Finder stared at me as if she couldn't quite believe it.

"I have to get to the lab as soon as I can."

"Did you talk to the judges?"

I tried for about one second to recall the frenzied moments as the judges reviewed our project. They needed to ask questions of both of us. I told them my partner was sick and they sighed and checked a box. I'm sure the one that said LOSER. After a few cursory questions, and some talking amongst themselves, they moved on. No way could we place. Rules were rules.

"I don't remember what I said. I was busy working on this." I showed her my list. Everything we needed, everything we didn't already have. And the impossibly short time we had to put it all together.

"Let's go home," I said to Jill as paper bag lunches were rolled out on carts. "Finder says she'll bring my project back to her house. We didn't win, so let's go. I have a lot of work to do today for, um, Julian. I have to get to the lab right away."

"Dad and Steve are still at the Science Center," Jill said. "They were planning to be back here for the ceremony at 2:00."

"Can we call them? Can we leave early?" If I had to stay here the rest of the afternoon and not get to Richmond until 5:00, that left only four hours to get ready.

"I guess we can see if they're ready to go," Jill said. "Don't you want to tour the other projects and see who wins? It still could be you and Judy. I heard some judges talking- your project has made quite a splash."

"I'm sure we're disqualified," I said. "Finder will win and she can tell me all about it later. Or those Asian kids from Newport News will win and then I don't care. Their project is amazing."

"Okay, well, we can try." She took out her cell phone.

I shifted my weight from foot to foot.

Judy's mutations were transversions or mispairings. If I could use the same predator protein, thank you Terrence, to weaken the bond, I could use another substrate of the protein to trigger a new mutation, to convert them to transitions, the bond we had mastered repairing. If I could repair her mutation that way, then the Man with No Face wouldn't be interested in eating her. Her or any of the werewolves.

"No, it's fine," Jill said into the phone, "take your time. We can do everything as planned."

No, no, no, we could NOT.

I held my hand out and she gave me the phone. "Hey, Dad. Can I please talk to Steve?" I closed my eyes and took a breath. This was going to have to be veiled. I hoped he would catch on. "Hey, Muppet," I said when he got on the line. "Are you having fun?"

"Yes! It's awesome! Wait, why are you on the phone?"

"You know how at Dad's birthday you smelled some new candy in Mrs. Macy's bag and got really excited about it?"

He got quiet. Thinking. "Um. Yeah."

"Well, I am going to the lab for an experiment. On the candy. Would you like to go with me?"

He was with Dad so couldn't talk freely either. Come on Steve, I thought. Come on. Figure it out.

"Is it the . . . wolf-shaped candy?" he asked.

"Yes! Yes, it is, and I could really use your help."

"So you want me to leave the museum so we can go home early and you can do this experiment?"

"Yes."

"You're supposed to baby-sit me tonight."

"I am. So you would be going to the lab with me and getting to help."

"OHHHH, okay. I get to help with the wolf candy. Gotcha. Let's go, Daddy! Stacy needs me to come home so I can help her do some science." He handed the phone back to my dad.

"Stacy, what's the rush? These tickets were expensive."

"Daddeeeeeeee pleeeeeeeeease?"

Good work Captain Kiddo. I was gonna owe him.

"Good grief, child! Yes, fine, but let go of my shirt. I want to at least see the shark thing. So we have one more exhibit to walk through and then we'll come back. Maybe 1:15?"

It was better than 3:00. I scarfed down a lunch and half of Jill's since she didn't like the egg salad sandwich or the cookie. I wasn't super hungry when I ate her second half, but whatever was coming tonight, I knew I'd need the calories. Plus, come on. Are you ever really so full that one little half a cookie is going to push you over the edge? Not to mention moonrise was well after dinner time. My money said that sitting down to a meal was not going to be high on our priority list.

Mama had brought Finder to the science fair this morning. Her sister lived nearby and came to the hotel to visit while Finder did her thing. I got up and went over to the table where they had just sat down to eat. Mama stood and gave me a big hug, then introduced me to her sister, her doppleganger except shorter and heavier set.

"Mama, I need a favor," I said. "Layla and I are going to be out tonight helping a friend with a . . . problem she's having."

Mama locked eyes with me. "Judy?"

I nodded. "I'm supposed to babysit Steve but I don't think this, um, this thing that we're helping with is a good— "

"Bring him to my house, baby. We'll watch movies and play Dance Party 143. I am harder to beat than you think." She leaned over and whispered in my ear. "Pajamas, toothbrush etc- him and you. Just in case."

"Thank you so much!" I hugged her again, gratitude pouring through me. That was a huge weight off my mind. No matter what was going on, Steve had to be safe. Finder went up to her mom and excused her from her aunt for a minute. They went off toward the exhibit hall where the projects were displayed. A few minutes later they came back.

"Baby, where's your mama?"

"You mean Jill?" I nodded toward where she sat chatting with a group of other moms. I don't know how she did that, but wherever she went she found a cluster of moms to chat with. It was weird.

"Jill," Mama said coasting up to her group like she owned it.

"Go with her on this," Finder said, smiling. She gave me a wink.

Letitia Jackson was as smooth as creamy peanut butter on a cracker. She gave Jill one of her best hugs, greeted the other mothers who she didn't know as if they were old friends and then stunned me into utter adoration.

"I hope it's not an inconvenient night," said Mama, "but I am having a group of people over this evening from work and I would love to borrow Stacy to help serve and clean up. I know she's in charge of Steven this evening so he can just come right along. My cousin will be there and she has two boys about his age, so he'll have plenty to do."

Mama kept going as if Jill's look of surprise was complete agreement.

"Teularen will be there helping, and of course so will Layla. It's kind of a big deal and her grown cousin who I also asked to help had to cancel last minute. Stacy said she thought it would be fine with you. It is fine with you, right? They'll have a great dinner from my caterer and then can spend the night."

"She's like a living statue in Times Square," I said. "You aren't really sure what you're looking at, but you can't look away."

"I know," said Finder, arms crossed over her chest. "It's crazy. She can sell ice to Eskimos."

I introduced Steve and Mama before we left the science fair and it was love at first sight. I thought he'd never get out of her lap.

He took my hand as we walked down the hallway. Most of the time walking down hotel hallways came with victory. Now, I felt lopsided and nervous, wondering what I had left out, what detail was missing that would prove crucial before the night ended. "Are you going to leave me with Finder's mom when you go fight the wolves?"

"We're not going to fight the wolves, we're going to save them."

He stopped, hand tight around mine. He looked up at me and popped his other tiny hand onto his hip.

"Do you think I'm dumb?"

"Of course not," I said. "But you have to be safe, Steve. I can't risk you."

"I'm a very good shot," he said. "Better than you. You'll all be safer if I'm there."

"That might be true, but if anything happens to you, I'd never forgive myself. Never ever. So you have to stay with Mrs. Jackson."

"She told me to call her Mama."

"Then you're staying with Mama."

"Stacy," he said looking up at me with those wide, soft eyes. "You owe me."

6:35 p.m.

The bright orange sunset hovered in the pickup's rear view mirror. I blinked away from its brilliance, breathing deep as it turned Tully's mane Irish Setter red. It tinged Nick's short shiny black with streaks of fire. Fire I knew would be soft and feathery on my fingers if I touched it. My chest still ached with sadness and disappointment. It wasn't fair, wanting to tousle his hair.

Finder stared ahead, her eyes following the light show in her boyfriend's golden red cascade.

"Do you ever just wanna run your fingers through it?" I said, next to her in the truck's jump seat.

"All the time."

I nodded. Me too. Stupid boys with pretty hair.

"Judy's mom said there was a bridge," Finder said leaning up between the guys, map of the reservation in her hand. "But it's not on the map."

I looked over, but she was right. No bridge marked.

"Did anyone ask why she was tied up?" I said.

Finder shifted the two wooden katanas on her lap. "Sis, if you haven't learned this already, when boyfriends and girlfriends tie each other up, don't ask."

"I don't think it was like that," Nick said.

"Can we change the subject?" Tully adjusted his mirror as the sun began to sink behind the trees, lighting the cab in a deeper crimson glow.

"Keep Tully sweet," Finder said patting his shoulder.

Ha, I thought. As if. What I said was: "I just want to know if he tied her up because her daughter was in a cage and she objected, or because she was being left out as bait, too."

"She wouldn't be left out as bait," said Nick. "Irene was very clear. He only eats wolves."

"Her house is close," Finder said. "We could ask."

She was teasing me now.

"This is not time for teasing!" I said. "We already know Julian's hiding something massive. What if she knows what it is?"

"The big unknown right now," Nick said, "is whether or not the serum changed Judy into a monster or not."

"Nasty surprise," Finder said.

"And if they already caught her," I said.

"You made the plan, Chess Team," Finder said. "We stick to the plan unless you change it. We keep our minds on the mate."

"If we hike in the way Julian showed us last night," Nick said, "we can track the pack from there."

"Track the pack how?" Finder said. "Sniffing branches?"

Nick shrugged. "At least on that path we'd know where we are. And we'd be on the sacred land already according to Julian, which eliminates at least one threat."

Everyone in this truck was really smart. They would stop me if my plan was bad, right? Right? Still. Monster Judy would eat us if she had the opportunity. The sacred land would do nothing to protect us from her.

The night felt soft and cool even as anxiety dampened my armpits. The bridge was not what we'd expected.

"Are you sure there isn't a driving bridge?" I said, eyeing the narrow wooden crossing. Maybe we should go in the way Julian showed us. But we couldn't trust him. Had he shown us that way because tonight there would be a trap there? Maybe it was the farthest point from where Judy would be. Would we find her? Could we find her? Or would we find a litter of bodies? I shut the truck door.

The track ended here. The parking area was a swath of dirt ruts, I guessed used by only the most hardcore hikers and fishers. Tully stripped off his sweatshirt. He dug in his bag and handed something to Finder.

She slid the forest green leather cuff over his forearm, then tightened and knotted it.

He turned the tied one so I could admire it as Finder fastened the other. A metal plate hammered with Celtic knots was riveted to the leather, covering where a swordsman would be most vulnerable.

"Arm guards," Finder said. "We got 'em at Virginia Ren Faire. A wolf could still break his arm," she said, "but these might make it harder."

Finder looked complete, wooden katanas from her lap now strapped across her back. The two blades I'd given her at New Year's were now tucked into forearm holsters, her equivalent of Tully's arm guards.

"I'm already regretting not snagging one of those righteous huge dog crates from Judy's mom's place," she said, "for when we catch her. Should we roll back and do that?"

"I don't think she'd fit," Nick said.

"She fit last night."

"As a human," Nick said.

"True." Finder warmed up, doing side lunges and tossing her staff from hand to hand. "She's too big as a wol- Holy moly, boy!" Finder said. "What is *that?*"

Nick practically danced with excitement as he fastened a carry strap to a gun longer than his arm. "You're welcome, you're welcome," he said. "This is a *tranquilizer rifle*. Check this thing out." Finder held out her hands to hold it.

"Four darts can go in this little thingie here, and you load them one at a time like this, here. Accurate shots from thirty yards away. Awesome, right?"

Not awesome. Terrifying, I thought. What if one of us got shot with a tranquilizer dart by mistake? "I'm not touching it," I said.

"It's not a real gun, Stacy," Nick said. "Nothing to be scared of. You made me the weapons guy. I'm doing my job." He slung the big gun across his back like Finder had her katanas.

"I pulled a favor from a fraternity brother who works for a vet that treats the animals at the zoo," Nick told Finder. "I have one vial of ketamine," Nick said, patting his cargo pants pocket. "We can maybe get two more darts out of it, besides these four I already loaded. Hopefully that'll do the job."

The plan was simple.

Find monster Judy, knock her out with ketamine, inject her with serum and schlep her regular wolfy self home. Totally doable. Right?

The moon crested the edge of the trees as we descended the ridge, walking single file on a narrow path running like a hairpin back and forth between tight turns.

"Love a good switchback," Nick said, enjoying this night hike way too much. We'd had enough twilight to cross the rickety footbridge without flashlights, but that was nearly an hour ago. I caught up to Nick as we hit the bottom of the trail.

"Is that the ridge we were on last night?" I said, looking up at the moonlit rock face above the trees.

He nodded. "We've come all the way around from the southern part of the river, if Finder's map is right."

Low grass came up in uneven patches underfoot. Though the air was cool, sweat stuck my T-shirt to my skin. I thought about stripping off my top-layer sweatshirt and tying it around my waist.

"Can you *find* werewolves?" I asked Finder.

"I can try. I don't know what they feel like," she said.

"They feel like Judy."

She stood for a few seconds, eyes closed. Three long breaths. Four. Five. The skin on her brow crinkled in concentration.

"Should be more animal noises," Nick said, voice low. "Deer, rabbits, owls." I paused to listen. The woods behind us were quiet, the field in front of us eerie and still. I didn't hear anything except a slight wind in the trees behind us.

"Just feels empty," Finder said, opening her eyes.

"Empty of vampires? Or empty of everything?" Nick said. Finder shrugged. "Well, no vampires is a plus."

Ugh. We needed information.

"Maybe imagine her?" I said. "Imagine her shifting. Try again." We all stood, closing our own eyes. Maybe we could give some energy and help?

Finder opened her eyes a solid few minutes later. "Sorry. Nothing."

I stood still and asked my own body, where is Judy? I pictured her in my mind. Almost immediately, my body leaned strongly to the right. Urgency made my heart beat faster.

"I think she's that way," I said.

Tully spoke for the first time in almost two hours. "I do, too." He nodded and shifted his pack.

And then I said two words I thought would never in a million years come out of my mouth.

"Let's run."

49.

April 27, continued.

We jogged along the edge of the field, a downhill slope toward where Julian said the stolen land began. Tully led us into the tree line. Looking across the field he raised his hand in warning. We slowed. He lowered it and we all sank down behind him. The bow I carried with my backpack hadn't felt so heavy before, but it dragged on me now. I wanted to take it off and give my shoulders a rest.

A man's voice, angry and loud, came from across the field to our left. His shout carried vowels only. I strained but couldn't make out words. Nick knelt close beside me.

We'd decided on a buddy system before we came out. I'd suggested Finder and Nick, Tully and me, so each pair had a good fighter. Tully had found one excuse after another why that was a bad idea. I guess he thought I'd be wanting to talk about last night and didn't want the stress. Or maybe he felt guilty. And part of me, maybe the mean part, agreed that he should.

I don't need to explain why Nick with Tully and Finder with me, though technically accomplishing the one fighter per pair result, was not my first choice.

Tully gestured to Finder and she went up beside him. They exchanged one of those wordless, 'a dot on a page in Pictionary means banana' kind of glances. Finder signaled to me and they took off together at a run. Barely ten steps into the field, a wolf stood up out of the tall grass. They stopped short.

It was the gray wolf with the red dorsal stripe down his spine. The heavy-set animal bared his teeth, blocking their path. This is not your fight, his expression seemed to say. Go back.

Finder started to move toward him, to go around him, I guess, but he lunged and snapped at her. She leveled her staff for a strike.

"Stop!" I said.

The big wolf growled. His head was level with my chest. I stepped in between Finder and Tully holding out my hand. I made eye contact then looked away. I knew that much from dog walking. The guy with the longest eye contact is in charge.

"We're here to help," I said. I looked at the wolf, then away, submitting just like Mrs. Finkelmeyer had taught me never to do with her dog. "Judy's in trouble. She's been given a poison that makes her violent. A big monster wants to eat her. The people who poisoned her think if she dies, you'll give up your land." I looked at him again, his golden eyes wide and determined. "We want you to keep your alpha female and your land. Let. Us. Help. You."

"It doesn't understand you," Finder said.

"You understand, don't you?" The wolf cocked his head to the side. He stopped snarling.

"We brought things to help. Medicine for Judy." Moving very slowly so as not to startle him, I pulled a filled syringe out of my pack and laid it steady and sideways on my open palm. He stuck his nose forward for a sniff. The wolf leaned in closer to me. He opened his mouth. I braced for a bite, not wanting to move and show weakness. A thick pink tongue shot out of his mouth. He licked my hand. A smear of saliva clung to the plastic syringe cap.

"Can you show us where Judy is?" I said. Behind us a twig snapped. All our heads shot around. The smallest wolf we'd seen last night plopped down in the bramble and scratched his ear. He stayed several yards away. He'd sneaked around behind us while we were distracted. Gotten himself into position to escort us, bring up the rear.

"Brilliant," I whispered, a thrill of excitement raising goosebumps along my arms. "We're not playing chess anymore. We're playing Bughouse. Team chess," I explained, walking fast beside Finder. "Super fun. Two boards. Played with partners. It's a fast capture game. I'll explain it for real if you ever want to play."

Leading us toward the woods on the other side of the field, the Red Dorsal Stripe wolf looked over his shoulder and grinned at me, tongue lolling. He glanced at Finder, licked his chops appreciatively, then turned and padded into the trees.

"Did that wolf just check me out?" she said, voice low. "'Cuz I think that wolf just checked me out."

"Us," I said with a sly smile. "He checked *us* out."

I wondered who he was when it wasn't the full moon. Finder might be up for a new boyfriend at some point sooner rather than later. Given her issues, a werewolf might be just the thing.

Red Dorsal wolf found a track wide enough for us to follow and loped forward, paws a whisper on the pine needle carpet. The path ended at a fallen tree.

The wolf veered off into raw woods. He led us zig zagging through trees, checking over his shoulder to note our progress. He avoided rocky tripping spots and heavily rooted areas, guiding us over the easiest route. The little wolf followed behind. He ran past us now and then to nip at the neck fur of Red Dorsal. At one of these check-ins, the bigger wolf stopped and sniffed the air. The wolves dropped to their bellies. Following their lead, we crouched low.

This time, I made out words. Land. Ours. The little wolf skirted a wall of fallen branches to our left. I lost sight of him as he melted into the damp night. Nick came in close, questions on his moonlight grey face. Shadows of pine needles patterned him.

Not far off, the moonlight seemed brighter, maybe a clearing? I raised my eyebrows at Finder. She nodded, yes.

I slid out of the knapsack and bow strap, leaning them against the branch wall. Then I clipped on my borrowed fanny pack loaded with three syringes of my new Judy serum. I only needed to get one into her, but I knew better than to not prepare for mistakes.

Finder pointed left. She came in toward my ear.

"We'll go around that way. If it's a clearing we'll meet you on the other side and we can keep looking for her. This spot will be six o'clock."

I nodded. Armed only with science, I crept forward, crouched low. Finder and Tully went left, following the path the little wolf had taken.

Red Dorsal stayed near Nick and I. We veered right, the most direct route toward the voices. Moonrise brightened the open space beyond the tree line. Ed faced our direction, cheek marred from being bitten the night before. Another man stood, back to us. A man holding a big stick, lit in silhouette. Half way around the clearing, a mass of white fur lay on the ground by a tree. Oh no. Oh no, no, no. Were we too late?

We crept tree-to-tree stepping low and quiet toward the massive white wolf until I could see her eyes. Open, alive. Too bright and blue. She panted, tongue dipping into the dirt. But the venom serum had worked. Her legs were sprawled and stretched; her muzzle misshapen, too long and square, like Luke's dog after its change. Monster Judy was bound by a heavy chain, throat cuffed to the tree behind her, belly exposed. Her ear was staked to the trunk. A sacrifice waiting for smoke and teeth.

Ed raised his hands to the sky. One was bright and clean, the other had a shadow on it. Blood, maybe? Judy's? His own? Maybe Judy had bitten him. I hoped she had.

"Come out, wolves!" he shouted, no fear of being overheard. How far into the woods were we? "Come out and surrender or fight for your land!"

"The land belongs to the tribe." I recognized Julian's voice immediately. "You are not going to get it, not tonight, not with the lawsuit, not ever," Julian said. What I had thought was a stick in his hand, I now saw was not. I recognized the object's true identity from this angle, as clearly as I had seen it in his dining room, leaning into the corner. He held it almost casually at his side, aimed at the ground. "We know who is hunting you. The pack offers you sanctuary, but none may hunt here. None may kill here." Julian shifted his weight. "None may . . . eat here."

Ed looked for a moment like he was considering Julian's offer. Moonlight crossed over him as the clouds rolled across the indigo sky. Ed moaned and leaned back like he was offering his chest to the moon.

"I only negotiate with the alpha," he said to the sky. "Tell him, come out. If he fears to face me, the land is mine."

"He's not afraid of you Ed, you nor any of your- "

"If he doesn't fear us, he doesn't understand what we are! Make him face me!"

"You know that's impossible," Julian said, voice like a hostage negotiator, calm and underscored. He shifted his weight foot-to-foot, betraying his confidence. "The offer is final. Sanctuary without violence. I suggest you accept."

The moon centered itself over the clearing, glowing bright and round at the peak of the sky.

Ed let out a low moan and doubled over. Holding his stomach, he looked up at Julian and hissed, "It is our right to have it."

"Your ancestors' crime grants you nothing. The people here before you have blessed and buried their beloveds on this land- "

"How do you know what lies beneath this dirt? If all that's needed to make sacred ground is to bury someone, we can- " Ed fell to his knees as if an invisible force shoved him down, his face a cruel mask.

Ed cried out, a strange, otherworldly scream. He threw his arms open to the moon. Black liquid spilled from his lips, shimmery in the moonlight, like an oil slick on the ocean. The dark iridescence slid over his chest and belly. The stench of sulphur and rotting toilets washed over my face. Nick sucked in a breath beside me. I stuffed my nose in the crook of my elbow.

The liquid bubbling out of Ed's mouth stifled his cries. It paused, then pulsed, congealing. And then the thick, black shimmer moved. It slid around his torso and oozed down to wrap his legs. It spread thin, crawling against gravity up his arms and over his shoulders.

Ed fell forward onto his hands as the blackness dug into his flesh. It made a popping sound, like when you break bubble wrap bubbles. But it wasn't bubble wrap popping. It was Ed's skin.

The popping sound got louder and faster. Ed shrieked as the sludge perforated his chest. It split open. The stench hit us like a physical blow, knocking me out of my crouch. Nick caught me with one strong arm, holding me to his side. He gasped.

Folds of Ed's flesh peeled back and over itself in a flood of dark bile. Bones snapped like sticks in a fire as his ribcage split. Bone followed the flesh in an impossible backward arc. Ed's chest heaved toward the moon. His head fell back toward his heels. Darkness slithered over him, tipping him backwards into the grass. We were spared the final visual because of our crouched position behind the trees. But we heard it. A wet sound, ripping and tearing. Ed was turning inside out.

Behind Ed, the trees shook. Twigs snapped. I heard the bear before I saw it. Its deep, rumbling growl parted the pines before it slammed though them, trampling saplings. This was so out of my wheelhouse. Meredith read a lot of fiction, so she might know what to do if a bear surprised her in the woods. I did not. The hugeness of the thing paralyzed me. It would snap me in half with one chomp of those massive jaws.

Across the clearing, Julian bolted for the nearest tree. The scientist grabbed hold of the lowest climbable branch, which, lucky for him, was pretty low. He scrambled up, gun bouncing on its strap against his back.

"Don't move," Nick whispered.

The bear's fur glistened with something shiny. It lumbered up to Ed and nudged him with a long, square snout. And whoa did it stink. I cupped my other hand over my nose and mouth, breathing in the scent of dirt and forest. Nick touched my arm. Don't. Move.

For a moment I didn't breathe. The beast stood on its hind legs sniffing the air. It raised paws bigger than my face. Paring knife claws glittered in the moonlight. Pictures of bears made their bodies look thick, but this bear was wider at the shoulder than the hip with deeper haunches, thickest at the thigh. I thought it was going to swing at Ed. I shut my eyes, braced for blood. The only sound was shuffling. I peeked. The bear laid flat on its dark belly. Every exhale pulsed a growl as it trembled, waiting, all its attention focused on the creature convulsing on all fours before it. Pointy ears flicked in the moonlight.

It was too much to process. I closed my eyes. My brain gifted me with an immediate and inappropriate thought of those reversible stuffed animals with happy faces on one side and sad or angry faces on the other. Meredith brought one to school to comment on how her day was going. I didn't like it.

If Nick hadn't been witnessing this madness, too, I might have thought I hallucinated it. Strong, rank air assaulted us as if Ed had been gutted. And then he rose, massive, hairy, horrible. Ed shook black wetness from his glistening fur.

He turned to face the other creature. It matched him in size and stench. My logical brain named it a bear for lack of a more accurate reference, but Matilda's definition came to me. Huge, hairy, horrible, violent. These were werewolves.

When I saw Luke's dog turn monster-y after getting the injection, I decided Matilda was super judgmental and her werewolf description a gross exaggeration. But she had told us the truth. Was Matilda evil? Yes. Was she a liar? Apparently not.

The creature that had been Ed/Loincloth Man howled a sound of bursting power that ripped air. My hands flew to my ears. The werewolf I mistook for a bear crawled forward on its belly. Thick, brown forelegs came off the ground as it stood to lick Ed's jaw. I saw its belly as it stood. No, not it. Her. Femaleness was unmistakeable with rows of teats low on her belly, like a dog. She sniffed Ed's snout with hers. He growled a deep, belly sound and she went back to four feet on the grass.

And then, to my utter horror, they mated.

Nick and I sat frozen, barely breathing. After a few seconds, I yanked myself out of fear paralysis and tugged his arm. I jerked my head to the right, toward Judy. This might be our only chance to free her. I wasn't sure how long the werewolves would . . . um, take, but it might be our only shot for them to be distracted enough to not attack us. It might be now or never to get the serum into Judy and get her freed.

The wolves of Judy's pack were here somewhere. Finder and Tully, even Julian were on our side. We had to get her free. Judy thrashed, struggling against her chain collar. Julian was closest, but he was up a tree and didn't know we were here.

Wait.

Julian had brought a gun.

A *real* gun.

Julian had *known*.

Fury filled me. This had to be what he'd been hiding.

He had not corrected us when we called Judy and John werewolves. Was that the first wrong information?

Judy's mom said the serum Ed used was from Julian. I had misread it. Julian had not created a serum to hold Judy's pack's monstrousness *back*. He'd used it to bring the werewolves monstrousness *forward*.

He'd stolen my science so the alphas of this foul pack could create creatures to take their places between the incorporeal jaws of the Man with No Face.

If that was true, then Judy and John and their pack were not monsters, they were shifters. Shifters with DNA mutations from birth. No need for a near death experience to make them unimaginables because their DNA already possessed the shifter sequencing.

I wanted to face palm. How could I not have seen this? Ed and Mrs. Macy and their fire dancers weren't a cult of witches summoning the Man with No Face. They were his werewolves, his 'cattle' Irene had called them. Safe from being eaten alive only on the sacred land, the land that belonged to the shifters. The fact that Irene had named a coven of witches who were also apparently real was information future me could process later.

Werewolf jigsaw complete. I saw the whole picture now.

When Michael and I banished the Man with No Face, its body disintegrated. Its/his essence did not. That essence knew how to rebuild a body for itself. Irene said the very marrow was sucked from all the oldest werewolves, the ones who no longer became human. That gave him enough energy and matter to begin the rebuild. Over the last several months, the Man with No Face had killed every full moon when his werewolves took shape. And the pack headed by Ed and Mrs. Macy, despite its very purpose being to feed the Man with No Face, had a mind of its own.

Self-preservation was inherent in the 'young' werewolves, since they still possessed enough humanity to remain people when the moon was not full. They'd gotten more desperate as their packmates got picked off. The sacred land was the only place the Man couldn't enter. That meant it was the only place the werewolves were safe on full moon nights. Now the land battle made sense.

The Man with No Face caught me last fall. I hadn't asked for that. Maybe Ed and Mrs. Macy hadn't asked for it, either. Killing them wasn't like staking vampires. It was murder. Tomorrow Ed and Mrs. Macy, loathsome as they were, would be making sandwiches and coffee and heading to work. Doing laundry. Feeding their cats. If Matilda told the truth, and it seemed she had, their vicious rottenness was a symptom of the venom. They might have been horrible people before the Man with No Face bit them, but I had to assume they were not. And I couldn't blame them for not wanting to be eaten alive.

Crap. Crap, crap, crap.

Time to change the plan.

We couldn't kill them, and we couldn't leave them werewolves. Not only for their sake, but for ours. If the Man with No Face ate them, he'd get his body back, but no food, no body. And we wanted him bodiless as long as possible. There was only one option now.

I had to undo the DNA change caused by the Man with No Face's venom. I had to save the werewolves.

50.

April 27, continued.

This was not what I had been prepared for at all. You'd think after the vampires I would've quit underestimating the power of stupid, stinkin' Richmond to deliver creatures I didn't expect. And what was worse? Steve had told me.

Mrs. Macy *was* a werewolf.

From now on, I told myself, I will believe my little brother. I will imagine every monster as bad as it can possibly be. I will never again let myself be surprised by the inconceivable hugeness of what is possible. And I will always, *always* listen to Steve.

Project number one. Get Judy her antidote and set her free. She'd have to run away on her own.

I jerked my head toward the bound white wolf again. Nick nodded. On our hands and knees, we crawled back to the thicker tree line. Once there, we got up and picked our way as fast and quiet as we could around the tree edge toward Judy. Nick paused and pressed against a tree side. He loaded the tranquilizer rifle.

"Not Judy," I whispered barely more than a breath. Nick pointed to the werewolves. I worried. What if ketamine didn't work on werewolves? What if their hide was too thick and the darts bounced off?

I closed my eyes and leaned into the tree at my back. My heart slammed in my chest so hard my ribs vibrated. It's Bughouse, I told myself. And the other guy has three queens. Queens one and two: werewolves. Queen number three: Julian's gun. I was scared of them all. How could I get a message to Julian that we were here and not to shoot us?

Werewolves were not monsters we could fight. They were too big, to physically powerful. And all we had brought was a handful of tranquilizer darts and some big sticks. Except Finder. She had blades. Matilda said werewolves ate people. I was people. Finder and Tully and Nick were people. Even lying, gun-toting Julian was people. If they killed us would there be anything left but bones? My stomach turned in my belly. Short, panicky breaths stormed my chest.

Keep it together, Goldman, I told myself. Don't imagine outcomes. Don't fabricate what the other player might do. Look at your own game. Get to Judy. Just get to Judy. You'll figure out the next move there.

Nick pointed up. Did I want to hide in the tree? I shook my head. Thick, sturdy branches, evenly enough spaced, started close enough to the ground to make a tree climb conceivable, but the thought of climbing far enough up to not be vulnerable made my head swim. What if a branch broke? Besides, I had the serum.

I pointed to Judy. Nick pressed against the bark, so close to me I could smell his skin. He held the tranquilizer gun out to me, pointing again, up. He pointed to himself and to Judy. He would stay on the ground to free her and I could climb to safety and try to tranq the werewolves. Keyword: Try.

I had never pulled a gun trigger in my life. I pointed to him then pointed up.

He shook his head. No. He wanted me to be safe. Well, safer.

Sweet, but no. I made an 'are you crazy?' face at the gun. I hoped he understood my expression. In case he didn't, I held out my hands. They were shaking.

His brow wrinkled in concern.

No, I thought, you don't have to worry. I can think. I just can't shoot.

New York City, Nick, I thought. Upper middle class Jewish teenagers in New York City shot movies, not guns. And let's talk about trees. Would he like to know how many times I had climbed a tree in my life? Even a tree like a ladder? Exactly never. I would probably slip, fall and break my ankle. Unless my life truly depended on it, I was not going up a tree. I was gonna free Judy, stab her with my antidote serum, and figure out how to get my two bonus doses into the two bonus monsters. Survive the night. Checkmate.

Nick of the excellent perception seemed to understand my silent monologue. He took hold of my shaking hands. Stepping in close to me, he placed them on his chest. His heart beat hard and fast. He was scared, too. He cupped my cheek with his free hand.

Oh no, I thought. Not now. This is absolutely not going to be the next kiss. No way. Kiss or death and you choose kiss now? I wanted to be chosen over something awesome like chocolate fudge brownie ice cream, please and thank you. Choose kiss over chocolate and win the game. But kiss over death? Duh. Definitely not. He leaned forward, touching his forehead to mine. His breath warmed my lips. A tiny lean forward and we would be kissing. Hands on his chest, I felt his heart slamming, too. I was so desperate for that kiss, it burned me from the inside out. He leaned forward.

I turned my cheek the other way. He backed up ever so slightly. Message received. A flicker of hurt crossed his face. A flicker of defiance crossed mine. At least he wanted to kiss me. That was good. I reached up to where his palm cradled my cheek. I covered his hand with mine.

Try again later, I thought. Live through this with me and try again. His expression changed from resignation to determination. That's my Adorable Goth Boy, I thought. That's my Nick. Let's go.

Stepping out of his closeness, I crept to the next tree, and then the next, keeping my eye on the white wolf choking herself on her restraint. I glanced over my shoulder. Nick's sneakered feet disappeared up into the branches.

A noise from the clearing caught my attention. The werewolves stood on all fours, separated now, and sniffing the air. I bet they were sniffing me.

A throaty, high-pitched howl, an animal siren, shook my bones close and resonant. I was shocked Judy could make that sound, bound by her neck as she was to the tree. She scrambled on her back, trying to right herself, twisting her neck in the heavy chain.

Wait. If she was tied, it was so the Man with No Face could *eat* her. *This was not the sacred land.* The boundary might be close, maybe even this clearing. But wherever the boundary was, Judy and now likely Nick and I, were on the wrong side of it. We were on the eating side.

The white wolf howled another piercing cry. This time, she got a response. Her father, the silver alpha wolf, bounded out of the forest. He was so much bigger up close than from the ridge last night. Crimson staining his bib fur, John Forest Stalker ran up the side of a cluster of boulders. He hit the top and launched himself at the alpha male werewolf. Ed stood on his hind legs as if to grab his adversary out of the air. The shifter crashed into the werewolf's neck. They tumbled to the ground.

Go, I said to myself. Go now!

I ran. When I hit open space, I dropped flat on my belly. I commando crawled to the base of Judy's tree. I could not, in that moment, have been luckier. Judy's chain was fastened to itself by a carabiner. The links strained as Judy pulled, trying to yank her neck free.

I grabbed the carabiner, the kind you unscrewed. It easily unlocked, but the chain was too tight for me to slide the end link over the carabiner's curve.

I almost didn't see the other shifter wolves circling in, waiting for a signal from their leader to enter the fray. The Red Dorsal wolf came up on John's right, the small wolf on his left. At the top of the boulder the Sandy female angled herself, ready to spring.

Judy barked, pulling harder. If she would relax for just a minute, she'd be free! Once I had slack, I could get her loose. Two seconds was all I needed.

An icy breeze raised the hairs on the back of my neck.

Oh *no*. Not the Man. Not now!

I stopped trying to free Wolf Judy. I grabbed my syringe of antidote and yanked off the cap. I reached around and jammed the needle into her thigh.

I heard the teeth clicking before I saw them. The Man with No Face's presence touched me like an icy caress. All the wolves went still.

Hurry! shouted Michael in my mind.

I yanked the chain binding Judy's throat tight. She gasped, choking. I anchored my foot against the tree trunk and yanked with all my might. It took all my strength to fight her pull and slide the chain off the carabiner. I fell back onto my behind as the heavy chain fell.

Judy was free. She yiped as her ear tore from where the werewolves had staked it to the tree. She scrambled to her feet. She shook herself. Blood from her ear hit me in the face.

Judy was still a monster. She turned and snarled and leaped. At me.

51.

April 27, continued.

Chain still in my hand, I rolled backward over my shoulder aikido style and came up in a crouch, on my feet. I had no weapons except the chain.

"Judy," I said, icy wind circling my legs. "It's me. It's Stacy. I'm here to help y- "

She sprung again. I dodged to the side swinging the chain as hard as I could. It cracked over her square, wrong-looking muzzle. She shook her head and drew down on me once more. That should have broken something, I thought. Come on, serum. Work!

It works on everything else, she'd said, but not on me. I'd adjusted it with that in mind, but still. Nothing.

Why?

I ran toward Nick's tree. In my peripheral vision, I saw something grab Judy and toss her to the side. I heard a thump and grunt as she made contact with a tree and fell to the ground. An icy fist grabbed my ankle and yanked. I hit the ground hard, throwing my arms out to brace my fall. I tried to roll onto my back, but my ankle was pinned to the ground. A shattering pain travelled up my leg and into my spine.

I screamed. And screamed.

You have caused a lot of trouble for me, said the Man with No Face.

Icy numbness spread, so cold, so hot it hurt. My vision went spotty. I had never felt pain like this, not breaking my tailbone, not being bitten by vampires. This pain consumed me. It spread up my spine to the back of my head. I screamed like I have never screamed before. He spoke again, a resonant smear of agony in my forehead.

Why are you interfering now? Was my bird message unclear?

A pair of sneakers landed in the dirt by my face. Nick. He held a knife out in front of him. Two pairs of hands grabbed under my arm pits and tried to pull me off the ground, but I was stuck, frozen to the ground, or maybe weighted. I couldn't tell. A searing ice so cold it burned filled my mouth, my lungs and everything was pain.

*

I dreamed Nick stood beside me. He was canting, like at temple, singing and chanting words I knew. Beautiful, powerful words. Hebrew words. In my mind's eye, they appeared in the air. Around them he traced my six-pointed star. It glowed bright with white magickal fire. Starlight filled his drawing and a wall of blackness pushed against it. Taller in my dream than in real life, Nick drew a circle around us. It, too, glowed with white fire. I saw my body on the ground, limp. Maybe dead. It was okay. Dreaming wasn't a bad thing. I'd wake eventually. If this body was gone, I would choose another one. I was starlight. I was soul.

The star floating above my body flamed bright. Nick's chest filled with brilliance. It traveled into his arms, his legs, his head. He was calling, calling names, calling for help. Four luminous figures materialized around him. There was Michael fully in his wings. Hello, Michael! I drifted above them all, the crystal clear luminosity of all consciousness opening before me, welcoming me into the vastness of the space after life. This was it. This was death.

A sickly blackness, a scar on the beautiful swath of light that held me in its embrace, reached toward Nick with tentacles of shadow, cuts of darkness. It shook a body against the ground trying to break it. Oh. That body had been mine. So tiny. So fragile. The necklaces around my neck glowed with brilliance, tiny stars from here. Below me, the land itself began to hum. The four figures, three plus Michael, placed their hands on Nick. Nick took the knife he'd been using as a sky pencil, aimed it straight out from his shoulder into the slices of darkness and cut sharply down.

*

I slammed back into my body. My head felt cracked and split, like a melon. Maybe it was? Grass and twigs grabbed at me, bit my searing skin as hands dragged me across the ground. I tried to tell them to stop, but I couldn't speak. My tongue was so thick. My limbs too heavy to control. And everything hurt, worse than anything, worse than death. I hurt.

"She's breathing," Tully said when they laid me flat on the pine needles. He put his fingers on my neck pulse.

"What did he do?" Finder said. "Why is she so heavy?"

"I don't know."

"But you felt it right? Whatever it was?"

"I felt something. Stay with her. I'll get Judy."

The pain turned from fire to tingling to ice, like when your foot falls asleep and 'wakes up'. My whole body felt it, but the tingling wasn't the usual pins and needles, it was sharp shocks. The sounds of melee were close, but I couldn't see, my head still turned to the side, cheek heavy in the pine needles. They smelled good. They smelled like angels.

I groaned.

"Ready, sis?"

I was not. Finder reached her arm under my side. I made the sound a person makes when a broken bone gets moved, though as far as I knew, I had no broken bones. Maybe they were all shattered. I couldn't tell. Finder shifted her position and we tried again. After a few labored breaths, she got me sitting, propped up against a tree.

"Look at me, Stacy," she said. "Can you move your head?"

It took effort, but I turned my head toward her voice. And then, there she was, skin glistening with sweat. Beyond Finder everything was blurry, but she was close and I could focus.

She wiped my forehead with her hand.

"Just dirt," she said, "not blood. Whew. I was afraid he'd broken your neck the way he slammed you to the ground."

Had I been slammed to the ground? I didn't remember that.

"I don't know how one little math nerd can make so many supernatural creatures so angry, but you sure do."

I tried to smile.

"I saw that lip twitch. That was my test to see how brain damaged you were, but I think you're gonna be okay." She leaned forward and kissed the top of my head. "Scare me to death. No dying," she pointed a finger in my face. "Do you hear me? No dying." She crouched beside me and steadied my shoulders. "The sacred land boundary must be there." Finder pointed.

A line of smoke blew back and forth, stalking, hungry, just past where the wolves and werewolves fought, a great white shark swimming on the other side of the glass. The sacred land was a tiny aquarium in the shark-infested Richmond waters. A massive pile of white fur lay on the ground, trapped between the combat and the invisible barrier protecting against the drifting smoke.

"It threw her and went for you. Then it let go of you and went after her, again," Finder said, holding a water bottle to my lips. I swallowed. "It caught her, but Nick pulled her back across the line."

"No . . . change?" I choked. She gave me more water. Had my antidote not worked?

"See for yourself," Finder said.

Tully skirted John and Ed's fight, diving out from the tree line to scoop up Judy before the melee got her stepped on or killed.

Ed climbed to his feet, black ooze dripping from gashes and bites. At a bark from John, the Sandy female and the little wolf attacked. Ed fought them as John, bleeding clean, red blood, leapt for his enemy's underbelly.

Halfway across the clearing, Red Dorsal wolf lunged at the alpha female's shin. She was huge, a foot taller than him with all four paws on the ground. She swung round to greet him, jaw snapping. He dodged.

Tully emerged from the trees beside us, Nick on his heels. He laid wolf Judy on the ground; a stunning, pure white wolf, marred only by a burn on one hind leg in the shape of human hand. Nick crouched beside me. All traces of monster Judy had vanished. My serum had worked after all. It just took time.

Time we didn't have. How could I make the serum work faster? How could I make it stronger to treat the werewolves?

"What now?" Tully said. "Do we run for the truck?"

"We save them," I said, my voice dry and rough.

"*Save* them?" Finder said.

In as few words as possible, I made them understand.

"We can't leave the sacred land," Nick said. "And we don't know the borders. They weren't parked back by the bridge, so there has to be a closer road. We're gonna need a way out if we have people who can't walk. A way that stays inside the sacred land as long as possible." He spoke to me. "We need to get you and Judy as far out of this as we can. Then we'll decide what's next."

"No. We need to get close. To give Ed and Mrs. Macy shots," I said.

"Can the serum go in the tranq gun darts?" Finder asked, helping Nick carry me further out of the danger zone.

The tranq gun was a good idea. My hands wouldn't move.

Setting me down behind the tree line, Nick rubbed my arms to get blood moving again. Finder rubbed my legs. I cried out. It felt like they were rolling my limbs in glass.

To distract myself from pain after they stopped, I talked Tully through filling a tranq dart from the syringe I had prepared.

"Who can go to Judy's house?" I said. "There's serum in her fridge. I need it. My Judy-sized doses won't work on the monsters."

Finder nodded. "I got it."

"Take Tully with you. He can drive," said Nick.

"Faster and quieter on my own. And I know how to drive." Finder took off into the woods.

In the center of the clearing, the five shifter wolves fought the two werewolves. The werewolves moved slower than the shifters, but their size and weight gave them the advantage. The Man with No Face, embodied by the smoke, slithered back and forth between the trees on the other side of the sacred land border. Ed, the alpha male werewolf, loosed a howl. He swung at the wolf nearest his feet, Red Dorsal. The wolf dashed between the monster's legs and came up behind him. He jumped up and bit Ed's rear end. John Forest Stalker, silver moonlight lighting his fur, crouched and leaped. He collided with Ed's chest, knocking the tall monster backwards. Wolf and werewolf landed hard on the ground and John, on top, lunged for the bigger creature's throat. But not fast enough. The werewolf intercepted, sinking claws into John's side. John tumbled off the monster. Bleeding from fresh claw wounds, he dragged himself to his feet.

The Sandy female dove for Ed's knees. Red Dorsal now danced with the werewolf alpha female. It had to be Mrs. Macy. He kept her attention by weaving back and forth as he drew her away from the alpha male fight. He dodged her blows, left and right and left again. She roared, but left the males' fight alone.

Beside me, wolf Judy stirred. The burn on her leg was already healing. She climbed gingerly to all four feet. She stretched, more like a dog waking from a nap than a fighter recovering from a blow. I'd thought she would be German Shepherd or maybe Labrador Retriever sized. Wrong. Standing on all four feet, Judy's back was higher than my head sitting down. Great Dane. Mastiff. She shook herself all over. I struggled to make my own limbs work.

The werewolf screamed as a chunk of foul flesh came away in John's mouth. Judy ran for her dad. Wolf John lunged forward, clamping his jaws again into the werewolf's thigh. The werewolf grabbed John with both clawed hands. It threw him hard. John flew through the air and smacked spine first into a tree. He fell to the ground, limp.

Judy howled, sharp and piteous.

Julian was on the ground running toward John's crumpled form when the enraged werewolf stepped into his path. Julian raised his shotgun. The werewolf snatched it out of his hands. The gun strap broke across the scientist's back with a snap. Julian staggered forward.

Ed, not even seeming to register what he held, threw the gun to the side. He raised his fist to strike Julian.

A roar erupted beside me. The werewolf paused his blow and looked our way. Tully, staff drawn and ready, launched himself toward the fight.

"No!" I shouted. Tully shoved Julian aside, then struck the monster's raised fist with his staff.

Beside me, Nick aimed the tranquilizer rifle and shot.

The dart buried itself in Ed's thigh. Intent on his prey, Ed didn't even acknowledge it.

"Come on!" Tully shouted. "Come and get me!" What was he doing? The werewolf swung. Tully blocked with his staff. It splintered.

The Sandy wolf snapped at Ed's achilles. Red Dorsal left Mrs. Macy and ran to help fight Ed. He jumped and bit the werewolf male on the arm. Judy stood over her father's limp form. She howled again.

"Will your arms work yet?" Nick said to me, desperation in his voice. I moved them both, heavy, but not unresponsive. Yes, my arms worked.

I felt my legs try to obey. Try and fail. Nick winced at my struggle, then tucked the tranquilizer rifle under my arm and put his remaining darts in my lap. Four.

"I love you," he said. "Don't die." He took off across the clearing to where John Forest Stalker lay still.

You love me? I thought. Like, *love* love?

A deep throated snarl caught my attention. The alpha female werewolf, all four feet on the ground, had moved to her mate and was backing Judy away from guarding her father's body, backing her toward the invisible sacred land border where the icy, dark smoke continued to roil. Judy must've felt the chill, because she stopped, snarled at Mrs. Macy, and darted forward under the bigger female's chest. Macy dropped to the dirt to crush Judy, but the fast, nimble shifter shot between her legs, forcing the werewolf to turn to fight again. Judy growled and pushed forward, pressing Mrs. Macy backwards toward the border, toward the starving smoke that was the Man with No Face.

Path now clear, Julian bolted to where John lay. Nick was already beside him, crouched and professional.

Tully pulled his bat out from its across-the-back holder. He swung at Ed. The baseball bat slammed across the werewolf's shoulder. Ed flung an arm to fend off the next blow. Red Dorsal leaped and caught the monster's arm in his jaws. At the same time, Sandy wolf dove in for another ankle bite. Ed lifted his huge foot to stomp her. She darted away. Ed stepped forward, blocking my view of Nick, Julian and John. He tried again to stomp Sandy wolf, slamming his foot down so hard the ground vibrated, but she was fast. He missed. She bit him again. He shrieked. This time she held on a second too long.

The werewolf turned. He grabbed Sandy by the scruff of her neck and her tail. He lifted her into the air. She thrashed to escape. He smashed her to the earth like a toddler throwing a toy to the ground. Red Dorsal leaped in and crashed into Ed's knee. Tully swung with all his might at the other. The werewolf wobbled but stayed upright. Tully struck again, strong and fast. Red Dorsal bit down hard. Ed roared and fell to his battered knees, his wet maw now eye level with Tully.

Hands trembling, I lined up my shot.

"Do it," Tully said, looking the monster in the eyes. He held his bat at the ready. "I dare you."

I took a breath and squeezed the trigger.

Ed flinched as the tranquilizer dart embedded itself in his meaty side. Focused on his prey, he ignored it and swung again. Tully blocked with the bat. Ed's foot landed on the Sandy wolf. She yiped as his foot crushed her paw. He didn't even notice, concentrating on backing Tully toward the shark tank wall. The second his foot was off her, Sandy righted herself to her belly. She tried to crawl out of the way. Red Dorsal and the smallest wolf grabbed her by the scruff and dragged her out of the fray.

Judy leaped and teased in front of Mrs. Macy like a fox fascinating prey. They had changed direction, no longer headed for the sacred land border. The werewolf lunged. Judy dodged. Judy and Mrs. Macy traded blows as Red Dorsal and the smallest wolf ran in to attack the werewolf's legs and feet.

Behind the fight, Nick and Julian were arguing.

Guns are scary. Guns are dangerous. Guns are effective. Unless one of your friends is in the way. Nick grabbed Julian's gun up off the ground.

"Tully! Move!"

Tully did not move. Tully whacked the werewolf's massive skull with the bat so hard it rang. Tully loosed another battle cry and flung himself into the werewolf beating and flailing like how I imagined a berserker would fight. Tully screamed as the werewolf scored a blow. The werewolf bit his shoulder. Something crunched. Tully screamed. The werewolf threw Tully on the ground. Tully rolled to his feet, weaponless, but miraculously standing. Why wasn't he running? Ed swiped those claws at Tully. The Southern Scotsman looked at his attacker and did not dodge. What was he doing? The werewolf struck, digging his claws deep into Tully's side.

Nick's words from the night before came back to me. *Do you know how many men kill themselves because they can't be who they are?*

"Tully! No!"

After too many seconds, the dart I struggled to load snapped into the slide. I didn't remember shaking so hard during the vampire fight. I braced myself, rifle butt tight to the inside of my shoulder. I lined up my target. I exhaled, squeezing the trigger. By a miracle I cannot name, my shot landed.

Tully smacked at what stung him, driving the needle in his arm deeper. He looked up and our eyes met. He looked like I had betrayed him.

Tully swayed as the ketamine, enough for a wolf, made him dizzy. He opened his arms and flung himself toward the werewolf. Ed lifted him off the ground.

BOOM! Nick stood behind the werewolf, gun raised. Ed howled, vicious and furious. He staggered, unable to turn with the weight of Tully dragging him forward. The Southern Scotsman grabbed the monster's head and slammed it into his own. Together they fell.

The Man with No Face shrieked in rage from the shark tank. The trees blew hard in unnatural, icy wind.

A streak of pain shot up my legs. Like a switch in my body had flipped, I could move. I could move! My legs were hard to feel, but they were moving. I fell twice getting to my feet.

Nick had dropped Julian's gun and was trying to roll Ed off Tully when Finder's shout cracked the air from outside the melee. Her skin shone with sweat in the silver light as she bolted into the clearing.

"Run!" she screamed. "Run!"

52.

April 27, continued.

The moving shadows behind Finder roared.

Three more werewolves summoned by Ed's howl came too fast into view. Seven to eight feet tall each, they lumbered after her.

Finder recognized Tully's feet sticking out from under the alpha werewolf and screamed a scream I hope never to hear the like of again. It's said that mothers can lift cars when their babies are trapped underneath. The brain releases a dose of adrenaline so powerful it can make a superhero out of anyone. It must've been adrenaline fueling my friends, because there's no other way Finder and Nick could've lifted what had to be five hundred pounds of werewolf off Tully. But they did.

I ran to my friends, clumsy but moving, forcing my still heavy limbs to go.

Tully lay, eyes closed, mouth open. Blood stained his hair from open gashes in his forehead where he'd smashed it into the jaws of the werewolf. His chest was an awkward squashed shape on the right. I reached to get the dart out of his arm, but Nick got there first.

"I hit him with ketamine," I said. Nick placed a hand on Tully's chest and then felt again, face rumpling in confusion. Pulling down the collar of Tully's shirt he saw what puzzled him.

"Help me," he said. We pulled Tully's shirts up to reveal a plastic chest plate. Fencing armor. It was all kinds of bent and punctured by teeth.

Finder thrust a paper bag at me. The serum from Judy's fridge. Ed was down. I needed to inject him now.

I dug for the other syringes of Judy's serum. I realized in a flash that Judy's serum had the right messenger enzyme, but was combined for the wrong mutation. This serum was for transversions. I needed to get the protein from Judy's serum into Evia's serum for non-hereditary mutations.

Julian cradled John in his arms.

"Did you add anything other than the venom?" I demanded.

Julian looked stricken. "Tell me now!" I screamed in his face.

"Yes," he cried. "I added a stimulant. The werewolf venom is too weak. It takes months for them to fully take form and we needed to change the shifter wolves into werewolves fast."

"So the Man with No Face could eat them instead?" I shouted.

"Who's the Man with No Face?" Julian said. "Ed and all these people got bitten by the *Famelicus*. Its venom gets into their blood and consumes the healthy cells. The take over isn't instantaneous, it can take months."

That's why the werewolves took so long before they fully wolfed out.

"The predator blood cell sample you brought to the lab," Julian said. "I thought it was from the Famelicus. I thought you knew."

I'd heard that term before. Where? Was that the 'real' name of the Man with No Face? Was it what he was? Were there other Famelicuses? Famelici? That was terrifying. I put it out of my mind. If there was more than one Man with No Face, I did not want to know.

"Werewolves can't create other werewolves," Julian said, looking at Ed lying still in the dirt. "He tried, but the second generation venom they produce isn't strong enough. We thought maybe if we mixed their venom with serum designed to alter mutated DNA, we could create a werewolf hybrid out of the shifters the Famelicus could eat instead."

So much to unpack here.

"Ed wanted to save his pack. He told me he would spare John and Lea Macy would drop the lawsuit if I helped them. I tried to negotiate!"

"Negotiate? You decided it was okay to kill people! You decided to steal someone else's science and use it for your own evil ends!"

"I'm not evil! I just want John to be happy. And this lawsuit has been making him miserable, stressed and worried and working all the time. He's lost weight."

I could not believe what I was hearing. Julian was willing to be the catalyst for other people *dying* because his honey muffin was *losing weight?*

"Julian!" I shouted. "How much venom is in this?"

"I don't know. Ed got impatient when my serum didn't work and started adding to it himself."

Crap. My perfect plan was now a complete long shot.

"Which base did you use? Judy's or Evia's"

"I don't know! Whatever you left at the lab."

Ugh. Idiot. How could he not know this? I took a breath. There had been samples of both serums at the lab. One marked blue, one with red. These tubes were marked red. That should mean it was Evia's base. No wonder it wasn't working on Judy. I emptied one syringe into a tube from Finder's bag and swirled to mix it.

I turned my attention to the downed werewolf. My hands shook as I got a syringe out of my fanny pack and loaded it. I uncapped the syringe.

"Where do I- ?" I said, never having stuck a needle into a werewolf before.

Nick took the syringe from me then felt in the gross fur under the stirring monster's chin. Ed groaned and moved. Nick opened a spot in the fur and jammed the needle into Ed's neck. The monster stiffened.

The smallest shifter wolf barked and growled. The three fresh, new werewolves readied themselves to attack. I had counted eight people at the fire last night. If these were them, and I suspected they were, where were the other three? Maybe not fully changed enough to hunt with the others? I hoped that was the case. Ed stirred on the ground but wasn't changing back to human. Crap. The serum wasn't strong enough. It took too long to work. Then I had an idea.

"Nick! Are there heart attack supplies in your med kit? Adrenaline shots to restart someone's heart! Do you have them?"

He nodded.

I grabbed Finder's arm. "Can you- ?"

"Med bag. Got it." She ran across the clearing to the branch wall where we had stashed our stuff.

Behind us, Julian knelt, cradling his love in his arms.

"I told you, don't!" Nick said, making Julian lay John back on the ground. Nick put his hands, cautious, respectful, on wolf John's ribcage and belly. "Internal injuries. Like I said before," he said. "He needs a vet. Right now. Who do you call?"

Julian's eyes went wide. "They heal so fast. He's only been badly hurt once."

Nick pulled down one of the wolf's eyelids. "He's not healing now," Nick said. "If an organ's burst, he might bleed out inside before rapid healing can kick in."

Behind us, the shifters were keeping the new werewolves busy. Using their superior speed and team work, they led the heavier, less agile beasts striking and missing back and forth, back and forth. How long could they keep it up before they tired?

Finder arrived and slung my pack from her shoulder. She chucked the bow at my feet and dropped the med kit into the grass. I found what I needed, ripped open the wrapping and tore off the cap. Ed's fur was wet with black ooze. I hesitated. I didn't want to touch it. The monster moaned and stirred.

"If this works, you owe me." The fur was still slightly parted from the first shot. I slid the needle into Ed's neck and pushed the plunger. My hands came away smelling like I'd given a bad diaper change.

Please work, I silently begged. Please. Work.

Nothing happened.

Finder spilled her last bottle of water over my hands. "Ed's truck is over the hill," she said as I wiped my fingers in the grass. "Quarter mile. Maybe less. Keys are in it. Full of dog stealing stuff, too. Crates, leashes the whole bit. I brought you this." She handed me a second bottle of ketamine and a handful of tranquilizer darts. "Couldn't find the gun."

My mind spun. Should I give Ed another shot of ketamine to keep him down or would it counter the adrenaline shot I'd given him to speed my serum? As if in answer, the black ooze still coating Ed's fur trembled and coagulated toward his heart. After having seen what happened the last time that ooze moved on its own, I backed off. I nearly tripped on Julian.

"You knew and you didn't tell us," I accused the scientist as he met my gaze. "You've led us all to the slaughter."

Ed's body spasmed as the black ooze dug deeper into his fur. His legs kicked out as if caught in a nightmare. The werewolf groaned.

Please work.

"Can't move either of them," Nick said, looking up from Judy's dad and Tully. "Help's gotta come to us."

"Take me to the truck," Julian said to Finder.

"The trail splits," she said. "Go right. I'm not leaving my friends."

Saying nothing, Julian took off at a run.

"What if he doesn't come back?" Finder said.

"Good riddance," I said.

Nick said, "He'll come back for John."

The werewolf's body in front of me trembled as if the ground below him vibrated with an earthquake. Boy did he stink.

Across the clearing, Judy held Mrs. Macy at the tree line where she used her smaller size and the proximity of trees to keep Mrs. Macy pinned at the sacred land border. The werewolf howled a throaty, piercing sound.

Red Dorsal blocked the three new werewolves from coming our way. A steel gray wolf I hadn't seen before lurked at the tree line. A member of the shifter pack late to the party? Or a real wolf?

The smallest wolf dove between the werewolves' legs. Steel Grey, gorgeous like a nature magazine's photograph, did the same in the opposite direction. As if in a planned formation, the three wolves began a patterned dance, diving between the legs of their adversaries. Each move forced the monsters to pivot, turning side-to-side to strike. The shifter wolves repeated their bite-leap-snap-then-twist choreography. The center werewolf lost her balance. She hit the male and they tumbled to the ground.

Mrs. Macy shrieked in fury at the tree line. Judy was latched onto her arm.

"Don't feed her to him!" I shouted to Judy.

Red Dorsal turned to me and yipped.

Help, please.

Finder, as if she could also read the wolf's bark, unleashed her blades, letting them slide into her palms like the professional she was. Her face was set, her gaze deadly. She had practiced with the long, silver daggers daily since New Year's. As she readied to engage, they sat in her hands like natural extensions of her arms.

"No killing!" I shouted to my friends.

Something rumbled from the trees on our left. Two more enormous werewolves came crashing on all fours into the field.

Mrs. Macy's summons had not gone unheard. Finder's blades gleamed in the moonlight. I readied my bow as Nick raised the tranquilizer rifle. What if kill or be killed were the only options we had left?

The melee burst into a blur. I shot my bow as Nick hit any werewolf he could with ketamine darts.

Ketamine, the stuff that might slow their change back to human and undo my serum.

"Stop!" I shouted to Nick. I threw him my bow and dropped to my knees. I yanked the tranq darts I still had out of my fanny pack and emptied the ketamine on the ground. I filled the darts with my newly doctored serum. If this didn't work, we were done for. I shoved the darts into Nick's hand.

Judy yiped from the tree line as Mrs. Macy gouged her with those endless claws. Red spread across white fur. Judy backed off, sinking low to the ground. The smallest wolf leaped in the air and slammed into Mrs. Macy. She staggered to the side. Red Dorsal rose on his hind legs. He rammed his head into the exact spot to throw the werewolf off balance.

I snatched up my bow and nocked an arrow. My shot pierced the alpha female's leg. Mrs. Macy shrieked. She reached to yank out the arrow. I ran. Red Dorsal wolf ran beside me, a shield. He matched my pace and together we got half way around the clearing to where Finder swung the silver blades, dodging blows from one of the two new werewolves. She was bleeding.

Nick had dropped the tranquilizer gun and was fending off blows from the other new wolf with Tully's discarded baseball bat.

Had he shot them all with serum? Surely, yes.

I couldn't get a clear arrow shot without risking hitting Nick or Finder. I had a few syringes and some serum left. How could I get close enough to jam a needle into one of these monsters?

Red Dorsal wolf looked at the fight and looked at me. Was I okay?

I was. Technically speaking. I nodded.

"Thanks, wolf." The massive wolf stuck his nose in my ear, took a big sniff and licked the entire side of my face in one lop. He crouched and leaped toward the werewolf attacking Finder. He hit the monster in the chest and sent it reeling.

Finder used both blades to cut the werewolf across the jaw on both sides. The monster yowled. The wounds sizzled and smoked. The smell of fouled meat filled the air. Red Dorsal wolf chomped the monster in the knee. Finder ducked a clawed swipe then sliced across the werewolf's chest as she came up. She whirled her blade to stabbing position.

"Legs!" I shouted. "No killing blows!" Black blood smoked off the silver. I had no time to wonder.

Finder stabbed her werewolf's thigh. The werewolf screamed and leaped back taking Finder's weapon with her, stuck and smoking in the thick muscle.

Red Dorsal wolf crouched and leaped. Mid-leap, he closed his jaws over Finder's blade handle. Turning his head he yanked it out. He tossed his head as his feet hit the ground. Finder reached up. She snatched the handle out of the air in time to swipe her blade across the face of the werewolf attacking Nick. Sizzle. Smoke. Finder's werewolf limped back toward the trees, maybe with a broken knee.

Nick's werewolf shook off the sting of Finder's blade. Smoke rose from the cut. He grabbed the business end of Nick's bat and forced Nick to his knees. Finder and Red Dorsal attacked at once, a blur of blows as they tried to get the werewolf to back away. Finder cut him deep in the arm. Sizzle. Smoke. The werewolf howled in rage and swung his huge fist. Finder and Nick both dove to the ground.

Red Dorsal wolf pivoted on his back feet. He skidded to a halt blocking Mrs. Macy's way to the bigger fight. He nodded at me. I ran forward and stabbed Nick's werewolf with one of my last two

DNA reversing syringes. How much longer could we hold out against six werewolves?

I've never seen Finder look genuinely scared. Except for now. Rolling to her feet, she repositioned her blades, ready for the alpha female to spring. Finder and Red Dorsal wolf made eye contact. Fighters side by side. The shifter bared his teeth at Mrs. Macy. Judy appeared at the top of the boulders, a moonlit pale ghost dripping red and holding one back paw off the ground. Mrs. Macy sprung.

She swiped down fast and dug her claws into Red Dorsal's chest. She roared, lifting the heavy wolf up on her claws like a skewer. She flung him off. I heard a slick sound, raw meat sliding off knives.

Finder landed a blade in the werewolf's arm. Sizzling black juice spat up from the wound. Mrs. Macy ignored it. One sign of adrenaline overload is taking damage without noticing it. Mrs. Macy's arm was cooking where the silver was lodged. She should have been screaming. How much adrenaline was in these werewolves?

Mrs. Macy grabbed Finder's shoulder and pressed down. Finder's knees started to crumple. The werewolf roared as she gripped Finder's wrist. I ran forward and slammed my last syringe into her back. I couldn't reach her neck.

Finder, arm trapped by the werewolf, tried yanking the monster off balance. When that didn't work, she kicked Mrs. Macy in the chest. Mrs. Macy clamped down harder on Finder's shoulder and twisted her arm. She yanked it away from the socket. Finder screamed.

A bird flew into the monster's face. The werewolf swung her head in avoidance, but the tiny attacker persisted, diving at Mrs. Macy's eyes and screaming a tiny "scree" sound.

Wait. Not a bird. A *bat*.

53.

April 27, continued.

Mrs. Macy dropped Finder. She shielded her eyes.

The wind blew, sudden and hard, shapeshifting wind that sucked at the air in my lungs, then let go. The sound of ripping echoed across the clearing.

Darcy Jackson clung to the werewolf's chest. His jacket was split up the back. Pushing off with his feet, he threw himself over Mrs. Macy's shoulder, catching her jaw in the crook of his arm. Darcy's fangs gleamed in the moonlight.

"Shoot, Stacy!" he yelled. I aimed and fired. Mrs. Macy stumbled to the side, unprepared for the weighted drag on her neck. My arrow hit her in the side. "Again!" Darcy's voice rang out in the clearing. I loaded another arrow. I ran to get a better shot. It stank worse over here. I aimed. The bow shattered out of my arms as the missing werewolf, monster number eight, slammed a hairy arm down and grabbed me up off the ground.

My ribs creaked as the werewolf squashed me to her chest. I kicked backward and grabbed the arm anchoring me. I dug my spiked wristband into her fur, but it was like shoving it into thick, filthy carpet. I screamed "Let go!" slamming my elbow backward over and over into the thing's chest. The werewolf reached around and grabbed me by the collar. She dangled me out in front of her, razor claws making tiny cuts in the side of my neck. Fabric dug into my throat and I choked for air.

The werewolf's head was twice the size of mine, her eyes glistening with runny slime. Pointy ears laid flat against her matted fur. Her breath, hot and foul, smelled like a toilet explosion as she opened her jaw for a bite.

The average bite of a natural wolf is 406 psi. That means four hundred and six *pounds* of pressure per square *inch*. Wolves in distress have been recorded biting at closer to 1200 psi. Pit Bulls, dogs feared for their powerful bites, clamp down at about 235 psi. A bite from the werewolf currently strangling me, averaging standard wolf bite with distressed wolf bite, comes in at around 800 psi. In other words, it would chomp/slice straight to the bone. My living flesh would rip away like cooked chicken off a drumstick.

The werewolf leaned in and by some miracle did not bite me. She ran her foul cold nose along my cheek as the shirt digging into my throat stifled my breath. She pulled back and growled. I flailed, trying to land a kick. She licked her chops, splattering my face with thick, sour saliva. I kicked harder. She shook me like a dog toy. I tried to suck in air, but choked on my own collar. Gravity dragged me into the fabric and toward the ground. I wriggled, desperate to get free. I slid just a little. My vision filled with red and black spots. The monster shook me again, harder, trying to snap my neck.

Gravity yes, I thought. Gravity! Yes! One more shake from the werewolf and my left arm slid free of the hoodie. Wedging my fingers under the collar of my shirt, I tore it away from my throat. My collar loosened just enough. A breath ripped through me. Not a full breath but enough to clear my vision. I slid out from inside my shirts. I fell sideways, landing on my hip, not graceful, not at all like Finder had taught me. I laid there for half a second as breath filled my lungs. Half a second too long. The werewolf swiped. My fanny pack severed as her claws sliced the pack strap and cut the bare skin above my jeans. Then she stepped on my legs. She leaned down, and searing pain ripped into my side where she had sliced me. I screamed. Something hot and wet dripped onto my back.

A creature, huge and black, tore out of the trees and leaped toward me. I screamed, pain exploding further across my middle.

The black animal, too big for a wolf, sailed over me and landed on the other side of the werewolf. Her stench was choking as she crouched low over me. Defending me. Defending her meal. I tried to crawl backward, but she stepped on me again, claws piercing my shoulder through muscle and bone. All I could see of my rescuer was massive black paws the size of ramen bowls.

"Get off her!" screamed a far-away voice. One second ticked by as the owner of the massive paws and the werewolf who wanted to eat me growled into a standoff. Two seconds, three. It might have been an hour for how long I lay there blood pumping out of my shoulder, wondering if I was going to be dead the next minute. The werewolf lay down, dead weight on top of me. I couldn't breathe. I wasn't sure if what I heard was my ribs cracking, but it felt like it. Stabbing pain rocked my chest. I was being crushed.

And then the weight was gone. I opened my eyes, gasping for air. The owner of the ramen bowl paws was a wolf, the biggest I'd ever seen. The black wolf from last night. He was the size of a small pony up close. He licked my face and I sputtered. Something clung to his back, but my vision was blurry from pain.

"Stacy! Stacy! Are you alive? Are you?"

I'm hallucinating, I thought. This is not possible. "Stacy, say something!" The big wolf dug his nose under my chest and rolled me over. The pain from my ribs was excruciating. Flat on my back in the dirt, I groaned in pain. Somewhere in the clearing, a werewolf shrieked. An object whizzed over my face as I struggled to recover. A dart. Something moved on the big wolf's back. No. Not something. *Someone.*

"Stacy! Look at me!"

A desperate panic filled me as Steve leaned over the black wolf's back. His little face was lit with moonlight and worry. I blinked up at him.

"Yay! You're alive! I'll get you help. Let's go, Sensei!" The black wolf launched.

Steve could NOT be here. I had trusted Mama to keep him safe. I was going to kill her. How could she let him out like this with the level of danger and guaranteed bodily harm? I was scared, I was furious. I was in so much pain, but I had to get up. I had to get Steve out of here.

A werewolf roared. My little brother's victory whoop echoed among the trees.

My head swam as I rolled from my back to my belly. I wanted to crawl to all fours, but that was not happening. My chest felt spiked to the ground.

Is this what it's like to be staked? I thought.

I felt a gentle, cool hand on my back.

"Stop trying to get up," said Darcy Jackson. "Your ribs are all broken and one of your lungs is punctured. I can hear it. You've lost a lot of blood from that shoulder. What a waste. Stay still, baby." The contents of my stomach roiled for one brief second, then left my body in one agonizing heave.

There are a lot of things I do not like in this world, besides being told I am dying. Bad coffee, weak milk chocolate, the fact that vampires exist, losing chess. But until right now, throwing up had topped them all. It's the throat and mouth acid burn aftermath that's the worst part. More miserable even than the actual moment of meal eviction. All I'd had had before we came out to spend a nice quiet evening breaking up a wolf territory battle and saving our friend was what I'd eaten off the science fair lunch cart. A snack pack of potato chips, Jill's cookie, a nice coffee and one and a half egg salad sandwiches. There are a lot of things you can choose to eat before going into an uncertain situation that may or may not include melee. Egg salad should not be one of them. Never. Never, ever.

Darcy Jackson moved me away from my mess. I let him, hardly concerned for myself at all. I lay there acknowledging the one thing I now hated more than anything else I'd experienced to date. I hated seeing my baby brother in combat.

Darcy Jackson laid down beside me in the dirt. His eyes were filled with regret. He held my gaze for a moment. Before I had time to realize what was happening and panic, his expression softened.

"Thanks for looking me in the eyes," he said. "And for being a friend to Layla. She's needed someone like you for a long time."

Maybe against my better judgement, I did not look away. I was dying. How could a vampire make that worse? I stayed calm, stayed still, stayed looking in his eyes, like he was human. Like we were friends.

She's a good person, I wanted to say, but I was in so much pain, nothing came out. He must've been an okay dad before he vamped out. And maybe, considering he came to save her, he could be a worse dad even now.

"Don't tell Matilda, but I miss . . . I miss looking people in the eyes." He sighed. "I know we are enemies," Darcy said, "and you have no reason to trust me, but you have two choices right now. Die or don't."

I blinked up at him.

"Option one, hospital. You will most likely die in the half hour between here and there whether I remain in human form and fly or run with you or go find a vehicle and drive you." He looked reluctant, as if even saying whatever he was about to say was a huge mistake. "Or, and I know I'm going to regret offering this, option two. I can feed you my blood and you can heal."

I sucked in a rattling breath to say something along the lines of No Way Possible will I agree to that, but, ow. Breathing hurt.

"It will not make you what I am, but it will bind us," Darcy said. "Matilda will likely kill me for doing it, which for you is a plus because if I'm truly dead, any binding we do will be moot. The other con for me is that you will be able to detect my whereabouts and my danger alarm will not go off when you are near. So if you really wanted to sneak into my apartment and stake me, I'd be vulnerable to that. Also not good for me. The advantage for me is that I can call you whenever I want and you will feel strongly compelled to come. And do what I ask you to do." I felt my eyes go wide. "The advantage for you is if you drink my blood on a regular basis, you will have a longer life span than the average person and you will heal very quickly. I think you see how quick healing could be a huge bonus in your new line of work." He paused, thinking. "This is not without risk for either of us." That was true.

"I am not trying to manipulate you," he said. "Do you feel that?" Yes, I did. He was not using any powers on me at all.

"Layla has needed a friend like you for a long time. I'd rather you not get taken away from her, too. I'm gone. Teularen is about to be gone in his own way. Will you let me heal you? We'd need an agreement of course, you agree not to kill me and I agree not to call you. Fair enough?"

I couldn't speak my chest hurt so badly. I wheezed in a breath. Breathing was getting harder.

I wasn't actually considering this, was I?

"I should also mention that werewolf left her venom in your skin when she clawed you. Even if you weren't already broken, that infection could kill you by itself."

Michael, I said in my mind. *Michael!*

Yes?

Can you heal me?

Mmm, no.

What? Why?

Twice in one night is not allowed.

Wait, I died already once?

Yes. Have you forgotten? It was when the Famelicus tried to suck your life.

I had no idea what he was talking about.

The dream you had?

I had a dream?

Sorry, I don't remember.

The angel sighed.

I could go with you to the hospital and jump start your body after you die, but that won't heal your injuries. They will take weeks to heal. And surgery, likely, on your lung.

So Darcy Jackson isn't lying? I'm broken enough to die?

You are. And he's not wrong about that infection. It's nasty.

What's the point of having an angel watch over you if you can't do anything useful?

I did already save your life once tonight.

I struggled for memory. I knew the Man with No Face had grabbed me, and I remembered the blistering pain. The next memory in my timeline was Finder and Tully pulling me across the grass. What had happened between those things? I had a near death experience and didn't even know it? That seemed unfair.

Is Tully okay?

Sound asleep. Saved by his friend Stacy. He's having some very odd, ketamine-induced dreams. His shoulder will be bruised and cut and sore, but he's not broken anywhere.

Finder?

Still fighting. Her dad put her dislocated arm back in place. She'll be fine.

Healing my tailbone had been enough of a lesson in getting hurt while saving my friends. I didn't want to go through that again.

"'Kay," I wheezed.

Darcy Jackson wiped a clump of dirt away from my eye. "Are you sure?"

I gave the smallest nod. It was the most effort I could manage.

"Death is quite peaceful. And the hospital is still an option. I promise I won't make you a vampire. Unless you die first. If you die and then I feed you my blood, you'll become a vampire. If my blood's strong enough. Matilda thinks it might be. It's why my leash is so short."

Oh, interesting. Did that mean the predator blood cells we'd observed in Terrence's blood only affected cells in the process of dying or that had just died? Goldman! Stop that! I told myself. This is not the time for scientific inquiry! Make a decision. Blood or death.

I thought of the little kid riding a big, black wolf.

My choice was obvious.

"There is one little matter we need to agree on first," he said. "You are dying. It's going to take a lot of blood to heal you. I'm going to be, ah, very hungry when this is over."

What was he asking?

"Animal blood won't cut it," he said. "I might need some soul, too. Obviously, I can't feed on you."

He was asking me who to feed on. He was asking me who I could spare.

"Not the vet," I choked.

"Very well. You understand who's left," he said.

"Yeh," I gasped. I was trading someone else's life for my own. I was telling Darcy Jackson it was okay to maybe *kill* someone.

Michael?

Yes?

I wasn't sure I could make this decision.

You saved eight lives tonight, said the angel.

That doesn't make it right.

It doesn't.

Silence.

"Stacy," Darcy Jackson said, "your heart is slowing. I have to know."

"Idgh . . . " I said. I couldn't get any words out.

"I'm gonna take that as a yes."

Darcy Jackson's fangs gleamed in the moonlight. He bit his wrist and two lines of blood ran toward his cuff. He tipped my head and held his wrist where I could reach.

"Until you heal," he said.

I looked at the lines of blood. Could I do this? What about AIDS? I thought. Or hepatitis? There were a million bloodborne pathogenic diseases this could give me.

"I don't have anything bad," he said. What was with people replying like they could hear my thoughts? Gah.

"I'm a vampire," Darcy Jackson said. "My blood is as pure as it comes."

I've read enough vampire books to know two things. 1. Drinking blood is supposed to be somehow seductive. 2. Blood is supposed to taste metallic yet delicious, like you're drinking the most nutritious and luxurious food ever.

Neither of those things are true.

Sucking blood from someone's wrist is not only messy and staining, it's work. My head ached from the effort of sucking with my lips slipping on a flat surface. It was not easy to get enough blood in my mouth to swallow, and then force it down. And for the record, blood tastes terrible.

My stomach flipped in my belly, nauseated by the heavy metal flavor. The thickness of the blood in my mouth made me dizzy. Or maybe that was just my lungs trying to kill me from where I'd been squashed by a werewolf.

It felt like an hour went by as I drank and drank. At one point, I realized I wasn't in pain anymore. I took a few more swallows to be sure, and then I let Darcy's wrist go. His eyes were shut, his fangs buried in his lower lip. The second I released him, he bolted into the woods. Had I taken too much? Was he going to kill someone else to feed?

No, but I had taken more than he had bargained I would need.

I knew it for certain. I felt him running through the woods. I felt his hunger.

There it was. The bond. Darcy Jackson had to find blood somewhere and come back. He did not intend to kill. It was bad for business leaving a trail of corpses. He was glad I was alive.

I climbed to my hands and knees, then stood. I took a deep breath and touched all my ribs. Everything felt fine. Fixed and a little tender, but healed.

I wasn't sure how long I'd been drinking, but the scene before me was not as I had left it.

54.

April 27, continued.

Outside the boundary, the black smoke shrieked. Four werewolves were down; Ed, Nick's first one, Finder's first one, and the one who had tried to squash me. None were fully still, but none were getting up either. Good enough. The werewolf that had broken me had a dart stuck in her neck.

Nick bled from one arm. Finder staved off Mrs. Macy with the silver blades. Red Dorsal, Steel Grey and the smallest shifter wolf kept the two standing werewolves confused and blundering. I swear they used chess moves. The smallest wolf and the Steel Gray wolf ran diagonal bishop cuts through the werewolves' legs driving them to hit each other as Red Dorsal ran straight rook attacks backing the monsters toward each other.

Judy stood on top of the boulders, fur stained red. She held a back paw off the ground.

Steve and the black wolf sailed through the fray, Steve shooting and scoring, shooting and scoring. Another werewolf fell. What was *in* those darts? Steve and the wolf he rode turned to Finder's fight. Judy barked a command and the black wolf slid to a stop and backpedaled. Judy leaped in from the boulders, knocking the other alpha female to the ground.

The big black wolf carried his rider close enough to shoot Mrs. Macy in the neck and shoulders. By the time she saw where the stings were coming from, Steve, the black wolf and Judy were all out of range. The alpha female went down.

The black wolf gave a warning bark followed by a short whine. The shifter wolves scattered, clearing the way. Steve shot four more darts; two each into the remaining pair of standing werewolves as the black wolf wove around them. The littlest wolf ran to the tree line and came back dragging a thick branch. Red Dorsal grabbed the other end of it and together they ran at the remaining upright werewolves, toppling them as they rammed the branch like a trip wire into their shins. Steel Grey wolf bit each monster in the forehead, opening cuts and blinding them with their own black blood. The monsters dug at their eyes and rolled onto their bellies. Heads down, they slowed, panting and rubbing their faces. Fighting to stay alert, they lay on their bellies like filthy monster rugs and conked out.

For a long moment, the clearing was quiet.

What had Steve put in those darts?

The sound of a vehicle and bright headlights through the trees caught all of our attention.

It stopped too far away for us to see who it brought, but the forest was so dense a vehicle couldn't get any closer. Doors slammed shut, flashlight beams lit the night. Julian's voice, tense, desperate.

I felt Darcy Jackson hovering. I felt his hunger.

A square, brown-skinned man in a cowboy hat ran into the clearing. He stopped short, absorbing the scene in front of him. Eight massive werewolves were on the ground, some still, some stirring and pawing at the dirt.

Two shifter wolves and one teenager lay still. Finder crouched on Tully's outside, cradling her arm. Nick bled from his side and arm and face as he knelt between John and Tully. I have no idea what I looked like standing in a sports bra covered in werewolf spit, blood and filth.

"I know you, Snow Forest. Remember? I'm a friend." The man focused on Judy, meeting her eyes then looking deliberately away.

He spoke in a kind voice. "It's safe, girl. You can let me help him." Judy yipped. Her wolves, two limping and all blooded, slinked behind her into a protective 'V' formation around John Forest Stalker and by default, Nick, Finder and Tully.

The black wolf and his rider had vanished. I wasn't sure if that made me relieved or nervous.

"Julian," the man called quietly. "I'm gonna need the tarp."

My head spun. My breath turned thick as I felt Darcy Jackson catch his prey.

"I'll get it for you," I said. "Julian is . . . busy."

I listened for sounds of a fight as I moved away from the clearing and deeper into the woods. Was Julian resisting? Had Darcy caught him by surprise? I stopped to listen and heard nothing. No sign of Julian.

I had never in my life been alone in the woods this far from everything. I ran in the direction of the truck headlights. I'd stood on the beach solo when we went down the shore, I'd spent plenty of time by myself in Central Park. But alone at the beach meant there was a boardwalk full of people behind you and alone in Central Park meant there was someone else right over there. Gray light glowed through the trees lighting everything around me like muted daylight.

The silence clung to me in an eerie way, like the rattle of the subway clings when you're riding alone at midnight. Technically, you're safe because you're alone. Is it eerie because it's empty? Because it's midnight? Or because you don't know who'll get on when the doors open next? I mean come on. You can't get mugged or murdered by an empty train car. It's you and the train rumbling along, the train doing its thing with or without you. All the rest is imagination.

The forest stood as I moved through it, taking that break that allows plants to not grow as fast while photosynthesis isn't happening. I couldn't get hurt by a quiet forest. I stood for a moment, not moving, not deciding. Standing. Clean, damp air pulled in and out of my healed lungs. My heart echoed in my chest, beating against blood sewn ribs. I moved one hand to my side. Bruised for sure, but not broken. The bones pulsed a little.

If every time I went out with my friends at night I came home with an injury, my dad would quit letting me leave the house. Or worse, he'd make up a series of my-daughter-is-a-klutz jokes I'd never outgrow. Like the chess jokes I couldn't silence. Why did the chess playing shrimp get a job? It was looking for prawn promotion. Ugh. It would be a disaster. Speaking of disaster, Steve coming out of tonight unhurt and emotionally unscarred by what he'd seen would be a miracle.

I got to the truck, found the tarp, and turned around into the quiet forest. Tully was the biggest problem. How were we going to explain his injuries? I had no idea. He couldn't die. Just, no. It sure looked like dying was what he meant to do. Was that why he'd thrown himself into the fight with such abandon? He hadn't intended be around to explain anything when it was over.

Around me the silence thickened. The trees seemed to close in, tightening my space, making it harder for me to breathe. I told my feet to move, but they refused.

Don't be scared of trees, I told myself. Pretend it's the Park. Only emptier. And with no paved paths or trash cans. You can do this.

I was no longer the city-only, brain-only girl I'd been when I got to Richmond seven months ago. I'd kissed a boy. I'd yanked a knife out of his hand. I'd captured a vampire and saved my friends' lives. I'd been fed on by that vampire and his boss, and tonight I had crossed a major line to save my own life. I had drunk Darcy Jackson's blood. And I was going to stand here scared of *trees*?

I can do this, I told myself. I can walk alone in the woods and come out okay. If a werewolf stalks me, I'll climb a tree. Just because I never have doesn't mean I can't.

Trees are not scary, I told myself. As if to prove it, I reached out and put a hand on the nearest trunk. I closed my eyes for a moment to pull myself together. I turned around and pressed my spine into the tree.

I'm not sure how to describe the moment that came next because it was so un-me. When I leaned against the tree, I *felt* the forest. The ground moved up through my legs, creating stability. My chest energy opened, similar to when Archangel Michael had come to me at Maymont; cool and calm, like water pouring into a vessel (me) from every living thing around me. The forest breathed me in, alive, full and delicious as it made space for me to be part of it. It held me. I synched up with that flow, that energy, the living, powerful forest; the twigs on the ground not obstacles, but supports. The earth itself had guidance for me if I could hear it. If I agreed to release my resistance and allow myself to listen.

An image of Hank popped into my mind, a flash of our conversation at the tournament. This was what he meant. This was 'grokking'. I closed my eyes and grokked.

I took a long breath letting the forest air, the forest life, fill my lungs. Trees whispered in a gentle chorus around me as if my breath had triggered the breeze. My feet began to tingle. The crown of my head hummed. A wave of an unfamiliar emotion anchored me to the tree I leaned on, to the ground I stood on. Full and complete, quiet and open. Not anger. Not even love.

Joy. The forest filled me with joy. The sense of fullness, of not needing anything but what was already provided. I was fully supported by the living earth, the thing I lived on, lived with. The thing I was an integral part of. A thought came to me so loud and strong I thought it was Michael in my head.

I am you.

I AM YOU.

It was not Michael. It wasn't even a voice. It was bigger than that. It was *everything*.

The spark of epiphany thrilled through my body.

I was not an outsider in this forest, I was *part* of this forest. I *belonged*. My body was part of nature. I was part of nature. Nature fought when it had to. Nature didn't cultivate fear and weakness, it eliminated them in its progress. Even prey animals were as strong as they could be. Just because you were the strongest, fastest rabbit didn't mean you wouldn't get caught by the hawk or the lion. Or the wolf.

Werewolves were not natural. They were not part of nature, of the harmonious paring of life and earth. They were death bringers in a very unnatural sense. It wasn't that the tribe needed the land and wanted the werewolves off it. They had offered for the werewolves to stay, but the werewolves couldn't accept that.

Maybe on some level the land battle was about this-is-mine-and-not-yours. The Mattaponi held stewardship for the land long before the white man arrived and said, 'I want that.' But digging deeper, this war wasn't about borders and territory in the way I had thought. It was about the shifter wolves protecting and preserving the nature that birthed them.

In that moment, I understood why we were fighting, why Judy and her father and the wolves would die to keep the werewolves from owning this land and what a dangerous and selfish game Julian had played offering power and violence the chance to rule a place intended for growth and joy.

The shifter wolves' existence was amazing, but under this lens, it was a miracle. They were nature's most integrated creatures, fully able to walk both sides of animal and human experience. Transformation in nature was normal, egg to animal, chrysalis to butterfly. Starting as one thing and becoming something else was not unthinkable in any way, in fact it was predictable. But shifting entirely from one creature into another changed the rules, rules about mass and density, growth and maybe even procreation. How many doors of possibility did that open on a scientific platform?

How heavy was Darcy Jackson in bat form? Did his mass just condense into that itty bitty shape? What I thought of as permanent, for example height and even species, now became malleable.

The Man with No Face corrupted that malleability. He had taken a natural mutation and made it monstrous. Why? And what did that even mean under the lens of science? If the permanence of bone and sinew was no longer a rule of nature, what was? That every being had the potential to transform into something completely different?

I had thought until this very moment, that astrophysics or rocket science would be good career paths for me, but now? Hmmm. Maybe genetics and cellular biology were the way to fly.

I don't know how I navigated my way back through the gray and silver light to the clearing, but my body knew exactly where to go, where to step so my feet were quiet, how to breathe so I didn't disturb the sleeping creatures, when to duck to avoid getting the spider webs in my face and upsetting their owners' night's work.

It wasn't fair. Tully was hurt, Judy's dad might be dying and I was on a nature hike filled with curiosity and a profound bliss that made my every step more purposeful and beautiful than the last.

Was it because I had died and come back, according to Michael? Was it because Darcy Jackson had fed me his blood? Or was it because the forest was teaching me to listen?

I might never know.

I thought back to sticking my hand in that fishbowl and hoping I drew Finder's number. Well. Hmm. Maybe there was some "meant to be-ness" about that moment. Again, not sure I was willing to give Sister Mary Chemistry the benefit of the doubt when she said it was 'God's will' who we got as our partners, but pulling Judy's number certainly had made life more interesting.

Moonlight highlighted the crouched figure of the vet hunched over John Forest Stalker's wolf body as I arrived back in the clearing. Judy, white fur matted in dark patches on her chest, side, and muzzle, stood across from the vet, intent on his task. Behind her, her pack watched the vet's every move.

The Sandy wolf had joined them, keeping watch toward the shark tank wall. Her muzzle looked crooked as it lay on her paws, broken jaw maybe? The black wolf had rejoined the group, standing between the vet, John, and now Julian, not letting Julian near. Where was Steve?

Julian held onto a tree. It looked like standing was hard. Served that betrayer right. Where was Darcy Jackson?

"Psst! Stacy!" Steve waved from a tree branch. He was really high up. Relief flooded me. Grinning, he hung over the fat limb, lying on his belly, legs and arms dangling free. In one hand he held his plastic bow. Monster's head stuck out from his backpack.

"I don't think we have much time," he said. "That one has been moving like he wants to get up." He pointed to Ed, on the ground not far from where the vet worked on Judy's dad. The alpha werewolf lay groaning, eyes shut like in a nightmare. The Man with No Face, in smoke form, prowled the invisible border to the sacred land directly in line with his werewolf captain.

"We have to get him to the Jeep," the vet said, meaning Judy's dad. "I stopped the worst of it but I have to get everything repaired and get him some antibiotics for at least 12 hours before he shifts back. And I can't do it here. I need anesthesia. I need light and electricity. Where is that girl with my tarp?"

"I'm here," I said. The men looked up, startled. They hadn't noticed me come back. The vet started to stand. The wolves got to their feet. Anchored by Judy, they closed in, circling the vet. I went to hand him his stuff. Judy bared her teeth. Her pack followed her lead. If it was up to the wolves, John Forest Stalker wasn't going anywhere. The vet froze.

Julian, outside the circle, raised his gun.

"Julian, stop!"

"Get out of his way," Julian said to Judy, ignoring me.

"Julian, put down the gun. You can't shoot her."

"I won't let him die." He sighted on Judy. "If she stands in the way of him getting help- "

"You can't shoot her," I repeated. "We came to save lives, not take them. Look in her eyes and look away."

"It won't work."

"It will. Do it." Tension filled my body.

"She understands me," he said. Wolf Judy growled low and deep in her chest.

"You said last night they think like wolves when they're like this," I said. "All she understands is how you feel. And right now you feel like a threat."

"And how do you suggest I change that?" he snapped.

"Look away," I said. "Be a submissive wolf to her alpha."

"Why?" he said. "She doesn't respect me as a human or a wolf. Why shouldn't I shoot her and have John all to myself?"

Ah. So *that's* what this was about. And he'd told me as much before, I just missed it. He was willing to let the whole pack die to protect John. I didn't realize that he wanted Judy out of the way on purpose.

Julian locked eyes with Judy.

"Rethink it, Julian," I said, lowering my voice. My body dropped its energy, going calm and still. "What will John say if he finds out you killed his daughter? What will his grief be like?" I let that settle.

Julian hadn't thought of that. Comprehension dawned in his eyes. I thought of something I'd heard Bubbe say many times: Selfishness blinds reason.

"Your selfishness is blinding your reason," I said. Julian's stare turned to a glare. Whoops, I'd said the wrong thing. Try again.

"Think about it," I said, stalling. "His loyalty to you c- " A clutch in my belly clipped those words before they could come out.

I was going to say 'his loyalty to you can never be as strong as it is to her.' Bad idea. Recover, recover . . . "His loyalty to you will never break if *she* loves you, too," I said.

"I'm not afraid of her," Julian said, eyes narrowing at the white wolf.

"You're afraid John is going to die. And you're right to be afraid. But Judy needs to know you can save him before she will let you leave." Absolute certainty filled me, filled my body. "You have to be more determined to save him than afraid you will lose him."

Huh? Where did that come from? It came from me. From my *body*. My very muscles felt linked to the white wolf, as if I could feel in me what was going on with her, thin and defensive in her furred frame. Still snarling, her gaze stayed locked on Julian.

Julian's eyes flicked from me to the wolf and back to me as if he was deciding which of us to shoot first.

"She doesn't care what your fear is about, Julian. None of the wolves do. She knows you're dangerous if you're afraid."

"How do you know what she knows? I've lived with these things for five years. Five! Every month they go and I stay behind. And this ungrateful wretch doesn't even want it! And do you know why? Because she doesn't like killing. She thinks killing is wrong. Even the deer she hunts in the woods. Do you know what she does? She collects the skulls and buries them. She takes the buck antlers and puts them in the trees for birds to build nests in. It's ridiculous. You know what I would give to have her power? Do you? But I can never have it. Never. I will always be just a regular human. Every month, every turn cycle, every full moon . . . left behind while they run and hunt and howl. And she starves herself so her body will be too light, too frail to change. But is it? No! No matter what she refuses to eat, she's never frail enough and when the moon comes, boom! Wolf! Now, when I'm trying to save her father's life, she dares to stand in my way?" Julian leveled the muzzle of his weapon.

"If he could make you what he is, he would. Please Julian," I said. "Killing her won't make you a wolf. Put down the gun."

Judy's hackles raised, a ripple of dirty white fur rising along her spine. Her pack stood at the ready. One cue from her and they would leap. The thin scientist would not make it twenty feet.

Julian braced his weapon against his shoulder.

"Julian. Do. Not. Shoot. That. Gun," I said, channeling my BFF. Meredith had stopped a mugger when she was twelve by pretending she didn't understand what he meant when he said for her to give him her money, and then telling him he was making a wrong decision. Admittedly, she had gotten lucky. Her assailant was a teenager who had smoked the wrong plant and had never mugged anybody before. It was kind of impossible; scrawny tween Meredith caught in a raging growth spurt defeating a fully grown teenager with a knife in the subway, but she did it. Meredith the Impossible, I called her.

I needed to be her right now. I shivered, as if my body understood and could help me transform.

"Julian!" I said, in my best impersonation of my friend. "What is wrong with you? You are aiming a *gun* at your lover's daughter! At the reason he gets up in the morning."

"*I* am the reason he gets up in the morning!" Julian said. Whoa. Narcissistic, much?

"She's his *flesh and blood*," I said. "You can't replace her. It's a different relationship. Of course he loves you, but if you hurt her, you are ending your relationship. And for what?" Julian was not relenting. I needed a new approach. I took a long breath. I was not Meredith, the kind of person who could sell a pigeon a park bench. I reached.

I am you. Speak from your own heart.

"We're scientists," I said. "We discover life. We treasure it. That's what you told me, right? Every living cell has the breath of perfection in it somewhere? The physical model of possibility that we may not even have discovered yet?"

Judy started a low growl. Her packmates picked it up.

"Stop that," I said. "You're not helping." She ignored me. She had honed in on his scent, his intention. He needed to change it.

"Call them off," he said, shifting his weight as the wolves encroached.

"They don't obey me! You have to change your scent." He had to change his whole body chemistry away from being terrified the man he loved was going to die. Then, I had an idea.

"Decide John is going to be okay," I said. "Pretend if you have to." Judy's growl deepened.

"Quiet, you." She turned to me and snapped her jaws. I smacked her across the nose. "No ma'am!" I said like I would to any dog I watched. "You do *not* bite me." As we faced off, snick. A dart flew from the tree across the clearing and landed in Judy's side. She startled when it hit. She broke my gaze and tried to nose the dart out of her ribs. Tully's staff lay a few feet from me on the ground. I bent and grabbed it.

Judy shook her whole body trying to release the dart. She lowered her head and laid her ears flat.

Julian kept the gun trained. Moving it a few degrees would land its sight on me. I was not going to get lucky a third time in one night. If I wanted to win this exchange, I had to defend my piece more times than he attacked it.

"You have to change your scent, Julian. You have to relax." The wolves crept closer, narrowing the distance between each other and the scientist.

"The girl is right, Julian," said the vet. "I'd do as she says."

Judy and her pack closed in.

"Julian! Judy! STOP!" He didn't. She didn't. Couldn't they see what was coming? The moves were obvious! Neither would relent, they would throw all their material at each other in the sloppy way untrained players do when they want to feel like they are winning and are scared. They would both lose in a big, fat stalemate as I scraped them all off the grass.

"Judy, back off! Leave him alone!" I raised my staff to smack her on the butt and get her to turn to me. If she quit attacking him maybe he would put the gun down. Something in his expression changed. Julian gripped his rifle. His face went tight in determination.

"Julian!" I shouted. "Stop! Killing her isn't- "

BOOM! My hands flew to my ears. A scream from behind me. I whirled. Darcy Jackson stood, a fresh hole ripped in his shirt, Steve riding piggy back. My little brother had his face buried in the vampire's shoulder, one arm flung around his neck. His toy bow was clutched in his tiny fist. Julian's eyes met Darcy Jackson's as he lined up for another shot.

I was about to run for Steve, when Darcy spoke.

"Put it down."

Julian blinked, eyes captive. He put the gun on the ground.

"Sit down."

Julian sat. Relief flooded me. I had never been so happy to see a vampire use his powers in all my life.

"There you go, buddy," Darcy said, setting Steve gently down. "Safe on the ground with Sis. Maybe don't climb quite so high next time, huh?" He patted Steve on the head.

"Thanks, Mr. Jackson," Steve said, like he chatted with vampires all the time. "I was kind of stuck."

"Oh, you were more than kind of stuck, little sprout. You were *stuck* stuck."

Steve rushed into my arms. I hugged him hard.

"What're you even doing here?!" I said. "You were supposed to be with Mama, home and safe."

"She kept knocking over her dominoes. She said it was a sign so we packed up lots of stuff and got in her car. She has a whole hospital set up at Judy's dad's house."

Of course Mama would set up a makeshift hospital. Of course she would.

Darcy winced as he dug his fingers into a hole in his smoking shirt. He pulled a small object out from where his shoulder met his chest and flicked it to the ground.

"Hate those." He crushed the bullet into the dirt like a cigarette butt.

It was then Darcy noticed that he was full on surrounded by shifter wolves. And they did not look happy.

"I just took the bullet that fool was gonna put in your alpha," he said, voice stern. "Now, ya'll be nice."

He aimed a finger at Judy's face and did not break her gaze. Their eyes locked in a stare-down for dominance, but being dead, Darcy Jackson didn't have to blink. After what felt like very long minutes, Judy relented. The pack backed off.

"Thank you," Darcy said, straightening his loosened tie. "Talk about ungrateful. If you weren't a friend of my daughter's in school, I'd have minded my business." Judy shook out her mane of dirty fur like a retort.

Darcy searched, his eyes landing on Finder.

"I'm sorry, Layla," Darcy Jackson said. "I just want you to be safe. And happy. I thought if you were like me you would be unbeatable and you'd like that. I mean, I like it." He took a step back, as if he was about to turn and walk off. But he paused, a thoughtful expression crossing his face. "You have to understand, I've needed one eye over my shoulder my whole life. You know. It's why Flying Eagle started. To help any person who walked though that door feel like they could defend themselves. So being . . . like this . . ." He looked toward the sky and his face glowed in appreciation and gratitude. "I never look over my shoulder now.

No cop, no white man, no crazy person with a gun can touch me. I can stop fights before they begin. I'm like . . . a superhero. Speed. Strength. I can turn into a bat. The whole blood thing is a small price to pay for fearlessness.

"You'd think that now in 2002, our world would be safe for everyone, but it's not. That boy from Columbine, that's just the beginning. The beginning of something ugly in this world. But imagine this, Layla. Imagine if I could have found that boy *before* he shot all those children. If you could have. If one of us could have found him and smelled his intention. I can smell what you plan to do, did you know that? It's the most interesting thing. Like tonight. Why Teularen was trying to do himself in I have no idea, but y'all should be aware. That boy needs help." He made a small, very southern hmph noise. "You would enjoy being what I am, Layla. And you would be . . . so beautiful at it."

Finder scowled. Whether from what he was saying, or what she thought he was going to say next, I didn't know.

"But, I understand," Darcy went on. "You don't want what I want. I see that now."

A high pitched moan came from the spinning smoke. The Man with No Face was hungry. His food was everywhere, ripe and ready. Werewolves lay strewn around the clearing, a cornucopia, just out of reach.

The vet, headlamp battery flickering, had bent again over John Forest Stalker, still working. Around him the pack watched, ears pricked in alertness.

I thought about the big wolf being jostled over gravel roads all the way back to the vet's office or Mama's makeshift hospital.

"Mr. Jackson," I said. "Before you go, can you . . . help the vet?" Out of habit, I looked away right before Darcy Jackson met my eyes.

"I probably shouldn't tell you this," he said so only I could hear him, "but once you drink my blood I can't command you with my eyes. Dumb, right? Logic would dictate I get more control over you with my blood running through your organs. I can compel you to come to me from miles away, and even bring me someone to feed on, but I can't make you sit and stay. No vampire can. My blood grants you some immunity to our influence."

"What? Why?" That didn't make any sense.

He shrugged.

"You're supposed to want to help instead of being forced." This was too much information. I had eight werewolves to turn back human and thinking about vampire powers was distracting. You're playing a simul, I told myself. One board, one reply, then on to the next board. Play the board in front of you.

"Think of it this way," said Darcy Jackson, "I just gave you a good card. Maybe you should hold it close to your chest."

My whole world had done a 180.

"Sensei Bolo came and got me while we were setting up the first aid," Steve said, waving at his big wolf ride. "Mama knew he wouldn't let anything happen to me so thought it would be okay if I came to help. We didn't know there'd be guns and stuff."

Steve looked toward the massive black wolf sitting near the stirring werewolf alpha. Bolo gave me a big grin, tongue lolling out of his mouth.

Darcy Jackson glanced at his watch. "If you got this under control for real now," he said taking stock of the clearing, "I'll get Teularen and the wolf loaded, then I gotta get back to work. Overnight trades in Asia."

"I was trying to turn the werewolves back human," I said. "But it's not working."

"That might be my fault," Steve said, clutching my hand. "My darts."

I stared at him. What could be in those darts that reversed my serum?

"Xavier at the dojo is diabetic," Steve said. "Remember how his mom wants him to increase his adrenaline so he doesn't need as much insulin?"

Yes. But what did that have to do with werewolves? I raised an eyebrow. Darcy Jackson crossed his arms over his chest.

"Mama told me a story about Mr. Jackson when they first got married. He was diabetic, too, right, Mr. Jackson?" Darcy nodded. "And he was fighting in a tournament so his adrenaline was really high and- "

"Oh yeah. Boy, that was a long time ago. I drank a sports drink full of sugar and passed out mid-fight," Darcy said, the light of understanding dawning behind his eyes.

I wasn't seeing the connection.

"The darts were full of sugar syrup," Steve said.

I stared at my little brother. Hair flopped into his face.

"I knew you were gonna give the wolves ketamine and I thought that sugar might help it get into their blood faster and work better. But when we saw what you were really fighting, I doubled the amounts." He showed me a plastic bottle still half full of clear liquid.

"Sugar water?"

He nodded.

"You figured out the werewolves were hyped on adrenaline?"

"Bolo and I saw one of them change way back in the woods on our way to help you. I tried to think like you, Stacy. I said what would Stacy think of? And I thought she would wonder how the change could happen. What made it possible? And then I figured it out," he said brightly. "We saw the lady turn into a monster and Bolo took me straight back to the house. I was gonna stay there, but then I saw it. I saw the solution. I was just like you, Stace! It was like a cloud cleared from in front of my eyes and poof I knew what the answer was! So Mama made me the extra sugar water. I hoped it would make them pass out like Mr. Jackson in his tournament fight." He gave me a massive grin. "And it worked!"

My baby brother had just saved my life. With sugar.

Around me eight werewolves lay conked out in the equivalent of diabetic comas.

I took a big breath.

"Did I do okay?" he said, looking worried. I grabbed him up off the ground and clutched him to my chest. He wrapped his legs around my waist, hugging me back.

"I could not love you any more if I tried," I said into his hair. "You are a stupid genius."

"That's an oxymoron," he said. I squeezed him so hard he squeaked.

55.

Sunday, April 28, 2002. 12:04 a.m.

Despite the warm spring midnight, the fire in the Forest Stalker wood stove felt absolutely necessary.

The night hadn't ended when Darcy Jackson left. Not by a long shot. Only Steve and I had witnessed the final bloodbath, the part I never wanted to think about ever again. I held my hands out to the fire, holding this new secret in my palms, like I'd held so many others since I left New York. It rolled and twisted inside me, wanting to get out, wanting to stay hidden. I closed my eyes, utterly unprepared to say the words out loud, to tell the story of what had happened next. Steve snuggled down into my lap. We had lived. Yet, my gratitude for our survival was curbed by this new secret, curbed by what I knew.

I had asked to stay behind to make sure the werewolves changed back, make sure my serum worked. I wanted to make sure the Man with No Face was deprived of a victim this full moon.

The outcome I wished for most, the outcome that was most impossible, was to erase what Steve had seen. The werewolves' return to their human forms was almost as horrendous as the change in, slick with evil. I snuggled my face down into Steve's soft, muppet hair. He smelled like baby shampoo. Maybe I should ask Darcy Jackson to wipe his memory. A selfish part of me refused to ask for that help, though. I wasn't sure I could handle being the only one who knew.

*

"I'm not leaving you here," Nick argued. Finder held her injured arm at her side.

"Hell no, sis. You gotta come with us."

Behind them, Darcy Jackson helped the vet and Julian get John and Tully up the path to the truck.

"There's not enough room with all the equipment he has in that thing," I said, meaning the vet's pickup. "With everyone injured, we can't just pile in." When I went to get the tarp, there was only one vehicle parked. Julian must've left Ed's truck at the vet's. "I need to know if my serum works, if they change back or not."

I nodded toward the black smoke pulsing just beyond the tree line. "He can't touch me here. You're both hurt. You go in the first trip. Steve can sit in your laps."

"No! It's my science, too," said Steve. "I'm staying to see them change back."

"I don't like it, Stacy," Nick said. "I don't feel good leaving you behind."

"It'll be fine. I'll hide in a tree, watch for the change back and wait for you to come get me."

"I'm staying with you," Steve said.

"Absolutely not." I scowled down at him. "You are going with Nick and Finder." I looked back at my friends. "Julian can get Ed's truck after John and Tully are set and come back for me."

"Julian? You trust Julian?"

"No. But I don't think he'll have energy for any more betrayal tonight." I didn't offer that he'd been heavily fed on by Darcy Jackson and was probably incapable of anything more devious than a nap. "Or, if it makes you feel better," I said to Nick, "let Mama shoot some venom-killing antibiotics into your behind and come get me yourself."

"Let's go, kids," called the vet, standing on the path.

"Not leaving," Steve said, arms crossed, lower lip out in a determined pout. I understood why he wanted to stay. As useful as he'd proven himself tonight, I didn't have it in me to lord his age over him and 'make' him go in. My stamina for fighting was all used up.

"Please go," I said to Nick and Finder. "I'm not hurt. Steve's not hurt. You'll be back to get us in no time."

"I can stay," Finder said to Nick, like they were my parents. "My arm's not that bad. She's right- you need antibiotics for the venom. You ride first."

"Your shoulder was dislocated, and you're bleeding from, like five places," Nick said. "I'd rather you stay because you're the fighter, but right now you need ice or that joint is gonna kill for days."

"Both of you, go! Please! We're FINE!"

Judy and her pack watched us argue.

"They will stay with us. They'll keep us safe. Right, wolves?" I said. Every single wolf was bleeding or favoring a paw or leg except the big, black one, Bolo. He sat, ears pricked forward, as if he understood every word.

"He stays with me," said Steve. "He won't let anything happen to us."

Expressions still skeptical, but having seen the shifter wolf carry and protect Steve, Nick and Finder started up the path behind the vet.

We could still hear the truck heading away when Ed started thrashing.

"Go," I said to Steve, aiming him toward the trees. "Go!"

The alpha werewolf was on all fours before we even got to the base of the pine where Steve had hidden before.

"Not so high this time!" I said, as he started climbing. Ignoring the deep growl from behind me, I grabbed the lowest branch and hauled myself onto it. I would have to ask Darcy Jackson if his blood did more than heal me. I didn't struggle to climb. I pulled myself up one branch at a time, my body lithe and strong. I screamed when something caught my shoe. Ed slavered below me, a tooth snagged in the rubber bottom of my sneaker. Just as he snapped his jaw shut, I yanked my foot free of the shoe. He stood, massive forepaws on the pine's branches, claws slicing into the wood like knives into butter. Black stain crusted his chest and legs from the earlier fight. Darts were still embedded in his fur. And he stank.

Werewolves, however foul, were built for endurance and slow brawling, not climbing. Ed ripped his claws out of the pine's trunk and reached to grip a branch. Hunger shone in his runny eyes. He was starving. We were food. He dug his hind claws into the trunk. Oh no.

"Go higher!" I cried to Steve. "Go!"

How had I failed? Why wasn't Ed changing back?

Bolo came up behind the werewolf. He snarled a low, menacing threat. Ed yanked his claws from the tree and dropped to all fours, turning to face the shifter wolf.

The two beasts came together with a thud that shook our tree. Bolo sank his teeth into Ed's shoulder. The monster stood up on his hind feet to shake the shifter off. They traded bites and blows. The shifter knocked the werewolf to the ground, then backed up, teeth still bared.

A wet, splitting sound filled the air. Bolo backed further away.

Ed convulsed. The dark ooze under his fur rose to the surface, coming together like hot oil in a frying pan. The tearing of skin and fur off muscle made a sound I felt in my gut, the split starting at the base of his spine. Ed's jaw opened wide, too wide, sucking the fur into its black depth, lubricated by the dark, oily film. His belly distended as layers sucked off his bones. Skin and fur. Then, muscle. Then, sinew. It was fast. And loud. Steve barfed over the branch beside him. I put an arm out to steady him. When I looked down, Ed's chest cavity hung empty and bare, the bones of the werewolf skeleton crumbling into a slick, grey gravel. Dark sludge crawled up the werewolf's head covering the whole mess like a slimy tent. Green-brown veins ran through the stinky pile. Like a water ballon exploding, an adult, human hand ripped its way out of a slime-filled, 'amniotic' sack.

It was disgusting. It was scary.

It was science.

"Yes!" I shouted. "Yes! Judy! We did it!"

Ed, uninjured, even after the damage he'd taken in his werewolf body, crawled out of the slick, foul membrane. He stayed on all fours, panting. He fell onto his side, curling fetal. I looked away. Shifting out of werewolf form did not come with wardrobe.

How come vampires got to keep their clothes when they shifted, but woodland creatures, and now werewolves, did not? I added this question to my list for Darcy Jackson.

The downed werewolves began to stir. Bolo returned to his pack, staying between the injured shifter wolves and the werewolves.

A shriek of fury tore through the air from the roiling smoke, the Man with No Face.

"Lea!" Ed cried. "Lea, what's happening?"

Mrs. Macy, still in werewolf form, had fully awakened. She rose to all fours, swung around and saw her mate, now human. She leaped toward our tree. I screamed and climbed one branch closer to Steve. Mrs. Macy skidded to a halt. I thought she was coming for us, but she dove for Ed. She landed on him with both front paws. Still curled fetal, he did not even try to defend himself. She shook her head, long yellow teeth baring to the sky. Thrusting her heavy muzzle forward, Mrs. Macy's merciless jaw clamped down on Ed's arm.

With one powerful head jerk, she ripped it out of the socket.

And ate it, bones and all.

I may never forget the sound of his screaming. Or the moist crunching of bones and meat as she ate.

"Stop! Stop!" I shrieked. She did not.

My body moved before I could make a different decision. I landed on the ground, knees bent, having jumped down from my branch. The splinter-tipped half of Tully's bat lay on the ground. I grabbed it and ran for the werewolf. The shifter wolves were suddenly beside me, limping and injured, but led by Judy and Red Dorsal. I swung, slamming the bat stump into the side of Mrs. Macy's head. She kicked out with her hind leg.

Something grabbed the back of my pants. Hot breath wet my skin as I was snatched off the ground for the second time that night and flung into the air. I landed with a thump on my belly, across Bolo's broad wolf back. He really was the size of a small pony. Even slung like a crooked saddle over his back, I was far from the ground. I grabbed his fur to keep from falling.

How Ed got up from having his arm ripped off, I will never know. The man flung himself at his werewolf mate, clinging to her fur with his one arm as she tried to shred him with her claws. Ed bit and snarled as if he didn't know he was in human form, naked and helpless. Maybe he didn't know. He'd had a lot of ketamine.

Ed held on to her bib fur with his one arm. He slammed his head over and over into Mrs. Macy's jaw and chest. She failed to grab him, but succeeded in raking her claws across his back. His skin was slick with red, human blood.

The shifter wolves ran me back to the base of Steve's tree. The air slid over us, cool and comforting, like we'd stepped into the shade on a sunny day. Don't ask me how I knew, but I knew. The shifter wolves were hiding us from the werewolves.

Four of the sleepy monsters had gotten up. Two were still on their knees. Two of the standing werewolves were females. The one that had squashed me dropped to all fours and ran for her alphas. She grabbed Ed by the shoulder. She bit down. He screamed. She tore him off Mrs. Macy, then shook him like a dog trying to snap the neck of a rabbit. He shrieked. She dropped him, stepped on his chest with one massive paw and grabbed his left leg in her jaw. With two sharp pulls, she ripped it off. He screamed then went silent. His foot was still twitching as she dug in her claws and began to eat.

Mrs. Macy roared in fury at the thief. She dropped to all four feet and pulled back into a crouch. The small brown female dove into the fight, knocking her feasting packmate to the ground. She grabbed the severed limb out of the other werewolf's jaws. The two monsters fought. One of the males stood on his hind legs and roared. He backed Mrs. Macy closer to the border, keeping her away from her prey.

"No!" I shouted. The stink of meat and blood was in the air. Behind Mrs. Macy, the Man with No Face throbbed, teeth clacking in anticipation. I flung myself off the black wolf's back. I hit the ground and rolled to my feet. The shifter wolves pressed against me, their backs as high as my ribs.

"Let me out!" I cried, slamming my hands into the thick fur. I couldn't let them push her over the edge.

The Man with No Face, the Famelicus, could not get his body back. And I hadn't made that serum to *kill* the werewolves, I made it to *save* them. Ed was horribly maimed, but maybe still clung to life? Even vicious Mrs. Macy deserved a life without the Man with No Face's poison. Who had she been before he caught her? Caught her like he'd caught me so many months ago? Maybe she was only cruel because she had his venom in her. Could she return to her regular self once his venom was gone? Could my serum reverse the effects of years of poisoning? I didn't know.

The werewolves, all now defending the same food, backed Mrs. Macy toward the border. I screamed "No!" again, as loud as I could. I shoved against the Red Dorsal wolf who blocked me from going forward. Blood soaked my hands where I pushed him. The small shifter wolf and Judy grabbed me with their jaws. Teeth sank into my skin. The pain of bites on my arm and legs did not stop me. I fought, struggling to get loose, but there were five of them, and one of me.

A splitting, ripping sound made me look to my left. Another werewolf was shedding its skin like Ed had. In moments, it would be human. Would it also become food for its monstrous pack?

The smoke thickened and grew as the werewolves pressed Mrs. Macy toward the border. She drew her arm back to swing. That was her mistake. Her claws went too far. The smoke caught the end of her finger. Caught and kept. She shrieked in pain. The smoke pulled her, drew her one step, one single step, over the border of the sacred land.

The sound was jarring, like shattering glass, as the thick smoke engulfed her. The werewolf screamed in agony. Black blood splattered. The Man with No Face fed.

The werewolves backed away as their master and creator stoked his dark hunger. They turned to their own meal, ripping, tearing and fighting amongst themselves, one eye on the border, aware of the bigger predator. One by one, they fell back, sated. One by one, tents of amniotic blackness covered them. I turned away, burying my face in the fur of the black wolf.

The unnatural crash of shattering glass filled the air, again.

*

John Forest Stalker, still in wolf form, lay on thick blankets by the fire sleeping off his anesthesia. The vet, Dr. Edward Riverstone, also Mattaponi, divorced twice, two daughters both grown, owner of four rescue cats and six dogs abandoned at his vet practice, and one of the few people outside the immediate circle of shifter wolves who knew what was what in the unimaginables world, sat across from Mama at the kitchen table unable to stop talking.

"She'll heal by the time she shifts back," the vet said. "They all will. Probably curled up in their den right now licking each other's wounds. As long as one of them can hunt, they'll be fine."

"Tell me more," Nick said, indicating John. "Why couldn't he heal?"

"Some injuries will claim a life before even an enhanced healing body can regenerate enough cells to get the job done. See how his fur is already coming back where I shaved him for fluids? He is healing." The vet finished his beer and set the bottle on the table. Mama palmed the empty and slid a fresh one into its place. "He'd be gone if it weren't for Julian coming for me when he did." The vet tipped his new beer in Nick's direction.

"Would you like one?"

Nick eyed it, sighed and shook his head. "No thank you, sir." Nick smiled at me. "I have to drive this young lady home."

"Plus you aren't twenty-one yet," I said, amazed that I could make small talk under the circumstances.

Nick smiled slyly. "Well, actually I am."

The room went silent, many teenaged ears perking toward this surprise information.

"You lied?" I said. "You told my dad you were twenty."

"I was twenty. Then."

"Hang on," I said. "You had your birthday? Your *twenty-first* birthday and you didn't tell me?" A gory image jumped into my mind. I should tell them what I saw. Nope. Ignore and move on. "What is it with you people and secret birthdays?" I said. "You're all a bunch of freaks. You'll tell me your birthday, right?" I asked Tully, laid out on the couch, his head in Finder's lap. She put her hand over her mouth.

"Why are you smirking?" I said. No one would smile if I told them. How could I be so blithe, actually offended that my friends didn't tell me about their birthdays when there was something so much more important in my pocket. They don't need to know, yet,

I told myself. The people who do need to know are wolves right now. This was best kept to myself. Reframe thought, move on.

I looked at Tully. "Seriously? Did you have a secret birthday, too?"

"Mine wasn't a secret," Nick said, drawing the heat away from Tully. "I forgot to mention it. It was the weekend of Regionals. You were busy winning things. I was out of town with my fraternity."

"An Aries," Finder said. "I knew it!"

I glared at Nick. They'd find out sooner or later. It didn't have to be from me. Me, who had failed to prevent it from happening. Me, who might be to blame.

"Well, it's not like we could go get a drink together and celebrate," Nick said. "Besides, the less your dad knows about my age, the better."

"Do you think he's going to forget and think you're twenty forever?"

Mama chuckled. "Not impossible, baby," she said.

"My mom still thinks I'm twelve," Nick said. "I'm hoping your dad could fall into the frozen-at-the-age-I-met-you category."

Tully laughed and then stopped. "Ow, ow. Don't make me laugh," he said. "It hurts."

Laughter. How long would it be before there was laughter again in this room if I told them? Put it out of your mind, I told myself. Just for now. Focus on the present.

Tully had split his skull open when he rammed heads with the werewolf. Mama had given him a numbing injection, then Nick had stitched that wound and his massive shoulder gash. Tully did in fact, look terrible. His eyes were sunken, his face as ghastly pale as Judy's the night before the full moon.

"Do you need a real hospital?" I asked.

"And explain to them what happened to me how?" Tully said.

Mama intervened. "A hospital isn't practical. We have to watch for venom poisoning. A hospital won't know what to do with that."

Darcy Jackson had said something about me dying from a venom infection, too.

"John fought this same land battle with Ed's predecessor," said Dr. Riverstone. "The old alpha was a vicious bastard. Owned the bar just off the res. He lost his humanity over about five years and when the Famelicus finally ate him, Ed took over. That was, I think, three years ago now?" The vet looked up as Julian came down the hall, pale and unsteady on his feet. Julian paused and leaned on the hall doorframe.

"How was your nap?" said the vet.

I did not care about Julian's nap. "All of these injuries are your fault," I said.

"What was I supposed to do? Would you have gone in if you'd known?"

I ignored that. "You knew Judy was messing with my serums? That she was taking them?"

"Of course. Why do you think I agreed to be your advisor?"

Fury rose in me. Knowledge kept secret is the world's worst enemy. Oh. The last half of the night burned in my mind. Knowledge kept secret.

I would tell them. Soon. I would.

Was this how Julian felt when he didn't tell us the truth? Was I like him?

No, I thought. I am not like him. I am going to tell them. But not yet. I have to wait for the wolves. I have to wait for Judy.

Had we known what we were up against tonight, we could have started with Steve's darts. Maybe no one would even have gotten hurt. Or . . . worse.

I thought about Judy's pack, licking their wounds apart from their alpha who lay here in front of the fire. None of them knew if he had survived or not. Were they worried? Or had he already been replaced?

"Judy's mom got bit two years ago," said Dr. Riverstone. "I treated her between forms, still new. It's how we learned the difference between shifters and werewolves. Especially the transformation pattern. Cathy's really committed to making sure we learn everything we can about werewolves."

Steve snored softly in my lap. Cathy was really committed to learning about werewolves. After everyone else had left, she had taught me and Steve more than we wanted to know.

Dr. Riverstone finished his second beer, gave John a final once over and, satisfied that the wolf would be absolutely fine, left just after 1:00 a.m.

Cuddling sleeping Steve, I calmed my seething anger toward Julian. I did not trust him and part of me was sad about that. I hadn't disliked Julian. We had a lot in common. But, I couldn't justify him putting all of us at risk for his own selfish interests.

He set the kitchen timer for 5:30 a.m. to let John out to be with his pack for the day and shift back with them in the wee hours of Monday morning when the moon phased to waning. He went to the back of the house to set his own bedroom alarm and came back carrying a duffel bag. John and I shared the space closest to the fire. Julian set the duffel between us.

"Put this in the shed before you sleep in case the injuries make them shift out early," Julian said as if everything was fine between us. "They don't magically get clothes when they shift. There's an emergency box for each in our shed."

"Why can't you do it?" I said. "It's your shed."

Julian literally rolled his eyes at me and sighed. "I feel like I've been hit by a truck. Would you rather do the dishes?"

No, I would not. He headed for the kitchen where plates, mugs and other remnants of all of us having come in from the fight lay strewn. He was so lucky Darcy Jackson hadn't killed him. Speaking of being killed, I was not going out to that creepy shed by myself. Tully lay sacked out on Finder's leg. I handed her a pillow to stuff under his head. "Come with me," I said.

"You're not scared to go out to that shed alone, are you?" Mama said, clearing the last of the mugs to the sink.

"No," I lied. "But martial artists never get whacked in horror movies. Taking her with me is purely precautionary."

Mama smiled.

"I do not understand what it is about you that I like so much," Mama said. "But you're special, Stacy." She walked over and wrapped her arms around me. She kissed my head and held me in a long hug. "You are the best friend a mother could want for her unruly daughter. Cautious in all the right ways, gutsy and full of piss and vinegar. And honest. You tell it like it is and don't keep secrets." She pulled back and looked into my eyes. "Not ones that people should know. Right?"

It took me a minute to figure out which secret she was referring to.

"You forgot to mention, I'm perceptive," I said. "And ferociously loyal to *all* of my friends." I knew loud and clear what she wanted me to tell Finder. No, Mama. I know you know, but it's not my secret to tell.

Finder made me go first because the arm she'd use to push the door open was tied up in a sling. We walked out the back door of the house. The shed, like the porch, glowed with a string of fairy lights. The indigo sky looked black against the little orbs, and green paint peeled off the shed as if it had been painted that way on purpose.

"I'm not opening this one," I said. A breeze moved the wind chimes on the front porch. Horror movie 101. Finder shook her head and used her good hand to let us in. She pulled the string on the light bulb in the middle, revealing a tidy garden shed with a curtain strung across the back to separate a make shift dressing room. It was pulled aside and tucked into a curved curtain holder so you could see behind it. On a shelf, half way up the wall were seven clear plastic tubs, each labeled with initials, JFS, JFSjr, BJR, HR, DS, RR and BXZ. I opened the one labeled JFS and put in what were obviously Judy's dad's clothes. Soft jeans, socks, man underwear and a green T-shirt. JFSjr held a pair of purple crocs and a towel. I added a bralette, some lacy undies (Judy really?), a clean pair of flannel comfy pants and a St. Ignatius sweatshirt.

"These people are like, prepared," I said. Each tub was also stocked with granola bars, a bottle of water, a pack of baby wipes, and a plastic baggie with keys and some cash.

"I guess they've had time to figure this out," Finder said. "Come in wet once, realize you need a towel. Come in after a bad hunt, realize you need to eat before you see people. Extra keys and cash in case you're low on gas or lost your stuff when you shifted in."

I nodded. A first aid kit hung on the wall beside what Jill would call a slop sink. A little shelf above the sink was stocked with washcloths. Below the sink sat a bucket, placed probably for the dirty washcloths or towels.

"I wouldn't mind being a wolf shifter," Finder said. "It seems cool. Do you think Tully's gay?"

I am so grateful I was not drinking anything at that moment because I might've done a spit take. You know, when you take a drink and the water sprays out of your mouth in surprise.

I took a long minute. Crap. Mama had basically asked me to tell her, which I couldn't do without violating Tully's trust. But if she asked? My opinion wasn't an opinion tho, it was fact. Crap, crap, crap.

"So, yes," she said. "You have that panicked look on your face. The what-do-I-do look."

"I do not."

"You do. It's okay. I think I've known for a while, I just didn't wanna *know*. You know?"

"I walked in on him and Nick kissing at the formal," I said, the words busting out of me in horrible relief.

"Kissing Nick, like *your* Nick or super gay Nick Johnson from math?"

"*My* Nick. I was so mad. I'm still mad. It's not fair, Finder, he won't even kiss me but he'll kiss Tully? It makes no sense and he says it's no biggie for him because it was just to prove a point, to help Tully be who he is and I totally hate them both right now. I mean what am I supposed to do?"

She took my shoulder in her good hand. "You're supposed to tell me. You're supposed to tell me because you trust me and because the truth is that even though we both think we can do everything on our own, we're stronger together. And not just where unimaginables are concerned."

I looked into her face. Resignation, defiance and-

Finder sniffed and the gloss spilled over and out.

"I love him, Stacy." She let go of my arm and plopped down on an overturned five gallon bucket. "I thought I was going to marry him. There's no one else I want like that. That I trust to . . . Nobody at all." And Finder the unbreakable, Finder the brilliant, Finder the girl with a broken heart sat there, dropped her face in her hand and sobbed.

And stayed sobbing for a long time. Minutes. I turned over the dirty washcloth bucket and sat down beside her. When she finally looked up, I handed her one of the washcloths from the shelf. And then, she reached over my head and handed one to me.

Tears flowed hot and strong down my face, too. Tears for her, tears of release after the night we'd had, tears for my own romantic expectations not being met. Tears for Judy's mom and the secret I still hadn't told.

"I can't tell my mom," she said. "I've defended him to her so many times. Stupid denial. He should've told me. I just don't want to see her give me that I told you so look."

"She knows," I said. "I mean she really knows. She was all hoping I would tell you when we came out here."

"Of course you couldn't tell me," Finder said. "That would totally betray his trust. Not that you shouldn't have found some way to give me a hint, tho. I mean, some clue would have been good."

"I've known for, like twenty-six hours."

"Oh yeah. I guess that didn't leave much time for processing."

I blew my nose in my washcloth. She did, too.

"Is it wrong to leave these in the bucket?" I said.

"After what Julian did to us tonight? Sis, he owes us. Big time. Snotty laundry is the least he can do." She threw her cloth in the sink since I was sitting on the bucket. "Never going to trust him again."

I shook my head. "No way." I sighed. I wished I could change that. And speaking of things I wished I could change, "Meredith hates your guts, you know."

She nodded. "I hate her, too."

"Good," I said. "Then it's even. Enemies to lovers trope, here we go."

"Unlike my unofficial ex-boyfriend, I'm not gay, so it's not really enemies to lovers."

"I'm not thinking about it like dating. I choose to live with the microscopic hope that you two can hate each other in a way that eventually lets you be friends."

"Don't count on it."

I shrugged. "I am happy counting tiny, tiny things. I love calculus. "

"You are so weird, Chess Team."

I could do worse for a friend than Finder. She squinted at my neck.

"I never noticed that before. Do you have a scar?" She pointed to the spot where my Star hung, now joined by the silver disc necklace from Nick. I looked in the mirror hanging over the slop sink. So strange. It looked like someone had drawn an equation on me with a thin, white marker; only no numbers, only math-y looking symbols connected by ultra thin white lines, and all in a tiny circle under where my necklaces fell. I tried to rub it off. Nope.

We washed our sobby faces and my weird mark which didn't come off (two more washcloths into the bucket) and stayed in the shed until we approved each other looking normal enough to face any still awake people. I wondered about my 'scar', but honestly, with everything else, I was too tired to do anything other than pull my T-shirt over it and ignore it for now.

Mama had blown up an air mattress for Finder and I to share in the living room. She would take Judy's room. Steve had gotten up and fallen back asleep cuddling Monster, both of them tucked beneath his superhero cape on a pile of cushions under the kitchen table. Tully still slept on the couch and Nick sat in the arm chair reading a book he'd probably pulled off the living room shelf.

"I think hit by a car while taking the trash out after the party is going to be the best option," Mama said, face serious as she handed us sleeping bags to unroll. She appraised us both, noticing, I'm sure, our scrubbed and washy faces. She gave me a small nod of approval. "A hit and run, maybe," she nodded toward the Southern Scotsman. Finder sat down on the air mattress.

"But there would be police involved if that happened. We would have taken him to the hospital," Finder said.

"And they would have called his parents," Nick said. "So would we."

Julian was finishing the clean-up, wiping down the homey butcher block counter.

"I'd keep it simple," Julian said. "You were hosting some people from work for a get together, correct? That's what you told Stacy's parents?"

Mama nodded.

"The simplest and most believable thing is that someone brought a guest who was already in a bad way. When you asked the guest to leave, they got violent. It is totally realistic for Tully and your daughter to have defended you and helped throw the guy out. Tully can keep the shoulder injury hidden. Nick stitched up the cut where the bad guest threw the bottle at Tully's head and you fixed up his bruised ribs. Nobody realized how bad the injuries were until this morning, because Tully is such a hero about it and plays rugby so didn't give the bruising too much thought. If they want him to see a doctor, you can meet them wherever they want him seen in the morning."

"You are scary good at that," Mama said, arms crossed over her chest.

"It's a good story," Finder said. "Let's use that."

"How are you feeling?" Mama said to me. I thought about showing her the mark on my chest, but stopped before I did it. The scrapes I'd gotten climbing the tree were already healed.

"Fine." Compared to twice possibly dead, I felt physically unscathed. Inside, though. Ugh.

"Thank you, Stacy," Mama said too quietly for anyone else to hear.

She'd made it clear to Nick by not providing a bed for him that he could go home any time. Nick made is clear to Mama that he would not be leaving until I left and, as promised, would return me to my domicile in person. So when he pulled his own sleeping bag out of the Hulk's trunk and alerted her that he'd be sleeping across his back seat, she went ahead and set up an extra coffee cup for him for the morning since she was "plumb out" of air mattresses.

April 28, continued.

Sunday was quiet as most of us were still hurt, healing, or just plain old processing the night before. Wolf John was gone. Tension with Julian was high so Nick, Finder and I went out for a walk in the spring sunshine after I called my parents to ask if Steve and I could spend one more night with Finder. Tomorrow was a teacher workday at St. Ignatius, so there was no school. Steve was way ahead of his class, so Jill was cool letting him miss. We decided not to mention Tully's injuries to his parents yet, hoping maybe we could get him looking and moving better by tomorrow.

Steve had spent the morning outdoors playing with rocks by the river so decided to stay in now to keep Tully company, bouncing on the air mattress and watching whatever the Southern Scotsman wanted on John and Julian's wide screen TV. Steve liked the TV because it hung on the wall like art.

Nick, Finder and I found ourselves on the path to the clearing. I did not want to go there. I stopped before we hit the switchback.

"Let's stop here," I said. "Or go down that other path."

"We should go to the clearing," Finder said. Nick agreed.

"I got all the syringes," I said. "I counted. It looked pretty innocuous when I left." What I didn't say was: 'And I don't want you to find what I hid.'

"A second look won't hurt," Nick said. I struggled for an excuse. I failed.

56.

April 28, continued.

The clearing looked different in daylight. Peaceful, typical. Trees. Dirt. Saplings reaching for sun.

"Eww," Finder said as her foot slipped in a puddle of slime. "It stinks."

Nick stepped in it too, on the other side of the clearing. Nick was too close to what I didn't want him to find. Okay chess girl, I thought. Time to redirect your opponent's attention.

"You can see it in the light better here," I stood by the wide pile of tendril filled slime that had rebirthed Ed. "When the serum kicked in, they changed back," I said, unwilling to describe it in detail.

"Why does it smell so bad?" Finder asked.

"I think the tendrils are from their bodies purging the venom."

"Purge? Like poop?" Finder said.

"Well, you can smell it," I said. She backed up and wiped her sneaker in the grass.

"It looks like a membrane," Nick said poking it with a stick. "It's pretty solid. Oh yuck. Except that. Yeah. That's poop."

It was also warm today, the hint of summer coming.

We moved around the clearing picking up all leftover human made objects. I stayed carefully between Nick, Finder and what I'd hidden. At one point Finder looked at me and said, "Hey, you got the mark off."

"I did?" She moved my necklaces aside with her finger.

"Yup," she said. "Gone." That was weird, but I had bigger things to worry about right now. We gathered up a few darts to return to Nick's zoo friend, the pieces of chain that had bound Judy to the tree, and some plastic from the vet supplies.

We headed back up the path after covering the piles of werewolf slime with leaves.

"Hey guys?" I said. "Can you go ahead of me for a minute? I need to pee."

I ran back to the clearing and went straight to the hollow behind the rocks. I moved aside my branches. What I had hidden was there, just as I had left it. I thought back to Finder showing me the deer skull on our run that one time. How far I had come, I thought. How very, very far.

Behind me, something whined. I turned. Standing feet away was a grey and white dog that looked remarkably like a wolf. It had a sock-like marking on its front foot.

"Hi dog," I said. "I don't remember your name, but your daddy is going to be so happy to see you." I crouched down and the dog came right up. He sniffed my hand and let me touch his thick fur. "Come on, buddy," I said. "You've got to be starved."

Monday, April 29, 2002.

I woke well after 8:30 Monday morning to the smell of cooking bacon. Opening my eyes, I found Mama, Tully and Finder already at the table playing cards, drinking coffee and cocoa and discussing Julian's fictional story that we would tell. Steve sat in Finder's lap drawing on a legal pad. Grendel slept under the table, his head on Tully's feet. Where was Nick?

"Rummy," said Mama. She scooped a bunch of cards off the table and put one down. "There's my play."

"Curse you, Mother," Finder said. "I wanted that card." Grendel stood up under the table and growled. Tully took him by the collar and walked him right out the front door.

The back door opened. I sat up, pulling my sleeping bag around me against the chill.

A warm, male voice said "Oh. I wondered about the cars in the driveway on a Monday. Um, good morning." John Forest Stalker, wearing the clothes I had put in his emergency tub and bare feet, looked pretty sound for someone who'd been bleeding to death twenty-four hours ago.

"Let's get that fire going again," he said. "Where's Julian?"

"He's in bed," Mama said. "Not feeling too well. We weren't expecting to spend another night but Layla and Teularen were hurt enough that it seemed a good idea. We wanted everyone to have some rest and get checked on one more time." What she didn't say was, 'and we don't trust Julian so we wanted to keep an eye on him, too.'

"Nick's going to be a doctor, so if any of y'all pack wolves feel like you want a once over or you have any questions, Nick will be happy to field them once he gets back with the rest of breakfast."

"I got a question," said a familiar, southern accented voice. "How do ya count cows?" He paused. I tried to place his voice. "You use a cow-culator."

Tully came back in the front door.

"Hi Stay-cee," Bradley Joe said as he came around the corner into the tiny dining room. "You sure did good helping get them werewolves down off us," he said voice full of odd pride. "You're a pretty boss fighter for such a little thing."

"Stacy? Which Stacy?" Another familiar voice. This was getting weird. "I don't remember much of anything about the weekend except getting a face full of- oh holy queens and bishops!"

Hank, my chess friend, came up behind Bradley Joe.

Caught in astonishment, I found myself without words. Bradley Joe and Hank, *Hank*, were shifter wolves? Huh? Judy poked her head around the corner and the boys made way for her. Their alpha female.

"Hike Club," Judy said at an almost normal human volume. She looked brighter than usual, her skin had a healthy glow about it despite her thinness.

Finder whooped in the kitchen and a big voice boomed "Heeey baby! Great job kicking ass last night! Oh sorry- I shouldn't say ass because my boy is here somewhere. Where's my dart man?" Steve launched from the living room where he'd come to bounce on my air mattress.

He leaped into Bolo's arms for a hug that made him look like a marmoset on the man's chest. "You did so good, Bolo!" Steve said. "Carrying me around and then fighting the werewolves like that! You are amazing!"

"Did I fight anybody? I remember seeing her do it, but whatever I did is a blur."

This kind of chat went on for several minutes as everybody shared their little slice of what happened.

No one mentioned Mrs. Macy attacking Ed or her own pack pushing her into the jaws of the Man with No Face. Only Steve and I had seen that part.

Nick arrived with two boxes of donuts which vanished almost before he even got them open, three dozen eggs, and who knows how many pounds of sausage and potatoes. After he and Mama managed the cooking, Nick stayed quietly by my side through the whole breakfast, bringing me coffee while I picked at some food, and letting the air out of my mattress to get it put away. When breakfast was nearly done, Grendel, tied on the front porch, began to bark.

A woman stood just off the front porch, the one with dreadlocks from the Tattooed Angel. Daja. She was a shifter, too?

And then I placed her. The Sandy wolf. Good grief! Was there anyone in Richmond unconnected to someone weird? One was still missing. Bradley Joe had to be the Red Dorsal stripe wolf who licked me, Hank the smallest one who ran the fight like a chess game. Bolo was obvious and Judy and John. If Daja was the Sandy wolf, who was the gorgeous silver wolf who had arrived late?

Judy stepped close to me, her face tense and tight. She came closer than she'd ever been and I thought for a moment she was going to slap me. She knows, I thought. She knows and she blames me.

She grabbed me to her in a fierce hug. I felt every rib.

"Thank you," she whispered, "for saving my pack. I owe you."

"No, you don't."

It was time. Waiting would only make this worse.

"Can we go outside?" I said. "Alone?"

57.

Sunday, May 12, 2002. Two weeks later. New moon.

We stood side by side, my family and Nick, Mama and Finder, Tully's family, all of them, John Forest Stalker and Julian. Judy, known to her packmates as Junior, stood next to her dad. Dr. Riverstone was there with his daughter who anchored a small collection of other women who, from the outside edges of their conversation, were all Cathy's birth clients. Sister Elizabeth Religion stood with Sister Mary Medical as the representatives from St. Ig's.

Five people I'd only seen at night by fire and moonlight stood in a small clump, furthest from the grave. I recognized one from the scars on his cheeks. Scars Finder had put there. I guess wounds inflicted by silver didn't heal the same way. We had learned that her new knives were not just any silver blades. Glaringly absent were the former werewolf alphas, Ed and Mrs. Macy.

The minister blessed the simple wooden coffin. Steve's tiny paw gripped mine.

Other than my grandfather's, this was my first funeral. Tonight would be my second. Tonight, I would help bury someone I'd watched die. Steve tugged my hand and I leaned over.

"Why is the box so big?" Steve whispered. I pressed my mouth close to his ear.

"So it looks like her body is in there."

We had seen her head struck from her shoulders, guillotined by a wisp of acrid smoke. Steve alone had seen the Man with No Face call her, draw her in her weakened state, depleted by ketamine and sugar syrup. My face had been buried in Bolo's fur. But when I heard the sound of shattering glass, I'd broken through the wall of shifter wolves. I'd grabbed her, tried to hold her back from violating the border of the sacred land to feed him, though I hadn't known who she was. I had been so sure of victory, so sure I had gotten them all with my antidote. But I missed one. I had missed Judy's mom.

I didn't know it was her until her head landed too close to my feet. He ripped her werewolf body apart as he ate it, but once severed from the heart pumping the venom through her, Cathy's face, hands and feet had returned to hers. Mrs. Macy's had done the same. I had picked them up and hidden them.

Beside me Steve shuddered, in tears. My dad reached down and picked him up, but Steve wouldn't let go of my hand. I knew why he was crying. He was crying because he was remembering. Reliving the moment when his big sister had carried human hands and feet, and heads, behind a rock and covered them with pine needles. He'd slept in my bed every night since. I was the only one who understood his nightmares, the only one who could get him quiet when he woke in a sweaty, tearful panic having relived the scene in his sleep. Which was worse? Asking Darcy Jackson to take the memory from him, or leaving him to carry this burden his whole life?

I squeezed my eyes shut, trying to chase away the wet flesh bending sounds and the screams as the werewolves resumed their human forms, forced by my serum.

Now, on a cloud-covered new moon morning, we all stood in shades of grey, black and navy, holding space as Judy buried a box of nothing but dirt.

7:36 p.m.

The sunset left licks of pink above the trees as indigo settled around us, around our fire. This was no blazing bonfire. Contained in a metal dish no bigger than a hubcap, it burned small and low, crackling as each herb landed in its flickering hands. John and Judy wore tribal garb, pale deer skins decorated with beads and feathers and paint. Their heads were covered with the simple beaded adornment of those in mourning.

Bradley Joe, Hank, Daja, and Bolo made a tight circle around their alphas. Where was the other wolf, the gorgeous silver grey? John and Judy alternated sprinkling blessed salt, herbs and powders from pouches into the bowl of burnt remains.

There hadn't been much left of Cathy to burn, but we had done it immediately that day, once I told Judy what had happened and shown her and John where I had hidden what was left to gather. We had burned Mrs. Macy's remains, too, and buried them with respect to whoever she was before the venom took her over. There was nothing left of Ed. In explaining the "car accident" we learned that Mrs. Macy's husband had died a few years back and they'd had no kids, and Ed had no family at all.

Now, Julian stood near Mama who held hands with Steve. Tully, Nick, Finder and I stood together, all in white as requested.

John and Judy moved slowly, raising and lowering their arms in small pulsing waves as they circled the small fire three times, then stopped.

The blessing was in Algonquian, the original Mattaponi language, but we all understood what John said from his tone.

This person had been loved. This person had been human. Her mistakes were now forgotten, all missteps forgiven. This person belonged to the Great Spirit, to the earth and to the consciousness of One that claimed us all.

"May nothing in her life or death be wasted," John said in English, "and may we all hold her in love and peacefulness in our hearts."

Judy said the rest, strong and clear, her voice resonating against the rocks behind us and the trees all around.

"May she rest in oneness with all things on this sacred land. We now return you, release you, Cathy Ellen Dobbs Forest Stalker, mother, wife and sister of earth, to the Great Mother that births, blesses and waits to keep us all."

And from somewhere outside, far outside our clearing, a screech of fury erupted and lingered in the air carried by a cold breeze touched with malice.

Steve fell asleep as soon as his head lay down on the back seat of the Hulk on the way home. It had been a long fourteen hours with the formal funeral this morning and the burial ceremony tonight. Steve could have gone home with Dad and Jill, but he refused. He had seen Cathy Forest Stalker die and it was only right for him to see her properly blessed and laid to rest.

Julian had made meals for us all and brought them as we spent the hours between ceremonies in work clothes emptying and scrubbing Cathy's trailer, car and Ed's SUV. We also smudged them with thick bundles of dried sage. They would sit empty from tonight's new moon to the full moon, be smudged again, and then at the next new moon, be blessed and given to Judy. Smudging was new to me, lighting bundles of sage and letting the smoke fill the space to cleanse it of unwanted energy and vibrations. John had shown Tully how to do it for the third round (that nasty place took multiple smudgings) and had insisted that we all be smudged ourselves before heading home.

Mama was my personal hero of the day. She had cleaned the fridge.

Nick, Steve and I drove in a close silence. We were all three smash down tired.

"Can we make a stop before I drop you off?" Nick said as we pulled into Wilton. "Do you feel up to it?" I did not, but I agreed, curiosity winning over exhaustion. Nick pulled over at the park near my house, unoccupied at this late hour. He unrolled the windows for Steve in the unlikely case he woke up.

Nick led me to the pirate ship part of the playground and we climbed up inside. I sat on the aft deck, facing the car.

Nick knelt on the deck beneath where I sat.

We hadn't touched at all since the not-kiss while rescuing Judy.

"I am so sorry, Stacy. You were right."

"About what?" I said.

"About me. I know I've apologized a hundred times, but it still doesn't feel like enough. I shouldn't have kissed Tully. It was thoughtless and hurtful to you and- " he took a long breath. "I shouldn't be trying to control what we do together like I have been. You are capable of making decisions for yourself and I'm sorry I've tried to run the show. It's not respectful, me trying to be all in charge of it. I was selfish, looking out for my own interests, trying to be the hero. But, I'm not the hero here. You are. Finder is. Tully is. Not me. I'm so sorry."

I sat speechless.

The truth was, he was right to apologize. I *was* capable of making my own decisions, he *had* been a jerk to try to control everything and if he had to live with some physical discomfort and patience as I got slowly into these waters then so be it.

"You don't have to say anything," he said, looking like he very much wished I would say something. "I just wanted to say what I had to say to you in private."

I slid off the deck steps and sat facing him on the pirate ship floor. I reached up and slid my hands behind his neck and up into his soft hair.

"Thank you," I said, pressing my forehead to his. "It was dumb, and you were a jerk. And, I love Tully, too, so I understand why you did it. And I forgive you. And him. If it happens again, I'll stake you both in your sleep."

Nick smiled and laughed a little.

"I hope that's a nervous laugh," I said. "Because I'm not really kidding." And I leaned forward. Ever so gently, as if he might vanish, I reached for his mouth. I kissed him, long and slow and deep as if I could tell him everything with one kiss.

"Stacy," he said as we came up for air.

"Nope," I said. "Stop right there. I'll let you know when it's too much." And on the playground in the pitch dark of the new moon, I kissed him. And kissed him. He pulled me up into his lap and held me as if we could melt into each other through all our clothes. My body woke up from its tiredness into a state of electricity that made every breath we took more needful than the one before. Being connected to him, kissing him was the only thing on earth that mattered in that moment. When we finally came apart, I wasn't the only one panting.

"This," he said, lower lip curving in mischief, "is going to be difficult."

"Eww," said Steve, standing high up on the ship's ledge. "Were you guys making out?"

Nick looked at me and blushed. Blushed!

"Yes," I said. "Now go play for five minutes so we can finish."

"It's dark and too late to play. Kissing is gross and you're going to get in trouble."

"Steven! Go. Sit. In the car!"

And bless his little heart, he did.

58.

Thursday, May 30, 2002.

"What's happening right now?" I asked Judy, jogging a few steps to match her pace toward the principal's office. "What did we do?"

She shrugged, took the last bite of her apple and chucked the core into a trash can. Judy always seemed small to me, but walking beside her now, I realized she was almost as tall as Finder. She'd cut her hair during her mom's ceremony and now ran her fingers through the hairdresser modified tousle.

"Probably my grief counsellor. I think she wants to talk to us together since you 'saw the accident'."

Oh, I thought. Got it.

"Remember it's a *car* accident," Judy said leaning down to talk right in my ear. "Macy didn't look, pulled out, and rammed into her side killing them both instantly."

"Instantly," I said. If only it had been.

"I have to see Sister every day for the next month," Judy went on. "She's not bad. You won't have to talk or anything. She's fine with me just sitting there if that's what I want. Yesterday I finished my history homework. She tries not to 'dictate what form my grief should be taking.'"

It sounded very Jill.

"The hard part is *not* talking, if you can believe that. It's not like I can tell her the truth."

We rounded the corner and opened the door to the principal's office. The school secretary, a wizened little lady with bling on her glasses dinged a bell. "They're here, Father," she said. A bell dinged in reply.

Judy and I were ushered into the office of a wiry priest a little older than my dad. I hadn't been in this office since presenting my petition to take junior and senior classes as a sophomore. Three buttoned up adults, all but one with glasses, stood with Father Jacob as we entered. The secretary shut the door behind us.

My first thought was lawyers. But their suits weren't high-end enough. And these people lacked law firm polish.

"Please, girls," said Father Jacob, the Principal at St. Ig's, "I'd like to introduce you to Dr. Smythe, Dr. Mandivala and Dr. Rubenstein." Judy and I exchanged a look. I hoped she wouldn't freak out having to meet and talk to so many people. We all shook hands. The stout and scowling doctor looked familiar.

"Miss Goldman," she said. "Dr. Smythe. I reviewed your project at the Statewide Science Fair. Miss Forest was ill that day and unable to be present."

Oh yes, this was the judge who'd been super rude.

"You look a little confused," said the doctor next to her in a soft Indian accent. "Please don't worry. This meeting is nothing bad."

"We interviewed Professor Windworth after seeing your work," said Dr. Smythe. "He shared some," she paused and took a big breath, "interesting information with us."

Oh no. *Oh. No.* Hank once told me that in his family the word interesting was a curse. Nerves bunched in my belly. Dr. M-something's assurances were nice, but this was Richmond. If this wasn't something bad, why did Dr. Scowly-face Smythe look like a bug was crawling up her pants leg?

A knock on the door and the secretary popped her head back in. "Father Jacob, the parents are here."

The parents? I thought. Dread made my heart race. Were we going to be expelled? I grabbed Judy's hand and squeezed. We stepped closer together. She squeezed right back, then let go.

"Send them in."

Jill, wearing a worried expression entered in a flurry of coat, tote bag and Steve, John Forest Stalker on her heels. My little brother was stuffing his face with Swedish fish and looking entirely unconcerned. Father gestured for us all to sit. The tiny office had been crammed with chairs. Judy and I took the two sandwiched between the doctors and the parents.

"I'm not sure if you girls understand the gravity of this situation," said Dr. Smythe "but your project could generate some serious consequences."

A strain of panic slid up my spine. I focused on the beatific Jesus painting behind Father Jacob's desk.

Dude, I thought, I promise I'll go to confession or whatever you want if you help me not get crucified right now.

Judy and I exchanged a look. What had happened? Did all the werewolf people die and they traced the cause of death to me? To my serum? They were alive two weeks ago at the funeral.

"I don't know how you did it," said Dr. Smythe. (Go me, remembering names.) "And frankly I'm not happy my team of professionals missed what you found." She sighed again and shook her head. "We have a strong reason to believe that your research may be some of the most important science done in the last decade. It's far above where you should be academically and touches fields beyond genetics. Dr. Mandivala, would you . . . ?"

He leaned forward in his heavy carved chair. "Yes, thank you, Dr. Smythe. Miss Goldman, Miss Forest, it is a pleasure and an honor to meet you both. I am a geneticist at the Teluride Mason Science Group and we have been working on a DNA mutation project for quite some time." I'd read about Teluride Mason, the most avant-garde science group in the U.S., and one of the top five private research institutions in the world. The Wall Street Journal had done a huge spread on them which I had devoured last year word by word. Dad bought me three shares of their stock as my birthday present since we'd just moved. My jaw literally dropped open for a whole second before I got ahold of myself.

"Miss Goldman, you are familiar with Teluride Mason?"

I swallowed. "Um. I've read. Articles."

"Excellent. Dr. Windworth confirmed for us that one hundred percent of the research, activity and conclusions in your science fair project were your own and not based on his prior research. Dr. Smythe and Dr. Rubenstein and I are colleagues in a collective genetics research consortium. Dr. Smythe told me about your project after she was unable to award it because of your absence," he looked at Judy. "Dr. Rubenstein and I independently reviewed all of your work and in fact, replicated your research in our own labs. The work you girls did is extraordinary." He exchanged looks with the other doctors. "We wanted to ask you some questions."

The next half hour passed in a blur. I answered question after question about our research as the scientists exchanged astonished glances. Judy answered questions too, speaking at a regular, humanly hearable volume. By the end, I was breathless. These people not only understood what we had done, they had replicated my science! They had shown that my hypothesis was legit. Jill and John sat beaming with pride.

"The bottom line here," said Dr. Rubenstein, "is that your research needs to be written and published. The potential of this breakthrough to unlock missing elements of cures for hereditarily caused diseases is huge. We, at the consortium, want to make sure there are no obstructions to either of your education and future career choices, so we asked Father Jacob to invite you and your parents to meet with us. The consortium would like to offer both of you full scholarship funding to the college of your choice assuming you major in a research based science with a minimum of a minor in genetics. We will pay all your expenses including room and board, books and a small stipend of spending money for a four year bachelor's degree first and then, as long as you agree to work for the consortium either at Teluride Mason or my company, Alto Technologies for the first five years of your career, we will also support your Master's degree efforts and fully fund you through a Ph.D."

A stunned silence electrified the room.

Steve, being Steve, broke it. "Well, that's gonna be a yes." The adults laughed.

"Thank you, young man," said Dr. Mandivala. "I hope you are right!"

"We will discuss the particulars with your parents and Father Jacob," said Dr. Smythe, "You all can sleep on it and give us an answer next week. It is a big commitment to make as sophomores in high school."

Dr. Mandivala continued. "But it is clear to us that you are going to accomplish extraordinary things in your careers and we want to make sure you stay on the right path."

Jill grabbed me into a huge hug in the hall outside.

"Stacy! This is amazing! Your father is going to be so proud! And so sorry he missed this. He is going to wet his pants when we tell him!" Steve stood beside her, a thoughtful expression on his face. I'd put money on him thinking exactly what I was thinking.

Something was up. We just didn't know yet what it was.

John stood talking quietly with Judy, who had broken the spell of excitement at the end by telling the scientists all the work was mine and she did not deserve the offer. They had pooh-poohed that and told her that time would prove her worthiness.

We shook hands again with all the doctors on their way out, accepting their congratulations and hopes for our acceptance of their offer.

Steve's parting words to me were, "Judy smells like jellybeans."

I pulled my candy-scented friend into the bathroom on our way back to class.

"What was that?" I whispered after making sure we were alone.

"I don't know."

"It's weird, right? I'm not the only guy who thinks that was totally weird?"

"It's totally right," Judy said. "For you. You deserve every penny of that offer."

"That's not what I'm talking about," I said. "I'm talking about how they found our research and re-ran our experiments. They were missing a massive element unless they were working on shifters, too. What do those people *know?*"

"Maybe they are real scientists with real research needs. Maybe you're a real genius, Stacy. Maybe the world needs you. You saved my life. Who knows how many millions more you could save if you had a bigger platform?"

I didn't know what to say to that. The unspoken truth hung in the air. I had maybe saved her life. But I had let her mom die.

We stood looking into each other's eyes.

"I will never forgive myself," I said. "I can't ever- "

She held up her hand. "Stop. Don't apologize. Not to me, not to anyone. What happened to her was Ed's responsibility. And the Man. He's the one I hold accountable. Not you." She grabbed my hand and held it hard. "I vow two things," she said, "With you as my witness because you are the only person who can understand. I vow I will never deny or resist what I am again. I will eat, I will get strong and I will learn to shift without pain. I will never again be victimized by pigs like Ed and I will never let the people I love be harmed," her eyes welled. She pressed my hand to her heart. "And I swear on my own heart, Stacy, I swear on the pack of wolves that follow me that I will avenge my mother's hideous . . . horrible . . ." a tear trickled down her face, "unspeakable . . . death if it's the last thing I do."

Judy's breath heaved under my hand.

"Are you my witness?" she said.

"I am," I said as quiet as Judy when I first met her.

She looked at me, calm and clear and held together with pent up rage. For the first time in her human form, she was letting me truly see her. It was as if the night in my kitchen in the moonlight had been a curtained window into the deep chasm that was the true Judy.

"Are we friends?" she said. "I'm fine if we're not. I'm not the person you- "

"We are," I said.

"Good." She dropped my hand. "Because you're going to need me. Something is definitely up with those scientists."

59.

Saturday, June 8, 2002.

"I came to give you my news," Luke said, an expression of excitement on his face. He sat down across from us, coffee and free biscotti in hand. "And to have the best cup of coffee in Richmond one last time."

"Ooo, I love news!" Nick said, delight sweeping his face. "Wait. One *last* time? You aren't moving are you?"

"Nina and I are officially separated," Luke began. "One year from today we'll be divorced. And no, I'm not moving. I'm," he paused, "giving up caffeine." Nick looked surprised.

"Divorced? I didn't see that coming."

"I did," I said before I could stop myself. "When we were at your house and she didn't know about your gaming and you were all hush hush about how we met, I was like, oh yeah, this relationship cannot possibly last."

"She did know about the gaming," Luke said, sipping. "Just not the depth of it. Or of the . . . relationships I formed while doing it."

"You mean your affair with Matilda," I said. I'd had E-nough of untrustworthy men. Luke and Julian were running neck-and-neck for my least favorite.

"It was not an affair."

"It was a something," I said.

"What about the dogs?" Nick said. "Who gets custody of Bitsy and Grendel?"

"She does." Luke's brow dropped, sad maybe. Or missing them already.

"You can get dog time though, surely," I said.

"Nope. I said my goodbyes this afternoon at the house." Luke put down his coffee. "I have something big to tell you guys," he said. "After everything we've been through, I've thought long and hard about who I am and what I want out of life. Being married in a suburban house with dogs and a jealous wife who doesn't understand me isn't it."

Nick sat forward, elbows on his knees. "Yeah. But you can't live forever and have superpowers with a wackadoodle vampire girlfriend who might torture you for fun."

Luke gave Nick a hard look.

"I think I can."

Nick nearly dropped his cup.

"What?" I said, louder than I meant. The couple at the next table looked up.

"You can't talk me out of it, so don't even try," Luke whispered. "I know she nearly killed me, I know you think she's evil, but I don't have anything better to do with my life. We owe her two Gentlemen Butlers and she is not going to give up until she has them. I'd pay half that debt."

Nick and I together overlapping: "No, no! Absolutely not. We got that debt reversed at New Year's. That is a terrible idea. You can't give in to her! You cannot turn into a Bat Suit! That is a huge mistake." We talked fast and over each other.

Luke stood. "I've made up my mind. I've been thinking about it for months and have gone over everything very carefully. This past weekend cinched it for me."

Fury grabbed me. I grabbed Luke's arm. I squeezed. Hard.

"I have been *feeding* a Bat Suit, Luke. Feeding him with my own blood." It was hard to yell at someone while whispering, but I figured it out. I let go of Luke and shoved up my sleeve. I shook the bruise from Terrence's last bite from two nights ago in his face. "This, my *blood* has been the *price* for saving your sorry pathetic useless, idiotic life! *This* is how you pay me back? This is what I've been paying for? For you to give up being human and go be one of them? No. No! Absolutely not."

Luke looked bewildered. "What do you mean?"

Nick reached out his arm and drew his friend gently back into a seat.

"So you remember how Matilda ripped your throat open to save her own life and drained you nearly to a husk?"

"Yeah, but she healed me. I was fine the next day."

"Do you know why she healed you? *How* you came to be 'fine' the next day?"

I could not, absolutely not stand and listen to this garbage. I walked over to the counter and stared at the desserts. I counted them, to calm my mind.

Roberto tapped on the glass. "What would you like, Miss Stacy?" He was wearing a very tight T-shirt.

"Do you get better tips when you wear shirts that let people see your nipple ring?" My conversational appropriateness filter was gone.

He grinned. "No, but I get more dates."

I stared at him in shock. "Aren't you engaged?"

He laughed. "I'm teasing you!" He dropped his voice to a whisper. "Yes, I get better tips when I wear tight T-shirts."

"That's so wrong," I said.

"It's so life."

"Have you ever saved someone's life and then they committed suicide anyway?"

"Can't say I have. Is that why Dr. Nick is holding hands with the old, straight guy there?"

I turned. Nick was leaning forward, Luke's wrists in his hands. I stalked over.

"I hear you," Nick was saying. "I hear that you want the cool powers and- "

"I want a life I can fully live," Luke said, pulling his hands away. "I'll have forever. I'll have loyal, long term relationships. I'll be able to affect the world over time. I won't feel guilty about being who I am and wanting things above and beyond what other men expect from this life. Look, Nick, you're young, you can't probably even comprehend this, but waking up every day next to someone who resents you for what you love is horrible. Impossible, really. It makes you not even a man anymore, it rips you up inside and makes you feel like less than a person. I never want to feel like that again. Even if I wake up," he lowered his voice nearly to a whisper. "Even if I wake up in a coffin knowing my former friends want to stake me, at least I can do it knowing that I have something that I want, the ability to live my life for myself."

"Enjoy it fast," I said, "because you are going to get staked. You are. I promise. And it is going to be me who stakes you. And you want to know what? I'm going to enjoy every stab I put through your ungrateful chest because of how much," I poked him in the chest once for each word. "Being. Fed. On. *Hurts!*"

"I can spy for you guys. I'll keep you informed about what happens at Maymont."

"Oh my god! LUKE!" Nick gave me a warning glance and I lowered my voice. "Your humanity will be GONE. You won't be friends with us. You'll smell our blood and think of us as smoothies! This is not okay. You cannot do this!" I looked at Nick. "Do we knock him out and tie him up somewhere until he comes to his senses?" I wondered how hard my fist would have to hit his temple to make that happen. The calculus started in my head. If a fist travels twelve inches at eighteen miles per hour . . .

"What if Matilda rejects you?" Nick asked.

"She won't. Why are you so righteous?" Luke said. "Why are you so sure that you have the answers? I don't care about anything other than how I am going to feel for the rest of my life and I would love for you, my true and real friends to understand and give me your blessing on this . . . transition. I didn't come for you to talk me out of it. And thanks for feeding Terrence or whatever but I had no idea that was happening. I didn't ask you to save my life or get a vampire to come and brainwash doctors to give me a blood transfusion. I thought she was going to turn me that night. That is what I wanted. That is why I showed up to help you. I'm a grown man and I can make these decisions for myself. I am here because I respect you and I want you to know that I'm about to help you in a very big way by paying off half the debt you incurred saving my life- "

"Which was clearly pointless," I said, bitter.

"It wasn't! I am so grateful for that wake-up call. For the months of problems with Nina, and my ability to see my life for what I want from it. I'm not asking you to agree with me, and I would rather do this with your approval and partnership, but I'm doing it whether you like it or not. Now, I am going to finish my final coffee before it gets cold and you can say whatever you want."

"It's suicide," Nick said. "It's emotional and physical suicide."

"Does Nina know you're going to vanish?"

"That's just it. I'm not. Do you have any idea how much Matilda pays her Gentleman Butlers? And how much they earn on investments through Darcy Jackson? Not only can I pay alimony and make sure that Nina and the dogs are looked after, but my own lifestyle is going to dramatically improve. No more crappy car, no more bargain jeans on sale. I am going to have a beautiful apartment for my days off and enough money to do whatever I like as long as I walk this earth."

"Money, superpowers, community, I can see the appeal," I said. "Needing to suck souls to not become a zombie, depriving other humans of their precious memories and relationships so you can wake up with consciousness, drinking the blood of humans, which hurts by the way, a *lot*, so you can be fed, needing to use your powers to manipulate people to get what you want."

"She has human servants who love giving blood, giving soul. I will, too."

"She asked *me* to be one of those human servants, Luke. She begged me that night at Third Rock and it was *not* all Little House on the Prairie. She wanted something from me. Something big." I stopped myself before I went any further. Nick's eyes were wide. This was a secret I had told no one.

"Her servants are like cattle. Like the way," I paused I didn't want to mention his name or whatever we call him that isn't his name so I gave a pointed look instead, "the way you-know-what eats werewolves. In his eye they are willing, but as we know, they are *not*."

"It's not the same with our kind."

"Our kind?" I shrieked. "You're *human*, Luke! You're a *person!*" People around us started stirring. I was making us a spectacle and I was beyond caring who heard me say what. This was Richmond. They were all probably related to something supernatural anyway.

Luke dipped his biscotti, took a bite, then chugged the contents of his cup. "I love you guys, I thank you for everything and I'm headed to Maymont where I am expected this evening. I'll try to talk her into me paying off the full debt. It's the least I can do."

"The debt is already PAID!" I shouted. More people minding their own business looked over.

I felt flabbergasted. This could not be happening. Nick stood and walked to Luke. The two men hugged. A long, honest farewell hug.

They did their fist knocking goodbye thing. "See you around, Dr. Nick," Luke said. "I know you're gonna do great things. You, too," he said, looking at me.

"How are you giving up this easily?" I said to Nick. "Are you going to let him do this?"

"We don't have a choice. He's made up his mind."

Luke looked at me. "Thank you for saving my life. I will always owe you. And Finder and Tully," he added, "for that." Luke met my gaze, though I did not respond to his invite for a goodbye hug. "Every day I wake up and look at the tattoo on my arm. I am a false thing. And I realize that is not what I want. I want to be real. Whatever that means. I hope you can find clarity about what you want to be, too, Stacy Goldman. Take good care of my friend if he lets you. He's a keeper."

Luke picked up his cup, put his last bite of biscotti into his mouth savoring. "God, that's good," he said. Then he turned and walked away, clearing his cup to the bussing station as he left. The door shut behind him with a finality I felt in my bones.

We sat, said nothing. After what I think was a lot of minutes, I spoke.

"That didn't really happen, did it?"

"I think it did." Nick's voice was so sad. "I really love that guy, you know?"

"Yeah," I said. "I know."

"I hate losing a patient."

"I hate losing a game."

"It's why you're magic, Stacy," Nick said. "Games aren't just playtime to you. They are how you tick. How you interact with the world. Nothing is unbeatable to you. No win is impossible. When you open a game, you stay with it until it's done. I feel like that with my work, too. I love people, I want them to be well, but if one isn't and they come to me for help, I won't stop until we solve the mystery. I feel like I lost Luke. I could have saved him, but he wouldn't take the advice. I feel like a failure."

"You're not a failure. Luke is a failure."

We finished our coffees listening to our own thoughts and the clatter and hush of Chapter & Mercy, maybe now the best coffee shop in the whole world. I heard Roberto laugh behind the counter as a customer flirted. Dishes clanked as the new kid emptied the bussing station. Pages turned behind us, friends chatted on our left. The bookstore side door opening and closing brought a breeze every so often.

Was Luke really doing this? Was he going to become a Bat Suit? Was there anything we could do to stop him? And if we could stop him, should we? Could he be right? Could this be a decision he had thought long and carefully about? Could it be the thing he wanted over all other things?

I looked at Nick, brow furrowed, shoulders hunched. I bet he was thinking/wondering the same things.

I got up and went over to the bookstore side. I felt Nick's eyes on my back, but didn't turn. Inhaling the distinctive smell of ink and paper, I negotiated the narrow aisles to the languages section. I ran my finger along the spines. Was it a good thing Finder and Tully weren't here? They could easily overpower Luke. French, German. He would not be on his way to his doom if they would have been here. Finder would have stopped him. Hebrew, Ingles. Or would she? I thought. Maybe she would buy the idea that he could spy for us, that he would stay somehow on our side? Maybe Darcy would gain an ally? Everything felt so uncertain.

Latin. Latin Grammar, Latin for Dummies. Latin Dictionary. I took it off the shelf and flipped to F.

'Famelicus: Hungry; starved; famished. Adj. feminine famelica, neuter, famelicum.'

Of course.

I was wondering how long it would take you to do some research, said Michael. *There's more to be done, you know. Being a wielder is a responsibility. You should read that book Nick gave you.*

I'm not a wielder, whatever that is, and I'm not taking assignments right now, I said. *And why didn't you tell me the Man with No Face had a name?*

I did. I told you in your school gymnasium. You weren't listening. But you are now. That's good. Nothing like dying once to wake a girl up, right?

You could be a nice angel and give me my memories back about all that.

You remember what you need to remember. I guess that was something you don't need to know.

Well, until the next time my life is in danger, I thought.

A little listening, a little faith, said Michael.

As Nick and I left Chapter & Mercy, a car beeped behind us.

"Stacy!"

I turned to see a navy-blue sedan pulling into an empty parking space by the bike rack.

"Stacy!" Finder waved furiously from the driver's side.

"You got a car?" I said. "Congratulations!" I had no idea this was on her agenda.

"It's Christopher's. He's getting a new one so he's selling this to me. Why weren't you answering your phone? I called and called. I finally figured you guys were here so I came over." She got out of the car and came around to where Nick and I stood. Her white shirt gleamed in the streetlight and the colorful scarf wrapping her hair gave her a random voodoo priestess kind of look.

She grabbed my shoulders. "I was doing this meditation Miss Joanne gave me and this idea came," she said. "I think I know what's next!" Her broad smile was contagious and I smiled back. Was there a new college thing or a science fair she could win without a partner?

"What? What do you mean what's next?"

"I need you to do it with me." Excitement emanated from her like it was Passover and she had found the afikomen.

"Okay, but what are we doing?"

"What I've wanted to do from the beginning." She paused as if I was supposed to know what this meant.

"Win world championships in tae kwon do? I don't think I can help you there."

"No, duh. You're the only person I know who has summoned an angelic being. So I need you."

"Why?"

"Because I think we can do it."

"Do what?"

"On the sacred ground. He apologized! There is something left inside him, Stacy, something good we can restore. We just have to figure out how to summon the piece that got broken off."

"Oh no," I said. "No. No, no."

Had everyone in my world suddenly gone completely bonkers?

Finder put her arm around me and gave me a squeeze.

"We've got this," she said. "Just a little more research to do. Think of it as a righteous new project. 'Cuz we, Chess Team, you and me, we are going to re-alive my dad."

To be continued . . .

in

MAGICK SQUARED

The Unimaginables
Book III

Acknowledgements

Thank you for reading this book! I am truly so grateful to you for reading, for sharing, for reviewing and for spending many of your precious hours with me. There's more to come.

I am grateful also to the following: My adult editor, Deborah Hawkins, whose insight, miraculous brain-sharing and no small amount of last-minute texting was critical to making this book shine, my teen editor, Emma Fandey who not only has read the whole book multiple times from awkward beta-reads to full polish, and who sat on a six-hour car ride listening to me read a huge chunk of it aloud, but who, along with her mom, Charlotte Fandey puts up with emergency texts, endless character hashing phone calls, run-on sentences and oh, so much more. You are magic! I would be remiss to not mentioning my own teenaged daughter, Roane Furlong, who lives with book chaos and who makes me keep it real, especially where the romance is concerned. Her hugs are the best. Thanks to my son, Clark, who hears this more often than he wants, "Hey Clark, can you- oh sorry for interrupting- can you just listen to this paragraph and tell me if it's too (brutal, boring, long, short, etc.)?"

Thank you to my beautiful beta readers, Robin Long, Robyn Dow, Mara Barnhart and again, Char and Emma. Your willingness to read drafts that are so far from perfect helps me more than you can possibly know. Thank you also to my emergency copy edit crew, who at the last minute, each took some chapters and dove in for a final nitpick; the ladies above, plus Melanie Bartenstein, Beth Mason, and Rebagrace Lee.

Thanks to my sensitivity readers who help me fill in the gaps where they have lived what I have not, Carolyn Faye Kramer, Bryan Coffee, Caitlin Barton-Landfield, Michael Sugar, James Tedeschi, Coffee Polk, and assistant librarians Lisha Payne & Julie Dixon who gave this book approval on the high-school library spice-o-meter. It's very important to me that we talk intelligently about real stuff in a way that still allows people to find this book in their school libraries!

Extra special thanks goes to Coffee Polk who, soul-offended by the sad, internet print out map I took to signings, made you the utterly perfect map at the opening of this book. What's a fantasy book without a map, right?

Thank you to every teacher and librarian who offers this book to their people, especially the librarians and teachers in Stafford County, VA where The Unimaginables was born. Thank you to all the people whose names are not here, but have answered random questions that seem completely out of the blue but which make this book juicer and more correct. Thank you to Tracey Ramsey & Books International for making sure the copies you get out of my hands are beautiful, Kasun2050 for a cover that fills me with joy, and my writing buddies, authors Tara Taffera and screenwriter Bryan Coffee for showing up! Thank you to Ashley Welch, Mike Maxon, Deb Beutel, Emilie Mason, Gene Allen and all you other book lovers who have invited me to speak at your schools and bookclubs and/or who have shared posts, and told your friends, put in library requests or just asked more than once when this book would be out.

Thanks to Mike Curry and the Powder Puff Poker League who inspired the card games in this book, and who kept me playing and not just working, and Lesa Carter and Mariel Iezzoni whose kitchens provided much needed sanctuaries when the work was a must.

And thank you, thank you, to James, Tiffany, Jane, Tania, Cristina and all the brilliant Barnes & Noble teams who have helped me reach so many more people with these stories than I could have on my own. Thank you for the signings, the events, the face-out shelf space, the personal recommendations to your customers and for being kind and wonderful humans! Your love for books is evident and I am so grateful to you for championing a debut author, and for teaching me so much about how bookselling works. I am always here to help make your job easier.

Last, but not least, the pillars of my life are my husband Shaun, thank you, darling, for actually reading these books, I'm sure you will find every in-joke (and every typo,) my kids, Wyatt, Emmet, Clark and Roane; all four of you bring me so much joy every day just being who you are and especially when you play all the music. Last but not least, thanks Char. You inspire me to be more truthful, more open, braver, more badass and, of course, funnier. Thank you for coming out to play even when you'd rather be napping, and for laughing at my jokes.

Independent publishing is a fascinating road. I am grateful for every bump and curve. And I'm grateful for you, being here with me. Thanks. Big hugs to you!   ~Jen

About the Author

J.S. (Jen Selby) Furlong has told stories all her life. She has written, performed, produced and directed for theatre, circus, film and television. Under her maiden name, Jennifer Albright, she is the author of *Antagonists* for Mind's Eye Theatre, the LARP version of *Vampire: The Masquerade,* and once played a small, but pivotal role, on *Buffy: The Vampire Slayer.* Her family of six now knows way more about book creation and publishing than they ever wanted to.

Follow Jen on socials:

IG @iamjenfurlong
BookTok @jenwritesvampirebooks.
FB @J.S. Furlong
If you leave her a message or comment, she will probably follow you back.

For more, visit jsfurlong.com, or scan this code with your smartphone.